Upon this barrow rode resplendent, with crosier, cope, and miter, the new Pope of Fools, the bell-ringer of Notre-Dame, Quasimodo the Hunchback. (page 67)

The trunk of the tree is fixed; the foliage is variable.

(page 117)

Say if you know of anything on earth richer, more joyous, more mellow, more enchanting than this tumult of bells and chimes; than this furnace of music; than these ten thousand brazen voices singing together through stone flutes three hundred feet in length; than this city which is but an orchestra; than this symphony which roars like a tempest.

(page 143)

"This foundling, as they call it, is a regular monster of abomination." (page 145)

The poor little imp had a wart over his left eye, his head was buried between his shoulders, his spine was curved, his breastbone prominent, his legs crooked; but he seemed lively; and although it was impossible to say in what language he babbled, his cries proclaimed a certain amount of health and vigor. (pages 152–153)

It was Quasimodo, bound, corded, tied, garotted, and well guarded. The squad of men who had him in charge were assisted by the captain of the watch in person, wearing the arms of France embroidered on his breast, and the city arms on his back. (page 205)

"Come and see, gentlemen and ladies! They are going straightway to flog Master Quasimodo, the bell-ringer of my brother the archdeacon of Josas, a strange specimen of Oriental architecture, with a dome for his back and twisted columns for legs." (page 239)

The people, particularly in the Middle Ages, were to society what the child is to a family. So long as they remain in their primitive condition of ignorance, of moral and intellectual nonage, it may be said of that as of a child,—

"It is an age without pity."

(page 241)

"A man must live; and the finest Alexandrine verses are not such good eating as a bit of Brie cheese." (page 268)

The cathedral seemed somber, and given over to silence; for festivals and funerals there was still the simple tolling, dry and bare, such as the ritual required, and nothing more; of the double noise which a church sends forth, from its organ within and its bells without, only the organ remained. It seemed as if there were no musician left in the belfry towers.

(page 274)

Lovers' talk is very commonplace. It is a perpetual "I love you." A very bare and very insipid phrase to an indifferent ear, unless adorned with a few grace-notes; but Claude was not an indifferent listener. (page 312)

It was but too truly Esmeralda. Upon this last round of the ladder of opprobrium and misfortune she was still beautiful; her large black eyes looked larger than ever from the thinness of her cheeks; her livid profile was pure and sublime.

(page 368)

"A drop of water and a little pity are more than my whole life can ever repay." (page 395)

The heart of man cannot long remain at any extreme.

(page 396)

"Fate has delivered us over to each other. Your life is in my hands; my soul rests in yours. Beyond this place and this night all is dark." (page 502)

THE HUNCHBACK
OF NOTRE DAME

Victor Hugo

With an Introduction and Notes
by Isabel Roche
Translated anonymously

George Stade
Consulting Editorial Director

BARNES & NOBLE CLASSICS
NEW YORK

_JB_

BARNES & NOBLE CLASSICS
NEW YORK

Victor Hugo first published _Notre-Dame de Paris_ in 1831; the present
anonymous translation was contemporaneous with the French edition.

Introduction, Notes, and For Further Reading
Copyright © 2004 by Isabel Roche.

Note on _The Hunchback of Notre Dame_, The World of Victor Hugo and _The
Hunchback of Notre Dame_,
Inspired by _The Hunchback of Notre Dame_, and Comments & Questions
Copyright © 2004 by Fine Creative Media, Inc.

The Hunchback of Notre Dame
ISBN 1-59308-047-6
LC Control Number 2003112456

Produced by:
Fine Creative Media, Inc.
322 Eighth Avenue
New York, NY 10001

President & Publisher: Michael J. Fine
Consulting Editorial Director: George Stade
Editor: Jeffrey Broesche
Editorial Research: Jason Baker
Vice-President Production: Stan Last
Senior Production Manager: Mark A. Jordan
Production Editor: KB Mello

Printed in the United States of America
QB
3 5 7 9 10 8 6 4 2

VICTOR HUGO

Novelist, poet, dramatist, essayist, idealist politician, and leader of the French Romantic movement from 1830 on, Victor-Marie Hugo was born the youngest of three sons in Besançon, France, on February 26, 1802. Victor's early childhood was turbulent: His father, Joseph-Léopold, traveled frequently as a general in Napoléon Bonaparte's army, forcing the family to move throughout France, Italy, and Spain. Weary of this upheaval, Hugo's wife, Sophie, separated from her husband and settled with her three sons in Paris. Victor's brilliance declared itself early in the form of illustrations, plays, and nationally recognized verse. Against his mother's wishes, the passionate young man fell in love and secretly became engaged to his neighbor, Adèle Foucher. Following the death of Sophie Hugo, and self-supporting thanks to a royal pension granted for his first book of odes, Hugo wed Adèle in 1822.

In the 1820s and 30s, Hugo came into his own as a writer and figurehead of the new Romanticism, a movement that sought to liberate literature from its stultifying classical influences. His preface to the play *Cromwell*, in 1827, proclaimed a new aesthetics inspired by Shakespeare and Velázquez, based on the shock effects of juxtaposing the grotesque with the sublime (for example, the deformed hunchback inhabiting the magnificent cathedral of Notre Dame). The play *Hernani* incited violent public disturbances among scandalized audiences in 1830. The next year, the great success of *Notre-Dame de Paris* (*The Hunchback of Notre Dame*) confirmed Hugo's primacy among the Romantics.

By 1830 the Hugos had four children. Exhausted from her pregnancies and Hugo's insatiable sexual demands, Adèle began to sleep alone, and soon fell in love with Hugo's best friend, the critic Charles-Augustin Sainte-Beuve. They began an affair. The Hugos stayed together as friends, and in 1833 Hugo met the actress Juliette Drouet, who would remain his primary mistress until her death fifty years later.

Personal tragedy pursued Hugo relentlessly. His jealous brother Eugène went permanently insane at Victor's wedding to Adèle. Three of Victor's children died before him. His favorite, Léopoldine, together with her unborn child and her devoted husband, died at nineteen in a boating accident on the Seine. The one survivor, Adèle (named after her mother), would be institutionalized for more than thirty years.

Hugo's early royalist sympathies shifted toward liberalism during the late 1820s under the influences of the fiery liberal priest Félicité de Lamennais; of his close friend Charles Nodier, an ardent opponent of capital punishment; and of his father, a general under Napoléon I. He first held political office in 1843, and as he became more engaged in France's social troubles, he was elected to the Constitutional Assembly following the February Revolution of 1848. A lifetime advocate of freedom and justice, often at his own peril, Hugo's work linked art to the political realm. After Napoléon III's coup d'état in 1851, Hugo's open opposition created hostilities that ended in his flight abroad from the new government.

Hugo's exile took him first to Belgium, and then to the Channel Islands of Jersey and Guernsey. Declining at least two offers of amnesty—which would have meant curtailing his opposition to the Empire—Hugo remained abroad for nineteen years, until Napoléon's fall in 1870. Meanwhile, the seclusion of the islands enabled Hugo to write some of his most famous verse and his masterpiece, the novel *Les Misérables*. When he returned to Paris, the country hailed him as a hero. Hugo then weathered, within a brief period, the siege of Paris, the institutionalization of his daughter for insanity, and the death of his two sons. Despite this personal anguish, the aging author remained committed to political change. He became an internationally revered figure who helped to preserve and shape the Third Republic and democracy in France. Hugo's death on May 22, 1885, generated intense national mourning; more than two million people joined his funeral procession in Paris from the Arc de Triomphe to the Panthéon, where he was buried.

TABLE OF CONTENTS

The World of Victor Hugo and
The Hunchback of Notre Dame
ix

Introduction by Isabel Roche
xix

THE HUNCHBACK OF NOTRE DAME
1

Endnotes
545

Inspired by *The Hunchback of Notre Dame*
551

Comments & Questions
555

For Further Reading
561

THE WORLD OF VICTOR HUGO AND
THE HUNCHBACK OF NOTRE DAME

1797   Hugo's parents, Joseph-Léopold Hugo and Sophie Trébuchet, marry. They will have three sons: Abel (1798), Eugène (1800), and Victor-Marie (1802), who is born in Besançon on February 26. An officer in the army of Napoléon Bonaparte (Napoléon I), Léopold must travel constantly during Victor's youth.

1803–   Marital problems occur as Sophie cannot tolerate the
1812   transience of army life; finally, she settles in Paris with her three children. Both parents start extramarital affairs. The family travels to Corsica and Elba, where Léopold is stationed. He later commands the troops that will suppress freedom fighters in occupied Italy and Spain, sometimes nailing their severed heads above church doors.

1804   Napoléon proclaims himself Emperor of the French. Literary critic Charles-Augustin Sainte-Beuve is born.

1807   Léopold Hugo receives a post in Naples, where his family soon joins him.

1808   Léopold Hugo follows a cortege of Napoléon's brother, Joseph, to Spain. Weary of travel, Sophie returns with her young sons to Paris, where she begins an affair with General Victor Lahorie, a conspirator against Napoléon.

1809   Napoléon promotes Major Hugo to general, and honors him with the title of count.

1810   The police arrest Lahorie in Mme. Hugo's house on December 30.

1811   Sophie journeys to Spain to save her marriage, but problems in the relationship persist. Léopold, knowing of his wife's infidelity, asks for a divorce. Sophie and her sons return to Paris.

1812   General Lahorie is executed for plotting against Napoléon.

1814   Napoléon abdicates and is banished to the island of Elba. The monarchy is reinstated, and Louis XVIII is named king.

1815   Napoléon returns from exile. The "Hundred Days" of his renewed reign ends when he is defeated at Waterloo. Louis XVIII returns to power.

1816   A marvelously gifted and precocious writer, Victor Hugo proclaims his ambition to rival François-René de Chateaubriand, the most famous Romantic author of his generation. Estranged from his father and influenced by his mother, a royalist by expediency, he skillfully curries favor with the conservative literary establishment and the King, whom he praises in odes.

1817   Hugo wins honorable mention in the national poetry contest sponsored by l'Académie française (the French Academy).

1818   Sophie and Léopold are legally separated (divorce was illegal in France between 1816 and 1886). Victor composes a first, brief version of his novel *Bug-Jargal*, an account of a slave revolt in the Caribbean after the French Revolution; this version will appear in 1820.

1819   Despite his mother's wishes for a more ambitious union, Victor falls in love with—and secretly asks the hand of—his neighbor, Adèle Foucher. But as a minor, he cannot marry her without his mother's consent, which is denied. The three Hugo brothers found a literary journal called *Le Conservateur littéraire*.

1820–   Hugo writes over one hundred essays and more than
1821   twenty poems for *Le Conservateur*.

1821   Victor becomes friends with the famous priest Félicité de Lamennais, who preaches a socially committed Christianity. Victor's mother dies on June 27. In July his father marries his mistress, Catherine Thomas. Victor becomes reconciled with his father, who does not oppose Victor's marriage to Adèle.

1822   Granted a small pension by Louis XVIII for his first volume of *Odes* praising the monarchy, Victor marries Adèle Foucher on October 12. Eugène Hugo, who also loves her, has a psychotic breakdown at the wedding; he will never recover.

1823   Hugo publishes a pioneering historical novel, *Han d'Islande* (*Han of Iceland*, sometimes translated as *The Demon Dwarf*), a bloodthirsty melodrama. He helps found the periodical *La Muse française* and attends weekly gatherings hosted by the then leader of the French Romantic movement, Charles Nodier (1780–1844).

1824   Hugo publishes the *Nouvelles Odes*. His first child, a daughter, Léopoldine, is born. Charles X assumes the throne, and Victor serves as the historian of the coronation.

1826   *Odes et Ballades* is published, as is the full version of *Bug-Jargal*, noteworthy for its altruistic black hero. Adèle gives birth to Hugo's second child, Charles-Victor.

1827   Hugo becomes best friends with the critic Sainte-Beuve. The play *Cromwell* is published; its famous preface proposes a Romantic aesthetic that contrasts the sublime with the grotesque, in emulation of Shakespeare. Hugo declares his independence from the conservative, divine-right royalists.

1828   General Léopold Hugo dies unexpectedly on January 29. Hugo's third child, François-Victor, is born.

1829   Hugo's prodigious literary output includes the picturesque verse collection *Les Orientales* (*The Orientals*), the tale *Le Dernier Jour d'un condamné à mort* (*The Last Day of a Condemned Man*), opposing capital punishment, and the historical play *Marion de Lorme*, censored by the French monarchy because it portrays the sixteenth-century ruler François I as a degenerate.

1830   Hugo's fourth child, a daughter, named Adèle after her mother, is born. Mme. Hugo wants no more children, and from then on sleeps alone. Sainte-Beuve betrays his best friend, Victor, by telling Adèle he loves her. Hugo's play *Hernani* (which served as the basis for the libretto to Italian composer Giuseppe Verdi's 1844 opera *Ernani*), defiantly Romantic in its use of informal language and its violation of the classical "three unities" of time, place, and action, causes riots in the theater where it is performed.

1831   *Notre-Dame de Paris: 1482* (*The Hunchback of Notre Dame*), a tale of the era of the cruel, crafty Louis XI, is published and becomes a best-seller. The visionary poetry collection *Les Feuilles d'automne* (*The Leaves of Autumn*) is published. In it Hugo displays a profundity and a mastery of the art of verse that rival the greatest European poets of the era, Johann Wolfgang von Goethe and Percy Bysshe Shelley.

1832   Hugo's play *Le Roi s'amuse* (*The King's Fool*), which will inspire Giuseppi Verdi's great opera *Rigoletto* (1851), is banned after opening night owing to its disrespectful portrayal of a king. Hugo occupies an apartment in what is today called la place des Vosges, where he will remain until 1848.

1833   The minor actress Juliette Drouet enters Hugo's life. He provides her with an apartment near him, forbids her to go out alone, and occupies her with making fair copies of his manuscripts. The couple will continue their liaison until her death fifty years later. The first version of George Sand's feminist novel *Lelia* is published.

1834   Hugo ends his friendship with Sainte-Beuve.

1835   Hugo's great verse collection *Les Chants du crépuscule* (*Songs of Twilight*) appears.

1837   Hugo is made an officer of the Légion d'honneur (Legion of Honor). *Les Voix intérieures*, the third of four collections of visionary poetry during Hugo's middle lyric period (1831–1840), appears. Victor's brother Eugène, confined in the Charenton madhouse, dies.

1838   *Ruy Blas*, Hugo's best play, outrages the monarchists by depicting a queen and a valet in love.

1840   *Les Rayons et les Ombres* (*Sunlight and Shadows*), the last great poetic collection before Hugo's exile, is published.

1841   After several failed attempts, Hugo is elected to the French Academy, the body of "Forty Immortals"—the greatest honor a French writer can receive.

1843   A tragic year is punctuated by the failure of Hugo's play *Les Burgraves* and the drowning of his beloved elder daughter, Léopoldine, her unborn child, and her husband, a strong swimmer who tried to save her after a boating accident. Hugo will dedicate his poetic masterpiece, *Les Contemplations*, to her.

1844   Alexandre Dumas's *Le Comte de Monte Cristo* (*The Count of Monte Cristo*) appears.

1845   Hugo is made a *pair de France*, an appointive position in a body roughly equivalent to the British House of Lords. Ten weeks later, his affair with Mme. Léonie Biard (from 1844 to 1851) comes to light when they are arrested in their love nest and charged with adultery. She goes to prison. Hugo's rank saves him from prosecution.

1847   Honoré de Balzac publishes *La Cousine Bette*.

1848   The monarchy is overthrown and the Second Republic proclaimed. Hugo is elected to its Constitutional Assembly, with the support of the conservatives. With his son Charles he founds and edits *L'Événement*, a liberal paper that unwisely campaigns to have Louis-Napoléon Bonaparte, the nephew of the former Emperor, elected president.

1849   Hugo presides over the International Peace Conference in Paris and delivers the first public speech that proposes the creation of a United States of Europe. Eugène Delacroix paints the ceiling of the Louvre's Salon d'Apollon.

1849–   Hugo increasingly criticizes the government's poli-
1851   cies, making fiery speeches on poverty, liberty, and

the church. His positions provoke the ire of the government.

1851   The government briefly imprisons Hugo's two sons in June for having published disloyal articles in *L'Événement*. Soon after Louis-Napoléon's coup d'état (actually, a legal election that creates the Second Empire) in early December, Hugo learns that the imperial police have issued a warrant for his arrest. He flees with his family and mistress to Belgium and then to the Isle of Jersey, a British possession in the English Channel.

1852–   In 1852 Louis-Napoléon declares himself emperor as
1853   Napoléon I. Hugo writes a scathing satire, *Napoléon le petit*. From 1853 to 1855 he attends séances at which the spirits of both the living and the dead (including Shakespeare, Jesus, and a cowering Napoléon I) seem to communicate by tapping on the table. They explain that all living beings must expiate their sins through a cycle of punitive reincarnations, but that all, even Satan, will finally be pardoned and merge with the Godhead. These ideas figure prominently in Hugo's visionary poetry for the remainder of his life. Georges Haussmann (1809–1891) begins the urban renewal of Paris.

1853   Hugo publishes *Les Châtiments* (*The Punishments*), powerful anti-Napoleonic satire.

1855   Hugo moves to the Channel island of Guernsey.

1856   Hugo's *Les Contemplations*, his poetic masterpiece, appears. Profits from its sales allow him to purchase Hauteville House on Guernsey, today a museum.

1857   Gustave Flaubert's novel of adultery, *Madame Bovary*—the work most influential on Western novelists until after World War II—is published in book form, as is the first edition of Charles Baudelaire's poetry, *Les Fleurs du mal* (*The Flowers of Evil*). Both men and their publishers are placed on trial for offenses to public morals. Baudelaire's publisher is fined and must remove seven poems treating lesbianism and sadism.

1859   The first volume of Hugo's poetic history of the world, *La Légende des siècles* (*The Legend of the Centuries*), appears.

1861   The danger of arrest having subsided, Hugo's wife, Adèle, and her sons begin leaving him to stay in Paris during the winter months. She secretly meets with Sainte-Beuve there.

1862   *Les Misérables*, a 1,200-page epic completed in fourteen months, is published on the heels of a fertile period during which Hugo wrote many political speeches and creative works. Hugo's famous novel gains an enormous popular audience, although the book is panned by critics and banned by the government. He begins hosting a weekly banquet for fifty poor children.

1866   Guernsey provides the setting for Hugo's regional novel *Les Travailleurs de la mer* (*The Toilers of the Sea*). Edgar Degas commences his series of ballet paintings. Works of Cézanne, Renoir, Monet, and other Impressionists appear. The next year Émile Zola's novel *Thérèse Raquin* is published.

1868   Hugo's wife, Adèle, dies unexpectedly in Brussels. She had been living apart from Victor for several years, but the two had remained friends.

1869   Hugo publishes the historical novel *L'Homme qui rit* (*The Man Who Laughs*). He declines a second offer of amnesty from Napoléon III. Sainte-Beuve dies.

1870   Defeated by the Prussians at Sedan, Napoléon III surrenders to them and is deposed. France's Third Republic is proclaimed. Hugo returns to Paris in triumph after nineteen years in exile.

1871   Hugo is elected to the National Assembly, but resigns due to the opposition of right-wing members. His son Charles dies.

1872   Consumed by madness, Hugo's daughter Adèle is in-

stitutionalized until her death, in 1915. Jules Verne's
Le Tour du Monde en quatre-vingts jours (*Around the
World in Eighty Days*) is published.

1873   Hugo's younger son, François-Victor, dies. French
Symbolist poet Arthur Rimbaud publishes *Un Saison
en enfer* (*A Season in Hell*).

1874   Hugo publishes *Quatrevingt-treize* (*Ninety-three*), a
historical novel about the counter-revolutionary rebellion in la Vendée (in eastern France) and events
leading to the Reign of Terror in 1793. He provides
nuanced portraits of both sides.

1876   Hugo is elected to the Senate.

1877   As senator, Hugo plays a leading role in preventing
Marshal Marie Edmé Patrice de MacMahon, president of the Third Republic from 1873 to 1879, from
becoming dictator of France. Because the monarchists have split their support among various
claimants to the throne, the republicans achieve a
working majority. The second volume of Hugo's poetic history of the world, *La Légende des siècles*,
appears.

1878   A stroke leaves Hugo incapable of composing additional literary works.

1880   After years of efforts, Hugo arranges amnesty for the
Communards, popular-front rebels in the Paris of
1871 opposed to surrender to the Prussians. Some
20,000 of them, including women and children, had
been slaughtered by French government troops—
more than the total of those guillotined during the
Reign of Terror in 1793. Guy de Maupassant's collected *Contes* (*Stories*) are published.

1881   On February 26, Hugo's birthday, a national holiday
is proclaimed, and 600,000 marchers pass his windows. The street where he lives is renamed L'avenue
Victor-Hugo.

1882   Hugo is reelected to the Senate. His play *Torquemada*
(1869) is performed.

1883 Juliette Drouet, Hugo's mistress since 1833, dies after a prolonged struggle with cancer. The final volume of Hugo's poetic history of the world, *La Légende des siècles*, appears.

1885 Victor Hugo dies May 22. Two million mourners pass his coffin underneath the Arc de Triomphe. Hugo is entombed in the Panthéon, the first of a series of culture heroes and great leaders to be placed there. June 1 is declared a day of national mourning. Posthumous publications will enhance his reputation for decades—notably, the verse collections *La Fin de Satan* (*The End of Satan*, 1886), *Toute la lyre* (1888, 1893), and *Dieu* (1891). His experimental plays, eventually published in a Pléïade edition as "Le Théâtre en liberté," brilliantly anticipate the Theater of the Absurd in the 1950s.

1902 On the centenary of his birth, the French government opens the Maison de Victor Hugo museum in the apartment where he once lived on the place des Vosges.

1912– In collaboration with André Antoine, the director of
1918 the naturalistic Théatre-Libre, the filmmaker Albert Capellani, with the Pathé firm, produces a series of movies based on Hugo's works: *Les Misérables* (1912), *Marie Tudor* (1912), *Quatrevingt-treize* (1914), and *Les Travailleurs de la mer* (1918).

1923 Wallace Worsley's silent film version of *The Hunchback of Notre Dame* appears, starring Lon Chaney as Quasimodo.

1926 The Buddhist sect Cao Dai originates in Vietnam. It now has about 2,000 temples and several million followers worldwide. The worshipers venerate Hugo and his two sons, whom they believe return to earth, reincarnated.

1939 William Dieterle's film version of *The Hunchback of Notre Dame*, with Charles Laughton as Quasimodo and Maureen O'Hara as Esmeralda, is released.

1975   François Truffaut's film *Adèle H.*, retelling the tragedy
       of Hugo's second daughter, wins Le Grand Prix du
       Cinéma Français.
1996   Walt Disney issues an animated, freely altered film
       version of *The Hunchback of Notre Dame*, distinctive
       in its politically correct treatment of gypsies, women,
       and persons with disabilities.

INTRODUCTION

With the Eiffel Tower and the Arc de Triomphe, the cathedral of Notre Dame figures among the most visited monuments of Paris. Famous for its Gothic facade, great portals, rose window, and looming towers, the cathedral—built principally in the twelfth century—is one of the most enduring symbols of the French capital and its medieval heritage. Aiding in the transmission of the cathedral's symbolic importance is the novel it inspired: Victor Hugo's 1831 *Notre-Dame de Paris: 1482*, better known in English as *The Hunchback of Notre Dame*. In it, Hugo brings to life the cathedral of Notre Dame as it existed at the end of the fifteenth century. Many critics and readers have seen the great church as the novel's true hero, as it takes an active role in the narrative and resides at the core of the ideological message Hugo seeks to project on collective and individual destiny, the passage of time, and the nature of progress. Indeed, Hugo's novel is perhaps as well known today as the cathedral itself and is, alongside its main characters—Claude Frollo, the fiery priest; Quasimodo, the hideously deformed bell ringer; Phoebus, the golden guardsman; and Esmeralda, the beautiful gypsy girl—firmly implanted in cultural consciousness. From the written page to the stage and screen, the tale has been told and retold countless times, its impact and capacity for reinvention rivaled only by that of another of Hugo's novels, the ever-popular *Les Misérables* (1862). If the flurry of recent reprintings and adaptations—including two Disney films and a new musical version—are any indication, generations to come will continue to be enthralled by Hugo's story of love rendered impossible.

Yet did Hugo set out to immortalize Notre Dame? As much myth surrounds the origin and writing of the novel as surrounds the cathedral itself. If the publicly presented version is to be believed, *The Hunchback of Notre Dame* was written from July 1830 to January 1831. This account is furnished in *Victor Hugo raconté par un témoin de sa vie* (*Victor Hugo: A Life Related by One Who Has Witnessed It*, 1863; henceforth cited as *A Life Related*), a testimonial written by Hugo's wife, Adèle, with, as it often has been observed, more than a helping hand from her husband. The novel had been under contract with the publisher Gosselin since 1828, but the theatrical success of Hugo's play *Hernani* (1830) distracted the writer from the project. In April 1830 Hugo still had not begun the novel and was threatened by Gosselin with financial sanctions if he failed to deliver the manuscript. A new deadline of December 1830 was agreed upon but was then jeopardized by the political and social upheaval of July 1830, during which the restored Bourbon monarchy was toppled and Louis-Philippe, duke of Orleans, ascended the throne. Consumed by these events and their impact, and additionally troubled by a book of notes that had "disappeared" during his family's move to a new apartment, Hugo, who had only begun to compose his novel, lost weeks of writing time. Gosselin grudgingly agreed to another extension, pushing back the due date to February 1, 1831. It was at this point, according to Adèle's explanation, that her husband entered into his novel as into "a prison," stopping only to eat and sleep. In one of the most famous anecdotes of *A Life Related*, she recounts how Hugo, upon returning to writing *The Hunchback*, bought a new bottle of ink. He plunged himself into his work, using this bottle alone, which ran out only on the day he completed the manuscript—January 14, 1831—at the precise moment he marked the novel's final word on the page. As the story goes, Hugo, reflecting on this "remarkable" coincidence, considered renaming his novel "Ce qu'il y a dans une bouteille d'encre" (What Is Inside a Bottle of Ink).

This tale of the writing process, and particularly the prodigious circumstances surrounding the novel's completion, cannot, however, be taken at face value. Even in the early years of his career, Hugo was a master shaper of his own image and rarely failed to seize the opportunity to market himself, to spin reality into legend. The truth behind the composition of *The Hunchback* is in all likelihood more complex, and is certainly less of a good story. What is clear is that Hugo had a difficult time beginning the novel. Gosselin's threats were genuine: Hugo had engaged in a contract with the publisher and had received a sizable advance, yet in spite of the rather extensive research he undertook, the manuscript did not materialize. What is also clear is that his recent triumph in the theater kept his attention elsewhere: Not only was *Hernani* an overwhelming success, but by 1830 Hugo was widely considered the leader of the growing Romantic movement in France. The preface he wrote to his 1827 historical play *Cromwell* was nothing short of a manifesto that boldly sought to redefine the aesthetics of French theater; it raised the Romantic flag against the constraining tenets of classical drama. *Hernani*, with its revolutionary use of poetic language and mixture of dramatic modes, put this new vision to the test, and the spectacular polemic that swirled around the play brought Hugo, despite past failures such as *Amy Robsart* (1828), to the forefront of the theater scene. In addition, poetry (the genre in which Hugo had first distinguished himself by winning, at age seventeen, a prestigious award for his ode on the re-erection of a statue of Henri IV, and which put bread on his table with one of the last royal pensions in the 1820s) continued to occupy him, as did the literary criticism in which he increasingly engaged.

What is less evident in Adèle's account of *The Hunchback*'s composition are the events of Hugo's personal life, which undoubtedly had an effect on his concentration—be they salutary, such as the birth of the couple's second daughter, Adèle, in late July 1830, or troubling, such as problems in the Hugo marriage that stemmed from his wife's nascent affair with Hugo's close friend, the poet and literary critic Charles-Augustin Sainte-Beuve. Equally unaddressed—or at the very least underaddressed—is a certain hesitancy on Hugo's part regarding the genre of the novel. Although writing *The Hunchback* was appealing in that it would bring money to the growing family's coffer, Hugo was keenly aware that the novel was generally considered a frivolous literary form. Even as it was already showing by its suppleness to be the genre perhaps best suited to reflect the concerns of the new society born of the French Revolution, and in spite of efforts in the form undertaken in the first decades of the nineteenth century by respected writers such as Benjamin Constant, François-René de Chateaubriand, and Madame de Staël, the novel was nonetheless still perceived in the 1820s as a minor genre and lagged in importance far behind poetry and theater, which were both steeped in classical tradition and prestige.

Prior to *The Hunchback of Notre Dame* Hugo had already written and published three novels—*Han d'Islande* (*Han of Iceland*, 1823), *Bug-Jargal* (1826), and *Le Dernier Jour d'un condamné à mort* (*The Last Day of a Condemned Man*, 1829). Yet each of these examples was more a response to personal or growing social preoccupations than an effort to practice or elevate the genre: *Han of Iceland*, a Gothic tale of thwarted young lovers, plays out Hugo's own love story with Adèle (he once said that she was the only person who was meant to understand it). *Bug-Jargal*, which centers on an episode from the then recent past—a violent 1791 slave revolt in Santo Domingo (present-day Haiti)—had its origins in a school bet in which Hugo was challenged to compose a novel in a period of two weeks. *The Last Day of a Condemned Man*, a first-person narrative that follows a man through prison to the guillotine, was a polemically charged effort to bring awareness to the horrors of the death penalty. Hugo's first novelistic endeavors can be understood as rather isolated attempts to give voice to private or socially oriented concerns. One unifying influence on Hugo's early novel writing is, however, indisputable—that of the Scottish novelist Sir Walter Scott, author of *Waverley* (1814), *Rob Roy* (1818), *Ivanhoe* (1819), and *Quentin Durward* (1823). Scott's mastery of the historical novel brought the genre quickly into vogue and helped, in the 1820s, to advance the merits of the novel as a literary form. Staunch and fervent admirers—among them Honoré de

Balzac, the future author of *La Comédie humaine* (*The Human Comedy*)—declared themselves, and French historical novels, such as Alfred de Vigny's *Cinq-Mars* (1826) and Prosper Mérimée's *Chronique du règne de Charles IX* (*Chronicle of the Reign of Charles the Ninth*, 1829), began to appear and garner attention. In the same way that nature inspired introspection and reflection in Romantic poetry, history served as the fertile terrain of the Romantic novel. Whether this renewed interest in French history was the result of reawakened national sentiment or sought to exalt and glorify the ideals of the distant past in an effort to soothe the still-open wounds of the Revolution, the historical backdrop and content lent legitimacy and weight to the form, and was the push the novel needed to propel it forward.

Both *Han of Iceland* and *Bug-Jargal* drew heavily on Scott's expansive vision and his techniques of novel writing, adopting in particular his trademark use of *couleur locale*—local color—to bring the depiction of the historical period alive through attention to the picturesque. The 1823 preface to *Han of Iceland* playfully points out the care that went into reproducing the atmosphere of the tale's exotic location, down to the near-abusive use of the letters k, y, h, and w in the characters' names. In *Bug-Jargal* the island of Santo Domingo is also replete with an exoticism produced by vivid details, from the extremes of the tropical landscape to the mysterious language (a mixture of Spanish and Creole) spoken by the rebelling slaves. In a review of Scott's *Quentin Durward* that appeared in the July 1823 issue of *La Muse française* (a periodical Hugo helped found), Hugo openly lauded Scott's epic and colorful conception of the novel, hailing him as the catalyst of a literary renaissance and praising him for his all-encompassing exploration of the past, for the truth behind his fiction, and for his ability to diffuse a didactic message artfully. Yet Hugo stops short of extolling Scott's achievements as the apogee of the form; instead he uses his approbation of Scott as a springboard to elaborate his own conception of the novel. Indeed, despite the critical failure of *Han of Iceland*,

Hugo was in no way deterred from introducing and promoting his idea(l) of a yet nonexistent form of the novel: "After the picturesque but prosaic novel of Walter Scott, there remains another novel to be created, more beautiful and still more complete. This novel is at once drama and epic, is picturesque but is also poetic, is real, yet also ideal, is true, but also grand—it will enshrine Walter Scott in Homer" (see, in "For Further Reading," Victor Hugo, *Oeuvres complètes*, vol. 5, p. 131; translation mine).

It is this "new" novel that Hugo undertook to create with *The Hunchback of Notre Dame*, incorporating as organizing principles many of the artistic conceptions already presented relative to theater in his preface to *Cromwell*, such as man's inherent duality, the coexistence of antitheses in the universe, the tension between cyclical and progressive notions of time and history, and the essential and prophetic role of the poet-author. Hugo was also aware that this new novel belonged to a new time—both in terms of the political climate following the regime change of 1830, in which the period and the purpose of the Restoration were redefined as a constitutional monarchy came to power; and in terms of the literary climate, as literature was shifting more and more from the patronage model to a business model in which commercial concerns and the emergence of a new and more literate middle-class reading public had, for the first time, an impact on writers and their craft. Hugo's exclusion of several chapters from the first edition of *The Hunchback* can be understood in this context. Although Hugo claims in the "Author's Note Added to the Definitive Edition" (1832) that these three chapters—"Unpopularity" (book 4, chapter 6), "*Abbas Beati Martini*" (book 5, chapter 1), and "The One Will Kill the Other" (book 5, chapter 2)—were "lost" prior to the printing of the first edition, the truth is more likely that Hugo purposefully held them back to ensure his novel's commercial success, fearing that the latter two, which are strong in ideological content but do not advance the narrative, might compromise the rhythm of the story. Added incentive for waiting to include these chapters was the realization that the contract with Gosselin specified royalties for only two volumes, and that Gosselin — firm in his stance and already exasperated with Hugo's delays — would pay no more if Hugo went beyond the agreed-upon length of the manuscript. Retaining them for inclusion in a later edition (with a different publisher once his deal with Gosselin expired) granted Hugo the possibility of maximizing his profit.

Although such reasoning and negotiations may seem commonplace in today's world, Hugo's business savvy helped him avoid the financial and artistic dependence on the new reading public that many of his contemporaries faced. Indeed, the novel proved its worth in the 1830s with a number of successes — among them Stendhal's *Le Rouge et le Noir* (*The Red and the Black*, 1830) and Balzac's *La Peau de chagrin* (*The Magic Skin*, 1831) — increasingly validating the capacities of the form. As realism gradually emerged as the aesthetic and literary movement that would transform the novel into the principal literary genre, and as the serial publication of novels in newspapers spurred on the industrialization of literature, the novelist of the nineteenth century — well known or not — had to live by his or (much less often) her pen, and with this reality often came practical and artistic constraints. In Hugo's case, however, his careful management of the publication and republication of not only *The Hunchback of Notre Dame* but also his theatrical works and poetry resulted in a financial independence that ultimately allowed him to avoid the same kinds of concerns about content and style; he could write what he wanted, when he wanted. With regard to his fiction, which subsequently included *Les Misérables* (1862), *Les Travailleurs de la mer* (*The Toilers of the Sea*, 1866), *L'Homme qui rit* (*The Man Who Laughs*, 1869), and *Quatrevingt-treize* (*Ninety-three*, 1874), this freedom gave Hugo the space he needed to continue pursuing the concept of the novel outlined in his review of *Quentin Durward*, one in which core, universal truths are transmitted through an expansive exploration of the human condition.

While the majority of French novelists of the nineteenth century who are still read and studied today—Stendhal, Balzac, Gustave Flaubert, Émile Zola—focused their gaze inward on the workings of contemporary society and the ways the political turmoil of their recent past affected their present and the social behavior that defined it, and while the most celebrated French historical novelists, such as Alexandre Dumas—author of *Les Trois Mousquetaires* (*The Three Musketeers*, 1844) and *Le Comte de Monte Cristo* (*The Count of Monte Cristo*, 1844)—looked to the distant past as a way of distracting from the uncertainties of the here and now, Hugo wrote during the course of his career a decidedly different kind of novel. Hugo's novel viewed history—from long-ago medieval France in *The Hunchback of Notre Dame*, to the more recent post-Revolutionary and Restoration France in *Les Misérables* and *The Toilers of the Sea*, to the seemingly immaterial history of seventeenth-century England in *The Man Who Laughs*, to the haunting history of Revolutionary France in *Ninety-three*—as neither an explanation for the present nor an escape from it, but rather as a catalyst for grappling with ideological and philosophical questions of the highest order relative to the passage of time itself and the nature of progress. Each of Hugo's novels tells and retells the same story of universal man and his struggles; in this larger context we can understand Hugo's surprising assertion, in an 1868 letter, that although he considered the historical novel a very good genre because Walter Scott had distinguished himself with it, he had "never written . . . a historical novel" (*Oeuvres complètes*, vol. 14, p. 1,254; translation mine). If, strictly speaking and by modern definition, this declaration rings false, since all of Hugo's novels do meet the criteria to qualify as "historical," it is more significant that this disavowal—which was made while Hugo was in self-imposed exile in protest of the unfolding history of the Second Empire and its emperor, Napoléon III—underscores the complex understanding of and relationship to history that characterizes all of Hugo's work.

In *The Hunchback of Notre Dame*, Hugo's first real attempt to tell this universal story, this complexity finds its ideal expression in the symbol of the cathedral. Firmly planted in the historical moment of the crepuscule of the Middle Ages—the year 1482, as the subtitle to the French edition clearly specifies—the novel showcases one of the medieval period's great architectural achievements, the cathedral of Notre Dame, which is literally and figuratively at the center of all action (no wonder, then, that Hugo condemned the English translation of the title for shifting the focus from the cathedral to its bell ringer). This choice was undoubtedly affected by the zeal of the Romantic age for all things medieval. Ever since Chateaubriand's *Génie du Christianisme* (*The Genius of Christianity*, 1802), in which Chateaubriand sought to rehabilitate Gothic art and architecture as well as the Christian faith, there had been a renewed and even frenzied interest in this underappreciated period of history. Hugo himself had jumped enthusiastically on the bandwagon with an 1825 article titled "Sur la destruction des monuments en France" (see endnote 28), in which he calls for an end to the demolition and mutilation of the monuments of the Middle Ages, pieces of a collective past in which history was inscribed. This idea of the monument as living history is developed and magnified in *The Hunchback of Notre Dame*, as the cathedral serves as the transitional marker both in art, between Roman and Gothic architecture, and in history, between the periods of the Middle Ages and the Renaissance. Yet this role of the monument as witness bearer, as "carved" history, is destined to be supplanted by the advent of a different kind of record, the printed page.

In "The One Will Kill the Other," one of the three chapters Hugo reintegrated into the definitive edition of the novel, the narrator seeks to elucidate the enigmatic words spoken by the Faustian priest Claude Frollo, who, during a mysterious visit from King Louis XI, makes, while looking alternately at an open book and the great cathedral, the melancholy assertion that "the book will kill the building" (p. 183). Frollo and the narrator, however, view the relationship between architecture and the written word in quite opposite ways. While Frollo, a high-ranking representative of the Church, laments the invention of the printing press in predicting that it will reduce the Church's theocratic stronghold, the narrator sees the printing press positively as a democratic invention that will serve to enlighten the masses. Implicit in this notion of inevitable enlightenment are the political dimensions of the more accessible printed word, a form of progress that will propel the masses out of the darkness and tyranny of the Middle Ages. The novel, in which the fictional trajectories and events are shadowed by the major political events of the year 1482—the final full year of the reign of the dying Louis XI—depicts in this way a world on the cusp of change. Using a technique opposite to that employed by most writers of the historical novel, in which the author strives to render time timeless, to transport the reader in a way that makes him unaware of the temporal abyss, Hugo, through his narrator, a man of 1830, repeatedly draws attention to the differences between these two eras, to the great divide between "then" and "now."

It is the representation of the masses—the people, who are at the height of their religious, judicial, social, economic, and political oppression—that best incarnates the essence of this transitional moment. First seen during Gringoire's mystery play at the Palace of Justice, the assembled throng (indistinct in its motivations and distinct in its restlessness) has a decidedly moblike quality. This menacing aspect is heightened through the development of the Parisian underworld of "vagrants" (thieves, beggars, vagabonds) in the "Court of Miracles." The cruelty, superstition, and barbaric ways that govern medieval Paris are mirrored and magnified in this city within the city, presided over by its own ruffian leaders. This group is characterized by its dynamic aspects, by a constant state of motion, yet motion in no way signifies movement in a forward direction or, figuratively, evolution; on the contrary, this group is equally defined by its inherent confusion and blindness. Just as its chosen "Pope of Fools," Quasimodo, is only "partially made," the vagrants are without any kind of ideological shape: They are ruled entirely by instincts of base survival and by their own self-interest. At no moment in the novel is this central lack of a guiding ideology more evident than in the scene in which the vagrants storm the cathedral to "save" Esmeralda, as this noble effort quickly degenerates into a frenzied desire to rebel and to pillage the cathedral of its treasures, and results in a staggering loss of lives. At the very heart of the vagrants' defeat is a chaos rooted in the breakdown of any common linguistic understanding ("There was an awful howl, intermingled with all languages, all dialects, all accents" [p. 455]). Indeed, in an ironic twist that highlights their inability to communicate, the vagrants and Quasimodo work at cross purposes, each believing the other to be the enemy. The vagrants' capacity to bring about change is dormant, and those not killed in the assault on Notre Dame are quickly brought down by the king's men.

Yet this effort itself, the bold and subversive action of attacking a church—that is to say, the house of God and, by divine right, that of the king—can be seen as a clear indication of things to come. For while the king succeeds in quelling and even erasing all traces of the vagrants' failed uprising (the narrator specifies that "Kings like Louis XI are careful to wash the pavement quickly after a massacre" (p. 531), in the larger framework of history another, more significant uprising is referenced, and the potential of this group to bring about change is deferred to a future moment. As Master Jacques Coppenole announces directly to the king, who comfortably oversees the brief mutiny from his apartment above the newly constructed Bastille prison, "The people's hour has not yet come" (p. 484). This direct allusion to the year 1789—when the French Revolution erupted violently with the storming of that same prison—reminds us that the people will in time become a (political) force great enough to bring down the monarchy. The march of time alone, however, is not enough to ensure progress. Written during the Restoration, a period that sought to turn time backward in wiping out all traces of the Revolution, First Republic, and Napoleonic Empire, the novel is ripe with unease relative to the notion of advancement. Through the numerous narrative interventions that refer the reader to recent or "present" history—including the July Revolution of 1830 (during which Hugo was at work on the novel)—the dangers of blind temporal progress, of the unfolding of one regime into the next, are underscored. While much attention has been given to the shift in Hugo's political views over the course of his lifetime, from royalist to republican, and of his political engagement (witnessed, for example, by his nineteen-year exile in reaction to the regression of Napoléon III's regime), progress for Hugo is, above all, ideological. In this way, the memorable dates of 1789, 1793, 1815, and 1830 (and later 1848 and 1870) are all steps on the way to a future sublime moment in which progress would be realized, a moment in which he unfailingly believed but that had not yet come to fruition.

In this conception of history, the roles played by destiny and fate are of capital importance. As the novel's epigraph informs us, the book is based upon the word *anankè* (the French rendition of the Greek word for "fate"), which had been "carved" on a wall of one of the towers and was "discovered" by the author during a visit to the cathedral. The word, however, as Hugo signals, has since "vanished," scraped away into nothingness by time or human effort. The story is thus placed from its outset under fate's implication of destruction and death, which is further reinforced during the course of the novel by the recurrent image of an innocent fly caught in a spider's toxic web. Both individual and collective destiny hang under the iron, immutable weight of *anankè*, as witnessed by the characters' trajectories and the social and moral stagnancy that asphyxiates the world of the novel. As we come to learn, it is Claude Frollo, who is at once archdeacon and occult scientist, torn by the impossibility of a different situation ("Oh, to love a woman! to be a priest! [p. 351]), who has traced these letters, but their significance applies to all of the novel's principal characters, themselves trapped in a web of impossible existence. Frollo loves Esmeralda, who despises him; Quasimodo also loves Esmeralda, who is horrified by the hunchback; and, in turn, Esmeralda loves Phoebus, who, morally bankrupt, is incapable of love. Maternal love and fraternal love are no less spared in this novel of unfulfilled passion: The suffering Paquette is reunited with Esmeralda, her long-lost daughter, only to have the girl immediately ripped away and put to death for her "crimes"; and Jehan Frollo, Claude's adored brother, who rebuffs his sibling's affection, meets his death at Quasimodo's hand during the assault on the cathedral, as Frollo himself will when his "adopted" son holds him responsible for Esmeralda's death. The oppressive hand of fate operates, by the novel's close, a mass liquidation of characters—Dom Frollo, Esmeralda, Paquette, Jehan Frollo, and Quasimodo are all dead—while, in a contrast that underscores the irony of destiny, those of mediocre moral substance survive: Phoebus gets out unscathed and marries, as planned, Fleur-de-Lys de Gondelaurier; and Gringoire, perhaps the wisest of all in the area of self-preservation, finds companionship with a goat preferable to the perils of human contact.

To translate this vision of impossible love in an impossible world, Hugo creates a new kind of character to populate his new novel or, at the very least, a different kind of character than the one put in place by his contemporaries. Void of the psychological depth and unity of composition that was increasingly valorized over the course of the nineteenth century, Hugo's characters, drawn from an archetypal model, are pure symbol. From Esmeralda, who is defined by her sublime state of physical and moral purity, to Paquette, on whom the primal maternal qualities of instinctive love and protection are transposed, to Phoebus, who, as his name implies, is brilliant on the exterior but lacks any true substance, they are larger-than-life representations. The characters of Claude Frollo and Quasimodo are larger than life as well, but they are complicated by the presence of a central duality through which universal man's struggle is figured. In the case of Frollo, in whom the opposing forces of good and evil engage in a fierce and debil-

Introduction

itating combat as he struggles with his growing obsession with Esmeralda, this duality has no possibility for resolution or transcendence: Simultaneously attracted and repelled by the enchanting gypsy, Frollo is the spider *and* the fly, rigidly trapped in a tortured state between priest and demon. This internal turmoil manifests itself not only mentally, as Frollo loses all interest in his intellectual pursuits and in his much-loved brother, but physically, as Frollo passes during the course of the novel from human to beast to monster, as witnessed by his reaction to Esmeralda's hanging: "At the most awful moment a demoniac laugh—a laugh impossible to a mere man—broke from the livid lips of the priest" (p. 533). Just as occurs in the alchemy that Frollo investigates, he is literally transformed (changed from one form to another) by the novel's end, his body, as the narrator notes following Frollo's fall from the cathedral, found "without a trace of human shape" (p. 536).

In the case of Quasimodo, the central duality is that of the opposing poles of the sublime and the grotesque. From the beginning to the end of the novel, his physical incompleteness leaves him hopelessly suspended between the states of man and animal. Quasimodo is defined by his animal-like strength (proven in numerous scenes such as the early, failed abduction of Esmeralda and the assault on the cathedral) and by his animal-like mentality, which is at once a result of his incomplete intellectual faculties and a conditioned response to the (unkind) way he has been treated by those around him, save his "adopted" father, Claude Frollo, to whom he is completely devoted ("Quasimodo loved the archdeacon as no dog, no horse, no elephant, ever loved its master" [p. 162]). But unlike the archdeacon, who is rigidly locked into his dual(ing) nature, Quasimodo is transfigured by Esmeralda's simple gesture of kindness to him during his torture on the pillory. All the difference is there. Indeed, from that moment on, Quasimodo undergoes an awakening, during which his dormant soul comes alive and expands exponentially, as witnessed in the scene in which Quasimodo—proud and glorious—swoops down from the top of the cathedral to save

Esmeralda from being hanged: "For at that instant Quasimodo was truly beautiful. He was beautiful,—he, that orphan, that foundling, that outcast; he felt himself to be august and strong; he confronted that society from which he was banished . . . he,—the lowliest of creatures, with the strength of God" (pp. 375–376). Quasimodo's devotion to Esmeralda supplants the cherished role previously held for Frollo, and he subsequently does everything in his power to ensure her safety and happiness. In attempting to repair her relationship with Phoebus, in warding off Frollo's unwanted visits, and in endeavoring to save Esmeralda from the "attackers," in whom he mistakenly perceives a threat to her safety, Quasimodo risks everything in Esmeralda's name.

Yet in the end this transfiguration, this conversion from grotesque to sublime—unobserved by Esmeralda, so caught up is she in Phoebus's aura of false brilliance—is of a profoundly personal nature and passes virtually unnoticed. It is the reader who is charged with recognizing its final expression in the account given in the novel's last chapter of two anonymous skeletons found sometime later in the vault at Montfaucon, locked in an embrace. Without naming them, the description leaves no doubt that one is Esmeralda (identifiable by the remnants of her white gown and the empty bag that once contained her childhood shoe) and the other is Quasimodo (identifiable by the remains of his hideously deformed body), who disappeared from the cathedral the day of Esmeralda's death. More remarkable than the embrace, however, is that the male skeleton's neck is intact, leading to the irrefutable conclusion that he came to the cave not already dead, but to die. The self-imposed nature of Quasimodo's death thus implies that the completion of this conversion must necessarily occur outside the boundaries of the social and historical world of the novel. For the only place where his opposing poles can be truly reconciled is in the cosmic whole; it is in leaving his shell of a body behind (it significantly crumbles into dust when separated from that of Esmeralda) that this awakened soul can take flight.

This message that redemption and salvation are possible, but never in the world as it exists *now*, is the thread that binds all of Hugo's novels together like a quilt whose squares, when viewed carefully, each reveal the same intricate pattern. Everything that is in *The Hunchback of Notre Dame* will be retraced, retold, reinvented in Hugo's four subsequent novels. Quasimodo's dilemma, his struggle between two opposing poles, will become that of Jean Valjean in *Les Misérables*, that of Gilliatt in *The Toilers of the Sea*, that of Gwynplaine—another "monster" horrific on the outside and pure within—in *The Man Who Laughs*, and that of Gauvain in *Ninety-three*. Only through their deaths and a corresponding cosmic expansion or rebirth are Hugo's fictional heroes able to find acceptance, transcendence, reconciliation of their internal oppositions, and affirmation of their individual moral potential. Time and again, the message of Hugo's "new" novel is that historical existence as depicted, with its blindness, failures, and shortcomings, is incompatible with, or at the very least less significant than, the realization of this personal and often private promise.

In spite of Hugo's lingering hesitancy surrounding the genre—a thirty-year period of novelistic silence separates the wildly successful *Hunchback of Notre Dame* from *Les Misérables*—it is without a doubt the form best suited to the scope and breadth of his all-encompassing vision, one that, to his own mind, was not at all fatalistic. On the contrary, Hugo preferred to view his novels as a "series of affirmations of the soul" (*Oeuvres complètes*, vol. 14, p. 387; translation mine). While contemporary readers and critics did not always agree—citing *The Hunchback of Notre Dame* as particularly ambiguous in its meaning—Hugo's profound and overwhelming belief in both individual and collective man's potential for progress is perhaps more evident to us today. Indeed, while the inadequacies of each past society that he examines and of the present in which he wrote pervade Hugo's fiction, his presentation of core, universal truths relative to the human condition show an unwavering faith in the future, in our future, to which his aspirations for the historical and social worlds are deferred.

This continued relevance of Hugo's vision to our world finds its confirmation in the amazing capacity for reinvention that his fiction has shown, in a resilience that has granted it a life and mythology all its own in popular culture, particularly in the genres of film (Lon Chaney's and Charles Laughton's impressive interpretations of Quasimodo come immediately to mind) and theater, in which Hugo's unforgettable, larger-than-life characters have continued to mesmerize. While this in some ways implies that Hugo's prediction that the book will kill the monument has been surpassed, and that it is now the book's turn to be rivaled by and perhaps supplanted by other creative mediums, it is difficult to argue that Hugo would not be in favor of this evolution. During his own lifetime Hugo authorized, encouraged, and even participated in the adaptation of several of his works for the stage (including an 1836 opera based on *The Hunchback of Notre Dame*), reflecting a desire to give his timeless message the momentum it needed to ensure it an afterlife in fresh contexts and mediums. It is thus that, more than two hundred years after Hugo's birth, the vision he sought to project has, far beyond the boundaries of the novel, continued to leave its indelible mark on each new generation.

ISABEL ROCHE has a Ph.D. in French literature from New York University. Her dissertation explores the creation and role of character in the novels of Victor Hugo. Her research interests include Hugo, his fiction, and French Romanticism. She has published articles in *The French Review* and *French Forum*. Roche teaches at Bennington College in Vermont.

THE HUNCHBACK OF
NOTRE DAME

PREFACE

Some years ago, while visiting, or rather exploring, Notre-Dame, the author of this book discovered in an obscure corner of one of the towers this word, carved upon the wall:

'ANÁTKH*

These Greek characters, black with age and cut deep into the stone with the peculiarities of form and arrangement common to Gothic calligraphy that marked them the work of some hand in the Middle Ages, and above all the sad and mournful meaning which they expressed, forcibly impressed the author.

He questioned himself, he tried to divine what sad soul was loath to quit the earth without leaving behind this brand of crime or misery upon the brow of the old church.

Since then the wall has been whitewashed or scraped (I have forgotten which), and the inscription has vanished; for this is the way in which, for some two hundred years, we have treated the wonderful churches of the Middle Ages. They are mutilated in every part, inside as well as out. The priest whitewashes them, the archdeacon scrapes them; then come the people, who tear them down.

So, save for the frail memory which the author of this book here dedicates to it, nothing now remains of the mysterious word engraved upon the dark tower of Notre-Dame, nothing of the unknown fate which it summed up so sadly. The man who wrote that word upon the wall faded away, many ages since, amidst passing generations of men; the word in its turn has faded from the church wall; the church itself, perhaps, will soon vanish from the earth.

Upon that word this book is based.[1]

MARCH, 1831.

---

*Greek word that signifies "fate."

CONTENTS

Book I

I.	The Great Hall	1
II.	Pierre Gringoire	17
III.	The Cardinal	27
IV.	Master Jacques Coppenole	34
V.	Quasimodo	43
VI.	Esmeralda	51

Book II

I.	From Charybdis to Scylla	54
II.	The Place de Grève	57
III.	*Besos para Golpes*	59
IV.	The Inconveniences of Following a Pretty Woman in the Street at Night	70
V.	The Continuation of the Inconveniences	75
VI.	The Broken Pitcher	77
VII.	A Wedding Night	98

Book III

I.	Notre-Dame	108
II.	A Bird's-Eye View of Paris	117

Book IV

I.	Kind Souls	144
II.	Claude Frollo	148
III.	*Inmanis Pecoris Custos, Immanior Ipse*	153

IV.	The Dog and his Master	161
V.	More about Claude Frollo	162
VI.	Unpopularity	170

Book V

| I. | *Abbas Beati Martini* | 172 |
| II. | The One Will Kill the Other | 183 |

Book VI

I.	An Impartial Glance at the Ancient Magistracy	199
II.	The Rat-Hole	210
III.	The Story of a Wheaten Cake	215
IV.	A Tear for a Drop of Water	236
V.	End of the Story of the Cake	246

Book VII

I.	On the Danger of Confiding a Secret to a Goat	248
II.	Showing that a Priest and a Philosopher Are Two Very Different Persons	264
III.	The Bells	273
IV.	'ANÁTKH	276
V.	The Two Men Dressed in Black	291
VI.	The Effect Produced by Seven Oaths in the Public Square	297
VII.	The Spectre Monk	302
VIII.	The Advantage of Windows Overlooking the River	310

Book VIII

| I. | The Crown Piece Changed to a Dry Leaf | 320 |
| II. | Continuation of the Crown Piece Changed to a Dry Leaf | 330 |

III. End of the Crown Piece Changed to a Dry
Leaf   336
IV. *Lasciate Ogni Speranza*   339
V. The Mother   354
VI. Three Men's Hearts, Differently Constituted   359

Book IX

I. Delirium   377
II. Deformed, Blind, Lame   389
III. Deaf   393
IV. Earthenware and Crystal   396
V. The Key to the Porte-Rouge   407
VI. The Key to the Porte Rouge (*continued*)   409

Book X

I. Gringoire Has Several Capital Ideas in
Succession in the Rue des Bernardins   413
II. Turn Vagabond!   424
III. Joy Forever!   426
IV. An Awkward Friend   436
V. The Retreat Where Louis of France Says
His Prayers   456
VI. "The Chive in the Cly"   489
VII. Châteaupers to the Rescue   490

Book XI

I. The Little Shoe   493
II. *La Creatura Bella Bianco Vestita*   527
III. Marriage of Phœbus   536
IV. Marriage of Quasimodo   537

Author's Note Added to the Definitive Edition   540

BOOK I

CHAPTER I

The Great Hall

Three hundred and forty-eight years, six months, and nineteen days ago today the Parisians were awakened by the sound of loud peals from all the bells within the triple precincts of the City, the University, and the Town.

And yet the 6th of January, 1482, is not a day of which history takes much note. There was nothing extraordinary about the event which thus set all the bells and the citizens of Paris agog from early dawn. It was neither an attack from the Picards or the Burgundians, nor some shrine carried in procession, nor was it a student revolt in the vineyard of Laas, nor an entry of "our greatly to be dreaded Lord the King," nor even the execution of thieves of either sex at the Palace of Justice. Neither was it the arrival, so frequent during the fifteenth century, of some plumed and laced embassy. It was scarcely two days since the last cavalcade of this sort, that of the Flemish ambassadors empowered to arrange a marriage between the Dauphin* and Margaret of Flanders, had entered Paris, to the great annoyance of Cardinal Bourbon, who, to please the king, was forced to smile upon all this rustic rout of Flemish burgomasters, and to entertain them at his own mansion with "a very fine morality and

---

*The king's eldest son; used as a title from 1349 to 1830.

farce," while a driving rain-storm drenched the splendid tapestries at his door.

That which "stirred the emotions of the whole populace of Paris," as Jehan de Troyes expresses it, on January 6, was the double festival, celebrated from time immemorial, of Epiphany and the Feast of Fools.[2]

Upon that day there was to be a bonfire at the Place de Grève, a Maypole at the Braque chapel, and a mystery or miracle play at the Palace of Justice. All these things had been proclaimed in the streets, to the sound of trumpets, by the provost's men, in fine coats of purple camlet, with big white crosses on the breast.

A crowd of citizens with their wives and daughters had therefore been making their way from every quarter, towards the places named, ever since early dawn. Each had decided for himself, in favor of the bonfire, the Maypole, or the mystery. It must be confessed, to the glory of the proverbial good sense of Parisian idlers, that the majority of the crowd turned towards the bonfire, which was most seasonable, or towards the miracle play which was to be performed in the great hall of the Palace of Justice, well roofed in and between four walls; and that most of the pleasure-seekers agreed to leave the poor Maypole with its scanty blossoms to shiver alone beneath the January sky, in the cemetery of the Braque chapel.

The people swarmed most thickly in the avenues leading to the Palace, because it was known that the Flemish ambassadors who arrived two nights before proposed to be present at the performance of the miracle play and election of the Pope of Fools, which was also to take place in the great hall.

It was no easy matter to make a way into the great hall upon that day, although it was then held to be the largest enclosure under cover in the world (at that time, Sauval* had

---

*Reference to Henri Sauval, a seventeenth-century historian whose study *Histoire et recherches des antiquités de la ville de Paris* (*Antiquities of Paris*) Hugo draws upon frequently in the novel for descriptions of the period depicted.

not yet measured the great hall of the castle at Montargis).
The courtyard, filled with people, looked to the spectators
at the windows like a vast sea into which five or six streets,
like the mouths of so many rivers, constantly disgorged new
waves of heads. The billowing crowd, growing ever greater,
dashed against houses projecting here and there like so many
promontories in the irregular basin of the courtyard. In
the middle of the lofty Gothic façade of the Palace was
the great staircase, up and down which flowed an unending
double stream, which, after breaking upon the intermediate
landing, spread in broad waves over its two side slopes; the
great staircase, I say, poured a steady stream into the courtyard, like a waterfall into a lake. Shouts, laughter, and the
tramp of countless feet made a great amount of noise and
a great hubbub. From time to time the hubbub and the
noise were redoubled; the current which bore this throng towards the great staircase was turned back, eddied, and
whirled. Some archer had dealt a blow, or the horse of some
provost's officer had administered a few kicks to restore
order,—an admirable tradition, which has been faithfully
handed down through the centuries to our present Parisian
police.

At doors, windows, in garrets, and on roofs swarmed thousands of good plain citizens, quiet, honest people, gazing at
the Palace, watching the throng, and asking nothing more; for
many people in Paris are quite content to look on at others,
and there are plenty who regard a wall behind which something is happening as a very curious thing.

If it could be permitted to us men of 1830 to mingle in
imagination with those fifteenth-century Parisians, and to
enter with them, pushed, jostled, and elbowed, into the vast
hall of the Palace of Justice, all too small on the 6th of January, 1482, the sight would not be without interest or charm,
and we should have about us only things so old as to seem
brand-new.

With the reader's consent we will endeavor to imagine the
impression he would have received with us in crossing the

threshold of that great hall amidst that mob in surcoats, cassocks, and coats of mail.

First of all there is a ringing in our ears, a dimness in our eyes. Above our heads, a double roof of pointed arches, wainscotted with carved wood, painted in azure, sprinkled with golden *fleur-de-lis*; beneath our feet, a pavement of black and white marble laid in alternate blocks. A few paces from us, a huge pillar, then another,—in all seven pillars down the length of the hall, supporting the spring of the double arch down the center. Around the first four columns are tradesmen's booths, glittering with glass and tinsel; around the last three, oaken benches worn and polished by the breeches of litigants and the gowns of attorneys. Around the hall, along the lofty wall, between the doors, between the casements, between the pillars, is an unending series of statues of all the kings of France, from Pharamond down,—the sluggard kings, with loosely hanging arms and downcast eyes; the brave and warlike kings, with head and hands boldly raised to heaven. Then in the long pointed windows, glass of a thousand hues; at the wide portals of the hall, rich doors finely carved; and the whole—arches, pillars, walls, cornices, wainscot, doors, and statues—covered from top to bottom with a gorgeous coloring of blue and gold, which, somewhat tarnished even at the date when we see it, had almost disappeared under dust and cobwebs in the year of grace 1549, when Du Breuil admired it from hearsay alone.

Now, let us imagine this vast oblong hall, lit up by the wan light of a January day, taken possession of by a noisy motley mob who drift along the walls and ebb and flow about the seven columns, and we may have some faint idea of the general effect of the picture, whose strange details we will try to describe somewhat more in detail.

It is certain that if Ravaillac had not assassinated Henry IV, there would have been no documents relating to his case deposited in the Record Office of the Palace of Justice; no accomplices interested in making off with the said documents, accordingly no incendiaries, forced for want of better means to burn the Record Office in order to burn up the documents, and to burn the Palace of Justice in order to burn the Record Office; consequently, therefore, no fire in 1618. The old Palace would still be standing, with its great hall; I might be able to say to my reader, "Go and look at it," and we should thus both of us be spared the need,—I of writing, and he of reading, an indifferent description; which proves this novel truth,—that great events have incalculable results.

True, Ravaillac may very possibly have had no accomplices; or his accomplices, if he chanced to have any, need have had no hand in the fire of 1618. There are two other very plausible explanations: first, the huge "star of fire, a foot broad and a foot and a half high," which fell, as every one knows, from heaven upon the Palace after midnight on the 7th of March; second, Théophile's verses:—*

> "In Paris sure it was a sorry game
> When, fed too fat with fees, the frisky Dame
> Justice set all her palace in a flame."

Whatever we may think of this triple explanation,—political, physical, and poetical,—of the burning of the Palace of Justice in 1618, one unfortunate fact remains: namely, the fire. Very little is now left, thanks to this catastrophe, and thanks particularly to the various and successive restorations which have finished what it spared,—very little is now left of this first home of the King of France, of this palace, older than the Louvre, so old even in the time of Philip the Fair that in it they sought for traces of the magnificent buildings erected by King Robert and described by Helgaldus. Almost everything is gone. What has become of the chancery office, Saint Louis' bridal chamber? What of the garden where he administered justice, "clad in a camlet coat, a sleeveless surcoat of

---

*Reference to Théophile de Viau (1590–1626), poet who was imprisoned with Ravaillac.

linsey-woolsey, and over it a mantle of black serge, reclining upon carpets, with Joinville?" Where is the chamber of the Emperor Sigismond, that of Charles IV, and that of John Lackland? Where is the staircase from which Charles VI issued his edict of amnesty; the flag-stone upon which Marcel, in the dauphin's presence, strangled Robert of Clermont and the Marshal of Champagne? The wicket-gate where the bulls of Benedict the antipope were destroyed, and through which departed those who brought them, coped and mitred in mockery, thus doing public penance throughout Paris? And the great hall, with its gilding, its azure, its pointed arches, its statues, its columns, its great vaulted roof thickly covered with carvings, and the golden room, and the stone lion, which stood at the door, his head down, his tail between his legs, like the lions around Solomon's throne, in the humble attitude that befits strength in the presence of justice, and the beautiful doors, and the gorgeous windows, and the wrought-iron work which discouraged Biscornette, and Du Hancy's dainty bits of carving? What has time done, what have men done with these marvels? What has been given to us in exchange for all this,—for all this ancient French history, all this Gothic art? The heavy elliptic arches of M. de Brosse, the clumsy architect of the St. Gervais portal,—so much for art; and for history we have the gossipy memories of the big pillar still echoing and re-echoing with the gossip of the Patrus.

This is not much. Let us go back to the genuine great hall of the genuine old Palace.

The two ends of this huge parallelogram were occupied, the one by the famous marble table, so long, so broad, and so thick, that there never was seen, as the old Court Rolls express it in a style which would give Gargantua an appetite, "such another slice of marble in the world;" the other by the chapel in which Louis XI had his statue carved kneeling before the Virgin, and into which, wholly indifferent to the fact that he left two vacant spaces in the procession of royal images, he ordered the removal of the figures of Charlemagne and Saint Louis, believing these two saints to be in high favor with Heaven as being kings of France. This chapel, still quite new, having been built scarcely six years, was entirely in that charming school of refined and delicate architecture, of marvellous sculpture, of fine, deep chiselling, which marks the end of the Gothic era in France, and lasts until towards the middle of the sixteenth century in the fairy-like fancies of the Renaissance. The small rose-window over the door was an especial masterpiece of delicacy and grace; it seemed a mere star of lace.

In the center of the hall, opposite the great door, a daïs covered with gold brocade, placed against the wall, to which a private entrance was arranged by means of a window from the passage to the gold room, had been built for the Flemish envoys and other great personages invited to the performance of the mystery.

This mystery, according to custom, was to be performed upon the marble table. It had been prepared for this at dawn; the superb slab of marble, scratched and marked by lawyers' heels, now bore a high wooden cage-like scaffolding, whose upper surface, in sight of the entire hall, was to serve as stage, while the interior, hidden by tapestry hangings, was to take the place of dressing-room for the actors in the play. A ladder placed outside with frank simplicity formed the means of communication between the dressing-room and stage, and served the double office of entrance and exit. There was no character however unexpected, no sudden change, and no dramatic effect, but was compelled to climb this ladder. Innocent and venerable infancy of art and of machinery!

Four officers attached to the Palace, forced guardians of the people's pleasures on holidays as on hanging days, stood bolt upright at the four corners of the marble table.

The play was not to begin until the twelfth stroke of noon rang from the great Palace clock. This was doubtless very late for a theatrical performance; but the ambassadors had to be consulted in regard to the time.

Now, this throng had been waiting since dawn. Many of these honest sightseers were shivering at earliest daylight at the foot of the great Palace staircase. Some indeed declared that they had spent the night lying across the great door, to be sure of getting in first. The crowd increased every moment, and, like water rising above its level, began to creep up the walls, to collect around the columns, to overflow the entablatures, the cornices, the window-sills, every projection of the architecture, and every bit of bold relief in the carvings. Then, too, discomfort, impatience, fatigue, the day's license of satire and folly, the quarrels caused incessantly by a sharp elbow or a hobnailed shoe, the weariness of waiting gave, long before the hour when the ambassadors were due, an acid, bitter tone to the voices of these people, shut up, pent in, crowded, squeezed, and stifled as they were. On every hand were heard curses and complaints against the Flemish, the mayor of Paris, Cardinal Bourbon, the Palace bailiff, Madame Margaret of Austria, the ushers, the cold, the heat, the bad weather, the Pope of Fools, the columns, the statues, this closed door, that open window,—all to the vast amusement of the groups of students and lackeys scattered through the crowd, who mingled their mischief and their malice with all this discontent, and administered, as it were, pin-pricks to the general bad humor.

Among the rest there was one group of these merry demons who, having broken the glass from a window, had boldly seated themselves astride the sill, distributing their glances and their jokes by turns, within and without, between the crowd in the hall and the crowd in the courtyard. From their mocking gestures, their noisy laughter, and the scoffs and banter which they exchanged with their comrades, from one end of the hall to the other, it was easy to guess that these young students felt none of the weariness and fatigue of the rest of the spectators, and that they were amply able, for their own private amusement, to extract from what they had before their eyes a spectacle quite diverting enough to make them wait patiently for that which was to come.

"By my soul, it's you, Joannes Frollo de Molendino!" cried one of them to a light-haired little devil with a handsome but mischievous countenance, who was clinging to the acanthus leaves of a capital; you are well named, Jehan du Moulin (of the mill), for your two arms and your two legs look like the four sails fluttering in the wind. How long have you been here?"

"By the foul fiend!" replied Joannes Frollo, "more than four hours, and I certainly hope that they may be deducted from my time in purgatory. I heard the King of Sicily's eight choristers intone the first verse of high mass at seven o'clock in the Holy Chapel."

"Fine choristers they are!" returned the other; "their voices are sharper than the points of their caps. Before he endowed a Mass in honor of Saint John, the king might well have inquired whether Saint John liked his Latin sung with a southern twang."

"He only did it to give work to these confounded choristers of the King of Sicily!" bitterly exclaimed an old woman in the crowd beneath the window. "Just fancy! a thousand pounds Paris for a Mass! and charged to the taxes on all salt-water fish sold in the Paris markets too!"

"Silence, old woman!" said a grave and reverend personage who was holding his nose beside the fishwoman; "he had to endow a Mass. You don't want the king to fall ill again, do you?"

"Bravely spoken, Master Gilles Lecornu, master furrier of the king's robes!" cried the little scholar clinging to the capital.

"Lecornu! Gilles Lecornu!" said some.

"*Cornutus et hirsutus,*"* replied another.

"Oh, no doubt!" continued the little demon of the capital. "What is there to laugh at? An honorable man is Gilles Lecornu, brother of Master Jehan Lecornu, provost of the king's palace, son of Master Mahiet Lecornu, head porter of

---

*Horned and hairy (Latin).

the Forest of Vincennes,—all good citizens of Paris, every one of them married, from father to son!"

The mirth increased. The fat furrier, not answering a word, strove to escape the eyes fixed on him from every side, but he puffed and perspired in vain; like a wedge driven into wood, all his efforts only buried his broad apoplectic face, purple with rage and spite, the more firmly in the shoulders of his neighbors.

At last one of these neighbors, fat, short, and venerable as himself, came to his rescue.

"Abominable! Shall students talk thus to a citizen! In my day they would have been well whipped with the sticks which served to burn them afterwards."

The entire band burst out:—

"Oh! who sings that song? Who is this bird of ill omen?"

"Stay, I know him," said one; "it's Master Andry Musnier."

"He is one of the four copyists licensed by the University!" said another.

"Everything goes by fours in that shop," cried a third,— "four nations, four faculties, four great holidays, four proctors, four electors, four copyists."

"Very well, then," answered Jehan Frollo; "we must play the devil with them by fours."

"Musnier, we'll burn your books."

"Musnier, we'll beat your servant."

"Musnier, we'll hustle your wife."

"That good fat Mademoiselle Oudarde."

"Who is as fresh and as fair as if she were a widow."

"Devil take you!" growled Master Andry Musnier.

"Master Andry," added Jehan, still hanging on his capital, "shut up, or I'll fall on your head!"

Master Andry raised his eyes, seemed for a moment to be measuring the height of the column, the weight of the rascal, mentally multiplied that weight by the square of the velocity, and was silent.

Jehan, master of the field of battle, went on triumphantly:—

"I'd do it, though I am the brother of an arch-deacon!"

"Fine fellows, our University men are, not even to have insisted upon our rights on such a day as this! For, only think of it, there is a Maypole and a bonfire in the Town; a miracle play, the Pope of Fools, and Flemish ambassadors in the City; and at the University—nothing!"

"And yet Maubert Square is big enough!" answered one of the scholars established on the window-seat.

"Down with the rector, the electors, and the proctors!" shouted Joannes.

"We must build a bonfire tonight in the Gaillard Field," went on the other, "with Master Andry's books."

"And the desks of the scribes," said his neighbor.

"And the beadles' wands!"

"And the deans' spittoons!"

"And the proctors' cupboards!"

"And the electors' bread-bins!"

"And the rector's footstools!"

"Down with them!" went on little Jehan, mimicking a droning psalm-tune; "down with Master Andry, the beadles, and the scribes; down with theologians, doctors, and decretists; proctors, electors, and rector!"

"Is the world coming to an end?" muttered Master Andry, stopping his ears as he spoke.

"Speaking of the rector, there he goes through the square!" shouted one of those in the window.

Every one turned towards the square.

"Is it really our respectable rector, Master Thibaut?" asked Jehan Frollo du Moulin, who, clinging to one of the inner columns, could see nothing of what was going on outside.

"Yes, yes," replied the rest with one accord, "it is really he, Master Thibaut, the rector."

It was indeed the rector and all the dignitaries of the University going in procession to meet the ambassadors, and just at this moment crossing the Palace yard. The scholars, crowding in the window, greeted them, as they passed, with sarcasms and mock applause. The rector, who walked at the head of his company, received the first volley, which was severe:—

"Good-morning, Sir Rector! Hello there! Good-morning, I say!"

"How does he happen to be here, the old gambler? Has he forsaken his dice?"

"How he ambles along on his mule! The animal's ears are not as long as his own."

"Hello there! Good-day to you, Master Rector Thibaut! *Tybalde aleator!** old fool! old gambler!"

"God keep you! did you throw many double sixes last night?"

"Oh, look at his lead-colored old face, wrinkled and worn with love of cards and dice!"

"Whither away so fast, Thibaut, *Tybalde ad dados,*† turning your back on the University and trotting straight towards town?"

"He's probably going to look for a lodging in Tybaldice Street," shouted Jehan du Moulin.

The entire band repeated the silly joke in a shout like thunder, and with frantic clapping of hands.

"You're going to look for a lodging in Tybaldice Street, are you not, Sir Rector, you devil's advocate?"

Then came the turn of the other officials.

"Down with the beadles! down with the mace-bearers!"

"Say, you Robin Poussepain, who's that fellow yonder?"

"That's Gilbert de Suilly, *Gilbertus de Soliaco,* Chancellor of the College of Autun."

"Here's my shoe; you've got a better place than I; fling it in his face."

"*Saturnalitias mittimus ecce nuces.*"‡

"Down with the six theologians in the white surplices!"

---

*Thibaut the gamester (Latin).

†Thibaut of the dice (Latin).

‡Here are the Saturnalian nuts that we send thee (Latin).

"Are those theologians? I thought they were six white geese given to the city by Saint Geneviève for the fief of Roogny."

"Down with the doctors!"

"Down with all the pompous and jocose disputations."

"Take my cap, Chancellor of St. Geneviève! You did me an injustice,—and that's the truth; he gave my place in the nation of Normandy to little Ascanio Falzaspada, who belongs to the province of Bourges, being an Italian."

"Rank injustice," exclaimed all the students. "Down with the Chancellor of St. Geneviève."

"Ho there, Master Joachim de Ladehors! Ho there, Louis Dahuille! Hollo, Lambert Hoctement!"

"May the devil smother the proctor of the German nation!"

"And the chaplains of the Holy Chapel, with their grey amices, *cum tunicis grisis!*"

"Seu de pellibus grisis fourratis!" *

"Ho there! you Masters of Arts! See all the fine black copes! See all the fine red copes!"

"That makes a fine tail for the rector!"

"You would think it was a Venetian doge on his way to wed the sea."

"I say, Jehan! look at the Canons of St. Geneviève!"

"To the devil with all Canons!"

"Abbot Claude Choart! Doctor Claude Choart! Are you looking for Marie la Giffarde?"

"She lives in Glatigny Street."

"She's bedmaker to the king of scamps."

"She's paying her four farthings, *quatuor denarios.*"

"Aut unum bombum." †

"Would you like her to pay you in the nose?"

"Comrades! there goes Master Simon Sanguin the Elector from Picardy, with his wife behind him!"

---

*Lined with gray fur (Latin).

†Four farthings—or a fart (Latin).

*"Post equitem sedet atra cura."**

"Cheer up, Master Simon!"

"Good-day to you, Sir Elector!"

"Good-night to you, Madame Electress!"

"How lucky they are to see so much!" sighed Joannes de Molendino, still perched among the foliage of his column.

Meanwhile, the licensed copyist to the University, Master Andry Musnier, leaned towards the ear of the furrier of the king's robes, Master Gilles Lecornu.

"I tell you, sir, this is the end of the world. The students never were so riotous before; it's the cursed inventions of the age that are ruining us all,—artillery, bombards, serpentines, and particularly printing, that other German pestilence. No more manuscripts, no more books! Printing is death to bookselling. The end of the world is at hand."

"So I see by the rage for velvet stuffs," said the furrier.

At this instant the clock struck twelve.

"Ha!" cried the entire throng with but a single voice.

The students were silent. Then began a great stir; a great moving of feet and heads; a general outbreak of coughing and handkerchiefs; everybody shook himself, arranged himself, raised himself on tiptoe, placed himself to the best advantage. Then came deep silence; every neck was stretched, every mouth was opened wide, every eye was turned towards the marble table. Nothing was to be seen there. The four officers still stood stiff and motionless as four coloured statues. Every eye turned towards the daïs reserved for the Flemish ambassadors. The door was still shut and the daïs empty. The throng has been waiting since dawn for three things: noon, the Flemish ambassadors, and the mystery. Noon alone arrived punctually.

Really it was too bad.

They waited one, two, three, five minutes, a quarter of an

---

*Behind the rider sits black worry (Latin; from Roman lyric poet Horace [65–8 B.C.], *Odes*, book 3, ode 1).

hour; nothing happened. The daïs was still deserted, the theater mute. Rage followed in the footsteps of impatience. Angry words passed from mouth to mouth, though still in undertones, to be sure. "The mystery! the mystery!" was the low cry.

Every head was in a ferment. A tempest, as yet but threatening, hung over the multitude. Jehan du Moulin drew forth the first flash.

"The mystery! and to the devil with the Flemish!" he shouted at the top of his voice, writhing and twisting around his capital like a serpent.

The crowd applauded.

"The mystery!" repeated the mob; "and to the devil with all Flanders!"

"We insist on the mystery at once," continued the student; "or else it's my advice to hang the Palace bailiff by way of a comedy and morality."

"Well said," cried the people; "and let us begin the hanging with his men."

Loud cheers followed. The four poor devils began to turn pale and to exchange glances. The mob surged towards them, and the frail wooden railing parting them from the multitude bent and swayed beneath the pressure.

It was a critical moment.

"Down with them! Down with them!" was the cry from every side.

At that instant the hangings of the dressing-room, which we have already described, were raised, giving passage to a personage the mere sight of whom suddenly arrested the mob, changing rage to curiosity as if by magic.

"Silence! Silence!"

This person, but little reassured, and trembling in every limb, advanced to the edge of the table, with many bows, which, in proportion as he approached, grew more and more like genuflections. However, peace was gradually restored. There remained only that slight murmur always arising from the silence of a vast multitude.

"Sir citizens," said he, "and fair citizenesses, we shall have the honor to declaim and perform before his Eminence the Cardinal a very fine morality entitled, 'The Wise Decision of Mistress Virgin Mary.' I am to enact Jupiter. His Eminence is at this moment escorting the very honorable ambassadors of his Highness the Duke of Austria, which is just now detained to listen to the speech of the Rector of the University at the Donkeys' Gate. As soon as the most eminent Cardinal arrives, we will begin."

It is plain that it required nothing less than the intervention of Jupiter himself to save the poor unfortunate officers of the bailiff. If we had had the good luck to invent this very truthful history, and consequently to be responsible for it to our lady of Criticism, the classic rule, *Nec deus intersit,** could not be brought up against us at this point. Moreover, Lord Jupiter's costume was very handsome, and contributed not a little to calm the mob by attracting its entire attention. Jupiter was clad in a brigandine covered with black velvet, with gilt nails; on his head was a flat cap trimmed with silver-gilt buttons; and had it not been for the paint and the big beard which covered each a half of his face, had it not been for the roll of gilded cardboard, sprinkled with spangles and all bristling with shreds of tinsel, which he carried in his hand, and in which experienced eyes readily recognized the thunder, had it not been for his flesh-colored feet bound with ribbons in Greek fashion, he might have sustained a comparison for his severity of bearing with any Breton archer in the Duke of Berry's regiment.

---

*Never let a god intervene (Latin; from Horace, *Ars Poetica*, c. 13 C.).

CHAPTER II

Pierre Gringoire

But as he spoke, the satisfaction, the admiration excited by his dress, were destroyed by his words; and when he reached the fatal conclusion, "as soon as the most eminent Cardinal arrives, we will begin," his voice was drowned in a storm of hoots.

"Begin at once! The mystery! the mystery at once!" screamed the people. And over all the other voices was heard that of Joannes de Molendino piercing the uproar, like the fife in a *charivari* at Nîmes. "Begin at once!" shrieked the student.

"Down with Jupiter and Cardinal Bourbon!" shouted Robin Poussepain and the other learned youths perched in the window.

"The morality this instant!" repeated the mob; "instantly! immediately! The sack and the rope for the actors and the Cardinal!"

Poor Jupiter, haggard, terrified, pale beneath his paint, let his thunderbolt fall, and seized his cap in his hand. Then he bowed, trembled, and stammered out: "His Eminence—the ambassadors—Madame Margaret of Flanders—" He knew not what to say. In his secret heart he was mightily afraid of being hanged.

Hanged by the populace for waiting, hanged by the Cardinal for not waiting,—on either hand he saw a gulf; that is to say, the gallows.

Luckily, some one appeared to extricate him from his embarrassing position and assume the responsibility.

An individual, standing just within the railing, in the vacant space about the marble table, and whom nobody had as yet observed,—so completely was his long slim person hidden from sight by the thickness of the pillar against which he leaned,—this individual, we say, tall, thin, pale, fair-haired, still young, although already wrinkled in brow and cheeks, with bright eyes and a smiling mouth, clad in black serge, worn and shining with age, approached the table and made a sign to the poor victim. But the latter, in his terror and confusion, failed to see him.

The newcomer took another step forward.

"Jupiter!" said he, "my dear Jupiter!"

The other did not hear him.

At last the tall fair-haired fellow, growing impatient, shouted almost in his ear,—

"Michel Giborne!"

"Who calls me?" said Jupiter, as if suddenly wakened.

"I," replied the person dressed in black.

"Ah!" said Jupiter.

"Begin directly," continued the other. "Satisfy the public; I take it upon myself to pacify the Provost, who will pacify the Cardinal."

Jupiter breathed again.

"Gentlemen and citizens," he shouted at the top of his lungs to the crowd who continued to hoot him, "we will begin at once."

"*Evoe, Jupiter! Plaudite, cives!*"* cried the students.

"Noël! Noël!"† cried the people.

Deafening applause followed, and the hall still trembled with acclamations when Jupiter had retired behind the hangings.

But the unknown person who had so miraculously changed "the tempest to a calm," as our dear old Corneille says, had modestly withdrawn into the shadow of his pillar, and would doubtless have remained there invisible, motionless, and mute as before, had he not been drawn forward by

---

*Hail Jupiter! Citizens, applaud! (Latin).

†The populace's shout of joy in the Middle Ages.

two young women, who, placed in the foremost rank of the spectators, had observed his colloquy with Michel Giborne-Jupiter.

"Master," said one of them, beckoning him to come nearer.

"Be quiet, my dear Liénarde," said her neighbor, pretty, fresh, and emboldened by all her Sunday finery. "That is no scholar, he is a layman; you must not call him *Master*, but *Sir*."

"Sir," said Liénarde.

The stranger approached the railing.

"What do you wish of me, young ladies?" he asked eagerly.

"Oh, nothing!" said Liénarde, much confused; "it is my neighbor Gisquette la Gencienne who wants to speak to you."

"Not at all," replied Gisquette, blushing; "it was Liénarde who called you Master; I told her that she should say Sir."

The two young girls cast down their eyes. The stranger, who desired nothing better than to enter into conversation with them, looked at them with a smile.

"Then you have nothing to say to me, young ladies?"

"Oh, nothing at all!" answered Gisquette.

The tall fair-haired youth drew back a pace; but the two curious creatures did not want to lose their prize.

"Sir," said Gisquette hastily, and with the impetuosity of water rushing through a floodgate or a woman coming to a sudden resolve, "so you know that soldier who is to play the part of Madame Virgin in the mystery?"

"You mean the part of Jupiter?" replied the unknown.

"Oh, yes," said Liénarde, "isn't she silly? So you know Jupiter?"

"Michel Giborne?" replied the unknown. "Yes, madame."

"He has a fine beard!" said Liénarde.

"Will it be very interesting—what they are going to recite up there?" asked Gisquette, shyly.

"Very interesting indeed," replied the stranger, without the least hesitation.

"What is it to be?" said Liénarde.

"'The Wise Decision of Madame Virgin Mary,' a morality, if you please, madame."

"Ah, that's another thing," replied Liénarde.

A short pause followed. The stranger first broke the silence:—

"It is quite a new morality, which has never yet been played."

"Then it is not the same," said Gisquette, "that was given two years ago, on the day of the legate's arrival, and in which three beautiful girls took the part of—"

"Sirens," said Liénarde.

"And all naked," added the young man. Liénarde modestly cast down her eyes; Gisquette looked at her, and did the same. He continued with a smile,—

"That was a very pretty sight. This, now, is a morality, written expressly for the young Flemish madame."

"Will they sing pastorals?" asked Gisquette.

"Fie!" said the stranger, "in a morality! You must not mix up different styles. If it were a farce, that would be another thing."

"What a pity!" replied Gisquette. "That day there were wild men and women at the Ponceau Fountain, who fought together and made all sorts of faces, singing little songs all the while."

"What suits a legate," said the stranger, somewhat drily, "will hardly suit a princess."

"And close by them," added Liénarde, "were several bass instruments which played grand melodies."

"And to refresh the passers-by," continued Gisquette, "the fountain streamed wine, milk, and hippocras,* from three mouths, for all to drink who would."

"And a little way beyond that fountain," went on Liénarde, "at the Trinity, there was a passion-play, performed by mute characters."

---

* Cordial made from wine and flavored with spices.

"How well I remember it!" exclaimed Gisquette,—"God on the cross, and the two thieves to right and left."

Here the young gossips, growing excited at the recollection of the arrival of the legate, both began to talk at once.

"And farther on, at the Painters' Gate, there were other persons richly dressed."

"And at the Fountain of the Holy Innocents, that hunter chasing a doe, with a great noise of dogs and hunting-horns!"

"And at the Paris slaughter-house, those scaffolds representing the fortress at Dieppe!"

"And when the legate passed by, you know, Gisquette, there was an attack, and all the English had their throats cut."

"And over against the Châtelet Gate there were very fine persons!"

"And on the Money-brokers' Bridge, which was hung all over with tapestries!"

"And when the legate passed by, they let loose more than two hundred dozen birds of all sorts; it was very fine, Liénarde."

"It will be finer today," replied their listener at last, seeming to hear them with some impatience.

"Then you promise us that this play will be a fine one?" said Gisquette.

"To be sure," he answered. Then he added with a certain emphasis: "Young ladies, I am the author of it!"

"Really?" said the young girls, much amazed.

"Really!" replied the poet, drawing himself up; "that is, there are two of us: Jehan Marchand, who sawed the planks and built the frame and did all the carpenter's work, and I, who wrote the piece. My name is Pierre Gringoire."[3]

The author of the *Cid* could not have said "Pierre Corneille" with any greater degree of pride.

Our readers may have noticed that some time had already passed since Jupiter had gone behind the hangings, and before the author of the new morality revealed himself so abruptly to the simple admiration of Gisquette and Liénarde. Strange to say, all that multitude, which a few instants previ-

ous was so furiously uproarious, now waited calmly for the ful-
fillment of the actor's promise, which proves that enduring
truth, still verified in our own theatres, that the best way to
make your audience wait patiently is to assure them that you
will begin right away.

However, the young scholar Joannes was not asleep.

"Hello, ho!" he cried out suddenly, in the midst of the
calm expectation which followed the confusion. "Jupiter,
Madame Virgin, devilish mountebanks! are you mocking us?
The play! the play! Begin, or we will stir you up again!"

This was quite enough.

The sound of musical instruments pitched in various keys
was heard from the interior of the scaffolding. The tapestry
was raised; four characters painted and clad in motley garb
came out, climbed the rude stage ladder, and, gaining the
upper platform, ranged themselves in line before the public,
bowing low; then the symphony ceased. The mystery was
about to begin.

These four personages, having been abundantly repaid for
their bows by applause, began, amid devout silence, a prologue which we gladly spare the reader. Moreover, as happens
even nowadays, the audience was far more interested in the
costumes of the actors than in the speeches which they re-
cited; and, to tell the truth, they were quite right. They were
all four dressed in gowns partly yellow and partly white, which
only differed from each other in material; the first was of gold
and silver brocade, the second of silk, the third of wool, the
fourth of linen. The first of these characters had a sword in his
right hand, the second two golden keys, the third a pair of
scales, the fourth a spade; and to aid those indolent understandings which might not have penetrated the evident meaning of these attributes, might be read embroidered in big
black letters — on the hem of the brocade gown, "I AM NOBIL-
ITY," on the hem of the silk gown, "I AM RELIGION," on the
hem of the woollen gown, "I AM COMMERCE," and on the
hem of the linen gown, "I AM LABOR." The sex of the two
male allegories was clearly shown to every sensible beholder

by their shorter gowns and by their peculiar headdress, — a flat cap called a *cramignole*; while the two feminine allegories, clad in longer garments, wore hoods.

One must also have been wilfully dull not to gather from the poetical prologue that Labor was wedded to Commerce, and Religion to Nobility, and that the two happy pairs owned in common a superb golden dolphin,* which they desired to bestow only on the fairest of the fair: They were therefore journeying through the world in search of this beauty; and having in turn rejected the Queen of Golconda, the Princess of Trebizond, the daughter of the Chain of Tartary, etc., Labor and Religion, Nobility and Trade, were now resting on the marble table in the Palace of Justice, spouting to their simple audience as many long sentences and maxims as would suffice the Faculty of Arts for all the examinations, sophisms, determinances, figures, and acts required at the examinations at which the masters took their degrees.

All this was indeed very fine.

But in the crowd upon whom the four allegorical personages poured such floods of metaphor, each trying to outdo the other, there was no more attentive ear, no more anxious heart, no more eager eye, no neck more outstretched, than the eye, the ear, the neck, and the heart of the author, the poet, the worthy Pierre Gringoire, who could not resist, a moment previous, the delight of telling his name to two pretty girls. He had withdrawn a few paces from them, behind his pillar; and there he listened, looked, and enjoyed. The kindly plaudits which greeted the opening lines of his prologue still rang in his innermost soul, and he was completely absorbed in that kind of ecstatic contemplation with which an author watches his ideas falling one by one from the actor's lips amid the silence of a vast assembly. Happy Pierre Gringoire!

---

*A play on words; "dolphin," the ocean-dwelling, whale-like mammal, and "dauphin," a French king's eldest son, are spelled identically in French as *dauphin*.

We regret to say that this first ecstasy was very soon disturbed. Gringoire had scarcely placed his lips to this intoxicating draught of joy and triumph, when a drop of bitterness was blended with it.

A ragged beggar, who could reap no harvest, lost as he was in the midst of the crowd, and who doubtless failed to find sufficient to atone for his loss in the pockets of his neighbors, hit upon the plan of perching himself upon some conspicuous point, in order to attract eyes and alms. He therefore hoisted himself, during the first lines of the prologue, by the aid of the columns of the daïs, up to the top of the high railing running around it; and there he sat, soliciting the attention and the pity of the multitude, by the sight of his rags, and a hideous sore which covered his right arm. Moreover, he uttered not a word.

His silence permitted the prologue to go on without interruption, and no apparent disorder would have occurred if ill luck had not led the student Joannes to note the beggar and his grimaces, from his own lofty post. A fit of mad laughter seized upon the young rogue, who, regardless of the fact that he was interrupting the performance and disturbing the general concentration of thought, cried merrily,—

"Just look at that impostor asking alms!"

Any one who has thrown a stone into a frog-pond or fired a gun into a flock of birds, can form some idea of the effect which these incongruous words produced in the midst of the universal attention. Gringoire shuddered as at an electric shock. The prologue was cut short, and every head was turned, in confusion, towards the beggar, who, far from being put out of countenance, regarded this incident as a good occasion for a harvest, and began to whine, with an air of great distress, his eyes half closed, "Charity, kind people!"

"Why, upon my soul," continued Joannes, "it is Clopin Trouillefou! Hello there, my friend! Did you find the wound on your leg inconvenient, that you have transferred it to your arm?"

So saying, with monkey-like skill he flung a small silver

coin into the greasy felt hat which the beggar held with his invalid arm. The beggar accepted the alms and the sarcasm without wincing, and went on in piteous tones, "Charity, kind people!"

This episode greatly distracted the attention of the audience; and many of the spectators, Robin Poussepain and all the students at their head, joyfully applauded the odd duet, improvised, in the middle of the prologue, by the student with his shrill voice and the beggar with his imperturbable whine.

Gringoire was much displeased. Recovering from his first surprise, he began shouting to the characters on the stage: "Go on! Why do you stop? Go on!" not even condescending to cast a look of scorn at the two interrupters.

At this moment he felt himself pulled by the hem of his surcoat; he turned, in rather an ill-humor, and had hard work to force a smile. It was the fair arm of Gisquette la Gencienne, which, passed through the rails, thus entreated his attention.

"Sir," said the young girl, "will they go on?"

"Of course," replied Gringoire, quite shocked at the question.

"In that case, sir," she went on, "would you have the kindness to explain to me—"

"What they are going to say?" interrupted Gringoire. "Well! listen."

"No," said Gisquette, "but what they have already said."

Gringoire started violently, like a man touched on a sensitive spot.

"Plague take the foolish, stupid little wench!" he muttered between his teeth.

From that moment Gisquette was lost in his estimation.

However, the actors had obeyed his command, and the public, seeing that they had begun to speak again, again began to listen, not without necessarily losing many beauties from this kind of rough joining of the two parts of the piece, so abruptly dissevered. Gringoire brooded bitterly over this fact in silence. Still, quiet was gradually restored, the student was silent, the beggar counted a few coins in his hat, and the play went on.

It was really a very fine work, and one which it seems to us might well be made use of today, with a few changes. The plot, somewhat long and somewhat flat,—that is, written according to rule,—was simple; and Gringoire, in the innocent sanctuary of his innermost soul, admired its clearness. As may be imagined, the four allegorical characters were rather fatigued after traversing three quarters of the globe without managing to dispose of their golden dolphin suitably. Thereupon ensued fresh eulogies of the marvellous fish, with a thousand delicate allusions to the young lover of Margaret of Flanders, then very sadly secluded at Amboise, and little suspecting that Labor and Religion, Nobility and Commerce, had just travelled around the world for his sake. The aforesaid dauphin was young, was handsome, was strong, and especially (magnificent source of all royal virtues!) he was the son of the Lion of France. I declare that this bold metaphor is admirable; and that the natural history of the theater, on a day of allegories and royal epithalamia, is not to be alarmed at the thought of a dolphin being the son of a lion. It is just these rare and Pindaric mixtures which prove the degree of enthusiasm. Nevertheless, to play the critic, we must confess that the poet might have managed to develop this beautiful idea in less than two hundred lines. True, the mystery was to last from noon until four o'clock, by the order of the provost; something must be done to fill up the time. Besides, the people listened patiently.

All at once, in the very middle of a quarrel between Mademoiselle Commerce and Madame Nobility, just as Master Labor pronouced this wonderful line,—

"Ne'er saw the woods a beast more beautiful,"

the door leading to the platform, which had hitherto remained so inopportunely closed, was still more inopportunely opened, and the ringing voice of the usher abruptly announced: "His Eminence, Monseigneur the Cardinal de Bourbon!"

CHAPTER III

The Cardinal

Poor Gringoire! The noise of all the big cannon crackers fired on St. John's day, the discharge of twenty crooked arquebuses, the thunder of that famous serpentine of the Tower of Billy, which, during the siege of Paris, on Sunday, Sept. 29, 1465, killed seven Burgundians at one shot, the explosion of all the gunpowder stored at the Temple Gate, would have assailed his ears less rudely, at that solemn and dramatic moment, than did those few words dropping from the mouth of an usher: "His Eminence, Monseigneur the Cardinal de Bourbon!"

Not that Pierre Gringoire feared the Cardinal or scorned him; he was neither so weak nor so conceited. A genuine eclectic, as he would be called nowadays, Gringoire was one of those firm and lofty, calm and temperate souls, who always contrive to choose a happy medium (*stare in dimidio rerum*), and who are full of sense and liberal philosophy, although they have a high regard for cardinals. Precious and perpetual race of philosophers, to whom, as to another Ariadne, wisdom seems to have given a bell of thread which they have gone on unwinding from the beginning of the world, as they journeyed through the labyrinth of human things! They are to be found in every age, ever the same; that is, always in harmony with the age. And, to say nothing of our Pierre Gringoire, who would represent them in the fifteenth century if we could succeed in portraying him as he deserves, it is assuredly their spirit which animated Father du Breuil in the sixteenth, when he wrote these simple and sublime words, worthy of all the ages: "I am a Parisian in nationality and parrhisian in speech; *parrhisia* being a Greek word signifying 'freedom of speech;' the which I have used even towards the cardinals, uncle and brother to the Prince of Conty; always with due respect for their greatness, and without offending any man among their followers, which is much."

The disagreeable effect which the Cardinal produced on Pierre Gringoire, therefore, partook neither of hatred nor of scorn. Quite the contrary; our poet had too much good sense and too threadbare a coat not to attach especial value to the fact that many an allusion in his prologue, and particularly those in glorification of the dauphin, son of the Lion of France, might be heard by a most eminent ear. But interest is not all-powerful in the noble nature of poets. Let us suppose the entity of the poet to be represented by the number ten: it is certain that a chemist, who should analyze and "pharma-copœize" it, as Rabelais says, would find it to be composed of one part self-interest to nine parts of self-esteem. Now, at the moment that the door was thrown open to admit the Cardinal, Gringoire's nine parts of self-esteem, swollen and inflated by the breath of public admiration, were in a state of abnormal development, before which the imperceptible molecule of self-interest, which we just now discovered in the constitution of poets, vanished and faded into insignificance, precious ingredient though it was,—the ballast of reality and humanity, without which they would never descend to earth. Gringoire enjoyed feeling, seeing, handling, as it were, an entire assembly,—of rascals, it is true, but what did that matter? They were stupefied, petrified, and almost stifled by the incommensurable tirades with which every portion of his epithalamium bristled. I affirm that he himself partook of the general beatitude, and that, unlike La Fontaine, who, on witnessing a performance of his own comedy, "The Florentine," inquired, "What clown wrote that rhapsody?" Gringoire would gladly have asked his neighbor, "Whose is this masterpiece?" You may judge the effect produced on him by the abrupt and untimely arrival of the Cardinal.

His fears were but too soon realized. The entrance of his Eminence distracted the audience. Every head was turned towards the platform. No one listened. "The Cardinal! the Cardinal!" repeated every tongue. The unfortunate prologue was a second time cut short.

The Cardinal paused for a moment on the threshold. While he cast an indifferent glance over the assembly, the uproar increased. Every one wished to get a better view of him. Every one tried to see who could best stretch his neck over his neighbor's shoulders.

He was indeed a great personage, and one the sight of whom was well worth any other spectacle. Charles, the Cardinal de Bourbon, Archbishop and Count of Lyons, Primate of the Gauls, was at the same time related to Louis XI through his brother, Pierre, Lord of Beaujeu, who had married the eldest daughter of the king, and related to Charles the Bold through his mother, Agnes of Burgundy. Now, the dominant feature, the characteristic and distinctive trait in the character of the Primate of the Gauls, was his courtier-like spirit and his devotion to those in power. It is easy to imagine the countless difficulties in which his double kinship had involved him, and all the temporal reefs between which his spiritual bark had been forced to manœuvre lest it should founder upon either Louis or Charles,—that Charybdis and that Scylla which had swallowed up the Duke of Nemours and the Constable of Saint-Pol. Heaven be thanked, he had escaped tolerably well from the voyage, and had reached Rome without accident. But although he was safe in port, and indeed because he was safe in port, he never recalled without a tremor the various haps and mishaps of his political life, so long full of alarms and labors. He was therefore wont to say that the year 1476 had been to him both black and white; meaning that in one and the same year he had lost his mother, the Duchess of Bourbonnais, and his cousin, the Duke of Burgundy, and that one loss had consoled him for the other.

However, he was a very good fellow; he led a joyous life as cardinal, cheered himself willingly with the royal wine of Chaillot, was not averse to Richarde de la Garmoise and Thomasse la Saillarde, preferred to bestow alms upon pretty maids rather than aged matrons, and for all these reasons was very agreeable to the populace of Paris. He always went surrounded by a small court of bishops and priests of lofty lineage, gallant, jovial, and fond of feasting on occasion; and more than once the good devotees of St. Germain d'Auxerre, as they passed by night beneath the brightly lighted windows of the Cardinal's residence, had been scandalized on hearing the same voices which had sung vespers for them that day, now chanting to the clink of glasses the Bacchic adage of Benedict III,—that pope who added a third crown to the tiara,—"*Bibamus papaliter.*"*

It was undoubtedly this popularity, so justly acquired, which saved him, on his entrance, from any unpleasant reception on the part of the mob, so dissatisfied but a moment before, and but little inclined to respect a cardinal on the very day when they were to elect a pope of their own. But Parisians are not given to hoarding up grudges; and then, by insisting that the play should begin, the good citizens had shown their authority, thus getting the better of the Cardinal: and this triumph sufficed them. Besides, the Cardinal was a remarkably handsome man; he had a very gorgeous red robe which was most becoming; which is as much as to say that all the women, and consequently the better half of the audience, were on his side. Certainly, it would have been unjust, and in very bad taste, to boo a cardinal for being late for the play, when he is handsome and wears his red robe gracefully.

He entered, therefore, bowed to the assembly with that hereditary smile which the great have for the people, and walked slowly towards his scarlet velvet arm-chair with an air of being absorbed in thoughts of far other things. His escort,

_____

us drink like popes (Latin).

or what we should now call his staff of bishops and priests, flocked after him upon the daïs, not without renewed curiosity and confusion on the part of the spectators. Every man tried to point them out and name them; every man knew at least one among them: this one, the Bishop of Marseilles, Alaudet, if I remember rightly; that one, the Dean of St. Denis; another, Robert de Lespinasse, Abbot of St. Germain des Prés, the libertine brother of one of the mistresses of Louis XI,—all with endless mistakes and mispronunciations. As for the students, they swore heartily. It was their day, their Feast of Fools, their Saturnalia, the annual orgies of the basoche* and the schools. No iniquity but was allowable and sacred upon that day. And then there were plenty of giddy girls in the crowd,—Simone Quatrelivres, Agnès la Gadine, Robine Piédebou. Was it not the least that they could do to swear at their ease and blaspheme a little on so fine a day, in so goodly a company of churchmen and courtesans? Neither were they slow to seize the opportunity; and in the midst of the uproar came a terrific outburst of oaths and obscenities from their lawless lips,—the lips of a set of students and scholars restrained all the rest of the year by their dread of the hot iron of Saint Louis. Poor Saint Louis! how they set him at defiance in his own Palace of Justice! Each of them selected from the newcomers on the daïs a black or grey, a white or purple gown for his own victim. As for Joannes Frollo de Molendino, in his quality of brother to an archdeacon he boldly attacked the red cassock, and bawled at the top of his voice, fixing his impudent eyes full on the Cardinal, *"Cappa repleta mero!"*†

All these details, boldly set down here for the edification of the reader, were so covered by the general noise and confusion, that they were lost before they reached the daïs; besides which, the Cardinal would have paid but little heed to them, had he heard them, the license of that particular day was so

---

*Company of clerks of the Parliament of Paris.
†Cassock full of wine! (Latin).

ell established a fact in the history of public morals. He had, moreover,—and his countenance showed how fully it absorbed him,—quite another cause of concern following him closely, and stepping upon the platform almost at the same moment as himself; namely, the Flemish ambassadors.

Not that he was much of a politician, or that he troubled himself much about the possible results of the marriage of his cousin, Lady Margaret of Burgundy, with his cousin Charles, Dauphin of Vienna; he cared very little about the duration of the friendship patched up between the Duke of Austria and the King of France, or about the King of England's opinion of the slight put upon his daughter! and he tested the royal vintage of Chaillot every evening, without suspecting that a few flasks of that same wine (slightly doctored and improved by Doctor Coictier, to be sure), cordially presented to Edward IV by Louis XI would one fine day rid Louis XI of Edward IV. The very honorable embassy of the Duke of Austria brought none of these cares to the Cardinal's mind, but it troubled him in another way. It was indeed rather hard, and we have already spoken a word in regard to it in an earlier page of this book, to be forced to welcome and entertain—he, Charles of Bourbon—these nondescript citizens; he, a cardinal, to condescend to aldermen; he, a Frenchman and a *bon-viveur*, to befriend Flemish beer-drinkers, and in public too! This was assuredly one of the most painful farces he had ever been compelled to play for the King's pleasure.

Still, he turned to the door with the best grace in the world (so well had he trained himself) when the usher announced in ringing tones, "The envoys from the Duke of Austria!" Needless to say, the entire audience did the same.

Then entered, two by two, with a gravity in vivid contrast to the lively ecclesiastical escort of the Cardinal, the forty-ght ambassadors of Maximilian of Austria, headed by the rend father in God, Jehan, Abbot of Saint-Bertin, Chan- of the Golden Fleece, and Jacques de Goy, Lord of high bailiff of Ghent. A profound silence fell upon embly, followed by stifled laughter at all the absurd

names and all the commonplace titles which each of these personages calmly transmitted to the usher, who instantly hurled names and titles pell-mell, and horribly mangled, at the heads of the crowd. There were Master Loys Roelof, alderman of the city of Louvain; Master Clays d'Etuelde, alderman of Brussels; Master Paul de Baeurst, Lord of Voirmizelle, president of Flanders; Master Jehan Coleghens, burgomaster of the city of Antwerp; Master George de la Moere, head sheriff of the Court of Law of the town of Ghent; Master Gheldolf van der Hage, head sheriff of the court of equity of the same town; and the Lord of Bierbecque, and Jehan Pinnock, and Jehan Dymaerzelle, etc., etc., etc.: bailiffs, aldermen, burgomasters; burgomasters, aldermen, bailiffs; all stiff, starched, and strait-laced, dressed in their Sunday best of velvet and damask, wearing flat black velvet caps on their heads, with large tassels of gold thread from Cyprus; honest Flemish figures after all, severe and dignified faces, of the race of those whom Rembrandt portrayed so gravely and forcibly against the dark background of his "Night Watch,"—personages every one of whom bore it written upon his brow that Maximilian of Austria was right in "confiding fully," as his proclamation had it, "in their good sense, valor, experience, loyalty, and good qualities."

But there was one exception. This was a man with a cunning, intelligent, crafty face, the face of a monkey combined with that of a diplomatist, to meet whom the Cardinal stepped forward three paces, bowing low, and yet who bore a name no more high sounding than "Guillaume Rym, councillor and pensionary of the town of Ghent."

Few persons there knew what Guillaume Rym was,—a rare genius, who in time of revolution would have appeared with renown in the foremost rank, but who in the fifteenth century was reduced to the lowest intrigues, and to "living by sapping and mining," as the Duke of St. Simon expresses it. However, he was appreciated by the greatest "sapper" in Europe; he planned and plotted with Louis XI on familiar terms, and often laid his hand on the king's secret necessities.

All these things were utterly unknown to this throng, who marvelled at the politeness shown by the Cardinal to this scurvy Flemish bailiff.

CHAPTER IV

Master Jacques Coppenole

As the pensionary of Ghent and his Eminence were exchanging very low bows, and a few words in still lower voices, a tall, broad-faced, square-shouldered man entered boldly after Guillaume Rym; he reminded one of a dog in pursuit of a fox. His felt hat and leather jerkin looked very shabby in the midst of the velvet and silk which surrounded him. Supposing him to be some groom who had lost his way, the usher stopped him.

"Hey, my friend! there's no passing here."

The man in the leather coat shouldered him aside.

"What does the fellow mean?" he said in a tone which made the entire hall aware of this strange colloquy. "Don't you see that I belong to the party?"

"Your name?" asked the usher.

"Jacques Coppenole."

"Your titles?"

"Hosier at the sign of the Three Little Chains, at Ghent."

The usher started back. It was bad enough to have to announce aldermen and burgomasters; but a hosier, that was hard indeed! The Cardinal was on thorns. Every one was looking and listening. For two days his Eminence had been laboring to lick these Flemish bears into some presentable shape, and this outburst was hard upon him. However, Guillaume Rym, with his crafty smile, leaned towards the usher.

"Announce Master Jacques Coppenole, clerk to the aldermen of the town of Ghent," he whispered softly.

"Usher," added the Cardinal in a loud voice, "announce Master Jacques Coppenole, clerk to the aldermen of the illustrious town of Ghent."

This was a mistake. Guillaume Rym, if left to himself, would have evaded the difficulty; but Coppenole had overheard the Cardinal.

"No, by God's cross!" he cried in his voice of thunder. "Jacques Coppenole, hosier. Do you hear me, usher? Nothing more, nothing less. By God's cross! a hosier is good enough for me. The archduke himself has more than once sought his glove* in my hose."

There was a burst of laughter and applause. A pun is always instantly appreciated in Paris, and consequently always applauded.

Let us add that Coppenole was a man of the people, and that the audience about him consisted of the people only; thus the sympathy between them was prompt, electric, and they were at once on an equal footing. The proud exclamation of the Flemish hosier, while it mortified the courtiers, stirred in every humble soul a certain sense of dignity still vague and indistinct, in the fifteenth century. This hosier, who had just held his own before the Cardinal himself, was their equal! A very pleasant thought for poor devils who were wont to respect and obey the servants of the officers of the bailiff of the Abbot of St. Geneviève, train-bearer to the Cardinal.

Coppenole bowed haughtily to his Eminence, who returned the salutation of the all-powerful citizen dreaded by Louis XI. Then, while Guillaume Rym, "a wise and wily man," as Philippe de Comines has it, watched them both with a smile full of mocking and superiority, they took each his

---

*In the original French, *gant*, meaning glove, is used as a play on words with the name of the Belgian city of Ghent.

place,—the Cardinal troubled and disconcerted, Coppenole calm and erect, doubtless thinking that after all his title of hosier was quite as good as any other, and that Mary of Burgundy, mother of that Margaret whose marriage he was now negotiating, would have feared him less as cardinal than as hosier; for no cardinal would have led on the men of Ghent against the favorites of the daughter of Charles the Bold; no cardinal could have hardened the hearts of the masses against her tears and her prayers, by a single word, when the heiress of Flanders besought her people to grant their pardon, at the very foot of their scaffold; while the hosier had but to lift his leathern elbow to cause both your heads to fall, O ye illustrious lords, Guy d'Hymbercourt and Chancellor Guillaume Hugonet!

But all was not over yet for the poor Cardinal, who was to drink the dregs of the bitter cup of association with such low company.

The reader may perhaps recall the impudent beggar who clung to the fringes of the Cardinal's daïs at the opening of the prologue. The arrival of the distinguished guests did not cause him to relax his hold; and while prelates and ambassadors were packed as close as Dutch herrings in the seats upon the platform, he made himself quite comfortable, and coolly crossed his legs upon the architrave. Such insolence was unusual, and no one noted it at the moment, attention being fixed elsewhere. He for his part saw nothing in the hall; he swayed his head to and fro with the careless ease of a Neapolitan, repeating ever and anon amid the din, as if mechanically, "Charity, kind people!" and certainly he was the only one in the entire audience who did not deign to turn his head to listen to the altercation between Coppenole and the usher. Now, as chance would have it, the master hosier of Ghent, with whom the people already sympathized strongly, and upon whom all eyes were fixed, seated himself in the front row upon the platform, just above the beggar; and they were not a little amazed to see the Flemish ambassador, after glancing at the rascal beneath him, give him a friendly slap upon his tattered shoulder. The beggar turned; surprise, recognition, delight, were visible in both faces, then, without paying the slightest heed to the throng of spectators, the hosier and the scurvy knave fell to talking in low tones, clasping each other's hands; while the rags of Clopin Trouillefou, displayed against the cloth of gold of the daïs, produced the effect of a caterpillar upon an orange.

The novelty of this strange scene excited such an outburst of mirth in the hall that the Cardinal quickly perceived it; he bent forward, and, unable from his position to catch more than a glimpse of Trouillefou's disgraceful garments, he quite naturally supposed that the beggar was asking alms, and, indignant at his audacity, he exclaimed, "Sir Bailiff of the Palace, throw that rascal into the river!"

"By God's cross! Sir Cardinal," said Coppenole, without releasing Clopin's hand, "he is my friend."

"Noël! Noël" cried the mob. From that instant Master Coppenole was "in high favor with the people," in Paris as in Ghent; "for men of his cut always are," says Philippe de Comines, "when they are thus disorderly."

The Cardinal bit his lip. He bent towards his neighbor, the Abbot of St. Geneviève, and said in an undertone:—

"Pleasant ambassadors are these sent us by the arch-duke to announce the coming of Lady Margaret!"

"Your Eminence," replied the abbot, "wastes his courtesies upon these Flemish grunters,—*Margaritas ante porcos.*"*

"Say rather," replied the Cardinal with a smile, "*Porcos ante Margaritam.*"†

All the little court in priestly robes went into ecstasies over the joke. The Cardinal felt slightly comforted: he was quits with Coppenole; his pun also had been applauded.

Now, let those of our readers who have the power of gen-

---

*Pearls before swine (Latin).

†Swine before a pearl (Latin); a pun on the name Margaret, which means "pearl."

eralizing an image and an idea, as it is the pleasant fashion to express it, allow us to ask them if they have a distinct conception of the spectacle afforded, at the moment that we claim their attention, by the vast parallelogram of the great hall of the Palace: In the center of the hall, against the western wall, a broad and magnificent platform covered with gold brocade, upon which stepped in procession, through a small arched doorway, a number of grave and reverend personages successively announced by the nasal voice of an usher; on the foremost benches, already seated, various venerable figures wrapped in ermine, velvet, and scarlet; around the daïs, where all was dignity and silence, below, in front, everywhere, a great crowd and a great uproar; a thousand eyes from the crowd fixed upon every face on the platform, a thousand murmurs upon the announcement of every name. Certainly the sight is a strange one, and well worthy the attention of the spectators. But below there, at the extreme end, what is that kind of trestle-work with four motley puppets above and four more below? Who is that pale-faced man in a black coat beside the boards? Alas! dear reader, that is Pierre Gringoire and his prologue.

We had all entirely forgotten him.

This was precisely what he feared.

From the instant that the Cardinal entered, Gringoire had never ceased working for the salvation of his prologue. He at first enjoined the actors, who remained in suspense, to go on, and to raise their voices; then, seeing that no one was listening, he stopped them; and then, after the interruption had lasted nearly fifteen minutes, he began to stamp, to struggle, to question Gisquette and Liénarde, and to encourage his neighbors to call for the prologue. All in vain; not an eye would move from the Cardinal, the ambassadors, and the daïs,—the sole center of that vast circle of visual rays. We must therefore believe, and we say it with regret, that the prologue was beginning to be somewhat tedious to the audience at the moment that his Eminence caused so terrible a diversion. After all, the spectacle was the same upon the daïs as upon the marble table,—the conflict between Labor and Religion, Nobility and Commerce; and many people preferred to see them simply, in living, breathing reality, elbowing and pushing, in flesh and blood, in this Flemish embassy, in this Episcopal court, beneath the Cardinal's robe, beneath the jacket of Coppenole, rather than painted and decked out, speaking in artificial verse, and as it were stuffed with straw beneath the white and yellow tunics in which Gringoire had arrayed them.

However, when our poet saw that peace was beginning to reign once more, he hit upon a stratagem which might have saved all.

"Sir," said he, turning towards one of his neighbors, a good fat fellow with a patient face, "suppose they begin again?"

"Begin what?" said the neighbor.

"Why, the mystery!" said Gringoire.

"If you like," responded his neighbor.

This lukewarm approval was enough for Gringoire, and acting for himself he began to shout, mixing with the crowd as much as he could, "Go on with the miracle-play! Go on!"

"The devil!" said Joannes de Molendino, "what are they bawling about over there?" (For Gringoire made noise enough for four.) "Say, boys, isn't the play done? They want to have it all over again; it's not fair."

"No, no!" cried the students. "Down with the mystery! down with it!"

But Gringoire seemed ubiquitous, and shouted louder than before, "Go on! go on!"

These outcries attracted the attention of the Cardinal.

"Bailiff," he said to a tall dark man seated near him, "are those devils caught in a font of holy water, that they make such an infernal noise?"

The Bailiff of the Palace was a species of amphibious magistrate, a sort of bat of the judicial order, partaking at once of the nature of the rat and the bird, the judge and the soldier.

He approached his Eminence, and, not without serious fears of his displeasure, stammered out an explanation of the popular misconduct,—that noon had come before his Eminence, and that the actors were obliged to begin without awaiting his Eminence.

The Cardinal burst out laughing.

"Upon my word, the Rector of the University had better have done as much. What say you, Master Guillaume Rym?"

"My lord," replied Guillaume Rym, "let us be content that we have escaped half the play. It is just so much gained."

"May those rascals go on with their performance?" asked the bailiff.

"Go on, go on," said the Cardinal; "it's all the same to me. I will read my breviary in the meantime."

The Provost advanced to the edge of the platform and cried aloud, after imposing silence by a wave of his hand: "Citizens, commoners, and residents: to satisfy those who wish the play to begin again and those who wish it to end, his Eminence orders that it be continued."

Both parties were forced to submit. However, the author and the audience long cherished a grudge against the Cardinal.

The characters on the stage accordingly resumed their recital, and Gringoire hoped that the rest of his work at least would be heard. This hope soon proved as illusory as all the rest. Silence was indeed restored to a certain extent among the audience; but Gringoire had not remarked that, at the moment when the Cardinal gave the order to go on, the daïs was far from being filled, and that in the train of the Flemish embassy came other personages forming part of the procession, whose names and titles, shouted out in the midst of his prologue by the intermittent cry of the usher, made many ravages in it. Imagine the effect, in the midst of a play, of the shrill voice of an usher uttering between two rhymes, and often between two hemistichs, such parentheses as these:—

"Master Jacques Charmolue, king's attorney in the Ecclesiastical Court!"

"Jehan de Harlay, esquire, keeper of the office of captain of the watch of the city of Paris!"

"Master Galiot de Genoilhac, knight, Lord of Brussac, chief of the king's ordnance!"

"Master Dreux-Raguier, inspector of the woods and waters of our lord the king, in the lands of France, Champagne, and Brie!"

"Master Louis de Graville, knight, councillor, and chamberlain to the king, admiral of France, keeper of the forest of Vincennes!"

"Master Denis le Mercier, guardian of the Home for the Blind of Paris!" etc.

This at last became insufferable.

This strange accompaniment, which made it very hard to follow the play, enraged Gringoire all the more because he could not blind himself to the fact that the interest was constantly increasing, and that all his work needed was to be heard. It was indeed difficult to conceive of a more ingenious and more dramatic context. The four characters of the prologue were lamenting their terrible embarrassment, when Venus in person (*vera incessu patuit dea*) appeared before them, clad in a fine coat of mail, emblazoned with the ship from the seal of the city of Paris. She came herself to claim the dolphin promised to the fairest of the fair. Jupiter, whose thunder was heard muttering in the dressing-room below, supported her claim, and the goddess was about to triumph,—that is, speaking without metaphor, to marry the Dauphin,—when a young child, habited in white damask and holding a daisy (an obvious allusion to the Lady of Flanders), came to contest the prize with Venus. Theatrical effect and sudden change of affairs! After some controversy, Venus, Margaret, and those behind the scenes agreed to refer the matter to the wise decision of the Holy Virgin. There was also another fine part, that of Don Pedro, King of Mesopotamia; but amid so many interruptions it was difficult to discover the object of his introduction. All these characters came up the ladder.

But it all was in vain; none of these beauties were appreciated or understood. With the Cardinal's entrance, an invisible and magical cord seemed suddenly to draw all eyes from the marble table to the daïs, from the southern to the western portion of the hall. Nothing could free the audience from the spell; every eye was fixed, and the newcomers and their accursed names, and their faces and their dresses, were a perpetual source of distraction. It was heartrending. Save for Gisquette and Liénarde, who occasionally turned away when Gringoire pulled them by the sleeve; save for the patient fat neighbor, no one listened to, no one looked at, the poor forsaken morality. Gringoire saw nothing but profiles.

With what bitterness he saw his whole framework of fame and poetry crumble away bit by bit! And to think that this very mob had been on the point of revolting against the bailiff, from sheer impatience to hear his work! Now that they had it, they cared nothing for it,—this same performance which began amid such universal applause! Eternal ebb and flow of popular favor! To think that they had come so near hanging the bailiff's men! What would he not have given to recover that golden hour!

The usher's brutal monologue ceased at last; every one had arrived, and Gringoire breathed again; the actors went bravely on.

But then what should Master Coppenole, the hosier, do but rise suddenly; and Gringoire heard him utter, amid universal attention, this abominable speech:—

"Citizens and squires of Paris, I know not, by God's cross! what we are doing here. I do indeed see in yonder corner, upon those boards, people who look as if they were spoiling for a fight. I don't know whether that is what you call a 'mystery,' but it is not at all amusing: they abuse one another, and get no farther. For full fifteen minutes I have been waiting for the first blow; nothing comes; they are cowards, who deal in no other weapons than insults. You ought to fetch a few wrestlers from London or Rotterdam, and then you'd have a treat! You would see blows that could be heard all over the place; but those fellows yonder are a disgrace. They might at least give us a Morris-dance or some other mummery! This is

not what I was told I should see; I was promised a Feast of
Fools and the election of a Pope. We have our Pope of Fools
in Ghent, too; and we're not behind you in that, by God's
cross! But this is how we do it: we collect a crowd, as you do
here; then every man in his turn puts his head through a hole
and pulls a face at the rest; he who makes the ugliest is chosen pope by popular acclaim; there! It's very amusing. Would
you like to choose your pope after the fashion of my country?
At least it would be better than listening to those chatterboxes.
If they will come and make their grimaces through the window, they can join the game. What say you, Sir Citizens?
There are quite enough absurd specimens of both sexes here
to give us a good Flemish laugh, and we have ugly mugs
enough to hope for some fine grimaces."

Gringoire longed to answer; but amazement, anger, indignation, robbed him of speech. Moreover, the proposal of the
popular hosier was greeted with such enthusiasm by those
plain citizens who were flattered at being dubbed "Squires,"
that all opposition was useless. Nothing remained but to follow the current. Gringoire hid his face in his hands, not being
lucky enough to have a cloak to cover his head, like Agamem-
non of Timanthes.

CHAPTER V

Quasimodo

In the twinkling of an eye, all was ready for the execution
of Coppenole's idea. Citizens, students, and lawyers'
clerks set briskly to work. The little chapel opposite the
marble table was chosen as the stage for the grimaces. A broken pane in the pretty rose-window over the door left free a

circle of stone, through which it was agreed that the contest-
ants should thrust their heads. To reach it, all were obliged to
climb upon a couple of barrels, which had been discovered
somewhere and set one upon the other. It was settled that all
candidates, men or women (for a papess might be chosen),
lest the effect of their grimaces should be weakened, should
cover their faces and remain hidden in the chapel until the
proper moment to appear. In less than an instant the chapel
was filled with aspirants, upon whom the door was closed.

Coppenole, from his seat, directed everything, arranged
everything. During the confusion, the Cardinal, no less disconcerted than Gringoire, withdrew with all his train, feign-
ing business and vespers; the same crowd which had been so
stirred by his coming, showing not the least emotion at his de-
parture. Guillaume Rym was the only one who observed his
Eminence's flight. Popular attention, like the sun, pursued its
course; starting from one end of the hall, after pausing for
some time in the center, it was now at the other end. The
marble table, the brocaded daïs, had had their day; it was the
turn of Louis XI's chapel. The field was now clear for every
kind of folly. No one remained but the Flemings and the vulgar herd.

The grimaces began. The first to appear at the window,
with eyelids inverted until they showed the red, a cavernous
mouth, and a forehead wrinkled like the boots of a hussar
under the Empire, produced such inextinguishable laughter,
that Homer would have taken all these clowns for gods. And
yet, the great hall was anything but an Olympus, and
Gringoire's poor Jupiter knew this better than any one. A second, a third wry face followed, then another, and another;
and still the shouts of laughter and stamps of delight increased. There was a certain peculiar intoxication in the spectacle, a certain potent ecstasy and fascination which it would
be hard to explain to the reader of our own day and society.
Let him imagine a series of faces presenting in turn every geometric form, from the triangle to the trapezium, from the
cone to the polyhedron; every human expression, from rage

to lust; every age, from the wrinkles of the new-born babe to the furrows of the old and dying; every religious phantasmagoria, from Faunus to Beelzebub; every animal profile, from the jaws of the dog to the beak of the bird, from the boar's head to the pig's snout. Let him picture to himself all the grotesque heads carved on the Pont Neuf, those petrified nightmares from the hand of Germain Pilon, taking breath and life, and coming in turn to gaze at you with fiery eyes; all the masks from a Venetian carnival passing before your glass,—in one word, a human kaleidoscope.

The revelry became more and more Flemish. Téniers could have given but an imperfect idea of it! Imagine Salvator Rosa's battle-piece turned into a bacchanal feast. There were no longer students, ambassadors, townspeople, men, or women; no longer a Clopin Trouillefou, a Gilles Lecornu, a Simone Quatrelivres, or a Robin Poussepain. All distinctions died in the common license. The great hall ceased to be anything but a vast furnace of effrontery and mirth, wherein every mouth was a cry, every face a grimace, every individual a posture; the sum total howled and yelled. The strange faces which took their turn in gnashing their teeth through the rose-window were like so many brands cast into the flames; and from this effervescent mob arose, like steam from a furnace, a sharp, shrill, piercing sound, like the buzz of a gnat's wings.

"Oh, confound it!"

"Just look at that face!"

"That's nothing!"

"Let's have another!"

"Guillemette Maugerepuis, do look at that bull's head! it only lacks horns. It is not your husband."

"Another!"

"By the Pope's head! what's the meaning of that contortion?"

"Well there! that's not fair. You should show only your face."

"That damned Perrette Callebotte! She is just capable of such a thing."

"Noël! Noël!"

"I'm smothering!"

"There's a fellow whose ears are too big to go through!"

But we must do justice to our friend Jehan. Amidst this uproar he was still to be seen perched upon his pillar, like a cabin-boy on a topsail. He exerted himself with incredible fury. His mouth was opened wide, and there issued from it so a yell which no one heard,—not that it was drowned by the general clamor, tremendous though it was; but because it undoubtedly reached the limit of audible shrillness,—the twelve thousand vibrations of Sauveur or the eight thousand of Biot.

As for Gringoire, the first moment of depression over, he recovered his composure. He braced himself to meet adversity. "Go on!" he cried for the third time to his actors, whom he regarded as mere talking-machines; then, as he strode up and down in front of the marble table, he was seized with a desire to appear in his turn at the chapel window, were it only for the pleasure of making faces at that ungrateful mob. "But no, that would be unworthy of us; no vengeance. Let us struggle on to the end," he murmured; "the power of poetry over the people is great; I will bring them back. Let us see whether grimaces or polite learning will triumph."

Alas! he was left the only spectator of his play.

It was even worse than before. Now he saw nothing but people's backs.

I am wrong. The patient fat man, whom he had already consulted at a critical moment, was still turned towards the theater. As for Gisquette and Liénarde, they had long since deserted.

Gringoire was touched to the heart by the fidelity of his only listener. He went up to him and addressed him, shaking him slightly by the arm; for the worthy man was leaning against the railing in a light doze.

"Sir," said Gringoire, "I thank you."

"Sir," replied the fat fellow with a yawn, "for what?"

"I see what annoys you," resumed the poet; "it is all this noise which prevents you from hearing readily. But be calm! your name shall be handed down to posterity. Your name, if you please?"

"Renauld Château, Keeper of the Seals of Châtelet, at Paris, at your service."

"Sir, you are the sole representative of the muses here," said Gringoire.

"You are too kind, sir," replied the Keeper of the Seals of Châtelet.

"You are the only man," added Gringoire, "who has paid proper attention to the play. How do you like it?"

"Ha, ha!" replied the fat magistrate, who was but half awake, "jolly enough, in truth!"

Gringoire was forced to content himself with this eulogy; for a storm of applause, mingled with prodigious shouts, cut short their conversation. The Pope of Fools was elected.

"Noël! Noël! Noël!" shouted the people on all sides.

That was indeed a marvelous grin which now beamed through the hole in the rose-window. After all the pentagonal, hexagonal, and heteroclitic faces which had followed one another in quick succession at the window without realizing that ideal of the grotesque constructed by imagination exalted by revelry, it required nothing less to gain the popular vote than the sublime grimace which had just dazzled the assembly. Master Coppenole himself applauded; and Clopin Trouille-fou, who had competed for the prize (and Heaven knows to what intensity of ugliness his features could attain), confessed himself conquered. We will do the same. We will not try to give the reader any idea of that tetrahedron-like nose, of that horseshoe-shaped mouth; of that small left eye overhung by a bushy red eyebrow, while the right eye was completely hidden by a monstrous wart; of those uneven, broken teeth, with sad gaps here and there like the battlements of a fortress; of that callous lip, over which one of these teeth projected like an elephant's tusk; of that forked chin; and especially of the expression pervading all this, that mixture of malice, amazement, and melancholy. Imagine, if you can, that comprehensive sight.

The vote was unanimous; the crowd rushed into the chapel. They returned leading the fortunate Pope of Fools in triumph. But it was then only that surprise and admiration reached their highest pitch; the grimace was his natural face.

Or rather the entire man was a grimace. A large head bristling with red hair; between his shoulders an enormous hump, with a corresponding prominence in front; legs and thighs so singularly crooked that they touched only at the knees, and, seen from the front, resembled two reaping-hooks united at the handle; broad feet, huge hands; and, with all this deformity, a certain awe-inspiring air of vigor, agility, and courage; strange exception to the rule which declares power, as well as beauty, to be the result of harmony,—such was the pope whom the fools had chosen to reign over them.

He looked like a giant broken to pieces and badly cemented together.

When this species of Cyclop appeared upon the threshold of the chapel, motionless, thickset, almost as broad as he was long, "the square of his base," as a great man once expressed it, the people recognized him instantly, by his party-colored red and purple coat spangled with silver, and particularly by the perfection of his ugliness, and cried aloud with one voice:—

"It is Quasimodo, the bell-ringer! It is Quasimodo, the hunchback of Notre-Dame! Quasimodo, the one-eyed! Quasimodo, the bandy-legged! Noël! Noël!"

The poor devil evidently had an abundance of nicknames to choose from.

"Let all pregnant women beware!" cried the students.

"Or all those who hope to be so," added Joannes.

In fact, the women hid their faces.

"Oh, the ugly monkey!" said one of them.

"As wicked as he is ugly," added another.

"He's the very devil," added a third.

"I am unlucky enough to live near Notre-Dame. I hear him prowling among the gutters by night."

"With the cats."

"He's always on our roofs."

"He casts spells upon us through the chimneys."

"The other evening he came and pulled a face at me through the window. I thought it was a man. He gave me such a fright!"

"I'm sure he attends the Witches' Sabbath. Once he left a broomstick on my leads."

"Oh, what a disagreeable hunchback's face he has!"

"Oh, the villainous creature!"

"Faugh!"

The men, on the contrary, were charmed, and applauded. Quasimodo, the object of this uproar, still stood at the chapel door, sad and serious, letting himself be admired.

A student (Robin Poussepain, I think) laughed in his very face, and somewhat too close. Quasimodo merely took him by the belt and cast him ten paces away through the crowd; all without uttering a word.

Master Coppenole, lost in wonder, approached him.

"By God's cross and the Holy Father! you are the most lovely monster that I ever saw in my life. You deserve to be pope of Rome as well as of Paris."

So saying, he laid his hand sportively upon his shoulder. Quasimodo never budged. Coppenole continued:—

"You're a rascal with whom I have a longing to feast, were it to cost me a new douzain of twelve pounds Tours. What say you?"

Quasimodo made no answer.

"By God's cross!" said the hosier, "you're not deaf, are you?"

He was indeed deaf.

Still, he began to lose his temper at Coppenole's proceedings, and turned suddenly towards him, gnashing his teeth so savagely that the Flemish giant recoiled, like a bull-dog before a cat.

Then a circle of terror and respect, whose radius was not less than fifteen geometric paces, was formed about the strange character. An old woman explained to Master Coppenole that Quasimodo was deaf.

"Deaf!" said the hosier, with his hearty Flemish laugh. "By God's cross! but he is a perfect pope!"

"Ha! I know him now," cried Jehan, who had at last descended from his capital to view Quasimodo more closely; "it's my brother the archdeacon's bell-ringer. Good-day, Quasimodo!"

"What a devil of a fellow!" said Robin Poussepain, still aching from his fall. "He appears: he's a hunchback; he walks: he's bandy-legged; he looks at you: he is blind of one eye; you talk to him: he is deaf. By the way, what use does this Polyphemus make of his tongue?"

"He talks when he likes," said the old woman; "he grew deaf from ringing the bells. He is not dumb."

"That's all he lacks," remarked Jehan.

"And he has one eye too many," said Robin Poussepain.

"Not at all," judiciously observed Jehan. "A one-eyed man is far more incomplete than a blind one. He knows what he lacks."

But all the beggars, all the lackeys, all the cutpurses, together with the students, had gone in procession to fetch, from the storeroom of the basoche, the pasteboard tiara and mock robes of the Pope of Fools. Quasimodo submitted to be arrayed in them without a frown, and with a sort of proud docility. Then he was seated upon a barrow painted in motley colors. Twelve officers of the fraternity of fools raised it to their shoulders; and a sort of bitter, scornful joy dawned upon the morose face of the Cyclop when he saw beneath his shapeless feet the heads of so many handsome, straight, and well-made men. Then the howling, tatterdemalion train set out, as was the custom, to make the tour of the galleries within the Palace before parading the streets and public squares.

CHAPTER VI

Esmeralda

We are delighted to be able to inform our readers that during the whole of this scene Gringoire and his play had stood their ground. His actors, spurred on by him, had not stopped spouting his verses, and he had not given over listening. He had resigned himself to the uproar, and was determined to go on to the bitter end, not despairing of recovering some portion of public attention. This ray of hope revived when he saw Quasimodo, Coppenole, and the deafening escort of the Pope of Fools leave the hall with a tremendous noise. The crowd followed eagerly on their heels. "Good!" said he to himself; "now we have got rid of all the marplots." Unfortunately, all the marplots meant the whole audience. In the twinkling of an eye, the great hall was empty.

To be exact, there still remained a handful of spectators, some scattered, others grouped around the pillars, women, old men, or children, who had had enough of the tumult and the hurly-burly. A few students still lingered, astride of the window-frames, gazing into the square.

"Well," thought Gringoire, "here are still enough to hear the end of my mystery. There are but few, but it is a picked public, an intellectual audience."

A moment later, a melody meant to produce the greatest effect at the appearance of the Holy Virgin was missing. Gringoire saw that his musicians had been borne off by the procession of the Pope of Fools. "Proceed," he said stoically.

He went up to a group of townspeople who seemed to him to be talking about his play. This is the fragment of conversation which he caught:—

"You know, Master Cheneteau, the Hôtel de Navarre, which belonged to M. de Nemours?"

"Yes, opposite the Braque Chapel."

"Well, the Treasury Department has just left it to Guillaume Alexandre, the painter of armorial bearings, for six pounds and eight pence Paris a year."

"How high rents are getting to be!"

"Well, well!" said Gringoire with a sigh; "the rest are listening."

"Comrades!" shouted one of the young scamps in the window; "Esmeralda! Esmeralda is in the square!"

This cry had a magical effect. Every one in the hall rushed to the windows, climbing up the walls to get a glimpse, and repeating, "Esmeralda! Esmeralda!"

At the same time a great noise of applause was heard outside.

"What do they mean by their 'Esmeralda'?" said Gringoire, clasping his hands in despair. "Oh, heavens! I suppose the windows are the attraction now!"

He turned back again to the marble table, and saw that the play had stopped. It was just the moment when Jupiter should have appeared with his thunder. Now Jupiter stood motionless at the foot of the stage.

"Michel Giborne!" cried the angry poet, "what are you doing there? Is that playing your part? Go up, I tell you!"

"Alas!" said Jupiter, "one of the students has taken away the ladder."

Gringoire looked. It was but too true. All communication was cut off between his plot and its solution.

"The rascal!" he muttered; "and why did he carry off that ladder?"

"That he might see Esmeralda," piteously responded Jupiter. "He said, 'Stay, there's a ladder which is doing no one any good!' and he took it."

This was the finishing stroke. Gringoire received it with submission.

"May the devil seize you!" said he to the actors; "and if I am paid, you shall be too."

Then he beat a retreat, with drooping head, but last to leave, like a general who has fought a brave fight.

And as he descended the winding Palace staircase, he muttered between his teeth: "A pretty pack of donkeys and clowns these Parisians are! They come to hear a miracle-play, and then pay no heed to it! Their whole minds are absorbed in anybody and everybody,—in Clopin Trouillefou, the Cardinal, Coppenole, Quasimodo, the devil! but in Madame Virgin Mary not a whit. If I had known, I'd have given you your fill of Virgin Marys. And I,—to come to see faces, and to see nothing but backs! to be a poet, and to have the success of an apothecary! True, Homer begged his way through Greek villages, and Naso died in exile among the Muscovites. But may the devil flay me if I know what they mean by their 'Esmeralda'! What kind of a word is that, anyhow? It must be Egyptian!"

BOOK II

CHAPTER I

From Charybdis to Scylla

Night falls early in January. The streets were already dark when Gringoire left the Palace. This nightfall pleased him. He longed to find some dark and solitary alley where he might meditate at his ease, and let the philosopher apply the first healing balm to the poet's wounds. Besides, philosophy was his only refuge; for he knew not where to find shelter. After the total failure of his first theatrical effort he dared not return to the lodging which he had occupied, opposite the Hay-market, in the Rue Grenier-sur-l'Eau, having reckoned upon what the provost was to give him for his epithalamium to pay Master Guillaume Doulx-Sire, farmer of the taxes on cloven-footed animals in Paris, the six months' rent which he owed him, namely, twelve Paris pence,—twelve times the worth of everything that he owned in the world, including his breeches, his shirt, and his hat. After a moment's pause for reflection, temporarily sheltered under the little gateway of the prison of the treasurer of the Sainte-Chapelle, as to what refuge he should seek for the night, having all the pavements of Paris at his disposition, he remembered having noticed, the week before, in the Rue de la Savaterie, at the door of a Parliamentary Councillor, a stone block for mounting a mule, and having said to himself that this stone would, on occasion, make a very excellent pillow for a beggar or a poet. He thanked Providence for sending him so good an idea; but as he prepared to cross the Palace courtyard on his way to the crooked labyrinth of the city, formed by the windings of all those antique sisters, the Rues de la Barillerie, de la Vieille-Draperie, de la Savaterie, de la Juiverie, etc., still standing at the present day with their nine-story houses, he saw the procession of the Pope of Fools, which was also just issuing from the Palace and rushing across the courtyard, with loud shouts, an abundance of glaring torches, and his (Gringoire's) own music. This sight opened the wound to his self-esteem; he fled. In the bitterness of dramatic misfortune, all that recalled the day's festival incensed him, and made his wound bleed afresh.

He meant to cross the Pont Saint-Michel; some children were careering up and down there with rockets and crackers.

"A plague on all fireworks!" said Gringoire; and he turned towards the Pont-au-Change. The houses at the head of the bridge were adorned with three large banners representing the king, the dauphin, and Margaret of Flanders, and six little bannerets with portraits of the Duke of Austria, the Cardinal de Bourbon, M. de Beaujeu, and Madame Jeanne de France, the Bastard of Bourbon, and I know not who besides,— all lighted up by torches. The mob gazed in admiration.

"Lucky painter, Jehan Fourbault!" said Gringoire, with a heavy sigh; and he turned his back on banners and bannerets. A street opened directly before him: it looked so dark and deserted that he hoped it would afford a way of escape from every echo as well as every reflection of the festival: he plunged down it. In a few moments he struck his foot against something, stumbled, and fell. It was the big bunch of hawthorn which the members of the basoche had that morning placed at the door of a president of the Parliament, in honor of the day. Gringoire bore this new misfortune bravely; he rose and walked to the bank of the river. Leaving behind him the civil and criminal towers, and passing by the great walls of the royal gardens, along the unpaved shore where the mud was ankle-deep, he reached the western end of the city, and for some time contemplated the islet of the Passeur-aux-

Vaches, which has since vanished beneath the bronze horse on the Pont Neuf. The islet lay before him in the darkness, — a black mass across the narrow strip of whitish water which lay between him and it. The rays of a tiny light dimly revealed a sort of beehive-shaped hut in which the cows' ferryman sought shelter for the night.

"Lucky ferryman!" thought Gringoire; "you never dream of glory, and you write no wedding songs! What are the marriages of kings and Burgundian duchesses to you? You know no Marguerites save those which grow upon your turf in April for the pasturage of your cows! and I, poet that I am, am hooted, and I shiver, and I owe twelve pence, and the soles of my shoes are so thin that you might use them for glasses in your lantern. Thanks, ferryman! Your hut rests my eyes and makes me forget Paris."

He was roused from his almost lyric ecstasy by a huge double-headed rocket, which was suddenly sent up from the blessed cabin. The ferryman was taking his part in the festivities of the day, and setting off a few fireworks.

The explosion set Gringoire's teeth on edge.

"Accursed festival!" he exclaimed, "will you pursue me forever, — oh, my God! even to the ferryman's house?"

He gazed at the Seine at his feet and a horrible temptation overcame him.

"Ah!" said he, "how cheerfully I would drown myself if the water were not so cold!"

Then he took a desperate resolve. It was, since he could not escape from the Pope of Fools, Jehan Fourbault's flags, the bunches of hawthorn, the rockets, and squibs, to plunge boldly into the very heart of the gaiety and go directly to the Place de Grève.

"At least," thought he, "I may find some brands from the bonfire to warm myself, and I may sup on some crumbs from the three great sugar escutcheons which were to be served on the public sideboard."

CHAPTER II

The Place de Grève

But very slight traces now remain of the Place de Grève as it existed at the time of which we write; all that is left is the picturesque little tower at the northern corner of the square; and that, already buried beneath the vulgar whitewash which incrusts the sharp edges of its carvings, will soon disappear perhaps, drowned in that flood of new houses which is so rapidly swallowing up all the old facades of Paris.

People who, like ourselves, never pass through the Place de Grève without giving a glance of sympathy and pity to the poor little tower, choked between two hovels of the time of Louis XV, may readily reconstruct in fancy the entire mass of buildings to which it belonged, and as it were restore the old Gothic square of the fifteenth century.

It was, as it still is, an irregular square, bounded on one side by the quay, and on the other three by a number of tall, narrow, gloomy houses. By day one might admire the variety of its edifices, all carved in stone or wood, and presenting perfect specimens of the various kinds of mediæval domestic architecture, going back from the fifteenth to the eleventh century, from the casement window which was beginning to supersede the pointed arch, to the semi-circular arch of the Romance period, which gave way to the pointed arch, and which still occupied below it the first story of that old house called Tour de Roland, on the corner of the square nearest the Seine, close to the Rue de la Tannerie. At night, nothing could be seen of this mass of buildings but the dark indented line of the roofs stretching their chain of acute angles round the square. For it is one of the radical differences between modern and ancient towns, that nowadays the fronts of the houses face upon the squares and streets, and in old times it was the gable ends. In two centuries the houses have turned round.

In the middle of the eastern side of the square stood a heavy and hybrid construction composed of three houses together. It was known by three names, which explain its history, its purpose, and its architecture. The Maison au Dauphin, because Charles V occupied it while dauphin; the Marchandise, because it was used as the Town Hall; the Maison-aux-Piliers (*domus ad piloria*), on account of a series of thick columns which supported its three stories. There the city found everything required for a well-to-do town like Paris—a chapel in which to pray to God; a court of special pleas, where audience was given, and if necessary "the king's men put down;" and in the garrets an "arsenal" full of artillery. For the citizens of Paris, knowing that it is not always enough to pray and plead for the liberties of the town, always had a good rusty arquebus or two in reserve in an attic of the Town Hall.

Even then the Place de Grève had the same forbidding aspect which the detestable ideas clinging about it awaken, and the gloomy Town Hall built by Dominique Bocador, which has taken the place of the Maison-aux-Piliers, still gives it. It must be confessed that a permanent gibbet and pillory,—"a justice and a ladder," as they were then called,—standing side by side in the middle of the flagstones, largely contributed to make men turn away from that fatal square where so many beings full of life and health have died in agony; where the Saint Vallier's fever was destined to spring to life some fifty years later,—that disease which was nothing but dread of the scaffold, the most monstrous of all maladies, because it came not from God, but from man.

It is a consoling thought (let us say in passing) that the death penalty, which three hundred years ago still cumbered the Place de Grève, the Halles, the Place Dauphine, the Cross du Trahoir, the Marché-aux-Pourceaux, the hideous Montfaucon, the Porte Bandet, Place-aux-chats, the Porte Saint-Denis, Champeaux, and Barrière-des-Sergents, with its iron wheels, its stone gibbets, and all its machinery of torture, permanently built into the pavement; not to mention the countless pillories belonging to provosts, bishops, chapters, abbots, and priors administering justice; to say nothing of the legal drownings in the river Seine,—it is a consolation that in the present day, having successively lost all the pieces of her armor, her refinements of torture, her purely capricious and wilful penal laws, her torture for the administration of which she made afresh every five years a leather bed at the Grand-Châtelet, that ancient sovereign of feudal society, almost outlawed and exiled from our cities, hunted from code to code, driven from place to place, now possesses in all vast Paris but one dishonored corner of the Place de Grève, but one wretched guillotine, furtive, timid, and ashamed, seeming ever in dread of being taken in the very act, so swiftly does it vanish after it has dealt its deadly stroke!

CHAPTER III

*Besos Para Golpes**

When Pierre Gringoire reached the Place de Grève, he was benumbed. He had come by way of the Pont-aux-Meuniers to avoid the mob on the Pont-au-Change and Jehan Fourbault's flags; but the wheels of all the bishop's mills had bespattered him as he crossed, and his coat was soaked; moreover, it seemed to him that the failure of his play had made him more sensitive to cold than ever. He therefore made haste to draw near the bonfire which still

---

*A kiss brings pain (Spanish).

blazed gloriously in the middle of the square; but a considerable crowd formed a circle round about it.

"Damned Parisians!" said he to himself (for Gringoire, like all true dramatic poets, was given to monologues), "there they stand blocking my way to the fire! and yet I greatly need a good warm chimney-corner; my shoes leak, and all those cursed mills have dripped upon me! Devil take the Bishop of Paris and his mills! I would really like to know what a bishop wants with a mill! does he expect to turn miller? If he is merely waiting for my curse, I give it to him cheerfully, and to his cathedral and his mills into the bargain! Now just let's see if any of those boors will disturb themselves for me! What on earth are they doing there? Warming themselves indeed; a fine amusement! Watching to see a hundred fagots burn; a fine sight, truly!"

Looking more closely, he saw that the circle was far larger than was necessary for the crowd to warm themselves at the royal bonfire, and that the large number of spectators was not attracted solely by the beauty of the hundred blazing fagots.

In the vast space left free between the crowd and the fire a young girl was dancing.

Whether this young girl was a human being, or a fairy, or an angel, was more than Gringoire, cynic philosopher and sarcastic poet though he was, could for a moment decide, so greatly was he fascinated by the dazzling vision.

She was not tall, but seemed to be, so proudly erect did she hold her slender figure. Her skin was brown, but it was evident that by daylight it must have that lovely golden gleam peculiar to Spanish and Roman beauties. Her tiny foot was Andalusian too, for it fitted both snugly and easily into its dainty shoe. She danced, she turned, she twirled, upon an antique Persian carpet thrown carelessly beneath her feet; and every time her radiant figure passed, as she turned, her great black eyes sent forth lightning flashes.

Upon her every eye was riveted, every mouth gaped wide; and in very truth, as she danced to the hum of the tambourine which her round and graceful arms held high above her head, slender, quick and active as any wasp, with a smoothly fitting golden bodice, her many-colored full skirts, her bare shoulders, her shapely legs, from which her skirts now and then swung away, her black hair, her eyes of flame, she seemed more than mortal creature.

"Indeed," thought Gringoire, "she is a salamander, a nymph, a goddess, a bacchante from Mount Mænalus!"

At this moment one of the salamander's tresses was loosened, and a bit of brass which had been fastened to it fell to the ground.

"Alas, no!" said he, "she's a gipsy."

All illusion had vanished.

She began to dance once more. She picked up two swords, and balancing them by their points on her forehead, she twirled them in one direction while she herself revolved in another; she was indeed but a gipsy girl. But great as was Gringoire's disenchantment, the picture was far from being destitute of all charm and beauty; the bonfire lit it up with a crude red light, which flickered brightly upon the circle of surrounding figures and the young girl's brown face, casting wan reflections, blended with alternating shadows, into the farthest corners of the square,—on one side upon the black and weather-beaten front of the Maison-aux-Piliers, and on the other upon the cross-beam of the stone gibbet.

Among the myriad of faces dyed scarlet by the flames, there was one which seemed absorbed even beyond all the rest in gazing at the dancer. It was the face of a man, austere, calm, and somber. This man, whose dress was hidden by the crowd about him, seemed not more than thirty-five years old, and yet he was bald; he had but a few grey and scanty locks of hair about his temples; his broad, high forehead was already beginning to be furrowed with wrinkles, but in his deep-set eyes sparkled an extraordinary spirit of youth, an ardent love of life and depth of passion. He kept them fixed on the gipsy; and while the giddy young damsel danced and fluttered to the delight of all, his thoughts seemed to become more and more melancholy. From time to time a smile and a sigh met upon his lips, but the smile was far sadder than the sigh.

The young girl stopped at last, breathless, and the people applauded eagerly.

"Djali!" said the gipsy.

Then Gringoire saw a pretty little white goat, active, alert, and glossy, with gilded horns, gilded hoofs, and a gilded collar, which he had not before observed, and which had hitherto remained quietly crouching on a corner of the carpet, watching its mistress as she danced.

"Djali," said the dancer, "it's your turn now."

And sitting down, she gracefully offered the goat her tambourine.

"Djali," she added, "what month in the year is this?"

The goat raised its fore-foot and struck once upon the tambourine. It was indeed the first month of the year. The crowd applauded.

"Djali," resumed the young girl, turning her tambourine another way, "what day of the month is it?"

Djali lifted his little golden hoof and struck it six times upon the tambourine.

"Djali," continued the daughter of Egypt, with still another twist of the tambourine, "what time of day is it?"

Djali gave seven blows, and at the same instant the clock on the Maison-aux-Piliers struck seven.

The people were lost in wonder.

"There is sorcery in this," said a forbidding voice from the throng. It was the voice of the bald man, who had never taken his eyes from the gipsy.

She trembled, and turned towards him; but fresh applause broke out, and drowned the surly exclamation.

They even effaced it so completely from her mind that she went on questioning her goat.

"Djali, how does Master Guichard Grand-Remy, the captain of the city pistoleers, walk in the procession at Candlemas?"

Djali rose on his hind-legs and began to bleat, walking as

he did so with an air of such polite gravity that the whole ring of spectators burst into a laugh at this parody of the selfish devotion of the captain of pistoleers.

"Djali," continued the young girl, encouraged by her increasing success, "show us how Master Jacques Charmolue, the king's attorney in the Ecclesiastical Court, preaches."

The goat sat up and began to bleat, waving his fore-feet in so strange a fashion that, except for the bad French and the bad Latin, Jacques Charmolue himself stood before you,—gesture, accent, and attitude.

And the crowd applauded louder than before.

"Sacrilege! Profanation!" exclaimed the voice of the bald-headed man.

The gipsy turned again.

"Ah!" said she, "it is that ugly man!" Then projecting her lower lip beyond the upper one, she made a little pout which seemed habitual with her, pirouetted on her heel, and began to collect the gifts of the multitude in her tambourine.

Big pieces of silver, little pieces of silver, pennies, and farthings, rained into it. Suddenly she passed Gringoire. He put his hand in his pocket so heedlessly that she stopped. "The devil!" said the poet, as he found reality at the bottom of his pocket,—that is to say, an empty void. But there stood the pretty girl, looking at him with her big eyes, holding out her tambourine, and waiting. Gringoire was in an agony.

If he had had the wealth of Peru in his pocket, he would certainly have given it to the dancing-girl; but Gringoire did not possess the wealth of Peru, and moreover America had not then been discovered.

Luckily an unexpected event came to his rescue.

"Will you be gone, you gipsy grasshopper?" cried a sharp voice from the darkest corner of the square.

The young girl turned in terror. This was not the voice of the bald-headed man; it was a woman's voice,—the voice of a malicious and bigoted person.

However, the cry which alarmed the gipsy delighted a band of roving children.

"It's the recluse of the Tour-Roland," they shouted with riotous laughter. "It's the *sachette** scolding! Hasn't she had her supper? Let's carry her some bits from the city sideboard!"

All rushed towards the Maison-aux-Piliers.

Gringoire seized the occasion of the dancer's distress to disappear. The children's shouts reminded him that he too had not supped. He therefore hastened to the sideboard. But the little scamps had better legs than he; when he arrived, they had swept the table clear. There was not even a paltry cake at five cents the pound remaining. Nothing was left on the wall but the delicate *fleurs-de-lis*, twined with rose branches, painted in 1434 by Mathieu Biterne. That was a meager repast.

It's a tiresome matter to go to bed without supper; it is still less agreeable to have no supper and not to know where to find a bed. This was Gringoire's condition. No bread, no shelter; he was goaded on every hand by necessity, and he found necessity very crabbed and cross. He had long since discovered the truth that Jupiter created mankind in a fit of misanthropy, and that throughout a wise man's life fate keeps his philosophy in a state of siege. As for himself, the blockade had never been so complete. He heard his stomach sounding a parley, and he thought it very improper for an evil destiny to overcome his philosophy by famine.

He was becoming more and more absorbed in these melancholy reflections, when a peculiar although melodious song suddenly roused him from them. The young gipsy girl was singing.

Her voice was like her dancing, like her beauty. It was charming, and not to be defined,—possessing a pure and sonorous quality, something ethereal and airy. There was a constant succession of bursts of melody, of unexpected cadences, then of simple phrases mingled with shrill sibilant

---

*Nun of the Order of the "Sack," a name derived from the sack-like garment members of this group wore.

notes: now runs and trills which would have baffled a nightin-
gale, but which never ceased to be harmonious; then softly
undulating octaves rising and falling like the bosom of the
youthful singer.

Her fine features expressed every caprice of her song with
singular flexibility, from the most lawless inspiration to the
chastest dignity. At one instant she seemed a mad woman, at
the next a queen.

The words which she sang were in a language unknown to
Gringoire, and apparently one with which she was not herself
familiar, so little connection had the expression which she
lent her song with the meaning of the words. Thus these four
lines in her mouth became wildly gay:—

> "Un cofre de gran riqueza
> Hallaron dentro un pilar,
> Dentro del, nuevas banderas
> Con figuras de espantar."*

And a moment later, the tone in which she uttered the words,—

> "Alarabes de cavallo
> Sin poderse menear,
> Con espadas, y los cuellos,
> Ballestas de buen echar."†

brought the tears into Gringoire's eyes. And yet her song was
full of joy, and she seemed to sing like a bird, from sheer happiness and freedom from care.

The gipsy's song had troubled Gringoire's reverie, but as
the swan troubles the water. He listened in a sort of ecstasy

---

*A chest richly decorated / They found in a well, / And in it new ban-
ners / With figures most terrifying (Spanish).

†Arab horsemen they are / Looking like statues, / With swords, and
over their shoulders / Crossbows that shoot well (Spanish).

which rendered him oblivious of all else. It was the first instant, for some hours, in which he had felt no pain.

The moment was brief.

The same woman's voice which had cut short the girl's
dance now interrupted her song.

"Will you hold your tongue, you infernal cricket?" she
cried, still from the same dark corner of the square.

The poor "cricket" stopped short. Gringoire clapped his
hands to his ears.

"Oh," he exclaimed, "cursed be that rusty saw, which
breaks the lyre!"

And the other listeners grumbled with him.

"To the devil with the crazy nun!" said more than one. And
the invisible old marplot might have had reason to repent of
her aggressions, had not their thoughts been diverted at that
very moment by the procession of the Pope of Fools, which,
having traversed many a street and square, now appeared in
the Place de Grève with all its torches and all its noise.

This procession, which our readers saw as it started from
the Palace, had taken shape as it marched, enlisting all the
available vagabonds and scamps and idle thieves in Paris; so
that it presented quite a respectable appearance when it
reached the Place de Grève.

First came Egypt at the head, on horseback, with his aids
on foot, holding his stirrup and bridle. Behind walked the rest
of the Egyptians, male and female, with their little ones
clamoring on their backs; all, men, women, and children, in
rags and tatters. Then came the thieves' brotherhood:[4] that is,
all the robbers in France, ranged according to their degree,
the least expert coming first. Thus they filed along four by
four, armed with the various insignia of their degrees. In this
singular faculty, most of them maimed, some halt, some with
but one arm, were shoplifters, mock pilgrims, housebreakers,
sham epileptics, sham Abrams,* street rowdies, sham crip-

---

*Men who feigned insanity.

ples, the card sharpers, the fakely infirm, the hawkers, rogues pretending to have been burned out, cadgers, old soldiers, high-flyers, swell mobsmen, and thieves of the highest order—a list long enough to weary Homer himself. In the center of the high thieves might dimly be distinguished the head of the thieves' brotherhood, the "Grand Coëre," or king of rogues, squatting in a small cart, drawn by two big dogs. After the fraternity of thieves came the Empire of Galilee.* Guillaume Rousseau, Emperor of the Galilees, marched majestic in his purple robes stained with wine, preceded by mountebanks fighting and dancing Pyrrhic dances, surrounded by his mace-bearers, tools, and the clerks of the Court of Exchequer. Last came the basoche (the corporation of lawyers' clerks), with their sheaves of maize crowned with flowers, their black gowns, their music worthy of a Witches' Sabbath, and their huge yellow wax candles. In the midst of this throng the high officials of the fraternity of fools bore upon their shoulders a barrow more heavily laden with tapers than the shrine of St. Geneviève in time of plague; and upon this barrow rode resplendent, with crosier, cope, and miter, the new Pope of Fools, the bell-ringer of Notre-Dame, Quasimodo the Hunchback.

Each division of this grotesque procession had its own peculiar music. The Gipsies drew discordant notes from their balafos and their African tabors. The thieves, a far from musical race, were still using the viol, the cow-herd's horn, and the quaint rubeb of the twelfth century. Nor was the Empire of Galilee much more advanced; their music was almost wholly confined to some wretched rebec dating back to the infancy of the art, still imprisoned within the *re-la-mi*. But it was upon the Pope of Fools that all the musical riches of the period were lavished in one magnificent cacophony. There were treble rebecs, counter-tenor rebecs, tenor rebecs, to say nothing

---

*The Realm of Gamblers.

of flutes and brass instruments. Alas! our readers may remember that this was Gringoire's orchestra.

It is difficult to convey any idea of the degree of proud and
sanctimonious rapture which Quasimodo's hideous and
painful face had assumed during the journey from the Palace
to the Place de Grève. This was the first thrill of vanity which
he had ever felt. Hitherto he had known nothing but humilia-
tion, disdain of his estate, and disgust for his person. Therefore,
deaf as he was, he enjoyed, like any genuine pope, the applause
of that mob which he had hated because he felt that it hated
him. What mattered it to him that his subjects were a collection of fools, cripples, thieves, and beggars! They were still subjects and he a sovereign! And he took seriously all the mock
applause, all the satirical respect with which, it must be confessed, there was a slight mixture of very real fear in the hearts
of the throng. For the hunchback was strong; for the bow legs
were nimble; for the deaf ears were malicious,—three qualities
which tempered the ridicule.

Moreover, we are far from fancying that the new Pope of
Fools realized clearly either his own feelings or those which
he inspired. The mind lodged in that imperfect body was necessarily something dull and incomplete. Therefore what he
felt at this instant was absolutely vague, indistinct, and confused to him. Joy only pierced the cloud; pride prevailed. The
somber and unhappy face was radiant.

It was not therefore without surprise and fright that, at the
moment when Quasimodo in this semi-intoxication passed
triumphantly before the Maison-aux-Piliers, the spectators
saw a man dart from the crowd and snatch from his hands,
with a gesture of rage, his gilded crosier, the badge of his
mock papacy.

This man, this rash fellow, was no other than the bald-
headed character who, the instant before, mingling with the
group about the gipsy girl, had chilled her blood with his
words of menace and hatred. He was clad now in ecclesiastical garb. Just as he stepped forward from the crowd,
Gringoire, who had not noticed him until then, recognized

him. "Why!" said he with an exclamation of amazement, "it is my master in Hermetics, Dom Claude Frollo, the archdeacon! What the devil does he want with that ugly one-eyed man? He'll be swallowed up alive!"

Indeed, a cry of terror rose. The terrible Quasimodo flung himself headlong from his barrow, and the women turned away their eyes that they might not see the archdeacon torn limb from limb.

He made but one bound towards the priest, gazed at him, and fell on his knees.

The priest tore from him his tiara, broke his crosier and broke his tinsel cope.

Quasimodo still knelt, with bowed head and clasped hands. Then followed between them a strange dialogue in signs and gestures, for neither spoke,—the priest, erect, angry, threatening, imperious; Quasimodo, prostrate, humble, suppliant. And yet it is very certain that Quasimodo could have crushed the priest with his thumb.

At last the archdeacon, rudely shaking Quasimodo's powerful shoulder, signed to him to rise and follow.

Quasimodo rose.

Then the fraternity of fools, their first stupor over, strove to defend their pope, so abruptly dethroned. The thieves, the Galilees, and all the lawyers' clerks yelped about the priest.

Quasimodo placed himself before the priest, put the muscles of his fists in play, and glared at his assailants, gnashing his teeth like an enraged bear.

The priest resumed his somber gravity, beckoned to Quasimodo, and withdrew silently.

Quasimodo walked before him, scattering the crowd as he passed.

When they had made their way through the people and the square, a swarm of curious idlers attempted to follow them. Quasimodo then took up the position of rearguard, and followed the archdeacon backwards, short, thickset, crabbed, monstrous, bristling, gathering himself together, licking his tusks, growling like a wild beast, and driving the crowd before him in waves, with a gesture or a look.

They vanished down a dark, narrow street, where none dared venture after them; so effectually did the mere image of Quasimodo grinding his teeth bar the way.

"Strange enough!" said Gringoire; "but where the devil am I to find supper?"

CHAPTER IV

The Inconveniences of Following a Pretty Woman in the Street at Night

Gringoire determined to follow the gipsy girl at any risk. He had seen her go down the Rue de la Coutellerie with her goat; he therefore went down the Rue de la Coutellerie.

"Why not?" said he to himself.

Gringoire, being a practical philosopher of the streets of Paris, had observed that nothing is more favorable to reverie than the pursuit of a pretty woman when you don't know where she is going. In this voluntary surrender of your own free will, this caprice yielding to another caprice, all unconscious of submission, there is a mixture of odd independence and blind obedience, a certain happy medium between slavery and liberty, which pleased Gringoire, a mind essentially mixed, undetermined, and complex, carrying everything to extremes, forever wavering betwixt all human propensities, and neutralizing them the one by the other. He frequently compared himself to Mahomet's tomb, attracted in opposite directions by two loadstones, and perpetually trembling between top and bottom, between the ceiling and the pavement, between descent and ascent, between the zenith and the nadir.

If Gringoire were living now, what a golden mean he would observe between the classic and romantic schools![5]

But he was not sufficiently primitive to live three hundred years, and 't is a pity. His absence leaves a void but too deeply felt today.

However, nothing puts a man in a better mood for following people in the street (especially when they happen to be women), a thing Gringoire was always ready to do, than not knowing where he is to sleep.

He accordingly walked thoughtfully along behind the young girl, who quickened her pace and urged on her pretty goat, as she saw the townspeople were all going home, and the taverns—the only shops open upon this general holiday—were closing.

"After all," thought he, "she must have a lodging somewhere; gipsies are generous. Who knows—"

And there were some very pleasant ideas interwoven with the points of suspension that followed this mental reticence.

Still, from time to time, as he passed the last belated groups of citizens shutting their doors, he caught fragments of their talk, which broke the chain of his bright hypotheses.

Now, it was two old men chatting together.

"Master Thibaut Fernicle, do you know it is cold?"

(Gringoire had known this since the winter first set in.)

"Yes, indeed, Master Boniface Disome! Are we going to have another winter like the one we had three years ago, in '80, when wood cost eight pence the measure?"

"Bah! that's nothing, Master Thibaut, to the winter of 1407, when it froze from St. Martin's Day to Candlemas, and with such fury that the parliamentary registrar's pen froze, in the Great Chamber, between every three words, which was a vast impediment to the registration of justice!"

Farther on, two neighbor women gossiped at their windows; the candles in their hands flickered faintly through the fog.

"Did your husband tell you of the accident, Mademoiselle la Boudraque?"

"No. What was it, Mademoiselle Turquant?"

"The horse of M. Gilles Godin, the notary from the Châtelet, took fright at the Flemish and their procession, and knocked down Master Philippot Avrillot, lay brother of the Celestines."

"Is that really so?"

"Indeed it is."

"And such a plebeian animal! It's a little too much. If it had only been a cavalry horse, it would not be so bad!"

And the windows were closed. But Gringoire had already lost the thread of his ideas.

Luckily, he soon recovered and readily resumed it, thanks to the gipsy girl, thanks to Djali, who still went before him,— two slender, delicate, charming creatures, whose tiny feet, pretty forms, and graceful manners he admired, almost confounding them in his contemplation; thinking them both young girls from their intelligence and close friendship; considering them both goats from the lightness, agility, and grace of their step.

But the streets grew darker and more deserted every instant. The curfew had long since sounded, and it was only at rare intervals that a passenger was seen upon the pavement or a light in any window. Gringoire had involved himself, by following in the footsteps of the gipsy, in that inextricable labyrinth of lanes, cross-streets, and blind alleys, which encircles the ancient sepulcher of the Holy Innocents, and which is much like a skein of thread tangled by a playful kitten.

"Here are streets with but little logic!" said Gringoire, lost in the myriad windings which led back incessantly to their original starting-point, but amid which the damsel pursued a path with which she seemed very familiar, never hesitating, and walking more and more swiftly. As for him, he would not have had the least idea where he was, if he had not caught a glimpse, at the corner of a street, of the octagonal mass of the pillory of the Markets, whose pierced top stood out in sharp, dark outlines against a window still lighted in the Rue Verdelet.

A few moments before, he had attracted the young girl's attention; she had several times turned her head anxiously towards him; once she had even stopped short, and taken advantage of a ray of light which escaped from a half-open bakeshop, to study him earnestly from head to foot; then, having cast that glance, Gringoire saw her make the little pouting grimace which he had already noted, and then she passed on.

It gave Gringoire food for thought. There was certainly a leaven of scorn and mockery in that dainty grimace. He therefore began to hang his head, to count the paving-stones, and to follow the young girl at a somewhat greater distance, when at the turn of a street which hid her from his sight, he heard her utter a piercing scream.

He hastened on.

The street was full of dark shadows. Still, a bit of tow soaked in oil, which burned in an iron cage at the foot of the image of the Holy Virgin at the street corner enabled Gringoire to see the gipsy girl struggling in the arms of two men who were trying to stifle her cries. The poor little goat, in great alarm, lowered its horns and bleated piteously.

"This way, gentlemen of the watch!" shouted Gringoire; and he rushed boldly forward. One of the men who held the girl turned towards him. It was the formidable figure of Quasimodo.

Gringoire did not take flight, but neither did he advance another step.

Quasimodo approached him, flung him four paces away upon the pavement with a single back stroke, and plunged rapidly into the darkness, bearing the girl, thrown over one arm like a silken scarf. His companion followed him, and the poor goat ran behind, with its plaintive bleat.

"Murder! murder!" shrieked the unfortunate gipsy.

"Halt, wretches, and let that wench go!" abruptly exclaimed, in a voice of thunder, a horseman who appeared suddenly from the next cross-street.

It was a captain of the King's archers, armed from head to foot, and broadsword in hand.

He tore the gipsy girl from the arms of the astounded Quasimodo, laid her across his saddle, and just as the redoubtable hunchback, recovering from his surprise, rushed upon him to get back his prey, some fifteen or sixteen archers, who were close behind their captain, appeared, two-edged swords in hand. They were a squadron of the royal troops going on duty as extra watchmen, by order of Master Robert d'Estouteville, the Provost's warden of Paris.

Quasimodo was surrounded, seized, garotted. He roared, he foamed at the mouth, he bit; and had it been daylight, no doubt his face alone, made yet more hideous by rage, would have routed the whole squadron. But by night he was stripped of his most tremendous weapon,—his ugliness.

His companion had disappeared during the struggle.

The gipsy girl sat gracefully erect upon the officer's saddle, placing both hands upon the young man's shoulders, and gazing fixedly at him for some seconds, as if charmed by his beauty and the timely help which he had just rendered her.

Then breaking the silence, she said, her sweet voice sounding even sweeter than usual:

"What is your name, Mr. Officer?"

"Captain Phœbus de Châteaupers, at your service, my pretty maid!" replied the officer, drawing himself up.

"Thank you," said she.

And while Captain Phœbus twirled his moustache, cut in Burgundian fashion, she slipped from the horse like an arrow falling to the earth, and fled.

A flash of lightning could not have vanished more swiftly.

"By the Pope's head!" said the captain, ordering Quasimodo's bonds to be tightened, "I would rather have kept the wench."

"What would you have, Captain?" said one of his men; "the bird has flown, the bat remains."

CHAPTER V

The Continuation of the Inconveniences

Gringoire, still dizzy from his fall, lay stretched on the pavement before the figure of the Blessed Virgin at the corner of the street. Little by little he regained his senses; at first he was for some moments floating in a sort of half-drowsy reverie which was far from unpleasant, in which the airy figures of the gipsy and her goat were blended with the weight of Quasimodo's fist. This state of things did not last long. A somewhat sharp sensation of cold on that part of his body in contact with the pavement roused him completely, and brought his mind back to realities once more.

"Why do I feel so cold?" said he, abruptly. He then discovered that he was lying in the middle of the gutter.

"Devil take the hunchbacked Cyclop!" he muttered; and he tried to rise. But he was too dizzy and too much bruised; he was forced to remain where he was. However, his hand was free; he stopped his nose and resigned himself to his fate.

"The mud of Paris," thought he (for he felt very sure that the gutter must be his lodging for the night,

"And what should we do in a lodging if we do
    not think?")*

"the mud of Paris is particularly foul; it must contain a vast amount of volatile and nitrous salts. Moreover, such is the opinion of Master Nicolas Flamel and of the Hermetics—"

The word "Hermetics" suddenly reminded him of the

---

*Reference to "The Hare and the Frogs," a fable by Jean de la Fontaine (1621–1695).

archdeacon, Claude Frollo. He recalled the violent scene which he had just witnessed,—how the gipsy struggled with two men, how Quasimodo had a companion; and the morose and haughty face of the archdeacon passed confusedly through his mind. "That would be strange!" he thought. And he began to erect, upon these data and this basis, the fantastic edifice of hypothesis, that card-house of philosophers; then suddenly returning once more to reality, "But there! I am freezing!" he exclaimed.

The situation was in fact becoming more and more unbearable. Every drop of water in the gutter took a particle of heat from Gringoire's loins, and the temperature of his body and the temperature of the gutter began to balance each other in a very disagreeable fashion.

An annoyance of quite another kind all at once beset him.

A band of children, those little barefoot savages who have haunted the streets of Paris in all ages under the generic name of "gamins," and who, when we too were children, threw stones at us every day as we hastened home from school because our trousers were destitute of holes,—a swarm of these young scamps ran towards the cross-roads where Gringoire lay, with shouts and laughter which seemed to show but little regard for their neighbors' sleep.[6] They dragged after them a shapeless sack, and the mere clatter of their wooden shoes would have been enough to rouse the dead. Gringoire, who was not quite lifeless yet, rose to a sitting position.

"Olé, Hennequin Dandèche! Olé, Jehan-Pincebourde!" they bawled at the top of their voices; "old Eustache Moubon, the junk-man at the corner, has just died; we've got his mattress; we're going to build a bonfire. This is the Flemings' day!"

And lo, they flung the mattress directly upon Gringoire, near whom they stood without seeing him. At the same time one of them snatched up a wisp of straw which he lighted at the good Virgin's lamp.

"Christ's body!" groaned Gringoire, "am I going to be too hot next?"

It was a critical moment. He would soon be caught betwixt

fire and water. He made a supernatural effort,—such an effort as a coiner of false money might make when about to be boiled alive and struggling to escape. He rose to his feet, hurled the mattress back upon the little rascals, and fled.

"Holy Virgin!" screamed the boys; "the junk-dealer has returned!"

And they too took to their heels.

The mattress was left mistress of the battlefield. Belleforêt, Father le Juge, and Corrozet affirm that it was picked up next day with great pomp by the clergy of the quarter, and placed in the treasury of the Church of the Holy Opportunity, where the sacristan earned a handsome income until 1789 by his tales of the wonderful miracle performed by the statue of the Virgin at the corner of the Rue Mauconseil, which had by its mere presence, on the memorable night of Jan. 6, 1482, exorcised the spirit of the defunct Eustache Moubon, who, to outwit the devil, had, in dying, maliciously hidden his soul in his mattress.

CHAPTER VI

The Broken Pitcher

After running for some time as fast as his legs would carry him, without knowing whither, plunging headlong around many a street corner, striding over many a gutter, traversing many a lane and blind alley, seeking to find escape and passage through all the windings of the old streets about the markets, exploring in his panic fear what the elegant Latin of the charters calls *tota via, cheminum et viaria,**

---

*Every way, highway, and byway (Latin).

our poet came to a sudden stop, partly from lack of breath,
and partly because he was collared as it were by a dilemma
which had just dawned upon his mind. "It strikes me, Pierre
Gringoire," said he to himself, laying his finger to his forehead, "that you are running as if you had lost your wits. Those
little scamps were quite as much afraid of you as you were of
them. It strikes me, I tell you, that you heard the clatter of
their wooden shoes as they fled to the south, while you took
refuge to the north. Now, one of two things: either they ran
away, and then the mattress, which they must have forgotten
in their fright, is just the hospitable bed which you have been
running after since morning, and which Our Lady miraculously sends you to reward you for writing a morality in her
honor, accompanied by triumphal processions and mummeries; or else the boys did not run away, and in that case they
have set fire to the mattress; and there you have just exactly
the good fire that you need to cheer, warm, and dry you. In
either case, whether as a good fire or a good bed, the mattress
is a gift from Heaven. The Blessed Virgin Mary, at the corner
of the Rue Mauconseil, may have killed Eustache Moubon
for this very purpose; and it is sheer madness in you to betake
yourself to such frantic flight, like a Picard running before a
Frenchman, leaving behind what you are seeking before you;
and you are a fool!"

Then he retraced his steps, and fumbling and ferreting his
way, snuffing the breeze, and his ear on the alert, he strove to
find the blessed mattress once more, but in vain. He saw nothing but intersecting houses, blind alleys, and crossings, in the
midst of which he doubted and hesitated continually, more
hindered and more closely entangled in this confusion of dark
lanes than he would have been in the very labyrinth of the
Hôtel des Tournelles. At last he lost patience, and exclaimed
solemnly: "Curse all these crossings! The devil himself must
have made them in the likeness of his pitchfork."

This outburst comforted him somewhat, and a sort of reddish reflection which he observed at this instant at the end of
a long, narrow lane, quite restored his wonted spirits. "Heaven

be praised!" said he; "yonder it is! There's my mattress burning briskly." And comparing himself to the boatman foundering by night, he added piously: "*Salve, salve, maris stella!*"*

Did he address this fragment of a litany to the Holy Virgin, or to the mattress? That we are wholly unable to say.

He had taken but a few steps down the long lane, which was steep, unpaved, and more and more muddy and sloping, when he remarked a very strange fact. It was not empty: here and there, along its length, crawled certain vague and shape-less masses, all proceeding towards the light which flickered at the end of the street, like those clumsy insects which creep at night from one blade of grass to another towards a shep-herd's fire.

Nothing makes a man bolder than the sense of an empty pocket. Gringoire continued to advance, and had soon over-took that larva which dragged itself most lazily along behind the others. As he approached, he saw that it was nothing but a miserable cripple without any legs, a stump of a man, hop-ping along as best he might on his hands, like a wounded spi-der which has but two legs left. Just as he passed this kind of human insect, it uttered a piteous appeal to him: "*La buona mancia, signor! la buona mancia!*"†

"Devil fly away with you," said Gringoire, "and with me too, if I know what you're talking about!"

And he passed on.

He came up with another of these perambulating masses, and examined it. It was another cripple, both lame and one-armed, and so lame and so armless that the complicated sys-tem of crutches and wooden limbs which supported him made him look like a mason's scaffolding walking off by itself. Gringoire, who loved stately and classic similes, compared the fellow, in fancy, to Vulcan's living tripod.

The living tripod greeted him as he passed, by holding his

---

*Hail, star of the sea! (Latin).

†Charity, kind sir! Charity! (Italian).

hat at the level of Gringoire's chin, as if it had been a barber's basin, and shouting in his ears: "*Señor caballero, para comprar un pedaso de pan!*"*

"It seems," said Gringoire, "that he talks too; but it's an ugly language, and he is better off than I am if he understands it."

Then, clapping his hand to his head with a sudden change of idea: "By the way, what the devil did they mean this morning by their 'Esmeralda'?"

He tried to quicken his pace; but for the third time something blocked the way. This something, or rather this some one, was a blind man, a little blind man, with a bearded Jewish face, who, feeling about him with a stick, and towed by a big dog, snuffled out to him with a Hungarian accent: "*Facitote caritatem!*"†

"That's right!" said Pierre Gringoire; "here's one at last who speaks a Christian tongue. I must have a very charitable air to make all these creatures come to me for alms when my purse is so lean. My friend [and he turned to the blind man], I sold my last shirt last week; that is to say, since you understand the language of Cicero, '*Vendidi hebdomade nuper transita meam ultimam chemisam!*'"

So saying, he turned his back on the blind man and went his way. But the blind man began to mend his steps at the same time; and lo and behold! the cripple and the stump hurried along after them with a great clatter of supports and crutches over the pavement.

Then all three, tumbling over each other in their haste at the heels of poor Gringoire, began to sing their several songs:—

"*Caritatem!*" sang the blind man.

"*La buona mancia!*" sang the stump.

And the lame man took up the phrase with, "*Un pedaso de pan!*"

---

*Kind sir, something with which to buy a piece of bread! (Spanish).
†Charity! (Latin).

Gringoire stopped his ears, exclaiming, "Oh, tower of Babel!"

He began to run. The blind man ran. The lame man ran. The stump ran.

And then, the farther he went down the street, the more thickly did cripples, blind men, and legless men swarm around him, with armless men, one-eyed men, and lepers with their sores, some coming out of houses, some from adjacent streets, some from cellar-holes, howling, yelling, bellowing, all hobbling and limping, rushing towards the light, and wallowing in the mire like slugs after a rain shower.

Gringoire, still followed by his three persecutors and not knowing what would happen next, walked timidly through the rest, going around the lame, striding over the cripples, his feet entangled in this ant-hill of deformity and disease, like that English captain caught fast by an army of land-crabs.

He thought of retracing his steps; but it was too late. The entire legion had closed up behind him, and his three beggars pressed him close. He therefore went on, driven alike by this irresistible stream, by fear, and by a dizzy feeling which made all this seem a horrible dream.

At last he reached the end of the street. It opened into a vast square, where a myriad scattered lights twinkled through the dim fog of night. Gringoire hurried forward, hoping by the swiftness of his legs to escape the three infirm specters who had fastened themselves upon him.

"*Onde vas, hombre?*"* cried the lame man, throwing away his crutches, and running after him with the best pair of legs that ever measured a geometric pace upon the pavements of Paris.

Then the stump, erect upon his feet, clapped his heavy iron-bound bowl upon Gringoire's head, and the blind man glared at him with flaming eyes.

"Where am I?" asked the terrified poet.

---

*Where do you go, man? (Spanish).

"In the Court of Miracles," replied a fourth specter, who had just accosted them.

"By my soul!" replied Gringoire; "I do indeed behold blind men seeing and lame men running; but where is the Savior?"

They answered with an evil burst of laughter.

The poor poet glanced around him. He was indeed in that fearful Court of Miracles, which no honest man had ever entered at such an hour; the magic circle within whose lines the officers of the Châtelet, and the Provost's men who ventured to penetrate it, disappeared in morsels; a city of thieves, a hideous wart upon the face of Paris; the sewer whence escaped each morning, returning to stagnate at night, that rivulet of vice, mendicity, and vagrancy, perpetually overflowing the streets of every great capital; a monstrous hive, receiving nightly all the drones of the social order with their booty; the lying hospital, where the gipsy, the unfrocked monk, the ruined scholar, the scapegrace of every nation, Spanish, Italian, and German, and of every creed, Jew, Christian, Mohametan, and idolater, covered with painted sores, beggars by day, were transformed into robbers by night,—in short, a huge cloak-room, used at this period for the dressing and undressing of all the actors in the everlasting comedy enacted in the streets of Paris by theft, prostitution, and murder.

It was a vast square, irregular and ill-paved, like every other square in Paris at that time. Fires, around which swarmed strange groups, gleamed here and there. People came and went, and shouted and screamed. There was a sound of shrill laughter, of the wailing of children and the voices of women. The hands, the heads of this multitude, black against the luminous background, made a thousand uncouth gestures. At times, a dog which looked like a man, or a man who looked like a dog, passed over the space of ground lit up by the flames, blended with huge and shapeless shadows. The limits of race and species seemed to fade away in this city as in some pandemonium. Men, women, beasts, age, sex, health, disease, all seemed to be in common among these people; all was blended, mingled, confounded, superimposed; each partook of all.

The feeble flickering light of the fires enabled Gringoire to distinguish, in spite of his alarm, all around the vast square a hideous framing of ancient houses whose worm-eaten, worn, misshapen fronts, each pierced by one or two lighted garret windows, looked to him in the darkness like the huge heads of old women ranged in a circle, monstrous and malign, watching and winking at the infernal revels.

It was like a new world, unknown, unheard of, deformed, creeping, swarming, fantastic.

Gringoire, more and more affrighted, caught by the three beggars, as if by three pairs of pincers, confused by the mass of other faces which snarled and grimaced about him,—the wretched Gringoire tried to recover sufficient presence of mind to recall whether it was Saturday or not. But his efforts were in vain; the thread of his memory and his thoughts was broken; and doubting everything, hesitating between what he saw and what he felt, he asked himself the unanswerable questions: "If I be I, are these things really so? If these things be so, am I really I?"

At this instant a distinct cry arose from the buzzing mob which surrounded him: "Take him to the King! take him to the King!"

"Holy Virgin!" muttered Gringoire, "the King of this region should be a goat."

"To the King! to the King!" repeated every voice.

He was dragged away. Each one vied with the other in fastening his claws upon him. But the three beggars never loosed their hold, and tore him from the others, howling, "He is ours!"

The poet's feeble doublet breathed its last in the struggle.

As they crossed the horrid square his vertigo vanished. After walking a few steps, a sense of reality returned. He began to grow accustomed to the atmosphere of the place. At first, from his poetic head, or perhaps, quite simply and quite prosaically, from his empty stomach, there had arisen certain fumes, a vapor as it were, which, spreading itself between him and other objects, prevented him from seeing anything save through a confused nightmare mist, through those dream-like shadows which render every outline vague, distort every shape, combine all objects into exaggerated groups, and enlarge things into chimeras and men into ghosts. By degrees this delusion gave way to a less wild and less deceitful vision. Reality dawned upon him, blinded him, ran against him, and bit by bit destroyed the frightful poetry with which he had at first fancied himself surrounded. He could not fail to see that he was walking, not in the Styx, but in the mire; that he was pushed and elbowed, not by demons but by thieves; that it was not his soul, but merely his life which was in danger (since he lacked that precious conciliator which pleads so powerfully with the bandit for the honest man,—a purse). Finally, examining the revels more closely and with greater calmness, he descended from the Witches' Sabbath to the tavern.

The Court of Miracles was indeed only a tavern, but a tavern of thieves, as red with blood as with wine.

The spectacle presented to his eyes when his tattered escort at last landed him at his journey's end was scarcely fitted to bring him back to poetry, even were it the poetry of hell. It was more than ever the prosaic and brutal reality of the tavern. If we were not living in the fifteenth century, we should say that Gringoire had fallen from Michael Angelo to Callot.

Around a large fire burning upon a great round flagstone, and lapping with its flames the rusty legs of a trivet empty for the moment, stood a number of worm-eaten tables here and there, in dire confusion, no lackey of any geometrical pretensions having deigned to adjust their parallelism, or at least to see that they did not cross each other at angles too unusual. Upon these tables glittered various pots and jugs dripping with wine and beer, and around these jugs were seated numerous Bacchanalian faces, purple with fire and wine. One big-bellied man with a jolly face was administering noisy kisses to a brawny, thickset woman. A rubbie, or old vagrant, whistled as he loosed the bandages from his mock wound, and rubbed his sound, healthy knee, which had been swathed all day in ample ligatures. Beyond him was a malingerer, preparing his "visitation from God"—his sore leg—with suet and ox-blood. Two tables farther on, a sham pilgrim, in complete pilgrim dress, was spelling out the lament of Sainte-Reine, not forgetting the snuffle and the twang. In another place a young scamp who imposed on the charitable by pretending to have been bitten by a mad dog, was taking a lesson of an old cadger in the art of frothing at the mouth by chewing a bit of soap. By their side a dropsical man was reducing his size, making four or five hags hold their noses as they sat at the same table, quarrelling over a child which they had stolen during the evening,—all circumstances which, two centuries later, "seemed so ridiculous to the court," as Sauval says, "that they served as diversion to the King, and as the opening to a royal ballet entitled 'Night,' divided into four parts, and danced at the Petit Bourbon Theatre." "Never," adds an eye-witness in 1653, "have the sudden changes of the Court of Miracles been more happily hit off. Benserade prepared us for them by some very fine verses."

Coarse laughter was heard on every hand, with vulgar songs. Every man expressed himself in his own way, carping and swearing, without heeding his neighbor. Some hobnobbed, and quarrels arose from the clash of their mugs, and the breaking of their mugs was the cause of many torn rags.

A big dog squatted on his tail, gazing into the fire. Some children took their part in the orgies. The stolen child cried and screamed; while another, a stout boy of four, sat on a high bench, with his legs dangling, his chin just coming above the table, and not speaking a word. A third was gravely smearing the table with melted tallow as it ran from the candle. Another, a little fellow crouched in the mud, almost lost in a kettle which he was scraping with a potsherd, making a noise which would have distracted Stradivarius.

A cask stood near the fire, and a beggar sat on the cask. This was the king upon his throne.

The three who held Gringoire led him up to this cask, and all the revellers were hushed for a moment, except the caldron inhabited by the child.

Gringoire dared not breathe or raise his eyes.

"*Hombre, quita tu sombrero!*"* said one of the three scoundrels who held him; and before he had made up his mind what this meant, another snatched his hat,—a shabby head-piece, to be sure, but still useful on sunny or on rainy days. Gingoire sighed.

But the king, from the height of his barrel, addressed him,—

"Who is this rascal?"

Gringoire started. The voice, although threatening in tone, reminded him of another voice which had that same morning dealt the first blow to his mystery by whining out from the audience, "Charity, kind souls!" He lifted his head. It was indeed Clopin Trouillefou.

Clopin Trouillefou, decked with his royal insignia, had not a tatter more or less than usual. The wound on his arm had vanished.

In his hand he held one of those whips with whit-leather thongs then used by sergeants of the wand to keep back the crowd, and called "boullayes." Upon his head he wore a circular bonnet closed at the top; but it was hard to say whether it was a child's cap or a king's crown, so similar are the two things.

Still, Gringoire, without knowing why, felt his hopes revive when he recognized this accursed beggar of the Great Hall in the King of the Court of Miracles.

"Master," stuttered he, "My lord—Sire— How shall I address you?" he said at last, reaching the culminating point of his crescendo, and not knowing how to rise higher or to redescend.

---

*Take off your hat, man! (Spanish).

"My lord, your Majesty, or comrade. Call me what you will; but make haste. What have you to say in your defense?"

"'In your defense,'" thought Gringoire; "I don't like the sound of that." He resumed stammeringly, "I am he who this morning—"

"By the devil's claws!" interrupted Clopin, "your name, rascal, and nothing more. Hark ye. You stand before three mighty sovereigns: me, Clopin Trouillefou, King of Tunis,* successor to the Grand Coëre, the king of rogues, lord paramount of the kingdom of Slang; Mathias Hungadi Spicali, Duke of Egypt† and Bohemia, that yellow old boy you see yonder with a clout about his head, Guillaume Rousseau, Emperor of Galilee,‡ that fat fellow who pays no heed to us, but caresses that wench. We are your judges. You have entered the kingdom of Slang, the land of thieves, without being a member of the confraternity; you have violated the privileges of our city. You must be punished, unless you be either prig, mumper, or cadger; that is, in the vulgar tongue of honest folks, either thief, beggar, or tramp. Are you anything of the sort? Justify yourself; state your character."

"Alas!" said Gringoire, "I have not that honor. I am the author—"

"Enough!" cried Trouillefou, not allowing him to finish his sentence. "You must be hanged. Quite a simple matter, my honest citizens! As you treat our people when they enter your domain, so we treat yours when they intrude among us. The law which you mete out to vagabonds, the vagabonds mete out to you. It is your own fault if it be evil. It is quite necessary that we should occasionally see an honest man grin ever through a hempen collar; it makes the thing honorable. Come, friend, divide your rags cheerfully among these young ladies. I will have you hanged to amuse the vagabonds, and

---

*Slang for King of the Beggars.

†King of the Gypsies.

‡Leader of the Gamblers.

you shall give them your purse to pay for a drink. If you have any mummeries to perform, over yonder in that mortar there's a capital God the Father, in stone, which we stole from the Church of Saint-Pierre-aux-Bœufs. You have four minutes to fling your soul at his head."

This was a terrible speech.

"Well said, upon my soul! Clopin Trouillefou preaches as well as any pope!" exclaimed the Emperor of Galilee, smashing his jug to prop up his table.

"Noble emperors and kings," said Gringoire with great coolness (for his courage had mysteriously returned, and he spoke firmly), "you do not consider what you're doing. My name is Pierre Gringoire; I am the poet whose play was performed this morning in the Great Hall of the Palace."

"Oh, is it you, sirrah?" said Clopin. "I was there, God's wounds! Well, comrade, because you bored us this morning, is that any reason why we should not hang you tonight?"

"I shall have hard work to get off," thought Gringoire. But yet he made one more effort. "I don't see," said he, "why poets should not be classed with vagabonds. Æsop was a vagrant; Homer was a beggar; Mercury was a thief—"

Clopin interrupted him: "I believe you mean to cozen us with your lingo. Good God! be hanged, and don't make such a row about it!"

"Excuse me, my lord King of Tunis," replied Gringoire, disputing every inch of the ground. "Is it worth while— An instant— Hear me— You will not condemn me unheard—"

"His melancholy voice was indeed lost in the uproar around him. The little boy scraped his kettle more vigorously than ever; and, to cap the climax, an old woman had just placed a frying-pan full of fat upon the trivet, and it crackled over the flames with a noise like the shouts of an army of children in chase of some masquerader.

However, Clopin Trouillefou seemed to be conferring for a moment with the Duke of Egypt and the Emperor of Galilee, the latter being entirely drunk. Then he cried out sharply, "Silence, I say!" and as the kettle and the frying-pan paid no heed, but kept up their duet, he leaped from his cask, dealt a kick to the kettle, which rolled ten paces or more with the child, another kick to the frying-pan, which upset all the fat into the fire, and then gravely reascended his throne, utterly regardless of the little one's stifled sobs and the grumbling of the old woman whose supper had vanished in brilliant flames.

Trouillefou made a sign, and the duke, the emperor, the arch thieves, and the dignitaries of the kingdom ranged themselves around him in the form of a horseshoe, Gringoire, still roughly grasped by the shoulders, occupying the center. It was a semicircle of rags, of tatters, of tinsel, of pitchforks, of axes, of staggering legs, of bare brawny arms, of sordid, dull, stupid faces. In the middle of this Round Table of beggary Clopin Trouillefou reigned pre-eminent, as the doge of this senate, the king of this assembly of peers, the pope of this conclave,— pre-eminent in the first place by the height of his cask, then by a peculiarly haughty, savage, and tremendous air, which made his eyes flash, and amended in his fierce profile the bestial type of the vagrant. He seemed a wild boar among swine.

"Hark ye," he said to Gringoire, caressing his shapeless chin with his horny hand; "I see no reason why you should not be hanged. To be sure, you seem to dislike the idea, and it's very plain that you worthy townsfolk are not used to it; you've got an exaggerated idea of the thing. After all, we wish you no harm. There is one way of getting you out of the difficulty for the time being. Will you join us?"

My reader may fancy the effect of this proposal upon Gringoire, who saw his life escaping him, and had already begun to lose his hold upon it. He clung to it once more with vigor.

"I will indeed, with all my heart," said he.

"Do you agree," resumed Clopin, "to enroll yourself among the gentry of the chive?"*

---

*Slang term signifying "Men of Slang."

"Of the chive, exactly," answered Gringoire.

"Do you acknowledge yourself a member of the rogues' brigade?" continued the King of Tunis.

"Of the rogues' brigade."

"A subject of the kingdom of Slang?"

"Of the kingdom of Slang."

"A vagrant?"

"A vagrant."

"At heart?"

"At heart."

"I would call your attention to the fact," added the King, "that you will be hanged none the less."

"The devil!" said the poet.

"Only," continued Clopin, quite unmoved, "you will be hanged later, with more ceremony, at the cost of the good city of Paris, on a fine stone gallows, and by honest men. That is some consolation."

"As you say," responded Gringoire.

"There are other advantages. As a member of the rogues' brigade you will have to pay no taxes for pavements, for the poor, or for lighting the streets, to all of which the citizens of Paris are subject."

"So be it," said the poet; "I consent. I am a vagrant, a man of Slang, a member of the rogues' brigade, a man of the chive,—what you will; and I was all this long ago, Sir King of Tunis, for I am a philosopher; *et omnia in philosophia, omnes in philosopho continentur,** as you know."

The King of Tunis frowned.

"What do you take me for, mate? What Hungarian Jew's gibberish are you giving us? I don't know Hebrew. I'm no Jew, if I am a thief. I don't even steal now; I am above that; I kill. Cutthroat, yes; cutpurse, no."

---

*All things are included in philosophy, all men in the philosopher (Latin).

Gringoire tried to slip in some excuse between these brief phrases which anger made yet more abrupt.

"I beg your pardon, my lord. It is not Hebrew, it is Latin."

"I tell you," replied Clopin, furiously, "that I am no Jew, and that I will have you hanged,—by the synagogue, I will!—together with that paltry Judean cadger beside you, whom I mightily hope I may some day see nailed to a counter, like the counterfeit coin that he is!"

So saying, he pointed to the little Hungarian Jew with the beard, who had accosted Gringoire with his *"Facitote caritatem,"* and who, understanding no other language, was amazed at the wrath which the King of Tunis vented upon him.

At last my lord Clopin became calm.

"So, rascal," said he to our poet, "you wish to become a vagrant?"

"Undoubtedly," replied the poet.

"It is not enough merely to wish," said the surly Clopin; "good-will never added an onion to the soup, and is good for nothing but a passport to paradise; now, paradise and Slang are two distinct things. To be received into the kingdom of Slang, you must prove that you are good for something; and to prove this you must search the manikin."*

"I will search," said Gringoire, "as much as ever you like."

Clopin made a sign. A number of Slangers stepped from the circle and returned immediately, bringing a couple of posts finished at the lower end with broad wooden feet, which made them stand firmly upon the ground; at the upper end of the two posts they arranged a crossbeam, the whole forming a very pretty portable gallows, which Gringoire had the pleasure of seeing erected before him in the twinkling of an eye. Nothing was wanting, not even the rope, which swung gracefully from the crossbeam.

"What are they going to do?" wondered Gringoire with

---

*Show one's skill at picking pockets.

some alarm. A sound of bells which he heard at the same moment put an end to his anxiety; it was a manikin, or puppet, that the vagrants hung by the neck to the cord,—a sort of scarecrow, dressed in red, and so loaded with little bells and hollow brasses that thirty Castilian mules might have been tricked out with them. These countless tinklers jingled for some time with the swaying of the rope, then the sound died away by degrees, and finally ceased when the manikin had been restored to a state of complete immobility by that law of the pendulum which has superseded the clepsydra and the hour-glass.

Then Clopin, showing Gringoire a rickety old footstool, placed under the manikin, said,—

"Climb up there!"

"The devil!" objected Gringoire; "I shall break my neck. Your stool halts like one of Martial's couplets; one foot has six syllables and one foot has but five."

"Climb up!" repeated Clopin.

Gringoire mounted the stool, and succeeded, though not without considerable waving of head and arms, in recovering his center of gravity.

"Now," resumed the King of Tunis, "twist your right foot round your left leg, and stand on tiptoe with your left foot."

"My lord," said Gringoire, "are you absolutely determined to make me break a limb?"

Clopin tossed his head.

"Hark ye, mate; you talk too much. I will tell you in a couple of words what I expect you to do: you are to stand on tiptoe, as I say; in that fashion you can reach the manikin's pockets; you are to search them; you are to take out a purse which you will find there; and if you do all this without ringing a single bell, it is well: you shall become a vagrant. We shall have nothing more to do but to baste you with blows for a week."

"Zounds! I shall take good care," said Gringoire. "And if I ring the bells?"

"Then you shall be hanged. Do you understand?"

"I don't understand at all," answered Gringoire.

"Listen to me once more. You are to search the manikin and steal his purse; if but a single bell stir in the act, you shall be hanged. Do you understand that?"

"Good," said Gringoire, "I understand that. What next?"

"If you manage to get the purse without moving the bells, you are a vagrant, and you shall be basted with blows for seven days in succession. You understand now, I suppose?"

"No, my lord; I no longer understand. Where is the advantage? I shall be hanged in the one case, beaten in the other?"

"And as a vagrant," added Clopin, "and as a vagrant; does that count for nothing? It is for your own good that we shall beat you, to harden you against blows."

"Many thanks," replied the poet.

"Come, make haste," said the king, stamping on his cask, which re-echoed like a vast drum.

"Make haste, and be done with it! I warn you, once for all, that if I hear but one tinkle you shall take the manikin's place."

The company applauded Clopin's words, and ranged themselves in a ring around the gallows, with such pitiless laughter that Gringoire saw that he amused them too much not to have everything to fear from them. His only hope lay in the slight chance of succeeding in the terrible task imposed upon him; he decided to risk it, but not without first addressing a fervent prayer to the manikin whom he was to plunder, and who seemed more easily moved than the vagrants. The myriad little bells with their tiny brazen tongues seemed to him like so many vipers with gaping jaws, ready to hiss and sting.

"Oh," he murmured, "is it possible that my life depends upon the slightest quiver of the least of these bells? Oh," he added with clasped hands, "do not ring, ye bells! Tinkle not, ye tinklers! Jingle not, ye jinglers!"

He made one more attempt to melt Trouillefou.

"And if a breeze spring up?" he asked.

"You will be hanged," answered the other, without hesitating.

Seeing that neither respite, delay, nor subterfuge was possible, he made a desperate effort; he twisted his right foot round his left leg, stood tiptoe on his left foot, and stretched out his arm, but just as he touched the manikin, his body, now resting on one foot, tottered upon the stool, which had but three; he strove mechanically to cling to the figure, lost his balance, and fell heavily to the ground, deafened and stunned by the fatal sound of the myriad bells of the manikin, which, yielding to the pressure of his hand, first revolved upon its own axis, then swung majestically to and fro between the posts.

"A curse upon it!" he cried as he fell; and he lay as if dead, face downwards.

Still he heard the fearful peal above his head, and the devilish laugh of the vagrants, and the voice of Trouillefou, as it said, "Lift up the knave, and hang him double-quick."

He rose. The manikin had already been taken down to make room for him.

The Canters made him mount the stool. Clopin stepped up to him, passed the rope round his neck, and clapping him on the shoulder, exclaimed,—

"Farewell, mate. You can't escape now, though you have the digestion of the Pope himself."

The word "mercy" died on Gringoire's lips. He gazed around him, but without hope; every man was laughing.

"Bellevigne de l'Etoile," said the King of Tunis to a huge vagrant who started from the ranks, "climb upon the crossbeam."

Bellevigne de l'Etoile nimbly climbed the crossbeam, and in an instant Gringoire, raising his eyes, with terror beheld him squatting upon it, above his head.

"Now," continued Clopin Trouillefou, "when I clap my hands, do you, Andry le Rouge, knock away the footstool from under him; you, Françoise Chante-Prune, hang on to the knave's feet; and you, Bellevigne, jump down upon his shoulders; and all three at once, do you hear?"

Gringoire shuddered.

"Are you ready?" said Clopin Trouillefou to the three Canters prepared to fall upon Gringoire. The poor sufferer endured a moment of horrible suspense, while Clopin calmly pushed into the fire with his foot a few vine-branches which the flame had not yet kindled. "Are you ready?" he repeated; and he opened his hands to clap. A second more, and all would have been over.

But he paused, as if struck by a sudden thought.

"One moment," said he; "I forgot! It is our custom never to hang a man without asking if there be any woman who'll have him. Comrade, it's your last chance. You must marry a tramp or the rope."

This gipsy law, strange as it may seem to the reader, is still written out in full in the ancient English codes. (See "Burington's Observations.")

Gringoire breathed again. This was the second time that he had been restored to life within the half-hour; so he dared not feel too confident.

"Holà!" cried Clopin, remounting his cask; "holà there, women, females! is there among you, from the old witch to her cat, a wench who'll take this scurvy knave? Holà, Colette la Charonne! Elisabeth Trouvain! Simone Jodouyne! Marie Piédebou! Thonne la Longue! Bérarde Fanouel! Michelle Genaille! Claude Ronge-Oreille! Mathurine Girorou! Holà! Isabeau la Thierrye! Come and look! a man for nothing! who'll take him?"

Gringoire, in his wretched plight, was doubtless far from tempting. The vagabond women seemed but little moved by the offer. The luckless fellow heard them answer: "No! no! hang him; that will make sport for us all."

Three, however, stepped from the crowd to look him over. The first was a stout, square-faced girl. She examined the philosopher's pitiable doublet most attentively. The stuff was worn, and more full of holes than a furnace for roasting chestnuts. The girl made a wry face. "An old clout!" she grumbled, and, addressing Gringoire, "Let's look at your cloak?"

"I have lost it," said Gringoire.

"Your hat?"

"Some one took it from me."

"Your shoes?"

"The soles are almost worn through."

"Your purse?"

"Alas!" faltered Gringoire, "I have not a penny."

"Be hanged to you then, and be thankful!" replied the tramp, turning her back on him.

The second, old, weather-beaten, wrinkled, and ugly, hideous enough to be conspicuous even in the Court of Miracles, walked round and round Gringoire. He almost trembled lest she should accept him. But she muttered, "He's too thin," and took her leave.

The third was a young girl, quite rosy and not very ugly. "Save me!" whispered the poor devil.

She looked at him a moment with a compassionate air, then looked down, began to plait up her skirt, and seemed uncertain. He watched her every motion; this was his last ray of hope. "No," said the young woman at last; "no! Guillaume Longuejoue would beat me," and she went back to the crowd.

"Comrade," said Clopin Trouillefou, "you're down on your luck."

Then, standing erect upon his cask, he cried, "Will no one take this lot?" mimicking the tone of an auctioneer, to the great entertainment of all; "will no one take it? Going, going, going!" and turning to the gallows with a nod, "Gone!"

Bellevigne de l'Etoile, Andry le Rouge, and François Chant-Prune approached Gringoire.

At this instant a shout rose from the thieves: "Esmeralda! Esmeralda!"

Gringoire trembled, and turned in the direction of the cry. The crowd opened and made way for a pure and radiant figure.

It was the gipsy girl.

"Esmeralda!" said Gringoire, astounded, amidst his contending emotions, at the suddenness with which that magic word connected all the various recollections of his day.

This rare creature seemed to exercise sovereign sway through her beauty and her charm even in the Court of Miracles. Thieves, beggars, and harlots stood meekly aside to let her pass, and their brutal faces brightened at her glance.

She approached the victim with her light step. Her pretty Djali followed her. Gringoire was more dead than alive. She gazed at him an instant in silence.

"Are you going to hang this man?" she gravely asked Clopin.

"Yes, sister," replied the King of Tunis, "unless you'll take him for your husband."

She pouted her pretty lower lip.

"I'll take him," said she.

Gringoire here firmly believed that he had been dreaming ever since morning, and that this was the end of the dream.

In fact, the sudden change of fortune, though charming, was violent.

The slip-noose was unfastened, the poet was helped from his stool. He was obliged to seat himself, so great was his agitation.

The Duke of Egypt, without uttering a word, brought forward an earthen pitcher. The gipsy girl offered it to Gringoire. "Throw it down," she said to him.

The pitcher was broken into four pieces.

"Brother," then said the Duke of Egypt, laying his hands on their heads, "she is your wife; sister, he is your husband. For four years. Go!"

CHAPTER VII

A Wedding Night

A few moments later our poet found himself in a small room with a vaulted roof, very snug, very warm, seated before a table which seemed to ask nothing better than to borrow a few stores from a hanging cupboard close by; with a good bed in prospect, and alone with a pretty girl. The adventure partook of the nature of magic. He began seriously to think himself the hero of some fairy-tale; now and then he gazed about him as if in search of the fairy chariot, drawn by two winged steeds, which could alone have transported him so swiftly from Tartarus to Paradise. Occasionally his eyes were riveted on the holes in his doublet, to bring himself back to actual things, and lest he should quite lose sight of land. His reason, floating in imaginary realms, had only this thread to cling to.

The young girl apparently took no notice of him: she came and went, moved a stool, chatted with her goat, smiled, and pouted. Finally she seated herself at the table, and Gringoire could study her at his leisure.

You were once a child, reader, and you may be lucky enough to be one still. You must more than once (and for my part I spent whole days at it,—the best days of my life) have pursued from bush to bush, on the brink of some brisk stream, in bright sunshine, some lovely green or azure dragon-fly, which checked its flight at sharp angles, and kissed the tip of every twig. You will remember the loving curiosity with which your mind and your eye followed that buzzing, whizzing little whirlwind, with blue and purple wings, between which floated an intangible form, veiled by the very swiftness of its motion. The airy creature, vaguely seen amid the quivering wings, seemed to you chimerical, imaginary, impossible to touch, impossible to see. But when the dragon-fly at last rested on the tip of a reed, and you could examine, holding your breath meanwhile, its slender gauzy wings, its long enameled robes, its crystal globe-like eyes, what amazement you felt, and what fear lest it should again fade to a shadow and the creature turn to a chimera! Recall these sensations, and you will readily appreciate what Gringoire felt as he beheld in visible, palpable form that Esmeralda of whom he had hitherto had but a glimpse amidst the eddying dance and song, and a confused mass of people.

Becoming more and more absorbed in his reverie, he thought: "This, then, is 'Esmeralda'! a celestial creature! a street dancer! So much and so little! It was she who put the finishing stroke to my play this morning; it was she who saved my life this evening. My evil genius! my good angel! A pretty woman, upon my word! And she must love me to distraction to take me in this fashion. By-the-by," said he, rising suddenly with that sense of truth which formed the basis of his character and his philosophy, "I don't quite know how it came about, but I am her husband!"

With this idea in mind and in his eyes, he approached the young girl in so military and lover-like a fashion that she shrank away from him.

"What do you want?" she said.

"Can you ask me, adorable Esmeralda?" replied Gringoire in such impassioned tones that he himself was astounded at his own accents.

The gipsy girl stared at him. "I don't know what you mean."

"Oh, come now!" added Gringoire, becoming more and more excited, and thinking that after all he was only dealing with the ready-made virtue of the Court of Miracles; "am I not yours, sweet friend? Are you not mine?"

And, quite innocently, he clasped her by the waist.

The girl's bodice slipped through his hands like a snake's skin. She leaped from one end of the little cell to the other, stooped, and rose with a tiny dagger in her hand, before

Gringoire had time to see whence this dagger came,—proud, angry, with swelling lips, dilated nostrils, cheeks red as crab-apples, and eyes flashing lightning. At the same time the white goat placed itself before her, and presented a battle-front to Gringoire, bristling with two pretty, gilded, and very sharp horns. All this took place in the twinkling of an eye.

The damsel had turned wasp, and asked nothing better than to sting.

Our philosopher stood abashed, glancing alternately at the girl and the goat in utter confusion. "Holy Virgin!" he exclaimed at last, when surprise allowed him to speak, "here's a determined pair!"

The gipsy girl broke the silence in her turn. "You must be a very bold rascal!"

"Forgive me, mademoiselle," said Gringoire with a smile. "But why did you marry me, then?"

"Was I to let them hang you?"

"So," replied the poet, somewhat disappointed in his amorous hopes, "you had no other idea in wedding me than to save me from the gibbet?"

"And what other idea should I have had?"

Gringoire bit his lips. "Well," said he, "I am not quite such a conquering hero as I supposed. But then, what was the use of breaking that poor pitcher?"

But Esmeralda's dagger and the goat's horns still remained on the defensive.

"Mademoiselle Esmeralda," said the poet, "let us come to terms. I am not clerk of the Châtelet, and I shall not pick a quarrel with you for carrying concealed weapons in Paris, in the face of the provost's orders and prohibition. Yet you must know that Noël Lescrivain was sentenced to pay ten Paris pence only a week ago for wearing a broadsword. Now, that is none of my business, and I will come to the point. I swear to you, by all my hopes of paradise, that I will not come near you without your sovereign leave and permission; but give me some supper."

To tell the truth, Gringoire, like Despréaux, was "very lit-

tle of a Don Juan." He was not one of the chivalric, muske-
teering kind who take girls by storm. In the matter of love, as
in all other matters, he was always for temporizing and compromising; and a good supper, in friendly society, struck him,
especially when he was hungry, as an excellent interlude between the prologue and the issue of an intrigue.

The gipsy made no answer. She gave her usual scornful little pout, cocked her head like a bird, then burst out laughing,
and the dainty dagger disappeared as it came, Gringoire being
still unable to discover where the bee hid her sting.

A moment later, a rye loaf, a slice of bacon, a few withered
apples, and a jug of beer were on the table. Gringoire began
to eat greedily. Judging by the fierce clatter of his iron fork
against his earthen-plate, all his love had turned to hunger.

The young girl seated near him looked on in silence, evidently absorbed in other thoughts, at which she occasionally
smiled, while her gentle hand caressed the intelligent head of
the goat as it rested idly against her knee.

A yellow wax candle lit up this scene of voracity and
reverie.

However, the first cravings of hunger appeased, Gringoire
felt somewhat ashamed to find that there was but one apple
left. "You don't eat, Mademoiselle Esmeralda?"

She answered by a shake of the head, and her pensive
gaze was fixed on the arched roof of the cell.

"What the devil is she thinking about?" thought Gringoire;
and, looking to see what she was looking at: "It can't be the
wry face of that stone dwarf carved upon yonder keystone
which so absorbs her attention. What the devil! I'm sure I can
stand the comparison!"

He raised his voice: "Mademoiselle!"

She did not seem to hear him.

He spoke still louder: "Mademoiselle Esmeralda!"

Labor lost. The girl's mind was elsewhere, and Gringoire's
voice had no power to call it back. Luckily the goat interfered,
by softly pulling her mistress by the sleeve.

"What do you want, Djali?" said the gipsy, hastily, as if roused suddenly.

"The creature is hungry," said Gringoire, delighted to open the conversation.

Esmeralda began to crumple some bread, which Djali nibbled daintily from the hollow of her hand.

However, Gringoire gave her no time to resume her reverie. He risked a delicate question:—

"Then you don't want me for your husband?"

The young girl looked steadily at him, and replied, "No."

"For your lover?" continued Gringoire.

She pouted, and answered, "No."

"For your friend?" went on Gringoire.

She looked at him fixedly once more, and after an instant's reflection, said, "Perhaps."

This "perhaps," so dear to philosophers, emboldened Gringoire.

"Do you know what friendship is?" he asked.

"Yes," answered the gipsy; "it is to be brother and sister; two souls which meet without mingling, two fingers of one hand."

"And love?" continued Gringoire.

"Oh, love!" said she, and her voice trembled and her eye brightened. "That is to be two and yet but one. A man and a woman blended into an angel. It is heaven itself."[7]

The street dancer assumed a beauty, as she spoke, which struck Gringoire strangely, and seemed to him in perfect harmony with the almost Oriental exaltation of her words. Her pure rosy lips half smiled; her serene and innocent brow was clouded for the moment by her thought, as when a mirror is dimmed by a breath; and from her long, dark, drooping lashes flashed an ineffable light, which lent her profile that ideal sweetness which Raphael has since found at the mystic meeting-point of the virgin, the mother, and the saint.

Nevertheless, Gringoire kept on,—

"What must one be to please you, then?"

"He must be a man."

"And I," said he,—"what am I?"

"A man with a helmet on his head, a sword in his hand, and golden spurs on his heels."

"Good!" said Gringoire; "dress makes the man. Do you love any one?"

"As a lover?"

"As a lover."

She looked pensive for a moment; then she said with a peculiar expression, "I shall know soon."

"Why not tonight?" said the poet, tenderly; "why not me?"

She cast a serious glance at him.

"I can only love a man who can protect me."

Gringoire flushed, and was silent. It was evident that the young girl alluded to the slight assistance which he had afforded her in the critical situation in which she had found herself a couple of hours previous. This memory, blotted out by the other adventures of the evening, returned to him. He struck his brow.

"By-the-bye, mademoiselle, I ought to have begun there. Forgive me my foolish distractions. How did you manage to escape from Quasimodo's claws?"

This question made the gipsy shudder.

"Oh, the horrid hunchback!" she cried, hiding her face in her hands.

And she shivered as if icy cold.

"Horrid, indeed," said Gringoire, not dropping the subject; "but how did you contrive to escape him?"

Esmeralda smiled, sighed, and was silent.

"Do you know why he pursued you?" continued Gringoire, trying to get an answer by a roundabout way.

"I don't know," said the girl. And she added quickly, "But you followed me too; why did you follow me?"

"In good faith," replied Gringoire, "I have forgotten."

There was a pause. Gringoire was scratching the table with his knife. The girl smiled, and seemed to be gazing at something through the wall. All at once she began to sing in a voice which was scarcely articulate,

> "Quando las pintadas aves
> Mudas estan, y la tierra—"*

She broke off abruptly, and began to fondle Djali.

"That's a pretty creature of yours," said Gringoire.

"It is my sister," she replied.

"Why do they call you 'Esmeralda?'" the poet ventured to ask.

"I've no idea."

"But why do they?"

She drew from her bosom a small oblong bag fastened to her neck by a string of red seeds. This bag gave forth a strong smell of camphor; it was made of green silk, and had in the center a large bit of green glass, in imitation of an emerald.

"Perhaps it is on account of that," said she.

Gringoire tried to take the bag. She drew back.

"Don't touch it! It's an amulet. You will injure the charm, or the charm you."

The poet's curiosity was more and more eagerly aroused.

"Who gave it to you?"

She put her finger to her lip and hid the amulet in her bosom. He tried her with other questions, but she scarcely answered him.

"What does the word 'Esmeralda' mean?"

"I don't know," said she.

"To what language does it belong?"

"I think it is a gipsy word."

"So I suspected," said Gringoire; "you are not a native of France?"

"I know nothing about it."

"Are your parents living?"

She began to sing, to an ancient air:—

> "A bird is my mother,
> My father another.

---

*When the bright-hued birds are quiet, / And the earth—(Spanish).

Nor boat nor bark need I
As over the sea I fly;
A bird is my mother,
My father another."

"Very good," said Gringoire. "At what age did you come to France?"

"When I was very small."

"To Paris?"

"Last year. Just as we entered the Papal Gate, I saw the reed warbler skim through the air; it was the last of August. I said: It will be a hard winter."

"So it has been," said Gringoire, charmed at this beginning of conversation; "I have spent it in blowing on my fingers to keep them warm. So you have the gift of prophecy?"

She fell back into her laconicism.

"No."

"Is that man whom you call the Duke of Egypt, the head of your tribe?"

"Yes."

"But it was he who married us," timidly remarked the poet.

She made her usual pretty grimace.

"I don't even know your name."

"My name? You shall have it, if you wish: Pierre Gringoire."

"I know a nicer one," said she.

"Cruel girl!" replied the poet. "Never mind, you shall not vex me. Stay; perhaps you will love me when you know me better; and then you told me your history so confidingly that I owe you somewhat of mine. You must know, then, that my name is Pierre Gringoire, and that I am the son of the notary of Gonesse. My father was hanged by the Burgundians and my mother ripped up by the Picards, at the time of the siege of Paris, now twenty years ago. At the age of six years, therefore, I was left an orphan, with no sole to my foot but the pavement of Paris. I don't know how I managed to exist from six to sixteen. A fruit-seller would give me a plum, a baker would throw me a crust; at nightfall I would contrive to be caught by the watch, who put me in prison, and there I found a bundle of straw. All this did not hinder me from growing tall and thin, as you see. In winter time I warmed myself in the sun, under the portico of the Hôtel de Sens, and I thought it very absurd that the bale-fires of St. John should be deferred until the dog-days. At the age of sixteen I wished to learn a trade. I tried everything in turn. I became a soldier, but I was not brave enough. I turned monk, but I was not pious enough; and then, I'm no drinker. In despair, I became a carpenter's apprentice, but I was not strong enough. I had more liking for the schoolmaster's trade; true, I did not know how to read, but that was no hindrance. After a time, I discovered that I lacked some necessary quality for everything; and seeing that I was good for nothing, I became a poet and composer of rhymes, of my own free will. That is a trade that one can always take up when one is a vagabond; and it is better than stealing, as certain thievish young friends of mine advised. By good luck, I one fine day encountered Dom Claude Frollo, the reverend archdeacon of Notre-Dame. He took an interest in me, and it is to him I owe it that I am now a genuine man of letters, knowing Latin, from Cicero's Offices to the necrology of the Celestine Fathers, and being ignorant of neither scholastics, poetry, nor rhythm, that sophism of sophisms. I am the author of the miracle-play performed today with great triumph, and before a great concourse of people, in the hall of the Palace. I have also written a book which will make six hundred pages, on the wonderful comet of 1465, which drove one man mad. I have also had other successes. Being somewhat of an engineer, I worked on Jean Maugue's great bomb, which you know burst on Charenton Bridge the day that it was to be tested, and killed twenty-four of the curious spectators. You see that I am by no means a bad match. I know a great many sorts of delightful tricks which I will teach your goat; for instance, how to take off the Bishop of Paris, that accursed Parisian whose mills bespatter all those who pass over the Pont-aux-Meuniers. And then, my miracle-play will bring me in plenty of ready money if they pay me. Finally, I am at your service, I and my wit and my science and my learning,—ready to live with you, lady, as it may please you: soberly or merrily; as husband and wife if you see fit; as brother and sister if you prefer."

Gringoire ceased, awaiting the effect of this speech upon the young girl. Her eyes were bent on the floor.

"'Phœbus,'" she said in an undertone. Then, turning to the poet, "'Phœbus;' what does that mean?"

Gringoire, scarcely comprehending the connection between his words and this question, was nothing loath to display his erudition. He answered, drawing himself up,—

"It is a Latin word signifying 'sun.'"

"'Sun'?" she repeated.

"It is the name of a certain handsome archer who was a god," added Gringoire.

"A god!" repeated the gipsy; and there was something pensive and passionate in her tone.

At this moment, one of her bracelets became unfastened and fell. Gringoire stooped quickly to pick it up; when he rose, the girl and the goat had disappeared. He heard a bolt slide across a small door, doubtless communicating with a neighboring cell, which was fastened on the other side.

"At least, I hope she has left me a bed!" said our philosopher.

He walked around the room. There was nothing fit to sleep upon except a long wooden chest; and even that had a carved lid, which gave Gringoire a feeling, when he stretched himself out upon it, very like that experienced by Micromegas* when he slept at full length upon the Alps.

"Come," said he, making himself as comfortable as he could, "I must submit to fate. But this is an odd wedding night. It is a pity; there was something simple and antediluvian about this marriage by a broken pitcher, which I liked."

---

*Reference to the giant who is the hero of a 1752 story of the same name by Voltaire (pen name of François Marie Arouet, 1694–1778).

BOOK III

CHAPTER I

Notre-Dame

The Cathedral of Notre-Dame de Paris is doubtless still a sublime and majestic building. But, much beauty as it may retain in its old age, it is not easy to repress a sigh, to restrain our anger, when we mark the countless defacements and mutilations to which men and Time have subjected that venerable monument, without respect for Charlemagne, who laid its first stone, or Philip Augustus, who laid its last.

Upon the face of this aged queen of French cathedrals, beside every wrinkle we find a scar. *"Tempus edax, homo edacior;"* which I would fain translate thus: "Time is blind, but man is stupid."

Had we leisure to study with the reader, one by one, the various marks of destruction graven upon the ancient church, the work of Time would be the lesser, the worse that of Men, especially of "men of art," since there are persons who have styled themselves architects during the last two centuries.

And first of all, to cite but a few glaring instances, there are assuredly few finer pages in the history of architecture than that façade where the three receding portals with their pointed arches, the carved and denticulated plinth with its twenty-eight royal niches, the huge central rose-window flanked by its two lateral windows as is the priest by his deacon and subdeacon, the lofty airy gallery of trifoliated arcades supporting a heavy platform upon its slender columns, and lastly the two dark and massive towers with their pent-house roofs of slate, harmonious parts of a magnificent whole, one above the other, five gigantic stages, unfold themselves to the eye, clearly and as a whole, with their countless details of sculpture, statuary, and carving, powerfully contributing to the calm grandeur of the whole; as it were, a vast symphony in stone; the colossal work of one man and one nation, one and yet complex, like the Iliad and the old Romance epics, to which it is akin; the tremendous sum of the joint contributions of all the forces of an entire epoch, in which every stone reveals, in a hundred forms, the fancy of the workman disciplined by the genius of the artist,—a sort of human creation, in brief, powerful and prolific as the Divine creation, whose double characteristics, variety and eternity, it seems to have acquired.

And what we say of the façade, we must also say of the whole church; and what we say of the cathedral church of Paris must also be said of all the Christian churches of the Middle Ages. Everything is harmonious which springs from that spontaneous, logical, and well-proportioned art. To measure a toe, is to measure the giant.

Let us return to the façade of Notre-Dame as we see it at the present day, when we make a pious pilgrimage to admire the solemn and mighty cathedral, which, as its chroniclers declare, inspires terror: *"Quæ mole sua terrorem incutit spectantibus."*

This façade now lacks three important things: first the eleven steps which formerly raised it above the level of the ground; next, the lower series of statues which filled the niches over the doors; and lastly, the upper row of the twenty-eight most ancient kings of France, which adorned the gallery of the first story, from Childebert down to Philip Augustus, each holding in his hand "the imperial globe."

The stairs were destroyed by Time, which, with slow and irresistible progress, raised the level of the city's soil; but while this flood-tide of the pavements of Paris swallowed one by one the eleven steps which added to the majestic height of the edifice, Time has perhaps given to the church more than it took away, for it is Time which has painted the front with that sober hue of centuries which makes the antiquity of churches their greatest beauty.

But who pulled down the two rows of statues? Who left those empty niches? Who carved that new and bastard pointed arch in the very center of the middle door? Who dared to insert that clumsy, tasteless wooden door, carved in the style of Louis XV, side by side with the arabesques of Biscornette? Who but men, architects, the artists of our day!

And if we step into the interior of the edifice, who overthrew that colossal figure of Saint Christopher, proverbial among statues by the same right as the Great Hall of the Palace among halls, as the spire of Strasburg among steeples? And those statues which peopled every space between the columns of the choir and the nave, kneeling, standing, on horseback, men, women, children, kings, bishops, men-at-arms, — of stone, of marble, of gold, of silver, of copper, nay, even of wax, — who brutally swept them away? It was not the hand of Time.

And who replaced the old Gothic altar, with its splendid burden of shrines and reliquaries, by that heavy marble sarcophagus adorned with clouds and cherubs, looking like a poor copy of the Val-de-Grâce or the Hôtel des Invalides? Who was stupid enough to fasten that clumsy stone anachronism into the Carlovingian pavement of Hercandus? Was it not Louis XIV, fulfilling the vow of Louis XIII?

And who set cold white panes in place of that stained glass of gorgeous hue, which led the wondering gaze of our fathers to roam uncertain 'twixt the rose-window of the great door and the ogives of the chancel? And what would a precentor of the sixteenth century say if he could see the fine coat of yellow wash with which our Vandal archbishops have smeared their cathedral? He would remember that this was the color with which the executioner formerly painted those buildings judged "infamous;" he would recall the hotel of the Petit-

Bourbon, bedaubed with yellow in memory of the Constable's treason; "a yellow of so fine a temper," says Sauval, "and so well laid on, that more than a hundred years have failed to wash out its color." He would fancy that the sacred spot had become accursed, and would turn and flee.

And if we climb higher in the cathedral, without pausing to note a thousand barbarous acts of every kind, what has become of that delightful little steeple which rested upon the point of intersection of the transept, and which, no less fragile and no less daring than its neighbor, the spire of the Sainte-Chapelle (also destroyed), rose yet nearer heaven than the towers, slender, sharp, sonorous, and daintily wrought? An architect of good taste (1787) amputated it, and thought it quite enough to cover the wound with that large leaden plaster which looks like the lid of a sauce pan. Thus was the marvelous art of the Middle Ages treated in almost every land, but particularly in France. We find three sorts of injury upon its ruins, these three marring it to different depths: first, Time, which has made insensible breaches here and there, mildewed and rusted the surface everywhere; then, political and religious revolutions, which, blind and fierce by nature, fell furiously upon it, rent its rich array of sculpture and carving, shivered its rose-windows, shattered its necklaces of arabesques and quaint figures, tore down its statues, —sometimes because of their miter, sometimes because of their crown; lastly, changing fashion, ever more grotesque and absurd, from the anarchic and splendid deviations of the Renaissance down to the necessary decline of architecture. Fashion did more harm than revolutions. Fashion cut into the living flesh, attacked the very skeleton and framework of art; it chopped and hewed, dismembered, slew the edifice, in its form as well as in its symbolism, in its logic no less than in its beauty. But fashion restored, —a thing which neither time nor revolution ever pretended to do. Fashion, on the plea of "good taste," impudently adapted to the wounds of Gothic architecture the paltry knick-knacks of a day, —marble ribbons, metallic plumes, a veritable leprosy of egg-shaped mouldings, of volutes, wreaths, draperies, spirals, fringes, stone flames, bronze clouds, lusty cupids, and bloated cherubs, which began to ravage the face of art in the oratory of Catherine de Médicis, and destroyed it, two centuries later, tortured and distorted, in the boudoir of Mme Dubarry.

There are thus, to sum up the points to which we have alluded, three sorts of scars now disfiguring Gothic architecture,—wrinkles and warts upon the epidermis (these are the work of time); wounds, brutal injuries, bruises, and fractures (these are the work of revolution from Luther to Mirabeau); mutilations, amputations, dislocations of the frame, "restorations" (these are the Greek, Roman, Barbaric work of professors according to Vitruvius and Vignole). Academies have murdered the magnificent art which the Vandals produced. To centuries, to revolutions which at least laid waste with impartiality and grandeur, are conjoined the host of scholastic architects, licensed and sworn, degrading all they touch with the discernment and selection of bad taste, substituting the tinsel of Louis XV for Gothic lace-work, for the greater glory of the Parthenon. This is the donkey's kick at the dying lion. It is the old oak, decaying at the crown, pierced, bitten, and devoured by caterpillars.

How different from the time when Robert Cenalis, comparing Notre-Dame at Paris to the famous temple of Diana at Ephesus, "so loudly boasted by the ancient pagans," which immortalized Erostrates, held the cathedral of the Gauls to be "more excellent in length, breadth, height, and structure!"*

Notre-Dame at Paris is not, however, what can be called a complete, definite monument, belonging to a class. It is neither a Roman nor a Gothic church. The edifice is not a typical one. It has not, like the abbey at Tournus, the sober massive breadth, the round expansive arch, the icy bareness, the majestic simplicity of those buildings based on the semi-

---

*Author's note: [from *Histoire Gallicane*] (*Gallican History*), book ii, period ii, fo. 130, p. 1, by Robert Cenalis.

circular arch. It is not, like the cathedral at Bourges, the magnificent, airy, multiform, bushy, sturdy, efflorescent product of the pointed arch. It is impossible to class it with that antique order of dark, mysterious, low-studded churches, apparently crushed by the semicircular arch,—almost Egyptian, save for the ceiling; all hieroglyphic, all sacerdotal, all symbolic, more loaded in their ornamentation with lozenges and zig-zags than with flowers, with flowers than with animals, with animals than with men: less the work of the architect than of the bishop: the first transformation of the art, bearing the deep impress of theocratic and military discipline, taking root in the Lower Empire, and ceasing with William the Conqueror. It is impossible to place our cathedral in that other family of lofty, aerial churches, rich in stained glass and sculpture; of pointed forms and daring attitudes; belonging to the commoners and plain citizens, as political symbols; free, capricious, lawless, as works of art; the second transformation of architecture, no longer hieroglyphic, unchangeable, sacerdotal, but artistic, progressive, and popular, beginning with the close of the Crusades and ending with Louis XI. Notre-Dame at Paris is not of purely Roman race like the former, nor of purely Arab breed like the latter.

It is a building of the transition period. The Saxon architect had just reared the pillars of the nave, when the pointed arch, brought back from the Crusades, planted itself as conqueror upon those broad Roman capitals which were never meant to support anything but semicircular arches. The pointed arch, thenceforth supreme, built the rest of the church. And still, inexperienced and shy at first, it swelled, it widened, it restrained itself, and dared not yet shoot up into spires and lancets, as it did later on in so many marvelous cathedrals. It seemed sensible of the close vicinity of the heavy Roman columns.

Moreover, these buildings of the transition from Roman to Gothic are no less valuable studies than the pure types. They express a gradation of the art which would otherwise be lost.

They represent the ingrafting of the pointed arch upon the semicircular.

Notre-Dame at Paris, in particular, is a curious example of this variety. Every face, every stone of the venerable monument is a page not only of the history of the country, but also of the history of science and art. Thus, to allude only to leading details, while the little Porte Rouge attains almost the extreme limit of the Gothic refinements of the fifteenth century, the pillars of the nave, in their size and gravity of style, go back to the Carlovingian Abbey of Saint-Germain-des-Prés. One would say that there was an interval of six centuries between that door and those pillars. Even the Hermetics find among the symbols of the great door a satisfactory epitome of their science, of which the Church of St. Jacques de la Boucherie formed so complete a hieroglyph. Thus, the Roman abbey, the philosophers' church, Gothic art, Saxon art, the clumsy round pillar, which recalls Gregory VII, the hermetic symbolism by which Nicolas Flamel paved the way for Luther, papal unity, schism, Saint-Germain-des-Prés, Saint-Jacques de la Boucherie, are all confounded, combined, and blended in Notre-Dame. This central and generative church is a kind of chimera among the old churches of Paris; it has the head of one, the limbs of another, the trunk of a third, something of all.

These hybrid constructions are, we repeat, by no means the least interesting to the artist, the antiquary, and the historian. They show us to how great an extent architecture is a primitive thing, in that they demonstrate (as the Cyclopean remains, the pyramids of Egypt, the vast pagodas of India demonstrate) that the greatest products of architecture are not so much individual as they are social works; rather the children of nations in labor than the inspired efforts of men of genius; the legacy of a race; the accumulated wealth of centuries; the residuum of the successive evaporations of human society,—in a word, a species of formation. Every wave of time adds its alluvium, every race leaves a fresh layer on the monument, every individual brings his stone. Thus the beavers work, thus work the bees, thus works man. The great symbol of architecture, Babel, is a beehive.

Great buildings, like great mountains, are the work of centuries. Art is often transformed while still pending completion, — *pendent opera interrupta;* they go on quietly, in harmony with the changes in the art. The new form of art takes up the monument where it finds it, becomes a part of it, assimilates it to itself, develops it according to its fancy, and finishes it if it can. The thing is done without effort, without reaction, in accordance with a natural and tranquil law. It is like a budding graft, like circulating sap, like renewed vegetation. Certainly, there is matter for many big books, and often for the universal history of humanity, in these successive weldings of various forms of art at various levels upon one and the same structure. The man, the artist, and the individual are obliterated in these huge anonymous piles; they represent the sum total of human intelligence. Time is the architect, the nation is the mason.

Considering here Christian European architecture only, that younger sister of the grand piles of the Orient, we may say that it strikes the eye as a vast formation divided into three very distinct zones or layers, one resting upon the other; the Roman zone,* the Gothic zone, the zone of the Renaissance, which may be called the Greco-Roman. The Roman stratum, which is the oldest and the lowest, is occupied by the semicircular arch, which reappears, together with the Greek column, in the modern and uppermost stratum of the Renaissance. The pointed arch is between the two. The build-

---

Author's note: This is also known, according to situation, race, or style, as Lombard, Saxon, or Byzantine; four sister and parallel architectures, each having its own peculiar characteristics, but all springing from the same principle: the circular arch. *"Facies non omnibus una / non diversa tamen, qualem,"* etc. ["Appearance not the same for all, not different however, such"; Latin, from Ovid's *Metamorphoses,* book 2, lines 13–14].

ings belonging to any one of these three strata are perfectly distinct, uniform, and complete. Such are the Abbey of Jumiéges, the Cathedral of Rheims, the Church of the Holy Cross at Orleans. But the three zones are blended and mingled at the edges, like the colors in the solar spectrum. Hence, we have certain complex structures, buildings of gradation and transition, which may be Roman at the base, Gothic in the middle, and Greco-Roman at the top. This is caused by the fact that it took six hundred years to build such a fabric. This variety is rare. The donjon-keep at Etampes is a specimen. But monuments of two formations are more frequent. Such is Notre-Dame de Paris, a structure of the pointed arch, its earliest columns leading directly to that Roman zone, of which the portal of Saint-Denis and the nave of Saint-Germain-des-Prés are perfect specimens. Such is the charming semi-Gothic chapter-house of Bocherville, where the Roman layer reaches midway. Such is the cathedral of Rouen, which would be wholly Gothic if the tip of its central spire did not dip into the zone of the Renaissance.*

However, all these gradations and differences affect the surface only of an edifice. Art has but changed its skin. The construction itself of the Christian church is not affected by them. The interior arrangement, the logical order of the parts, is still the same. Whatever may be the carved and nicely wrought exterior of a cathedral, we always find beneath it, if only in a rudimentary and dormant state, the Roman basilica. It rises forever from the ground in harmony with the same law. There are invariably two naves intersecting each other in the form of a cross, the upper end being rounded into a chancel or choir; there are always side aisles, for processions and for chapels, a sort of lateral galleries or walks, into which the principal nave opens by means of the spaces between the columns. This settled, the number of chapels, doors, steeples,

---

**Author's note:* This part of the spire, which was not made of timber, was destroyed by lightning in 1823.

and spires may be modified indefinitely according to the fancy of the century, the people, and the art. The performance of divine service once provided for and assured, architecture acts its own pleasure. Statues, stained glass, rose-windows, arabesques, denticulations, capitals, and bas-reliefs,—it combines all these flowers of the fancy according to the logarithm that suits it best. Hence the immense variety in the exteriors of those structures within which dwell such unity and order. The trunk of the tree is fixed; the foliage is variable.

CHAPTER II

A Bird's-Eye View of Paris

In the last chapter we strove to restore the wonderful Church of Notre-Dame de Paris for the reader's pleasure. We briefly pointed out the greater part of the charms which it possessed in the fifteenth century and which it now lacks; but we omitted the chief beauty,—the view of Paris then to be had from the top of its towers.

It was, indeed, when after long fumbling in the gloomy spiral staircase which pierces perpendicularly the thick wall of the steeples you finally emerged suddenly upon one of the two lofty platforms bathed in sunshine and daylight,—it was, indeed, a fine picture which lay unrolled before you on every hand; a spectacle *sui generis*, as those of our readers can readily imagine who have been so fortunate as to see one of the few Gothic cities still left entire, complete, and homogeneous, such as Nuremberg in Bavaria, and Vittoria in Spain; or even smaller examples, if they be but well preserved, like Vitré in Brittany, and Nordhausen in Prussia.

The Paris of three hundred and fifty years ago, the Paris of the fifteenth century, had already attained vast dimensions. We modern Parisians are apt to deceive ourselves in regard to the ground which we imagine we have gained since then. Paris has not grown much more than a third larger since the days of Louis XI. It has certainly lost far more in beauty than it has gained in size.

Paris was born, as every one knows, on that island of the City which is shaped like a cradle. The shores of that island were her first enclosure, the Seine her first moat. Paris remained for several centuries in the state of an island, with two bridges, one on the north, the other on the south, and two bridge-heads, at once her gates and her fortresses: the Grand-Châtelet on the right bank, the Petit-Châtelet on the left. With the first line of kings, being pressed for room in her island, back of which she no longer could return, Paris crossed the water. Then, beyond the two Châtelets, the first enclosing line of walls and towers began to encroach upon the country region on either side the Seine. Some traces of this ancient boundary wall still existed in the last century; now, nothing but the memory of it survives, and here and there a local tradition, like the Porte des Baudets or Baudoyer, *Porta Bagauda*. Little by little the flood of houses, perpetually driven from the center of the city, overflowed, made breaches in, and wore away this enclosure. Philip Augustus made a new embankment, and confined Paris within a circular chain of great towers, tall and solid. For more than a hundred years the houses pressed one upon the other, accumulated and raised their level within this basin, like water in a reservoir. They began to grow higher; they added story to story; they climbed one upon the other; they leaped up in height like any repressed fluid, vying each with the other in raising its head above its neighbors to get a little air. The streets became deeper and narrower; every vacant space was filled up and disappeared. The houses at last leaped the wall of Philip Augustus, scattered merrily over the plain irregularly and all awry, like so many school-boys let loose. There they strutted proudly about, cut themselves gardens from the fields, and took their ease. By 1367 the city had extended so far into the suburbs that a new boundary wall was needed, particularly on the right bank of the river; Charles V built it. But a city like Paris is in a perpetual state of growth. It is only such cities which ever become capitals. They are funnels into which flow all the geographical, political, and intellectual watersheds of a country, all the natural tendencies of a nation; wells of civilization, as it were, and also sewers, into which trade, commerce, intellect, population, all the vigor, all the life, all the soul of a nation unceasingly filter and collect, drop by drop, century after century. Charles V's boundary wall followed in the footsteps of that of Philip Augustus. By the end of the fifteenth century, it was overtaken, left behind, and the suburbs advanced yet farther. In the sixteenth, the wall seemed to recede visibly, and to be more and more deeply buried in the old city, so thickly did the new town spring up outside it. Thus, in the fifteenth century, to stop there, Paris had already worn out the three concentric circles of walls, which in the time of Julian the Apostate were, as we may say, in embryo, in the Grand-Châtelet and the Petit-Châtelet. The mighty city burst its four girdles of ramparts in succession, like a child outgrowing his last year's clothes. Under Louis XI, groups of the ruined towers belonging to the old enclosure rose here and there from the sea of houses like hill-tops after a flood,—archipelagoes, as it were, of the old Paris submerged beneath the new.

Since then Paris has, unfortunately for us, undergone another transformation, but has crossed only one more wall, that of Louis XV,—that miserable rampart of lath and plaster, worthy of the king who built it, worthy of the poet who celebrated it in a verse defying translation:—

Le mur murant Paris rend Paris murmurant."*

---

*"The dam damning Paris set Paris free" (French).

In the fifteenth century, Paris was still divided into three quite distinct and separate cities, each possessing its own physiognomy, peculiar features, manners, customs, privileges, and history,—the City, the University, and the Town. The City, which occupied the island, was the oldest, the smallest, and the mother of the other two, crowded in between them (if we may be allowed the comparison) like a little old woman between two tall, handsome daughters. The University covered the left bank of the Seine, from the Tournelle to the Tour de Nesle,—points corresponding in the Paris of today to the Wine-market and the Mint. Its precincts infringed boldly upon the region where Julian built his baths. The mountain of St. Geneviève was included in this division. The culminating point of this curve of walls was the Porte Papale; that is, just about where the Pantheon now stands. The Town, which was the largest of the three parts of Paris, held possession of the right bank of the river. Its quay, broken and interrupted at various points, ran along the Seine, from the Tour de Billy to the Tour du Bois; that is, from the present site of the Public Granaries to the present site of the Tuileries. These four points, at which the river intersected the precincts of the capital, the Tournelle and the Tour de Nesle on the left, the Tour de Billy and the Tour du Bois on the right, were called the "Four Towers of Paris," by way of distinction. The Town extended even farther into the country than the University. The extreme limits of the Town (in the time of Charles V) were the Portes Saint-Denis and Saint-Martin, the situation of which has not been changed.

As we have just observed, each of these three great divisions of Paris was a city in itself, but a city too individual to be complete,—a city which could not dispense with the aid of the other two. Thus, they were utterly unlike in aspect. Churches abounded in the City, palaces in the Town, and colleges in the University. To pass over the minor eccentricities of old Paris and the caprices of those persons holding right of road, we may make the general statement—speaking only of the great masses in the chaos of communal jurisdictions—

that the island was subject to the bishop, the right bank of the
river to the provost, and the left bank to the rector; the Provost
or Mayor of Paris, a royal and not a municipal officer, having
authority over them all. The City contained Notre-Dame; the
Town, the Louvre and the Hôtel de Ville; and the University
the College of the Sorbonne. The Town contained Les
Halles, the City Hôtel-Dieu, the University the Pré-aux-
Clercs.* For any offence committed by a student on the left
bank of the river, he was tried upon the island at the Palace of
Justice, or law courts, and punished on the right bank, at
Montfaucon, unless the rector, finding the University strong
and the king weak, interfered; for it was one of the privileges
of the students to be hanged in their own domain.

(The majority of these privileges, it may be noted in passing,—and there were many more desirable than this,—had
been extorted from various kings by riots and revolts. This is
the traditional course of things: a French proverb declares
that the king only grants what the people wrest from him.
There is an ancient charter which states the fact with much
simplicity; speaking of loyalty, it says: "*Civibus fidelitas in
reges, quæ tamen aliquoties seditionibus interrupta, multa
peperit privilegia.*"†)

In the fifteenth century, the Seine washed the shores of five
islets within the precincts of Paris: the Ile Louviers, where there
were then trees, and where there is now nothing but wood; the
Ile-aux-Vaches and the Ile Notre-Dame, both deserted, save for
a single structure, both held in fee by the bishop (in the seventeenth century, these two islands were made into one, now
known as the Ile Saint-Louis); and lastly, the City, and at its extreme end the islet of the Passeur-aux-Vaches, since submerged
beneath the platform of the Pont-Neuf. The City had then five

---

*Stomping ground of Parisian students, the present Faubourg Saint-
Germain.

†Fidelity to kings, though broken at times by revolts, has procured
many privileges for citizens (Latin).

bridges: three on the right,—the Pont Notre-Dame and Pont-au-Change, of stone, the Pont-aux-Meuniers, of wood; two on the left side,—the Petit-Pont, of stone, the Pont Saint-Michel, of wood: all built over with houses. The University had six gates, built by Philip Augustus; starting from the Tournelle, there were the Porte Saint-Victor, the Porte Bordelle, the Porte Papale, the Porte Saint-Jacques, the Porte Saint-Michel, the Porte Saint-Germain. The Town had six gates, built by Charles V; starting from the Tour de Billy, there were the Porte Saint-Antoine, the Porte du Temple, the Porte Saint-Martin, the Porte Saint-Denis, the Porte Montmartre, and the Porte Saint-Honoré. All these gates were strong, and handsome also, which does not detract from strength. A broad, deep moat, whose waters ran rapidly during winter floods, washed the foot of the walls all around Paris, the Seine providing the water. At night the gates were closed, the river barred at each end of the town by great iron chains, and Paris slept in peace.

A bird's-eye view of these three boroughs—the City, the University, and the Town—presented an inextricable network of streets strangely entangled. But still, even at first sight, it was apparent that these three fragments of a city formed but one body. One saw at once two long parallel streets, without break or deviation, running almost in a straight line, and traversing the three towns from end to end, from north to south, perpendicular to the Seine, connecting them, uniting them, infusing, pouring, and incessantly decanting the people of the one into the precincts of the other, and making of the three but one. One of these two streets led from the Porte Saint-Jacques to the Porte Saint-Martin; it was known as Rue Saint-Jacques in the University, Rue de la Juiverie in the City, Rue Saint-Martin in the Town; it crossed the water twice under the name of the Petit-Pont and the Pont Notre-Dame.

The other, known as Rue de la Harpe on the left bank of the river, Rue de la Barillerie on the island, Rue Saint-Denis on the right bank, Pont Saint-Michel over one arm of the Seine, Pont-au-Change over the other, ran from the Porte Saint-Michel in the University to the Porte Saint-Denis in the

Town. And yet, under all these various names, they were still the same two streets, the two parent streets, the two original streets, the two arteries of Paris. All the other veins of the triple town proceeded from or emptied into them.

Independently of these two diametrical main streets, traversing the entire breadth of Paris, and common to the whole capital, the University and Town had each its individual street, traversing its length, parallel to the Seine, and crossing the two arterial streets at right angles. Thus, in the Town, one could go in a straight line from the Porte Saint-Antoine to the Porte Saint-Honoré; in the University, from the Porte Saint-Victor to the Porte Saint-Germain. These two great roads, crossing the two first mentioned, made the canvas upon which was wrought the knotted and tangled web of the streets of Paris. By careful study of the unintelligible design of this network, one might also distinguish—like two sheaves of wheat stretching, one into the University, the other into the Town—two bunches of great streets leading from the bridges to the gates. Something of this geometric plan still exists.

We shall now attempt to give some idea of the general view seen from the top of the towers of Notre-Dame.

To the spectator who reached this pinnacle in a breathless condition, all was at first a dazzling sea of roofs, chimneys, streets, bridges, squares, spires, and steeples. Everything burst upon his vision, at once,—the carved gable, the steep roof, the turret hanging from the angles of the walls, the eleventh-century stone pyramid, the fifteenth-century slate obelisk, the round bare tower of the donjon-keep, the square elaborately wrought tower of the church, the great, the small, the massive, and the light. The eye wandered for a time, plunging deep down into this labyrinth, where there was no one thing destitute of originality, purpose, genius, and beauty, nothing uninspired by art, from the tiniest house with carved and painted front, outside timbers, surbased door, and overhanging stories, to the royal Louvre, which then had a colonnade of towers. But the principal masses to be seen when the eye became accustomed to this medley of buildings were as follows:

First, the City. "The island of the City," as says Sauval, who, in spite of his nonsense, sometimes hits upon a happy phrase, — "the island of the City is shaped like a huge ship buried in the mud and stranded in the current towards the middle of the Seine." We have just explained that in the fifteenth century this ship was moored to the shores of the stream by five bridges. This likeness to a vessel also struck the heraldic scribes; for it is thence, and not from the Norman siege, say Favyn and Pasquier, that the ship blazoned on the ancient shield of Paris is taken. To him who can decipher it, the science of heraldry is another algebra, the science of heraldry is a language. The whole history of the second half of the Middle Ages is written out in heraldry, as is the history of the first half in the symbolism of the Roman Church. The hieroglyphs of feudalism follow those of theocracy.

The City, then, first fell upon the eye with its stern to the east and its prow to the West. Facing the prow, the spectator saw a countless collection of ancient roofs, above which rose, broad and round, the leaden bolster of the Sainte-Chapelle, like an elephant's back laden with its tower. Only in this case the tower was the most daring, the most daintily wrought, the most delicately carved spire that ever gave glimpses of the sky through its lace-like cone. In front of Notre-Dame, close at hand, three streets emptied into the space in front of the cathedral, — a beautiful square lined with old houses. Over the southern side of this square hung the wrinkled and frowning front of the Hospital, or Hôtel-Dieu, and its roof, which seemed covered with warts and pimples. Then to the left, to the right, to the east, to the west, throughout the City limits, narrow as they were, rose the steeples of its one-and-twenty churches of every age, of every form and every size, from the low, worm-eaten Roman campanile of Saint-Denis du Pas (*carcer Glaucini*) to the slender spires of Saint-Pierre-aux-Bœufs and Saint-Landry. Behind Notre-Dame were revealed, on the north, the cloisters with their Gothic galleries; on the south, the semi-Roman palace of the bishop; on the east, the borders of the Terrain, a plot of waste land. Amid this accumulation of houses, by the tall miters made of openwork stone, which crowned the highest windows of the palace, then placed even in the very roof, the eye could also distinguish the hotel given by the town in the reign of Charles VI to Juvénal des Ursins; a little farther away, the tarred booths of the Palus Market; elsewhere, again, the new chancel of Saint-Germain le Vieux, pieced out in 1458 with a bit of the Rue aux Febves; and then, at intervals, a square crowded with people; a pillory set up at some street corner; a fine fragment of the pavement of Philip Augustus, — superb flagging laid in the middle of the road, and furrowed to prevent horses from slipping, which was so ill replaced in the sixteenth century by the wretched flints and pebbles known as the "pavement of the League;" a deserted back yard with one of those open turret staircases which were common in the fifteenth century, and an example of which may still be seen in the Rue des Bourdonnais. Finally, to the right of the Sainte-Chapelle, towards the west, the Palace of Justice reared its group of towers on the water's edge. The tall trees of the royal gardens, which covered the western end of the City, hid the Ile du Passeur. As for the water, from the top of the towers of Notre-Dame it was barely visible on either side of the City: the Seine was concealed by bridges, the bridges by houses.

And if the spectator looked beyond those bridges, the roofs of which were of a greenish tint, mouldy before their time by the damp vapors rising from the water, if he turned to the left in the direction of the University, the first building which attracted him was a broad, low group of towers, the Petit-Châtelet, whose wide-mouthed porch swallowed up the end of the Petit-Pont; then, if his eye followed the shore from east to west, from the Tournelle to the Tour de Nesle, he saw a long line of houses with carved beams and stained-glass windows, overhanging the pavement story upon story, an endless zig-zag of homely gables, often interrupted by the mouth of some street, and sometimes also by the front or the projecting corner of a huge stone mansion, spreading out its courtyards and gardens, its wings and its main buildings, quite at its ease amid this mob of narrow crowded houses, like a great lord in a rabble of rustic clowns. There were five or six of these mansions on the quay, from the house of Lorraine, which shared the great monastery enclosure next the Tournelle with the Bernardines, to the family mansion of the de Nesles, the main tower of which bounded Paris on that side, and whose painted roofs for three months in the year slivered the scarlet disk of the setting sun with their dark triangles.

This side of the Seine, moreover, was the less commercial of the two; students were noisier and more numerous than laborers, and, properly speaking, the quay extended only from the Pont Saint-Michel to the Tour de Nesle. The rest of the river-bank was now a bare beach, as beyond the Bernardine monastery, and then again a mass of houses washed by the water, as between the two bridges.

There was a vast clamor of washerwomen; they shouted, chattered, and sang from morning till night along the shore, and beat the linen hard, as they do in our day. This is not the least part of the gaiety of Paris.

The University presented a huge mass to the eye. From one end to the other it was a compact and homogeneous whole. The myriad roofs, close-set, angular, adherent, almost all composed of the same geometrical elements, looked from above like a crystallization of one substance. The fantastic hollows of the streets divided this pasty of houses into tolerably equal slices. The forty-two colleges were distributed about quite evenly, there being some in every quarter. The delightfully varied pinnacles of these fine structures were the product of the same art as the simple roofs which they crowned, being really but a multiplication of the square or cube of the same geometrical figure. In this way they made the sum total more intricate without rendering it confused, and completed without overloading the general effect. Geometry is harmony. Certain handsome mansions here and there stood out superbly among the picturesque garrets on the left bank of the river,—the Nevers house, the house of Rome, the Rheims house, which have all disappeared; the Hôtel de Cluny, still

standing for the consolation of artists, and the tower of which
was so stupidly lowered some years since. That Roman palace
near Cluny, with its beautiful arches, was formerly the Baths
of Julian. There were also a number of abbeys of a beauty
more religious, a grandeur more severe, than the mansions,
but no less splendid, no less spacious. Those first attracting
the eye were the monastery of the Bernardines, with its three
spires; Sainte-Geneviève, whose square tower, still standing,
makes us regret the rest so much; the Sorbonne, half college,
half monastery, of which the fine nave still remains; the elegant quadrangular cloister of the Mathurin friars; its neighbor, the cloister of St. Benedict, within the walls of which a
theater has been knocked up in the interval between the sev-
enth and eighth editions of this book; the Franciscan abbey,
with its three enormous gables side by side; the house of the
Austin friars, whose graceful spire was, after the Tour de
Nesle, the second lofty landmark on this side of Paris, looking
westward. The colleges, which are in fact the connecting link
between the convent and the world, formed the central point
in the series of buildings between secular and religious
houses, with a severity full of elegance, their sculptures being
less meaningless than those of the palaces, their architecture
not so sober as that of the monasteries. Unfortunately,
scarcely anything is left of these monuments in which Gothic
art hit so happy a medium between richness and economy;
the churches (and they were many and splendid in the University quarter, representing every period of architecture,
from the semicircular arches of St. Julian to the painted
arches of St. Severius) predominated over everything else;
and, like one harmony the more in that mass of harmonies,
they broke through the varied sky-line of gables with their
sharp spires, their open steeples, and their slender pinnacles,
whose line was but a magnificent exaggeration of the steep
pitch of the roofs.

The ground on which the University stood was hilly. The
mountain of St. Geneviève formed a huge mound to the
southeast; and it was a sight well worth seeing, to look down

from the top of Notre-Dame upon that crowd of narrow, winding streets (now the Latin Quarter), and those close clusters of houses which, scattered in every direction from the summit of the height, seemed hurrying haphazard and almost perpendicularly down its sides to the water's edge, some apparently falling, others climbing up again, all clinging together for mutual support. The constant ebb and flow of a myriad of black dots crossing and recrossing each other on the pavement lent a shimmering and indistinct look to everything: these were the people seen from a height and a distance.

Lastly, in the spaces between these roofs, these spires, these unnumbered and irregular structures which curved and twisted and indented the outline of the University in so odd a fashion, might be seen at intervals a big bit of mossy wall, a thick round tower, or an embattled city gate, representing the fortress: this was the wall of Philip Augustus. Beyond were the green fields, and beyond these ran the roads, along which stretched a few suburban houses, becoming fewer in number as the distance increased. Some of these suburbs were of considerable importance: there was first, starting from the Tournelle, the borough of Saint-Victor, with its single arched bridge across the Bièvre; its abbey, where one might read the epitaph of Louis the Fat,—*epitaphium Ludovici Grossi*; and its church with an octagonal steeple flanked by four eleventh-century belfries (there is a similar one at Etampes, which has not yet been destroyed); then the borough of Saint-Marceau, which possessed three churches and a convent; then, leaving the Gobelins factory and its four white walls on the left, came the suburb of Saint-Jacques, with the beautiful carved cross in the market-place; the Church of Saint-Jacques du Haut-Pas, which was then Gothic, pointed and delightful; Saint-Magloire, with a fine fourteenth-century nave, which Napoleon turned into a hayloft; Notre-Dame-des-Champs, where there were Byzantine mosaics; lastly, leaving in the open country the Carthusian monastery, a rich edifice of the same date as the Palace of Justice, with its little private gardens, and the ill-famed ruins of Vauvert, the eye fell, to the westward, upon the three Roman spires of Saint-Germain-des-Prés. The borough of Saint-Germain, even then a large parish, included fifteen or twenty streets in the rear; the sharp spire of Saint-Sulpice formed one of the boundaries of the borough. Close beside it might be seen the square enclosure of the Saint-Germain fair-ground, where the market now stands; then the abbot's pillory, a pretty little round tower neatly capped with a leaden cone; the tile-kiln was farther on, as were the Rue du Four, leading to the town ovens, the mill on its knoll, and the hospital for lepers,—a small isolated building shunned by all. But the thing which particularly attracted and held attention was the abbey itself. It is certain that this monastery which held high rank both as a church and as a manor, this abbatial palace where the bishops of Paris held themselves happy to be allowed to pass a night, that refectory to which the architect had given the air, the beauty, and the splendid rose-window of a cathedral, that elegant Lady Chapel, that vast dormitory, those great gardens, that portcullis, that drawbridge, the battlements which intrenched upon the verdure of the surrounding fields, the courtyards glittering with men-at-arms mingled with golden copes, all grouped and combined around the three tall spires with their semicircular arches, firmly planted upon a Gothic chancel, made a magnificent figure on the horizon.

When at length, after close study of the University, the spectator turned towards the right bank of the river, towards the Town, the character of the view changed abruptly. The Town, in fact, though much larger than the University, was less of a unity. At the first glance it seemed to be divided into several strangely distinct masses. First, to the east, in that part of the town which still retains the name of the Marais, derived from the marsh in which Camulogenes mired Cæsar, there were a number of palaces. The buildings extended to the water's edge. Four mansions, so close together as to be almost connected,—the homes of the Jouy, Sens, Barbeau families, and the queen's residence,—mirrored their slated roofs, bro-

ken by slender turrets, in the Seine. These four buildings occupied the region between the Rue des Nonaindières and the
Celestine Abbey, whose spire formed a graceful contrast to
their line of battlements and gables. Certain moss-grown
structures, overhanging the water in front of these sumptuous
mansions, did not hide the fine outlines of their façades, their
broad square windows with stone casements, their porches
with pointed arches overloaded with statues, the sharp clear-
cut edges of their walls, and all those dainty architectural ac-
cidents which make Gothic art seem as if it began a fresh
series of combinations with every new building. Behind these
palaces, stretched on every hand, here broken, palisaded, and
crenelated like a citadel, here concealed amid tall trees like a
monastery, the vast and varied wall around that marvelous
Hôtel Saint-Pol, where the king had sufficient space to lodge
luxuriously twenty-two princes of the rank of the Dauphin
and the Duke of Burgundy, with their servants and suites, to
say nothing of great lords, and the Emperor himself when he
visited Paris, and the lions, which had a separate residence in
the royal establishment. Let us say here that the apartment of
a prince at this period comprised no less than eleven rooms,
from the audience chamber to the oratory, not to mention the
galleries, baths, stove-rooms, and other "superfluous places"
with which each apartment was provided; not to mention the
private gardens for each guest of the king; not to mention the
kitchens, cellars, offices, and general refectories of the house;
the servants' quarters, where there were twenty-two offices,
from the bakehouse to the wine-cellars; the games of various
sorts, mall, tennis, riding at the ring, etc.; aviaries, fish-ponds,
poultry-yards, stables, cow-houses, libraries, arsenals, and
foundries. Such was a royal palace of that period, a Louvre, a
Hôtel Saint-Pol,—a city within a city.

From the tower where in fancy we stand, the Hôtel Saint-
Pol, almost half concealed by the four great mansions just
mentioned, was yet very vast and very wonderful to behold. Although skilfully joined to the main building by long glazed
and columned galleries, the three residences which Charles V

had added to his palace were readily to be distinguished: the Hôtel du Petit-Muce, with the open-work balustrade so gracefully bordering its roof; the house of the Abbot of St. Maur, having the aspect of a stronghold, a great tower, bastions, loopholes, iron cowls, and over the wide Saxon gateway, the abbot's escutcheon between the two grooves for the drawbridge; the residence of the Count d'Etampes, whose donjon-keep, in ruins at the top, was round and notched like a cock's comb; here and there three or four low bushy old oak-trees grew close together, looking like huge cauliflowers; swans sported in the clear waters of the fish-ponds, rippled with light and shade; numerous courtyards afforded picturesque glimpses; the Hôtel des Lions, with its low pointed arches resting upon short Saxon pillars, its iron portcullises and its never-ending roar; rising above all this, the scaly spire of the Ave-Maria; to the left, the house of the provost of Paris, flanked by four delicately designed turrets; in the center, in the background, the Hôtel Saint-Pol itself, properly so called, with its multiplicity of façades, its successive embellishments from Charles V's day down, the hybrid excrescences with which the caprice of architects had loaded it during the lapse of two centuries, with all the chancels of its chapels, all the gables of its galleries, its endless weathercocks, and its two tall adjacent towers, whose conical roofs, bordered with battlements at their base, looked like cocked hats.

Still climbing the various stages of this amphitheater of palaces rising in the distance, after crossing a deep ravine cut through the house-roofs of the Town, which marked the passage of the Rue Saint-Antoine, the eye fell upon the D'Angoulême mansion, a vast structure built at different periods, and containing very new and shining portions, which harmonized with the general effect no better than a red patch with a blue doublet. Still, the oddly steep, high roof of the modern palace, bristling with carved gutters, covered with sheets of lead over which rolled sparkling incrustations of gilded copper in a thousand fanciful arabesques,—the curiously damascened roof soared airily and gracefully aloft in the midst of the dark ruins of the ancient edifice, whose antique towers, bulging like casks, from old age, were bowed down by the weight of years and sinking from top to bottom. Behind them rose the forest of spires of the Palace of the Tournelles. No view in the world, not even from Chambord or the Alhambra, could be more magical, more airy, more enchanting than this wilderness of spires, steeples, chimneys, vanes, winding staircases, wrought lanterns which looked as if struck out with a die, pavilions and spindle-shaped turrets, or tournelles, all varying in form, height, and position. It might well be compared to a gigantic stone chess-board.

That group of enormous inky-black towers, one melting into the other, and as it were bound together by a circular moat; that donjon-keep more thickly pierced with loopholes than with windows; that drawbridge forever raised and that portcullis forever down, to the right of the Tournelles, is the Bastille. Those black muzzles peering from the battlements, and which from this distance might pass for gutter-spouts, are cannon.

Within gunshot, below the terrible edifice, is the Porte Saint-Antoine, quite hidden between its two towers.

Beyond the Tournelles, as far as the wall of Charles V, stretched an expanse of beds of shrubs and flowers, and velvety lawns, the royal parks, amidst which the Dædalus garden, given by Louis XI to Coictier, was easily to be distinguished by its labyrinth of trees and winding walks. The doctor's laboratory rose from the maze like a great solitary column with a tiny house for capital. In this small dwelling dread predictions of astrology were concocted.

The Place Royale now stands upon this spot.

As we have just observed, the region of the Palace—some idea of which we have striven to give the reader, although alluding to its principal features only—filled up the angle formed on the east by the Seine and the boundary wall of Charles V. The heart of the Town was occupied by a group of common houses. There the three bridges leading from the City discharged themselves upon the right bank; and bridges lead to the building of houses rather than of palaces. This collection of ordinary houses, crowded together like cells in a hive, was not without a beauty of its own. The roofs of a great city have a certain grandeur, like the waves of the sea. In the first place, the streets, crossed and intertangled, formed a hundred droll figures; around the markets, they looked like a myriad-rayed star. The Rues Saint-Denis and Saint Martin, with their endless ramifications, climbed the hill side by side, like two great trees with intermingling branches; and then crooked lines, like the Rues de la Plâtrerie, de la Verrerie, de la Tixeranderie, etc., twisted and wound in and out among the whole. There were also fine structures piercing through the fixed swell of this sea of gables. At the end of the Pont-aux-Changeurs, behind which the Seine foamed beneath the wheels of the Pont-aux-Meuniers, there was the Châtelet, no longer a Roman tower, as in the days of Julian the Apostate, but a feudal tower of the thirteenth century, and constructed of a stone so hard that three hours' work with the pick would not remove a piece the size of a man's fist; there was the superb square bell-tower of Saint-Jacques de la Boucherie, all its angles softened by sculptures, even then worthy of admiration, although it was not finished in the fifteenth century. (It lacked particularly those four monsters which even yet, perched on the corners of its roof, look like four sphinxes giving modern Paris the riddle of the ancient Paris to solve. Rault the sculptor put them up in 1526, and he was paid only twenty francs for his pains!) There was the Maison-aux-Piliers, opening on the Place de Grève, of which we have already given the reader some idea; there was Saint-Gervais, which a porch "in good taste" has since spoiled; Saint-Méry, whose old pointed arches were a close approach to the semi-circular; Saint-Jean, whose magnificent spire had passed into a proverb; there were at least twenty other edifices, which did not disdain to bury their marvels in this wilderness of deep, dark, and narrow streets. Add to this the carved stone crosses, even more abundant at cross-roads than gibbets; the Cemetery of the Innocents, whose wall, a fine specimen of architecture, was visible from a distance, over the house-tops; the pillory of les Halles, the top of which peeped between two chimneys in the Rue de la Cossonnerie; the "ladder" of the Croix-du-Trahoir at the cross-roads, always black with people; the circular booths of the Corn-market; the remains of the ancient wall of Philip Augustus, visible here and there, lost among the houses, towers overgrown with ivy, ruined gates, crumbling, shapeless fragments of masonry; the quay with its countless shops and its bloody knackers' yards; the Seine, covered with boats, from the Port au Foin to For-l'Evêque,— and you will have a dim idea of what the central portion of the town was in 1482.

Together with these two quarters,—the one of princely mansions, the other of ordinary houses,—the third element in the view of the Town was a long belt of abbeys bordering almost its entire circumference from east to west, and forming a second inner circle of convents and chapels in addition to the circle of fortifications enclosing Paris. Thus, close beside the Tournelles Park, between the Rue Saint-Antoine and the old Rue du Temple, there was Sainte-Catherine with its immense grounds, bounded only by the city walls. Between the old and the new Rue du Temple there was the Temple,—a gloomy group of towers, tall, straight, lonely in the midst of a vast battlemented enclosure. Between the Rue Neuve du Temple and the Rue Saint-Martin there was the Abbey of Saint-Martin, in its gardens, a superb fortified church, whose engirdling towers, whose coronet of spires, only yielded in strength and splendor to those of Saint-Germain-des-Prés. Between the Rues Saint-Martin and Saint-Denis were the precincts of the Convent of the Trinity. Lastly, between the Rue Saint-Denis and the Rue Montorgueil was the Convent of the Daughters of God. Close by might be seen the rotting roofs and unpaved district of the Court of Miracles. This was the only profane link in this pious chain of convents.

Lastly, the fourth division clearly outlined in the conglomeration of house-tops on the right bank of the river, and occupying the western angle formed by the boundary wall and the shore down stream, was still another cluster of palaces, and elegant residences, nestling in the shadow of the Louvre. The old Louvre of Philip Augustus, that overgrown structure around whose great tower were grouped twenty-three towers almost as large, to say nothing of smaller turrets, seemed from a distance to be framed in the Gothic summits of the Hotel d'Alençon and of the Petit-Bourbon. This hydra of towers, the giant guardian of Paris, with its twenty-four heads always reared aloft, with its monstrous cruppers covered with lead or scaly with slates, all dimpling and rippling with metallic reflections, made a surprising finish to the outline of the Town on the west.

An immense mass, therefore,—what the Romans called an *insula,*—of plain, homely houses, flanked on either hand by blocks of palaces, crowned, the one by the Louvre, the other by the Tournelles, bounded on the north by a long line of abbeys and cultivated fields, blending and mingling together as one gazed at them; above these countless buildings, whose tiled and slated roofs stood out in such strange outlines one against the other, the crimped, twisted, ornamented steeples the forty-four churches of the right bank of the river; myriads of crooked streets, bounded on one side by a line of high walls with square towers (that of the University had round towers), on the other by the Seine intersected by bridges, and bearing along a wilderness of boats,—such was the Town in the fifteenth century.

Outside the walls, some few suburbs crowded to the gates; but there were not so many houses, nor were they so close together, as in the University quarter. There were, behind the Bastille, some twenty huts, built close around the Cross of Faubin with its curious carvings, and the Abbey of Saint-Antoine des Champs with its buttresses; then came Popincourt, hidden in wheat-fields; then Courtille, a jolly village of taverns; the borough of Saint-Laurent, with its church, whose steeple at a distance seemed to be a part of the pointed towers of the Porte Saint-Martin; the Faubourg Saint-Denis, with the vast enclosure of Saint-Ladre; outside the Porte Montmartre,

Grange-Batelière, surrounded by white walls; behind it, with its chalky slopes, Montmartre, which then held almost as many churches as windmills, and which has kept only the mills,—for society now prefers material to spiritual bread. Lastly, beyond the Louvre the Faubourg Saint-Honoré, even then of considerable extent, stretched away into the fields, and Little Britain looked green in the distance, and the Pig-market was plainly visible, in the midst of it the horrible caldron for boiling alive coiners of counterfeit money. Between Courtille and Saint-Laurent the eye noted, on the summit of a height situated in the midst of bare plains, a sort of structure looking from a distance like a ruined colonnade standing upon bare foundations. It was neither a Parthenon nor a temple to Olympian Jove; it was Montfaucon.*

Now, if the list of so many buildings, brief as we have tried to make it, has not destroyed, as fast as we constructed it, in the reader's mind the general outlines of old Paris, we will sum up our description in a few words. In the center, the island of the City, shaped like a huge turtle, and protruding its bridges, scaly with tiles, like feet, from under its grey shell of roofs. To the left, the close, compact, crowded, monolithic trapezium of the University; to the right, the vast semicircle of the Town, where houses and gardens were much more mingled,—the three districts, City, University, and Town, veined with countless streets. In and out, through the whole, ran the Seine,—"the nourishing Seine," as Father du Breuil calls it,—obstructed with islands, bridges, and boats; all around an immense plain, green with a thousand different crops, and sprinkled with lovely villages: to the left, Issy, Vanvres, Vaugirard, Montrouge, Gentilly with its round tower and its square tower, etc.; to the right, a score of others, from Conflans to Ville-l'Evêque; on the horizon, a line of hills arranged in a circle like the rim of the basin. Finally, in the distance, to the

---

*Place of execution and/or burial of the executed that will figure prominently in the outcome of the novel.

eastward, Vincennes and its seven quadrangular towers; to the south, Bicêtre, and its pointed turrets; to the north, Saint-Denis and its spire; to the west, Saint-Cloud and its donjon. Such was Paris as seen from the top of the towers of Notre-Dame by the ravens who lived in 1482.

And yet it was of this city that Voltaire said that "before the time of Louis XIV it possessed but four handsome public buildings": the dome of the Sorbonne, the Val-de-Grâce, the modern Louvre, and the fourth I have forgotten,—possibly the Luxembourg. Fortunately, Voltaire wrote "Candide" all the same, and is still, in spite of this criticism, of all men who have succeeded one another in the long series of humanity, the one who was most perfect master of sardonic laughter. This proves, moreover, that one may be a great genius and yet understand nothing of other people's art. Did not Molière think he honored Raphael and Michael Angelo when he called them "those Mignards of their age"?*

Let us return to Paris and the fifteenth century.

It was not only a beautiful city; it was a uniform, consistent city, an architectural and historic product of the Middle Ages, a chronicle in stone. It was a city formed of two strata only,—the bastard Roman and the Gothic; for the pure Roman stratum had long since disappeared, except in the Baths of Julian, where it still broke through the thick crust of the Middle Ages. As for the Celtic stratum, no specimen was to be found even in the digging of wells.

Fifty years later, when the Renaissance added to this severe and yet varied unity the dazzling luxury of its fantasy and its systems, its riotous wealth of Roman semicircular arches, Greek columns, and Gothic foundations, its tender and ideal sculpture, its peculiar taste for arabesques and acanthus-leaves, its architectural paganism, contemporary with Luther,

---

*Reference to Pierre Mignard (1610–1695), a well-known French painter and contemporary of the comic dramatist Molière (1622–1673).

Paris was perhaps still more beautiful, although less harmonious to the eye and intellect. But this splendid moment was of brief duration, the Renaissance was not impartial; not content with building up, it desired to pull down: true, it needed space. Thus Gothic Paris was complete for an instant only. Saint-Jacques de la Boucherie was scarcely finished when the destruction of the old Louvre began.

Since then the great city has grown daily more and more deformed. Gothic Paris, which swallowed up the Paris of the bastard Roman period, vanished in its turn; but who can say what manner of Paris has replaced it?

There is the Paris of Catherine de Médicis, at the Tuileries;* the Paris of Henry II, at the Hôtel de Ville, or Town Hall,—two buildings still in the best taste; the Paris of Henry IV, at the Place Royale,—brick fronts, with stone corners and slated roofs, tricolored houses; the Paris of Louis XIII, at the Val-de-Grâce,—a squat, dumpy style of architecture, basket-handle vaults, something corpulent about the columns, something crook-backed about the dome; the Paris of Louis XIV, at the Invalides,—grand, rich, gilded, and cold; the Paris of Louis XV, at Saint-Sulpice,—volutes, knots of ribbon, clouds, vermicelli, and chiccory, all in stone; the Paris of Louis XVI, at the Pantheon,—a poor copy of St. Peter's at Rome (the

---

Author's note added to the fifth edition of May 1831: It is with grief mingled with indignation that we hear that there is a project to enlarge, alter, reconstruct—that is, to destroy—this beautiful palace. Modern architects are too clumsy to touch the delicate work of the Renaissance. We still hope that they dare not attempt the task. Besides, the demolition of the Tuileries now would be not only a brutal deed at which a drunken vandal might blush, it would be an act of treason. The Tuileries is not just an artistic masterpiece of the sixteenth century, it is a page in the history of the nineteenth century. This palace no longer belongs to the king, but to the people. Let us leave it as it is. The French revolution has twice marked its brow. In one façade are the bullets of August 10; in the other, the bullets of July 29. It is sacred.

building has settled awkwardly, which has not corrected its lines); the Paris of the Republic at the School of Medicine,— a poor bit of Greek and Roman taste, no more like the Coliseum or the Parthenon than the Constitution of the year III is like the laws of Minos; it is known in architecture as "the Messidor style;"* the Paris of Napoleon, at the Place Vendôme: this is sublime,—a bronze column made from captured cannon; the Paris of the Restoration, at the Exchange,—a very white colonnade supporting a very smooth frieze; the whole thing is square, and cost twenty million francs.

For each of these characteristic structures we find a certain number of houses, similar in taste, style, and attitude, scattered through different quarters of the city, and easily to be recognized and dated by a trained observer. Any one who has the art of seeing can trace the spirit of a century and the physiognomy of a king even in a door-knocker.

Paris of the present day, therefore, has no general character of its own. It is a collection of specimens of various ages, and the best ones have disappeared. The capital increases in houses only, and what houses! At the rate at which Paris moves, it will be renewed every fifty years. Thus the historic significance of its architecture dies daily. Monuments of art are becoming more and more rare, and it seems as if we saw them swallowed up by degrees, lost among the houses. Our fathers had a Paris of stone; our children will have a Paris of plaster.

As for the modern monuments of new Paris, we would gladly forbear to speak of them. This is not because we do not admire them as they deserve. M. Soufflot's Sainte-Geneviève is assuredly the best fancy cake that was ever made of stone. The Palace of the Legion of Honor is also a very elegant piece of confectionery. The dome of the Corn-market is an English jockey-cap on a large scale. The towers of Saint-Sulpice are

---

*From the period of the French Revolution, when imitation of antiquity was in vogue.

two big clarionets, and that is a very good shape in its way; the telegraph wire, twisting and wriggling, makes a pretty diversity upon their roof. Saint-Roch has a doorway only comparable in magnificence to that of the church of Saint-Thomas d'Aquin. It has also a Calvary in high relief in a cellar, and a sun made of gilded wood. These are very marvelous matters. The lantern in the labyrinth of the Botanical Garden, too, is very ingenious. As for the Exchange, which has a Greek colonnade, Roman semicircular arches over its doors and windows, and a great elliptic vault of the period of the Renaissance, it is undoubtedly a very correct and very pure piece of architecture: the proof being, that it is crowned with an attic such as Athens never saw,—a beautiful straight line gracefully broken here and there by chimney-pots. Let us add, that if it be the rule that the architectural design of a building should be adapted to its purpose, so that this purpose shall be self-evident from one look at the edifice, we cannot too much wonder at a public building which might be indifferently a royal palace, a House of Commons, a town-hall, a college, a riding-school, a warehouse, a courthouse, a museum, a barrack, a tomb, a temple, or a theater. And, after all, it is an Exchange! Moreover, a building should be appropriate to the climate. This is evidently built for our cold and rainy sky. It has a roof almost as flat as if it were in the Orient, so that in winter, when it snows, the roof can be swept; and it is evident that roofs were made to be swept. As for that purpose to which we alluded just now, it fulfils it marvellously well; it is an Exchange in France, as it would have been a temple in Greece. True, the architect took great pains to hide the face of the clock, which would have destroyed the purity of the fine lines of the front; but, to make amends for this, there is that colonnade which runs round the building, and under which, on high holidays or religious festivals, the theories of stockbrokers and exchange-agents may be solemnly unfolded.

These are doubtless very superb structures. Add any number of fine streets, entertaining and diversified like the Rue de Rivoli, and I am not without hope that Paris, seen from a balloon, may yet present that richness of outline, that wealth of detail, that diversity of aspect, that union of the grandiose and simple, of the unexpected and the beautiful, which characterize a checker-board.

Nevertheless, admirable as Paris of the present day may seem to you, recall Paris of the fifteenth century; reconstruct it in imagination; gaze at the sky through that amazing thicket of spires, steeples, and towers; let the Seine flow through the center of the vast city, interrupt its course with islands, let it curve around the arches of its bridges in broad pools of green and yellow more variable than a serpent's skin; draw distinctly on the blue horizon the Gothic profile of old Paris; let its outlines shimmer in the fog which clings about its many chimneys; drown it in profound darkness, and watch the strange play of lights and shadows in this gloomy labyrinth of buildings; throw a moonbeam upon it which shall reveal it dimly and lift the great heads of the towers above the fog; or recall that dark picture, light up the myriad of sharp angles of spire and gable as they lurk in the shadow, and make them all stand out, more indented than a shark's jaw, against the coppery sunset sky,—and then compare the two.

And if you would receive an impression from the old city which the modern one can never give you, climb, some holiday morning, say at sunrise on Easter or Whitsunday,—climb to some high point whence you overlook the whole town, and listen to the call of the chimes. See, at a signal from the sky,—for it is the sun that gives it,—those countless churches quiver simultaneously. At first a scattered tolling passes from church to church, as when musicians give notice that they are about to begin. Then, all at once, see,—for at certain moments it seems as if the ear had also its vision,—see as it were a column of sound, a vapor of harmony rise at one and the same moment from every tower. At first the vibrations of each bell ascend straight, pure, and as it were apart from the rest, into the clear morning sky; then, little by little, as they increase, they melt into one another, are blended, united, and combined into one magnificent harmony. It ceases to be anything but a

mass of sonorous vibrations incessantly set loose from countless spires, floating, undulating, bounding, whirling over the
city, and prolonging the deafening circle of its oscillations far
beyond the horizon. Yet that sea of harmonies is not a chaos.
Deep and wide as it may be, it has not lost its transparency;
you may see each group of notes, as it escapes from the several chimes of bells, take its own meandering course. You
may follow the dialogue, by turns solemn and shrill, between
the small bell and the big bell; you may see the octaves bound
from spire to spire; you watch them spring winged, light, and
sibilant from the silver bell, fall maimed and halting from the
wooden bell; you admire in their midst the rich gamut perpetually running up and down the seven bells of Saint-
Eustache; you behold quick, clear notes dart through the
whole in three or four luminous zig-zags, and then vanish like
lightning flashes. Yonder is the Abbey of Saint-Martin, shrill
and cracked of voice; here is the surly, ominous voice of the
Bastille; at the other end the great tower of the Louvre, with
its counter-tenor. The royal peal of the Palace flings resplendent trills on every hand, without a pause; and upon them fall
at regular intervals dull strokes from the belfry of Notre-
Dame, which strike sparks from them as the hammer from
the anvil. At intervals you see passing tones of every form,
coming from the triple peal of Saint-Germain-des-Prés. Then
again, from time to time this mass of sublime sounds half
opens and makes way for the *stretto* of the Ave-Maria, which
twinkles and flashes like a starry plume. Below, in the very
heart of the harmony, you vaguely catch the inner music of
the churches as it escapes through the vibrating pores of their
vaulted roofs. Certainly, this is an opera worth hearing. Usually, the noise which rises up from Paris by day is the talking
of the city; by night, it is the breathing of the city; but this,—
this is the singing of the city. Hearken then to this *tutti* of the
steeples; over all diffuse the murmur of half a million men,
the never-ending murmur of the river, the endless sighing of
the wind, the grave and distant quartet of the four forests
ranged upon the hills in the horizon like huge organ-cases;

drown, as in a demi-tint, all that would otherwise be too harsh and shrill in the central chime,—and then say if you know of anything on earth richer, more joyous, more mellow, more enchanting than this tumult of bells and chimes; than this furnace of music; than these ten thousand brazen voices singing together through stone flutes three hundred feet in length; than this city which is but an orchestra; than this symphony which roars like a tempest.

BOOK IV

CHAPTER I

Kind Souls

It was some sixteen years previous to the date of this story, on a fine morning of the first Sunday after Easter, known in France as Quasimodo Sunday, that a living creature was laid, after Mass, in the Church of Notre-Dame, upon the bedstead fixed in the square outside, to the left of the entrance, opposite that "great image" of Saint Christopher, which the carven stone figure of Master Antoine des Essarts, knight, had contemplated on his knees until the year 1413, when it was thought proper to pull down both saint and believer. Upon this bed it was customary to expose foundlings to public charity. Whoever chose to take them, did so. In front of the bedstead was a copper basin for alms.

The sort of living creature lying on the board upon this Sunday morning, in the year of our Lord 1467, seemed to excite in a high degree the curiosity of the somewhat numerous group of people who had gathered around the bed. This group was largely composed of members of the fair sex. They were almost all old women.

In the foremost rank, and bending over the bed, were four who by their grey hoods and gowns seemed to belong to some religious community. I know no reason why history should not hand down to posterity the names of these four discreet and venerable dames. They were Agnès la Herme, Jehanne de la Tarme, Henriette la Gaultière, and Gauchère la Violette, all four widows, all four good women from the Etienne Haudry Chapel, who had come out for the day by their superior's permission, and conformably to the statutes of Pierre d'Ailly, to hear the sermon.

However, if these worthy Haudriettes were, for the time being, obeying the statutes of Pierre d'Ailly, they were certainly wilfully violating those of Michel de Brache and the Cardinal of Pisa, which so barbarously condemned them to silence.

"What on earth is it, sister?" said Agnès to Gauchère, gazing at the little foundling as it shrieked and writhed upon its bed, terrified by so many observers.

"What is the world coming to," said Jehanne, "if that is the way the children look nowadays?"

"I don't know much about children," added Agnès; "but it must surely be a sin to look at this thing."

"It's no child, Agnès."

"It's a deformed monkey," remarked Gauchère.

"It's a miracle," continued Henriette la Gaultière.

"Then," observed Agnès, "it's the third since Lætare Sunday; for it's not a week since we had the miracle of the mocker of pilgrims divinely punished by Our Lady of Aubervilliers, and that was the second miracle of the month."

"This foundling, as they call it, is a regular monster of abomination," added Jehanne.

"He howls fit to deafen a chorister," said Gauchère. "Will you hold your tongue, you little screamer!"

"To think that the Bishop of Rheims should send this monstrosity to the Bishop of Paris," went on La Gaultière, clasping her hands.

"I believe," said Agnès la Herme, "that it's a beast, an animal, a cross between a Jew and a pig; something, in fact, which is not Christian, and should be burned or drowned."

"I'm sure I hope," exclaimed La Gaultière, "that no one will offer to take it."

"Oh, good gracious!" cried Agnès, "I pity those poor nurses in the Foundling Hospital at the end of the lane, as you go down to the river, just next door to his lordship the bishop, if this little monster is given to them to suckle. I'd rather nurse a vampire."

"What a simpleton you are, poor La Herme!" cried Jehanne; "don't you see, sister, that this little wretch is at least four years old, and that he would have less appetite for your breast than for a piece of roast meat."

In fact, "the little monster" (for we ourselves should find it hard to describe him otherwise) was no new-born baby. He was a very bony and very uneasy little bundle, tied up in a linen bag marked with the monogram of M. Guillaume Chartier, then Bishop of Paris, with a head protruding from one end. This head was a most misshapen thing; there was nothing to be seen of it but a shock of red hair, an eye, a mouth, and teeth. The eye wept, the mouth shrieked, and the teeth seemed only waiting a chance to bite. The whole body kicked and struggled in the bag, to the amazement of the crowd, which grew larger and changed continually around it.

Dame Aloïse de Gondelaurier, a rich and noble lady, leading a pretty girl of some six years by the hand, and trailing a long veil from the golden horn of her headdress, stopped as she passed the bed, and glanced for an instant at the miserable creature, while her lovely little daughter Fleur-de-Lys de Gondelaurier, arrayed in silk and velvet, spelled out with her pretty little finger the permanent inscription fastened to the bedstead: "For Foundlings."

"Really," said the lady, turning away in disgust, "I thought they only put children here!"

She turned her back, throwing into the basin a silver coin which jingled loudly among the copper pence, and made the four good women from the Etienne Haudry Home stare.

A moment later, the grave and learned Robert Mistricolle, prothonotary to the king, passed with a huge missal under one arm and his wife under the other (Damoiselle Guillemette la Mairesse), being thus armed on either hand with his spiritual and his temporal advisers.

"A foundling," said he, after examination, "found apparently on the shores of the river Phlegethon!"

"It sees with but one eye," remarked Damoiselle Guillemette; "there is a wart over the other."

"That is no wart," replied Master Robert Mistricolle; "that is an egg which holds just such another demon, who also bears another little egg containing another demon, and so on *ad infinitum.*"

"How do you know?" asked Guillemette la Mairesse.

"I know it for very good reasons," answered the prothonotary.

"Mr. Prothonotary," inquired Gauchère la Violette, "what do you predict from this pretended foundling?"

"The greatest misfortunes," replied Mistricolle.

"Ah, good heavens!" said an old woman in the audience; "no wonder we had such a great plague last year, and that they say the English are going to land at Harfleur!"

"Perhaps it will prevent the queen from coming to Paris in September," added another; "and trade's so bad already!"

"It is my opinion," cried Jehanne de la Tarme, "that it would be better for the people of Paris if this little sorcerer here were laid on a fagot rather than a board."

"A fine flaming fagot!" added the old woman.

"That would be more prudent," said Mistricolle.

For some moments a young priest had been listening to the arguments of the Haudriettes and the sententious decrees of the prothonotary. His was a stern face, with a broad brow and penetrating eye. He silently put aside the crowd, examined the "little sorcerer," and stretched his hand over him. It was high time; for all the godly old women were already licking their lips at the thought of the "fine flaming fagot."

"I adopt this child," said the priest.

He wrapped it in his cassock and bore it away. The spectators looked after him with frightened eyes. A moment later he had vanished through the Porte Rouge, which then led from the church to the cloisters.

When their first surprise was over, Jehanne de la Tarme whispered in La Gaultière's ear,—

"I always told you, sister, that that young scholar Monsieur Claude Frollo was a wizard."

CHAPTER II

Claude Frollo

Indeed, Claude Frollo was no ordinary character. He belonged to one of those middle-class families called indifferently, in the impertinent language of the last century, the better class of citizens, or petty nobility. This family had inherited from the brothers Paclet the estate of Tirechappe, which was held of the Bishop of Paris, and the twenty-one houses belonging to which had been the subject of so many suits before the judge of the bishop's court during the thirteenth century. As holder of this fief, Claude Frollo was one of the one hundred and forty-one lords and nobles claiming manorial dues in Paris and its suburbs; and his name was long to be seen inscribed, in that capacity, between those of the Hôtel de Tancarville, belonging to Master François le Rez, and the College of Tours, in the cartulary deposited for safe keeping at Saint-Martin des Champs.

Claude Frollo had from early childhood been destined by his parents to enter the ranks of the clergy. He was taught to read in Latin; he was trained to look down and speak low. While still very young his father put him at the convent School of Torchi in the University. There he grew up on the missal and the lexicon.

He was moreover a sad, serious, sober child, who loved study and learned quickly. He never shouted at play, took little part in the riotous frolics of the Rue du Fouarre, knew not what it was to "*dare alapas et capillos laniare*,"* and had no share in the mutiny of 1463, which historians gravely set down as the "sixth disturbance at the University." It seldom occurred to him to tease the poor scholars of Montaigu about their capotes,—the little hoods from which they took their name,—or the bursars of the College of Dormans about their smooth tonsure, and their motley garb of grey, blue, and violet cloth, "*azurini coloris et bruni*," as the charter of Cardinal des Quatre-Couronnes words it.

But, on the other hand, he was faithful to the great and little schools in the Rue Saint-Jean de Beauvais. The first scholar to be seen by the Abbot of Saint-Pierre de Val, as he began his lecture on canon law, was always Claude Frollo, glued to a column in the Saint-Vendregesile School, directly opposite the speaker's chair, armed with his inkhorn, chewing his pen, scribbling on his threadbare knee, and in winter blowing on his fingers to keep them warm. The first auditor whom Master Miles d'Isliers, doctor of decretals, saw hurrying up all out of breath every Monday morning at the opening of the doors of the Chef-Saint-Denis School, was Claude Frollo. Accordingly, at the age of sixteen the young scholar was quite able to argue matters of mystical theology with a father of the Church, of canonical theology with a father of the Councils, and of scholastic theology with a doctor of the Sorbonne.

Theology mastered, he plunged into decretals. After the "Master of Sentences," he fell upon the "Capitularies of Charlemagne;" and devoured in turn, in his appetite for knowledge, decretal after decretal,—those of Theodore, Bishop of Hispala; those of Bouchard, Bishop of Worms; those of Yves, Bishop of Chartres; then the decree of Gratian, which followed the "Capitularies of Charlemagne;" then the collection of Gregory IX; then the epistle "*Super Specula*," of Honorius III. He gained a clear idea of, he became familiar

---

*Deal out blows and pull out hair (Latin).

with, that vast and bewildering period when civil law and canon law were struggling and laboring amid the chaos of the Middle Ages,—a period beginning with Bishop Theodore in 618, and ending with Pope Gregory in 1227.

Decretals digested, he turned to medicine and the liberal arts. He studied the science of herbs, the science of salves; he became skilled in fevers and bruises, in wounds and sores. Jacques d'Espars would have given him the degree of doctor of medicine; Richard Hellain, that of surgeon. He also took all the degrees in all the other arts. He studied languages, Latin, Greek, and Hebrew,—a triple shrine then but little worshipped. His was a genuine thirst for acquiring and treasuring the facts of science. At eighteen, he had done with the four faculties; life seemed to the youth to have but one purpose,—to gain knowledge.

It was about this time that the excessive heat of the summer of 1466 caused an epidemic of the plague, which carried off more than forty thousand souls in the viscounty of Paris, and among others, says Jehan de Troyes, "Master Arnoul, astrologian to the king, who was a very virtuous, wise, and pleasant man." A rumor spread through the University that the Rue Tirechappe was especially subject to the disease. There Claude's parents lived, in the heart of their estate. The young scholar hastened in alarm to the paternal mansion. On entering, he found that his father and mother had died the night before. A baby brother was still living, and lay crying in his cradle. He was all that was left to Claude of his family. The youth took the child in his arms and walked thoughtfully away. Hitherto, he had lived for science only; he now began to live in the present.

This catastrophe marked a turning point in his existence. An orphan, the eldest, the head of a family at the age of nineteen, he was rudely recalled from scholastic dreams to actual realities. Then, moved by pity, he was filled with love and devotion for this child, his brother; and human affection was a strange sweet thing to him who had loved nothing but books before.

This affection grew to a singular degree; in so virgin a soul it was like a first love. Parted in infancy from his parents, whom he scarcely knew, cloistered and as it were immured among his books, eager to study and to learn everything, hitherto paying exclusive attention to his intellect, which delighted in literature, the poor student had had no time to learn that he had a heart. This little fatherless, motherless brother, this baby dropped unawares from heaven into his arms, made a new man of him. He saw that there were other things in the world than the speculations of the Sorbonne and the verses of Homer; that man required affection; that life without tenderness and without love was only a noisy, miserable, unfeeling machine. Only he fancied—for he was at the age when illusions are still replaced by illusions only—that the ties of family and kindred were all that was necessary, and that a little brother to love was enough to fill up a whole life.

He therefore yielded to his love for little Jehan with the passion of a character which was already energetic, ardent, and concentrated. The poor frail creature, a pretty, fairhaired, rosy, curly-locked child, an orphan with none to look to for support but another orphan, stirred him to the very soul; and like the serious thinker that he was, he began to meditate about Jehan with infinite compassion. He thought and cared for him as for something very fragile and very precious. He was more than a brother to the boy; he became a mother to him.

Little Jehan was not yet weaned when he lost his mother; Claude put him out to nurse. Besides the estate of Tirechappe, he had inherited from his father the fief of Moulin, which was held of the square tower of Gentilly; it consisted of a mill upon a hill, near the Château de Winchestre (now Bicêtre). The miller's wife was just then nursing a fine child; it was not far from the University. Claude himself carried little Jehan to her.

Henceforth, feeling that he had a burden to bear, he took life very soberly. The thought of his little brother became not only the refreshment, but the object of his studies. He resolved to devote himself wholly to the future of one for whom he must be answerable to God, and to have no other wife, no other child, than the happiness and prosperity of his brother. He accordingly became more than ever attached to his clerical calling. His merits, his learning, his position as the direct vassal of the Bishop of Paris, opened wide all the doors of the Church to him. At the age of twenty, by a special dispensation from the Holy See, he was a priest, and served as the youngest of the chaplains of Notre-Dame at the altar called, from the lateness of the Mass said at it, *altare pigrorum.* *

There, more than ever buried in his dear books, which he only left to make a hasty visit to the mill, this mixture of wisdom and austerity, so rare at his age, soon made him respected and admired by the cloisters. From the convent, his reputation as a learned man spread to the people, among whom it had been somewhat changed—a frequent occurrence in those days—to the renown of a sorcerer.

It was as he was returning, on Quasimodo, or Low Sunday, from saying the sluggards' mass at their altar, which was close by the gate of the choir leading into the nave, to the right, near the image of the Virgin, that his attention was aroused by the group of old women chattering round the bed for foundlings.

He approached the unfortunate little being who seemed to be so much hated and so much threatened. Its distress, its deformity, its desertion, the thought of his own little brother, the wild dread, which at once struck him, that if he should die his dear little Jehan might also be flung upon that board to suffer,—all this rushed into his heart at once; a great wave of pity swept over him, and he carried off the child.

When he took the child from the sack, he found it terribly deformed indeed. The poor little imp had a wart over his left eye, his head was buried between his shoulders, his spine was curved, his breastbone prominent, his legs crooked; but he

---

*Sluggard's altar (Latin).

seemed lively; and although it was impossible to say in what language he babbled, his cries proclaimed a certain amount of health and vigor. Claude's pity increased at the sight of so much ugliness; and he vowed in his inmost soul that he would educate this child for love of his own brother, so that whatever faults little Jehan might in the future commit, he might always have to his credit this charitable deed done for his benefit. It was a sort of investment of good works in his little brother's name; it was part of the stock of good deeds which he decided to lay up for him in advance, in case the young rascal should one day run short of this sort of money, — the only coin which will be accepted at the tollgate of paradise.

He baptized his adopted child, and named him Quasimodo, either because he wished to mark in this way the day upon which the child was found, or because he wished to show by this name how imperfect and incomplete the poor little creature was. Indeed, Quasimodo, one-eyed, hunchbacked, and knock-kneed, was hardly more than half made.

CHAPTER III

*Immanis Pecoris Custos, Immanior Ipse**

Now, in 1482, Quasimodo had grown up. He had been made, some years previous, bell-ringer of Notre-Dame, thanks to his adopted father, Claude Frollo, who had become archdeacon of Josas, thanks to his liege lord

---

*The guardian of a monstrous herd, and himself more monstrous (Latin).

Sir Louis de Beaumont, who had become Bishop of Paris in 1472, on the death of Guillaume Chartier, thanks to his patron Olivier le Daim, barber to Louis XI, king by the grace of God.

Quasimodo, therefore, was ringer of Notre-Dame.

In time, a peculiar bond of intimacy grew between the ringer and the church. Cut off forever from the world by the double fatality of his unknown birth and his deformity, confined from infancy in this doubly insuperable circle, the poor wretch became used to seeing nothing of the world outside the religious walls which had received him into their shadow. Notre-Dame had been to him by turns, as he grew and developed, egg, nest, home, country, universe.

And it is certain that there was a sort of mysterious and preexisting harmony between this creature and the structure. When, still a child, he dragged himself tortuously and jerkingly along beneath its gloomy arches, he seemed, with his human face and animal-like limbs, to be some reptile native to that damp dark pavement upon which the Roman capitals cast so many grotesque shadows.

Later on, the first time that he mechanically grasped the bell-rope in the tower, and clung to it, and set the bell ringing, he seemed to Claude, his adopted father, like a child whose tongue is loosed, and who begins to talk.

It was thus, little by little, growing ever after the pattern of the cathedral, living there, sleeping there, seldom leaving its precincts, forever subject to its mysterious influence, he came to look like it, to be imbedded in it, to form, as it were, an integral part of it. His sharp angles (if we may be pardoned the simile) fitted into the re-entering angles of the building, and he seemed not only to inhabit it, but to be its natural tenant. He might almost be said to have assumed its form, as the snail assumes the form of its shell. It was his dwelling, his hole, his wrapper. There was so deep an instinct of sympathy between him and the old church, there were so many magnetic affinities between them, that he in some sort clung to it, as the tortoise to its shell. The rugged cathedral was his shell.

It is useless to warn the reader not to take literally the figures of speech which we are forced to use here to express this singular, symmetrical, direct, almost consubstantial union of a man and an edifice. It is also useless to speak of the degree of familiarity with the whole cathedral which he had acquired during so long and intimate a cohabitation. This dwelling was his own. It contained no depth which Quasimodo had not penetrated, no heights which he had not scaled. He often climbed the façade several stories high by the mere aid of projecting bits of sculpture. The towers upon the outer face of which he was frequently seen crawling like a lizard gliding over a perpendicular wall (those twin giants, so lofty, so threatening, so terrible) had no vertigoes, no terrors, no giddiness for him; they were so docile to his hand, so easily climbed, that he might be said to have tamed them. By dint of jumping, clambering, sporting amid the abysses of the huge cathedral, he had become, as it were, a monkey and a goat, like the Calabrian child who swims before he walks, and plays with the sea while but an infant.

Moreover not only his body but also his spirit seemed to be moulded by the cathedral. What was the state of that soul? What bent had it assumed, what form had it taken under its knotty covering in this wild life? It would be hard to tell. Quasimodo was born blind of one eye, hunchbacked, lame. It was only by great patience and great painstaking that Claude Frollo had succeeded in teaching him to speak. But a fatality followed the poor foundling. Bell-ringer of Notre-Dame at the age of fourteen, a new infirmity soon put the finishing touch to his misfortunes; the bells had broken the drum of his ears: he became deaf. The only avenue which Nature had left him open to the world was suddenly closed forever.

In closing, it shut off the only ray of joy and light which still reached Quasimodo's soul. That soul relapsed into utter darkness. The miserable lad's melancholy became as complete and as hopeless as his deformity. Add to this that his deafness made him in some sort dumb; for that he might not be an object of laughter to others, from the moment that he realized his deafness he firmly resolved to observe a silence which he scarcely ever broke save when alone. Of his own free will he bound that tongue which Claude Frollo had worked so hard to set free. Hence it resulted that, when necessity constrained him to speak, his tongue was stiff and awkward, like a door whose hinges have rusted.

If now we strive to penetrate to Quasimodo's soul through this hard thick bark; could we sound the depths of that misshapen organism; could we hold a torch behind those nontransparent organs, explore the dark interior of that opaque being, illuminate its obscure corners, its absurd blind alleys, and cast a strong light suddenly upon the Psyche imprisoned at the bottom of this well, we should doubtless find the poor thing in some constrained attitude, stunted and rickety, like those prisoners under the leads of Venice, who grew old bent double in a stone coffer too short and too low for them either to lie down or to stand up.

The spirit certainly wastes away in a misshapen body. Quasimodo barely felt within him the blind stirring of a soul made in his own image. His impressions of objects underwent a considerable refraction before they reached his mind. His brain was a peculiar medium; the ideas which traversed it came forth greatly distorted. The reflection resulting from that refraction was necessarily divergent, and deviated from the right path.

Hence endless optical illusions, endless aberrations of opinion, endless digressions into which his thoughts, sometimes foolish, and sometimes idiotic, would wander.

The first effect of this unfortunate condition of things was to disturb his views of all outward objects. He had scarcely any direct perception of them. The external world seemed much farther away from him than it does from us.

The second effect of his misfortune was to make him mischievous.

He was mischievous because he was an untrained savage; he was a savage because he was ugly. There was a logic in his nature as in ours.

His strength, wonderfully developed as it was, was the cause of still greater mischief. *"Malus puer robustus,"** says Hobbes.

But we must do him the justice to say that this mischievous spirit was not innate. From his first intercourse with men he had felt, had seen himself despised, scorned, repulsed. To him, human speech meant nothing but mockery or curses. As he grew up, he encountered nothing but hate. He caught the infection. He acquired the universal malevolence. He adopted the weapon with which he had been wounded.

After all, he never turned his face to the world of men save with regret; his cathedral was enough for him. It was peopled with marble figures, kings, saints, and bishops who at least did not laugh at him, and never looked upon him otherwise than with peace and goodwill. The other statues, those of monsters and demons, did not hate Quasimodo; he looked too much like them for that. They rather mocked at other men. The saints were his friends, and blessed him. The monsters were his friends, and protected him. Thus he had long conversations with them. He would sometimes pass whole hours squatting before one of these statues, in solitary chat with it. If any one came by, he would fly like a lover surprised in his serenade.

And the cathedral was not only company for him, it was the universe; nay, more, it was Nature itself. He never dreamed that there were other hedge-rows than the stained-glass windows in perpetual bloom; other shade than that of the stone foliage always budding, loaded with birds in the thickets of Saxon capitals; other mountains than the colossal towers of the church; or other ocean than Paris roaring at their feet.

But that which he loved more than all else in the motherly building, that which awakened his soul and bade it spread its poor stunted wings folded in such misery where it dwelt in

---

*A sturdy boy is a naughty boy (Latin).

darkness, that which sometimes actually made him happy, was the bells. He loved them, he caressed them, he talked to them, he understood them. From the chime in the steeple over the transept to the big bell above the door, he had a tender feeling for them all. The belfry of the transept and the two towers were to him like three great cages, in which the birds, trained by him, sang for him alone; and yet it was these very bells which made him deaf. But mothers often love that child best which has cost them most pain.

To be sure, their voice was the only one which he could now hear. For this reason the big bell was his best beloved. She was his favorite of that family of noisy damsels who fluttered about his head on holidays. This big bell had been christened Marie. She hung alone in the south tower with her sister Jacqueline, a bell of less size enclosed in a smaller cage close beside her own. This Jacqueline was named for the wife of Jehan Montague, who gave the bell to the church; which did not prevent him from figuring at Montfaucon without a head. In the second tower there were six other bells; and lastly, the six smallest dwelt in the belfry over the transept with the wooden bell, which was only rung from the afternoon of Maundy Thursday till the morning of Holy Saturday or Easter Eve. Thus Quasimodo had fifteen bells in his harem; but big Marie was his favorite.

It is impossible to give any idea of his joy on those days when full peals were rung. When the archdeacon dismissed him with the word "Go," he ran up the winding staircase more rapidly than any one else could have gone down. He reached the aerial chamber of the big bell, breathless; he gazed at it an instant with love and devotion, then spoke to it gently, and patted it, as you would a good horse about to take a long journey. He condoled with it on the hard work before it. After these initiatory caresses he called to his assistants, stationed on a lower story of the tower, to begin. They then hung upon the ropes, the windlass creaked, and the enormous mass of metal moved slowly. Quasimodo, panting with excitement, followed it with his eye. The first stroke of the clapper upon its brazen wall made the beam on which he stood quiver. Quasimodo vibrated with the bell. "Here we go! There we go!" he shouted with a mad burst of laughter. But the motion of the great bell grew faster and faster, and as it traversed an ever-increasing space, his eye grew bigger and bigger, more and more glittering and phosphorescent. At last the full peal began; the whole tower shook: beams, leads, broad stones, all rumbled together, from the piles of the foundation to the trefoils at the top. Then Quasimodo's rapture knew no bounds: he came and went; he trembled and shook from head to foot with the tower. The bell, let loose, and frantic with liberty, turned its jaws of bronze to either wall of the tower in turn,— jaws from which issued that whirlwind whose roar men heard for four leagues around. Quasimodo placed himself before those gaping jaws! he rose and fell with the swaying of the bell, inhaled its tremendous breath, gazed now at the abyss swarming with people like ants, two hundred feet below him, and now at the huge copper clapper which from second to second bellowed in his ear. That was the only speech which he could hear, the only sound that broke the universal silence reigning around him. He basked in it as a bird in the sunshine. All at once the frenzy of the bell seized him; his look became strange; he waited for the passing of the bell as a spider lies in wait for a fly, and flung himself headlong upon it. Then, suspended above the gulf, launched upon the tremendous vibration of the bell, he grasped the brazen monster by its ears, clasped it with his knees, spurred it with his heels, doubling the fury of the peal with the whole force and weight of his body. As the tower shook, he shouted and gnashed his teeth, his red hair stood erect, his chest labored like a blacksmith's bellows, his eye flashed fire, the monstrous steed neighed and panted under him; and then the big bell of Notre-Dame and Quasimodo ceased to exist: they became a dream, a whirlwind, a tempest; vertigo astride of uproar; a spirit clinging to a winged crupper; a strange centaur, half man, half bell; a sort of horrid Astolpho, borne aloft by a prodigious hippogriff of living bronze.[8]

The presence of this extraordinary being pervaded the whole cathedral with a peculiar breath of life. It seemed, at least in the opinion of the grossly superstitious mob, as if mysterious emanations issued from him, animating every stone in Notre-Dame and making the very entrails of the old church throb and palpitate. His mere presence there was enough to lead the vulgar to fancy that the countless statues in the galleries and over the doors moved and breathed. And in very truth the cathedral seemed a creature docile and obedient to his hand: it awaited his pleasure to lift up its mighty voice; it was possessed and filled with Quasimodo as with a familiar spirit. He might be said to make the vast edifice breathe. He was indeed omnipresent in it, he multiplied himself at every point of the structure. Sometimes the terrified spectator saw an odd dwarf on the extreme pinnacle of one of the towers, climbing, creeping, writhing, crawling on all fours, descending head-first into the abyss, leaping from one projection to another, and diving deep into the maw of some sculptured gorgon: it was Quasimodo hunting for crows' nests. Sometimes a visitor stumbled over a sort of living nightmare, crouching and scowling in a dark corner of the church; it was Quasimodo absorbed in thought. Sometimes an enormous head and a bundle of ill-adjusted limbs might be seen swaying frantically to and fro from a rope's end under a belfry: it was Quasimodo ringing the Vespers or the Angelus. Often by night a hideous form was seen wandering along the frail, delicately wrought railing which crowns the towers and runs round the top of the chancel: it was still the hunchback of Notre-Dame. Then, so the neighbors said, the whole church took on a fantastic, supernatural, horrible air,—eyes and mouths opened wide here and there; the dogs and dragons and griffins of stone which watch day and night, with outstretched necks and gaping jaws, around the monstrous cathedral, barked loudly. And if it were a Christmas night, while the big bell, which seemed uttering its death-rattle, called the faithful to attend the solemn midnight mass, the gloomy façade assumed such an aspect that it seemed as if the great door were devouring the crowd while the rose-window looked on. And all this was due to Quasimodo. Egypt would have taken him for the god of the temple; the Middle Ages held him to be its demon: he was its soul.

So much so that to those who know that Quasimodo once existed, Notre-Dame is now deserted, inanimate, dead. They feel that something has gone from it. That immense body is empty; it is a skeleton; the spirit has left it, the abode remains, and that is all. It is like a skull; the sockets of the eyes are still there, but sight is gone.

CHAPTER IV

The Dog and His Master

There was, however, one human being whom Quasimodo excepted from his malice and hatred of mankind in general, and whom he loved as much as, perhaps more than, his cathedral: this was Claude Frollo.

This was very natural. Claude Frollo had taken him, adopted him, fed him, brought him up. While still a child, it was between Claude Frollo's legs that he found shelter when dogs and boys barked at him and tormented him. Claude Frollo taught him to speak, to read, and to write. Claude Frollo even made him bell-ringer; and, to give the big bell in marriage to Quasimodo was like giving Juliet to Romeo.

Therefore Quasimodo's gratitude was profound, passionate, boundless; and although the face of his adopted father was often clouded and severe, although his speech was usually brief, harsh, and imperative, this gratitude never for an instant failed him. In Quasimodo the archdeacon had the most submissive of slaves, the most docile of servants, the most watchful of guardians. When the poor bell-ringer became deaf, the two contrived a language of signs, mysterious and incomprehensible to every one else. Thus the archdeacon was the only human being with whom Quasimodo kept up any communication. He had relations with but two things in the world,—Notre-Dame and Claude Frollo.

There is nothing to which we can compare the archdeacon's empire over the ringer or the ringer's devotion to the archdeacon. One sign from Claude, and the idea that it would please him, would have been enough for Quasimodo to hurl himself from the top of the cathedral towers. It was wonderful to see so much physical strength brought to such rare development in Quasimodo, and blindly placed by him at the disposal of another. This was doubtless partly due to filial love, domestic affection; it was also due to the fascination exercised by one mind upon another. It was a poor, clumsy, awkward nature, with bowed head and suppliant eyes, before a profound and lofty, superior, and all-powerful intellect. Lastly, and above all, it was gratitude,—gratitude so pushed to its extremest limits that we know of nothing to which it may be compared. This virtue is not one of those which are to be found in the finest examples among men. Let us say therefore that Quasimodo loved the archdeacon as no dog, no horse, no elephant, ever loved its master.

CHAPTER V

More about Claude Frollo

In 1482 Quasimodo was about twenty years old, Claude Frollo about thirty-six. The one had grown up, the other had grown old.

Claude Frollo was no longer the simple scholar of the College of Torchi, the tender protector of a little child, the dreamy young philosopher who knew many things and was ignorant of many more. He was now an austere, grave, morose priest; a keeper of other men's consciences; the archdeacon of Josas, second acolyte to the bishop, having charge of the two deaneries of Montlhéry and Châteaufort, and one hundred and seventy-four of the rural clergy. He was a gloomy and awe-inspiring personage, before whom choir-boys in alb and petticoat, the precentors, the monks of St. Augustine, and those clerks who officiated at the early service at Notre-Dame, trembled when he passed slowly by beneath the lofty arches of the choir, majestic, pensive, with folded arms, and head so bent upon his bosom that nothing of his face could be seen but the high bald forehead.

Now, Dom* Claude Frollo had not given up either science or the education of his younger brother,—those two occupations of his life. But time had imparted a slight bitterness to these things once so sweet. "The best bacon in the world," says Paul Diacre, "grows rancid at last." Little Jehan Frollo, surnamed "du Moulin," from the place where he was put to nurse, had not grown up in the path in which Claude would have led him. The big brother expected him to be a pious, docile, studious, honorable pupil. Now, the little brother, like those young trees which foil the gardener's every effort, and turn obstinately towards the sun and air,—the little brother only grew and flourished, only put forth fine leafy and luxuriant branches, in the direction of idleness, ignorance, and debauchery. He was a perfect imp, utterly lawless, which made Dom Claude frown; but very shrewd and witty, which made the big brother smile. Claude had confided him to that same College of Torchi where he had passed his own early years in study and meditation; and it cost him many a pang that this

---

*Title given to a certain level of priesthood, roughly equivalent to "Reverend."

sanctuary once so edified by the name of Frollo should now
be scandalized by it. He sometimes read Jehan very long and
very severe lectures on this text, but the latter bore them without wincing. After all, the young scamp had a good heart, as
every comedy shows us is always the case. But the lecture
over, he resumed his riotous ways with perfect tranquillity.
Now it was a yellow beak (as newcomers at the University
were called) whom he mauled for his entrance fee,—a precious tradition which has been carefully handed down to the
present day. Now he headed a band of students who had
fallen upon some tavern in classic style, *quasi classico excitati*,
then beaten the landlord "with offensive cudgels," and merrily sacked the house, even to staving in the casks of wine in
the cellar; and then it was a fine report in Latin which the
submonitor of Torchi brought ruefully to Dom Claude, with
this melancholy marginal note: "*Rixa; prima causa vinum op-
timum potatum.*"* Lastly, it was reported—horrible to relate
of a sixteen-year-old lad—that his excesses often took him
even to the Rue de Glatigny.†

Owing to all this, Claude, saddened and discouraged in
his human affections, threw himself with all the greater ardor
into the arms of Science,—that lady who at least does not
laugh in your face, and always repays you, albeit in coin that
is sometimes rather hollow, for the attentions that you have
bestowed on her. He therefore became more and more
learned, and at the same time, as a natural consequence,
more and more rigid as a priest, more and more melancholy
as a man. With each of us there are certain parallelisms between our intellect, our morals, and our character, which are
developed continuously, and only interrupted by great up-
heavals in our life.

Claude Frollo having traversed in his youth almost the entire circle of human knowledge, positive, external, and legiti-

---

*A brawl, resulting directly from too liberal potations (Latin).
†A street of ill-fame, known for its gambling houses.

mate, was forced, unless he stopped *ubi defuit orbis*,* to go farther afield and seek other food for the insatiate activity of his mind. The antique symbol of the serpent biting its own tail is especially appropriate to science. It seemed that Claude Frollo had experienced this. Many worthy persons affirmed that having exhausted the *fas*† of human knowledge, he had ventured to penetrate into the *nefas*.‡ He had, so they said, successively tasted every apple on the tree of knowledge, and whether from hunger or disgust, had ended by biting into the forbidden fruit. He had taken his place by turns, as our readers have seen, at the conferences of the theologians of the Sorbonne, the assemblies of the philosophers at the image of Saint-Hilaire, at the disputes of the decretists at the image of Saint-Martin, at the meetings of the doctors at the holy-water font in Notre-Dame, *ad cupam Nostrœ-Dominœ*. All the permissible and approved meats which those four great kitchens called the four faculties could prepare and serve up to the understanding he had devoured, and satiety had ensued before his hunger was appeased. Then he had dug farther and deeper, beneath all this finite, material, limited science; he had possibly risked his soul, and had seated himself in the cavern at that mysterious table of the alchemists, astrologers, and hermetics, headed by Averroës, Guillaume de Paris, and Nicolas Flamel, in the Middle Ages, and prolonged in the East, by the light of the seven-branched candlestick, to Solomon, Pythagoras, and Zoroaster.

At least this is what people imagined, whether rightly or wrongly.

Certain it is that the archdeacon often visited the Cemetery of the Holy Innocents, where, to be sure, his father and mother were buried, with the other victims of the pest in 1466; but he seemed far less interested in the cross over their

---

*Where the world comes to an end (Latin).

†Lawful (Latin).

‡Unlawful (Latin).

grave than in the strange characters carved upon the tomb of Nicolas Flamel and Claude Pernelle, which stood close by.

Certain it is that he was often seen walking slowly along the Rue des Lombards and furtively entering a small house at the corner of the Rue des Ecrivains and the Rue Marivault. This was the house which Nicolas Flamel built, where he died about 1417, and which, having remained empty ever since, was now beginning to fall into decay: so badly had the hermetics and alchemists of every nation injured the walls merely by writing their names upon them. Certain of the neighbors even declared that they had once seen, through a vent-hole, archdeacon Claude, digging, turning over, and spading the earth in those two cellars whose buttresses were scribbled all over with endless rhymes and hieroglyphics by Nicolas Flamel himself. It was supposed that Flamel had buried the philosopher's stone in these cellars; and alchemists, for two centuries back, from Magistri down to Father Pacificus, never ceased delving at the soil, until the house, so severely rummaged and ransacked, ended by crumbling into dust beneath their feet.

Certain it is also that the archdeacon was seized with a singular passion for the symbolical doorway of Notre-Dame, that page of conjury written in stone by Bishop Guillaume de Paris, who was undoubtedly damned for having added so infernal a frontispiece to the holy poem perpetually sung by the rest of the structure. Archdeacon Claude also passed for having fathomed the mystery of the colossal figure of Saint Christopher, and that tall enigmatical statue then standing at the entrance to the square in front of the cathedral, which people called in derision, "Monsieur Legris." But what every one might have observed, was the interminable hours which he often passed, sitting on the parapet of this same square, gazing at the carvings of the porch, sometimes studying the foolish virgins with their lamps turned upside down, sometimes the wise virgins with their lamps upright; at other times calculating the angle of vision of the crow to the left of the porch and gazing at a mysterious point inside the church where the philosopher's stone must assuredly be hidden, if it be not in the cellar of Nicolas Flamel. It was, let us say in passing, a singular fate for the Church of Notre-Dame at this period to be so loved, in different degrees and with such devotion, by two beings so dissimilar as Claude and Quasimodo. Loved by the one, a sort of instinctive and savage half-man, for its beauty, for its stature, for the harmonies that proceeded from its magnificent mass; loved by the other, a man of scholarly and impassioned fancy, for its significance, for its myth, for its hidden meaning, for the symbolism scattered throughout the sculptures of its front, like the first text under the second in a palimpsest—in short, for the riddle which it forever puts to the intellect.

Certain it is, lastly, that the archdeacon had arranged for himself, in that one of the two towers which looks upon the Place de Grève, close beside the belfry a very secret little cell, where none might enter without his leave, not even the bishop, it was said. This cell, contrived in old times, had been almost at the very summit of the tower, among the crows' nests, by Bishop Hugh of Besançon,* who practiced sorcery there in his time. What this cell contained, no one knew; but from the shore of the Terrain there was often seen at night, through a small dormer-window at the back of the tower, a strange, red, intermittent light, appearing, disappearing, and reappearing at brief and regular intervals, and seeming to follow the blasts of a bellows, and to proceed rather from the flame of a fire than from the light of a candle. In the darkness, at that height, it produced a singular effect; and the gossips would say, "There's the archdeacon blowing again! Hell is sparkling up there!"

After all, there was no great proof of sorcery in all this; but still there was so much smoke that it might well be supposed there was a fire, and the archdeacon had quite a formidable fame. And yet we must say that Egyptian arts, necromancy,

---

*Author's note: Hugo II of Bisuncio, 1326–1332.

and magic, even of the whitest and most innocent kind, had no more relentless enemy, no more pitiless accuser than himself, before the officials of Notre-Dame. Whether this were genuine horror, or the game played by the robber who shouts, "Stop, thief!" it did not prevent the archdeacon from being considered by the wise heads of the chapter as a soul which had ventured into the outskirts of hell, as one lost in the dark caves of the Cabala,—groping in the obscurity of the occult sciences. Nor were the people deceived: with every one who had a grain of sense, Quasimodo passed for the devil, Claude Frollo for the sorcerer. It was plain that the bell-ringer was bound to serve the archdeacon for a given time, at the end of which he would carry off his soul by way of payment. The archdeacon was therefore, in spite of the extreme austerity of his life, in very bad repute with pious people; and there was no devout nose so inexperienced as not to smell in him the magician.

And if, as he grew old, there were voids in his science, there were others in his heart. At least, so one was led to believe on looking at that face in which his soul never shone forth save through a dark cloud. Whence came that broad bald brow, that head forever bowed, that breast forever heaved by sighs? What secret thought made his lips smile so bitterly at the very moment that his frowning brows met like two bulls about to tussle? Why were his few remaining hairs already grey? What was that inward fire which sometimes broke forth in his eye to such a degree that it looked like a hole pierced in the wall of a furnace?

These signs of intense moral preoccupation had acquired a high pitch of intensity at the very time of this story. More than once a choir-boy had taken to his heels in alarm on finding him alone in the church, so strange and wild was his look. More than once, in the choir, during divine service, his neighbor in the stalls had heard him mingle unintelligible parentheses with the church music. More than once the laundress of the Terrain, employed "to wash the chapter," had remarked, not without terror, marks of nails and clinched fingers in the surplice of the archdeacon of Josas.

In other respects he redoubled his severity, and had never been more exemplary. From disposition as well as by profession he had always held himself aloof from women; he seemed now to hate them more than ever. The mere rustle of a silk petticoat made him pull his hood over his eyes. He was so jealous of his austerity and reserve upon this point that when Madame de Beaujeu, daughter of the king, came, in the month of December, 1481, to visit the convent of Notre-Dame, he gravely opposed her entrance, reminding the bishop of that statute in the Black Book, dated on the eve of St. Bartholomew, 1334, which forbids all access to the cloister to every woman "whatsoever, old or young, mistress or maid;" upon which the bishop was constrained to quote to him the ordinance of the legate Odo, which excepts certain great ladies, "*aliquæ magnates mulieres, quæ sine scandalo vitari non possunt.*"* And the archdeacon still protested, objecting that the legate's decree, which went back to 1207, antedated the Black Book by one hundred and twenty-seven years, and was consequently annulled by it; and he refused to appear before the princess.

It was moreover remarked that his horror of the gipsies seemed to have increased for some time past. He had solicited from the bishop an edict expressly forbidding the tribe from coming to dance and play the tambourine in the square before the cathedral; and he had also searched the musty official papers, to collect all cases of witches and wizards condemned to be burned or hanged for complicity in witchcraft with goats, swine, or rams.

---

*Certain ladies of a high degree may not be turned away without offense (Latin).

CHAPTER VI

Unpopularity

The archdeacon and the bell-ringer, as we have already observed, were not held in much favor by the great and little folk about the cathedral. When Claude and Quasimodo went forth together, as they frequently did, and were seen in company, the man behind the master, traversing the cool, narrow, shady streets about Notre-Dame, more than one malicious speech, more than one satirical exclamation and insulting jest, stung them as they passed, unless Claude Frollo, though this was rare, walked with head erect, displaying his stern and almost majestic brow to the abashed scoffers.

Both were in their district like the "poets" of whom Régnier speaks:—

> "All sorts of folks will after poets run,
> As after owls song-birds shriek and fly."

Now a sly brat would risk his bones for the ineffable delight of burying a pin in Quasimodo's hump: and now a lovely young girl, full of fun, and bolder than need be, would brush against the priest's black gown, singing in his ear the sarcastic song,—

> "Hide, hide, for the devil is caught."

Sometimes a squalid group of old women, squatting in a row in the shade upon the steps of some porch, scolded roundly as the archdeacon and the bell-ringer went by, and flung after them with curses this encouraging greeting: "Well, one of them has a soul as misshapen as the other one's body!" Or else it would be a band of students and beetle-crushers* playing at hop-scotch, who jumped up in a body and hailed them in classic fashion with some Latin whoop and hoot: *"Eia! eia! Claudius cum Claudo!"*†

But usually all insults were unheeded by both priest and ringer. Quasimodo was too deaf and Claude too great a dreamer to hear them.

---

*Slang term for foot soldiers.
†Ho! Ho! Claude with the cripple! (Latin).

BOOK V

CHAPTER I

Abbas Beati Martini*

Dom Claude's renown had spread far and wide. It procured him, at about the period when he refused to see Madame de Beaujeu, the honor of a visit which he long remembered.

It was on a certain evening. He had just retired after divine service to his canonic cell in the convent of Notre-Dame. This apartment, aside from a few glass phials banished to a corner, and full of somewhat suspicious powder, which looked vastly like gunpowder, contained nothing strange or mysterious. There were inscriptions here and there upon the walls, but they were merely scientific statements, or pious extracts from well-known authors. The archdeacon had just seated himself, by the light of a three-beaked copper lamp, before a huge chest covered with manuscripts. His elbow rested on a wide-open book by Honorius d'Autun, *"De Præ-destinatione et libero arbitrio,"*† and he was very meditatively turning the leaves of a printed folio which he had brought upstairs with him,—the only product of the press which his cell

---

*The Abbot of Saint-Martin (Latin).

†*Of Predestination and Free Will* (Latin); Honorius of Autun was a theologian and philosopher who flourished in the first half of the twelfth century.

contained. In the midst of his reverie there was a knock at the door. "Who is there?" cried the sage in the gracious tone of a hungry dog disturbed while eating his bone.

A voice answered from without: "Your friend, Jacques Coictier." He at once opened the door.

It was indeed the king's physician,—a person of some fifty years of age, whose harsh expression was only corrected by a crafty look. Another man was with him. Both wore long slate-colored robes furred with minever, belted and clasped, with caps of the same stuff and color. Their hands were hidden in their sleeves, their feet under their gowns, their eyes beneath their bonnets.

"God help me, gentlemen!" said the archdeacon, showing them in; "I did not expect so honorable a visit at such an hour." And while speaking in this courteous fashion, he cast an anxious and searching glance from the physician to his companion.

"It is never too late to visit so distinguished a scholar as Dom Claude Frollo de Tirechappe," replied Doctor Coictier, who being a native of Franche-Comté, drawled all his sentences until they dragged as majestically as the long train of a lady's dress.

Then began between the doctor and the archdeacon one of those congratulatory prefaces with which it was at this period customary to precede every conversation between learned men, and which did not hinder them from hating each other most cordially. However, it is just so today: the lips of every learned man who compliments another scholar are like a cup of honeyed poison.

Claude Frollo's congratulations to Jacques Coictier dwelt particularly on the numerous worldly advantages which that worthy physician in the course of his much-envied career had contrived to extract from every royal malady,—the result of a better and surer alchemy than the search for the philosopher's stone.

"Truly, Doctor Coictier, I was delighted to hear of the promotion of your nephew, my reverend lord Pierre Versé. Has he not been made Bishop of Amiens?"

"Yes, archdeacon; by the favor and mercy of God."

"Do you know that you cut a very fine figure on Christmas Day, at the head of your associates of the Court of Exchequer, Mr. President?"

"Vice-president, Dom Claude. Nothing more, alas!"

"How is your superb house in the Rue Saint-André des Arcs getting on? It's another Louvre. I particularly admire the apricot-tree carved over the door, and the pleasing pun in the motto, '*A L'Abri Cotier.*'"*

"Alas! Master Claude, all that stone-work costs me dear. I am being ruined as fast as the house grows."

"Pooh! Haven't you your revenues from the jail and the Palace bailiwick, and the rent of all the houses, butchers' stalls, booths, and shops within the boundary wall? That's a fine milch-cow for you."

"My Poissy castellany brought me in nothing this year."

"But your toll-gates at Triel, Saint-James, and Saint-Germain-en-Laye are still good."

"A hundred and twenty pounds, and not even Paris pounds at that."

"But you have your place as Councillor to the King. That's a permanent thing."

"Yes, Brother Claude; but that confounded manor of Poligny, which people make such a talk about, doesn't bring me in sixty crowns, take it one year with another."

In the compliments paid to Jacques Coictier by Dom Claude there was the sarcastic, sour, slightly mocking tone, the cruel, acid smile of an unfortunate and superior person sporting for a moment, by way of amusement, with the fat prosperity of a vulgar fellow. The other did not observe this.

"By my soul," said Claude at last, pressing his hand, "I am glad to see you in such robust health!"

---

*A pun on the word *abricotier*, French for "apricot tree."

"Thank you, Master Claude."

"By the way," cried Dom Claude, "how goes it with your royal patient?"

"He does not pay his doctor enough," answered the physician, casting a side glance at his comrade.

"Do you think so, friend Coictier?" said his comrade.

These words, uttered in tones of surprise and reproach, drew the archdeacon's attention to the stranger, although, to tell the truth, he had not been wholly unobservant of him for a single instant since he had crossed his threshold. Had there not been a thousand reasons for his conciliating Doctor Jacques Coictier, the all-powerful physician of King Louis XI, he would never have admitted him in such company. Therefore his expression was anything but cordial when Jacques Coictier said,—

"By the way, Dom Claude, I bring you a brother worker, who was anxious to see you, being familiar with your fame."

"A gentleman of science?" inquired the archdeacon, fixing his piercing eye upon Coictier's companion. The stranger returned his gaze with an equally searching and defiant look.

As well as the feeble light of the lamp allowed one to judge, he was an elderly man of some sixty years, and of medium height, apparently quite ill and broken. His profile, although not at all aristocratic, was still strong and severe; his eye flashed from beneath a very prominent brow, like a light from the depths of a cave; and under the flat cap which drooped over his face, the broad forehead of a man of genius was visible.

He took upon himself to answer the archdeacon's question.

"Reverend sir," he said in grave tones, "your renown has reached me, and I desired to consult you. I am only a poor country gentleman, who takes off his shoes before venturing into the presence of learned men. You must know my name. I am Compère* Tourangeau."

---

*Name for a gossip.

"An odd name for a gentleman!" thought the archdeacon. Still, he felt that he had before him a strong and serious character. The instinct of his lofty intellect led him to guess that a spirit no less lofty lurked beneath the furred cap of Compère Tourangeau; and as he studied his grave face, the ironical smile which the presence of Jacques Coictier had forced to his sullen lips faded slowly, as twilight fades from the sky at night. He reseated himself silently and moodily in his great arm-chair, his elbow resumed its wonted place upon the table, and his head on his hand. After a few moments of meditation he signed to the two visitors to be seated, and addressed Compère Tourangeau:—

"You came to consult me, sir; and upon what branch of science?"

"Your reverence," replied Tourangeau, "I am ill; very ill. You are said to be a great doctor, and I come to you for medical advice."

"Medical advice!" said the archdeacon, shaking his head. He seemed communing with himself an instant, then added: "Compère Tourangeau, if that be your name, turn your head. You will find my answer ready written on the wall."

Tourangeau obeyed, and read this inscription on the wall above his head: "Medicine is the daughter of dreams.—JAMBLIQUE."

But Doctor Jacques Coictier listened to his comrade's question with a displeasure only increased by Dom Claude's answer. He bent to Tourangeau's ear and said, low enough not to be overheard by the archdeacon, "I told you he was a madman; but you insisted on seeing him!"

"Because this madman may well be right, Doctor Jacques!" replied the stranger, in the same tone, and with a bitter smile.

"As you please," answered Coictier, dryly. Then turning to the archdeacon: "You are an apt workman, Dom Claude, and you handle Hippocrates as deftly as a monkey does a nut. Medicine a dream, indeed! I doubt me the druggists and the old masters would stone you well, were they here. Then you deny the influence of philters on the blood, of ointments on the flesh! You deny that everlasting pharmacy of flowers and metals which we call the world, made expressly for that eternal sufferer whom we call man!"

"I deny," said Dom Claude, coldly, "neither drugs nor disease. I deny the physician."

"Then it is false," continued Coictier, with warmth, "that gout is an inward eruption, that a cannon-wound may be cured by the application of a roasted mouse, that young blood properly infused restores youth to old veins; it is false to say that two and two make four, and that emprostathonos follows opistathonos."

The archdeacon quietly replied, "There are certain things which I regard in a certain way."

Coictier turned red with rage.

"There, there, my good Coictier, don't be angry!" said Tourangeau. "The archdeacon is our friend."

Coictier calmed himself, muttering, —

"After all, he's a madman!"

"Odzooks, Master Claude!" continued Tourangeau, after a pause, "you embarrass me mightily. I had two pieces of advice to ask of you, — one concerning my health, the other concerning my star."

"Sir," responded the archdeacon, "if that be your object, you would have done as well not to waste your breath in climbing my stairs. I am no believer in medicine: I am no believer in astrology."

"Indeed!" said the stranger with surprise.

Coictier laughed a forced laugh.

"You see now that he's mad," he whispered to Compère Tourangeau. "He doesn't believe in astrology."

"How can any one imagine," continued Dom Claude, "that every star-ray is a thread which leads to some man's head!"

"Pray, in what do you believe, then?" exclaimed Tourangeau.

The archdeacon for an instant seemed uncertain, then with a gloomy smile, which seemed to belie his answer, said: "credo in Deum."

"Dominum nostrum," added Tourangeau, making the sign of the cross.

"Amen," said Coictier.

"Reverend sir," resumed the stranger, "I am delighted to find you so good a Christian. But, great scholar that you are, have you reached such a point that you no longer believe in science?"

"No," said the archdeacon, seizing Tourangeau by the arm, while a lightning flash of enthusiasm kindled his dull eye,—"no, I do not deny science. I have not crawled flat on my face all these years, digging the earth with my nails, amid the countless mazes of the cavern, without seeing far before me, at the end of the dark tunnel, a light, a flame, something, doubtless the reflection of the dazzling central laboratory where sages and patient souls have taken God by surprise."

"Come, then," interrupted Tourangeau, "what do you consider true and certain?"

"Alchemy."

Coictier cried out: "Good God, Dom Claude! alchemy has its good points, no doubt; but why should you blaspheme against medicine and astrology?"

"Your science of mankind is naught; your science of heaven naught!" said the archdeacon, authoritatively.

"You treat Epidaurus and Chaldea very cavalierly," replied the doctor with a sneer.

"Hear me, Master Jacques. I speak in good faith. I am not the king's physician, and his Majesty did not give me the Dædalus garden as a convenient spot whence I might study the constellations. Don't be angry, and listen to me. What new truth did you ever derive,—I don't say from medicine, which is far too foolish a matter, but from astrology? Tell me the virtues of the vertical boustrophedon,* the discoveries of the number Ziruph and the number Zephirod."

"Would you deny," said Coictier, "the sympathetic power of the clavicle, and that the Cabala is derived from it?"

---

*Writing from right to left and back again from left to right.

"An error, Master Jacques! None of your formulæ lead to reality; while alchemy has its indubitable discoveries. Can you contest such results as these,—ice buried beneath the ground for a thousand years is transformed to rock crystal; lead is the progenitor of all the metals,—for gold is not a metal, gold is light; lead requires but four periods of two hundred years each to pass successively from the state of lead to the state of red arsenic, from red arsenic to tin, from tin to silver? Are these facts or are they not? But to believe in clavicles, planets, and stars is as absurd as to believe with the natives of far Cathay that the golden oriole turns into a mole, and grains of wheat into mollusks of the genus Cypræa!"

"I have studied hermetics," cried Coictier, "and I affirm—"

The fiery archdeacon did not permit him to finish his speech. "And I have studied medicine, astrology, and hermetics. Here alone is truth [as he spoke he took from the press a phial filled with the powder of which we spoke some pages back], here alone is light! Hippocrates is a dream; Urania is a dream; Hermes is a mere idea. Gold is the sun; to make gold, is to become God. This is the only wisdom. I have sounded the depths of medicine and astrology, I tell you. They are naught, naught! The human body is a mere shadow; the stars are shadows!"

And he fell back upon his seat in a striking and imposing attitude. Tourangeau watched him in silence. Coictier forced himself to sneer, shrugged his shoulders slightly, and repeated in a low voice,—

"A madman!"

"And," said Tourangeau suddenly, "the splendid goal,—have you attained that? Have you made gold?"

"Had I made it," replied the archdeacon, pronouncing his words slowly, like a man who is reflecting, "the King of France would be called Claude, and not Louis."

The stranger frowned.

"What do I say?" added Dom Claude with a scornful smile. "What would the throne of France avail me when I could reconstruct the Empire of the East?"

"Well, well," said the stranger.

"Oh, poor fool!" muttered Coictier.

The archdeacon went on, apparently replying to his own thoughts only:—

"But no, I still crawl; I bruise my face and knees on the sharp stones of the subterranean way. I see dimly; I do not behold the full splendor! I do not read; I spell!"

"And when you can read," asked the stranger, "shall you make gold?"

"Who can doubt it?" said the archdeacon.

"In that case, Notre-Dame knows that I am in great need of money, and I would fain learn to read your books. Tell me, reverend master, is your science hostile or displeasing to Notre-Dame?"

To this question from the stranger Dom Claude merely answered with a quiet dignity,—

"Whose archdeacon am I?"

"True, my master. Well; will it please you to initiate me? Let me spell with you."

Claude assumed the majestic and pontifical attitude of a Samuel.

"Old man, it needs more years than still remain to you to undertake the journey through mysterious things. Your head is very grey! None ever leave the cavern without white hairs, but none enter save with dark hair. Science is skilled in furrowing, withering, and wrinkling human faces; it needs not that old age should bring to her faces ready wrinkled. Yet if you long to submit yourself to discipline at your age, and to decipher the dread alphabet of sages, come to me; it is well: I will try what I can do. I will not bid you, you poor old man, go visit the sepulchres in the Pyramids, of which ancient Herodotus speaks, nor the brick tower of Babylon, nor the huge white marble sanctuary of the Indian temple of Eklinga. Neither I nor you have seen the Chaldean edifices constructed after the sacred form of Sikra, or the Temple of Solomon, which is destroyed, or the stone doors of the tomb of the kings of Israel, which are shattered. We will be content with the fragments of the book of Hermes which we have at hand. I will explain to you the statue of Saint Christopher, the symbolism of the sower, and that of the two angels at the door of the Sainte-Chapelle, one of whom has his hand in a vase and the other in a cloud—"

Here Jacques Coictier, who had been disconcerted by the archdeacon's spirited replies, recovered himself, and interrupted in the triumphant tone of one wise man setting another right: "*Erras, amice Claudi.* The symbol is not the number. You take Orpheus for Hermes."

"It is you who err," gravely answered the archdeacon. "Dædalus is the basement; Orpheus is the wall; Hermes is the building itself,—is the whole. Come when you will," he added, turning to Tourangeau; "I will show you the particles of gold remaining in the bottom of Nicolas Flamel's crucible, and you may compare them with the gold of Guillaume de Paris. I will teach you the secret virtues of the Greek word *peristera*. But first of all, you must read in turn the marble letters of the alphabet, the granite pages of the book. We will go from the porch of Bishop Guillaume and of Saint-Jean le Rond to the Sainte-Chapelle, then to the house of Nicolas Flamel in the Rue Marivault, to his tomb, which is in the Cemetery of the Holy Innocents, to his two almshouses in the Rue Montmorency. You shall read the hieroglyphics which cover the four great iron andirons in the porch of the Hospice Saint-Gervais, and those in the Rue de la Ferronnerie. We will spell over together once more the façades of Saint-Côme, Sainte-Geneviève des Ardents, Saint-Martin, Saint-Jacques de la Boucherie—"

For some time Tourangeau, intelligent though his appearance was, had seemed as if he failed to follow Dom Claude. He now interrupted him with the words,—

"Odzooks! What sort of books can yours be?"

"Here is one of them," said the archdeacon.

And opening the window of his cell, he pointed to the vast Church of Notre-Dame, which, with its two towers outlined in black against a starry sky, its stone sides and monstrous hiproof, seemed like some huge double-headed sphinx crouching in the heart of the town.

The archdeacon silently gazed at the gigantic edifice; then

with a sigh, stretching his right hand towards the printed book which lay open on the table, and his left hand towards Notre-Dame, with a melancholy glance from book to church, he said, "Alas! the one will kill the other."

Coictier, who had eagerly approached the book, could not repress the words, "Why! But what is there so terrible about this: '*Glossa in epistolas D. Pauli. Norimbergæ, Antonius Koburger.* 1474.' This is nothing new. It is a book by Pierre Lombard, the Master of Maxims. Is it because it is printed?"

"That's it," replied Claude, who seemed absorbed in deep meditation, and stood with his forefinger on the folio from the famous presses of Nuremberg. Then he added these mysterious words: "Alas! alas! Small things overcome great ones: the Nile rat kills the crocodile, the swordfish kills the whale, the book will kill the building."

The convent curfew rang just as Doctor Jacques once more whispered in his comrade's ear his perpetual refrain: "He is mad." To which his comrade now made answer, "I believe he is."

No stranger was allowed to linger in the convent at this hour. The two visitors withdrew. "Master," said Compère Tourangeau as he took leave of the archdeacon, "I like scholars and great minds, and I hold you in singular esteem. Come tomorrow to the Palace of the Tournelles, and ask for the Abbot of Saint-Martin de Tours."

The archdeacon returned to his cell in amazement, realizing at last who this Compère Tourangeau really was, and calling to mind this passage from the cartulary of Saint-Martin de Tours: "*Abbas beatti Martini,* SCILICET REX FRANCIÆ, *est canonicus de consuetudine et habet parvam præbendam quam habet sanctus Venantius et debet sedere in sede thesaurarii.*"*

It is said that from this time forth the archdeacon held fre-

---

*The Abbot of Saint-Martin, that is to say the King of France, is canon, according to custom, and has the small benefice which Saint-Venantis had, and shall sit in the seat of the treasurer (Latin).

quent meetings with Louis XI, when his Majesty came to Paris, and that Dom Claude's credit much eclipsed that of Oliver le Daim and Jacques Coictier, the latter of whom, as was his custom, roundly reproached the king on this score.

CHAPTER II

The One Will Kill the Other

Our fair readers will pardon us for pausing a moment to search for the hidden meaning of those enigmatical words of the archdeacon: "The one will kill the other. The book will kill the building."

In our opinion this thought had two phases. In the first place it was the thought of a priest. It was the terror of a true ecclesiastic at sight of a new agent,—printing. It was the fear and confusion of the man of the sanctuary at sight of Gutenberg's light-giving press. It was the pulpit and the manuscript, the spoken word and the written word, taking fright at the printed word; something similar to the stupor of a sparrow who should see the angel Legion spread his six million wings. It was the cry of the prophet who already hears the busy noise and stir of humanity set free, who sees in the future intellect undermining faith, opinion superseding belief, the world shaking off the yoke of Rome; the presage of the philosopher who sees human ideas, volatilized by the press, evaporated from the theocratic receiver; the dread of the soldier who examines the iron battering-ram and says: The tower must fall. It meant that one power was about to succeed another power. It meant: The press will kill the church.

But underlying this idea, doubtless the first and simplest, there was, to our thinking, another and more recent one, a corollary of the first, less easily seen and more easily contested; a point of view quite as philosophic, but not that of the priest alone,—that of the scholar and the artist as well. It was the presentiment that human thought, in changing its form, would also change its mode of expression; that the leading idea of each generation would no longer be written with the same material and in the same fashion; that the book of stone, so solid and so enduring, must make way for the book of papers still more solid and enduring. Looked at in this light, the archdeacon's vague statement had another meaning; it meant that one art would dethrone another art. It meant: Printing will destroy architecture.

Indeed, from the beginning of things down to the fifteenth century of the Christian era inclusive, architecture was the great book of humanity, the chief expression of man in his various stages of development, whether as force or as intellect.

When the memory of the earliest races became surcharged, when mankind's burden of recollections became so great and so bewildering that mere speech, naked and winged, was in danger of losing a part on the road, men wrote them upon the ground in the way which was at once plainest, most enduring, and most natural. Every tradition was sealed beneath a monument.

The first monuments were mere fragments of rock "which the iron had not touched," says Moses. Architecture began like all writing. A stone was placed on end, and it was a letter, and each letter was a hieroglyph; and upon each hieroglyph rested a group of ideas, like the capital on a column. Thus did the first races, everywhere, at the same moment, over the entire surface of the world. We find the "cromlech" of the Celts in Asiatic Siberia and in American pampas.

Later on, words were formed; stone was added to stone, these granite syllables were coupled together, the verb essayed a few combinations. The Celtic dolmen and cromlech, the Etruscan tumulus, the Hebrew galgal, are words. Some of them, particularly the tumulus, are proper names. Sometimes, when there was plenty of stone and a vast stretch of coast, a phrase was written. The immense pile of Karnac is an entire formulary.

Finally, men made books. Traditions gave birth to symbols, which hid them as the leaves hide the trunk of a tree; all these symbols, in which humanity believed, grew, multiplied, crossed one another, became more and more complicated; the first monuments were no longer sufficient to contain them; they overflowed them on every side; these monuments barely sufficed to express the primitive tradition, as bare, as simple, and as plain as themselves. Symbolism must needs expand into an edifice. Architecture, therefore, was developed parallel with human thought; it became a thousand-headed, thousand-armed giantess, and fixed all that floating symbolism in an eternal, visible, palpable form. While Dædalus, that is, force, measured; while Orpheus, which is to say, intellect, sang, the column, which is a letter, the arcade, which is a syllable, the pyramid, which is a word, set in motion alike by a geometric and a poetic law, grouped, combined, blended, rose, fell, were juxtaposed upon the ground, placed in rows one above another in air, until they had written, at the dictation of the universal idea of an epoch, those marvelous books which were also marvelous buildings,—the pagoda at Eklinga, the Egyptian Rhamseïon, the Temple of Solomon.

The original idea, the word, was not only at the base of all these buildings, but also in their form. Solomon's Temple, for instance, was not merely the binding of the Holy Book, it was the Holy Book itself. In each of its concentric halls the priests could read the Word translated and made manifest; and thus they followed its transformations from sanctuary to sanctuary, until they grasped it in its innermost tabernacle in its most concrete form, which was again architectural,—the arch. Thus the Word was contained within the edifice; but its image was upon its exterior as the human figure is upon the case of a mummy.

And not only the form of the structure, but the site which was chosen for it, revealed the thought which it represented. According as the symbol to be expressed was graceful and

pleasing or gloomy and severe, Greece crowned her mountains with a temple harmonious to the eye; India excavated
hers, to carve within them those misshapen subterranean
pagodas upborne by gigantic rows of granite elephants.

Thus, for the first six thousand years of the world's history,
from the most immemorial pagoda of Hindustan to the
Cologne Cathedral, architecture was the great writing of
mankind. And this is so true that not only every religious symbol, but even each human thought, has its page and its monument in this vast book.

All civilization begins with theocracy and ends with
democracy. This law of liberty succeeding to unity is written
in architecture. For,—let us dwell upon this point,—we must
not suppose that the mason's work is only potent to build the
temple, to express myth and priestly symbols, to transcribe the
mysterious tables of the law in hieroglyphic characters upon
its pages of stone. Were it so, as in every human society there
comes a moment when the sacred symbol is worn away and
obliterated by free thought, when the man slips away from the
priest, when the excrescences of philosophies and systems eat
away the face of religion, architecture could not reproduce
this new state of the human mind; its leaves, closely written
on the right side, would be blank upon the other, its work
would be mutilated, its book would be imperfect. But it is
not so.

Let us take for example the Middle Ages, which we see
more clearly from their being nearer to us. During its first period, while theocracy was organizing Europe, while the Vati-
can rallied and reclassified around it the elements of a Rome
made up from the Rome which lay crumbling about the
Capitol, while Christianity was seeking the various stages of
society amid the rubbish-heaps of previous civilizations, and
was rebuilding from its ruins a new hierarchic universe whose
high priest was the keystone of a vault, there was first heard
springing into place amid this chaos, then little by little seen
arising beneath the inspiration of Christianity, under the
hand of the barbarians, fragments of dead schools of archi-

tecture, Greek and Roman,—that mysterious Roman architecture, the sister of the theocratic edifices of Egypt and India,
the unalterable emblem of pure Catholicism, the unchang-
ing hieroglyph of papal unity. All the thought of that time, in
fact, is written in this somber Roman style. Authority, unity,
the impenetrable, the absolute, Gregory VII, are everywhere
evident; everywhere we find the priest, never the man; everywhere the caste, never the people. Next came the Crusades.
This was a great popular movement; and every great popular
movement, whatever its cause and purpose, always releases
the spirit of liberty from its final precipitate. Novelties are at
hand. Here begins the stormy period of the Jacqueries, the
Pragueries, and the Leagues. Authority is shaken, unity is divided. Feudality insists upon sharing with theocracy, until the
people shall inevitably rise, and, as usual, seize the lion's portion: *Quia nominor leo*. The nobility then penetrate the ranks
of the priesthood, the commonalty those of the nobility. The
face of Europe is changed. Well! the face of architecture is
also changed. Like civilization, it has turned the page, and the
new spirit of the times finds architecture ready to write at its
dictation. It returned from the Crusades with the pointed
arch, as the nations did with liberty. Then, while Rome was
being slowly dismembered, Roman architecture died. The hieroglyph forsook the cathedral, and went forth to emblazon
the donjon and lend a glory to feudalism. The cathedral itself,
that edifice once so dogmatic, henceforth invaded by the
burghers, by the Commons, by liberty, escapes from the priest
and falls into the power of the artist. The artist builds it in his
own way. Farewell to mystery, myth, and law! Fancy and
caprice have full sway. If the priest have but his basilica and
his altar, he has nothing to say; the four walls belong to the
artist. The architectural book no longer belongs to the priesthood, to religion, to Rome; it is the property of the imagination, of poetry, of the people. Hence the rapid and
innumerable changes in this style of architecture which has
existed but for three centuries, and which are so striking after
the stagnant immobility of the Roman school, which has

lived through six or seven. But art advances with giant pace. The genius and originality of the people do the work formerly assigned to the bishops. Each race, as it passes, writes its line in the book; it erases the old Roman hieroglyphs from the frontispiece of the cathedrals, and barely permits the dogma to peep here and there from beneath the new symbolism overlying it. The popular drapery scarcely permits us to guess at the religious framework. No idea can be given of the liberties then taken by architects even in regard to the Church. We find capitals interwoven with monks and nuns in shameful attitudes, as in the Salle des Cheminées of the Palace of Justice at Paris; we find Noah's adventures carved at full length, as under the great porch at Bourges; or we find a tipsy monk, with the ears of an ass, and a glass in his hand, laughing in the face of an entire community, as in the lavatory of the Abbey of Bocherville. There was at this time a license for thoughts written in stone, comparable only to the present freedom of the press. It was the freedom of architecture.

This liberty was carried to great lengths. Sometimes a doorway, a façade, an entire church, offers a symbolic meaning absolutely foreign to religion, nay, even hostile to the Church. Guillaume de Paris in the thirteenth century, Nicolas Flamel in the fifteenth, wrote such seditious pages. Saint-Jacques de la Boucherie was a church of opposition throughout.

In those days thought was free in this direction only; it was therefore never written out in full except upon those books called buildings. Accepted in the form of a building, it would have been burned in the market-place by the executioner had any one been rash enough to risk it in the manuscript form; the thought expressed in the porch of a church would have witnessed the torture of the same thought expressed in the shape of a book. Thus, having only this one way, mason-work, to see the light, it bloomed forth in this way on every hand. Hence the vast quantity of cathedrals which once covered Europe,—a number so prodigious that we can hardly credit it even after verifying it. All the material and all the intellectual forces of society tended to one and the same end,—architecture. In this way, under pretext of building churches to God, the art grew to magnificent proportions.

Then, whoever was born a poet, turned architect. The genius scattered through the masses, repressed on every hand by feudalism as beneath a carapace of iron bucklers, finding no issue save in the direction of architecture, emerged through that art, and its Iliad took the form of cathedrals. All the other arts obeyed and submitted to the sway of architecture. They were the workmen who executed the great work. The architect, the poet, the master singer, summed up in his own person the sculpture which carved his façades, the painting which lit up his window-panes, the music which set his bells in motion and blew his organs. Even the poor poetry, properly so called, which persisted in vegetating in manuscript, was obliged to take some part, to enter into the structure in the form of canticle or prose hymn,—the same part, after all, played by the tragedies of Æschylus at the sacerdotal feasts of Greece, by the book of Genesis in Solomon's Temple.

So, down to the days of Gutenberg, architecture was the principal, the universal writing. In this granite volume, begun by the East, continued by Greek and Roman antiquity, the Middle Ages wrote the final page. Moreover, this phenomenon of an architecture of the people taking the place of an architecture of caste and rank, which we have observed in the Middle Ages, is reproduced with every analogous movement of the human intellect in the other great epochs of history. Thus, to state but briefly here a law which requires volumes for its development, in the Orient, the cradle of the primitive races, after Hindu architecture came Phœnician architecture, that opulent mother of Arab architecture; in antiquity, after Egyptian architecture, of which the Etruscan style and cyclopean monuments are but one variety, came Greek architecture, whose Roman style is but an overloaded prolongation of the Carthaginian dome; in modern times, after Roman architecture, came Gothic architecture. And by dividing these three series, we shall find in the three elder sisters (Hindu architecture, Egyptian architecture, Roman architecture) the same symbolism, that is to say, theocracy, caste, unity, dogma, myth, God; and in the three younger sisters (Phœnician architecture, Greek architecture, Gothic architecture), whatever may be the diversity of form inherent in their nature, the meaning is always the same,—that is to say, liberty, humanity, mankind.

Whether he be known as Brahmin, Magian, or Pope, we are always conscious of the priest, nothing but the priest, in Hindu, Egyptian, or Roman structures. It is not so with the architecture of the people; their work is richer and less saintly. In the Phœnician school we are conscious of the tradesman; in the Grecian, of the republican; in the Gothic, of the burgess.

The general characteristics of all theocratic architecture are immutability, a horror of progress, a retention of traditional lines, a consecration of primitive types, a constant tendency of all human and natural forms towards the incomprehensible caprices of symbolism. These are obscure books, which only the initiated can decipher. Moreover, in them every form, every deformity even, has a meaning which makes it inviolable. Do not ask the Hindu, Egyptian, or Roman edifices to change their design or correct their statues. All perfection is to them impious. In these pieces of architecture the rigor of the dogma seems to overlie the stone like a second petrifaction. The general characteristics of popular edifices, on the contrary, should be variety, progress, originality, opulence, perpetual motion. They are sufficiently removed from religion to think of their beauty, to care for it, continually to alter and improve their adornment of statues or arabesques. They belong to this age. They have a human quality which they perpetually mingle with the divine symbolism under whose inspiration they are still produced. Hence edifices pervious to every soul, every intellect, and every imagination, still symbolical, but as easy to understand as Nature herself. Between theocratic architecture and this there is the difference that there is between a sacred language and a profane one, between hieroglyphics and art, between Solomon and Phidias.

If we sum up what we have thus far very hastily shown, omitting countless minor evidences and objections, we are led to these conclusions,—that architecture was, up to the fifteenth century, the chief register of humanity; that during this space of time no idea of any elaboration appeared in the world without being built into masonry; that every popular idea as well as every religious law has had its monument in fact, that the human race has never had an important thought which it has not written in stone. And why? It is because every thought, whether religious or philosophic, is interested in its own perpetuation; because an idea which has stirred one generation desires to stir others, and to leave its trace. Now, what a precarious immortality is that of the manuscript! How far more solid, lasting, and enduring a book is a building! A torch and a Turk are enough to destroy the written words; it takes a social or a terrestrial revolution to destroy the constructed word. The barbarians passed over the Coliseum, the Deluge perhaps over the Pyramids.

In the fifteenth century everything changed.

Human thought discovered a means of perpetuation, not only more durable and more resisting than architecture, but also simpler and easier. Architecture was dethroned. To the stone letters of Orpheus succeeded the leaden letters of Gutenberg.

"The book will destroy the building."

The invention of printing was the greatest event in history. It was the primal revolution. It was the renewed and renovated form of expression of humanity; it is human thought laying off one form and assuming another; it is the entire and final changing of the skin of that symbolic serpent which ever since Adam has represented intellect.

Under the form of printing, thought is more imperishable than ever; it is volatile, intangible, indestructible. It is mingled with the air. In the day of architecture it became a mountain, and took armed possession of a century and a place. Now it becomes a flock of birds, is scattered to the four winds, and occupies at once all points of the horizon and all space.

We repeat it; who does not see that in this way it is far more indelible than before? From being solid, it has become perennial. It has passed from duration to immortality. A great body may be demolished, but how can ubiquity be rooted out? Had a flood come, the mountain would have disappeared beneath the waves long before the birds ceased to fly above it; and if but a single ark should float on the surface of the cataclysm, they would rest upon it, survive with it, watch with it the going down of the waters; and the new world which rose from that chaos would, on awakening, behold hovering aloft, winged and living, the thought of the world which had been swallowed up.

And when we see that this mode of expression is not only the most preservative, but also the simplest, most convenient, and most practicable of all; when we consider that it entails no great amount of luggage, and requires no cumbrous apparatus; when we compare a thought obliged, in order to translate itself into an edifice, to set in motion four or five other arts, tons of gold, a whole mountain of stone, a whole forest of timber, a whole nation of workmen,—when we compare this with the thought which is made into a book, and which needs nothing but a little paper, a little ink, and a pen, why should we wonder that the human intellect gave up architecture for printing? Cross the original bed of a stream by a canal dug below its level, the stream will forsake its bed.

So, too, see how from the time of the discovery of printing, architecture gradually decayed, withered, and dried away. How plainly we can see the water sinking, the sap drying up, the thought of the time and of the people withdrawing from it! The sense of chill is almost imperceptible in the fifteenth century; the press was still too weak, and could only draw off somewhat of the superabundant life of mighty architecture. But with the dawn of the sixteenth century the disease of architecture becomes apparent; it has ceased to be the essential expression of society; in distress, it becomes classic art; from being Gallican, European, indigenous, it becomes Greek and Roman; from being real and modern, it becomes pseudo-antique. It is this decline which is known as the Renaissance, or revival. And yet it is a magnificent decline; for the old Gothic genius, that sun which is setting behind the gigantic press of Mayence, for some time longer pierces with its last rays all this hybrid heap of Latin arcades and Corinthian columns.

It is this setting sun which we take for the light of dawn. And yet, from the moment that architecture becomes an art, like any other art, that it ceases to be the sum total of art, the supreme, the tyrant art, it loses the power to hold the other arts. They therefore gain their liberty, break the yoke of the architect, and go each its own way. Each of them gains by this divorce. Isolation enlarges everything. Carving becomes sculpture, picture-making becomes painting, the canon becomes music. It might be compared to an empire torn limb from limb at the death of its Alexander, whose provinces become kingdoms.

Hence Raphael, Michael Angelo, Jean Goujon, Palestrina, — those splendors of the dazzling sixteenth century.

At the same time with the arts, thought gained freedom in all directions. The heresiarchs of the Middle Ages had already made large inroads upon Catholicism. The sixteenth century destroyed religious unity. Before the invention of printing, the Reformation would have been but a schism; the invention of printing made it a revolution. Take away the press, and heresy is unnerved. Whether it be due to Providence or to fate, Gutenberg was the precursor of Luther.

But when the sun of the Middle Ages had wholly set, when Gothic genius had forever faded from the horizon of art, architecture grew daily dimmer, duller, and fainter. The printed book, that undying worm of the great edifice, sucked its life-blood and devoured it. It grew visibly thinner, barer, and poorer. It was commonplace, it was paltry, it was null. It ceased to express anything, even the memory of the art of former ages. Reduced to itself, abandoned by the other arts be-

cause human thought has abandoned it, it calls in journey-
men for lack of artists; plain glass takes the place of painted
windows; the stonecutter succeeds the sculptor. Farewell to
all vigor, originality, life, and intellect. Architecture now
crawled, like a pitiful beggar of the studios, from copy to copy.
Michael Angelo, who had doubtless foreseen its death from
the dawn of the sixteenth century, had a last inspiration,—the
inspiration of despair. That Titan of art piled the Pantheon
upon the Parthenon, and created St. Peter's Church at Rome.
It is a great work, which deserved to remain unique,—the last
original creation of architecture, the signature of a colossal
artist at the foot of the vast registry of stone which it closed.
Michael Angelo dead, what did this wretched architecture do,
which survived itself in a spectral, ghost-like state? It took St.
Peter's at Rome, copied it, and parodied it. It was mere mania.
It was pitiable. Every century had its St. Peter's; in the seventeenth century it was the Val-de-Grâce, in the eighteenth,
Sainte-Geneviève. Every country had its St. Peter's; London
had its own; St. Petersburg had its own; Paris had two or
three,—a worthless legacy, the last unmeaning drivel of a
great art grown old and reduced to dotage before it died!

If in place of characteristic monuments, such as those to
which we have just referred, we examine the general aspect of
art from the sixteenth to the eighteenth centuries, we observe
the same phenomena of decline and decay. From Francis II
down, the architectural form of the edifice becomes less and
less apparent, the geometric form growing more and more
prominent, like the skeleton of an emaciated invalid. The
beautiful lines of art give way to the cold and inexorable lines
of geometry. A building ceases to be a building: it is a polyhedron. Architecture, however, struggles to disguise this nakedness. We have the Greek pediment put down upon the
Roman pediment, and *vice versa*. We still have the Pantheon
within the Parthenon; we still have St. Peter's. We have the
brick houses of the reign of Henry IV with brick corners, as in
the Place Royale and Place Dauphine. We have the churches
of the reign of Louis XIII, heavy, clumsy, surbased, short, and

broad, loaded with a dome as with a hump. We have the Mazarin architecture,—the wretched Italian Pasticcio of the "Four Nations." We have the palaces of the reign of Louis XIV,—long barracks built for courtiers, stiff, cold, and stupid. Lastly, we have the style of Louis XV, with its chiccory and vermicelli, and all the warts and fungi which disfigure that decrepit, toothless, coquettish old architecture. From the days of Francis II to those of Louis XIV the evil increased in geometrical ratio. Art was nothing but skin and bones. It was dying a wretched, lingering death.

But what was printing doing? All the life which architecture lost, flushed its veins. In proportion as architecture degenerated, printing throve and flourished. The capital of forces which human thought had expended in building, it henceforth expended in books. So from the dawn of the sixteenth century onward, the press, grown to the level of the declining architecture, wrestled with it and slew it. In the seventeenth century it was already sufficiently supreme, sufficiently triumphant, sufficiently sure of victory, to give the world the spectacle of a great literary age. In the eighteenth century, after a long interval of rest at the court of Louis XIV, it once more grasped the old sword of Luther, armed Voltaire with it, and hastened tumultuously forth to attack that ancient Europe whose architectural expression it had already destroyed. When the eighteenth century closed, it had uprooted everything. In the nineteenth, it will reconstruct.

Now, we ask which of the two arts has really represented human thought for three centuries past? Which translates it? Which expresses, not only its literary and scholastic fancies, but its vast, profound, universal movement? Which constantly superposes itself, without rupture or void, upon mankind, which moves apace, a thousand-footed monster,— Architecture, or Printing?

Printing. Let no one be deceived: architecture is dead, irrevocably dead; killed by the printed book; killed because it was less enduring; killed because it was more costly. Every cathedral represents a thousand million francs. Think, then, of the sum required to rewrite the architectural book; to make thousands of structures once more cover the earth as thick as ant-hills; to bring back the days when the number of monumental works was such that, in the words of an eye-witness, "You would have thought that the world had shaken off her old garments, to clothe herself in a white array of churches," *"Erat enim ut si mundus, ipse excutiendo semet, rejecta vetustate, candidam ecclesiarum vestem indueret."* —GLABER RADULPHUS.

A book is so soon made, costs so little, and may go so far! Why should we be surprised that all human thought flows that way? We do not mean to say that architecture may not yet produce a fine specimen here and there, a single masterpiece. We may still, I suppose, have from time to time, under the reign of printing, a column made by an entire army, of molten cannon, as during the reign of architecture we had Iliads and Romanceros, Mahâbhâratas, and Nibelungen-Lieds made by a whole nation, out of collected and blended rhapsodies.

The great accident of an architect of genius may occur in the twentieth century, as that of Dante did in the thirteenth; but architecture will never again be the social art, the collective art, the dominant art. The great poem, the great edifice, the great work of humanity, will no longer be built; it will be printed.

And in the future, should architecture accidentally revive, it will never again be supreme. It must bow to the sway of literature, formerly subject to it. The respective positions of the two arts will be reversed. It is certain that the rare poems to be found during the architectural period are like monuments. In India, Vyâsa was as manifold, strange, and impenetrable as a pagoda. In Egypt, poetry had, like the buildings, a grandeur and quietness of outline; in ancient Greece, beauty, serenity, and calm; in Christian Europe, the Catholic majesty, popular simplicity, the rich and luxuriant vegetation of a period of renewal. The Bible is like the Pyramids, the Iliad like the Parthenon, Homer like Phidias. Dante in the thirteenth century is the last Roman church; Shakspeare in the sixteenth the last Gothic cathedral.

Thus, to sum up what we have so far said in a manner necessarily brief and imperfect, mankind has two books, two registers, two testaments: architecture and printing, — the Bible of stone and the Bible of paper. Undoubtedly, when we examine these two Bibles, so widely opened during the lapse of centuries, we may be permitted to regret the visible majesty of the granite writing, of those gigantic alphabets formed into colonnades, pylons, and obelisks, of those human mountains which covered the world of the past, from the pyramid to the belfry, from Cheops to Strasburg. We should re-read the past upon those marble pages. We should admire and unceasingly re-turn the leaves of the book written by architecture; but we should not deny the grandeur of the structure reared by printing in its turn.

That structure is colossal. I know not what maker of statistics has calculated that by placing one upon another all the volumes issued from the press since the days of Gutenberg, we might fill up the space between the earth and the moon; but this is not the sort of grandeur which we mean. Still, when we try to form a mental image of all the products of printing down to our own day, does not the sum total seem a vast construction, resting upon the entire universe, at which humanity labors without respite, and whose monstrous summit is lost in the thick mists of the future? It is the ant-hill of intellects. It is the hive where all wit and imagination, those golden bees, store up their honey. The structure has a thousand stories. Here and there, opening on its staircases, we see the dark caves of learning intersecting one another within it. All over its surface art has woven its arabesques, its rose-windows, and its lace-work, to captivate the eye. There each individual work, fanciful and unique as it may seem, has its place and its purpose. Harmony results from the union of all. From the cathedral of Shakspeare to the mosque of Byron, a myriad spires are heaped pell-mell upon this metropolis of universal thought. At its base are inscribed some antique titles of humanity which architecture failed to register. At the left of the entrance is fastened the old white marble bas-relief of Homer; at the right the polyglot Bible rears its seven heads. The hydra of the Romancero bristles up beyond, with certain other hybrid forms, like the Vedas and the Nibelungen. Moreover, the vast edifice remains forever unfinished. The press, that gigantic machine which untiringly sucks up all the intellectual sap of society, unceasingly vomits forth fresh material for its work. All mankind are on the scaffolding. Every mind is a mason. The humblest stops up his hole or lays his stone. Every day a fresh course is laid. Independently of the original and individual contributions of each writer, there are collective supplies. The eighteenth century gave the *Encyclopædia*, the French Revolution gave the *Moniteur*. Assuredly, it is a structure which will gather and grow in unending spirals. Here, too, there is a confusion of tongues, an incessant activity, an indefatigable industry, a frantic co-operation of all humanity; it is the refuge promised to intellect against another deluge, against a flood of barbarians. It is the second Tower of Babel of the human race.

BOOK VI

CHAPTER I

An Impartial Glance at the Ancient Magistracy

A very lucky fellow, in the year of grace 1482, was that noble gentleman Robert d'Estouteville, knight, Lord of Beyne, Baron of Ivry and St. Andry in La Marche, councillor and chamberlain to the king, and keeper of the provosty of Paris. It was some seventeen years since he received from the king, Nov. 7, 1465, the year of the comet,* the handsome appointment of provost of Paris, which was regarded rather as a dignity than an office. "*Dignitas,*" says Joannes Lœmnœus, "*quæ cum non exigua potestate politiam concernente, atque præærogativis multis et juribus conjuncta est.*"† It was an extraordinary thing in 1482 for a gentleman to hold a commission from the king; and a gentleman, too, whose appointment dated back to the time of the marriage of Louis XI's natural daughter to the Bastard of Bourbon. On the same day that Robert d'Estouteville succeeded Jacques de Villiers as provost of Paris, Master Jehan Dauvet took the

---

*Author's note: This comet, for deliverance from which Pope Calixtus, uncle to Borgia, ordered a public prayer, is the same that reappeared in 1835.

†A dignity to which is attached no little power in dealing with public safety, together with many prerogatives and rights (Latin).

place of Master Hélye de Thorrettes as first president of the court of Parliament, Jehan Jouvenel des Ursins supplanted Pierre de Morvilliers in the office of Lord Chancellor of France, Regnault des Dormans deprived Pierre Puy of his place as referendary in ordinary to the king's household. Now, through how many hands had the presidency, chancellorship, and referendaryship not passed since Robert d'Estouteville was made provost of Paris! The office was "granted into his keeping," said the letters-patent; and certainly he kept it well. He clung to it, he identified himself with it, he made himself so much a part of it that he escaped that passion for change which possessed Louis XI, the suspicious, stingy, industrious king who insisted on keeping up the elasticity of his power by constant removals and appointments. Nay, more: the worthy knight had obtained the reversion of his office for his son, and for the last two years the name of the noble Jacques d'Estouteville, Esquire, had figured beside his own at the head of the ordinary of the provosty of Paris. Assuredly a rare and signal mark of favor! True, Robert d'Estouteville was a good soldier; he had loyally raised his standard against "the league of the public weal," and had offered the queen a very marvellous stag made of sweetmeats on the day she entered Paris, in 14—. Besides, he had a good friend in Master Tristan l'Hermite, provost of the marshals of the king's household. Master Robert, therefore, led a very smooth and pleasant life. In the first place, he had a capital salary, to which were attached and hung, like so many additional bunches of grapes to his vine, the revenues of the civil and criminal registries of the provostship, besides the civil and criminal revenues of the Inferior Courts of the Châtelet, not to mention some slight toll on the Pont de Mantes and Pont de Corbeil, the tax on all the onions, leeks, and garlic brought into Paris, and the tax on wood meters and salt measures. Add to this the pleasure of displaying his fine suit of armor within the city limits, and showing off among the party-colored red and tan robes of the sheriffs and district police which you may still admire carved upon his tomb at the Abbey of Valmont in Normandy, as you

may also see his embossed morion at Montlhéry. And then,—
was it nothing to have supreme power over the twelve sergeants, the porter and warder of the Châtelet, the two auditors
of the Châtelet (*auditores castelleti*), the sixteen commissaries
of the sixteen quarters of the city, the jailer of the Châtelet,
the four ennobled officers of the peace, the hundred and
twenty mounted police, the hundred and twenty vergers, the
captain of the watch, his under-watch, counter-watch, and
rear-watch? Was it nothing to administer high and low justice,
to exercise the right to turn, hang, and draw, to say nothing of
the minor jurisdiction "in the first instance" (*in prima instan-
tia*, as the charters say) of that viscounty of Paris, so gloriously
provided with seven noble bailiwicks? Can anything be imagined more agreeable than to give judgments and decrees, as
Master Robert d'Estouteville did daily at the Grand-Châtelet,
under the broad flat arches of Philip Augustus; and to return,
as he was wont to do every evening, to that charming house in
the Rue Galilée, within the precincts of the royal palace,
which he held by right of his wife, Madame Ambroise de
Loré, there to rest from the labor of sending some poor devil
to pass his night in "that little lodge in the Rue de l'Es-
corcherie, wherein the provosts and sheriffs of Paris frequently used as a prison,—the same measuring eleven feet in
length, seven feet and four inches in width, and eleven feet in
height?"*

And not only had Master Robert d'Estouteville his private
court as provost and viscount of Paris, but he also had his
share, both active and passive, in the king's own high justice.
There was no head of any note but had passed through his
hands before falling into those of the executioner. It was he
who went to the Bastille Saint-Antoine, in search of M. de
Nemours, to take him to the Halles; and he who conducted
M. de Saint-Pol to the Place de Grève, the latter gentleman

---

*Author's note: Crown accounts, 1383.

sulking and fretting, to the great delight of the provost, who
had no love for the constable.

Here, certainly, was more than enough to make life happy
and illustrious, and to justify in the future a memorable page
in the interesting history of the provosts of Paris, wherein we
learn that Oudard de Villeneuve had a house in the Rue des
Boucheries, that Guillaume de Hangest bought big and little
Savoy, that Guillaume Thiboust gave the nuns of Sainte-
Geneviève his houses in the Rue Clopin, that Hugues
Aubriot lived at Hôtel du Porc-Epic, and other domestic facts.

And yet, with all these motives for taking life patiently and
pleasantly, Master Robert d'Estouteville waked on the morning of Jan. 7, 1482, in a very sulky and disagreeable mood.
Whence came this ill-humor? He could not have told you
himself. Was it because the sky was overcast; because the
buckle of his old Montlhéry belt was fastened too tight, and
girt his provostship's goodly portliness in too military a fashion; because he had seen a band of ragamuffins march
through the street below his window, mocking him as they
passed in double file, wearing doublets without shirts, crown-
less hats, and wallet and flask at their side? Was it a vague presentiment of the three hundred and seventy pounds, sixteen
pence, and eight farthings which the future king, Charles
VIII, was to cut off from the revenues of the provosty? The
reader can take his choice; as for us, we incline to the belief
that he was out of temper simply because he was out of temper.

Besides, it was the day after a holiday,—a stupid day for
everybody, and especially for the magistrate, whose duty it was
to sweep away all the dirt, actual and metaphorical, caused by
a popular holiday in Paris. And then, he was to hold court at
the Grand-Châtelet. Now, we have noticed that judges usually so arrange matters that the day upon which they hold
court is also the day on which they are out of temper, in order
that they may always have some one upon whom to vent their
rage, in the name of the king, law, and justice.

However, the court had opened without him. His

deputies, in the civil, criminal, and private courts, were doing his work for him, as was the custom; and ever since eight o'clock in the morning some scores of citizens, men and women, crowded and crammed into a dark corner of the lower court-room of the Châtelet, between a stout oaken railing and the wall, had blissfully looked on at the varied and attractive spectacle of administration of civil and criminal law by Master Florian Barbedienne, examining judge of the Châtelet, and provost's deputy, whose sentences were delivered pell-mell and somewhat at random.

The hall was small and low, with a vaulted roof. A table branded with *fleur-de-lis* stood at the back of it, with a large carved oaken arm-chair, which belonged to the provost and was empty, and a stool on the left for Master Florian. Below sat the clerk, scribbling; opposite him were the people; and before the door and table were a number of the provost's officers, in frocks of purple camlet, with white crosses. Two officers from the Commonalty Hall, arrayed in party-colored red and blue kersey jackets, stood sentry before a half-open door, behind the table. A single arched window, deep set in the thick wall, cast a ray of pale January sunshine upon two grotesque figures,—the comical stone demon carved as a tailpiece to the keystone of the vaulted roof, and the judge seated at the end of the hall upon the *fleurs-de-lis*.

Now, picture to yourself at the provost's table, between two bundles of papers, leaning on his elbows, his feet on the train of his plain brown cloth gown, his face framed in its white lamb's-wool wig, of which his eyebrows seemed to be a fragment, red-faced, stern, winking and blinking, majestically bearing the burden of his fat cheeks, which met under his chin, Master Florian Barbedienne, examining judge of the Châtelet.

Now, the judge was deaf,—a slight defect for a judge. Master Florian gave judgment, nevertheless, without appeal, and very properly too. It is certainly quite enough if a judge look as if he were listening; and the venerable judge fulfilled this condition—the only one requisite to the due administration of justice—all the better for the fact that his attention was not to be distracted by any noise.

Moreover, he had a merciless comptroller of his sayings and doings, among the audience, in the person of our friend Jehan Frollo du Moulin, the little student of the previous day, that pedestrian who was sure to be found anywhere in Paris except in the lecture-room of his professors.

"Stay," he whispered to his comrade, Robin Poussepain, who was chuckling beside him while he commented on the scenes unrolled before them, "there's Jehanneton du Buisson,—the pretty daughter of that loafer from the New Market! Upon my soul, he has condemned her, the old wretch! Then his eyes can't be any better than his ears. Fifteen pence and four Paris farthings, for wearing two strings of beads! That's rather expensive. '*Lex duri carminis.*' Who's that fellow? Robin Chief-de-Ville, hauberk-maker,—for having been passed and received as a master of the said trade? It's his entrance-fee. Hollo! two gentlemen among these varlets,— Aiglet de Soins, Hutin de Mailly. Two esquires, *Corpus Christi!* Ah, ha! they've been playing at dice. When shall I see our rector here? A hundred Paris pounds fine to the king! Barbedienne hits hard, like a deaf man as he is! I wish I may be my brother the archdeacon if this prevent me from gambling,—gambling by day, gambling by night, living a gambler, dying a gambler, and gambling away my soul when my last rag's gone! Holy Virgin! what a lot of girls! One after the other, my lambs! Ambroise Lécuyère! Isabeau la Paynette! Bérarde Gironin! I know them all, by heaven! Fine 'em! fine 'em! That'll teach you to wear gilt belts! Ten Paris pence, coquettes! Oh, what an old dog of a judge! deaf and imbecile! Oh, Florian, you blockhead! Oh, Barbedienne, you booby! See him sit at table! He gobbles the suitor, he gobbles the suit, he minces, he munches, he stuffs himself, he fills himself full. Fines, unclaimed goods, taxes, expenses, legal costs, wages, damages, torture, prison and jail and stocks, are Christmas cakes and Saint John's marchpane to him! Just look at him, the pig! Now, then, good! Still another amorous dame!

Thibaud-la-Thibaude, and no one else,—for leaving the Rue Glatigny! Who is that fellow? Gieffroy Mabonne, bowman of the guard. He swore by the Holy Name, did he?—A fine, Thibaude! a fine, Gieffroy! Fine 'em both! Deaf old fool! he must have mixed the two charges up! Ten to one, he'll fine the woman for swearing, and the bowman for making love! Attention, Robin Poussepain! Whom are they bringing in now? What a lot of sergeants! By Jupiter! all the hounds in the pack are here. This must be the best head of game they've got,—a wild boar. It *is* one, Robin, it is indeed,—and a fine one too! By Hercules! it's our yesterday's prince, our Pope of Fools, our bell-ringer, our one-eyed, hunchbacked pet, our wry-face! It's Quasimodo!"

It was, indeed.

It was Quasimodo, bound, corded, tied, garotted, and well guarded. The squad of men who had him in charge were assisted by the captain of the watch in person, wearing the arms of France embroidered on his breast, and the city arms on his back. There was nothing, however, about Quasimodo, except his deformity, which could justify this display of halberds and arquebuses; he was somber, silent, and quiet. His solitary eye merely cast an occasional crafty, angry glance at the bonds which held him.

He gazed around him with the same expression, but so dull and sleepy was it that the women only pointed him out to each other to mock at him.

But Master Florian, the judge, was attentively turning over the brief containing the charge against Quasimodo, which the clerk had just handed him, and having examined the papers, seemed to be meditating for a moment. Thanks to this precaution, which he was always careful to take just before proceeding to an examination, he knew in advance the name, condition, and crimes of the prisoner, had his answer ready for the replies which he expected, and succeeded in extricating himself from all the intricacies of the examination without making his deafness too apparent. The brief therefore was to him like the blind man's dog. If he chanced to betray his infirmity by an occasional incoherent remark or an unintelligible question, it passed with some for profundity, and with others for imbecility. In either case, the honor of the magistracy was unimpeached; for it is much better that a judge should be considered stupid or profound than deaf. He accordingly took great pains to hide his deafness from all, and usually succeeded so well that he had actually come to deceive himself,—a thing, moreover, which is easier than you would think. All hunchbacks carry their heads high, all stammerers are fond of speechifying, all deaf people speak in low tones. As for him, at most he thought himself a little hard of hearing. This was the sole concession which he was willing to make to the public opinion upon this point, in his moments of perfect frankness and self-examination.

Having therefore thoroughly considered Quasimodo's case, he threw back his head and half closed his eyes, in order to look more majestic and impartial, so that for the time being he was both deaf and blind,—a twofold condition, without which there can be no perfect judge. In this magisterial attitude he began his cross-examination.

"Your name?"

Now, here was a case which had not been "provided for by the law,"—that of one deaf man questioning another.

Quasimodo, quite unconscious of the question, continued to gaze fixedly at the judge, and made no answer. The judge, deaf, and wholly unaware of the prisoner's deafness, supposed that he had answered, as all prisoners were wont to do, and went on, with his mechanical and stupid assurance,—

"Good! Your age?"

Quasimodo made no answer. The judge was satisfied, and continued,—

"Now, your business?"

Still the same silence. The audience began to whisper and look at each other.

"That will do," resumed the imperturbable judge, when he supposed that the prisoner had ended his third answer. "You are accused, before us: *primo*, of making a nocturnal disturbance; *secundo*, of an indecent assault upon the person of a light woman, *in præjudicium meretricis; tertio*, of rebellion and disloyalty towards the archers of the guard of our lord the king. What have you to say for yourself on all these points? Clerks, have you written down all that the prisoner has said thus far?"

At this unfortunate question a shout of laughter burst from both clerk and audience, so violent, so hearty, so contagious, so universal, that even the two deaf men could not fail to notice it. Quasimodo turned away, shrugging his hump in disdain; while Master Florian, equally surprised, and supposing the laughter of the spectators to be provoked by some irreverent reply from the prisoner, made apparent to him by that shrug, addressed him most indignantly,—

"Such an answer as that, you rascal, deserves the halter! Do you know to whom you speak?"

This sally was scarcely adapted to silence the outburst of merriment. It seemed to all so absurd and ridiculous that the contagious laughter spread to the very sergeants from the Commonalty Hall, the kind of men-at-arms whose stupidity is their uniform. Quasimodo alone preserved his gravity, for the very good reason that he understood nothing of what was going on around him. The judge, more and more indignant, felt obliged to proceed in the same strain, hoping in this way to strike the prisoner with a terror which would react upon the audience and restore them to a due sense of respect for him.

"So then, perverse and thievish knave, you venture to insult the judge of the Châtelet, the chief magistrate of the police courts of Paris, appointed to inquire into all crimes, offences, and misdemeanors; to control all trades and prevent monopoly; to keep the pavements in repair; to put down hucksters of poultry, fowl, and wild game; to superintend the measuring of logs and firewood; to cleanse the city of mud and the air of contagious diseases,—in a word, to watch continually over the public welfare, without wages or hope of salary! Do you know that my name is Florian Barbedienne, and that I am the lord provost's own deputy, and, moreover, commissary, comptroller, and examiner with equal power in provosty, bailiwick, court of registration, and presidial court?"

There is no reason why a deaf man talking to a deaf man should ever cease. Heaven knows when Master Florian, thus launched on the full flood of his own eloquence, would have paused, if the low door at the back of the room had not suddenly opened and admitted the provost himself.

At his entrance Master Florian did not stop short, but turning half round on his heel and abruptly addressing to the provost the harangue with which but a moment before he was overwhelming Quasimodo, he said: "My lord, I demand such sentence as it may please you to inflict upon the prisoner here present, for his grave and heinous contempt of court."

And he sat down again quite out of breath, wiping away the big beads of moisture which ran down his face like tears, wetting the papers spread out before him. Master Robert d'Estouteville frowned, and commanded Quasimodo's attention by a sign so imperious and significant that even the deaf man understood something of his meaning.

The provost addressed him severely: "What brings you here, scoundrel?"

The poor wretch, supposing that the provost asked his name, broke his habitual silence, and answered in a hoarse and guttural voice, "Quasimodo."

The answer had so little to do with the question that an irresistible laugh again ran round the room, and Master Robert cried out, red with rage, —

"Would you mock me too, you arrant knave?"

"Bell-ringer of Notre-Dame," replied Quasimodo, fancying himself called upon to explain to the judge who he was.

"Bell-ringer, indeed!" responded the provost, who, as we have already said, had waked in an ill enough humor that morning not to require any fanning of the flames of his fury by such strange answers. "Bell-ringer! I'll have a peal of switches rung upon your back through all the streets of Paris! Do you hear me, rascal?"

"If you want to know my age," said Quasimodo, "I believe I shall be twenty on Saint Martin's Day."

This was too much; the provost could bear it no longer.

"Oh, you defy the provost's office, do you, wretch! Vergers, take this scamp to the pillory in the Place de Grève; beat him well, and then turn him for an hour. He shall pay me for this, *tête-Dieu!* And I order this sentence to be proclaimed, by the aid of four sworn trumpeters, throughout the seven castellanies of the jurisdiction of Paris."

The clerk at once wrote down the sentence.

"A wise sentence, by God!" exclaimed the little student, Jehan Frollo du Moulin, from his corner.

The provost turned, and again fixed his flashing eyes upon Quasimodo: "I believe the scamp said 'By God!' Clerk, add a fine of twelve Paris pence for swearing, and let half of it go to the Church of Saint Eustache; I am particularly fond of Saint Eustache."

In a few moments the sentence was drawn up. It was simple and brief in tenor. The common law of the provosty and viscounty of Paris had not yet been elaborated by the president, Thibaut Baillet, and by Roger Barmue, the king's advocate; it was not then obscured by that mass of quirks and quibbles which these two lawyers introduced at the beginning of the sixteenth century. Everything about it was clear, expeditious, and explicit. It went straight to the mark, and at the end of every path, unconcealed by brambles or briers, the wheel, the gallows, or the pillory were plainly to be seen from the very outset. At least, you knew what was coming.

The clerk handed the sentence to the provost, who affixed his seal to it, and left the room to continue his round of the courts, in a state of mind which must have added largely that day to the population of the jails of Paris. Jehan Frollo and Robin Poussepain laughed in their sleeves. Quasimodo looked on with indifference and surprise.

But the clerk, just as Master Florian Barbedienne was reading the sentence in his turn before signing it, felt a twinge of pity for the poor devil of a prisoner, and in the hope of gaining some diminution of his punishment, leaned as close as he could to the judge's ear, and said, pointing to Quasimodo, "That fellow is deaf."

He hoped that their common infirmity might rouse Master Florian's interest in the prisoner's favor. But, in the first place, we have already observed that Master Florian did not care to have his deafness noticed. In the next place, he was so hard of hearing that he caught not one word of what the clerk said to him; and yet, he wanted to have it appear that he heard, and therefore answered. "Oho! that's a different matter; I did not know that. Give him another hour in the pillory, in that case."

And he signed the sentence with this modification.

"Well done!" said Robin Poussepain, who bore Quasimodo a grudge; "that will teach him to maltreat folks."

CHAPTER II

The Rat-Hole

With the reader's permission, we will return to the Place de Grève which we left yesterday with Gringoire, to follow Esmeralda.

It is ten o'clock in the morning; everything smacks of the day after a holiday. The pavement is covered with fragments,—ribbons, scraps, feathers from the plumes, drops of wax from the torches, crumbs from the public feast. A number of citizens are lounging here and there, occasionally stirring the dying embers of the bonfire with their feet, going into ecstasies in front of the Maison-aux-Piliers, as they recall the fine hangings of the previous day, and staring at the nails which held them, the last remnant of their pleasure. The venders of cider and beer roll their barrels through the various groups. A few busy passers come and go. The shop-keepers chat and gossip with one another at the door of their shops. The festival, the ambassadors, Coppenole, the Pope of Fools, are on every tongue, each vying with the other in the severity of his criticisms and the loudness of his laughter. And yet four mounted police, who have just stationed themselves at the four corners of the pillory, have already collected about them a goodly portion of the populace scattered about the square, and willing to stand stupidly still for any length of time, in the hope of witnessing some petty punishment.

If now the reader, having looked upon this lively and noisy scene enacting in every part of the square, will turn his gaze towards that ancient half-Gothic, half-Roman structure known as the Tour-Roland, which forms the western angle of the quay, he may perceive at the corner of its façade a large public breviary, ri hly illuminated, protected from the rain by a small pent-house, and from thieves by a grating, which, however, allows the passer-by to turn over its leaves. Beside this breviary is a narrow arched window, guarded by two iron bars placed crosswise, and looking out upon the square,—the only opening through which a little air and light reach a tiny cell without a door, built on the ground-floor, in the thickness of the wall of the old house, and filled with a peace made more profound, a silence made more melancholy, by the fact that a public square, the noisiest and most thickly peopled place in all Paris, swarms and shrieks just outside.

This cell has been celebrated throughout Paris for almost three centuries; since Madame Rolande, of the Tour-Roland, being in mourning for her father, who died while on a Crusade, had it hewed out of the wall of her own house and shut herself up in it forever, keeping no part of her palace but this one lodging, the door of which was walled up and the window open, in winter as in summer, giving all the rest of her property to God and the poor. The desolate dame did indeed await death for twenty years within this premature tomb, praying night and day for her father's soul, sleeping upon a bed of ashes, without even a stone for pillow, clad in black sack-cloth, and living on such portions of bread and water as the pity of the passers-by placed on her window-sill; thus accepting charity after having bestowed it. At her death, as she was about to pass to another tomb, she bequeathed this one in perpetuity to all afflicted women, mothers, widows, or daughters, who had great need to pray for others or themselves, and who wished to bury themselves alive in token of their great grief or great penitence. The poor of her time paid her the best of funeral rites in their tears and blessings; but, to their great regret, the pious dame could not be canonized a saint, for lack of patronage. Those of them who were inclined to be impious hoped that the matter might be more readily arranged in paradise than at Rome, and quite simply prayed to God instead of to the Pope, for the deceased. Most of them were satisfied with holding her memory sacred and making relics of her rags. The city, for its part, founded for the lady's sake a public breviary, which was fastened to the wall near the window of the cell, so that those who passed might occasionally stop, if only to pray, that so the prayer might lead them to think of alms, and that the poor recluses, the heirs of Madame Rolande's cell, might not die of hunger and neglect.

Nor was this sort of tomb a great rarity in the cities of the Middle Ages. There might frequently be found, in the most crowded street, in the most motley and clamorous market-place, in the very midst of the confusion, under the horses' feet, under the cart-wheels, as it were, a cellar, a well, a walled and grated cell, within which some human being prayed night and day, voluntarily vowed to everlasting lamentation, to some extraordinary expiation. And all the reflections which would be roused today by so singular a sight,—that horrid cell, a sort of connecting link between the house and the tomb, the cemetery and the city; that living creature cut off from human companionship and thenceforth reckoned with the dead; that lamp consuming its last drop of oil in darkness; that remnant of life flickering in a grave; that breath, that voice, that perpetual prayer, in a coffin of stone; that face forever turned towards the other world; that eye already illumined by another sun; that ear glued to the wall of the tomb; that soul imprisoned in that body; that body imprisoned in that dungeon; and beneath that double casing of flesh and stone the murmur of that suffering soul,—nothing of all this was noted by the crowd.

The unreasoning and far from subtile piety of that day could not conceive of so many sides to an act of religion. It viewed the thing as a whole, and honored, venerated, sanctified the sacrifice if need be, but did not analyze the suffering, and pitied it but slightly. It occasionally bestowed some pittance on the wretched penitent, looked through the hole to see if he were still alive, knew not his name, hardly knew how many years it was since he began to die, and to the stranger who asked about the living skeleton rotting in that cellar, the neighbors simply answered, "That is the recluse."

People saw things in this way then,—without metaphysics, without exaggeration, without magnifying-glass, with the naked eye. The microscope had not yet been invented, either for material or for spiritual things.

Besides, although people marvelled so little at them, instances of this kind of claustration in the heart of a town were really very frequent, as we just now observed. Paris contained a goodly number of these cells for praying to God and doing penance; they were almost all occupied. It is true that the clergy did not care to leave them empty, as that would imply luke-warmness among the faithful; and they therefore put lepers into them when they had no penitents. Besides the cell in the Place de Grève, there was one at Montfaucon, one at the charnel-house of the Cemetery of the Innocents, another,— I've forgotten just where,—at Clichon House, I believe; others again in many other places, traces of which may yet be found in popular tradition, for lack of monuments. The University had also cells of its own. On the mountain of St. Geneviève a kind of mediæval Job for thirty years sang the seven penitential psalms upon a dunghill, at the bottom of a cistern, beginning again whenever he reached the end, chanting louder by night,—*magna voce per umbras*; and even now the antiquary fancies that he hears his voice when he enters the street known as Rue Puits-qui-parle: the street of the Talking Well.

But to keep to the cell of the Tour-Roland, we should mention that it had never wanted for recluses. Since Madame Rolande's death, it had seldom been vacant for more than a year. Many women had gone thither to weep, until death, for parents, lovers, or sins. Parisian malice, which interferes with everything, even those things which concern it least, asserted that very few widows had ever been seen within its walls.

As was the fashion of that period, a Latin inscription on the wall informed the learned passers-by of the pious purpose of this cell. The custom was retained until the middle of the sixteenth century, of explaining the purpose of a building by a brief device inscribed above the door. Thus we still read in France, over the gate of the prison belonging to the manor of the Lord of Tourville: "*Sileto et spera*;"* in Ireland, under the escutcheon over the great door of Fortescue Castle: "*Forte scutum, salus ducum*;"† and in England, over the main entrance to the hospitable manor of Earl Cowper: "*Tuum est*."‡ In those days every edifice embodied a thought.

As there was no door to the walled cell in the Tour-Roland, some one had carved in Roman capitals over the window these two words:—

"TU, ORA."§

Hence the people, whose mind never grasps such nice distinctions, and who are quite ready to translate *Ludovico Magno* into the Porte Saint-Denis, gave this dark, damp,

---

*Be silent and hope (Latin).
†A strong shield is the safety of the leaders (Latin).
‡It is yours (Latin).
§Pray, thou (Latin).

gloomy cavern the name of the *"Trou-aux-Rats,"* or the Rat-Hole,—an explanation possibly less sublime, but certainly more picturesque than the other.

CHAPTER III

The Story of a Wheaten Cake

At the time of which this story treats, the cell in the Tour-Roland was occupied. If the reader wishes to know by whom, he has but to listen to the conversation of three worthy gossips, who, at the moment when we drew his attention to the Rat-Hole, were walking directly that way, going from the Châtelet towards the Place de Grève, along the water's edge.

Two of these women were dressed like good citizens of Paris. Their fine white gorgets; their petticoats of striped linsey-woolsey, red and blue; their white knitted stockings, with colored clocks, pulled well up over the leg; their square-toed shoes of tan-colored leather with black soles; and above all their head-dress,—a sort of tinsel horn overloaded with ribbons and lace, still worn by the women of Champagne and by the grenadiers of the Russian Imperial Guard,—proclaiming that they belonged to that class of rich tradesfolk occupying the middle ground between what servants call "a woman" and what they call "a lady." They wore neither rings nor gold crosses; and it was easy to see that this was not from poverty, but quite simply from fear of a fine. Their companion was attired in much the same style; but there was something in her appearance and manner which bespoke the country notary's wife. It was evident by the way in which her girdle was arranged high above her hips, that she had not been in Paris long; add to this a pleated gorget, knots of ribbon on her shoes, the fact that the stripes of her petticoat ran breadthwise and not lengthwise, and a thousand other enormities revolting to good taste.

The first two walked with the gait peculiar to Parisian women showing Paris to their country friends. The country-woman held by the hand a big boy, who grasped in his hand a large wheaten cake. We regret that we must add that, owing to the severity of the season, his tongue did duty as a pocket-handkerchief.

The child loitered (*"non passibus æquis,"* as Virgil has it), and stumbled constantly, for which his mother scolded him well. True, he paid far more attention to the cake than to the pavement. Undoubtedly he had some grave reason for not biting it (the cake), for he contented himself with gazing affectionately at it. But his mother should have taken charge of the cake. It was cruel to make a Tantalus of the chubby child.

But the three damsels (for the term "dame" was then reserved for noble ladies) were all talking at once.

"Make haste, Damoiselle Mahiette," said the youngest of the three, who was also the biggest, to the country-woman. "I am mightily afraid we shall be too late; they told us at the Châtelet that he was to be taken directly to the pillory."

"Nonsense! What do you mean, Damoiselle Oudarde Musnier?" replied the other Parisian. "He is to spend two hours in the pillory. We have plenty of time. Did you ever see any one pilloried, my dear Mahiette?"

"Yes," said the country-woman, "at Rheims."

"Pooh! What's your pillory at Rheims? A miserable cage, where they turn nothing but peasants! A fine sight, truly!"

"Nothing but peasants!" said Mahiette, "in the Clothmarket! at Rheims! We've seen some very fine criminals there,—people who had killed both father and mother! Peasants, indeed! What do you take us for, Gervaise?"

The country-lady was certainly on the verge of losing her temper in defense of her pillory. Fortunately the discreet Damoiselle Oudarde Musnier changed the subject in time:—

"By-the-bye, Damoiselle Mahiette, what do you say to our Flemish ambassadors? Have you any as fine at Rheims?"

"I confess," answered Mahiette, "that there is no place like Paris for seeing such Flemings as those."

"Did you see among the embassy that great ambassador who is a hosier?" asked Oudarde.

"Yes," responded Mahiette. "He looks like a regular Saturn."

"And that fat one with the smooth face?" added Gervaise. "And that little fellow with small eyes and red lids, as ragged and hairy as a head of thistle?"

"Their horses were the finest sight," said Oudarde, "dressed out in the fashion of their country."

"Oh, my dear," interrupted the rustic Mahiette, assuming an air of superiority in her turn, "what would you say if you had seen, in 1461, at the coronation at Rheims, now eighteen years ago, the horses of the princes and of the king's escort? Housings and trappings of every description: some of damask cloth, of fine cloth of gold, trimmed with sable; others, of velvet, trimmed with ermines' tails; others, loaded down with goldsmiths' work and great gold and silver bells! And the money that it must have cost! And the lovely page-boys that rode on them!"

"That does not alter the fact," drily responded Damoiselle Oudarde, "that the Flemings have very fine horses, and that they had a splendid supper last night given them by the Provost at the Hôtel-de-Ville, where they were treated to sugar-plums, hippocras, spices, and other rarities."

"What are you talking about, neighbor!" cried Gervaise. "It was at the Petit-Bourbon, with the Cardinal, that the Flemings supped."

"Not at all. At the Hôtel-de-Ville!"

"Yes, indeed. At the Petit-Bourbon!"

"So surely was it at the Hôtel-de-Ville," returned Oudarde, sharply, "that Doctor Scourable made them a speech in Latin with which they seemed mightily pleased. It was my husband, who is one of the licensed copyists, who told me so."

"So surely was it at the Petit-Bourbon," replied Gervaise, with no whit less of animation, "that I can give you a list of what the Cardinal's attorney treated them to: Twelve double quarts of hippocras, white, yellow, and red; twenty-four boxes of double-gilt Lyons marchpane; as many wax torches of two pounds each, and six half-casks of Beaune wine, red and white, the best to be found. I hope that's decisive. I have it from my husband, who is captain of fifty men in the Commonalty Hall, and who was only this morning comparing the Flemish ambassadors with those sent by Prester John and the Emperor of Trebizond, who came from Mesopotamia to Paris during the reign of the last king, and who had rings in their ears."

"It is so true that they supped at the Hôtel-de-Ville," replied Oudarde, but little moved by this display of eloquence, "that no one ever saw such an exhibition of meats and sugar-plums before."

"But I tell you that they were served by Le Sec, one of the city guard, at the Petit-Bourbon, and that's what misled you."

"At the Hôtel-de-Ville, I say!"

"At the Petit-Bourbon, my dear! For didn't they illuminate the word 'Hope,' which is written over the great entrance, with magical glasses?"

"At the Hôtel-de-Ville! at the Hôtel-de-Ville! Don't I tell you that Husson-le-Voir played the flute?"

"I tell you, no!"

"I tell you, yes!"

"And I tell you, no!"

The good fat Oudarde was making ready to reply, and the quarrel might have come to blows, if Mahiette had not suddenly exclaimed, "Only see those people crowding together at the end of the bridge! There's something in the midst of them, at which they're all looking."

"Truly," said Gervaise, "I do hear the sound of a tambourine. I verily believe it's that little Smeralda playing her tricks with her goat. Come quick, Mahiette! Make haste and pull your boy along faster. You came here to see all the sights of Paris. Yesterday you saw the Flemings; today you must see the gipsy girl."

"The gipsy," said Mahiette, turning back abruptly, and grasping her son's arm more firmly. "Heaven preserve us! She might steal my child!—Come, Eustache!"

And she set out running along the quay towards the Place de Grève, until she had left the bridge far behind her. But the child, whom she dragged after her, stumbled, and fell upon his knees; she stopped, out of breath. Oudarde and Gervaise rejoined her.

"That gipsy girl steal your child!" said Gervaise. "What a strange idea!"

Mahiette shook her head with a pensive air.

"The queer part of it is," observed Oudarde, "that the *sachette* has the same opinion of the gipsies."

"What do you mean by the *sachette*?" said Mahiette.

"Why!" said Oudarde, "Sister Gudule."

"And who," returned Mahiette, "is Sister Gudule?"

"You must indeed be from Rheims, not to know that!" replied Oudarde. "She is the recluse of the Rat-Hole."

"What!" asked Mahiette, "the poor woman to whom we are carrying this cake?"

Oudarde nodded.

"Exactly so. You will see her presently at her window on the Place de Grève. She feels just as you do about those gipsy vagabonds who go about drumming on the tambourine and telling people's fortunes. No one knows what gave her such a horror of gipsies. But you, Mahiette,—why should you take to your heels in such haste at the mere sight of them?"

"Oh," said Mahiette, clasping her child to her bosom, "I could not bear to have the same thing happen to me that happened to Paquette la Chantefleurie."

"Oh, do tell us the story, my dear Mahiette," said Gervaise, taking her arm.

"Gladly," answered Mahiette; "but you must indeed be from Paris, not to know that! You must know, then,—but we need not stand here to tell the tale,—that Paquette la Chantefleurie was a pretty girl of eighteen when I was one too; that is to say, some eighteen years ago, and it is her own fault if she is not now, like me, a happy, hale, and hearty mother of six-and-thirty, with a husband and a son. However, from the time she was fourteen, it was too late! She was the daughter of Guybertaut, minstrel to the boats at Rheims, the same who played before King Charles VII, at his coronation, when he sailed down the river Vesle from Sillery to Muison, and, more by token, the Maid of Orleans was in the boat with him. Her old father died when Paquette was still a mere child; then she had no one but her mother, a sister to Pradon, the master brazier and coppersmith at Paris, in the Rue Parin-Garlin, who died last year. You see that she came of an honest family. The mother was a good, simple woman, unfortunately, and taught Paquette nothing but a little fringe-making and toy-making, which did not keep the child from growing very tall and remaining very poor. The two lived at Rheims, on the water's edge, in the Rue Folle-Peine. Note this. I think this was what brought ill-luck to Paquette. In '61, the year of the coronation of our King Louis XI, —may Heaven preserve him!—Paquette was so merry and so pretty that every one knew her as Chantefleurie.* Poor girl! She had lovely teeth, and she liked to laugh, so that she might show them. Now, a girl who likes to laugh is on the high-road to weep; fine teeth spoil fine eyes. Such was Chantefleurie. She and her mother had hard work to earn a living; they were greatly reduced after the father's death; their fringe-making did not bring them in more than six farthings a week, which doesn't make quite two pence. Where was the time when Father Guybertaut earned twelve Paris pence at a single coronation for a single song? One winter (it was that same year of '61), when the two women had not a stick of firewood and it was bitterly cold, the cold gave Chantefleurie such a fine color that the men called her Paquette,—some called her

---

*Song blossom.

Pâquerette,*—and she went to the bad.—Eustache! don't you let me see you nibble that cake!—We soon saw that she was ruined, when she came to church one fine Sunday with a gold cross on her neck. At fourteen years of age! Think of that! First it was the young Vicomte de Cormontreuil, whose castle is about three quarters of a league away from Rheims; then M. Henri de Triancourt, the king's equerry; then something lower, Chiart de Beaulin, sergeant-at-arms; then, still lower, Guery Aubergeon, the king's carver; then, Macé de Frépus, the dauphin's barber; then, Thévenin-le-Moine, the king's cook; then, still descending to older and meaner men, she fell into the hands of Guillaume Racine, viol-player, and of Thierry-de-Mer, the lantern-maker. Then—poor Chantefleurie!—she became common property; she had come to the last copper of her gold piece. How shall I tell you, ladies? At the time of the coronation, in that same year '61, it was she who made the king of ribalds' bed,—that self-same year!"

Mahiette sighed, and wiped a tear from her cheek.

"No very uncommon story," said Gervaise; "and I don't see that it has anything to do with gipsies, or with children."

"Patience!" replied Mahiette: "we shall soon come to the child. In '66, sixteen years ago this very month, on Saint Paula's Day, Paquette gave birth to a little girl. Poor thing! Great was her joy; she had long wished for a child. Her mother, good woman, who never knew how to do anything but shut her eyes to her daughter's faults,—her mother was dead. Paquette had no one left to love, no one to love her. Five years had passed since her fall, and Chantefleurie was but a miserable creature. She was alone, alone in the world, pointed at, hooted after in the street, beaten by the police, mocked by little ragged boys. And then, she was now twenty years old; and twenty is old age to such women. Vice had ceased to bring her in much more than her fringe-making used to do; every fresh wrinkle took away another coin. Win-

---

*Daisy.

ter was once more a hard season for her; wood was again
scarce upon her hearth, and bread in her cupboard. She
could no longer work; for when she took to a life of pleasure
she learned to be lazy, and she suffered far more than before,
because in learning to be lazy she became accustomed to
pleasure,—at least, that's the way the priest of Saint-Remy explains it to us that such women feel cold and hunger more
than other poor folks do when they are old."

"Yes," remarked Gervaise; "but the gipsies?"

"One moment, Gervaise!" said Oudarde, whose attention
was less impatient. "What would there be left for the end, if
everything came at the beginning? Go on, Mahiette, please.
Poor Chantefleurie!"

Mahiette continued:—

"So she was very wretched, very unhappy, and her tears
wore deep furrows in her cheeks. But in her shame, her disgrace, and her misery, it seemed to her that she should feel
less ashamed, less disgraced, and less miserable, if she had
something to love or some one to love her. It must be a child;
for only a child could be innocent enough for that. She recognized this after trying to love a thief,—the only man who
would have anything to say to her; but after a little she saw
that even the thief despised her. Women of that sort must
have a lover or a child to fill up their hearts, otherwise they
are very unhappy. As she could not have a lover, she gave herself up to longing for a child; and as she had never given over
being pious, she prayed night and day that the good God
would give her one. The good God had pity on her, and gave
her a little girl. I cannot describe to you her delight; she covered it with a perfect rain of tears, kisses, and caresses. She
nursed her child herself, made swaddling-clothes for it of her
own coverlet,—the only one she had on her bed,—and no
longer felt cold or hungry. She grew handsome again. An old
maid makes a young mother.[9] She took to her former trade;
her old friends came back to see her, and she readily found
customers for her wares, and with the price of all these iniq-
uities she bought baby linen, caps, and bibs, lace gowns and

little satin bonnets, without ever thinking of buying herself another coverlet.—Master Eustache, didn't I tell you not to eat that cake?—It is certain that little Agnès,—that was the child's name, her given name; for as to a surname, Chantefleurie had long since ceased to have one,—it is certain that the little thing was more tricked out with ribbons and embroidery than a dauphiness from Dauphiny! Among other things, she had a pair of tiny shoes, the like of which even King Louis XI himself surely never had! Her mother sewed and embroidered them herself; she put all the dainty arts of her fringe-making into them, and as many intricate stitches as would make a gown for the Holy Virgin. They were the two sweetest little pink shoes imaginable. They were no longer than my thumb, and you must have seen the child's tiny feet slip out of them, or you would never have believed they could have gone in. To be sure, those little feet were so small, so pink, and so pretty!—pinker than the satin of the shoes!— When you have children of your own, Oudarde, you will know that there is nothing prettier than those little feet and hands!"

"I ask nothing better," said Oudarde, sighing; "but I must wait the good pleasure of Master Andry Musnier."

"Besides," resumed Mahiette, "Paquette's child had not merely pretty feet. I saw her when she was only four months old; she was a perfect love! Her eyes were bigger than her mouth, and she had the finest black hair, which curled already! She would have made a splendid brunette if she had lived to be sixteen. Her mother became more and more crazy about her every day. She fondled her, kissed her, tickled her, washed her, decked her out, almost ate her up! She lost her head over her; she thanked God for her. Her pretty little pink feet particularly were an endless wonder, the cause of a perfect delirium of joy! Her lips were forever pressed to them; she could never cease admiring their smallness. She would put them into the tiny shoes, take them out again, admire them, wonder at them, hold them up to the light, pity them when they tried to walk upon the bed, and would gladly have spent her life on her knees, putting the shoes on and off those feet, as if they had been those of an infant Jesus."

"A very pretty story," said Gervaise in a low voice; "but what has all this to do with gipsies?"

"This," replied Mahiette. "There came one day to Rheims some very queer-looking men on horseback. They were beggars and vagrants roaming about the country, under the lead of their duke and their counts. They were swarthy, all had curly hair, and silver rings in their ears. The women were even uglier than the men. Their faces were blacker, and always uncovered; they wore shabby blouses, with an old bit of cloth woven of cords tied over their shoulders, and their hair hung down like a horse's tail. The children wallowing under their feet would have frightened a monkey. A band of outlaws! They all came in a direct line from Lower Egypt to Rheims by way of Poland. People said that the Pope had confessed them, and ordered them, by way of penance, to travel through the world for seven years in succession, without ever sleeping in beds. So they called themselves penitents, and smelt horribly. It seems that they were once Saracens, so they must have believed in Jupiter; and they demanded ten Tours pounds from every crosiered and mitered archbishop, bishop, and abbot. It was a papal bull that gave them this right. They came to Rheims to tell fortunes in the name of the King of Algiers and the Emperor of Germany. You may imagine that this was quite enough reason for forbidding them to enter the town. So the whole band encamped near the Porte de Braine with a good grace, on that hill where there is a mill, close by the old chalk-pits; and every one in Rheims made haste to visit them. They looked into your hand and told you most marvellous things; they were quite capable of predicting to Judas that he should be pope! And yet there were evil reports of their having stolen children, cut purses, and eaten human flesh. Wise folks said to the simple, 'Keep away from them!' and then went themselves in secret. It was a perfect rage. The fact is, they said things that would have amazed a cardinal. Mothers boasted loudly of their children, after the gipsies had read all sorts of miracles written in their hands in Turkish and in heathen tongues. One had an emperor for her son, another a pope, and another a captain. Poor Chantefleurie was seized with curiosity; she longed to know what her child would be, and whether her pretty little Agnès would not one day be Empress of Armenia, or something of that sort. So she carried her to the gipsies; and the gipsies admired the child, caressed her, and kissed her with their black mouths, and wondered at her little hand, alas! to the great delight of her mother. They were particularly charmed with her pretty feet and her pretty shoes. The child was not a year old then. She already lisped a few words, laughed at her mother like a little madcap, was round and fat, and had a thousand enchanting little tricks like those of the angels in paradise. She was sorely afraid of the gipsy women, and cried. But her mother kissed her the harder, and went away charmed with the good luck which the fortune-tellers had promised her Agnès. She was to be beautiful, virtuous, and a queen. She therefore returned to her garret in the Rue Folle-Peine, quite proud of carrying a queen in her arms. Next day she took advantage of a moment while the child was asleep on her bed (for she always had it sleep in her own bed), softly left the door ajar, and ran out to tell a neighbor in the Rue de la Séchesserie that her daughter Agnès would one day have the King of England and the Duke of Ethiopia to wait upon her at table, and a hundred other surprising things. On her return, hearing no sound as she climbed the stairs, she said to herself, 'Good! baby is still asleep.' She found the door much wider open than she had left it; but she went in, poor mother! and ran to the bed. The child was gone; the place was empty. There was nothing left of the child but one of her pretty little shoes. She rushed from the room, flew down the stairs, and began to beat the walls with her head, crying, 'My child! my child! Where is my child? Who has taken away my child?' The street was deserted, the house stood alone; no one could give her any information. She went through the town, searched every street, ran up and down all day long, mad, distracted, terrible, staring in at doors and windows, like a wild beast that has lost its young. She was breathless, disheveled, fearful to look upon, and there was a fire in her eyes which dried her tears. She stopped the passers-by, and cried, 'My daughter! my daughter! my pretty little daughter! If any one will give me back my daughter, I will be his servant, the servant of his dog, and he shall devour my heart if he will.' She met the priest of Saint-Remy, and said to him: 'I will dig the ground with my nails, only give me back my child!' It was heartrending, Oudarde; and I saw a very hard-hearted man, Master Ponce Lacabre, the attorney, weep. Ah, poor mother! When night came, she went home. During her absence a neighbor had seen two gipsy women go slyly upstairs with a bundle in their arms, then shut the door again and hurry away. After they had gone, a child's cries were heard, coming from Paquette's room. The mother laughed wildly, flew over the stairs as if she had wings, burst open her door, and went in. A frightful thing had happened, Oudarde! Instead of her lovely little Agnès, so rosy and so fresh, who was a gift from the good God, there lay a hideous little monster, blind, lame, deformed, squalling, and crawling about the brick floor. She hid her eyes in horror. 'Oh!' she exclaimed, 'can the witches have changed my daughter into this horrible beast?' The little club-foot was hastily removed; he would have driven her mad. He was the monstrous offspring of some gipsy woman given over to the devil. He seemed to be about four years old, and spoke a language which was no human tongue; such words were quite impossible. Chantefleurie flung herself upon the little shoe,—all that was left her of all that she had loved. She lay there so long, motionless, silent, apparently not breathing, that the neighbors thought she must be dead. Suddenly she trembled from head to foot, covered her precious relic with frantic kisses, and burst into sobs as if her heart were broken. I assure you that we all wept with her. She said: 'Oh, my little girl! my pretty little girl! where are you?' And that would have wrung your hearts. I cry now when I think of it. Our children, you see, are the very marrow of our bones. My poor Eustache!

you are so handsome! If you only knew what a darling he is! Yesterday he said to me, 'I mean to be one of the city guard, I do.' Oh, my Eustache! if I were to lose you!—Chantefleurie got up all at once and began to run about Rheims, shouting, 'To the gipsy camp! to the gipsy camp! Guard, burn the witches!' The gipsies were gone. It was night. No one could follow them. Next day, two leagues away from Rheims, on a heath between Gueux and Tilloy, were found the remains of a great fire, some ribbons which had belonged to Paquette's child, drops of blood, and some goats' dung. The night just passed happened to be a Saturday night. No one doubted any longer that the gipsies had kept their Sabbath on that heath, and that they had devoured the child in company with Beelzebub, as the Mahometans do. When Chantefleurie heard these horrible things, she did not shed a tear; she moved her lips as if to speak, but could not. Next day her hair was grey. On the following day she had disappeared."

"A terrible story indeed," said Oudarde, "and one that would make a Burgundian weep!"

"I am no longer surprised," added Gervaise, "that the fear of the gipsies haunts you so."

"And you had all the more reason," continued Oudarde, "to run away with your Eustache just now, because these are also Polish gipsies."

"Not at all," said Gervaise; "they say they came from Spain and Catalonia."

"Catalonia? That may be," replied Oudarde; "Polonia, Catalonia, Valonia,—those places are all one to me; I always mix them up. There's one thing sure; they are gipsies."

"And their teeth are certainly long enough to eat little children. And I should not be a bit surprised if Smeralda ate a little too, for all her dainty airs. Her white goat plays too many clever tricks to be all right."

Mahiette walked on in silence. She was absorbed in that sort of reverie which seems to be the continuation of a painful story, and which does not cease until it has imparted its own emotion, throb by throb, to the innermost fibers of the heart.

Gervaise, however, addressed her: "And did no one ever know what became of Chantefleurie?" Mahiette made no answer. Gervaise repeated the question, shaking her arm and calling her by name as she did so. Mahiette seemed to wake from her dream.

"What became of Chantefleurie?" she said, mechanically repeating the words whose sound was still fresh in her ear; then, making an effort to fix her attention upon the meaning of the words, she said quickly, "Oh, no one ever knew."

She added, after a pause:—

"Some said they saw her leave Rheims at dusk by the Porte Fléchembault; others, at daybreak, by the old Porte Basée. A poor man found her gold cross hanging to the stone cross in the fair-grounds. It was that trinket which caused her ruin in '61. It was a gift from the handsome Vicomte de Cormontreuil, her first lover. Paquette never would part with it, however poor she might be. She clung to it like her own life. So when this cross was found, we all thought that she was dead. Still, there were people at Cabaret-les-Vautes who said they saw her pass by on the road to Paris, walking barefoot over the stones. But in that case she must have left town by the Porte de Vesle, and all these stories don't agree; or, rather, I believe she did actually leave by the Porte de Vesle, but that she left this world."

"I don't understand you," said Gervaise.

"The Vesle," replied Mahiette, with a melancholy smile, "is the river."

"Poor Chantefleurie!" said Oudarde, with a shudder; "drowned!"

"Drowned!" returned Mahiette; "and who could have told good father Guybertaut, when he floated down the river beneath the Pont de Tinquex, singing in his boat, that his dear little Paquette would one day pass under that same bridge, but without boat or song?"

"And the little shoe?" asked Gervaise.

"It disappeared with the mother," replied Mahiette.

"Poor little shoe!" said Oudarde.

Oudarde, a fat and tender-hearted woman, would have been quite content to sigh in company with Mahiette; but Gervaise, who was more curious, had not come to the end of her questions.

"And the monster?" she suddenly said to Mahiette.

"What monster?" asked the latter.

"The little gipsy monster left by the witches in Chantefleurie's room in exchange for her daughter. What did you do with it? I really hope you drowned it too."

"Not a bit of it," replied Mahiette.

"What! You burned it then? After all, that was better. A sorcerer's child!"

"Nor that either, Gervaise. My lord the archbishop took an interest in the gipsy child; he exorcised it, blessed it, carefully took the devil out of the boy's body, and sent him to Paris to be exposed upon the wooden bed at Notre-Dame, as a foundling."

"These bishops," grumbled Gervaise, "never do anything like other people, just because they are so learned. Just think, Oudarde, of putting the devil among the foundlings! For that little monster is sure to have been the devil. Well, Mahiette, what did they do with him in Paris! I'm sure no charitable person would take him."

"I don't know," replied the native of Rheims; "it was just at that very time that my husband bought the clerk's office at Beru, two leagues away from town, and we thought no more about the matter; particularly as near Beru there are the two hills of Cernay, which quite hide the spires of the Rheims cathedral."

While talking thus, the three worthy women had reached the Place de Grève. In their preoccupation, they had passed the public breviary of the Tour-Roland without stopping, and were proceeding mechanically towards the pillory, around which the crowd increased momentarily. Probably the sight which at this instant attracted every eye would have made them completely forget the Rat-Hole, and the visit which they meant to pay, if the sturdy six-year-old Eustache, whom Mahiette led by the hand, had not suddenly reminded them of it by saying, as if some instinct warned him that the Rat-Hole lay behind him, "Mother, may I eat the cake now?"

Had Eustache been more crafty, that is to say less greedy, he would have waited still longer, and would not have risked the timid question, "Mother, may I eat the cake now?" until they were safe at home again, at Master Andry Musnier's house, in the University, in the Rue Madame-la-Valence, when both branches of the Seine and the five bridges of the City would have been between the Rat-Hole and the cake.

This same question, a very rash one at the time that Eustache asked it, roused Mahiette's attention.

"By the way," she exclaimed, "we are forgetting the recluse! Show me your Rat-Hole, that I may carry her my cake."

"Directly," said Oudarde. "It's a true charity."

This was not at all to Eustache's liking.

"Oh, my cake! my cake!" he whined, hunching up first one shoulder and then the other,—always a sign of extreme displeasure in such cases.

The three women retraced their steps, and as they approached the Tour-Roland, Oudarde said to the other two:—

"It will never do for all three of us to peep in at the hole at once, lest we should frighten the *sachette*. You two must pretend to be reading the Lord's Prayer in the breviary while I put my nose in at the window; she knows me slightly. I'll tell you when to come."

She went to the window alone. As soon as she looked in, profound pity was expressed in every feature, and her bright frank face changed color as quickly as if it had passed from sunlight into moonlight; her eyes grew moist, her mouth quivered as if she were about to weep. A moment later, she put her finger to her lips and beckoned to Mahiette.

Mahiette silently joined her, on tiptoe as if by the bedside of a dying person.

It was indeed a sad sight which lay before the two women, as they gazed without moving or breathing through the grated window of the Rat-Hole.

The cell was small, wider than it was long, with a vaulted roof, and seen from within looked like the inside of an exaggerated bishop's miter. Upon the bare stone floor, in a corner, sat, or rather crouched a woman. Her chin rested on her knees, which her crossed arms pressed closely against her breast. Bent double in this manner, clad in brown sackcloth, which covered her loosely from head to foot, her long grey locks drawn forward and falling over her face, down her legs to her feet, she seemed at first sight some strange shape outlined against the dark background of the cell, a sort of blackish triangle, which the ray of light entering at the window divided into two distinct bands of light and shadow. She looked like one of those specters, half darkness and half light, which we see in dreams, and in the extraordinary work of Goya,—pale, motionless, forbidding, cowering upon a tomb or clinging to the grating of a dungeon. It was neither man nor woman, nor living being, nor any definite form; it was a figure; a sort of vision in which the real and the imaginary were blended like twilight and daylight. Beneath her disheveled hair, which fell to the ground, the outlines of a stern and emaciated profile were barely visible; the tip of one bare foot just peeped from the hem of her garment, seeming to be curled up on the hard, cold floor. The little of human form which could be dimly seen beneath that mourning garb made the beholder shudder.

This figure, which seemed rooted to the ground, appeared to have neither motion, thought, nor breath. In that thin sackcloth, in January, lying half naked on a granite floor, without fire, in the darkness of a dungeon, whose slanting window never admitted the sun, only the icy blast, she did not seem to suffer, or even to feel.

She seemed to have been turned to stone like her cell, to ice like the season. Her hands were clasped, her eyes were fixed. At the first glance, she seemed a specter, at the second, a statue.

And yet at intervals her blue lips were parted by a breath,

and trembled; but they seemed as dead and as destitute of will as leaves blowing in the wind.

Yet her dull eyes gazed with an ineffable expression, a deep, mournful, serious, perpetually fixed expression, on a corner of the cell hidden from those outside; her look seemed to connect all the somber thoughts of her distressed soul with some mysterious object.

Such was the creature who was called "the recluse" from her habitation, and "*sachette*" from her dress.

The three women—for Gervaise had joined Mahiette and Oudarde—peered through the window. Their heads cut off the faint light which entered the dungeon; but the wretched inmate seemed unconscious of her loss, and paid no attention to them. "Don't disturb her," said Oudarde in low tones; "she is in one of her ecstatic fits: she is praying."

But Mahiette still gazed with ever-increasing anxiety at the wan, wrinkled face, and those disheveled locks, and her eyes filled with tears. "How strange that would be!" she muttered.

She put her head through the iron bars, and at last contrived to get a glimpse of the corner upon which the unhappy woman's eyes were forever riveted.

When she withdrew her head from the window, her face was bathed in tears.

"What is that woman's name?" she asked Oudarde.

Oudarde answered,—

"We call her Sister Gudule."

"And I," returned Mahiette,—"I call her Paquette Chante-fleurie."

Then, putting her finger to her lip, she signed to the amazed Oudarde to put her head through the aperture and look.

Oudarde looked, and saw, in the corner upon which the recluse's eye was fixed in such sad ecstasy, a tiny pink satin shoe, embroidered with gold and silver spangles.

Gervaise looked in after Oudarde, and then the three women began to weep at the sight of that miserable mother.

However, neither their looks nor their tears disturbed the

recluse. Her hands were still clasped, her lips dumb, her eyes set; and to those who knew her story it was heartrending to see her sit and gaze at that little shoe.

The three had not yet breathed a word; they dared not speak, even in a whisper. This profound silence, this great grief, this entire oblivion of all but one thing, affected them like the high altar at Easter or at Christmas-tide. They were silent, absorbed, ready to fall upon their knees. They felt as if they had just gone into church on Holy Saturday and heard the *Tenebræ*.

At last Gervaise, the most curious, and consequently the least sensitive of the three, made an attempt to draw the recluse into conversation: "Sister! Sister Gudule!"

She repeated the call three times, raising her voice each time. The recluse did not stir; there was not a word, not a look, not a sign of life.

Oudarde, in her turn, in a gentler and more affectionate tone, said, "Sister! holy Sister Gudule!"

The same silence, the same absolute repose as before.

"What a strange woman!" cried Gervaise; "I don't believe she would mind a cannonade!"

"Perhaps she's deaf," said Oudarde.

"Maybe blind," added Gervaise.

"Perhaps dead," said Mahiette.

Certainly, if the soul had not already quitted that inert, torpid, lethargic body, it had at least withdrawn into it and concealed itself in depths to which the perceptions of the external organs did not penetrate.

"We shall have to leave the cake on the window-sill," said Oudarde; "but then some boy will steal it. How can we rouse her?"

Eustache, who had thus far been absorbed in a little wagon drawn by a big dog, which was just passing, suddenly noticed that his three companions were looking at something through the window, and, seized by curiosity in his turn, he scrambled upon a post, stood on tiptoe, and put his fat, rosy face to the opening, shouting,

"Mother, let me see, too!"

At the sound of this childish voice, clear, fresh, and ringing, the recluse trembled. She turned her head with the abrupt, quick, motion of a steel spring, her long, thin hands brushed the hair from her face, and she fixed her astonished, unhappy, despairing eyes upon the child. The look was like a flash of lightning.

"Oh, my God!" she instantly exclaimed, hiding her head upon her knees, and it seemed as if her hoarse voice tore her chest, "at least do not show me those of others!"

"Good-morning, madame," said the child, gravely.

But the shock had, as it were, aroused the recluse. A long shudder ran through her entire frame from head to foot; her teeth chattered; she half raised her head, and said, as she pressed her elbows to her sides and took her feet in her hands as if to warm them,—

"Oh, how bitterly cold!"

"Poor woman!" said Oudarde, pitifully; "would you like a little fire?"

She shook her head in token of refusal.

"Well," added Oudarde, offering her a bottle, "here is some hippocras, which will warm you; drink."

She again shook her head, looked steadily at Oudarde, and answered, "Water."

Oudarde insisted. "No, sister, water is no fit drink for January. You must drink a little hippocras, and eat this wheaten cake, which we have made for you."

She put aside the cake which Mahiette offered her, and said, "Some black bread."

"Come," said Gervaise, feeling a charitable impulse in her turn, and unfastening her woollen mantle, "here is a covering somewhat warmer than yours. Throw this over your shoulders."

She refused the mantle as she had the bottle and the cake, and answered, "A cloth."

"But," resumed the kind-hearted Oudarde, "you must have seen that yesterday was a holiday."

"I knew it," said the recluse; "for two days I have had no water in my jug."

She added after a pause: "On a holiday, every one forgets me. They do well. Why should people remember me, who never think of them? When the fire goes out, the ashes are soon cold."

And as if wearied by so many words, she let her head fall upon her knees once more. The simple and charitable Oudarde, who interpreted her last words as another complaint of the cold, answered innocently, "Then wouldn't you like a little fire?"

"Fire!" said the recluse in a singular tone; "and will you give me a little for the poor baby too,—the baby who has been under ground these fifteen years?"

She trembled in every limb, her voice quivered, her eyes flashed; she had risen to her knees; she suddenly stretched her thin white hand towards the child, who was looking at her in surprise.

"Take away that child!" she cried. "The gipsy woman will soon pass by."

Then she fell face downwards, and her forehead struck the floor, with the sound of one stone upon another. The three women thought her dead. But a moment later she stirred, and they saw her drag herself upon her hands and knees to the corner where the little shoe lay. They dared not look longer; they turned away their eyes; but they heard a thousand kisses and a thousand sighs, mingled with agonizing cries and dull blows like those of a head dashed against a wall; then after one of these blows, so violent that they all three started, they heard nothing more.

"Has she killed herself?" said Gervaise, venturing to put her head through the bars. "Sister! Sister Gudule!"

"Sister Gudule!" repeated Oudarde.

"Oh, heavens! She does not move!" exclaimed Gervaise. "Can she indeed be dead? Gudule! Gudule!"

Mahiette, until now so choked by emotion that she could not speak, made an effort. "Wait a minute," she said; then going to the window, she cried, "Paquette! Paquette Chante-fleurie!"

A child who innocently blows on an ill-lighted firecracker and makes it explode in his face, is no more alarmed than was Mahiette at the effect of the name so suddenly flung into Sister Gudule's cell.

The recluse trembled from head to foot, sprang to her bare feet, and rushed to the window with such flaming eyes that Mahiette, Oudarde, the other woman and the child retreated to the farthest edge of the quay.

But still the forbidding face of the recluse remained pressed against the window-bars. "Oh! oh!" she screamed with a terrible laugh, "the gipsy woman calls me!"

At this instant the scene which was passing at the pillory caught her wild eye. Her brow wrinkled with horror; she stretched her skeleton arms from her cell and cried in a voice which sounded like a death-rattle, "Have you come again, you daughter of Egypt? Is it you who call me, you child-stealer? Well! may you be accursed! accursed! accursed! accursed!"

CHAPTER IV

A Tear for a Drop of Water

These words were, so to speak, the connecting link between two scenes which up to this instant had gone on simultaneously, each upon its own particular stage: one, of which we have just read, at the Rat-Hole; the other, of which we shall now read, at the pillory. The former was witnessed only by the three women whose acquaintance the reader has just made, the spectators of the latter consisted of the crowd of people whom we saw some time since gathering in the Place de Grève, about the gibbet and the pillory.

This crowd, whom the sight of the four officers posted at the four corners of the pillory ever since nine in the morning led to expect an execution of some sort, perhaps not a hanging, but a whipping, cropping of ears, or something of the sort, this crowd had grown so rapidly that the four officers, too closely hemmed in, were more than once obliged to drive the people back by a free use of their whips and their horses' heels.

The populace, well accustomed to wait for public executions, betrayed no great impatience. They amused themselves by looking at the pillory,—a very simple structure, consisting of a cube of masonry some ten feet high, and hollow within. A very steep flight of stairs of unhewn stone, called the ladder, led to the upper platform, upon which was a horizontal wheel made of oak. The victim was bound to this wheel in a kneeling posture, with his hands behind him. A wooden shaft, set in motion by a capstan concealed inside the machine, made the wheel revolve horizontally, thus presenting the prisoner's face to each side of the square in turn. This was called "turning" a criminal.

It is evident that the pillory of the Place de Grève was far from possessing all the attractions of the pillory of the Halles. There was nothing architectural or monumental about it. It had no roof with an iron cross, no octagonal lantern, no slender columns expanding at the edge of the roof into capitals composed of acanthus-leaves and flowers, no huge fantastic gutter-spouts, no carved wood-work, no delicate sculpture cut deep into the stone.

Here the spectator must needs be content with the four rough walls, two stone facings, and a shabby stone gibbet, plain and bare.

The treat would have been a sorry one for lovers of Gothic architecture. It is true that no one was ever less interested in monuments than your good burghers of the Middle Ages, who paid very little heed to the beauty of a pillory.

The victim appeared at last, tied to the tail of a cart; and when he had been hoisted to the top of the platform, where he could be seen from all parts of the square bound to the wheel of the pillory with straps and ropes, a prodigious hooting, mingled with shouts and laughter, burst from the spectators. They had recognized Quasimodo.

It was indeed he. It was a strange reverse. He was now pilloried on the same place where he was the day before hailed, acclaimed, and proclaimed Pope and Prince of Fools, and attended by the Duke of Egypt, the King of Tunis, the Emperor of Galilee! One thing is certain; there was not a soul in the crowd, not even himself, in turn triumphant and a victim, who could distinctly draw a mental comparison between these two situations. Gringoire and his philosophy were lacking at spectacle.

Soon Michel Noiret, sworn trumpeter to our lord the king, imposed silence on all beholders, and proclaimed the sentence, according to the provost's order and command. He then retired behind the cart, with his men in livery coats.

Quasimodo, utterly impassive, never winked. All resistance on his part was rendered impossible by what was then called, in the language of criminal law, "the vehemence and firmness of the bonds;" which means that the chains and thongs probably cut into his flesh. This, by-the-bye, is a tradition of the jail and the convict prison which is not yet lost, and which the handcuffs still preserve as a precious relic among us, civilized, mild, and humane as we are (not to mention the guillotine and the galleys).

He allowed himself to be led, pushed, carried, lifted, tied, and re-tied. His face revealed nothing more than the surprise of a savage or an idiot. He was known to be deaf; he seemed to be blind.

He was placed upon his knees on the circular plank; he made no resistance. He was stripped of shirt and doublet to the waist; he submitted. He was bound with a fresh system of straps and buckles; he suffered himself to be buckled and bound. Only from time to time he breathed heavily, like a calf whose head hangs dangling from the back of the butcher's cart.

"The blockhead!" said Jehan Frollo du Moulin to his friend Robin Poussepain (for the two students had followed the victim, as a matter of course); "he understands no more about it than a cockchafer shut up in a box!"

A shout of laughter ran through the crowd when Quasimodo's hump, his camel breast, his horny, hairy shoulders, were bared to view. During this burst of merriment, a man in the city livery, short of stature, and strong, mounted the platform and took his place by the prisoner's side. His name was soon circulated among the spectators. It was Master Pierrat Torterue, sworn torturer of the Châtelet.

He began by placing on one corner of the pillory a black hour-glass, the upper part of which was full of red sand, which dropped slowly into the lower half; then he took off his party-colored coat, and there was seen hanging from his right hand a slim, slender whip with long white thongs, shining, knotted, braided, armed with metal tips. With his left hand he carelessly rolled his right shirt-sleeve up to his armpit.

Meanwhile Jehan Frollo shouted, lifting his fair curly head high above the crowd (he had climbed Robin Poussepain's shoulders for the express purpose), "Come and see, gentlemen and ladies! They are going straightway to flog Master Quasimodo, the bell-ringer of my brother the archdeacon of Josas, a strange specimen of Oriental architecture, with a dome for his back and twisted columns for legs."

All the people laughed, especially the children and the young girls.

At last the executioner stamped his foot. The wheel began to turn. Quasimodo reeled in spite of his bonds. The astonishment suddenly depicted upon his misshapen face redoubled the bursts of laughter around him.

Suddenly, just as the wheel in its revolution presented to Master Pierrat Quasimodo's mountainous back, Master Pierrat raised his arm; the thin lashes hissed through the air like a brood of vipers, and fell furiously upon the wretched man's shoulders.

Quasimodo started as if roused abruptly from a dream. He began to understand. He writhed in his bonds; surprise and pain distorted the muscles of his face, but he did not heave a sigh. He merely bent his head back, to the right, then to the left, shaking it like a bull stung in the flank by a gad-fly.

A second blow followed the first, then a third, and another, and another, and so on and on. The wheel did not cease from turning, or the blows from raining down.

Soon the blood spurted; it streamed in countless rivulets over the hunchback's swarthy shoulders; and the slender thongs, as they swung in the air, sprinkled it in drops among the crowd.

Quasimodo had resumed, apparently at least, his former impassivity. He had tried at first, secretly and without great visible effort, to burst his bonds. His eye kindled, his muscles stiffened, his limbs gathered all their force, and the straps and chains stretched. The struggle was mighty, prodigious, desperate; but the tried and tested fetters of the provosty held firm. They cracked; and that was all. Quasimodo fell back exhausted. Surprise gave way, upon his features, to a look of bitter and profound dejection. He closed his single eye, dropped his head upon his breast, and feigned death.

Thenceforth he did not budge. Nothing could wring a movement from him, neither his blood, which still flowed, nor the blows, which increased in fury, nor the rage of the executioner, who became excited and intoxicated by his work, nor the noise of the horrid lashes, keener and sharper than the stings of wasps.

At last an usher from the Châtelet, dressed in black, mounted on a black horse, who had been posted beside the ladder from the beginning of the execution of the sentence, extended his ebony wand towards the hour-glass. The executioner paused. The wheel stopped. Quasimodo's eye reopened slowly.

The flagellation was ended. Two attendants of the executioner washed the victim's bleeding shoulders, rubbed them with some salve which at once closed all the wounds, and threw over his back a piece of yellow cotton cloth cut after the pattern of a priest's cope. Meanwhile Pierrat Torterue let his red lashes soaked with blood drip upon the pavement.

But all was not over for Quasimodo. He had still to spend in the pillory that hour so judiciously added by Master Florian Barbedienne to the sentence of Master Robert d'Estouteville,—all to the greater glory of Jean de Cumène's old physiological and psychological pun: *"Surdus absurdus."**

The hour-glass was therefore turned, and the hunchback was left bound to the plank as before, in order that justice might be executed to the utmost.

The people, particularly in the Middle Ages, were to society what the child is to a family. So long as they remain in their primitive condition of ignorance, of moral and intellectual nonage, it may be said of that as of a child,—

"It is an age without pity."

We have already shown that Quasimodo was the object of universal hatred,—for more than one good reason, it is true. There was hardly a single spectator in the crowd who had not—or did not think he had—grounds for complaint against the malicious hunchback of Notre-Dame. Every one was delighted to see him in the pillory; and the severe punishment which he had just received, and the piteous state in which it had left him, far from softening the hearts of the populace, had made their hatred keener by adding to it a spice of merriment.

Thus, "public vengeance," as the legal jargon still styles it, once satisfied, a thousand private spites took their turn at revenge. Here, as in the Great Hall, the women made themselves especially conspicuous. All bore him a grudge,—some

---

*A deaf man is absurd (Latin).

for his mischief, others for his ugliness. The latter were the more furious.

"Oh, you image of Antichrist!" said one.

"Broomstick-rider!" cried another.

"What a fine tragic face!" yelled a third. "It would surely make you the Pope of Fools if today were only yesterday."

"That's right," added an old woman. "This is the pillory face. When shall we have the gallows face?"

"When shall we see you buried a hundred feet below ground, with your big bell upon your head, you cursed bell-ringer?"

"And to think that it's this demon that rings the Angelus!"

"Oh, you deaf man! you blind man! you hunchback! you monster!"

And the two students, Jehan du Moulin and Robin Pousse-pain, sang at the top of their voices the old popular refrain:—

> "A halter for the gallows-bird!
> A fagot for the ugly ape!"

Countless other insults rained upon him, mingled with hoots, curses, laughter, and occasional stones.

Quasimodo was deaf, but his sight was capital, and the fury of the mob was no less forcibly painted on their faces than in their words. Besides, the stones which struck him explained the peals of laughter.

He bore it for a time; but little by little his patience, which had resisted the torturer's whip, gave way, and rebelled against all these insect stings. The Asturian bull, which pays but little heed to the attacks of the picador, is maddened by the dogs and the banderillos.

At first he glanced slowly and threateningly around the crowd; but, bound fast as he was, his glance was impotent to drive away those flies which galled his wounds. Then he struggled in his fetters, and his frantic efforts made the old pillory wheel creak upon its timbers. All this only increased the shouts and derision of the crowd.

Then the wretched man, unable to break the collar which held him chained like a wild beast, became quiet again; only at intervals a sigh of rage heaved his breast. His face showed no trace of mortification or shame. He was too far removed from the existing state of society, and too nearly allied to a state of nature, to know what shame was. Besides, it is doubtful if infamy be a thing which can be felt by one afflicted with that degree of deformity. But rage, hate, despair, slowly veiled the hideous face with a cloud which grew darker and darker, more and more heavily charged with an electricity revealed by countless flashes from the eye of the Cyclop.

However, this cloud was lightened for a moment as a mule passed through the crowd, bearing a priest on his back. As soon as he saw that mule and that priest, the poor sufferer's face softened. The fury which convulsed it gave way to a strange smile, full of ineffable sweetness, affection, and tenderness. As the priest approached, this smile became more pronounced, more distinct, more radiant. It was as if the unhappy man hailed the coming of a Savior. Yet, when the mule was near enough to the pillory for his rider to recognize the prisoner, the priest cast down his eyes, turned back abruptly, spurred his animal on either side as if in haste to avoid humiliating appeals, and very far from anxious to be greeted and recognized by a poor devil in such a plight.

The priest was the archdeacon Dom Claude Frollo.

The cloud grew darker than ever upon the face of Quasimodo. The smile lingered for some time, although it became bitter, dejected, profoundly sad.

Time passed. He had been there at least an hour and a half, wounded, ill-treated, incessantly mocked, and almost stoned to death.

Suddenly he again struggled in his chains with renewed despair, which made all the timbers that held him quiver; and breaking the silence which he had hitherto obstinately kept, he cried in a hoarse and furious voice more like the bark of a dog than a human cry, and which drowned the sound of the hooting, "Water!"

This exclamation of distress, far from exciting compassion, only increased the amusement of the good Parisian populace who surrounded the ladder, and who, it must be confessed, taken in the mass and as a multitude, were at this time scarcely less cruel and brutish than that horrible tribe of Vagrant Vagabonds to whom we have already introduced the reader, and who were simply the lowest stratum of the people. Not a voice was raised around the wretched sufferer, except to mock at his thirst.

Certainly he was at this moment more grotesque and repulsive than he was pitiable, with his livid and streaming face, his wild eye, his mouth foaming with rage and suffering, and his tongue protruding. It must also be acknowledged, that, even had there been in the throng any charitable soul tempted to give a cup of cold water to the miserable creature in his agony, so strong an idea of shame and ignominy was attached to the infamous steps of the pillory, that this alone would have sufficed to repel the Good Samaritan.

In a few minutes Quasimodo cast a despairing look upon the crowd, and repeated in a still more heartrending voice, "Water!"

Every one laughed.

"Drink that!" shouted Robin Poussepain, flinging in his face a sponge which had been dragged through the gutter. "There, you deaf monster! I owe you something."

A woman aimed a stone at his head:—

"That will teach you to wake us at night with your cursed chimes!"

"Well, my boy!" howled a cripple, striving to reach him with his crutch, "will you cast spells on us again from the top of the towers of Notre-Dame?"

"Here's a porringer to drink out of!" added a man, letting fly a broken jug at his breast. "'Twas you who made my wife give birth to a double-headed child, just by walking past her."

"And my cat have a kitten with six feet!" shrieked an old woman, hurling a tile at him.

"Water!" repeated the gasping Quasimodo for the third time.

At this moment he saw the crowd separate. A young girl, oddly dressed, stepped from their midst. She was accompanied by a little white goat with gilded horns, and held a tambourine in her hand.

Quasimodo's eye gleamed. It was the gipsy girl whom he had tried to carry off the night before,—a feat for which he dimly felt that he was even now being punished; which was not in the least true, since he was only punished for the misfortune of being deaf, and having been tried by a deaf judge. He did not doubt that she too came to be avenged, and to take her turn at him with the rest.

He watched her nimbly climb the ladder. Rage and spite choked him. He longed to destroy the pillory; and had the lightning of his eye had power to blast, the gipsy girl would have been reduced to ashes long before she reached the platform.

Without a word she approached the sufferer, who vainly writhed and twisted to avoid her, and loosening a gourd from her girdle, she raised it gently to the parched lips of the miserable wretch.

Then from that eye, hitherto so dry and burning, a great tear trickled, and rolled slowly down the misshapen face, so long convulsed with despair. It was perhaps the first that the unfortunate man had ever shed.[10]

But he forgot to drink. The gipsy girl made her customary little grimace of impatience, and, then smilingly, pressed the neck of the gourd to Quasimodo's jagged mouth.

He drank long draughts; his thirst was ardent.

When he had done, the poor wretch put out his black lips, doubtless to kiss the fair hand which had helped him. But the girl, perhaps not quite free from distrust, and mindful of the violent attempt of the previous night, withdrew her hand with the terrified gesture of a child who fears being bitten by a wild animal.

Then the poor deaf man fixed upon her a look of reproach and unutterable sorrow.

It would anywhere have been a touching sight, to see this lovely girl, fresh, pure, charming, and yet so weak, thus devoutly hastening to the help of so much misery, deformity, and malice. Upon a pillory, the sight was sublime.

The people themselves were affected by it, and began to clap their hands and shout,—

"Noël! Noël!"

It was at this instant that the recluse saw, from the window of her cell, the gipsy girl upon the pillory, and hurled her ominous curse at her head:—

"May you be accursed, daughter of Egypt! accursed! accursed!"

CHAPTER V

End of the Story of the Cake

Esmeralda turned pale, and descended from the pillory with faltering steps. The voice of the recluse still pursued her:—

"Come down! come down, you gipsy thief! You will go up again!"

"The *sachette* has one of her ill turns today," muttered the people, and they said no more; for women of this sort were held in much awe, which made them sacred. No one liked to attack those who prayed night and day.

The hour had come to release Quasimodo. He was unbound, and the mob dispersed.

Near the Grand-Pont, Mahiette, who was returning home with her two companions, stopped suddenly:—

"By the way, Eustache, what have you done with the cake?"

"Mother," said the child, "while you were talking to the woman in that hole, there came a big dog and bit a piece out of my cake; so then I took a bite too."

"What, sir!" she continued, "did you eat it all?"

"Mother, it was the dog. I told him not to eat it, but he wouldn't mind me. So then I took a bite too; that's all!"

"What a bad boy you are!" said his mother, smiling and scolding at once. "Only think, Oudarde! he ate every cherry on the tree in our orchard at Charlerange; so his grandfather says that he is sure to be a soldier. Let me catch you at it again, Master Eustache! Get along, you greedy boy!"

BOOK VII

CHAPTER I

On the Danger of Confiding a Secret to a Goat

Several weeks had passed.[11]

It was early in March. The sun, which Dubartas,* that classic father of periphrase, had not yet dubbed "the grand duke of candles," was none the less bright and gay. It was one of those spring days which are so full of sweetness and beauty that all Paris, flocking into the squares and parks, keeps holiday as if it were a Sunday. On such clear, warm, peaceful days, there is one particular hour when the porch of Notre-Dame is especially worthy of admiration. It is the moment when the sun, already sinking towards the west, almost exactly faces the cathedral. Its rays, becoming more and more level, withdraw slowly from the pavement of the square, and climb the perpendicular face of the church, the shadows setting off the countless figures in high relief, while the great central rose-window flames like the eye of a Cyclop lighted up by reflections from his forge.

It was just that hour.

Opposite the lofty cathedral, reddened by the setting sun, upon the stone balcony built over the porch of a handsome

---

*Reference to Guillaume de Salluste du Bartas (1544–1590), popular French poet of the sixteenth century.

Gothic house at the corner of the square and the Rue du Parvis, a group of lovely young girls were laughing and chatting gracefully and playfully. By the length of the veil which hung from the peak of their pointed coif, twined with pearls, down to their heels, by the fineness of the embroidered tucker which covered their shoulders, but still revealed, in the pleasing fashion of the day, the swell of their fair virgin bosoms, by the richness of their under petticoats, even costlier than their upper garments (wonderful refinement!), by the gauze, the silk, the velvet in which they were arrayed, and especially by the whiteness of their hands, which proved that they led a life of idle ease, it was easy to guess that these were rich heiresses. They were in fact Damoiselle Fleur-de-Lys de Gondelaurier and her companions, Diane de Christeuil, Amelotte de Montmichel, Colombe de Gaillefontaine, and the little De Champchevrier, all daughters of noble houses, just now visiting the widowed Madame de Gondelaurier, on account of Monseigneur de Beaujeu and his wife, who were coming to Paris in April to choose maids of honor to meet the Dauphiness Marguerite in Picardy and receive her from the hands of the Flemings. Now, all the country squires for thirty miles around aspired to win this favor for their daughters, and many of them had already been brought or sent to Paris. The damsels in question were intrusted by their parents to the discreet and reverend care of Madame Aloïse de Gondelaurier, the widow of a former officer of the king's cross-bowmen, living in retirement, with her only daughter, in her house on the square in front of Notre-Dame.

The balcony upon which the young girls sat opened from a room richly hung with fawn-colored Flemish leather stamped with golden foliage. The transverse beams on the ceiling diverted the eye by countless grotesque carvings, painted and gilded. Splendid enamels glittered here and there upon sculptured presses. A boar's head made of earthenware crowned a superb sideboard, the two steps of which showed that the mistress of the house was the wife or widow of a knight banneret. At the end of the room, beside a tall

chimney-piece covered with armorial bearings and escutcheons, sat, in a rich red velvet arm-chair, Madame de
Gondelaurier, whose fifty-five years were as plainly written in
her garments as on her face. Near her stood a young man of
aristocratic though somewhat arrogant and swaggering
mien,—one of those fine fellows about whom all women
agree, although serious men and physiognomists shrug their
shoulders at them. This youthful cavalier wore the brilliant
uniform of a captain of the archers of the household troops,
which is too much like the dress of Jupiter, described in the
first part of this story, for us to inflict a second description of
it upon the reader.

The damsels were seated, some in the room, some upon
the balcony, the former upon squares of Utrecht velvet with
golden corner-pieces, the latter on oaken stools carved with
flowers and figures. Each held upon her knees a portion of a
large piece of tapestry, at which they were all working together, and a long end of which trailed over the matting that
covered the floor.

They talked together in the undertone and with the suppressed laughter common to a group of young girls when
there is a young man among them. The young man whose
presence sufficed to call forth all these feminine wiles
seemed, for his part, to pay but little heed to them; and while
these lovely girls vied with one another in trying to attract his
attention, he seemed chiefly occupied in polishing his belt-
buckle with his buckskin glove.

From time to time the elderly lady addressed some remark
to him in a very low voice, and he replied as best he could,
with awkward and forced courtesy. By Madame Aloïse's
smiles and little significant signs, as well as by the glances
which she cast at her daughter Fleur-de-Lys while she whispered to the captain, it was easy to see that she was talking of
the recent betrothal, and of the marriage, doubtless to come
off soon, between the young man and Fleur-de-Lys; and by
the officer's coldness and embarrassment, it was plain that on
his side at least there was no question of love. His whole man-

ner expressed a weariness and constraint such as the young officers of our day would aptly translate by saying that he was "horribly bored!"

The good lady, utterly infatuated with her daughter, like the silly mother that she was, did not perceive the officer's lack of enthusiasm, and did her best to point out to him in a whisper the infinite perfection with which Fleur-de-Lys plied her needle or wound her skeins of silk.

"There, cousin," she said, plucking him by the sleeve that she might speak in his ear, "just look at her now! See how gracefully she stoops!"

"To be sure," replied the young man; and he relapsed into his cold and careless silence.

A moment after, he was forced to bend anew, and Dame Aloïse said,—

"Did you ever see a merrier or more attractive face than that of your betrothed? Could any one have a fairer, whiter skin? Aren't those clever hands; and isn't her neck a perfect match in grace for a swan's? How I envy you at times! and how lucky it is for you that you are a man, wicked scamp that you are! Isn't my Fleur-de-Lys adorably lovely, and aren't you dead in love with her?"

"Of course," he replied, with his mind upon other things.

"But why don't you talk to her?" suddenly observed Madame Aloïse, giving him a push. "Say something to her; you are wonderfully shy all of a sudden."

We can assure our readers that shyness was neither one of the captain's failings nor good points; but he tried to do what was required of him.

"Fair cousin," said he, approaching Fleur-de-Lys, "what is the subject of your tapestry-work?"

"Fair cousin," answered Fleur-de-Lys in an injured tone, "I have told you three times already: it is Neptune's grotto."

It was plain that Fleur-de-Lys was far more clear-sighted than her mother in regard to the captain's cold and careless manners. He felt the necessity of making conversation.

"And what is all this Neptune-work for?" he asked.

"For the Abbey of Saint-Antoine des Champs," said Fleur-de-Lys, without raising her eyes.

The captain picked up a corner of the tapestry.

"And who, my fair cousin, is this fat fellow with puffy cheeks, blowing his trumpet so vigorously?"

"That is Triton," she answered.

There was still a somewhat offended tone about Fleur-de-Lys' brief words. The captain saw that he must absolutely whisper something in her ear,—a compliment, a bit of nonsense, never mind what. He bent towards her accordingly, but his imagination suggested nothing tenderer or more familiar than this: "Why does your mother always wear a petticoat wrought with coats-of-arms, such as our grandmothers wore in the time of Charles VII? Do tell her, fair cousin, that it is no longer the fashion, and that her laurel-tree and her hinges emblazoned all over her gown make her look like a walking mantelpiece. Really, nobody sits upon their banner in that way now, I swear they don't!"

Fleur-de-Lys raised her lovely eyes full of reproach.

"Is that all you have to swear to me?" she said in a low voice.

Meantime good Dame Aloïse, enchanted to see them chatting thus confidently, said, as she played with the clasps of her prayer-book,—

"What a touching picture of love!"

The captain, more and more embarrassed, fell back on the tapestry. "That really is a beautiful piece of work!" he exclaimed.

Upon this remark, Colombe de Gaillefontaine, another charming, fair-haired, white-skinned girl, in a high-necked blue damask gown, timidly ventured to address Fleur-de-Lys, in the hope that the handsome captain would reply: "My dear Gondelaurier, have you seen the tapestries at the Roche-Guyon house?"

"Isn't that the house with the garden, which belongs to the linen-dealer of the Louvre?" asked Diane de Christeuil with a laugh; for she had fine teeth, and consequently laughed on every occasion.

"And where there is that big old tower belonging to the ancient wall of Paris," added Amelotte de Montmichel, a pretty, curly-haired, rosy-cheeked brunette, who was as much given to sighing as the other was to laughing, without knowing why.

"My dear Colombe," put in Dame Aloïse, "are you talking of the house which belonged to M. de Bacqueville in the reign of King Charles VI? It does indeed contain some superb high-warp tapestries."

"Charles VI! Charles VI!" muttered the young captain, twirling his moustache. "Heavens! What a memory the good lady has for by-gone things!"

Madame de Gondelaurier went on: "Beautiful tapestries, indeed. Such magnificent work that it is thought to be unique!"

At this instant Bérangère de Champchevrier, a slender little girl of seven, who was gazing into the square through the trefoils of the balcony railing, cried out,—

"Oh, look, pretty godmother Fleur-de-Lys, see that dear dancing-girl dancing down there on the pavement, and playing on the tambourine among those common clowns!"

The shrill jingle of a tambourine was in fact heard by all.

"Some gipsy girl," said Fleur-de-Lys, turning nonchalantly towards the square.

"Let us see! let us see!" exclaimed her lively companions; and they all ran to the edge of the balcony, while Fleur-de-Lys, musing over her lover's coldness, followed them slowly, and her lover, relieved by this incident, which cut short an embarrassing conversation, returned to the farther end of the room with the satisfied air of a soldier released from duty. Yet it was a delightful and an easy duty to wait upon the fair Fleur-de-Lys, and so it had once seemed to him; but the captain had gradually wearied of it; the prospect of a speedy marriage grew less and less attractive day by day. Besides, he was of an inconstant humor, and—we must confess—his taste was somewhat vulgar. Although of very noble birth, he had contracted while in harness more than one of the habits of the common soldier. He loved the tavern and all its accompaniments. He was never at his ease except among coarse witticisms, military gallantries, easy-going beauties, and easy conquests. He had received some education and some polish from his family; but he had roamed the country too young, joined the garrison too young, and every day the veneer of the gentleman was worn away a little more by the hard friction of his military baldric. Although he still visited her occasionally, from a lingering spark of common respect, he felt doubly embarrassed in Fleur-de-Lys' presence: first, because by dint of distributing his love in all sorts of places he had very little left for her; and next, because amid so many stately, starched, and modest dames he trembled continually lest his lips, accustomed to oaths, should suddenly lose all restraint and break out into the language of the tavern. Fancy what the effect would be!

However, with all this were mingled great pretensions to elegance in dress and to a fine appearance. Let those who can reconcile these things. I am only the historian.[12]

He had been standing for some moments, thinking or not thinking, leaning silently against the carved chimney-piece, when Fleur-de-Lys, turning suddenly, spoke to him. After all, the poor girl only looked black at him in self-defense.

"Fair cousin, didn't you tell us of a little gipsy girl whom you rescued from a dozen robbers some two months since, while you were on the night patrol?"

"I think I did, fair cousin," said the captain.

"Well," she continued, "it may be that same gipsy girl who is dancing in the square below. Come and see if you recognize her, fair Cousin Phœbus!"

He perceived a secret desire for reconciliation in this gentle invitation to return to her side, and in the pains she took to call him by his Christian name. Captain Phœbus de Châteaupers (for it is he whom the reader has had before him from the beginning of this chapter) slowly approached the balcony. "There," said Fleur-de-Lys, tenderly, laying her hand upon Phœbus's arm, "look at that little thing dancing in the ring. Is that your gipsy girl?"

Phœbus looked, and said,—

"Yes; I know her by her goat."

"Oh, yes! what a pretty little goat!" said Amelotte, clasping her hands in admiration.

"Are its horns really, truly gold?" asked Bérangère.

Without moving from her easy-chair, Dame Aloïse took up the word: "Isn't it one of those gipsies who came here last year through the Porte Gibard?"

"Mother," said Fleur-de-Lys, gently, "that gate is now called Porte d'Enfer."

Mademoiselle de Gondelaurier knew how much her mother's superannuated modes of speech shocked the captain. In fact, he began to sneer, and muttered between his teeth: "Porte Gibard! Porte Gibard! That's to admit King Charles VI."

"Godmother," cried Bérangère, whose restless eyes were suddenly raised to the top of the towers of Notre-Dame, "what is that black man doing up there?"

All the girls looked up. A man was indeed leaning on his elbows on the topmost balustrade of the northern tower, overlooking the Place de Grève. He was a priest. His dress was distinctly visible, and his face rested on his hands. He was as motionless as a statue. His eye was fixed intently on the square.

There was something in his immobility like a kite which has just discovered a nest of sparrows, and gazes at it.

"It is the archdeacon of Josas," said Fleur-de-Lys.

"You have good eyes if you can recognize him from this distance!" remarked Mademoiselle Gaillefontaine.

"How he watches the little dancer," added Diane de Christeuil.

"The gipsy girl had better beware," said Fleur-de-Lys, "for he is not fond of gipsies."

"'T is a great pity the man should stare at her so," added Amelotte de Montmichel, "for she dances ravishingly."

"Fair Cousin Phœbus," suddenly said Fleur-de-Lys, "as you know this little gipsy girl, pray beckon to her to come up. It will amuse us."

"Oh, yes!" cried all the girls, clapping their hands.

"What nonsense!" replied Phœbus. "She has doubtless forgotten me, and I don't even know her name. Still, if you wish it, ladies, I will make an attempt;" and leaning over the balcony-rail, he called, "Little one!"

The dancer was not playing her tambourine at the moment. She turned her head towards the point whence this call came, her sparkling eye fell on Phœbus, and she stopped short.

"Little one!" repeated the captain; and he signed to her to come.

The young girl looked at him again; then she blushed as if her cheeks were on fire, and putting her tambourine under her arm, she moved through the astonished spectators towards the door of the house to which Phœbus called her, with slow, hesitating steps, and the troubled gaze of a bird yielding to the fascination of a snake.

A moment later, the tapestry hanging before the door was lifted, and the gipsy appeared on the threshold of the room, red, abashed, breathless, her large eyes cast down, and not daring to advance another step.

Bérangère clapped her hands.

But the dancer stood motionless at the door. Her appearance produced a strange effect upon the group of young girls. It is certain that a vague and indistinct desire to please the handsome officer animated them all alike; that his splendid uniform was the aim of all their coquetries; and that so long as he was present there was a certain secret lurking rivalry among them, which they hardly confessed to themselves, but which none the less appeared every instant in their gestures and words. Still, as they were possessed of an almost equal share of beauty, the contest was a fair one, and each might well hope for victory. The gipsy's arrival abruptly destroyed this equilibrium. Her beauty was so remarkable that when she appeared on the threshold of the room she seemed to diffuse a sort of light peculiar to herself. Shut into this room, in this dark frame of hangings and wainscotting, she was incomparably more beautiful and more radiant than in the public square. She was like a torch brought from broad daylight into darkness. The noble maidens were dazzled in spite of themselves. Each of them felt her beauty in some sort impaired. Therefore their battle-front (if we may be pardoned the expression) changed at once, without exchanging a word. Still, they understood one another to perfection. The instincts of women read and reply to one another more rapidly than the understandings of men. An enemy had arrived; all felt it, all rallied for mutual support. A drop of wine is enough to redden a whole glass of water; the entrance of a prettier woman than themselves is enough to tinge a whole party of pretty women with a certain amount of ill-humor,—especially when there is but one man present.

Thus their reception of the gipsy girl was marvelously cold. They examined her from head to foot, then looked at one another, and that was enough: they understood one another. But the young girl waited for them to speak, so much agitated that she dared not raise her eyes.

The captain was the first to break the silence.

"On my word," he said in his tone of bold assurance, "a charming creature! What do you think of her, fair cousin?"

The observation, which a more delicate admirer would at least have uttered in an undertone, was not adapted to soothe the feminine jealousies arrayed against the gipsy girl.

Fleur-de-Lys answered the captain with a sweet affectation of disdain: "She's not bad-looking."

The others whispered together.

At last Madame Aloïse, who was not the least jealous of the party since she was jealous for her daughter, addressed the dancer. "Come in, little one."

"Come in, little one!" repeated, with comic dignity, Bérangère, who would have reached about to the gipsy's waist.

Esmeralda approached the noble lady.

"My pretty child," said Phœbus with emphasis, taking a few steps towards her, "I don't know whether I have the supreme happiness of being recognized by you—"

She interrupted him with a smile and a glance of infinite sweetness,—

"Oh, yes!"

"She has a good memory," observed Fleur-de-Lys.

"Now, then," continued Phœbus, "you escaped very nimbly the other night. Did I frighten you?"

"Oh, no!" said the gipsy.

There was an indefinite something in the tone in which this "Oh, no!" was uttered directly after the "Oh, yes!" which wounded Fleur-de-Lys.

"You left me in your place, my beauty," resumed the captain, whose tongue was loosened when he talked to a girl from the streets, "a very surly knave, blind of one eye, and a hunchback, the bishop's bell-ringer, I believe. They tell me he's the archdeacon's son, and a devil. He has a droll name; they call him Ember Days, Palm Sunday, Shrove Tuesday, or something of the sort! He's named for some high holiday or other! He took the liberty of carrying you off; as if you were a mate for such as he! That was coming it rather strong. What the devil did that screech-owl want with you, eh? Tell me!"

"I don't know," answered she.

"Did any one ever hear of such insolence,—a bell-ringer to carry off a girl as if he were a viscount! a common fellow to poach the game of gentlemen! A pretty state of things, indeed! However, he paid dearly for it. Master Pierrat Torterue is the roughest groom that ever combed and curried a knave; and I can tell you, if it will please you, that he gave your bell-ringer's hide a most thorough dressing."

"Poor man!" said the gipsy, reminded by these words of the scene at the pillory.

The captain burst out laughing. "By the great horn-spoon! your pity is as much out of place as a feather on a pig's tail. May I be as fat as a pope, if—"

He stopped short. "Excuse me, ladies! I was just about to utter a folly."

"Fie, sir!" said Gaillefontaine.

"He speaks to that creature in her own tongue!" added Fleur-de-Lys in a low voice, her anger growing every instant. Nor was this wrath diminished when she saw the captain, charmed with the gipsy and above all with himself, turn on his heel, repeating with the coarse and frank gallantry of a soldier,—

"A lovely girl, upon my soul!"

"Very badly dressed," said Diane de Christeuil, smiling to show her fine teeth.

This remark was a ray of light to the others. It showed them the gipsy's vulnerable point: unable to carp at her beauty, they attacked her dress.

"Why, that's true, little one," said Montmichel; "where did you learn to run about the streets in this way, without a wimple or a neckerchief?"

"Your skirt is so short it fairly makes me shiver," added Gaillefontaine.

"My dear," continued Fleur-de-Lys, somewhat sharply, "you will be taken up one of these days, by the sergeants of the dozen, for your gilded belt."

"Little one, little one," resumed Christeuil with a pitiless smile, "if you wore a decent pair of sleeves upon your arms, they would be less sunburnt."

It was indeed a scene worthy of a more intelligent spectator than Phœbus, to see how these beautiful girls, with their angry, venomous tongues, glided and twisted and twined about the street dancer; they were cruel and yet gracious; they maliciously searched and scanned her shabby, fantastic garb of rags and tinsel. Their laughter, their mockery, and their sneers were endless. Sarcasms rained upon the gipsy, with wicked glances and a haughty pretence of benevolence. They were like those young Roman damsels who amused themselves by plunging golden pins into the bosom of a beautiful slave girl. They were like elegant greyhounds, hanging, with distended nostrils and fiery eyes, about a poor wood-deer which their master's eye forbids them to devour.

After all, what was a miserable street dancer to these daughters of noble houses? They seemed to pay no heed to her presence, and spoke of her, before her, to her, in loud tones, as of something rather dirty, rather low, but still rather pretty.

The gipsy was not insensible to these pin-pricks. Now and then a flush of shame, a flash of anger, kindled in her eyes or on her cheeks; a scornful word seemed trembling on her lips; she made that little pout with which the reader is familiar, in token of her contempt, but she stood motionless; she fixed a sad, sweet look of resignation upon Phœbus.

This look was also full of happiness and affection. She seemed to be restraining herself, for fear she should be turned out.

Phœbus also laughed, and took the gipsy's part with a mixture of impertinence and pity.

"Let them talk, little one," he repeated, jingling his golden spurs; "no doubt your dress is somewhat extravagant and peculiar; but what does that matter to such a charming girl as you are?"

"Good gracious!" exclaimed the fair-haired Gaillefontaine, straightening her swan-like neck with a bitter smile, "I see that the officers of the king's guard easily take fire at the bright eyes of a gipsy."

"Why not?" said Phœbus.

At this answer, carelessly uttered by the captain, like a stone cast at random, which falls unnoted, Colombe began to laugh, as did Diane and Amelotte and Fleur-de-Lys, into whose eyes tears started at the same time.

The gipsy, whose eyes had drooped at the words of Colombe de Gaillefontaine, now raised them beaming with pride and pleasure, and fixed them again upon Phœbus. She was beautiful indeed at this moment.

The old lady, who was watching this scene, felt offended, though she did not know why.

"Holy Virgin!" she suddenly exclaimed, "what is this thing poking about under my feet? Oh, the ugly beast!"

It was the goat, which had entered in search of its mistress, and which, in its haste to reach her, had caught its horns in the mass of folds which the noble dame's draperies formed about her feet when she was seated.

This caused a diversion. The gipsy girl, without speaking, released her pet.

"Oh, there's the little goat with the golden feet!" cried Bérangère, jumping with joy.

The gipsy girl crouched upon her knees and pressed her cheek against the goat's fond head. She seemed to be begging its pardon for having thus deserted it.

Diane whispered in Colombe's ear,—

"Gracious! why didn't I think of it before? It's the gipsy girl with the goat, of whom I have so often heard. They say she is a witch, and that her goat performs very marvelous tricks."

"Very well," said Colombe, "the goat must now amuse in its turn, by performing some miracle."

Diane and Colombe addressed the gipsy eagerly,—

"Little one, make your goat perform some miracle."

"I don't know what you mean," replied the dancer.

"A miracle, a piece of magic, some witchcraft."

"I don't understand;" and she began to fondle the pretty creature, repeating, "Djali! Djali!"

At this instant Fleur-de-Lys noticed an embroidered leather bag hanging from the goat's neck.

"What is that?" she asked.

The gipsy raised her large eyes to the girl's face and replied gravely, "That is my secret."

"I should very much like to know what your secret is," thought Fleur-de-Lys.

Meanwhile the good lady rose angrily, saying,—

"Come, gipsy, if neither you nor your goat can dance for us, why do you loiter here?"

The gipsy, without answering, moved slowly towards the door; but the nearer she came to it, the slower grew her steps.

An irresistible magnet seemed to hold her back. All at once she turned her eyes wet with tears upon Phœbus, and paused.

"Zounds!" cried the captain; "you mustn't go in that way. Come back, and dance something for us. By the way, my beauty, what is your name?"

"Esmeralda," said the dancer, without taking her eyes from his face.

At this strange name the young girls burst into a fit of laughter.

"A terrible name for a girl," said Diane.

"You see now," added Amelotte, "that she is an en-chantress."

"My dear," solemnly exclaimed Dame Aloïse, "your parents never fished out that name for you from the baptismal font."

Some moments previous, however, Bérangère, unheeded by the rest, had lured the goat into one corner of the room by a bit of marchpane. In an instant they were good friends. The curious child had removed the bag from the goat's neck, had opened it, and emptied its contents upon the matting; they consisted of an alphabet, each letter being written upon a sep-arate square of boxwood. No sooner were these playthings scattered over the floor, than the child was amazed to see the goat, one of whose "miracles" this undoubtedly was, select certain letters with her golden hoof and arrange them, by a se-ries of gentle pushes, in a particular order. In a moment a word was spelled out which the goat seemed to have been trained to write, so little did she hesitate in the task; and Bérangère exclaimed suddenly, clasping her hands in admi-ration,—

"Godmother Fleur-de-Lys, do see what the goat has just done!"

Fleur-de-Lys looked, and shuddered. The letters arranged upon the floor spelled this word:—

"PHŒBUS."[13]

"Did the goat do that?" she asked in an altered tone.

"Yes, godmother," answered Bérangère.

It was impossible to doubt her, for the child could not spell.

"This is her secret!" thought Fleur-de-Lys.

Meantime, at the child's shout, the whole party hastened to her side,—the mother, the girls, the gipsy, and the officer.

The gipsy saw the folly which her goat had committed. She turned first red, then pale, and trembled like a criminal before the captain, who regarded her with a smile of mingled satisfaction and surprise.

"Phœbus," whispered the astonished girls. "Why, that's the captain's name!"

"You have a marvellous memory!" said Fleur-de-Lys to the stupefied gipsy. Then bursting into sobs, she stammered out in an agony, hiding her face in her lovely hands, "Oh, she is a witch!" and she heard a voice more bitter yet, which said to her inmost heart, "She is your rival!"

She fell fainting to the floor.

"My daughter! my daughter!" screamed the terrified mother. "Begone, you devilish gipsy!"

Esmeralda picked up the unlucky letters in the twinkling of an eye, made a sign to Djali, and went out at one door as Fleur-de-Lys was borne away by another.

Captain Phœbus, left alone, hesitated a moment between the two doors; then he followed the gipsy.

CHAPTER II

Showing that a Priest and a Philosopher Are Two Very Different Persons

The priest whom the girls had noticed on the top of the north tower, leaning over to look into the square and watching the gipsy's dance so closely, was no other than Claude Frollo.

Our readers have not forgotten the mysterious cell which the archdeacon reserved to himself in that tower. (I do not know, let me observe by the way, whether or not this be the same cell, the interior of which may still be seen through a tiny grated loop-hole, opening to the eastward, at about the height of a man from the floor, upon the platform from which the towers spring; a mere hole, now bare, empty, and dilapidated, the ill-plastered walls "adorned" here and there, at the present time, with a few wretched yellow engravings, representing various cathedral fronts. I presume that this hole is conjointly inhabited by bats and spiders, and that consequently a double war of extermination is waged against flies.)

Every day, an hour before sunset, the archdeacon climbed the tower stairs and shut himself up in this cell, where he often passed whole nights. On this special day, just as, having reached the low door of his retreat, he was fitting into the lock the complicated little key, which he always carried about with him in the purse hanging at his side, the sound of tambourine and castanets struck upon his ear. The sound came from the square in front of the cathedral. The cell, as we have already said, had but one window looking upon the roof of the church. Claude Frollo hastily withdrew the key, and an instant later he was upon the top of the tower, in the gloomy and meditative attitude in which the ladies had seen him.

There he was, serious and motionless, absorbed in one

sight, one thought. All Paris lay beneath his feet, with its countless spires and its circular horizon of gently sloping hills, with its river winding beneath its bridges, and its people flowing through its streets, with its cloud of smoke and its mountainous chain of roofs crowding Notre-Dame close with their double rings of tiles; but of this whole city the archdeacon saw only one corner,—the square in front of the cathedral; only one figure in all that crowd,—the gipsy.

It would have been hard to explain the nature of his gaze, and the source of the fire which flashed from his eyes. It was a fixed gaze, and yet it was full of agitation and trouble. And from the perfect repose of his whole body, scarcely shaken by an occasional involuntary shiver, like a tree stirred by the wind; from the stiffness of his elbows, more stony than the railing upon which they rested; from the rigid smile which contracted his face, you would have said that there was nothing living about Claude Frollo but his eyes.

The gipsy danced; she twirled her tambourine upon the tip of her finger, and tossed it into the air as she danced her Provençal sarabands: light, alert, and gay, quite unconscious of the weight of that terrible gaze which fell perpendicularly upon her head.

The crowd swarmed about her. Now and then a man accoutred in a loose red and yellow coat waved the people back into a circle, then sat down again in a chair a few paces away from the dancer, and let the goat lay its head upon his knees. This man seemed to be the gipsy's comrade. From the lofty point where he stood, Claude Frollo could not distinguish his features.

From the moment that the archdeacon observed this stranger, his attention seemed to be divided between him and the dancer, and his face grew blacker and blacker. Suddenly he straightened himself up, and trembled from head to foot. "Who is that man?" he muttered between his teeth. "I have always seen her alone till now!"

Then he plunged down the winding stairs once more. As he passed the half-open belfry door, he saw something which struck him: he saw Quasimodo, who, leaning from an opening in one of those slate pent-houses which look like huge Venetian blinds, was also gazing steadily out into the square. He was so absorbed in looking that he paid no heed to his foster father's presence. His savage eye had a strange expression; it looked both charmed and gentle. "How strange!" murmured Claude. "Can he be looking at the gipsy?" He continued his descent. In a few moments the anxious archdeacon came out into the square through the door at the foot of the tower.

"What has become of the gipsy girl?" he said, joining the group of spectators called together by the sound of the tambourine.

"I don't know," answered one of his neighbors. "She has just vanished. I think she has gone to dance some sort of a fandango in the house over opposite, where they called her in."

In the gipsy's place, upon the same carpet whose pattern had but just now seemed to vanish beneath the capricious figures of her dance, the archdeacon saw no one but the red-and-yellow man, who, hoping to gain a few coppers in his turn, was walking round the ring, his elbows on his hips, his head thrown back, his face scarlet, his neck stretched to its utmost extent, and a chair between his teeth. Upon this chair was fastened a cat, lent by a neighboring woman, which spit and squalled in desperate alarm.

"By 'r Lady!" cried the archdeacon, as the mountebank, dripping with perspiration, passed him with his pyramid of chair and cat, "what is Master Pierre Gringoire doing here?"

The archdeacon's stern voice so agitated the poor wretch that he lost his balance, and his entire structure, chair, cat, and all, fell pell-mell upon the heads of the spectators, amid a storm of inextinguishable shouts and laughter.

Master Pierre Gringoire (for it was indeed he) would probably have had a serious account to settle with the mistress of the cat, and the owners of all the bruised and scratched faces around him, if he had not hastily availed himself of the confusion to take refuge in the church, where Claude Frollo had beckoned him to follow.

The cathedral was dark and deserted; the side aisles were full of shadows, and the lamps in the chapels began to twinkle like stars, so black had the arched roofs grown. Only the great rose-window in the front, whose myriad hues were still bathed in a ray from the setting sun, gleamed through the darkness like a mass of diamonds, and threw a dazzling reflection to the farther end of the nave.

When they had gone a few paces, Dom Claude leaned his back against a pillar and looked steadily at Gringoire. It was not such a look as Gringoire had dreaded, in his shame at being caught by a grave and learned person in this merry-andrew attire. The priest's glance had nothing mocking or ironical about it; it was serious, calm, and piercing. The archdeacon was first to break the silence.

"Come hither, Master Pierre. You have many matters to explain to me. And, first of all, how comes it that I have not seen you for these two months past, and that I now find you in the streets, in a pretty plight indeed,—half red and half yellow, like a Caudebec apple?"

"Sir," said Gringoire, in piteous tones, "it is in sooth a monstrous garb, and I feel as much abashed as a cat with a calabash on her head. 'Tis very ill done, I feel, to expose the gentlemen of the watch to the risk of cudgelling the shoulders of a Pythagorean philosopher under this loose coat. But what else could I do, my reverend master? The blame belongs entirely to my old doublet, which basely deserted me at the very beginning of winter, on the plea that it was falling to pieces, and must needs take a little rest in some rag-picker's basket. What could I do? Civilization has not yet reached the point where a man may go naked, as Diogenes of old desired. Besides, the wind blew very cold, and the month of January is not a good time to introduce such a new measure to mankind with any hope of success. This coat offered itself; I accepted it, and left behind my old black frock, which, for a Hermetic like myself, was far from being hermetically closed. So here I am in the dress of a mountebank, like Saint Genest. How can I help it? It is an eclipse; but even Apollo kept the swine of Admetus."

"A fine trade you have there," replied the archdeacon.

"I confess, master, that it is far better to philosophize and poetize, to blow the flame in the furnace, or to receive it from heaven, than to carry cats upon your shield; so, when you addressed me, I felt as silly as any donkey before a turnspit. But what was I to do, sir? A man must live; and the finest Alexandrine verses are not such good eating as a bit of Brie cheese. Now, I wrote that famous epithalamium for Margaret of Flanders, which you know all about, and the city has never paid me, under the pretext that it was not very good; as if one could furnish such tragedies as those of Sophocles for four crowns! I almost starved to death. Luckily, I discovered that I had rather a strong jaw. I said to this jaw of mine, 'Perform some feats of strength and balancing; feed yourself,'—*Ale te ipsam*. A lot of tatterdemalions, with whom I have made friends, taught me some score of Herculean tricks, and now I give my teeth every night the bread which I have earned through the day by the sweat of my brow. After all (*concedo*), I confess that it is a sad waste of my intellectual faculties, and that man was never made to spend his life in drumming on the tambourine and biting into chairs. But, reverend master, it is not enough to spend one's life; one must earn his living."

Dom Claude listened in silence. All at once his sunken eyes assumed so sagacious and penetrating an expression that Gringoire felt that the look searched his inmost soul.

"Very good, Master Pierre; but how comes it that you are now keeping company with that gipsy dancing-girl?"

"I' faith!" said Gringoire, "because she is my wife and I am her husband."

The priest's gloomy eyes blazed with wrath.

"Have you done this, miserable fellow?" cried he, furiously seizing Gringoire by the arm! "Can you have been so forsaken of God as to have laid your hands upon that girl?"

"By my hopes of paradise, my lord," replied Gringoire,

trembling in every limb, "I swear to you that I have never laid a finger upon her, if that is what disturbs you."

"Then, what do you mean by talking about husband and wife?" said the priest.

Gringoire hastily gave him as brief an account as possible of his adventure in the Court of Miracles, and his marriage with the broken jug, all of which the reader already knows. It seemed, moreover, that this marriage had as yet had no result, the gipsy always contriving to slip away and leave him as she had done on their wedding night. "It is very mortifying," said he in conclusion, "but that's the consequence of my being so unlucky as to marry a virgin."

"What do you mean?" asked the archdeacon, who had gradually grown calmer as he listened to this tale.

"That's not easy to explain," replied the poet. "It's a superstition. My wife, according to an old prig whom we call the Duke of Egypt, is a foundling or a lost child, which comes to the same thing in the end. She wears about her neck an amulet which they say will some day restore her to her parents, but which will lose its virtue should the young girl lose hers. Hence it follows that we are both leading the most virtuous of lives."

"Then," continued Claude, whose brow had cleared more and more, "you think, Master Pierre, that this creature has never been approached by any man?"

"What chance, Dom Claude, could any man have against a superstition? She has a mania upon this point. I certainly consider it a great rarity to find such nun-like prudery fiercely maintained in the midst of those gipsy girls, who are so easily tamed. But she has three safeguards,—the Duke of Egypt, who has taken her under his protection, perhaps intending to sell her to some gentleman priest; her whole tribe, who hold her in singular veneration, as if she were another Virgin Mary; and a certain dainty little dagger, which the hussy always carries somewhere about her, in spite of the provost's orders against wearing concealed weapons, and which always

springs into her hand if you do but clasp her waist. She's a regular wasp, I can tell you!"

The archdeacon pressed Gringoire with questions.

In Gringoire's opinion Esmeralda was a charming, harm-
less creature, pretty, if it were not for a grimace which she was
always making; a simple, affectionate girl, ignorant of all evil,
and enthusiastic about everything; particularly fond of dancing, of noise, of the open air; a sort of woman bee, with invisible wings to her feet, and living in a whirl. She owed this
nature to the wandering life which she had always led.
Gringoire had managed to find out that while still a child she
had traveled through Spain and Catalonia, to Sicily; he even
fancied that she was taken, by the caravan of gipsies to which
she belonged, to the kingdom of Algiers, a country situated in
Achaia, which Achaia, on one side borders Albania and
Greece, on the other the Sicilian sea, which is the road to
Constantinople. The gipsies, said Gringoire, are vassals of the
King of Algiers, in his capacity of chief of the nation of white
Moors. One thing is certain, that Esmeralda came to France
when very young, by way of Hungary. From all these coun-
tries the girl had gathered scraps of strange tongues, queer
songs and notions, which made her conversation as motley a
piece of patchwork as her dress, half Parisian and half African.
Moreover, the people of those quarters of the town which she
frequented, loved her for her gaiety, her gracefulness, her
lively ways, her dances, and her songs. She knew but two persons in the whole city who disliked her, of whom she often
spoke with terror,—the *sachette* of the Tour-Roland, a dreadful recluse who had some special spite against all gipsies, and
cursed the poor dancer every time she passed her window;
and a priest, who never met her without looking at her and
speaking to her in a way that frightened her. This latter circumstance greatly troubled the archdeacon, although
Gringoire paid but little heed to his agitation; so completely
had two months sufficed to blot from the careless poet's mind
the singular details of that evening upon which he first met
the gipsy, and the archdeacon's presence on that occasion.

Except for this, the little dancer feared nothing; she never told fortunes, which prevented all danger of a trial for witchcraft, such as was frequently brought against the other gipsy women. And then, Gringoire took the place of a brother, if not of a husband, to her. After all, the philosopher bore this kind of Platonic marriage very patiently. At any rate, it ensured him food and lodging. Every morning he set forth from the vagrant's headquarters, generally in Esmeralda's company; he helped her to reap her harvest of coin along the streets; every night he shared the same roof with her, allowing her to bolt herself into her tiny cell, and slept the sleep of the just. A very pleasant life, take it all in all, he thought, and very conducive to reverie. And then, in his innermost soul the philosopher was not so absolutely sure that he was desperately in love with the girl. He loved her goat almost as well. It was a charming animal, gentle, intelligent, quick,—a learned goat. Nothing was more common in the Middle Ages than these learned animals, at which men marveled vastly, and which often conducted their instructors to the stake. And yet, the sorceries of the goat with the golden hoofs were very innocent tricks. Gringoire explained them to the archdeacon, whom these particulars seemed to interest greatly. All that was necessary, in most cases, was to hold the tambourine out to the goat in such or such a fashion, to make the creature perform the desired trick. It had been trained to do all this by the gipsy girl, who had such rare skill as an instructor that it took her only two months to teach the goat to write the word "Phœbus" with movable letters.

"Phœbus," said the priest; "and why 'Phœbus'?"

"I don't know," answered Gringoire. "It may be a word which she thinks has some secret magic virtue. She often repeats it in an undertone when she thinks she is alone."

"Are you sure," returned Claude, with his penetrating glance, "that it is a word, and not a name?"

"Whose name?" said the poet.

"How do I know?" said the priest.

"This is what I believe, sir. These gipsies are a kind of fire-worshippers, and worship the sun. Hence, 'Phœbus.'"

"That is not so clear to me as to you, Master Pierre."

"Never mind; it doesn't concern me. Let her mumble her 'Phœbus' as much as she likes. I'm sure of one thing; and that is, that Djali is almost as fond of me as of her."

"Who is Djali?"

"That's the goat."

The archdeacon rested his chin on his hand, and seemed for a moment lost in thought. Suddenly he turned abruptly to Gringoire.

"And you swear that you have never touched her?"

"Who?" said Gringoire, — "the goat?"

"No, that woman."

"My wife? I swear I never have."

"And you are often alone with her?"

"A good hour every evening."

Dom Claude frowned.

"Oh! oh! *Solus cum sola non cogitabuntur orare Pater noster.*"*

"By my soul! I might repeat the *Pater*, and the *Ave Maria*, and the *Credo in Deum patrem omnipotentem*, without her taking any more notice of me than a hen would of a church."

"Swear to me by your mother's soul," repeated the archdeacon, vehemently, "that you have never laid the tip of your finger upon the girl."

"I will swear it by my father's head as well, if you like. But, my reverend master, let me ask one question in my turn."

"Speak, sir."

"What difference does it make to you?"

The archdeacon's pale face turned red as a girl's cheek.

---

*A man and a woman alone together do not think about paternosters (Latin); the Lord's Prayer is also known as the Pater Noster (Our Father).

For a moment he made no answer; then, with evident embarrassment, he said,—

"Hark ye, Master Pierre Gringoire. You are not yet damned, so far as I know. I am interested in you, and wish you well. Now, the slightest contact with that devilish gipsy girl would make you the slave of Satan. You know that it is always the body which destroys the soul. Woe betide you if you approach that woman! That is all."

"I tried it once," said Gringoire, scratching his ear. "That was the first day; but I got stung."

"Had you the effrontery, Master Pierre?"

And the priest's face clouded.

"Another time," said the poet, smiling, "I peeped through her keyhole before I went to bed, and I saw, in her shift, as delicious a damsel as ever made a bed creak beneath her naked foot."

"Go to the devil!" cried the priest, with a terrible look; and pushing away the amazed Gringoire by the shoulders, he was soon lost to sight beneath the gloomiest arches of the cathedral.

CHAPTER III

The Bells

Ever since the morning when he was pilloried, the people living in the neighborhood of Notre-Dame fancied that Quasimodo's zeal for bell-ringing had grown very cold. Up to that time he had pulled the bells upon every occasion and no occasion at all; their music sounded from prime to complines; the belfry rang a peal for high mass, or the bells sounded a merry chime for a wedding or a christen-

ing, mingling and blending in the air like a rich embroidery
of all sorts of melodious sounds. The old church, resonant
and re-echoing, was forever sounding its joy-bells. There
seemed to be an ever-present spirit of noise and caprice,
which shouted and sang through those brazen tongues. Now
that spirit seemed to have vanished; the cathedral seemed
somber, and given over to silence; for festivals and funerals
there was still the simple tolling, dry and bare, such as the ritual required, and nothing more; of the double noise which a
church sends forth, from its organ within and its bells without, only the organ remained. It seemed as if there were no
musician left in the belfry towers. And yet, Quasimodo was
still there. What had happened to him? Did the shame and
despair felt upon the pillory still rankle within him; did the
executioner's lashes still tingle in his soul; and had the agony
caused by such treatment killed all emotion within him, even
his passion for the bells? Or had big Marie a rival in the heart
of the ringer of Notre-Dame, and were the big bell and her
fourteen sisters neglected for a fairer and more attractive object?

It happened that in this year of grace 1482 the Feast of the
Annunciation fell upon Tuesday, the 25th of March. On that
day the air was so pure and so clear that Quasimodo felt some
slight return of his love for the bells. He therefore climbed up
into the north tower, while below, the beadle threw wide
open the church doors, which were then made of huge panels of hard wood covered with leather, edged with gilded iron
nails, and framed in carvings "very cunningly wrought."

The high belfry cage reached, Quasimodo gazed at the six
bells for some time with a sad shake of the head, as if mourning over the strange thing which had come between his heart
and them. But when he had set them swinging; when he felt
that cluster of bells vibrating beneath his touch; when he
saw—for he could not hear—the quivering octave run up and
down that sonorous scale as a bird hops from twig to twig;
when the demon of music, that demon which shakes a dazzling sheaf of runs, trills, and arpeggios, had taken possession

of the poor deaf fellow,—then he was happy again; he forgot everything; and as his heart swelled with bliss his face grew radiant.

He came and went, he clapped his hands, he ran from one rope to another, he encouraged the six singers with voice and gesture, as the leader of an orchestra spurs on intelligent performers.

"Go on," he cried; "go on, Gabrielle! Pour all your music into the public square; this is a high holiday. Thibauld, no laziness! your pace is slackening; go on, go on, I say! Are you growing rusty, sluggard? That's good! quick! quick! don't let me see the clapper. Make them all as deaf as I am. That's it, Thibauld! bravely done! Guillaume! Guillaume! you are the biggest of them all, and Pasquier is the smallest, and yet Pasquier rings the best. I'll wager that they who can hear, hear him better than they do you. Good! good! my Gabrielle! louder! louder! Hollo! what are you two doing up there, you Sparrows? I don't see you make the very least noise. What are those brazen beaks about yonder, that they seem to yawn when they should be singing? There, work away! 'Tis the Feast of the Annunciation. The sun shines bright; we want a fine peal of bells. Poor Guillaume! you're quite out of breath, my fat lad."

He was wholly absorbed in urging on his bells, all six of which bounded to and fro as best they could, and shook their shining sides, like a noisy team of Spanish mules goaded by the sharp voice of their driver.

All at once, as his gaze fell between the broad slate scales which covered the steep belfry wall up to a certain height, he saw in the square below a young girl quaintly attired, who paused, spread a carpet on the ground, upon which a little goat took its place, and a group of spectators formed about them. This sight suddenly changed the course of his ideas, and chilled his musical enthusiasm as a blast of wind chills melted resin. He stopped, turned his back on the chime of bells, and crouched behind the slated eaves, fixing on the dancing-girl that dreamy, tender, gentle look which had once before astonished the archdeacon. The neglected bells ceased suddenly and all at once, to the great disappointment of the lovers of chimes, who were eagerly listening to the peal from the Pont au Change, and who now went away as much amazed as a dog that has been shown a bone and then receives a stone.

CHAPTER IV

'Anátkh

It happened that on a fine morning in that same month of March,—I believe it was Saturday, the 29th,—Saint Eustache's Day, our young friend the student, Jehan Frollo du Moulin, noticed while dressing that his breeches, which contained his purse, gave forth no clink of metal. "Poor purse!" said he, pulling it from his pocket; "what! not the smallest coin! How cruelly have the dice, Venus, and mugs of beer gutted thee! How empty, wrinkled, and flat you are! You look like the breast of a Fury! I just ask you, Master Cicero and Master Seneca, whose dog's-eared works I see scattered over the floor, what does it avail me to know, better than any governor of the Mint or any Jew from the Pont au Change, that one golden crown-piece is worth thirty-five unzains at twenty-five pence and eight Paris farthings each, and that another is worth thirty-six unzains at twenty-six pence and six Tours farthings each, if I have not a paltry copper to stake upon the double-six? Oh, Consul Cicero! that is not a calamity to be overcome by periphrases,—by *quemadmodum* and *verum enim vero*."*

---

*Expressions such as "how" and "verily" (Latin).

He dressed himself sadly. A thought struck him as he laced his shoes, but he at first rejected it; however, it recurred to him, and he put on his waistcoat wrong side out,—an evident sign of some violent mental conflict. At last he dashed down his cap, exclaimed, "So much the worse! Come what will, I will go to my brother. I shall catch a lecture, but I shall also catch a crown piece."

Then he hastily put on his cassock with furred shoulder-pads, picked up his cap, and dashed out of the room.

He went down the Rue de la Harpe towards the City. As he passed the Rue de la Huchette, the smell of those wonderful spits perpetually revolving there tickled his olfactories, and he cast an affectionate glance at the gigantic cookshop which once drew from the Franciscan friar Calatagirone the pathetic exclamation,—"*Veramente, queste rotisserie sono cosa stupenda!*"* But Jehan had no money to pay for breakfast; and with a deep sigh he entered the door of the Petit-Châtelet,—that huge double trefoil of massive towers which guarded the entrance to the City.

He did not even take time to throw a stone as he passed, as was customary, at the wretched statue of that Périnet Leclerc who delivered over the Paris of Charles VI to the English,—a crime which his effigy, its surface defaced by stones and covered with mud, has expiated for three centuries, at the corner of the Rues de la Harpe and de Buci, as in a perpetual pillory.

Crossing the Petit-Pont, and striding down the Rue Neuve-Sainte-Geneviève, Jehan de Molendino found himself face to face with Notre-Dame. Then his former indecision overcame him, and he walked around the statue of Monsieur Legris for several moments, repeating in agony, "The lecture is a certainty; the crown-piece is doubtful!"

He stopped a beadle as he came from the cloister.

"Where is the archdeacon of Josas?"

---

*Truly these cookshops are wonderful places! (Spanish).

"I think that he is in his cell in the tower," said the beadle; "and I don't advise you to disturb him, unless you come from some such person as the pope or the king."

Jehan clapped his hands.

"The devil! what a splendid opportunity to see the famous abode of sorceries!"

Strengthened by this thought, he boldly entered the little black door, and began to climb the winding staircase of Saint-Gilles, which leads to the upper stories of the tower. "We'll see!" said he as he climbed. "By the Holy Virgin's shoestrings! it must be something very queer which my reverend brother keeps so closely hidden. They say that he lights the fires of hell up there, and cooks the philosopher's stone over the blaze. My word! I care no more for the philosopher's stone than for any common pebble; and I should rather find a good omelet of Easter eggs over his fire than the biggest philosopher's stone in the world!"

Reaching the gallery of little columns, he stopped a moment to take breath, and to swear at the interminable staircase by I know not how many millions of cartloads of devils; then he resumed his ascent by the little door of the north tower, now closed to the public. A few moments later, after passing the belfry cage, he reached a small landing-place built in a lateral recess, and under the arch, a low pointed door,—an opening cut through the circular wall of the staircase enabling him to see its enormous lock and strong iron framework. Persons desirous of visiting this door at the present time may recognize it by the inscription in white letters on the black wall, "I adore Coralie. 1823. Signed, Eugène." The word "signed" is in the original.

"Oho!" said the student; "this must be the place."

The key was in the lock. The door was ajar; he pushed it gently, and put his head through the opening.

The reader has doubtless seen the admirable works of Rembrandt, that Shakspeare of painting. Among many marvelous engravings, there is one special etching which is supposed to represent Doctor Faustus, and at which it is impossible to look without being dazzled. It represents a dark cell; in the foreground is a table covered with hideous objects,—skulls, globes, alembics, compasses, hieroglyphic parchments. The Doctor is at this table, dressed in his coarse great-coat, a furred bonnet pulled down to his eyebrows. He is painted at half-length. He has half risen from his vast arm-chair, his clinched fists rest on the table, and he stares with curiosity and terror at a large luminous circle, composed of magical letters, which gleams on the opposite wall like the solar spectrum in the camera obscura. This cabalistic sun seems to shimmer as we look, and fills the gloomy cell with its mysterious radiance. It is horrible, and the same time beautiful.

Something very similar to Faust's cell appeared to Jehan when he ventured to put his head in at the half-open door. This, too, was a dark and dimly lighted dwelling. Here, too, were the large chair and large table, the compasses and alembics, skeletons of animals hanging from the roof, a globe rolling over the floor, hippocamps pell-mell with glass jars in which quivered leaf gold, death's-heads lying on vellum scrawled over with figures and letters, thick manuscripts, open, and piled one upon another, without regard to the fragile corners of the parchment,—in short, all the rubbish of science, and over all this litter, dust and cobwebs; but there was no circle of luminous letters, no rapt doctor gazing at the flaming vision as the eagle looks upon the sun.

And yet the cell was not deserted. A man sat in the arm-chair, leaning over the table. Jehan, to whom his back was turned, could see only his shoulders and the back of his skull; but he found no difficulty in recognizing the bald head, which Nature had endowed with an enduring tonsure, as if wishing to mark by this outward symbol the archdeacon's irresistible clerical vocation.

Jehan recognized his brother; but the door had opened so softly that nothing warned Dom Claude of his presence. The curious student took advantage of this fact to examine the cell at his leisure. A large stove, which he had not at first observed, stood to the left of the arm-chair, under the dormer-window.

The rays of light which penetrated that aperture passed through a round cobweb covering the pointed arch of the window with its delicate tracery, in the center of which the insect architect lay motionless, like the nave of this wheel of lacework. Upon the stove were heaped in confusion all sorts of vessels,—earthen flasks, glass retorts, and charcoal matrasses. Jehan noticed, with a sigh, that there was not a single saucepan.

"The kitchen utensils are cold!" thought he.

Moreover, there was no fire in the stove, and it even seemed as if none had been lighted for a long time. A glass mask, which Jehan noted among the alchemist's tools, and doubtless used to protect the archdeacon's face when handling any dangerous substance, lay in one corner, covered with dust, and apparently forgotten. Beside it lay an equally dusty pair of bellows, upon the upper surface of which was the motto, inlaid in copper, "*Spira, spera.*"*

Other mottoes were written on the walls, after the manner of the Hermetics, in great number,—some in ink, others engraved with a metal point. Moreover, Gothic letters, Hebrew letters, Greek letters, and Roman letters were used indiscriminately,—the inscriptions overlapping each other haphazardly, the newest effacing the oldest, and all entangled together, like the branches in a thicket, like the pikes in an affray. There was a confused medley of all human philosophy, thought, and knowledge. Here and there one shone out among the rest like a flag among the spear-heads. They were for the most part brief Greek or Latin devices, such as the Middle Ages expressed so well: "*Unde? inde?*" "*Homo homini monstrum.*" "*Astra, castra, nomen, numen.*" "*Μέγα βιβλίον, μέγα κακόν.*" "*Sapere aude.*" "*Flat ubi vult,*"† etc. Sometimes

---

*I breathe; I hope (Latin).

†Whence thence? (Latin). Man is a monster to men (Latin). The stars, a fortress, the name, a wonder (Latin). A great book, great evil (Greek). Dare to be wise (Latin). [The spirit] blows where it wants (Latin).

a single word without any apparent meaning, "'Αναγκοφα-
γία," which possibly hid a bitter allusion to the monastic system; sometimes a simple maxim of clerical discipline in the
form of a regular hexameter, "*Cælestem dominum, terrestrem
dicito domnum.*"* There were also Hebrew hieroglyphics, of
which Jehan, who did not even know much Greek, could
make nothing; and the whole was crisscrossed in every direction with stars, figures of men and animals, and intersecting
triangles, which contributed not a little to make the blotted
wall of the cell look like a sheet of paper which a monkey had
bedaubed with an inky pen.

The entire abode, moreover, had a look of general desertion and decay, and the bad condition of the implements led
to the conjecture that their owner had for some time been distracted from his labors by other cares.

This owner, however, bending over a huge manuscript
adorned with quaint paintings, seemed tormented by a
thought which mingled constantly with his meditations,—at
least, so Jehan judged from hearing him exclaim, with the
pensive pauses of a man in a brown study thinking aloud:—

"Yes, Manu said it, and Zoroaster taught it,—the sun is the
offspring of fire, the moon of the sun; fire is the central soul
of the great whole; its elementary atoms perpetually overflow,
and flood the world in boundless currents! At the points
where these currents cross in the heavens, they produce light;
at their points of intersection on the earth, they produce gold.
Light, gold; the same thing! From fire to the concrete state.
The difference between the visible and palpable, between the
fluid and solid of the same substance, between steam and
ice,—nothing more. These are not mere dreams,—it is the
general law of Nature. But how are we to wrest from science
the secret of this general law? Why, this light which irradiates
my hand is gold! these self-same atoms, expanded in harmony
with a certain law, only require to be condensed in accor-

---

*Account the Lord of heaven thy ruler upon earth (Latin).

dance with another law. And how? Some have fancied it was by burying a sunbeam. Averroës,—yes, it was Averroës,— Averroës interred one under the first column to the left in the sanctuary of the Koran, in the great mosque of Cordova; but the vault may not be opened to see if the operation be successful, until eight thousand years have passed."

"The Devil!" said Jehan aside, "this is a long time to wait for a crown."

"Others have thought," continued the musing archdeacon, "that it was better to work with a ray from Sirius. But it is not easy to get such a ray pure, on account of the simultaneous presence of other stars which blend with it. Flamel! What a name for one of the elect, *Flamma!*—Yes, fire. That is all: the diamond lurks in the coal; gold is to be found in fire. But how to extract it? Magistri declares that there are certain feminine names possessing so sweet and mysterious a spell that it is enough to pronounce them during the operation. Let us read what Manu says under this head: 'Where women are reverenced, the divinities rejoice; where they are scorned, it is vain to pray to God. A woman's mouth is ever pure; it is like running water, it is like a sunbeam. A woman's name should be agreeable, soft, fantastic; it should end with long vowels, and sound like words of blessing.' Yes, the sage is right,—indeed, Maria, Sophia, Esmeral—Damnation! again that thought!"

And he closed the book violently.

He passed his hand across his brow, as if to drive away the idea which possessed him; then he took from the table a nail and a small hammer, the handle of which was curiously painted with cabalistic letters.

"For some time," said he with a bitter smile, "I have failed in all my experiments; a fixed idea possesses me, and is burned into my brain as with a red-hot iron. I have not even succeeded in discovering the lost secret of Cassiodorus, whose lamp burned without wick or oil. And yet it is a simple matter!"

"A plague upon him!" muttered Jehan.

"A single wretched thought, then," continued the priest,

"is enough to make a man weak and mad! Oh, how Claude Pernelle would laugh me to scorn,—she who could not for an instant turn Nicolas Flamel from his pursuit of the great work! Why, I hold in my hand the magic hammer of Ezekiel! At every blow which the terrible rabbi, in the seclusion of his cell, struck on this nail with this hammer, that one of his foes whom he had condemned, were he two thousand leagues away, sank an arm's-length into the earth, which swallowed him up. The King of France himself, having one night knocked heedlessly at the magician's door, sank knee-deep into the pavement of his own city of Paris. Well, I have the hammer and the nail, and they are no more powerful tools in my hand than a cooper's tiny mallet would be to a smith; and yet I only need to recover the magic word uttered by Ezekiel as he struck his nail."

"Nonsense!" thought Jehan.

"Let me see, let me try," resumed the archdeacon, eagerly. "If I succeed, I shall see a blue spark flash from the head of the nail. '*Emen-Hétan! Emen-Hétan!*' That's not it. '*Sigéani! Sigéani!*' May this nail open the gates of the tomb for every one who bears the name of Phœbus! A curse upon it! Always, always and forever the same idea!"

And he threw the hammer from him angrily. Then he sank so far forward over the table that Jehan lost sight of him behind the huge back of the chair. For some moments he saw nothing but his fist convulsively clinched upon a book. All at once Dom Claude rose, took up a pair of compasses, and silently engraved upon the wall, in capital letters, this Greek word:

'ANÁTKH.

"My brother is mad," said Jehan to himself; "it would have been much simpler to write *Fatum*; every one is not obliged to understand Greek."

The archdeacon resumed his seat in his arm-chair, and bowed his head on his hands, like a sick man whose brow is heavy and burning.

The student watched his brother in surprise. He, who wore

his heart on his sleeve, who followed no law in the world but the good law of Nature, who gave free rein to his passions, and in whom the fountain of strong feeling was always dry, so clever was he at draining it daily,—he could not guess the fury with which the sea of human passions bubbles and boils when it is denied all outlet; how it gathers and grows, how it swells, how it overflows, how it wears away the heart, how it breaks forth in repressed sobs and stifled convulsions, until it has rent its dikes and burst its bed. Claude Frollo's stern and icy exterior, that cold surface of rugged and inaccessible virtue, had always misled Jehan. The jovial student had never dreamed of the boiling lava which lies deep and fiery beneath the snowy front of Ætna.

We know not if he was suddenly made aware of these things; but, feather-brain though he was, he understood that he had seen what he was never meant to see, that he had surprised his elder brother's soul in one of its most secret moments, and that he must not let Claude discover it. Noting that the archdeacon had relapsed into his former immobility, he drew his head back very softly, and made a slight noise behind the door, as if he had just arrived, and wished to warn his brother of his approach.

"Come in!" cried the archdeacon from within the cell; "I expected you. I left the door on the latch purposely; come in, Master Jacques."

The student entered boldly. The archdeacon, much annoyed by such a visit in such a place, started in his chair. "What! is it you, Jehan?"

"It is a J, at any rate," said the student, with his merry, rosy, impudent face.

Dom Claude's features resumed their usual severe expression.

"Why are you here?"

"Brother," replied the student, trying to put on a modest, unassuming, melancholy look, and twisting his cap with an innocent air, "I came to ask you—"

"What?"

"For a little moral lecture, which I sorely need." Jehan dared not add aloud, "And a little money, which I need still more sorely." The last part of his sentence was left unspoken.

"Sir," said the archdeacon in icy tones, "I am greatly displeased with you."

"Alas!" sighed the student.

Dom Claude turned his chair slightly, and looked steadily at Jehan.

"I am very glad to see you."

This was a terrible beginning. Jehan prepared for a severe attack.

"Jehan, I hear complaints of you every day. How about that beating with which you bruised a certain little Viscount Albert de Ramonchamp?"

"Oh!" said Jehan, "that was nothing,—a mischievous page, who amused himself with spattering the students by riding his horse through the mud at full speed!"

"How about that Mahiet Fargel," continued the archdeacon, "whose gown you tore? '*Tunicam dechiraverunt*,'* the complaint says."

"Oh, pooh! a miserable Montaigu cape,—that's all!"

"The complaint says '*tunicam*,' and not '*cappettam*.' Do you know Latin?"

Jehan made no answer.

"Yes," resumed the priest, shaking his head, "this is what study and learning have come to now. The Latin language is hardly understood, Syriac is an unknown tongue, Greek is held in such odium that it is not considered ignorance for the wisest to skip a Greek word without reading it, and to say, '*Græcum est, non legitur*.'"†

The student boldly raised his eyes: "Brother, would you like me to explain in good every-day French that Greek word written yonder on the wall?"

---

*They tore the robe (Latin).
†It is in Greek, it is not read (Latin).

"Which word?"

"'ANÁTKH."

A slight flush overspread the archdeacon's dappled cheeks, like the puff of smoke which proclaims to the world the secret commotion of a volcano. The student scarcely noticed it.

"Well, Jehan!" stammered the elder brother with an effort, "what does the word mean?"

"Fate."

Dom Claude turned pale again, and the student went on carelessly,—

"And that word below it, written by the same hand, 'Αναγνεία, means 'impurity.' You see I know my Greek."

The archdeacon was still silent. This Greek lesson had given him food for thought.

Little Jehan, who had all the cunning of a spoiled child, thought this a favorable opportunity to prefer his request. He therefore assumed a very sweet tone, and began:—

"My good brother, have you taken such an aversion to me that you pull a long face for a few paltry cuffs and thumps distributed in fair fight to no one knows what boys and monkeys (*quibusdam marmosetis*)? You see, dear brother Claude, that I know my Latin."

But all this affectionate hypocrisy failed of its usual effect on the stern elder brother. Cerberus did not snap at the sop. The archdeacon's brow did not lose a single wrinkle.

"What are you driving at?" said he, drily.

"Well, then, to the point! This is it," bravely responded Jehan; "I want money."

At this bold declaration the archdeacon's face assumed quite a paternal and pedagogic expression.

"You know, Master Jehan, that our Tirechappe estate only brings us in, reckoning the taxes and the rents of the twenty-one houses, thirty-nine pounds eleven pence and six Paris farthings. It is half as much again as in the time of the Paclet brothers, but it is not much."

"I want money," stoically repeated Jehan.

"You know that it has been officially decided that our

twenty-one houses were held in full fee of the bishopric, and that we can only buy ourselves off from this homage by paying two silver gilt marks of the value of six Paris pounds to the right reverend bishop. Now, I have not yet been able to save up those two marks. You know this."

"I know that I want money," repeated Jehan for the third time.

"And what would you do with it?"

This question made the light of hope shine in Jehan's eyes. He resumed his demure, caressing manner.

"See here, dear brother Claude; I do not come to you with any evil intention. I don't want to cut a dash at the tavern with your money, or to walk the streets of Paris in garments of gold brocade with my lackey, *cum meo laquasio.* No, brother; I want the money for a charity."

"What charity?" asked Claude with some surprise.

"There are two of my friends who want to buy an outfit for the child of a poor widow in the Haudry almshouse. It is a real charity. It will cost three florins; I want to give my share."

"Who are your two friends?"

"Pierre l'Assommeur and Baptiste Croque-Oison."*

"Hum!" said the archdeacon; "those names are as fit for charity as a bombard for the high altar."

Certainly Jehan had chosen very suspicious names for his two friends, as he felt when it was too late.

"And then," added the sagacious Claude, "what kind of an outfit could you buy for three florins, and for the child of one of the women in the Haudry almshouse, too? How long have those widows had babies in swaddling-clothes?"

Jehan broke the ice once more:—

"Well, then, if I must tell you, I want the money to go to see Isabeau la Thierrye tonight, at the Val-d'Amour."

"Impure scamp!" cried the priest.

---

*The surnames signify Pierre as "the Slaughterer" and Baptiste as "the Rook."

"'Αναγνεία," said Jehan.

This quotation, borrowed, perhaps maliciously, by the student from the wall of the cell, produced a strange effect upon the priest. He bit his lip, and his rage was extinguished in a blush.

"Begone!" said he to Jehan. "I am expecting some one."

The student made another effort,—

"Brother Claude, at least give me a few farthings for food."

"How far have you got in Gratian's decretals?" asked Dom Claude.

"I've lost my copy-books."

"Where are you in the Latin humanities?"

"Somebody has stolen my copy of Horace."

"Where are you in Aristotle?"

"My faith, brother! what Father of the Church says that the errors of heretics have in all ages taken refuge in the brambles of Aristotle's metaphysics? Plague take Aristotle! I will not destroy my religion with his metaphysics."

"Young man," resumed the archdeacon, "at the king's last entry there was a gentleman called Philippe de Comines, who had embroidered on his horse's housings this motto, which I advise you to consider: '*Qui non laborat non manducet.*'"*

The student was silent for a moment, his finger to his ear, his eye fixed upon the ground, and an angry air.

Suddenly he turned to Claude with the lively quickness of a water wagtail,—

"So, good brother, you refuse to give me a penny to buy a crust from a baker?"

"'*Qui non laborat non manducet.*'"

At this reply from the inflexible archdeacon, Jehan hid his face in his hands like a woman sobbing, and exclaimed in accents of despair, "Οτοτοτοτοτοί!"

---

*He who will not work shall not eat (Latin).

"What do you mean by that, sir?" asked Claude, amazed at this outburst.

"Why," said the student,—and he looked up at Claude with impudent eyes into which he had just rubbed his fists to make them look red with crying,—"it is Greek! It is an anapæst of Æschylus which expresses grief perfectly."

And here he burst into laughter so absurd and so violent that it made the archdeacon smile. It was really Claude's fault; why had he so spoiled the child?

"Oh, good brother Claude," added Jehan, emboldened by this smile, "just see my broken buskins! Was there ever more tragic cothurnus on earth than boots with flapping soles?"

The archdeacon had promptly resumed his former severity.

"I will send you new boots, but no money."

"Only a paltry penny, brother," continued the suppliant Jehan. "I will learn Gratian by heart. I will believe heartily in God. I will be a regular Pythagoras of learning and virtue. But give me a penny, for pity's sake! Would you have me devoured by famine, which gapes before me with its jaws blacker, more noisome, deeper than Tartarus or a monk's nose?"

Dom Claude shook his wrinkled brow: "*'Qui non laborat,—'*"

Jehan did not let him finish.

"Well, then," he cried, "to the devil! Hurrah for fun! I'll go to the tavern, I'll fight, I'll drink, and I'll go to see the girls!"

And upon this, he flung up his cap and cracked his fingers like castanets.

The archdeacon looked at him with a gloomy air.

"Jehan, you have no soul!"

"In that case, according to Epicurus, I lack an unknown quantity composed of unknown qualities."

"Jehan, you must think seriously of reform."

"Oh, come!" cried the student, gazing alternately at his brother and at the alembics on the stove; "is everything crooked here,—ideas as well as bottles?"

"Jehan, you are on a very slippery road. Do you know where you are going?"

"To the tavern," said Jehan.

"The tavern leads to the pillory."

"It's as good a lantern as any other, and perhaps it was the one with which Diogenes found his man."

"The pillory leads to the gallows."

"The gallows is a balance, with a man in one scale and the whole world in the other. It is a fine thing to be the man."

"The gallows leads to hell."

"That's a glorious fire."

"Jehan, Jehan, you will come to a bad end!"

"I shall have had a good beginning."

At this moment the sound of footsteps was heard on the stairs.

"Silence!" said the archdeacon, putting his finger to his lip: "Here comes Master Jacques. Listen, Jehan," he added in a low voice; "take care you never mention what you may see and hear here. Hide yourself quickly under that stove, and don't dare to breathe."

The student crawled under the stove; there, a capital idea occurred to him.

"By the way, brother Claude, I want a florin for holding my breath."

"Silence! you shall have it."

"Then give it to me."

"Take it!" said the archdeacon, angrily, flinging him his purse.

Jehan crept farther under the stove, and the door opened.

CHAPTER V

The Two Men Dressed in Black

The person who entered wore a black gown and a gloomy air. Our friend Jehan (who, as may readily be supposed, had so disposed himself in his corner that he could see and hear everything at his good pleasure) was struck, at the first glance, by the extreme melancholy of the newcomer's face and attire. Yet a certain amiability pervaded the countenance, albeit it was the amiability of a cat or a judge,—a sickly amiability. The man was very grey, wrinkled, bordering on sixty years; had white eyebrows, hanging lip, and big hands. When Jehan saw that he was a mere nobody,—that is, probably a doctor or a magistrate, and that his nose was very far away from his mouth, a sure sign of stupidity,—he curled himself up in his hiding-place, in despair at having to pass an indefinite length of time in so uncomfortable a position and in such poor company.

Meantime, the archdeacon did not even rise from his chair to greet this person. He signed to him to be seated on a stool near the door, and after a few moments' silence, which seemed the continuation of a previous meditation, he said in a somewhat patronizing tone, "Good-morning, Master Jacques."

"Your servant, master," replied the man in black.

In the two ways of pronouncing,—on the one hand that "Master Jacques," and on the other that distinctive "master,"—there was the difference that there is between *domine* and *domne*. It bespoke the greeting of teacher and pupil.

"Well," resumed the archdeacon after a fresh pause, which Master Jacques took care not to break, "have you succeeded?"

"Alas! master," said the other, with a sad smile, "I am still blowing away. As many ashes as I choose; but not a particle of gold."

Dom Claude made an impatient gesture. "I'm not talking about that, Master Jacques Charmolue, but about the trial of your sorcerer, Marc Cenaine,—wasn't that what you called him?—the butler to the Court of Accounts. Does he confess his magic? Was the rack successful?"

"Alas! no," replied Master Jacques, still with the same sad smile, "we have not that consolation. The man is as hard as flint; we might boil him at the Pig-market before he would say a word. And yet, we have spared nothing to get at the truth; all his bones are out of joint already; we have left no stone unturned. As the old comic author, Plautus says:—

> *'Advorsum stimulos, laminas, crucesque, com-*
> *   pedesque,*
> *Nervos, catenas, carceres, numellas, pedicas,*
> *   boias.'**

All in vain; the man is terrible indeed. I can't make him out!"

"You've not found anything new at his house?"

"Yes, indeed," said Master Jacques, fumbling in his purse; "this parchment. There are words written on it which we cannot comprehend. And yet the criminal lawyer, Philippe Lheulier, knows a little Hebrew, which he picked up in that affair of the Jews in the Rue Kantersten at Brussels."

So saying, Master Jacques unrolled a parchment.

"Give it to me," said the archdeacon. And casting his eyes over the writing, he exclaimed, "Clear magic, Master Jacques! *'Emen-Hétan!'* that is the cry of the vampires as they appear at their Sabbath. *'Per ipsum, et cum ipso, et in ipso!'*— that is the word of command which rechains the devil in hell. *'Hax, pax, max!'* this belongs to medicine: a prescription

---

*Against goads, hot blades, torture, shackles, / straps, chains, dungeons, iron collars (Latin).

against the bite of mad dogs. Master Jacques, you are the king's attorney to the Ecclesiastical Court. This parchment is an abomination."

"We will return the man to the rack. Here again," added Master Jacques, rummaging in his wallet once more, "is something else which we found in Marc Cenaine's house."

It was a vessel similar to those which covered Dom Claude's stove.

"Ah!" said the archdeacon, "an alchemist's crucible."

"I must confess," replied Master Jacques, with his shy, awkward smile, "that I tried it on my furnace, but I succeeded no better than with my own."

The archdeacon began to examine the vessel.

"What has he inscribed upon his crucible? 'Och! Och!' — the word which drives away fleas! This Marc Cenaine is a dolt! I can easily believe that you will never make gold with this. Put it in your alcove in summer, for that's all it's fit for."

"Talking of mistakes," said the king's proxy, "I have just been studying the porch below before I came upstairs; is your reverence very sure that it is the opening of the book of physics which is represented there on the side towards the Hospital; and that, of the seven nude figures at the feet of the Virgin, the one with wings at his heels is meant for Mercury?"

"Yes," replied the priest; "it is so written by Augustin Nypho, that Italian doctor who had a bearded familiar spirit, which taught him everything. However, we will go down, and I will explain all this to you on the spot."

"Thanks, master," said Charmolue, bowing to the ground. "By the way, I forgot! When will it please you to have the little witch arrested?"

"What witch?"

"That gipsy girl whom you know well, who comes every day and dances in the square before the cathedral, despite the official prohibition. She has a goat which is possessed, and which has the devil's own horns; which reads and writes, and is as good a mathematician as Picatrix, and would be quite enough to hang an entire tribe of gipsies. The papers are

ready; the case will be a short one, I warrant! A pretty creature, by my soul,—that dancing-girl! The finest black eyes!
Two carbuncles! When shall we begin?"

The archdeacon was extremely pale.

"I will let you know," he stammered in a voice which was
scarcely articulate; then he added, with an effort, "Devote
yourself to Marc Cenaine."

"Never fear," said Charmolue, smiling; "I'll have him re-
strapped to the leather bed when I go back. But he's a devil of
a fellow; he would tire out Pierrat Torterue himself, and his
hands are bigger than mine. As the worthy Plautus says:—

> 'Nudus vinctus, centum pondo, es quando pen-
> des per pedes.'*

The torture of the wheel! That's the best thing we have. He
shall take a turn at that."

Dom Claude seemed absorbed in gloomy reverie. He
turned to Charmolue with the words,—

"Master Pierrat,—Master Jacques, I mean,—devote yourself to Marc Cenaine."

"Yes, yes, Dom Claude. Poor man! he must have suffered
like Mummol. But then, what an idea, to go to the Witches'
Sabbath,—a butler of the Court of Accounts, who must know
Charlemagne's text, '*Stryga vel masca!*'† As for that little
girl,—Smelarda, as they call her,—I will await your orders.
Ah! and as we pass through the porch you will also explain to
me the meaning of the gardener painted in relief at the entrance to the church. The Sower, isn't it? Eh! master, what are
you thinking about?"

Dom Claude, lost in his own thoughts, did not hear him.
Charmolue, following the direction of his gaze saw that it was

---

*Bound naked, you weigh a hundred pounds when you are hung up
by the feet (Latin).

†A witch or ghost! (Latin).

fixed mechanically upon the large cobweb which covered the window. At this instant a rash fly, in search of the March sun, plunged headlong into the trap and was caught in it. At the vibration of its web the huge spider made a sudden sally from its central cell, and with one bound fell upon the fly, which it doubled up with its front antennæ, while its hideous proboscis dug out the head. "Poor fly!" said the king's proxy to the Ecclesiastical Court; and he raised his hand to save it. The archdeacon, with a start, held back his arm with convulsive force.

"Master Jacques," he cried, "do not interfere with the work of Fate!"

The attorney turned in alarm; he felt as if iron pincers had seized his arm. The priest's eye was fixed, wild, and flaming, and was still fastened upon the horrible little group of the spider and the fly.

"Oh, yes," added the priest in a voice which seemed to come from his very entrails, "this is a universal symbol. The insect flies about, is happy, is young; it seeks the spring sun, the fresh air, freedom; oh, yes, but it runs against the fatal web; the spider appears,—the hideous spider! Poor dancing-girl! poor predestined fly! Master Jacques, do not interfere! it is the hand of Fate! Alas! Claude, you are the spider. Claude, you are the fly as well! You flew abroad in search of learning, light, and sun; your only desire was to gain the pure air, the broad light of eternal truth; but in your haste to reach the dazzling window which opens into the other world,—the world of intellect, light, and learning,—blind fly! senseless doctor! you failed to see that subtle spider's web woven by Fate between the light and you; you plunged headlong into it, wretched fool! and now you struggle in its meshes, with bruised head and broken wings, in the iron grasp of destiny. Master Jacques, Master Jacques, let the spider do its work!"[14]

"I assure you," said Charmolue, looking at him uncomprehendingly, "I will not touch it. But for mercy's sake, master, let go my arm! Your hand is like a pair of pincers."

The archdeacon did not hear him. "Oh, madman!" he resumed, without taking his eyes from the window. "And if you could have broken this dreadful web with your frail wings, do you think you could have reached the light? Alas! how could you have passed that pane of glass beyond it,—that transparent obstacle, that crystal wall harder than iron, which separates all philosophy from truth? Oh, vanity of science! How many sages have flown from afar to bruise their heads against it! How many contending systems have rushed pell-mell against that everlasting pane of glass!"

He ceased speaking. These last ideas, which had insensibly diverted his thoughts from himself to science, seemed to have calmed him. Jacques Charmolue completely restored him to a sense of reality by asking him this question: "Come, master, when are you going to help me to make gold? I long for success."

The archdeacon shook his head with a bitter smile:

"Master Jacques, read Michel Psellus, '*Dialogues de Energia et Operatione Dæmonum.*'* Our work is not altogether innocent."

"Not so loud, master! I fear you are right," said Charmolue. "But I must needs dabble a little in hermetics, being only the king's proxy to the Ecclesiastical Court, at a salary of thirty Tours crowns a year. But speak lower."

At this moment the sound of champing and chewing proceeding from under the stove, attracted Charmolue's anxious ear.

"What was that?" he asked.

It was the student, who, greatly cramped and much bored in his hiding-place, had contrived to find an old crust of bread and a bit of mouldy cheese, and had set to work to devour them without more ado, by the way of consolation and of breakfast. As he was ravenously hungry, he made a great deal

---

Dialogues upon the Powers and Works of Demons (Latin); written by Byzantine political figure and scholar Michel Psellus (1018–1078).

of noise, and smacked his lips loudly over every mouthful as to give the alarm to the lawyer.

"It is my cat," said the archdeacon, hastily, "feasting under there upon some mouse."

This explanation satisfied Charmolue.

"Indeed, master," he replied with a respectful smile, "every philosopher has had his familiar animal. You know what Servius says: '*Nullus enim locus sine genio est.*'"*

But Dom Claude, who feared some fresh outbreak from Jehan, reminded his worthy disciple that they had certain figures on the porch to study together; and the two left the cell, to the great relief of the student, who began seriously to fear that his knees would leave their permanent mark upon his chin.

CHAPTER VI

The Effect Produced by Seven Oaths in the Public Square

"*Te Deum laudamus!*" cried Master Jehan, as he stepped from his hiding-place; "the two screech-owls have gone. *Och! och! Hax! pax! max!* the fleas! the mad dogs! the devil! I've had enough of their talk! My head rings like a belfry. Mouldy cheese into the bargain! Now, then! let us be off; let us take our big brother's purse, and convert all these coins into bottles!"

He cast a look of tenderness and admiration into the interior of the precious purse, adjusted his dress, wiped his boots,

---

*There is no place without its genius (Latin).

dusted his poor shoulder-pads all grey with ashes, whistled a tune, frisked about, looked to see if there was nothing left in the cell which he might carry off, scraped up a few glass charms and trinkets from the top of the stove, thinking he might pass them off upon Isabeau la Thierrye for jewels, then gave a push to the door, which his brother had left ajar as a final favor, and which he left open in his turn as a final piece of mischief, and hopped down the winding stairs as nimbly as a bird.

In the midst of the shadows of the spiral staircase he elbowed something which moved aside with a growl; he took it for granted that it was Quasimodo, and this struck him as so droll that he held his sides with laughter all the rest of the way down. As he came out into the public square, he was still laughing.

He stamped his foot when he found himself on solid ground once more. "Oh," said he, "good and honorable pavement of Paris! Cursed stairs, which would put all the angels of Jacob's ladder out of breath! What was I thinking of when I poked myself into that stone gimlet which pierces the sky; and all to eat musty cheese, and to see the steeples of Paris through a garret window!"

He walked on a few paces, and saw the two screech-owls— that is to say, Dom Claude and Master Jacques Charmolue— lost in contemplation of a bit of carving on the porch. He approached them on tiptoe, and heard the archdeacon say in a very low voice to Charmolue, "It was Guillaume de Paris who had a Job graven on that lapis-lazuli colored stone, gilded at the edges. Job represents the philosopher's stone, which must also be tried and tortured before it can become perfect, as Raymond Lulle says: '*Sub conservatione formæ specificæ salva anima.*'"*

"That's all one to me," said Jehan. "'Tis I who hold the purse."

---

*By preserving it under a special form the soul is saved (Latin).

At this instant he heard a loud ringing voice pronounce a terrible string of oaths just behind him.

"Zounds! Odds bodikins! By the Rood! By Cock and pye! Damme! 'Sdeath! Thunder and Mars!"

"By my soul," exclaimed Jehan, "that can be no other than my friend Captain Phœbus!"

The name of Phœbus reached the archdeacon's ears, just as he was explaining to the king's proxy the dragon hiding his tail in a bath from which rise smoke and a king's head. Dom Claude shuddered, stopped short, to the great surprise of Charmolue, turned, and saw his brother Jehan talking to a tall officer at the door of the Gondelaurier house.

It was indeed Captain Phœbus de Châteaupers. He was leaning against the corner of his lady-love's house, and swearing like a pirate.

"My word! Captain Phœbus," said Jehan, taking him by the hand, "you swear with admirable spirit!"

"Thunder and Mars!" replied the captain.

"Thunder and Mars, yourself!" responded the student. "Now, then, my fine captain, what has caused such an outburst of elegant epithets?"

"Your pardon, good comrade Jehan," cried Phœbus, shaking him by the hand; "but a horse running at full speed cannot stop short. Now, I was swearing at full gallop. I have just come from those prudes; and when I leave them, I always have my mouth full of oaths; I must needs spit them out, or I should choke. Thunder and guns!"

"Will you take a drink?" asked the student. This proposition calmed the captain.

"With pleasure; but I've no money."

"But I have!"

"Pshaw! let me see!"

Jehan displayed the purse to the captain's eyes, with dignity and simplicity. Meanwhile the archdeacon, having left the amazed Charmolue, had approached them, and stood some paces distant, watching them both unobserved by them, so absorbed were they in looking at the purse.

Phœbus exclaimed, "A purse in your pocket, Jehan! That's like the moon in a pail of water. I see it, but it is not really there. It's only a shadow. By Heaven! I wager there's nothing but pebbles in it!"

Jehan answered coldly, "I'll show you the kind of pebbles that I pave my pocket with."

And without another word he emptied the purse upon a neighboring post, with the air of a Roman saving his country.

"Good God!" muttered Phœbus; "gold pieces, big silver pieces, little silver pieces, crowns, shillings, and pence! It is dazzling!"

Jehan remained dignified and unmoved. A few pennies had rolled into the mud; the captain, in his enthusiasm, stooped to pick them up. Jehan restrained him, saying,—

"Fie, Captain Phœbus de Châteaupers!"

Phœbus counted the money, and turning solemnly to Jehan, asked, "Do you know, Jehan, that you have here twenty-three crowns? Whom did you rob last night in the Rue Coupe-Gueule?"

Jehan threw back his fair curly head, and said, half closing his eyes in scorn,—

"I have a brother who is an archdeacon and a fool."

"Confound it!" cried Phœbus; "so you have, the worthy fellow!"

"Let us take a drink," said Jehan.

"Where shall we go?" said Phœbus; "to the Pomme d'Eve!"

"No, Captain; let us go to the Vieille Science."

"No, the wine is better at the Pomme d'Eve; and besides, at the door is a vine in the sun, which cheers me as I drink."

"So be it," said the student; and taking Phœbus by the arm, the two friends set out for that tavern. It is needless to say that they first picked up the money, and that the archdeacon followed them.

The archdeacon followed them, sad and worn. Was this the Phœbus whose accursed name, since his interview with Gringoire, had mingled with all his thoughts? He knew not;

but at any rate it was a Phœbus, and that magic name was enough to make the archdeacon follow the two heedless comrades with stealthy tread, listening to their every word and noting their least gesture with eager attention. Moreover, nothing was easier than to hear everything they said; for they spoke very loud, utterly regardless of the fact that they were taking the passers-by into their confidence. They talked of duels, women, drinking, and riots.

At the corner of a street the sound of a tambourine was heard from a neighboring cross-way. Dom Claude overheard the officer say to the student,—

"Thunder! We must hasten."

"Why, Phœbus?"

"I'm afraid the gipsy girl will see me."

"What gipsy girl?"

"That little thing with the goat."

"Smeralda?"

"Just so, Jehan. I always forget her devil of a name. Make haste; she would be sure to recognize me. I don't wish to have that girl accost me in the street."

"Do you know her, Phœbus?"

Here the archdeacon saw Phœbus chuckle, put his mouth to Jehan's ear, and whisper a few words to him; then he burst out laughing, and shook his head with a triumphant air.

"Really?" said Jehan.

"Upon my soul!" said Phœbus.

"Tonight?"

"Tonight."

"Are you sure she will come?"

"Are you mad, Jehan? How can there be any doubt in such matters?"

"Captain Phœbus, you are a lucky soldier!"

The archdeacon heard every word of this conversation. His teeth chattered; he shook from head to foot. He stood still a moment, leaned against a post like a drunken man, then followed in the track of the two jolly scamps.

When he rejoined them they had changed the subject. He heard them singing at the top of their voices the old refrain:—

> "The lads of Petty-Tiles, they say,
> Like calves are butchered every day."

CHAPTER VII

The Spectre Monk

The famous tavern known as the Pomme d'Eve was situated in the University, at the corner of the Rue de la Rondelle and the Rue du Bâtonnier. It was a large, low room on the ground-floor, with an arched roof, the central spring of which rested on a huge wooden pillar painted yellow; there were tables in every direction, shining pewter jugs hung on the wall; there were always plenty of topers, lots of girls, a window looking on the street, a vine at the door, and over the door a creaking piece of sheet iron, on which were painted a woman and an apple, rusted by the rain and swinging in the wind on an iron rod. This kind of weathercock, which overlooked the pavement, was the sign.

Night was falling; the streets were dark. The tavern, full of candles, flared from a distance like a forge in the gloom; a noise of glasses, of feasting, of oaths, and of quarrels escaped from the broken window-panes. Through the mist with which the heat of the room covered the glazed casement in front of the inn swarmed a myriad confused figures, and from time to time a ringing burst of laughter was heard. People passing, intent on their own affairs, hastened by that noisy window without a glance; but now and then some little ragged boy would raise himself on tiptoe to the window-sill, and scream into the tavern the old mocking cry with which drunkards were often greeted at this period:—

> "Back to your glasses,
> Ye drunken, drunken asses."

One man, however, marched imperturbably up and down in front of the noisy tavern, looking continually, and never stirring farther away from it than a pikeman from his sentry-box. His cloak was pulled up to his very nose. This cloak he had just bought from the old-clothes man who lived hard by the Pomme d'Eve, doubtless to shield himself from the chill of the March evening, perhaps to hide his dress. From time to time he paused before the dim panes set in lead, listened, looked, and stamped his feet impatiently.

At last the tavern door opened. This seemed to be what he was waiting for. Two tipplers came out. The ray of light which escaped through the door, for a moment reddened their jovial faces. The man with the cloak took up his position under a porch on the other side of the street.

"Thunder and guns!" said one of the two drinkers. "It will strike seven directly. It is the hour for my appointment."

"I tell you," resumed his companion, with a thick utterance, "that I do not live in the Rue des Mauvaises-Paroles, *indignus qui inter mala verba habitat.** My lodgings are in the Rue Jean-Pain-Mollet, *in vico Johannis-Pain-Mollet.* You are more unreasonable than a unicorn, if you say to the contrary. Everybody knows that he who has once climbed upon a bear's back is never afraid; but you've a fine nose for scenting out dainty bits like Saint-Jacques de l'Hôpital."

"Jehan, my friend, you are drunk," said the other.

He replied, staggering, "So it pleases you to say, Phœbus; but it is well proven that Plato had the profile of a hunting-dog."

---

*He is unworthy who dwelleth among evil words (Latin).

The reader has undoubtedly recognized our two worthy friends, the captain and the student. It seems that the man lurking in the shadow had also recognized them; for he followed with slow steps all the zig-zags which the student forced the captain to describe, the latter, a more hardened drinker, having preserved entire self-possession. By listening carefully, the man with the cloak was able to catch the whole of the following interesting conversation:—

"Body of Bacchus! do try to walk straight, Master Bachelor. You know that I shall have to leave you. Here it is seven o'clock. I have an appointment with a woman."

"Leave me then, do. I see fiery stars and spears. You are like the Château-de-Dampmartin, which burst with laughter."

"By my grandmother's warts, Jehan! your nonsense is rather too desperate. By-the-bye, Jehan, haven't you any money left?"

"Mr. Rector, there's no mistake: the little butcher's shop, *parva boucheria.*"

"Jehan, friend Jehan! you know that I made an appointment to meet that little girl at the end of the Pont Saint-Michel; that I can't take her anywhere but to La Falourdel,—the old hag on the bridge; and that I must pay for the room; the white-whiskered old jade gives no credit. Jehan, for pity's sake, have we drunk up the priest's whole purse? Haven't you a penny left?"

"The consciousness that you have spent the rest of your time well is a good and savoury table-sauce."

"Thunder and blazes! A truce to your nonsense! Tell me, Jehan, you devil! have you any money left? Give it to me, by Heaven! or I will rob you, were you as leprous as Job and as mangy as Cæsar!"

"Sir, the Rue Galiache is a street which runs from the Rue de la Verrerie to the Rue da la Tixeranderie."

"Yes, yes, good friend Jehan, my poor comrade, the Rue Galiache,—that's all right, quite right, but in Heaven's name, come to your senses! I want only a few pence, and my appointment is for seven o'clock."

"Silence all around, and pay attention to my song:

> 'When the rats have eaten every case,
> The king shall be lord of Arras' race.
> When the sea, so deep and wide,
> Is frozen o'er at Saint John's tide,
> Across the ice we then shall see
> The Arras men their city flee.'"

"There, then, scholar of Antichrist, the foul fiend fly away with you!" cried Phœbus; and he gave the tipsy student a violent push, which sent him reeling against the wall, whence he fell gently to the pavement of Philip Augustus. With a remnant of that brotherly compassion which never quite forsakes the heart of a toper, Phœbus rolled Jehan with his foot over upon one of those pillows of the poor which Providence keeps in readiness at every street corner in Paris, and which the rich scornfully stigmatize as dunghills. The captain arranged Jehan's head on an inclined plane of cabbage-stalks, and the student instantly began to snore in a magnificent bass. However, all rancor was not yet dead in the captain's heart. "So much the worse for you if the devil's cart picks you up as it passes!" said he to the poor sleeping scholar; and he went his way.

The man in the cloak, who had not ceased following him, paused for a moment beside the prostrate student, as if uncertain; then, heaving a deep sigh, he also departed in the captain's wake.

Like them, we will leave Jehan to sleep under the friendly watch of the bright stars, and we too will follow them, if it so please the reader.

As he emerged into the Rue Saint-André-des-Arcs, Captain Phœbus discovered that some one was following him. As he accidentally glanced behind him, he saw a kind of shadow creeping behind him along the walls. He stopped, it stopped;

he walked on again, the shadow also walked on. This troubled him but very little. "Pooh!" said he to himself, "I have not a penny about me."

In front of the Collége d'Autun, he came to a halt. It was at this college that he had passed through what he was pleased to call his studies, and from a habit learned in his student days he never passed the statue of Cardinal Pierre Bertrand without stopping to mock at it. He therefore paused before the statue as usual. The street was deserted, save for the shadow approaching slowly,—so slowly that he had ample time to observe that it wore a cloak and a hat. Coming close up to him, it stopped, and stood more motionless than the statue of Cardinal Bertrand itself; but it fastened upon Phœbus a pair of eyes full of that vague light seen at night in the pupil of a cat's eye.

The captain was brave, and would not have cared a farthing for a thief with a bludgeon in his hand; but this walking statue, this petrified man, froze his very blood. At that time there were current in society strange stories of the spectral monk, who prowled the streets of Paris by night. These tales now came confusedly to his mind, and for some moments he stood stupefied; at last he broke the silence with a forced laugh, saying,—

"Sir, if you are a robber, as I hope, you remind me of a heron attacking a nutshell; I am the son of a ruined family, my dear fellow. You've come to the wrong shop; you'd better go next door. In the chapel of that college there is a piece of the true cross set in silver."

The hand of the shadow was stretched from under the cloak, and swooped down upon Phœbus's arm with the grip of an eagle's talons. At the same time the shadow spoke:—

"Captain Phœbus de Châteaupers!"

"What! the devil!" said Phœbus; "do you know my name?"

"I not only know your name," replied the man in the cloak, with his sepulchral voice, "but I know that you have a rendezvous this evening!"

"Yes," answered the astonished Phœbus.

"At seven o'clock."

"In fifteen minutes."

"At La Falourdel's."

"Exactly so."

"The old hag of the Pont Saint-Michel."

"Saint Michel the archangel, as the Pater Noster says."

"Impious wretch!" muttered the spectre. "With a woman?"

"*Confiteor.*"

"Whose name is—"

"Esmeralda," said Phœbus, cheerfully. He had gradually recovered all his unconcern.

At this name the shadow's claws shook the captain's arm furiously.

"Captain Phœbus de Châteaupers, you lie!"

Any one who could at this moment have seen the captain's flaming face, his backward bound, so violent that it released him from the vise-like grasp that held him, the haughty air with which he clapped his hand to his sword-hilt, and the gloomy immobility of the man in the cloak in the presence of this rage,—any one who saw all this would have trembled with fear. It was something like the fight between Don Juan and the statue.

"Christ and Satan!" cried the captain; "that is a word which seldom greets the ears of a Châteaupers! You dare not repeat it!"

"You lie!" said the shadow, coldly.

The captain gnashed his teeth. Spectre monk, phantom, superstitions, all were forgotten at this instant. He saw nothing but a man and an insult.

"Ha! it is well!" he stammered in a voice stifled by rage. He drew his sword; then, stuttering,—for anger makes a man tremble as well as fear, "Here! on the spot! Now then! swords! swords! Blood upon these stones!"

But the other never stirred. When he saw his adversary on his guard, and ready to burst with wrath, he said,—

"Captain Phœbus,"—and his voice quivered with bitterness,—"you forget your rendezvous."

The fits of passion of such men as Phœbus are like boiling milk,—a drop of cold water is enough to check their fury. At these simple words the sword which glittered in the captain's hand was lowered.

"Captain," continued the man, "tomorrow, the day after tomorrow, in a month, in ten years, you will find me ready to cut your throat; but keep your rendezvous first."

"Indeed," said Phœbus, as if trying to compound with his conscience, "a sword and a girl are both charming things to encounter by appointment; but I do not see why I should miss one for the sake of the other, when I might have both."

He replaced his sword in his scabbard.

"Go to your rendezvous," replied the stranger.

"Sir," answered Phœbus with some embarrassment, "many thanks for your courtesy. You are right in saying that tomorrow will be time enough for us to cut slashes and button-holes in Father Adam's doublet. I am obliged to you for allowing me to pass another agreeable quarter of an hour. I did indeed hope to put you to bed in the gutter, and yet be in time for my fair one,—the more so that it is genteel to keep the women waiting a little in such cases. But you look to me like a determined dog, and it is safer to put the party off until tomorrow. I will therefore go to my appointment; it is for seven o'clock, as you know." Here Phœbus scratched his ear. "Ah, by my halidom! I forgot; I have not a penny to pay the toll for the use of the garret, and the old hag must be paid in advance. She won't trust me."

"Here is money to pay her."

Phœbus felt the stranger's cold hand slip a large piece of money into his. He could not help taking the money and squeezing the hand.

"By God!" he exclaimed, "you're a good fellow!"

"One condition," said the man. "Prove to me that I was wrong, and that you spoke the truth. Hide me in some corner where I can see whether this woman be really she whose name you mentioned."

"Oh," answered Phœbus, "with all my heart! We will take

Saint Martha's room; you can look in very easily from the kennel beside it."

"Come on, then!" said the shadow.

"At your service," replied the captain. "I don't know whether or no you are Master Diabolus in *propria persona*: but let us be good friends for tonight; tomorrow I will pay you all my debts, of purse and sword."

They set forth at a rapid pace. In a few moments the sound of the river warned them that they stood on Pont Saint-Michel, then covered with houses.

"I will first get you in," said Phœbus to his companion; "then I will go and fetch my charmer, who was to wait for me near the Petit-Châtelet."

His comrade made no answer; since they had walked side by side he had not said a word. Phœbus stopped before a low door and knocked loudly; a light appeared through the chinks of the door.

"Who is there?" cried a mumbling voice.

"By Saint Luke's face! By God's passion! By the Rood!" answered the captain.

The door opened instantly, and revealed to the new-comers an old woman and an old lamp, both in a very shaky state. The old woman was bent double, dressed in rags; her head shook; she had very small eyes, wore a kerchief on her head, and her hands, face, and neck were covered with wrinkles; her lips retreated under her gums, and she had tufts of white hair all around her mouth, which gave her the demure look of a cat.

The interior of the hovel was as dilapidated as its mistress; there were whitewashed walls, black beams running across the ceiling, a dismantled fireplace, cobwebs in every corner; in the middle of the room stood a rickety collection of tables and chairs; a dirty child played in the ashes; and in the background a staircase, or rather a wooden ladder, led to a trap-door in the ceiling.

On entering this den Phœbus's mysterious companion pulled his cloak up to his eyes. But the captain, swearing all the time like a Turk, hastened "to make the sun flash from a crown-piece," as our all-accomplished Régnier says.

"Saint Martha's room," said he.

The old woman treated him like a lord, and put the coin away in a drawer. It was the money which the man in the black cloak had given Phœbus. While her back was turned, the ragged, disheveled little boy who was playing in the ashes went adroitly to the drawer, took out the crown-piece, and put in its place a dried leaf which he had pulled from a fagot.

The old woman beckoned to the two gentlemen, as she called them, to follow her, and climbed the ladder before them. On reaching the upper floor, she placed her lamp upon a chest; and Phœbus, as one familiar with the house, opened a door leading to a dark hole. "Go in there, my dear boy," said he to his comrade. The man in the cloak obeyed without a word; the door closed behind him; he heard Phœbus bolt it, and a moment after go downstairs again with the old woman. The light had disappeared.

CHAPTER VIII

The Advantage of Windows Overlooking the River

Claude Frollo (for we presume that the reader, more clever than Phœbus, has discovered that this spectral monk was no other than the archdeacon), Claude Frollo groped about for some time in the gloomy hole into which the captain had bolted him. It was one of those nooks such as architects sometimes leave at the junction of the roof and outer wall. The vertical section of this kennel—as Phœbus had so aptly called it—would have formed a triangle. Moreover, there was neither window nor loop-hole, and the pitch of the roof was so steep that it was impossible to stand upright. Claude therefore squatted in the dust and mortar which crumbled beneath him. His head was burning; as he felt about him with his hands, he found upon the ground a bit of broken glass, which he pressed to his forehead, its coolness somewhat refreshing him.

What went on at this moment in the archdeacon's dark soul? God and himself alone knew.

According to what fatal order did he dispose in his thoughts Esmeralda, Phœbus, Jacques Charmolue, his young brother, so greatly loved, deserted by him in the mud, his archdeacon's gown, perhaps his reputation, dragged through the mire of La Falourdel's abode,—all these images, all these adventures? I cannot say; but it is certain that the ideas formed a horrible group in his mind.

He waited a quarter of an hour; he felt as if a century had been added to his age. All at once he heard the boards of the wooden staircase creak; some one was coming up. The trap-door opened; a light appeared. There was a considerable crack in the worm-eaten door of his prison; to this he glued his face. Thus he could see everything that happened in the next room. The cat-faced old woman first rose from the trap-door, lamp in hand; then came Phœbus, twirling his moustache; then a third person,—that lovely, graceful creature, Esmeralda. The priest saw her rise from below like a dazzling apparition. He trembled; a cloud came before his eyes; his veins swelled to bursting; everything swam before him; he saw and heard nothing more.

When he recovered his senses, Phœbus and Esmeralda were alone, seated on the wooden chest beside the lamp, whose light revealed to the archdeacon's eyes their two youthful figures, and a miserable pallet at the back of the garret.

Beside the pallet there was a window, through whose panes, shattered like a cobweb upon which rain has fallen, were seen a patch of sky, and the moon in the distance resting on a bed of soft clouds.

The young girl was blushing and trembling, and confused.

Her long, drooping lashes shaded her flushed cheeks. The officer, to whose face she dared not raise her eyes, was radiant. Mechanically, and with a charming awkwardness, she drew meaningless lines on the bench with her finger-tip, and then looked at her finger. Her feet were hidden, for the little goat was lying upon them.

The captain was very gallantly arrayed; at his wrists and neck he wore embroidery, then considered very elegant.

Dom Claude could scarcely hear what they said, for the throbbing of his temples.

Lovers' talk is very commonplace. It is a perpetual "I love you." A very bare and very insipid phrase to an indifferent ear, unless adorned with a few grace-notes; but Claude was not an indifferent listener.

"Oh," said the girl, without raising her eyes, "do not despise me, my lord Phœbus! I feel that I am doing very wrong."

"Despise you, pretty child!" replied the officer with an air of extreme gallantry,—"despise you! By God's passion! and why?"

"For coming here with you."

"On that point, my beauty, we are not agreed. I should not despise you, but hate you."

The young girl gazed at him in affright. "Hate me! What have I done?"

"For requiring so much urging."

"Alas!" said she, "that is because I am breaking a sacred vow. I shall never find my parents! The amulet will lose its virtue; but what does that matter? Why should I need father or mother now?"

So saying, she fixed upon the captain her large dark eyes, moist with love and joy.

"The Devil take me if I understand you!" exclaimed Phœbus.

Esmeralda was silent for a moment, then a tear fell from her eyes, a sigh from her lips, and she said, "Oh, my lord, I love you!"

There was such an odor of chastity, such a charm of virtue

about the young girl, that Phœbus did not feel wholly at his ease with her. But this speech emboldened him. "You love me!" said he, with transport; and he threw his arm around the gipsy's waist. He had only waited for such an opportunity.

The priest saw him, and tested with the tip of his finger the point of a dagger hidden in his bosom.

"Phœbus," continued the gypsy girl, gently removing the captain's stubborn hands from her girdle, "you are good, you are generous, you are kind; you saved me,—me, who am but a poor gipsy foundling. I have long dreamed of an officer who should save my life. It was of you I dreamed before I ever knew you, my Phœbus; the image of my dreams had a gorgeous uniform like yours, a grand air, a sword. Your name is Phœbus; it is a beautiful name. I love your name; I love your sword. Draw your sword, Phœbus, and let me see it."

"Child!" said the captain; and he unsheathed his rapier with a smile.

The gipsy girl studied the handle, the blade, examined the letters on the hilt with adorable curiosity, and kissed the sword, as she said,—

"You are a brave man's sword. I love my captain."

Phœbus again took advantage of the situation to imprint on her lovely bent neck a kiss which made the girl start up as red as a cherry. The priest ground his teeth in the darkness at the sight.

"Phœbus," resumed the gipsy, "let me talk to you. Walk about a little, so that I may have a good look at you, and hear your spurs jingle. How handsome you are!"

The captain rose to gratify her, while he scolded her with a smile of satisfaction:—

"What a child you are! By the way, my charmer, did you ever see me in my full dress uniform?"

"Alas, no!" she replied.

"Well, that is really fine!"

Phœbus came back and sat down beside her, but much nearer than before.

"Look here, my dear—"

"The gipsy gave him a few little taps on the lips with her pretty hand, with a childish playfulness full of gaiety and grace.

"No, no, I will not listen. Do you love me? I want you to tell me if you love me."

"Do I love you, angel of my life!" cried the captain, half kneeling before her. "My body, my soul, my blood, are yours. I am all yours,—all yours. I love you, and never loved any one but you."

The captain had so often repeated this phrase on many a similar occasion, that he uttered it in a breath, without making a single mistake. At this passionate declaration the gipsy turned towards the dirty ceiling, which took the place of heaven, a look of angelic happiness. "Oh," she murmured, "at such a moment one might well wish to die!"

Phœbus thought "the moment" a good one to steal another kiss, which inflicted fresh torment on the wretched archdeacon in his lair.

"To die?" exclaimed the amorous captain. "What are you talking about, my lovely angel? It is just the time to live, or Jupiter is but a paltry knave! Die at the beginning of such a pleasant thing! By Saint Luke's face, what a joke! that would never do! Listen, my dear Similar—Esmenarda—Forgive me! but you have such a vastly outlandish name that I can never get it straight. I'm forever getting entangled in it."

"Good Heavens!" said the poor girl, "and I thought the name pretty just for its oddness! But if you don't like it, I am quite ready to change it for anything you please."

"Ah, do not cry for such a trifle, my dearest! It's a name to which one has to get used, that's all. Once I have learned it by heart, it will be all right. Now listen, my dear Similar; I adore you passionately. I love you to such a degree that it is really marvelous. I know a little girl who is bursting with rage about it—"

The jealous damsel cut him short: "Who is she?"

"What difference does that make to us?" said Phœbus; "do you love me?"

"Oh!" said she.

"Well, then, that is all that is necessary. You shall see how I love you, too. May the great devil Neptune bestride me if I do not make you the happiest creature in the world. We will have a pretty little room somewhere! I will review my archers under your windows. They are all mounted, and make nothing of Captain Mignon's men. There are spear-men, cross-bowmen, and culverin men. I will take you to see the great Paris musters at the Grange de Rully. It's a very fine sight,— eighty thousand helmeted heads; thirty thousand bright harnesses, coats of mail, or brigandines; sixty-seven banners of the various guilds; the standards of the Parliament, the Chamber of Accounts, the Treasury, the Assistants in the Mint; in fact, the devil's own train! I will take you to see the lions at the king's palace, which are wild beasts; all the women like that."

For some moments the young girl, wrapped in her own delightful thoughts, had been dreaming to the sound of his voice, without heeding the meaning of his words.

"Oh, how happy you will be!" continued the captain; and at the same time he gently unclasped the gipsy's belt.

"What are you doing?" said she, quickly. This act of violence startled her from her reverie.

"Nothing," answered Phœbus; "I was merely saying that you must give up this ridiculous mountebank dress when you come to live with me."

"When I live with you, my Phœbus!" said the young girl, tenderly.

She again became pensive and silent.

The captain, made bold by her gentleness, took her by the waist without any resistance on her part, then began noiselessly to unlace the poor child's bodice, and so disarranged her neckerchief that the panting priest saw the gipsy's lovely shoulder issue from the gauze, plump and brown, like the moon rising through the mists on the horizon.

The young girl let Phœbus have his way. She did not seem conscious of what he was doing. The bold captain's eyes sparkled.

All at once she turned towards him.

"Phœbus," she said, with a look of infinite love, "instruct me in your religion."

"My religion!" cried the captain, bursting into laughter. "I instruct you in my religion! Thunder and guns! What do you want with my religion?"

"To be married to you," she answered.

The captain's face assumed an expression of mingled surprise, scorn, recklessness, and evil passion.

"Nonsense!" said he. "Why should we marry?"

The gipsy turned pale, and let her head sink sadly on her breast.

"My pretty love," tenderly added Phœbus, "what are all these foolish ideas? Marriage is nothing! Is any one less loving for not having spouted a little Latin in some priest's shop?"

So saying in his sweetest voice, he approached extremely near the gipsy girl; his caressing hands had resumed their place around the lithe, slender waist, and his eye kindled more and more, and everything showed that Master Phœbus was about to enjoy one of those moments in which Jupiter himself commits so many follies that the good Homer is obliged to call in a cloud to help him.

But Dom Claude saw all. The door was made of decayed puncheon staves, which left ample room between them for the passage of his hawk-like glance. The brown-skinned, broad-shouldered priest, hitherto condemned to the austere rule of the convent, shuddered and burned at this scene of love, darkness, and passion.

The young and lovely girl, her garments in disorder abandoning herself to this ardent young man, made his veins run molten lead. An extraordinary agitation shook him; his eye sought, with lustful desire, to penetrate beneath all these unfastened pins. Any one who had at this moment seen the face of the unhappy man glued to the worm-eaten bars, might have thought he saw a tiger glaring from his cage at some jackal devouring a gazelle. His pupils glowed like a candle through the cracks of the door.

Suddenly, with a rapid motion, Phœbus removed the gipsy's neckerchief. The poor child, who still sat pale and dreamy, sprang up with a start; she retreated hastily from the enterprising officer, and, glancing at her bare throat and shoulders, red, confused, and dumb with shame, she crossed her lovely arms over her bosom to cover it. But for the flame which mantled her cheeks, any one seeing her thus silent and motionless, might have thought her a statue of Modesty. Her eyes were downcast.

Meantime the captain's action had exposed the mysterious amulet which she wore about her neck.

"What's this?" said he, seizing this pretext to draw nearer to the beautiful creature whom he had alarmed.

"Do not touch it!" replied she, quickly, "it is my protector. It will help me to find my family, if I am still worthy of it. Oh, leave me, Mr. Captain! My mother! my poor mother! Mother, where are you? Help me now! For Heaven's sake, Mr. Phœbus, give me back my neckerchief!"

Phœbus drew back, and said in a cold tone,—

"Oh, young lady! I see very plainly that you do not love me!"

"I do not love him!" exclaimed the unhappy creature, and at the same time she hung upon the captain, whom she drew to a seat by her side. "I not love you, my Phœbus? How can you say so, you wicked man, to break my heart? Oh, come! take me, take everything! Do with me what you will; I am yours. What do I care for the amulet! What is my mother to me now! You are my mother, for I love you! Phœbus, my adored Phœbus, do you see me? It is I, look at me; it is that little girl whom you cannot repulse, who comes,—who comes herself in search of you. My soul, my life, my person, are yours; I am all yours, my captain. No, then, we will not marry; it would trouble you; and what am I? A miserable child of the gutter; while you, my Phœbus, are a gentleman. A fine thing, truly,—a dancing-girl to marry an officer! I was mad. No, Phœbus, no; I will be your mistress, your amusement, your pleasure, when you will; always yours. I am only made for that,—to be soiled, despised, dishonored; but what matter? I shall be loved. I shall be the proudest and happiest of women. And when I grow old or ugly, Phœbus, when I am no longer fit to love you, my lord, you will still suffer me to serve you. Others may embroider your scarves; but I, your servant, will take care of them. You will let me polish your spurs, brush your coat, dust your riding-boots. You will have this much pity for me, my Phœbus, will you not? Meantime, take me! There, Phœbus, all this belongs to you, only love me. We gipsy girls need nothing else,—nothing but air and love."

As she said this, she flung her arms around the officer's neck; she gazed up into his face imploringly, and with a lovely smile through her tears. Her delicate throat rubbed against his cloth doublet with its rough embroideries. She threw herself across his lap, her beautiful body half revealed. The enraptured captain pressed his burning lips to those beautiful brown shoulders. The young girl, her eyes fixed on the ceiling, her head thrown back, shuddered and trembled at his kiss.

All at once above the head of Phœbus she saw another head,—a livid, green, convulsed face, with the look of a soul in torment; beside this face there was a hand which held a dagger. It was the face and the hand of the priest; he had broken open the door, and he was there. Phœbus could not see him. The girl was motionless, frozen, mute, at the frightful apparition, like a dove which chances to raise its head at the instant when the sea-eagle glares into its nest with fiery eyes.

She could not even utter a cry. She saw the dagger descend upon Phœbus and rise again reeking.

"Malediction!" said the captain; and he fell.

She fainted.

As her eyes closed, as all consciousness left her, she fancied she felt a fiery touch upon her lips, a kiss more burning than the torturer's red-hot iron.

When she recovered her senses she was surrounded by the soldiers of the watch, some of whom were just carrying off the captain bathed in his own blood; the priest had vanished;

the window at the back of the room, which opened upon the river, was wide open; some one picked up a cloak which he supposed belonged to the officer, and she heard the soldiers say,—

"She is a sorceress who has stabbed a captain."

BOOK VIII

CHAPTER I

The Crown Piece Changed to a
Dry Leaf

Gringoire and the entire Court of Miracles were in a terrible state of anxiety. Esmeralda had not been heard from for a whole long month, which greatly grieved the Duke of Egypt and his friends the Vagrants; nor did any one know what had become of her goat, which redoubled Gringoire's grief. One night the gipsy girl had disappeared, and since then had given no sign of life. All search for her was vain. Some malicious sham epileptics told Gringoire that they had met her that same evening near the Pont Saint-Michel, walking with an officer; but this husband, after the fashion of Bohemia, was an incredulous philosopher, and besides, he knew better than any one else how chaste his wife was. He had been able to judge what invincible modesty resulted from the two combined virtues of the amulet and the gipsy, and he had made a mathematical calculation of the resistance of that chastity multiplied into itself. He was therefore quite easy on this point.

But he could not explain her disappearance. It was a great grief to him, and he would have grown thin from fretting had such a thing been possible. He had forgotten everything else,—even his literary tastes, even his great work, *"De figuris regularibus et irregularibus,"** which he intended to have

---

*Concerning Regular and Irregular Figures (Latin).

printed with the first money which he might have (for he raved about printing ever since he had seen the *Didascalon* of Hugues de Saint-Victor printed with the celebrated types of Wendelin de Spire).

One day, as he was walking sadly by the Tournelle, he noticed a crowd before one of the doors of the Palace of Justice.

"What's the matter?" he asked a young man who was just coming out.

"I don't know, sir," replied the young man. "I hear that they are trying a woman who murdered a man-at-arms. As it seems that there was witchcraft about it, the bishop and the judge of the Bishop's Court have interfered in the matter; and my brother, who is archdeacon of Josas, spends his entire time here. Now, I wanted to speak to him; but I could not get at him on account of the crowd, which annoys me mightily, for I am in need of money."

"Alas! sir," said Gringoire, "I wish I could lend you some; but if my breeches are full of holes, it is not from the weight of coins."

He dared not tell the young man that he knew his brother the archdeacon, whom he had not revisited since the scene in the church,—a neglect which embarrassed him.

The student went his way, and Gringoire followed the crowd, going up the stairs to the Great Hall. He considered that there was nothing like the sight of a criminal trial to dispel melancholy, the judges being generally most delightfully stupid. The people with whom he had mingled walked on and elbowed one another in silence. After a slow and tiresome progress through a long dark passage which wound through the Palace like the intestinal canal of the ancient edifice, he reached a low door opening into a hall, which his tall figure enabled him to examine over the moving heads of the mob.

The hall was huge and ill-lighted, which made it seem still larger. Evening was coming on; the long-pointed windows admitted but a faint ray of daylight, which faded before it reached the vaulted ceiling,—an enormous lattice-work of carved beams, whose countless figures seemed to move confusedly in the shadow. There were already several lighted candles here and there on the tables, and shining upon the heads of clerks bending over musty papers. The front of the hall was occupied by the crowd; to the right and left there were lawyers in their robes, and tables; in the background, upon a daïs, a number of judges, the last rows of whom were lost in the darkness; their faces were forbidding and unmoved. The walls were plentifully sprinkled with *fleurs-de-lis*. A huge crucifix was dimly visible over the heads of the judges, and everywhere there were pikes and halberds tipped with fire by the light of the candles.

"Sir," asked Gringoire of one of his neighbors, "who are all those people drawn up in line yonder, like prelates in council?"

"Sir," said the neighbor, "those are the councillors of the High Chamber on the right, and the councillors of inquiry on the left,—the referendaries in black gowns, and the masters in scarlet ones."

"Yonder, above them," added Gringoire, "who is that big red-faced fellow in such a perspiration?"

"That is the president."

"And those sheep behind him?" continued Gringoire, who, as we have already said, did not love the magistracy. This was perhaps partly due to the grudge which he had borne the Palace of Justice ever since his dramatic misadventure.

"Those are the masters of requests of the king's household."

"And that boar in front of them?"

"That is the clerk to the Court of Parliament."

"And that crocodile on the right?"

"Master Philippe Lheulier, advocate extraordinary to the king."

"And that big black cat on the left?"

"Master Jacques Charmolue, king's proxy to the Ecclesiastical Court, with the officials."

"Now, then, sir," said Gringoire, "what are all these worthy men doing here?"

"They are trying a case."

"Whom are they trying? I do not see the prisoner."

"It's a woman, sir. You cannot see her. She has her back to us, and is hidden from us by the crowd. Stay; there she is, where you see that group of halberds."

"Who is the woman?" asked Gringoire. "Do you know her name?"

"No, sir; I have only just got here. I merely suppose that there is sorcery in the case, because the judge of the Bishop's Court is present at the trial."

"Well," said our philosopher, "we will see all these men of the gown devour human flesh. It is as good a sight as any other."

"Sir," remarked his neighbor, "doesn't it strike you that Master Jacques Charmolue has a very amiable air?"

"Hum!" replied Gringoire. "I always suspect an amiability with pinched nostrils and thin lips."

Here their neighbors demanded silence from the two chatterers; an important piece of evidence was being heard.

"Gentlemen," said an old woman in the middle of the hall, whose face was so lost in the abundance of her garments that she looked like a walking rag-bag,—"gentlemen, the thing is as true as it is true that my name is La Falourdel, and that I have lived for forty years on the Pont Saint-Michel, paying my rent, lord's dues, and quit-rents punctually; and the door is just opposite the house of Tassin-Caillart the dyer, which is on the side looking up stream; a poor old woman now, a pretty girl once, gentlemen. Some one said to me only a few days ago, 'La Falourdel, don't sit at your wheel and spin too much of an evening; the devil loves to comb old women's distaffs with his horn. It is very certain that the spectre monk who roamed about the Temple last year now haunts the City. La Falourdel, beware lest he knock at your door.' One evening I was spinning at my wheel; there was a knock at the door. I asked who was there. Some one swore roundly. I opened. Two men came in,—one in black, with a handsome officer. I could only see the eyes of the one in black,—two burning coals; all the rest was hat and cloak. This is what they said to me: 'The Saint Martha room.' That is my upstairs room, gentlemen,—my nicest one. They gave me a crown piece. I put the crown in my drawer, and I said, 'That shall be to buy tripe tomorrow at the Gloriette shambles.' We went up. When we got to the upper room, while my back was turned the black man disappeared. This startled me a little. The officer, who was as handsome as any great lord, went downstairs again with me. He left the house. By the time I had spun a quarter of a skein he was back with a lovely young girl,—a puppet who would have shone like the sun if her hair had been well dressed. She had with her a goat,—a big goat. I have forgotten now whether it was black or white. That bothered me. As for the girl, she was none of my business; but the goat! I don't like those animals; they have a beard and horns. They look like men. And then, they savor of sorcery. However, I said nothing. I had the crownpiece. That was right, my lord judge, wasn't it? I took the captain and the girl to the upper room, and I left them alone,—that is, with the goat. I went down and began to spin again. You must know that my house has a ground-floor and a floor above; it overlooks the river at the back, like all the rest of the houses on the bridge, and the window on the ground-floor and the one above both open upon the water. As I say, I was spinning. I don't know how I fell to thinking of the goblin monk, of whom the goat had reminded me; and then, that pretty girl was so queerly rigged out. All at once I heard a scream upstairs, and something fell on the floor, and the window opened. I ran to my window, which is just under it, and I saw a dark mass fall past me into the water. It was a phantom dressed like a priest. It was bright moonlight. I saw as plainly as possible. He swam away towards the City. Then, all in a tremble, I called the watch. Those gentlemen entered, and being somewhat merry, and not knowing what the matter was, they fell to beating me. But I soon explained things to them. We went upstairs, and what did we find? My poor room all stained with blood, the captain stretched out at full length with a dagger in his throat, the girl pretending to be dead, and the goat in a terrible fright. 'Well done!' said I; 'it will take me more than a fortnight to scrub up these boards. I shall have to scrape them; it will be a dreadful piece of work!' They carried off the officer,—poor young man!—and the girl, all disheveled and in disorder. But stay; the worst of all is that next day, when I went to get the crown to buy my tripe, I found a withered leaf in its place."

The old woman paused. A murmur of horror ran round the room.

"The phantom, the goat, and all that, savor of sorcery," said one of Gringoire's neighbors.

"So does that withered leaf!" added another.

"No doubt," continued a third, "the girl was a witch, who was in league with the goblin monk to plunder officers."

Gringoire himself was inclined to consider the whole story both terrible and probable.

"La Falourdel," said the president, majestically, "have you nothing more to tell the court?"

"No, my lord," replied the old woman, "except that in the report my house was called a dirty, rickety hut, which is an outrageous way to talk. The houses on the bridge are not much to look at, because there are so many people there; but all the same even butchers don't scorn to live there, and some of them are rich folks, and married to very neat, handsome women."

The magistrate who had reminded Gringoire of a crocodile now rose.

"Silence!" said he. "I beg you, gentlemen, not to lose sight of the fact that a dagger was found upon the prisoner. La Falourdel, did you bring that leaf into which the crownpiece which the evil spirit gave you was changed?"

"Yes, my lord," replied she; "I found it. Here it is."

An usher handed the dead leaf to the crocodile, who shook his head mournfully, and passed it to the president, who sent it on to the king's proxy to the Ecclesiastical Court; and in this way it went the round of the room.

"It is a birch-leaf," said Master Jacques Charmolue. This was a fresh proof of magic.

A councillor next took up the word.

"Witness, two men went upstairs together in your house. The black man,—whom you first saw disappear, and afterwards swim the Seine in a priest's gown,—and the officer. Which of the two gave you the money?"

The old woman thought for a moment, and said, "It was the officer."

A confused clamor ran through the crowd.

"Ah!" thought Gringoire, "that shakes my conviction."

However, Master Philippe Lheulier, advocate extraordinary to the king, interfered afresh.

"I must remind you, gentlemen, that in his deposition, written at his bedside, the murdered officer, while he declares that he had a vague idea at the instant the man in black accosted him that it might easily be the goblin monk, added that the phantom had urged him to keep his rendezvous with the prisoner; and upon his remarking that he had no money, gave him the crown, which the said officer paid away to La Falourdel. Therefore, the crown was a coin from hell."

This conclusive observation seemed to dispel all the doubts of Gringoire and the other skeptics in the audience.

"Gentlemen, you have the brief," added the king's advocate, sitting down; "you can consult the statement of Phœbus de Châteaupers."

At the sound of this name the prisoner rose; her head appeared above the crowd. The terrified Gringoire recognized Esmeralda.

She was pale; her hair, once so gracefully braided and spangled with sequins, fell about her in disorder; her lips were livid; her hollow eyes were horrible. Alas!

"Phœbus!" said she, wildly, "where is he? Oh, gentlemen, before you kill me, in pity tell me if he still lives!"

"Be silent, woman!" replied the president; "that does not concern us."

"Oh, have mercy! Tell me if he is alive!" she repeated,

clasping her beautiful but emaciated hands; and her chains rattled as she moved.

"Well," said the king's advocate, drily, "he is dying! Are you satisfied?"

The wretched girl fell back upon her seat, voiceless, tearless, white as a waxen image.

The president leaned towards a man standing at his feet, with a golden cap and a black gown, a chain about his neck, and a wand in his hand.

"Usher, bring in the other prisoner."

All eyes were turned upon a small door which opened, and to Gringoire's great dismay a pretty goat, with gilded horns and hoofs, appeared. The dainty creature paused a moment on the threshold, stretching her neck as if, perched on the point of a rock, she had a vast horizon before her. All at once she saw the gipsy girl, and leaping over the table and the head of a clerk with two bounds, she was at her knees; then she curled herself gracefully at the feet of her mistress, imploring a word or a caress; but the prisoner remained motionless, and even poor Djali could not win a look from her.

"Why, but— That is the ugly beast I told you about," said La Falourdel; "and I recognize the pair of them well enough!"

Jacques Charmolue interrupted her.

"If it please you, gentlemen, we will proceed to examine the goat."

Such was indeed the other prisoner. Nothing was simpler at that time than to bring a suit for witchcraft against an animal. Among other details, we find in the provost's accounts for 1466 a curious item of the costs of the trial of Gillet-Soulart and his sow, "executed for their demerits," at Corbeil. Everything is set down,—the cost of the pen in which the sow was imprisoned, the five hundred bundles of short fagots brought from the port of Morsant, the three pints of wine and the bread for the victim's last repast, fraternally shared by the executioner; even the eleven days' feeding and keep of the sow, at eight Paris pence each. Sometimes they went even beyond animals. The capitularies of Charlemagne and Louis the Debonair inflict severe penalties upon those fiery phantoms who take the liberty of appearing in mid-air.

Meantime the king's proxy to the Ecclesiastical Court cried aloud, "If the devil possessing this goat, and which has resisted every exorcism, persist in his evil deeds, if he terrify the court with them, we warn him that we shall be compelled to send him to the gibbet or the stake."

Gringoire was in a cold perspiration. Charmolue took from a table the gipsy girl's tambourine, and presenting it to the goat in a particular way, he asked the creature:

"What time is it?"

The goat looked at him with an intelligent eye, lifted her gilded hoof, and struck seven blows. It was indeed seven o'clock. A movement of terror ran through the crowd.

Gringoire could not restrain himself.

"She is lost!" he cried aloud; "you see that she doesn't know what she is doing."

"Silence among the people at the end of the hall!" said the usher, sharply.

Jacques Charmolue, by the aid of the same maneuvers with the tambourine, made the goat perform various other tricks as to the day of the month, the month of the year, etc., which the reader has already witnessed. And, by an optical illusion common to judicial debates, those same spectators who had perhaps more than once applauded the innocent pranks of Djali in the public streets, were terrified by them within the walls of the Palace of Justice. The goat was clearly the devil.

It was still worse when, the king's proxy having emptied out upon the floor a certain leather bag full of movable letters, which Djali wore about her neck, the goat selected with her foot the separate letters spelling out the fatal name "Phœbus." The spells to which the captain had fallen a victim seemed to be irresistibly demonstrated; and, in all eyes, the gipsy girl—that enchanting dancer who had so often dazzled the passers-by with her grace—was nothing but a horrible witch.

Moreover, she gave no sign of life; neither the pretty pranks of Djali, nor the threats of the magistrates, nor the muttered curses of the audience seemed to reach her ear.

In order to rouse her, an officer was forced to shake her most unmercifully, the president raising his voice solemnly as he said:—

"Girl, you are of the gipsy race, addicted to sorceries. You, with your accomplice, the bewitched goat involved in the charge, did, upon the night of the 29th of March last, murder and stab, in league with the powers of darkness, by the aid of charms and spells, a captain of the king's troops, one Phœbus de Châteaupers. Do you persist in denying this?"

"Horrible!" cried the young girl, hiding her face in her hands. "My Phœbus! oh, this is indeed hell!"

"Do you persist in your denial?" coldly asked the president.

"Certainly I deny it!" said she, in terrible accents; and she rose to her full height, her eyes flashing.

The president continued bluntly:—

"Then how do you explain the facts alleged against you?"

She answered in a broken voice,—

"I have told you already. I do not know. It was a priest,—a priest whom I do not know; an infernal priest who has long pursued me!"

"There it is," said the judge; "the goblin monk."

"Oh, my lords, have pity! I am only a poor girl."

"A gipsy," said the judge.

Master Jacques Charmolue said gently,—

"In view of the prisoner's painful obstinacy, I demand that she be put to the rack."

"Agreed," said the president.

The wretched girl shuddered. Still, she rose at the order of the halberdiers, and walked with quite firm step, preceded by Charmolue and the priests of the Bishop's Court, between two rows of halberds, towards a low door, which suddenly opened and closed behind her, making the unhappy

Gringoire feel as if she had been devoured by some awful monster.

As she disappeared, a plaintive bleat was heard. It was the little goat mourning for her.

The hearing was over. A councillor remarked that the gentlemen were tired, and that it would be a long time for them to wait until the torture was over; and the president replied that a magistrate should be ever ready to sacrifice himself to his duty.

"What a disagreeable, tiresome jade," said an old judge, "to force us to send her to the rack when we have not supped!"

CHAPTER II

Continuation of the Crown Piece
Changed to a Dry Leaf

After going up a few steps and down a few steps in corridors so dark that they were lighted with lamps at midday, Esmeralda, still surrounded by her dismal escort, was pushed by the sergeants of the Palace into a room of forbidding appearance. This room, round in form, occupied the ground-floor of one of those great towers which still rise above the layer of modern structures with which the new Paris has covered the old city. There were no windows in this vault, nor was there any opening save the low entrance closed by a huge iron door. Still, there was no lack of light; a furnace was built in the thickness of the wall; a vast fire had been kindled in it, which filled the vault with its red glow, and robbed a paltry candle, placed in a corner, of all its radiance. The iron grating which served to close the furnace was just now raised, only showing, at the mouth of the flaming chasm against the dark wall, the lower edge of its bars, like a row of sharp black teeth set at regular intervals, which made the furnace look like the mouth of one of those legendary dragons that spit forth fire. By the light which it cast, the prisoner saw, all around the room, terrible instruments whose use she did not understand. In the middle of the room was a leather mattress laid almost flat upon the ground, over which hung a strap with a buckle, attached to a copper ring held by a flat-nosed monster carved on the keystone of the vaulted ceiling. Pincers, nippers, and broad plowshares filled the interior of the furnace, and glowed in a confused white-hot heap upon the living coals. The blood-red light of the furnace illuminated in the entire room nothing but a mass of horrible objects.

This Tartarus was known as "the torture-chamber."

Upon the bed sat carelessly Pierrat Torterue, the sworn torturer. His assistants, two square-faced gnomes with leather aprons and linen breeches, were stirring the iron instruments upon the coals.

In vain the poor girl strove to summon all her courage; as she entered the room a feeling of terror overcame her.

The sergeants of the Bailiff of the Palace ranged themselves on one side, the priests of the Bishop's Court on the other. A clerk, pen, ink, and paper, and a table were in one corner.

Master Jacques Charmolue approached the girl with a very sweet smile, saying, —

"Do you still persist in your denial, my dear child?"

"Yes," replied she in a faint voice.

"In that case," resumed Charmolue, "it will be our very painful duty to question you more urgently than we could wish. Be kind enough to take your seat on that bed. Master Pierrat, make room for the young lady, and close the door."

Pierrat rose with a grunt.

"If I close the door," he muttered, "my fire will go out."

"Very well, my dear fellow," replied Charmolue; "then leave it open."

But Esmeralda still stood. That leather bed, upon which so many wretches had writhed in torment, alarmed her. Terror froze the marrow in her bones; she stood there, stupefied and bewildered. At a sign from Charmolue, the two assistants took hold of her and seated her upon the bed. They did not hurt her; but when they touched her, when the leather touched her, she felt all the blood in her body flow back to her heart. She cast a desperate look around the room. She seemed to see all those monstrous tools of torture, which were to the instruments of every sort which she had hitherto seen, what bats, spiders, and wood-lice are to birds and insects, moving and advancing towards her from every direction, to crawl over her and bite her and pinch her.

"Where is the doctor?" asked Charmolue.

"Here," replied a black gown which she had not noticed before.

She shivered.

"Young lady," resumed the caressing voice of the king's proxy to the Ecclesiastical Court, "for the third time, do you persist in denying those things of which you are accused?"

This time she could only nod her head. Her voice failed her.

"You persist?" said Jacques Charmolue. "Then I am extremely sorry, but I must perform the duty of my office."

"Mr. Proxy," said Pierrat, abruptly, "with what shall we begin?"

Charmolue hesitated a moment, with the doubtful face of a poet in search of a rhyme.

"With the buskin," said he at last.

The unfortunate girl felt herself so wholly forsaken by God and man, that her head fell upon her breast like a lifeless thing destitute of all strength.

The torturer and the doctor approached her together. At the same time the two assistants began to rummage in their hideous arsenal.

At the clink of that frightful heap of iron, the unhappy creature trembled like a dead frog when galvanism is applied to it. "Oh," she murmured in so low a tone that no one heard it, "oh, my Phœbus!" Then she relapsed into her former immobility and marble-like silence. The sight would have wrung any heart save the hearts of judges. She seemed some poor sinning soul questioned by Satan at the scarlet gates of hell. Could it be that this gentle, fair, and fragile creature, a poor grain of millet given over by human justice to be ground in the fearful mills of torture, was the miserable body upon which that frightful array of saws, wheels, and racks was to fasten,—the being whom the rough hands of executioners and pincers were to handle?

But the horny fingers of Pierrat Torterue's assistants had already brutally bared that charming leg and that tiny foot, which had so often amazed the by-standers with their grace and beauty in the streets of Paris.

"'Tis a pity!" growled the torturer, as he looked at the dainty and delicate limb.

Had the archdeacon been present, he would certainly have recalled at this moment his symbol of the spider and the fly. Soon the wretched victim saw, through a cloud which spread before her eyes, the buskin approach; soon she saw her foot, locked between the iron-bound boards, hidden by the hideous machine. Then terror restored her strength.

"Take it off!" she cried frantically; and starting up all disheveled, "Mercy!"

She sprang from the bed to fling herself at the feet of the king's proxy; but her leg was held by the heavy mass of wood and iron, and she sank down upon the buskin, more helpless than a bee with a leaden weight upon its wing.

At a sign from Charmolue she was replaced upon the bed, and two coarse hands bound about her slender waist the strap which hung from the ceiling.

"For the last time, do you confess the facts in the case?" asked Charmolue with his unshaken benevolence.

"I am innocent."

"Then, young lady, how do you explain the circumstances brought against you?"

"Alas! sir, I do not know!"

"Then you deny everything?"

"Everything!"

"Proceed," said Charmolue to Pierrat.

Pierrat turned the handle of the screw-jack, the buskin contracted, and the wretched girl uttered one of those terrible shrieks which defy all orthography in any human language.

"Stop!" said Charmolue to Pierrat. "Do you confess?" said he to the gipsy.

"Everything!" cried the miserable girl. "I confess, I confess! Mercy!"

She had not calculated her strength when she braved the torture. Poor child! her life thus far had been so joyous, so sweet, so smooth, the first pang vanquished her.

"Humanity compels me to tell you," remarked the king's proxy, "that if you confess, you can look for nothing but death."

"I hope so, indeed!" said she. And she fell back upon the leather bed, almost fainting, bent double, suspended by the strap buckled around her waist.

"There, my beauty, hold up a little," said Master Pierrat, lifting her. "You look like the golden sheep which hangs on my Lord of Burgundy's neck."

Jacques Charmolue raised his voice,—

"Clerk, write. Young gipsy girl, you confess your complicity in the love-feasts, revels, and evil practices of hell, with wizards, demons, and witches? Answer!"

"Yes," said she, in so low a voice that it was scarcely more than a whisper.

"You confess that you have seen the ram which Beelzebub reveals in the clouds to summon his followers to the Witches' Sabbath, and which is only seen by sorcerers?"

"Yes."

"You confess that you have worshiped the heads of Bophomet, those abominable idols of the Templars?"

"Yes."

"That you have held constant intercourse with the devil in the shape of a tame goat, included in the trial?"

"Yes."

"And, finally, you acknowledge and confess that, with the help of the foul fiend and the phantom commonly called the goblin monk, on the night of the 29th of March last you did murder and assassinate a certain captain named Phœbus de Châteaupers?"

She raised her large steady eyes to the magistrate's face, and answered as if mechanically, without any effort or convulsion,—

"Yes."

It was plain that she was utterly broken.

"Write, clerk," said Charmolue; and addressing the torturers: "Release the prisoner, and lead her back to the courtroom."

When the prisoner was "unshod," the king's proxy examined her foot, still numb with pain.

"Come!" said he; "there is no great harm done. You screamed in time. You can dance yet, my beauty."

Then he turned to his companions from the Bishop's Court—

"So justice is enlightened at last! That's a comfort, gentlemen! The young lady will bear witness that we have acted with the utmost gentleness."

CHAPTER III

End of the Crown Piece Changed to a Dry Leaf

When she returned to the audience-chamber, pale and limping, she was greeted with a general buzz of pleasure. On the part of the audience, it was caused by that feeling of satisfied impatience which is felt at the theater, at the end of the final intermission, when the curtain rises and the last act begins. On the part of the judges, it came from a prospect of soon supping. The little goat also bleated with joy. She tried to run to meet her mistress, but she was tied to the bench.

Night had now fallen. The candles, whose number had not been increased, cast so little light that the walls of the court-room could not be seen. Shadows wrapped everything in a sort of mist. The apathetic faces of some of the judges could just be distinguished in the gloom. Opposite them, at the extreme end of the long hall, they could make out a vague white patch against the dark background. It was the prisoner.

She had dragged herself painfully to her place. When Charmolue had magisterially installed himself in his, he sat down, then rose, and said, without too great a show of vanity at his success, "The prisoner has confessed everything."

"Gipsy girl," began the president, "have you confessed all your crimes of sorcery, prostitution, and murder committed upon Phœbus de Châteaupers?"

Her heart sank within her, and she sobbed aloud in the darkness.

"Whatever you please," she replied feebly; "but kill me quickly!"

"Sir Proxy to the Ecclesiastical Court," said the president, "the court is ready to hear your requisitions."

Master Charmolue drew forth a tremendous bundle of papers, and began to read, with many gestures, and the exaggerated emphasis common to lawyers, a Latin speech, in which all the evidence produced during the trial was set forth in Ciceronian periphrases, flanked by quotations from Plautus, his favorite comic author. We regret that we cannot present our readers with this remarkable piece of oratory. The speaker delivered it with wonderful effect. Long before he had ended the exordium, the perspiration poured down his face, and his eyes seemed starting from his head.

All at once, in the very middle of a period, he paused, and his glance, usually mild enough and even stupid, became withering.

"Gentlemen," he exclaimed (but in French, for this was not set down in his manuscript), "Satan plays so large a part in this affair, that yonder he stands, listening to our discussions and making a mock of their majesty. Behold!"

As he spoke, he pointed to the little goat, which, seeing Charmolue gesticulate, sincerely thought that it was but right for her to do the same, and sitting up on her haunches, was imitating to the best of her ability, with her fore-feet and her bearded head, the pathetic pantomime of the king's proxy. This was, it may be remembered, one of her best tricks. This incident—this final proof—produced a great effect. The goat's feet were tied together, and the king's proxy resumed the thread of his eloquence.

His speech was very long, but the peroration was admirable. We give the concluding phrase; the reader may imagine Master Charmolue's hoarse voice and frantic gestures:—

"*Ideo, Domni, coram stryga demonstrata, crimine patente, intentione criminis existente, in nomine sanctæ ecclesiæ Nostræ-Dominæ Parisiensis, quæ est in saisina habendi omnimodam altam et bassam justitiam in illa hac intemerata Civitatis insula, tenore præsentium declaramus nos requirere, primo, aliquandam pecuniariam indemnitatem; secundo, amendationem honorabilem ante portalium maximum Nostræ-Dominæ, ecclesiæ cathedralis; tertio, sententiam in virtute cujus ista stryga cum sua capella, seu in trivio vulgariter dicto*

the Grève, *seu in insula exeunte in fluvio se canæ, juxta
pointam jardini regalis, executatæ sint!*"*

He put on his cap and sat down.

"*Eheu!*" said the agonized Gringoire; "*bassa latinitas!*"†

Another man in a black gown, near the prisoner, rose. This
was her lawyer. The judges, being hungry, began to murmur.

"Be brief, Sir Lawyer," said the president.

"Mr. President," replied the lawyer, "the defendant having
confessed her crime, I have but a few words to say to the
bench. It is laid down in the Salic law that 'If a witch have devoured a man, and she be convicted of the crime, she shall
pay a fine of eight thousand farthings, which make two hundred pence in gold.' May it please the court to sentence my
client to pay this fine."

"That law is obsolete," said the king's proxy.

"*Nego*,"‡ replied the lawyer.

"Put it to the vote!" said a councillor; "the crime is clear,
and it is late."

The question was put to the vote without leaving the hall.
The judges nodded assent; they were in haste. Their hooded
heads were uncovered one after the other in the darkness, in
response to the fatal question put to them in a low tone by the
president. The poor prisoner seemed to be looking at them,
but her dim eyes saw nothing.

---

*Therefore, Gentlemen, the witchcraft being proved and the crime
made manifest, as likewise the criminal intention, in the name of the
holy church of Notre-Dame de Paris, which is seized of the right of all
manner of justice high and low, within this inviolate island of the city,
we declare by the tenor of these presents that we require, firstly, a pe-
cuniary compensation; secondly, penance before the great portal of
the cathedral church of Notre-Dame; thirdly, a sentence, by the virtue
of which this witch, with her goat, shall either in the public square,
commonly called the Place de Grève, or in the island stretching out
into the Seine, adjacent to the royal gardens, be executed! (Latin).

†Oh, the monk's Latin! (Latin).

‡Term signifying "I say no!"

The clerk began to write; then he handed the president a lengthy parchment.

The unhappy girl heard a stir among the people, the pikes clashed, and an icy voice said:—

"Gipsy girl, upon such day as it shall please the lord our king, at the hour of noon, you shall be taken in a tumbrel, in your shift, barefoot, a rope around your neck, to the square before the great door of Notre-Dame, and shall there do proper penance, with a wax candle of the weight of two pounds in your hand; and thence you shall be taken to the Place de Grève, where you shall be hanged and strangled on the city gibbet; and likewise this your goat; and you shall pay to the judges of the Bishop's Court three golden lions, in atonement for the crimes by you committed and by you confessed, of sorcery, magic, prostitution, and murder, upon the person of Lord Phœbus de Châteaupers! And may God have mercy on your soul!"

"Oh, it is a dream!" she murmured; and she felt rude hands bear her away.

CHAPTER IV

*Lasciate Ogni Speranza**

I n the Middle Ages, when a building was finished, there was almost as much of it below as above ground. Unless built upon piles, like Notre-Dame, a palace, a fortress, a church, had always a double foundation. In the case of cathedrals, it

---

*Abandon all hope (Italian); this is the inscription on the doors to Hell in *The Divine Comedy* by Dante Alighieri (1265–1321).

was almost like another and subterranean cathedral, low, dark, mysterious, blind and mute, beneath the upper nave, which blazed with light and echoed with the sound of organ and bells day and night; sometimes it was a sepulcher. In palaces and fortresses it was a prison; sometimes, too, a tomb, sometimes a combination of both. These mighty structures, whose mode of formation and slow growth we have explained elsewhere, had not merely foundations, but as it were roots which extended under the earth, branching out into rooms, galleries, staircases, in imitation of the building above. Thus churches, palaces, and fortresses were buried midway in the earth. The cellars of an edifice formed another edifice, into which one descended instead of ascending, and whose subterranean stories were evolved below the pile of upper stories of the monument, like those forests and mountains seen reversed in the mirroring water of a lake beneath the forests and mountains on its shore.

In the Bastille Saint-Antoine, the Palace of Justice at Paris, and the Louvre, these underground structures were prisons. The various stories of these prisons as they sank deeper into the ground became darker and more contracted. They formed so many zones presenting various degrees of horror. Dante could have found no better image of his hell. These tunnel-like dungeons usually ended in a deep hole like a tub, such as Dante chose for the abode of Satan, and where society placed those condemned to death. When once any poor wretch was buried there, he bade farewell to light, air, life, all hope; he never left it save for the gallows or the stake. Sometimes he lay there and rotted. Human justice styled this "forgetting." Between mankind and himself the prisoner felt that a mountain of stones and jailers weighed him down; and the entire prison, the massive fortress, became but a huge complicated lock which shut him off from the living world.

It was in a dungeon-hole of this kind, in one of the oubliettes dug by Saint Louis, the *in pace* of the Tournelle, that

---

*Prison-tomb in which the prisoner is shut up for life.

Esmeralda was placed when condemned to the gallows, doubtless lest she should try to escape, with the colossal Palace of Justice above her head. Poor fly, which could not have stirred the smallest one of the unhewn stones!

Certainly Providence and mankind were equally unjust. Such a lavish display of misery and torment was needless to crush so frail a creature.

There she lay, lost in the darkness, buried, entombed, immured. Whoever had seen her in that state, after having seen her laugh and dance in the sunshine, must have shivered. Cold as night, cold as death, not a breath of air to flutter her hair, not a human sound in her ear, not a ray of daylight in her eyes, bent double, crushed beneath her chains, crouching beside a jug and a loaf of bread, upon a little straw, in the pool of water formed beneath her by the damp oozing of her cell, motionless, nearly breathless, she was almost beyond all sense of suffering. Phœbus, the sun, high noon, the fresh air, the streets of Paris, her dancing always hailed with applause, the sweet prattle of love with the officer; then the priest, the old hag, the dagger, the blood, the torture, and the gallows,—all these things had hovered before her, now like a gay and golden vision, now like a monstrous nightmare; but they were now naught but a vague and horrible struggle lost in the darkness, or like distant music played above, on the earth, and no longer heard in the depths to which the wretched girl had fallen.

Since she had been there she had neither waked nor slept. In her misery, in her dungeon, she could no more distinguish waking from sleeping, a dream from reality, than she could day from night. All was mingled, broken, vague, floating confusedly before her mind. She felt nothing, knew nothing, thought nothing; at best, she only dreamed. Never did living creature pierce so far into the realm of nothingness.

Thus benumbed, frozen, petrified, she had scarcely noted the sound of a trap-door which was twice or thrice opened somewhere above her without even admitting a ray of light, and through which a hand had thrown a crust of black bread.

And yet this was her only remaining means of communication with men,—the periodical visit of the jailer.

One thing only still mechanically caught her ear: over her head the dampness filtered through the moldy stones of the roof, and at regular intervals a drop of water fell. She listened stupidly to the noise made by this drop of water as it dripped into the pool beside her.

This drop of water falling into the pool was the only movement still stirring around her, the only clock which marked the time, the only sound of all the noises made upon the surface of the earth which reached her.

To be exact, she did also feel from time to time, in this sink of mire and gloom, something cold crawling hither and thither over her foot or her arm, and she shuddered.

How long had she been there? She did not know. She remembered a death sentence pronounced somewhere, against some one; then she was borne away, and she waked icy cold, in the midst of night and silence. She had dragged herself about on her hands and knees; then iron rings had cut her ankle, and chains had clanked. She discovered that there was a wall all about her, that there was a tiled floor under her, covered with water, and a bundle of straw; but neither lamp nor ventilator. Then she seated herself upon the straw, and occasionally, for a change of position, on the last step of some stone stairs in her cell.

At one time she tried to count the dark moments measured for her by the drop of water; but soon this sad task of a diseased brain ceased of its own accord, and left her in a stupor.

At last, one day, or one night,—for midnight and noon wore the same hue in this tomb,—she heard above her a noise louder than that usually made by the turnkey when he brought her bread and water. She raised her head, and saw a reddish ray coming through the cracks in the sort of trap-door made in the room of the "*in pace.*"

At the same time the heavy iron creaked, the trap-door grated on its rusty hinges, turned, and she saw a lantern, a hand, and the lower part of the bodies of two men, the door being too low for her to see their heads. The light hurt her so cruelly that she shut her eyes.

When she reopened them, the door was again closed, the lantern was placed on a step of the staircase, a man alone stood before her. A black gown fell to his feet; a cowl of the same color hid his face. Nothing of his person was visible, neither his face nor his hands. He looked like a long black winding-sheet standing bolt upright, under which something seemed to move. She gazed fixedly for some moments at this spectre. Still, neither she nor he spoke. They seemed two statues confronting each other. Two things only seemed to live in the cave,—the wick of the lantern, which crackled from the dampness of the atmosphere, and the drop of water from the ceiling, which interrupted this irregular crackle with its monotonous plash, and made the light of the lantern quiver in concentric rings upon the oily water of the pool.

At last the prisoner broke the silence,—

"Who are you?"

"A priest."

The word, the accent, the sound of his voice, made her tremble.

The priest added in a hollow tone,—

"Are you prepared?"

"For what?"

"To die."

"Oh," said she, "will it be soon?"

"Tomorrow."

Her head, which she had lifted with joy, again sank upon her breast.

"That is a very long time yet!" she murmured; "why did they not make it today?"

"Then you are very unhappy?" asked the priest, after a pause.

"I am very cold," replied she.

She took her feet in her hands,—a common gesture with those wretched people who suffer from cold, and which we have already observed in the recluse of the Tour-Roland,—and her teeth chattered.

The priest seemed to cast his eyes about the cell, from beneath his hood.

"No light! no fire! in the water! It is horrible!"

"Yes," she answered, with the look of surprise which misfortune had imprinted on her face. "Daylight is for every one. Why is it that they give me nothing but night?"

"Do you know," resumed the priest, after a fresh pause, "why you are here?"

"I think I did know once," said she, passing her thin fingers over her brow as if to help her memory, "but I don't know now."

All at once she began to cry like a little child.

"I want to get out, sir. I am cold, I am frightened, and there are creatures which crawl all over me."

"Well, follow me."

So saying, the priest took her by the arm. The unfortunate creature was frozen to the marrow; but still that hand gave her a sensation of cold.

"Oh," she murmured, "it is the icy hand of death. Who are you?"

The priest threw back his hood; she looked. It was that evil face which had so long haunted her; that demon head which had appeared to her at the house of La Falourdel above the adored head of her Phœbus; that eye which she had last seen sparkle beside a dagger.

This apparition, always so fatal to her, and which had thus urged her on from misfortune to misfortune and even to torture, roused her from her torpor. The veil which had clouded her memory seemed rent in twain. Every detail of her mournful adventure, from the night scene at the house of La Falourdel down to her condemnation at the Tournelle, rushed upon her mind at once, not vague and confused as heretofore, but clear, distinct, vivid, living, terrible. The somber figure before her recalled those half-effaced memories almost blotted out by excess of suffering, as the heat of the fire brings back in all their freshness invisible letters traced on white paper with sympathetic ink. She felt as if every wound in her heart were torn open and bled together.

"Ha!" she cried, pressing her hands to her eyes with a convulsive shudder, "it is the priest!"

Then her arms fell listlessly at her side, and she sat with downcast head and eyes, mute and trembling.

The priest gazed at her with the eye of a kite which has long hovered high in the heavens above a poor meadow-lark crouching in the wheat, gradually and silently descending in ever lessening circles, and, suddenly swooping upon his prey like a flash of lightning, grasps it panting in his clutch.

She murmured feebly,—

"Do your work! do your work! strike the last blow!" and her head sank between her shoulders in terror, like that of a lamb awaiting the butcher's axe.

"You look upon me with horror, then?" he asked at length.

She made no answer.

"Do you look on me with horror?" he repeated.

Her lips moved as if she smiled.

"Yes," said she, "the executioner jests with the prisoner. For months he has pursued me, threatened me, terrified me! But for him, my God, how happy I should have been! It is he who hurled me into this gulf of woe! Oh, heavens! it is he who killed,—it is he who killed *him*, my Phœbus!"

Here, bursting into sobs and raising her eyes to the priest, she cried,—

"Oh, wretch! who are you? What have I done to you? Do you hate me so much? Alas! what have you against me?"

"I love you!" exclaimed the priest.

Her tears ceased suddenly; she stared vacantly at him. He had fallen upon his knees, and devoured her face with eyes of flame.

"Do you hear? I love you!" he again exclaimed.

"What love!" said the miserable girl shuddering.

He replied,—

"The love of a damned man."

Both were silent for some moments, oppressed by the intensity of their emotions,—he mad, she stunned.

"Listen," said the priest at last, and a strange calm seemed to have taken possession of him. "You shall know all. I will tell you that which as yet I have hardly ventured to confess to myself, when I secretly questioned my own soul in those dead hours of the night when the darkness is so profound that it seems as if even God could no longer see us. Listen. Before I met you, girl, I was happy."

"And I!" she faintly sighed.

"Do not interrupt me! Yes, I was happy,—at least I thought so. I was pure; my soul was filled with limpid light. No head was held higher or happier than mine. Priests consulted me on chastity, doctors on doctrines. Yes, science was all in all to me; it was a sister,—and a sister was all I asked. Not but that, as I grew older, other ideas came to me. More than once my flesh thrilled as a woman's form passed by. That force of sex and passion which, although in the pride of youth, I had imagined I had stifled forever, more than once has rebelled against the chain of the iron vows which bind me,—wretch that I am!—to the cold stones of the altar. But fasting, prayer, study, and monastic mortifications again made my spirit ruler of my body. And then I shunned women. I had only to open a book, and all the impure vapors of my brain were banished by the glorious sunbeams of science. In a few moments I felt the gross things of earth fly far away, and I was once more calm and serene, bathed in the tranquil light of eternal truth. So long as the demon sent only vague shadows to attack me, passing singly before me, in church, in the streets, or in the fields, and scarcely recurring in my dreams, I conquered him easily. Alas! if the victory be not still mine, God is to blame, who failed to make man and the devil of equal strength. Listen! One day—"

Here the priest paused, and the prisoner heard him utter agonizing sighs.

He continued:—

"One day I was leaning from the window of my cell. What

book was I reading? Oh, all that is confused and vague to me
now. I had been reading. The window looked upon a public
square. I heard the sound of tambourine and music. Vexed at
being thus disturbed in my reverie, I looked out. What I saw
was seen by many others as well, and yet it was not a spectacle for mere mortal eyes. There, in the middle of the pavement,—it was noon, the sun shone brightly,—a creature was
dancing,—a creature so beautiful that God would have preferred her to the Virgin, and chosen her to be his mother, and
would have wished to be born of her, had she existed when he
was made man! Her eyes were black and lustrous; amidst her
black hair certain locks shone in the sun like threads of gold.
Her feet moved so swiftly that they faded from sight like the
spokes of a wheel revolving rapidly. About her head, in her
black braids, there were metallic plates which glittered in the
sun and made a crown of stars above her brow. Her gown,
sprinkled with spangles, scintillated, blue, and sown with a
thousand sparks like a summer night. Her pliant brown arms
waved and twined about her waist like two scarves. Her figure
was of surpassing beauty. Oh, how resplendent was that form
which stood out like something luminous even in the very
light of the sun itself! Alas! girl, it was you. Surprised, intoxicated, charmed, I suffered myself to gaze. I gazed so long that,
all at once, I shuddered with terror. I felt that Fate had overtaken me."

The priest, oppressed, again paused a moment. Then he
resumed:—

"Already half fascinated I tried to lay hold of something
and to stay myself from falling. I recalled the traps which
Satan had already laid for me. The creature before me possessed that superhuman beauty which could only proceed
from heaven or from hell. That was no mere girl made of
common clay, and dimly illumined within by the flickering
rays of a woman's soul. It was an angel,—but of darkness, of
flame, and not of light!

"Just as I was thinking thus, I saw close beside you a goat,
a devilish beast, which looked at me and laughed. The mid-

day sun made its horns seemed tipped with fire. Then I recognized the snare of the demon, and no longer doubted that you came from hell, and that you came for my perdition. I believed it."

Here the priest looked in the prisoner's face, and added coldly:—

"I believe so still. However, the charm worked little by little. Your dance went round and round in my brain; I felt the mysterious spell acting within me. All which should have waked slumbered in my soul, and, like men perishing in the snow, I found pleasure in the approach of this slumber. All at once you began to sing. What could I do, miserable man? Your singing was even more enchanting than your dancing. I strove to escape. Impossible. I was nailed, I was rooted to the spot. It seemed as if the marble of the floor had risen to my knees. I was forced to stay to the end. My feet were ice, my head burned. At last,—perhaps you pitied me,—you ceased to sing; you disappeared. The reflection of the dazzling vision, the echo of the enchanting music gradually faded from my eyes and ears. Then I sank into the corner of the window, stiffer and more helpless than a fallen statue. The vesper bell aroused me. I rose to my feet; I fled; but, alas! something within me had fallen which could never be raised up; something had overtaken me which I could not escape."

He paused once more, and then went on:—

"Yes, from that day forth there was another man within me, whom I did not know. I strove to apply all my remedies,— the cloister, the altar, work, books. Follies, all! Oh, how empty science seems when we beat against it in despair a head filled with frantic passion! Girl, do you know what I always saw between my book and me? You, your shadow, the image of the bright vision which had once passed before me. But that image was no longer of the same color; it was gloomy, funereal, somber as the black circle which long haunts the sight of the imprudent man who looks steadily at the sun.

"Unable to rid myself of it, forever hearing your song ring in my ears, forever seeing your feet dance over my breviary, forever feeling at night, in dreams, your form against mine, I longed to see you once more, to touch you, to know who you were, to see if you were indeed like the ideal image which I had formed of you,—to destroy perhaps my dream by confronting it with the reality. In any case, I hoped that a fresh impression might dispel the first, and the first had become unendurable. I sought you out; I saw you again. Misery! Having seen you twice, I longed to see you a thousand times,—I longed to see you forever. Then,—how may a man stop short upon that steep descent to hell?—then I ceased to be my own master. The other end of the cord which the demon had fastened to my wings was tied to his own foot. I became a wanderer and a vagrant like you. I waited for you beneath porches, I lurked at street corners, I watched you from the top of my tower. Every night I found myself more charmed, more desperate, more bewitched, nearer perdition!

"I had learned who you were,—a gipsy. How could I doubt your magic powers? I hoped that a criminal suit would set me free from your spell. A sorceress once enchanted Bruno d'Ast; he had her burned alive, and was cured. I knew it. I decided to try this remedy. I at first attempted to have you forbidden all access to the square in front of Notre-Dame, hoping that I might forget you if you no longer came thither. You paid no heed to the prohibition; you returned. Then I thought of carrying you off. One night, I tried to do so. There were two of us. We already had you in our grasp, when that miserable officer appeared. He rescued you. He thus began your misfortune, mine, and his own. Finally, not knowing what to do or what would become of me, I denounced you to the judges.

"I thought that I should be cured, like Bruno d'Ast. I also vaguely thought that a criminal trial would make you mine; that in a prison I should have you, should be able to hold you mine; that there you could not escape me; that you had possessed me so long that I might well possess you in my turn. When a man does wrong, he should do all the wrong he can; it is madness to stop half-way in crime! The extremity of guilt has its raptures of joy. A priest and a witch can mingle in delight upon the scanty straw of a cell!

"Accordingly I denounced you. It was then that I terrified you when we met. The plot which I was contriving against you, the storm which I was about to bring upon your head, burst from me in threats and in lightning flashes. And yet I still hesitated. My scheme had terrible sides which made me shrink.

"Perhaps I might have given it up; perhaps my odious thought might have withered in my brain, without bearing fruit. I thought that it would always be in my power to continue or to stay the prosecution; but every evil thought is inexorable, and insists upon becoming a deed. Where I supposed myself all-powerful, Fate was mightier than I. Alas, alas! it is she which captured you and delivered you over to the terrible wheels of the machine which I secretly constructed! Listen. I am near the end.

"One day—again the sun shone bright and warm—I saw a man pass who pronounced your name and laughed, and whose eyes were full of passion. Damnation! I followed him. You know the rest."

He ceased.

The young girl could only utter the words,—

"Oh, my Phœbus!"

"Not that name!" said the priest, seizing her angrily by the arm. "Do not utter that name! Oh, unhappy wretches that we are! it was that name which ruined us! or rather we have ruined each other by the inexplicable caprice of Fate! You suffer, do you not? You are cold, the darkness blinds you, the dungeon wraps you round; but perhaps you have still some ray of light in your innermost soul, were it but your childish love for that empty man who played with your heart, while I have a dungeon within me; within me all is winter, ice, despair; my soul is full of darkness.

"Do you know all that I have suffered? I was present at your trial. I sat upon the bench with the judges. Yes, beneath one of those priests' cowls were the contortions of the damned. When you were brought in, I was there; when you were cross-questioned, I was there. The den of wolves! It was my crime, it was my gibbet which I saw slowly rise above your head. At each witness, each proof, each plea, I was there; I counted your every step on the road of agony; I was there again when that savage beast— Oh, I did not foresee the torture! Listen. I followed you to the torture-chamber. I saw you stripped, and handled half naked by the infamous hands of the executioner. I saw your foot,—that foot upon which I would have given an empire to press a single kiss and die; that foot by which I would with rapture have been crushed,—I saw it enclosed in the horrid buskin which converts the limbs of a living creature into bleeding pulp. Oh, wretched me! As I saw these things, I grasped beneath my sackcloth a dagger, with which I slashed my breast. At the shriek which you uttered, I plunged it deep into my flesh; had you shrieked again, it would have pierced my heart. Look. I think it still bleeds."

He opened his cassock. His breast was indeed torn as if by a tiger's claw, and upon his side was a large, open wound.

The prisoner shrank from him in horror.

"Oh," said the priest, "have pity on me, girl! You think yourself unhappy. Alas! alas! You do not know the meaning of misery. Oh, to love a woman! to be a priest! to be abhorred! to love her with all the strength of your soul; to feel that you would give your blood, your life, your reputation, your salvation, immortality and eternity, this life and the next, for the least of her smiles; to regret that you are not a king, a genius, an emperor, an archangel, a god, to place at her feet a grander slave; to clasp her in your arms night and day, in your dreams and in your thoughts; and then to see her enamored of a soldier's uniform, and to have nothing to offer her but a priest's dirty gown, which would terrify and disgust her; to be present with your jealousy and your rage while she lavishes upon a miserable idiotic braggart the treasures of her love and beauty! To see that body whose form inflames you, that bosom which has so much sweetness, that flesh tremble and blush under the kisses of another! Oh, Heaven! to love her foot, her arm, her shoulder; to think of her blue veins, of her brown skin, until one has writhed whole nights on the floor of one's cell, and to see all the caresses which you have dreamed of bestowing upon her end on the rack; to have succeeded only in stretching her upon the leather bed,—oh, these are indeed tongs heated red-hot in the fires of hell! Oh, happy is he who is sawn asunder between two planks, or torn in quarters by four horses! Do you know what agony he feels through long nights, whose arteries boil, whose heart seems bursting, whose head seems splitting, whose teeth tear his hands,—remorseless tormentors which turn him incessantly, as on a fiery gridiron, over a thought of love, jealousy, and despair! Mercy, girl! One moment's truce! Cast a handful of ashes upon the coals! Wipe away, I conjure you, the big drops of sweat that trickle from my brow! Child, torture me with one hand, but caress me with the other! Have pity, maiden,—have pity upon me!"[15]

"The priest wallowed in the water which lay on the floor, and beat his head against the edge of the stone stairs. The girl listened to him, looked at him.

When he ceased speaking, panting and exhausted, she repeated in a low tone,—

"Oh, my Phœbus!"

The priest dragged himself towards her on his knees.

"I entreat you," he cried; "if you have any feeling, do not repulse me! Oh, I love you! I am a miserable wretch! When you utter that name, unhappy girl, it is as if you ground the very fibers of my heart between your teeth! Have mercy! If you come from hell, I will go there with you.

"I have done everything to that end. The hell where you are will be paradise to me; the sight of you is more blissful than that of God! Oh, speak! Will you not accept me? I should have thought that on the day when a woman could repel such love the very mountains themselves would move! Oh, if you would but consent! Oh, how happy we might be! We would fly,—I would help you to escape.

"We would go somewhere; we would seek out that spot of earth where there was most sunshine, most trees, most blue sky. We would love each other; we would pour our two souls one into the other, and we would thirst inextinguishably each for the other, quenching our thirst forever and together at the inexhaustible cup of love."

She interrupted him with a loud burst of terrible laughter.

"Only look, father! There is blood upon your nails!"

The priest for some moments stood petrified, his eyes fixed on his hands.

"Ah, yes!" he replied at length, with strange gentleness; "insult me, mock me, overwhelm me! But come, come. We must hasten. Tomorrow is the day, I tell you. The gallows in the Place de Grève, you know! It is ever ready. It is horrible,—to see you borne in that tumbrel! Oh, have mercy! I never felt before how much I loved you. Oh, follow me! You shall take your time to love me after I have saved you. You shall hate me, too, as long as you will. But come. Tomorrow! tomorrow! the gallows! your execution! Oh, save yourself! spare me!"

He seized her by the arm; he was frantic; he strove to drag her away.

She fixed her eyes steadily upon him.

"What has become of my Phœbus?"

"Ah!" said the priest, releasing her arm, "you are pitiless!"

"What has become of Phœbus?" she repeated coldly.

"He is dead!" cried the priest.

"Dead!" said she, still motionless and icy; "then why do you talk to me of living?"

He did not listen to her.

"Oh, yes," said he, as if speaking to himself, "he must indeed be dead. The blade entered very deeply. I think I touched his heart with the point. Oh, my very life hung upon that dagger!"

The young girl threw herself upon him like an angry tigress, and pushed him towards the stairs with supernatural strength.

"Begone, monster! begone, assassin! Leave me to die! May the blood of both of us forever stain your brow! Be yours, priest? Never! never! Nothing shall ever unite us,—not even hell! Go, accursed man! never!"

The priest had stumbled to the stairs. He silently freed his feet from the folds of his cassock, took up his lantern, and slowly ascended the steps leading to the door. He reopened the door and went out.

All at once the young girl saw his head reappear; his face wore a frightful expression, and he cried to her with a gasp of rage and despair,—

"I tell you he is dead!"

She fell face downwards on the ground, and no sound was heard in the dungeon save the sighing of the drop of water which rippled the water in the darkness.

CHAPTER V

The Mother

I do not think that there is anything in the world more delightful than the ideas aroused in a mother's heart by the sight of her child's little shoe, especially if it be a best shoe, a Sunday shoe, a christening shoe, a shoe embroidered down to the very sole, a shoe in which the child has never yet taken a step. That shoe is so dainty, so tiny, it is so impossible for it to walk, that it is to the mother as if she saw her child itself. She smiles at it, kisses it, talks to it; she asks it if there can really be so small a foot; and if the child be absent, the pretty shoe is quite enough to bring the sweet and fragile creature before her eyes. She fancies she sees it; she does see it, from head to foot full of life and laughter, with its delicate hands, its round head, its pure lips, its clear eyes, whose very white is blue. If it be winter, it is there; it crawls over the carpet; it laboriously climbs upon a stool, and the mother trembles lest it go too near the fire. If it be summer, it creeps about the court-yard or the garden, pulls up the grass which grows between the paving-stones, gazes innocently and fearlessly at the big dogs and horses, plays with shells and flowers, and makes the gardener scold when he finds sand on his borders and dirt in his paths. All is bright and gay; all is mirth around it like itself, even to the breeze and the sunbeam, which vie with each other in sporting among the light curls of its hair. The shoe shows the mother all this, and makes her heart melt within her like wax before the fire.

But if she has lost her child, these thousand images of bliss, delight, and love which hover around the little shoe become so many horrid visions. The pretty embroidered shoe ceases to be aught but an instrument of torture, forever rending the mother's heart. The same fiber still vibrates,—the deepest and most sensitive fiber; but instead of being caressed by an angel, it is wrenched by a demon.

One morning, as the May sun was rising in a deep-blue sky, such as Garofolo loved to use for the background of his "Descents from the Cross," the recluse of the Tour-Roland heard the noise of wheels, horses' hoofs, and the clink of iron in the Place de Grève. She paid but little heed to it, pulled her hair over her ears to drown it, and again fell to gazing, on her knees, at the inanimate object which she had thus adored for fifteen years. This little shoe, as we have already said, was the entire universe to her. Her every thought was bound up in it, never to be parted until death. The gloomy cavern of the Tour-Roland alone knew how many bitter curses, how many touching lamentations, prayers, and sobs, she had addressed to Heaven on behalf of that dainty pink satin toy. Never was greater despair lavished on a prettier, more graceful object.

On this particular morning it seemed as if her grief burst forth with even greater violence than usual; and those who passed by outside heard her wailing in a loud monotonous tone which pierced their very hearts.

"Oh, my daughter," she moaned, "my daughter! My poor,

dear little child, I shall never see you again, then! It is all over!
It always seems to me as if it were but yesterday that it happened! My God, my God, it would have been better never to
give her to me, if you meant to snatch her from me so soon!
Perhaps you did not know that our children are a part of ourselves, and that a mother who loses her child can no longer believe in God! Ah, wretch that I was, to go out that day! Lord!
Lord! to take her from me thus, you could never have seen me
with her when I warmed her, all rapture, at my fire; when she
laughed at my breast; when I helped her little feet to climb up
my bosom to my lips! Oh, if you had seen all this, my God,
you would have had pity on my joy; you would not have
robbed me of the only love left in my heart! Was I, then, so
miserable a creature, Lord, that you could not look upon me
before you condemned me? Alas! alas! here is the shoe, but
where is the foot; where is the rest; where is the child? My
daughter, my daughter! what have they done with you? Lord,
restore her to me! My knees have been bruised for fifteen years
in praying to you, my God! Will not that suffice? Restore her
to me for a day, an hour, a single instant,—one instant only,
Lord!—and then cast me to the devil for all eternity! Oh, if I
did but know where to find the skirts of your garment, I would
cling to them with both hands until you gave me back my
child! Have you no mercy, when you see her pretty little shoe,
Lord? Can you condemn a poor mother to fifteen years of torment? Kind Virgin, gracious Lady of Heaven! they have taken
away my child-Jesus; they have stolen her; they devoured her
flesh upon the heath, they drank her blood, they gnawed her
bones! Gracious Virgin, have pity upon me! My daughter! I
must have my daughter! What do I care if she is in paradise? I
don't want an angel; I want my child. I am a lioness, roaring
for my cub. Oh, I will writhe upon the ground, I will beat my
forehead against the stones, and I will be forever damned, and
I will curse you, Lord, if you keep my child from me! You see
that my arms are all bitten and torn, Lord! Has the good God
no compassion? Oh, give me nothing but salt and black bread,
but give me back my daughter, and she will warm me like the

sun! Alas! God, my Lord, I am but a vile sinner; but my daughter made me pious. I was full of religion from love of her; and I saw you through her smile as through an opening in the heavens. Oh, if I could only once, once more, just once more, put this shoe on her pretty little rosy foot, I would die, kind Virgin, blessing you! Ah! 'twas fifteen years ago. She would be almost a woman now! Unhappy child! What! then it is indeed true I shall never see her again, not even in heaven, for I shall never go there! Oh, what misery! to think that there is her shoe, and that is all I have left!"

The unhappy woman had flung herself upon the shoe, for so many years her consolation and her despair, and she burst into heartrending sobs as if it were the very day it happened; for to a mother who has lost her child, her loss is ever present. Such grief as that never grows old. The garments of mourning may rust and wear out; the heart remains forever darkened.

At this instant the fresh, gay voices of a band of children were heard outside, passing the cell. Every time that a child met her eye or ear, the poor mother rushed into the blackest corner of her tomb, and seemed trying to bury her head in the stone walls, that she might not hear or see them. But today, on the contrary, she sprang up hastily, and listened eagerly. One of the little boys said,—

"They are going to hang a gipsy girl today."

With the sudden leap of that spider which we saw rush upon a fly when her web quivered, she ran to her window, which looked, as the reader knows, upon the Place de Grève. A ladder was indeed erected close to the permanent gallows, and the hangman's assistant was arranging the chains rusted by the rain. A number of people stood about watching him.

The laughing group of children had already vanished. The recluse looked about for some passer-by, whom she might question. She noticed, close by her cell, a priest, who feigned to be reading the public breviary, but who was far less occupied with the "letters latticed with iron" than with the gibbet, towards which he cast repeated wild and gloomy glances. She recognized him as the archdeacon of Josas, a holy man.

"Father," she asked, "who is to be hanged yonder?"

The priest stared at her, and made no answer; she repeated her question. Then he said, —

"I do not know."

"The children said that it was a gipsy girl," continued the recluse.

"I believe it is," said the priest.

Then Paquette la Chantefleurie burst into a hyena-like laugh.

"Sister," said the archdeacon, "do you hate the gipsies so intensely?"

"Do I hate them!" cried the recluse; "they are witches, child-stealers! They devoured my little girl, my child, my only child! I have no heart now; they ate it!"

She was frightful to look upon. The priest gazed coldly at her.

"There is one whom I hate particularly, and whom I have cursed," she added; "she is young, —about the age that my daughter would have been if her mother had not eaten my girl. Every time that young viper passes my cell, my blood boils!"

"Well, then, sister, rejoice," said the priest, as cold as the statue on a monument; "it is that same girl whose death you are about to witness."

His head fell upon his breast, and he moved slowly away.

The recluse wrung her hands with joy.

"I told her she would mount those steps! Thanks, Sir Priest!" she cried.

And she began to stride up and down behind her barred window, with disheveled hair and flaming eyes, striking her shoulder against the wall as she moved, with the savage air of a caged wolf which has long gone hungry, and knows that feeding-time is at hand.

CHAPTER VI

Three Men's Hearts, Differently Constituted

Phœbus, however, was not dead. Men of his kind are hard to kill. When Master Philippe Lheulier, advocate extraordinary to the king, said to poor Esmeralda, "He is dying," he was either mistaken or joking. When the archdeacon, in pronouncing her sentence, repeated, "He is dead," the fact was that he knew nothing whatever about it, but that he supposed so, he reckoned upon it, had no doubt of it, sincerely hoped it was so. It would have been too much to expect of him, that he should carry good news of his rival to the woman he loved. Any man would have done the same in his place.

Not that Phœbus's wound was not severe, but it was less so than the archdeacon flattered himself. The surgeon, to whose house the soldiers of the watch had at once carried him, had for a week feared for his life, and even told him so in Latin. However, youth triumphed; and, as frequently happens, prognosis and diagnosis to the contrary, Nature amused herself by saving the patient in spite of the doctor. It was while he still lay upon his sick-bed that he underwent the first examination from Philippe Lheulier and the board of inquiry from the Bishop's Court, which annoyed him exceedingly. Accordingly, one fine morning, feeling better, he left his golden spurs in payment of the doctor, and slipped away. This circumstance, moreover, did not at all disturb the legal proceedings. Justice in those days cared little for precision and accuracy in a criminal suit. Provided the prisoner were hanged, that was all that was necessary. Now, the judges had proof enough against Esmeralda. They believed Phœbus to be dead, and that was the end of the matter.

Phœbus, for his part, had not gone far. He simply rejoined

his company, then in garrison at Queue-en-Brie, in the Ile-de-France, a few relays away from Paris.

After all, he had no desire to appear at the trial in person. He had a vague feeling that he should play a ridiculous part in it. In fact, he did not quite know what to think about the matter. Irreligious and superstitious, like most soldiers who are nothing but soldiers, when he questioned himself concerning the affair, he felt somewhat uneasy about the goat, about the strange fashion in which he first met Esmeralda, the no less strange fashion in which she had allowed him to guess her love for him, the fact of her gipsy blood, and lastly the goblin monk. He had a dim idea that there was far more magic than love in the story, that there was probably a witch, perhaps the devil, mixed up in it; it was a very disagreeable farce, or, to use the language of the day, a mystery, in which he played a most awkward part,—that of the butt for cuffs and laughter. He felt quite sheepish about it; he experienced that kind of shame which La Fontaine so admirably defines:—

"Shamefaced as a fox by timid chicken caught."

However, he hoped that the affair would not be noised abroad, and that he being absent, his name would scarcely be mentioned, and in any case would not be known outside the court-room. In this he was not mistaken; for there was no Police Gazette then; and as a week seldom passed but there was some coiner boiled, or witch hanged, or heretic burned, by one of the innumerable justices of Paris, people were so much accustomed to seeing the old feudal Themis at every street corner, with her sleeves tucked up and her arms bare, doing her work at the gibbet, the whipping-post, or the pillory, that they hardly noticed her. The aristocracy of that day scarcely knew the name of the victim who passed them on the street, and at most it was only the mob that regaled itself with this coarse meat. An execution was a common incident in the highways, like the baker's kneading-trough, or the butcher's shambles. The hangman was but a kind of butcher a shade more skillful than the other.

Phœbus accordingly soon set his mind at rest in regard to the enchantress Esmeralda, or Similar, as he called her; to the stab inflicted by the gipsy or the goblin monk (to him it mattered little which); and to the issue of the trial. But no sooner was his heart vacant on that score, than the image of Fleur-de-Lys re-entered it. The heart of Captain Phœbus, like the physics of that time, abhorred a vacuum.

Besides, Queue-en-Brie was a very tedious abode,—a village of farriers, and dairymaids with chapped hands; a long string of huts and hovels bordering the high-road on either side for half a league.

Fleur-de-Lys was his last passion but one,—a pretty girl with a delightful dowry; therefore, one fine morning, completely cured of his wound, and feeling sure that after a lapse of two months the gipsy matter must be past and forgotten, the amorous knight appeared in state at the door of the Gondelaurier house.

He paid no heed to a somewhat numerous crowd which had gathered in the square in front of Notre-Dame; he recollected that it was the month of May; he supposed there was some procession, that it was Pentecost or some other holiday, fastened his horse to the ring at the porch, and went joyously upstairs to see his fair betrothed.

She was alone with her mother.

Fleur-de-Lys ever had upon her mind the scene with the sorceress, her goat, her accursed alphabet, and Phœbus's long absence. Still, when her captain entered, he looked so handsome with his spick-and-span new uniform, his glittering baldric, and his impassioned air, that she blushed for pleasure.

The noble damsel herself was more lovely than ever. Her superb light hair was braided in the most ravishing manner; she was dressed from head to foot in that sky-blue which is so becoming to fair skins,—a piece of coquetry which Colombe had taught her; and her eyes swam in that languor of love which is still more becoming.

Phœbus, who had seen no beauties of any sort since he left the rustic wenches of Queue-en-Brie, was carried away by Fleur-de-Lys, and this lent such cordiality and gallantry to his manner that his peace was soon made. Madame de Gondelaurier herself, still seated maternally in her great armchair, had not the courage to scold him. As for the reproaches of Fleur-de-Lys, they died away in tender cooings.

The young girl sat by the window, still working away at her Neptune's cave. The captain leaned against the back of her chair, and she addressed her affectionate complaints to him in an undertone.

"Where have you been for these two months, you naughty fellow?"

"I swear," replied Phœbus, somewhat embarrassed by the question, "that you are handsome enough to disturb the dreams of an archbishop."

She could not help smiling.

"There, there, sir! Leave my beauty out of the question, and answer me. Fine beauty, indeed!"

"Well, dear cousin, I was sent back to garrison."

"And where, pray? And why didn't you come and take leave of me?"

"At Queue-en-Brie."

Phœbus was enchanted that the first question helped him to evade the second.

"But that is close by, sir. Why did you never come to see us?"

Here Phœbus was seriously embarrassed.

"Why—my duties— And then, fair cousin, I have been ill."

"Ill!" she repeated in alarm.

"Yes,—wounded."

"Wounded!"

The poor child was quite overcome.

"Oh, don't be frightened about that!" said Phœbus, indifferently; "it was nothing. A quarrel, a sword-thrust; why should that trouble you?"

"Why should that trouble me?" cried Fleur-de-Lys, raising her lovely eyes bathed in tears. "Oh, you do not really mean what you say! What was this sword-thrust? I insist upon knowing everything."

"Well, then, my dear, I had a row with Mahé Fédy,—you know whom I mean,—the lieutenant from Saint-Germain-en-Laye; and each of us ripped up a few inches of the other's skin. That's all there is about it."

The lying captain was well aware that an affair of honor always exalts a man in a woman's eyes. In fact, Fleur-de-Lys looked him in the face, quivering with terror, delight, and admiration. Still, she was not completely reassured.

"If you are sure that you are quite cured, dear Phœbus!" said she. "I don't know your Mahé Fédy, but he is a bad man. And what did you quarrel about?"

Here Phœbus, whose imagination was only tolerably active, began to wonder how he was to get out of the scrape.

"Oh, I don't know,—a trifle, a horse, a bit of gossip! Fair cousin," cried he, in order to change the conversation, "what can that noise be in the square?"

He stepped to the window.

"Heavens! fair cousin, what a crowd there is in the square!"

"I don't know," said Fleur-de-Lys, "but I heard that a witch was to do public penance this morning before the church, and to be hanged afterwards."

The captain felt so sure that Esmeralda's affair was well over, that he took very little interest in Fleur-de-Lys' words. Still he asked her one or two questions.

"What is this witch's name?"

"I do not know," replied she.

"And what do they claim that she has done?"

She again shrugged her white shoulders.

"I don't know."

"Oh, my sweet Savior!" said the mother, "there are so many sorcerers nowadays that they burn them, I verily believe, without knowing their names. You might as well try to find out the name of every cloud in the sky. After all, we may rest easy. The good God keeps his list." Here the venerable lady rose, and came to the window. "Good Lord!" said she, "you're right, Phœbus. What a rabble! Bless me! if they haven't climbed upon the house-tops! Do you know, Phœbus, it reminds me of my young days. When King Charles VII entered Paris, there was exactly such a crowd. I've forgotten, now, just what year that was. When I talk to you of such matters, it seems to you like ancient history, doesn't it, while to me it seems quite recent. Oh, that was a much finer-looking crowd than this is! They even hung upon the battlements of the Porte Saint-Antoine. The king had the queen on the crupper behind him, and after their Highnesses came all the ladies riding on the cruppers of all the lords. I remember people laughed well because beside Amanyon de Garlande, who was very short of stature, was my lord Matefelon, a knight of gigantic size, who had killed heaps of Englishmen. It was a splendid sight. A procession of all the gentlemen in France, with their oriflammes blazing in our very eyes. Some bore pennons and some bore banners. How can I tell you who they all were? There was the Lord of Calan, with his pennon; Jean de Châteaumorant with his banner; the Lord of Coucy, with his banner, and a showier one it was, too, than any of the others except that of the Duc de Bourbon. Alas! how sad it is to think that all that has been, and that nothing of it remains!"

The two lovers did not listen to the worthy dowager. Phœbus again leaned on the back of his sweetheart's chair,—a charming position, whence his impudent gaze pierced every opening in Fleur-de-Lys' neckerchief. This neckerchief gaped so opportunely, and permitted him to note so many exquisite things, and to divine so many others, that, dazzled by her skin with its satiny gloss, he said to himself, "How can anybody ever fall in love with any but a fair-skinned woman?"

Both were silent. The young girl occasionally looked up at him with rapture and affection, and their hair mingled in a spring sunbeam.

"Phœbus," suddenly said Fleur-de-Lys in a low voice, "we are to marry in three months; swear to me that you have never loved any other woman but me."

"I swear it, lovely angel!" replied Phœbus, and his passionate gaze combined with the truthful accent of his voice to convince Fleur-de-Lys. Perhaps he even believed himself at that instant.

Meanwhile the good mother, charmed to see the lovers on such excellent terms, had left the room to attend to some domestic detail. Phœbus perceived this, and solitude so emboldened the adventurous captain that his brain soon filled with very strange ideas. Fleur-de-Lys loved him; he was her betrothed; she was alone with him; his former fancy for her revived, not in all its freshness, but in all its ardor. After all, it is no great crime to eat some of your fruit before it is harvested. I know not whether all these thoughts passed through his mind, but certain it is that Fleur-de-Lys was suddenly frightened by the expression of his eyes. She looked about her, and saw that her mother had gone.

"Heavens!" said she, blushing and confused, "how warm I feel!"

"Indeed, I think," said Phœbus, "that it must be almost noon. The sun is very annoying; I had better close the curtains."

"No, no," cried the poor girl; "on the contrary, I want air."

And like a deer which feels the hot breath of the pack, she rose, ran to the window, opened it, and rushed out upon the balcony.

Phœbus, vexed enough, followed her.

The square before the cathedral of Notre-Dame, upon which, as we know, the balcony looked, at this moment offered a strange and painful spectacle, which quickly changed the nature of the timid Fleur-de-Lys' fright.

A vast throng, which overflowed into all the adjacent streets, completely blocked the square. The little wall, breast-high, which surrounded the central part, known as the Parvis, would not have sufficed to keep it clear if it had not been reinforced

by a thick hedge of sergeants of the Onze-Vingts and arquebusiers, culverin in hand. Thanks to this thicket of pikes and
arquebusiers, it remained empty. The entrance was guarded
by a body of halberdiers bearing the bishop's arms. The wide
church-doors were closed, in odd contrast to the countless
windows overlooking the square, which, open up to the very
gables, revealed thousands of heads heaped one upon the
other almost like the piles of cannon-balls in an artillery park.

The surface of this mob was grey, dirty, and foul. The spectacle which it was awaiting was evidently one of those which
have the privilege of extracting and collecting all that is most
unclean in the population. Nothing could be more hideous
than the noise which arose from that swarm of soiled caps and
filthy headgear. In that crowd there was more laughter than
shouting; there were more women than men.

Now and then some sharp, shrill voice pierced the general
uproar.

* * * * * * * * * * *

"Hollo! Mahiet Baliffre. Will she be hung yonder?"

"Fool! that is where she's to do penance in her shift. The
priest will spit a little Latin at her. It's always done here at
noon. If you are looking for the gallows, you must go to the
Place de Grève."

"I'll go afterwards."

* * * * * * * * * * *

"I say, Boucanbry, is it true that she has refused a confessor?"

"So it seems, Bechaigne."

"Look at that, the heathen!"

* * * * * * * * * * *

"Sir, it is the custom. The Palace bailiff is bound to deliver
over the malefactor, sentence having been pronounced, for
execution, if it be one of the laity, to the provost of Paris; if it
be a scholar, to the judges of the Bishop's Court."

"I thank you, sir."

* * * * * * * * * * *

"Oh, Heavens!" said Fleur-de-Lys, "the poor creature!"

The thought of the unfortunate victim filled with sadness the glance which she cast upon the crowd. The captain, far more absorbed in her than in that collection of rabble, amorously fingered her girdle from behind. She turned with the smiling entreaty, —

"For pity's sake, let me alone, Phœbus! If my mother returned, she would see your hand!"

At this instant the clock of Notre-Dame slowly struck twelve. A murmur of satisfaction burst from the crowd. The last vibration of the twelfth stroke had scarcely died away, when the sea of heads tossed like the waves on a windy day, and a vast shout rose from the street, the windows, and the roofs: —

"There she is!"

Fleur-de-Lys covered her eyes with her hands that she might not see.

"My charmer," said Phœbus, "will you go in?"

"No," replied she; and those eyes which she had closed from fear she opened again from curiosity.

A tumbrel, drawn by a strong Norman cart-horse, and entirely surrounded by cavalry in violet livery with white crosses, had just entered the square from the Rue Saint Pierre aux Bœufs. The officers of the watch made a passage for it through the people with lusty blows of their whips. Beside the tumbrel rode a number of officers of justice and of police who might be known by their black dress and their awkward seat in the saddle. Master Jacques Charmolue paraded at their head. In the fatal wagon sat a young girl, her arms bound behind her, and no priest at her side. She was in her shift; her long black locks (it was the fashion then not to cut them until the foot of the gibbet was reached) fell upon her breast and over her half-naked shoulders.

Through this floating hair, glossier than the raven's wing, a rough grey cord was twisted and knotted, chafing her delicate skin, and winding about the poor girl's graceful neck like an earthworm around a flower. Beneath this rope glittered a tiny amulet ornamented with green glass beads, which she had doubtless been allowed to keep, because nothing is refused to those about to die. The spectators posted at the windows could see at the bottom of the tumbrel her bare legs, which she tried to hide under her, as if by a last feminine instinct. At her feet was a little goat, also bound. The prisoner held in her teeth her shift, which was not securely fastened.

Even in her misery she seemed to suffer at being thus exposed almost naked to the public gaze. Alas! it is not for such tremors that modesty is made.

"Only see, fair cousin," said Fleur-de-Lys quickly to the captain, "it is that wicked gipsy girl with the goat."

So saying, she turned to Phœbus. His eyes were fixed upon the tumbrel. He was very pale.

"What gipsy girl with the goat?" he stammered.

"Why, Phœbus!" rejoined Fleur-de-Lys; "don't you remember—"

Phœbus interrupted her:—

"I don't know what you mean."

He took a step to re-enter; but Fleur-de-Lys, whose jealousy, already so deeply stirred by this same gipsy, was again revived, cast a suspicious and penetrating look at him. She now vaguely recalled having heard that there was a captain concerned in the trial of this sorceress.

"What ails you?" said she to Phœbus; "one would think that this woman had disturbed you."

Phœbus tried to sneer.

"Me! Not the least in the world! Me, indeed!"

"Then stay," returned she, imperiously; "let us see it out."

The luckless captain was forced to remain. He was somewhat reassured when he found that the prisoner did not raise her eyes from the bottom of her tumbrel. It was but too truly Esmeralda. Upon this last round of the ladder of opprobrium and misfortune she was still beautiful; her large black eyes looked larger than ever from the thinness of her cheeks; her livid profile was pure and sublime. She resembled her former self as one of Masaccio's Virgins resembles a Virgin by Raphael,—feebler, thinner, weaker.

Moreover, her whole being was tossed hither and thither,

and save for her sense of modesty, she had abandoned everything, so utterly was she crushed by stupor and despair. Her
body rebounded with every jolt of the cart, like some shattered, lifeless thing. A tear still lingered in her eye, but it was
motionless, and, as it were, frozen.

Meantime the mournful cavalcade had traversed the crowd
amid shouts of joy and curious stares. Still, we must confess, as
faithful historians, that many, even the hardest hearted, were
moved to pity at the sight of so much beauty and so much misery.

The tumbrel had entered the Parvis.

Before the central door it stopped. The escort was drawn
up in line on either side. The mob was hushed, and amidst
this solemn, anxious silence the two leaves of the great door
moved, as if spontaneously, upon their creaking hinges. Then
the entire length of the deep, dark church was seen, hung
with black, faintly lighted by a few glimmering tapers upon
the high altar, and opening like the jaws of some cavern in the
middle of the square, dazzling with light. At the very end, in
the shadows of the chancel, a huge silver cross was dimly visible, standing out in relief against a black cloth which hung
from the roof to the floor. The whole nave was empty; but
heads of priests were seen moving confusedly among the distant choir-stalls, and, at the moment that the great door was
thrown open, a loud, solemn, and monotonous chant proceeded from the church, casting fragments of dismal psalms,
like gusts of wind, upon the prisoner's head: —

"*Non timebo millia populi circumdantis me: exsurge,
Domine; salvum me fac, Deus!*

"*Salvum me fac, Deus, quoniam intraverunt aquæ usque ad
animam meam.*

"*Infixus sum in limo profundi; et non est substantia.*"*

---

*I shall not fear though thousands compass me about; arise, Lord,
and save me!

Save me, O Lord, for the waters have overwhelmed my very soul.

I am caught in deep mire, and my goods are gone from me
(Latin).

At the same time another voice, apart from the choir, intoned from the steps of the high altar this mournful offertory: —

"*Qui verbum meum audit, et credit ei qui misit me, habet vitam, æternam et in judicium non venit; sed transit a morte in vitam.*"*

This chant, sung afar off by a few old men lost in the darkness, over that beautiful being full of life and youth, caressed by the warm air of spring, bathed in sunshine, was a part of the mass for the dead.

The people listened quietly.

The wretched victim, in her terror, seemed to lose all power of sight and thought in the dark interior of the church. Her pale lips moved as if in prayer, and when the hangman's assistant approached to help her down from the cart, he heard her murmur in an undertone the word "Phœbus."

Her hands were untied, and she alighted, accompanied by her goat, which was also unbound, and which bleated with delight at regaining its freedom; and she was then led barefooted over the hard pavement to the foot of the steps leading to the porch. The cord about her neck trailed behind her, like a serpent pursuing her.

Then the chanting in the church ceased. A great gold cross and a file of tapers began to move in the gloom; the halberds of the beadles in their motley dress clashed against the floor; and a few moments later a long procession of priests in chasubles and deacons in dalmatics marched solemnly towards the prisoner, singing psalms as they came. But her eyes were fixed upon him who walked at their head, immediately after the cross-bearer.

"Oh," she whispered shudderingly, "there he is again! the priest!"

---

*Whoso heareth my words, and believeth in Him that sent me, He shall have everlasting life, and does not come to judgment, but passes from death to life (Latin).

It was indeed the archdeacon. On his left was the assistant precentor, and on his right the precentor himself, armed with the wand of his office. He advanced, with head thrown back, eyes fixed and opened wide, chanting in a loud voice:—

"*De ventre inferi clamavi, et exaudisti vocem meam.*

"*Et projecisti me in profundum in corde maris, et flumen circumdedit me.*"*

When he appeared in full daylight under the lofty pointed arch of the portal, wrapped in a vast cope of cloth of silver embroidered with a black cross, he was so pale that more than one of the crowd thought that he must be one of those marble bishops kneeling upon the monuments in the choir, who had risen and come forth to receive on the threshold of the tomb her who was about to die.

She, no less pale and no less rigid, hardly noticed that a heavy lighted taper of yellow wax had been placed in her hand; she did not hear the shrill voice of the clerk reading the fatal lines of the penance; when she was told to answer "Amen," she answered "Amen." Nor was she restored to any slight sense of life and strength until she saw the priest sign to her jailers to retire, and himself advance alone towards her.

Then the blood boiled in her veins, and a lingering spark of indignation was rekindled in that already numb, cold soul.

The archdeacon approached her slowly; even in this extremity she saw him gaze upon her nakedness with eyes glittering with passion, jealousy, and desire. Then he said to her aloud, "Young girl, have you asked God to pardon your faults and failings?"

He bent to her ear and added (the spectators supposed that he was receiving her last confession). "Will you be mine? I can save you even yet!"

---

*I called from the deep and Thou heardest my voice.

Thou did plunge me into the deep, in the heart of the sea, and the floods surrounded me (Latin).

She gazed steadily at him: "Begone, demon! or I will denounce you!"

He smiled a horrible smile. "No one will believe you; you would only add a scandal to a crime. Answer quickly! Will you be mine?"

"What have you done with my Phœbus?"

"He is dead!" said the priest.

At this moment the miserable archdeacon raised his head mechanically, and saw at the opposite end of the square, upon the balcony of the Gondelaurier house, the captain standing beside Fleur-de-Lys. He staggered, passed his hand over his eyes, looked again, murmured a curse, and all his features were violently convulsed.

"So be it! die yourself!" he muttered. "No one else shall possess you."

Then, raising his hand above the gipsy girl's head, he exclaimed in funereal tones, "*I nunc, anima anceps, et sit tibi Deus misericors!*"*

This was the awful formula with which these somber ceremonies were wont to close. It was the signal agreed upon between the priest and the executioner.

The people knelt.

"Kyrie, eleison," said the priests beneath the arch of the portal.

"Kyrie, eleison," repeated the multitude with a noise which rose above their heads like the roar of a tempestuous sea.

"Amen," said the archdeacon.

He turned his back upon the prisoner, his head again fell upon his breast, his hands were crossed, he rejoined his train of priests, and a moment later he disappeared, with cross, candles, and copes, beneath the dim arches of the cathedral, and his sonorous voice faded slowly down the choir, chanting these words of despair:

---

*Go, wavering soul! And may God be merciful unto thee! (Latin).

"*Omnes gurgites tui et fluctus tui super me transierunt!*" *

At the same time the intermittent echo of the iron-bound shaft of the beadles' halberds, dying away by degrees between the columns of the nave, seemed like the hammer of a clock sounding the prisoner's final hour.

Meantime the doors of Notre-Dame remained open, revealing the church, empty, desolate, clad in mourning, silent and unlighted.

The prisoner stood motionless in her place, awaiting her doom. One of the vergers was obliged to warn Master Charmolue, who during this scene had been studying the bas-relief upon the great porch, which represents, according to some, the Sacrifice of Abraham; according to others, the great Alchemical Operation, the sun being typified by the angel, the fire by the fagot, and the operator by Abraham.

He was with some difficulty withdrawn from this contemplation; but at last he turned, and at a sign from him, two men clad in yellow, the executioner's aids, approached the gipsy girl to refasten her hands.

The unhappy creature, as she was about to remount the fatal tumbrel and advance on her last journey, was perhaps seized by some poignant regret for the life she was so soon to lose. She raised her dry and fevered eyes to heaven, to the sun, to the silvery clouds here and there intersected by squares and triangles of azure; then she cast them down around her, upon the ground, the crowd, the houses. All at once, while the men in yellow were binding her elbows, she uttered a terrible shriek,—a shriek of joy. Upon yonder balcony, there, at the corner of the square, she had just seen him, her lover, her lord, Phœbus, the other apparition of her life.

The judge had lied! the priest had lied! It was indeed he, she could not doubt it; he was there, handsome, living, clad

---

*All thy whirlpools, O Lord, and all Thy waves, have gone over me (Latin).

in his splendid uniform, the plume upon his head, his sword at his side!

"Phœbus!" she cried; "my Phœbus!"

And she strove to stretch out her arms quivering with love and rapture; but they were bound.

Then she saw the captain frown, a lovely young girl who leaned upon him look at him with scornful lip and angry eyes; then Phœbus uttered a few words which did not reach her, and both vanished hastily through the window of the balcony, which was closed behind them.

"Phœbus," she cried in despair, "do you believe this thing?"

A monstrous idea had dawned upon her. She remembered that she had been condemned for the murder of Captain Phœbus de Châteaupers.

She had borne everything until now. But this last blow was too severe. She fell senseless upon the pavement.

"Come," said Charmolue, "lift her into the tumbrel, and let us make an end of it!"

No one had observed, in the gallery of statues of the kings carved just above the pointed arches of the porch, a strange spectator who had until now watched all that happened with such impassivity, with so outstretched a neck, so deformed a visage, that, had it not been for his party-colored red and violet garb, he might have passed for one of those stone monsters through whose jaws the long cathedral gutters have for six centuries past disgorged themselves. This spectator had lost nothing that had passed since noon before the doors of Notre-Dame. And at the very beginning, unseen by any one, he had firmly attached to one of the small columns of the gallery a strong knotted rope, the end of which trailed upon the ground below. This done, he began to look about him quietly, and to whistle from time to time when a blackbird flew by him.

All at once, just as the hangman's assistants were preparing to execute Charmolue's phlegmatic order, he bestrode the balustrade of the gallery, seized the rope with his feet, knees, and hands; then he slid down the façade as a drop of rain glides down a window-pane, rushed towards the two executioners with the rapidity of a cat falling from a roof, flung them to the ground with his two huge fists, seized the gipsy girl in one hand, as a child might a doll, and with one bound was in the church, holding her above his head, and shouting in a tremendous voice,—

"Sanctuary!"

All this was done with such speed that had it been night, one flash of lightning would have sufficed to see it all.

"Sanctuary! sanctuary!" repeated the mob; and the clapping of ten thousand hands made Quasimodo's single eye flash with pride and pleasure.

This shock restored the prisoner to her senses. She raised her eyelids, looked at Quasimodo, then closed them suddenly, as if alarmed by her savior.

Charmolue stood stupefied, and the hangman and all the escort did the same. In fact, within the precincts of Notre-Dame the prisoner was secure; the cathedral was a sure place of refuge; all human justice died upon its threshold.

Quasimodo had paused beneath the great portal, his broad feet seeming as firmly rooted to the pavement of the church as the heavy Roman pillars. His big bushy head was buried between his shoulders like the head of a lion which also has a mane and no neck. He held the young girl, trembling from head to foot, suspended in his horny hands like a white drapery; but he carried her as carefully as if he feared he should break or injure her. He seemed to feel that she was a delicate, exquisite, precious thing, made for other hands than his. At times he looked as if he dared not touch her, even with his breath. Then, all at once, he pressed her close in his arms, upon his angular bosom, as his treasure, his only wealth, as her mother might have done. His gnome-like eye, resting upon her, flooded her with tenderness, grief, and pity, and was suddenly lifted, flashing fire. Then the women laughed and wept, the mob stamped with enthusiasm, for at that instant Quasimodo was truly beautiful. He was beautiful,—he, that orphan, that foundling, that outcast; he felt himself to be august and strong; he confronted that society from which he was banished, and with whose decrees he had so powerfully interfered, that human justice from which he had wrested its prey, all those tigers with empty jaws, those myrmidons, those judges, those executioners, all that royal will which he had crushed, he,—the lowliest of creatures, with the strength of God.[16]

Then, too, how touching was the protection extended by so deformed a creature to one so unfortunate as the girl condemned to die, and saved by Quasimodo! It was the two extreme miseries of Nature and society meeting and mutually aiding each other.

However, after a few moments of triumph, Quasimodo plunged abruptly into the church with his burden. The people, lovers of all prowess, followed him with their eyes, regretting that he had so soon withdrawn from their plaudits. All at once he reappeared at one end of the gallery of the kings of France; he ran along it like a madman, holding his conquest aloft, and shouting, "Sanctuary!" The crowd broke into fresh applause. The gallery traversed, he again rushed into the interior of the church. A moment after, he reappeared upon the upper platform, the gipsy still in his arms, still running frantically, still shouting, "Sanctuary!" and the mob applauded. At last he appeared for the third time upon the summit of the tower of the big bell; from thence he seemed with pride to show the whole city her whom he had saved, and his thundering voice—that voice so rarely heard by any one, and never by himself—repeated thrice, with frenzy that pierced the very clouds: "Sanctuary! Sanctuary! Sanctuary!"

"Noël! Noël!" cried the people in their turn; and that vast shout was heard with amazement by the throng in the Place de Grève on the other bank of the river, and by the recluse, who still waited, her eyes riveted to the gallows.

BOOK IX

CHAPTER I

Delirium

Claude Frollo was no longer in Notre-Dame when his adopted son so abruptly cut the fatal knot in which the wretched archdeacon had caught the gipsy and was himself caught. Returning to the sacristy, he had snatched off his alb, cope, and stole, flung them all into the hands of the amazed sacristan, fled through the private door of the cloisters, ordered a boatman of the Terrain to set him over to the left bank of the Seine, and plunged in among the hilly streets of the University, not knowing whither he went, meeting at every turn bands of men and women hastening gaily towards the Pont Saint-Michel in the hope that they might yet be in time to see the witch hanged,—pale, haggard, more bewildered, blinder, and fiercer than a night-bird let loose in broad daylight and pursued by a troop of boys. He no longer knew where he was, what he did, whether he was dreaming or awake. He went on, he walked, he ran, taking any street at haphazard, but still urged forward by the Place de Grève, the horrible Place de Grève, which he vaguely felt behind him

In this way he passed the Montagne Sainte-Geneviève, and finally left the town by the Porte Saint-Victor. He continued to flee as long as he could see, on turning, the ring of towers around the University, and the scattered houses of the suburb; but when at last a ridge completely hid that odious Paris, when he could imagine himself a hundred leagues away in the fields, in a desert, he paused, and it seemed as if he breathed again.

Then frightful thoughts crowded upon him. Once more he saw into his soul as clear as day, and he shuddered at the sight. He thought of the unhappy girl who had destroyed him, and whom he had destroyed. He cast a despairing glance at the doubly-crooked path along which Fate had led their destinies, up to the meeting-point where it had pitilessly dashed them against each other. He thought of the folly of eternal vows, of the vanity of chastity, science, religion, virtue, and the uselessness of God. He indulged in evil thoughts to his heart's content, and as he yielded to them he felt himself giving way to Satanic laughter.

And as he thus searched his soul, when he saw how large a space Nature had reserved therein for the passions, he sneered more bitterly still. He stirred up all the hatred and malice from the very depths of his heart; and he recognized, with the cold gaze of a physician studying his patient, that this malice was nothing but love perverted; that love, the source of all virtue in man, turned to horrible things in the heart of a priest, and that a man formed like him, when he became a priest became a demon. Then he laughed fearfully, and all at once he again turned pale, as he considered the most forbidding side of his fatal passion,—of that corrosive, venomous, malignant, implacable love which led but to the gallows for one, to hell for the other: she condemned, he damned.

And then he laughed anew as he reflected that Phœbus was alive; that after all the captain lived, was light-hearted and content, had finer uniforms than ever, a new sweetheart whom he brought to see the old one hanged. His sneers were redoubled when he reflected that, of all the living beings whose death he had desired, the gipsy girl, the only creature whom he did not hate, was the only one who had not escaped him.

Then from the captain his mind wandered to the mob, and he was overcome with jealousy of an unheard-of kind. He thought that the mob, too, the entire mob, had had before their eyes the woman whom he loved, in her shift, almost naked. He writhed as he thought that this woman, whose form, half seen by him alone in darkness would have afforded him supreme delight, had been exposed in broad daylight at high noon to an entire multitude clad as for a night of pleasure. He wept with rage over all those mysteries of love profaned, soiled, exposed, withered forever. He wept with rage, picturing to himself the foul eyes which had reveled in that scanty covering; and that that lovely girl, that virgin lily, that cup of modesty and delight, to which he dared not place his lips without trembling, had been made common property, a vessel from which the vilest rabble of Paris, thieves, beggars, and lackeys, had come to quaff together a shameless, impure, and depraved pleasure.

And when he strove to picture the bliss which he might have found upon earth if she had not been a gipsy and he had not been a priest, if Phœbus had never lived, and if she had loved him; when he imagined the life of peace and love which might have been possible for him also; when he thought that there were even at that very instant here and there on the earth happy couples lost in long talks beneath orange-trees, on the border of streams, beneath a setting sun or a starry heaven; and that, had God so willed, he might have formed with her one of those blest couples, his heart melted within him in tenderness and despair.

Oh, she! it is she! She,—the one idea which returned ever and again, torturing him, turning his brain, gnawing his vitals. He regretted nothing, repented nothing; all that he had done he was ready to do again; he preferred to see her in the hangman's hands rather than in the captain's arms. But he suffered; he suffered so intensely that at times he tore out his hair by handfuls, to see if it had not turned white with anguish.

There was one moment among the rest when it occurred to him that this was possibly the minute when the hideous chain which he had seen that morning was drawing its iron noose closer and ever closer around that slender, graceful neck. This idea made the perspiration start from every pore.

There was another moment when, while laughing devil-
ishly at himself, he pictured at one and the same time Esmeralda as he had first seen her,—alert, heedless, happy, gaily
dressed, dancing, winged, and harmonious,—and Esmeralda
as he had last seen her, in her shift, with the rope about her
neck, slowly approaching with her bare feet the cruel gallows;
and this double picture was so vivid that he uttered a terrible
cry.

While this whirlwind of despair overwhelmed, crushed,
broke, bent, and uprooted everything in his soul, he considered the scene around him. At his feet some hens were peck-
ing and scratching among the bushes, enameled beetles
crawled in the sun; above his head, groups of dappled grey
clouds sailed over the blue sky; in the horizon, the spire of the
Abbey of Saint-Victor cut the curve of the hill with its slated
obelisk; and the miller of the Butte-Copeaux whistled as he
watched the busy wheels of his mill go round. All this active,
industrious, tranquil life, reproduced around him in a thousand forms, hurt him. He again tried to escape.

Thus he ran through the fields until nightfall. This flight
from Nature, life, himself, man, God, everything, lasted the
entire day. Sometimes he threw himself face downwards
upon the earth, and tore up the young corn with his nails:
sometimes he paused in some deserted village street; and his
thoughts were so unendurable that he seized his head in both
hands and tried to snatch it from his shoulders that he might
dash it to pieces upon the ground.

Towards sunset he examined himself anew, and found that
he was almost mad. The tempest which had been raging
within him from the instant that he lost all hope and will to
save the gipsy girl had not left a single sane idea, a single
sound thought, in his brain. His reason was laid low by it, was
almost wholly destroyed by it. His mind retained but two distinct images,—Esmeralda and the scaffold; all else was black.
Those two closely connected images presented a frightful
group; and the more he fixed upon them such power of attention and intellect as he still retained, the more they

seemed to grow, by a fantastic progression,—the one in grace, charm, beauty, light, the other in horror; so that at last Esmeralda appeared to him as a star, the gibbet as an enormous fleshless arm.

It was a remarkable thing that in spite of all this torment he never seriously thought of suicide. The wretch was so constituted. He clung to life. Perhaps he really saw hell lurking in the background.

Meantime, the day continued to decline. That spark of life which still burned within him dreamed dimly of returning home. He fancied himself remote from Paris; but on examination he discovered that he had merely made the circuit of the University. The spire of Saint-Sulpice and the three lofty pinnacles of Saint-Germain-des-Prés rose above the horizon on his right. He proceeded in that direction. When he heard the challenge of the abbot's men-at-arms around the battlemented walls of Saint-Germain he turned aside, took a footpath which he saw between the abbey mill and the lazaretto of the suburb, and in a few moments found himself at the edge of the Pré-aux-Clercs. This meadow was famous for the riots going on there continually, day and night; it was the "hydra-headed monster" of the poor monks of Saint-Germain: "*Quod monachis Sancti-Germani pratensis hydra fuit, clericis nova semper dissidiorum capita suscitantibus.*"* The archdeacon dreaded meeting some one there; he was afraid of any human face; he had shunned the University and the village of Saint-Germain; he was determined not to enter the city streets any earlier than he could help.

He skirted the Pré-aux-Clercs, took the deserted path dividing it from the Dieu-Neuf, and at last reached the bank of the river. There he found a boatman, who for a few farthings rowed him up the Seine as far as the City, where he landed him on that strip of waste land where the reader has already

---

*Because to the monks of Saint-Germain this meadow was a hydra ever raising its head anew in the brawls of the clerks (Latin).

seen Gringoire indulging in a reverie, and which extended beyond the king's gardens, parallel with the island of the Passeur-aux-Vaches.

The monotonous rocking of the boat and the ripple of the water had somewhat stupefied the unhappy Claude. When the boatman had gone, he stood upon the shore in a dazed condition, staring straight forward, and seeing everything in a sort of luminous mist which seemed to dance before his eyes. The fatigue of great grief often produces this effect upon the brain.

The sun had set behind the tall Tour de Nesle. It was twilight. The sky was silvery, the water in the river was silvery too. Between these two silver whites, the left bank of the Seine, upon which his eyes were riveted, stretched its somber length, and, tapering in the distance, faded away at last among the hazes of the horizon in the shape of a black spire. It was covered with houses, whose dark outlines only were visible, cast in strong relief against the bright background of cloud and water. Here and there windows began to glow like live embers. The vast black obelisk thus detached between the two white masses of sky and river, the latter very broad just here, produced a strange effect on Don Claude, — such as might be felt by a man lying flat on his back at the foot of the Strasburg cathedral, and gazing up at the huge spire piercing the twilight shadows over his head. Only here, Claude was standing and the obelisk lying low; but as the river, by reflecting the sky, prolonged the abyss beneath, the vast promontory seemed to shoot into space as boldly as any cathedral spire; and the impression produced was the same. The impression was made even stronger and more singular by the fact that it was indeed the Strasburg steeple, but the Strasburg steeple two leagues high, — something unheard-of, gigantic, immeasurable; a structure such as no human eye ever beheld; a Tower of Babel. The chimneys of the houses, the battlements of the wall, the carved gables of the roofs, the spire of the Augustine monastery, the Tour de Nesle, all these projections which marred the outline of the colossal obelisk, added to the illusion by grotesquely counterfeiting to the eye the indentations of some rich and fantastic carving.

Claude, in the state of hallucination in which he then was, believed that he saw—saw with his bodily eyes—the pinnacles of hell; the countless lights scattered from end to end of the awful tower appeared to him like so many doors leading to the vast furnace within; the voices and the sounds which arose from it, like so many shrieks and groans. Then he was terrified; he clapped his hands to his ears that he might not hear them, turned his back that he might not see, and hastened away from the fearful vision.

But the vision was within him.

When he once more entered the city streets, the passing people elbowing each other in the light of the shop windows affected him like the never-ending coming and going of specters. There were strange noises in his ears; extraordinary images troubled his senses. He saw neither houses, nor pavement, nor chariots, nor men and women, but a chaos of indeterminate objects which melted into one another. At the corner of the Rue de la Barillerie there was a grocer's shop, the sloping roof of which was, according to immemorial custom, hung with tin hoops, from each of which was suspended a circle of wooden candles, which clattered and clashed in the wind like castanets. He fancied he heard the heap of skeletons at Montfaucon knocking their bones against one another in the darkness.

"Oh," he muttered, "the night wind dashes them together, and mingles the sound of their chains with the rattle of their bones! Perhaps she too is there among them!"

Bewildered and distracted, he knew not where he went. After walking a few steps, be found himself upon the Pont Saint-Michel. There was a light at the window of a room on the ground-floor; he went up to it. Through a cracked pane he saw a dirty room, which roused a vague memory in his brain. In this room, dimly lighted by a small lamp, there was a fresh, fair-haired, merry-faced youth, who with loud bursts of laughter kissed a gaudily-dressed girl; and near the lamp sat an old woman spinning and singing in a cracked voice. As the young man occasionally ceased laughing, fragments of the old woman's song reached the priest; it was something unintelligible and frightful:—

> "Bark, Grève, growl, Grève!
> Spin, spin, my spindle brave,
> For the hangman spin a cord,
> As he whistles in the prison yard,
> Bark, Grève, growl, Grève!

> "The lovely hempen cord forevermore!
> Sow from Issy e'en to Vanvre's shore
> Hemp, and never of corn a grain.
> No thief will ever steal for gain
> The lovely hempen cord.

> "Growl, Grève, bark, Grève!
> To see the wanton and the knave
> Hanging on the gallows high,
> Every window is an eye.
> Growl, Grève, bark, Grève!"

Hereupon the young man laughed, and caressed the girl. The old woman was La Falourdel; the girl was a woman of the town; the young man was his brother Jehan.

He continued to gaze. As well this sight as another.

He saw Jehan go to a window at the back of the room, open it, cast a glance at the quay, where countless lighted windows gleamed in the distance, and he heard him say, as he closed the window,—

"By my soul! it is night already. The citizens have lighted their candles, and the good God his stars."

Then Jehan went back to the girl and broke a bottle which stood on the table, exclaiming,—

"Empty already, by Jove! and I have no more money! Isabeau, my love, I shall never feel content with Jupiter until he

turns your two white breasts into two black bottles, whence I
may suck Beaune wine night and day."

This witticism made the girl laugh, and Jehan sallied forth.

Dom Claude had barely time to throw himself on the
ground, lest he should be encountered, looked in the face,
and recognized by his brother. Luckily, the street was dark,
and the student was drunk. However, he noticed the archdeacon lying on the pavement in the mire.

"Ho! ho!" said he; "here's a fellow who has led a jolly life
today."

With his foot he stirred Dom Claude, who held his breath.

"Dead drunk," continued Jehan. "Well, he is full,—a regular leech dropped from a cask because he can suck no more.
He is bald," he added, stooping; "he is an old man! *Fortunate
senex!*"*

Then Dom Claude heard him move off, saying,—

"All the same, reason is a fine thing, and my brother the
archdeacon is very lucky to be both wise and rich."

The archdeacon then rose, and ran at full speed in the direction of Notre-Dame, whose enormous towers rose before
him in the darkness above the surrounding houses.

When, quite breathless, he reached the square in front of
the cathedral, he shrank back, and dared not raise his eyes to
the fatal building.

"Oh," said he in a low tone, "is it indeed true that such a
thing can have occurred here today,—this very morning?"

Still he ventured to look at the church. The front was dark;
the sky behind it glittered with stars. The crescent moon,
which had just risen above the horizon, had that instant
paused at the summit of the right-hand tower, and seemed to
have perched, like a luminous bird, on the edge of the railing,
which was cut into black trefoils.

The cloister door was closed, but the archdeacon always

---

*Fortunate old man! (Latin).

carried about him the key to the tower in which was his laboratory. He now used it to let himself into the church.

Inside, all was gloomy and silent as the tomb. By the heavy shadows falling on all sides in broad masses, he knew that the hangings put up for the morning's ceremonies had not yet been removed. The great silver cross gleamed through the darkness, dotted with sparkling points of light, like the milky way of this sepulchral night. The long choir windows showed the tops of their pointed arches above the black drapery, the panes, traversed by a moonbeam, wearing only the doubtful colors of the night,—a sort of violet, white, and blue, in tints which are found nowhere else save on the face of the dead. The archdeacon, seeing these pale points of arches all around the choir, fancied that he beheld the miters of bishops who had been damned. He shut his eyes, and when he reopened them, he imagined that there was a circle of ashen faces gazing at him.

He fled across the church. Then it seemed to him that the church, too, moved, stirred, breathed, and lived; that each big column became a monstrous leg, which pawed the ground with its broad stone hoof; and that the vast cathedral was only a sort of prodigious elephant, which panted and trampled, with pillars for feet, its two towers for tusks, and the immense black draperies for caparison.

Thus his fever, or mania, had attained such a degree of intensity that the external world had ceased to be to the unfortunate man anything more than a sort of Apocalypse, visible, tangible, terrifying.

For one moment he was comforted. As he entered the aisles, he perceived, behind a group of pillars, a reddish light, towards which he hastened as towards a star. It was the poor lamp which burned day and night above the public breviary of Notre-Dame, under its iron grating. He fell eagerly to reading the sacred book, in the hope of finding some consolation or some encouragement. The volume was open at this passage from Job, over which his fixed eye ran:—

"Then a spirit passed before my face; the hair of my flesh stood up."

On reading this melancholy passage, he felt as a blind man feels who is pricked by the staff which he has picked up. His knees gave way beneath him, and he sank to the ground, thinking of her who had that day perished. Such awful fumes rose up and penetrated his brain that it seemed to him as if his head had become one of the mouths of hell.

He remained some time in this position, incapable of thought, crushed and powerless in the hand of the demon that possessed him. At last, some measure of strength returned to him; it occurred to him to take refuge in the tower with his faithful Quasimodo. He rose, and as he was frightened, he took, to light his steps, the lamp from the breviary. This was a sacrilege, but he had ceased to heed such trifles.

He slowly climbed the tower stairs, full of secret terror, which must have been shared by the few passers-by outside in the square, who saw the mysterious light of his lamp moving at that late hour from loop-hole to loop-hole, to the top of the tower.

All at once he felt a freshness upon his face, and found himself under the door of the uppermost gallery. The air was cold; the sky was overcast with clouds, whose large white masses encroached one upon the other, rounding the sharp corners, and looking like the breaking-up of the ice in a river in winter. The crescent moon, stranded in the midst of the clouds, seemed a celestial ship caught fast among these icebergs of the air.

He cast down his eyes, and looked for a moment between the iron rails of the small columns which connect the two towers, far away, through a mist of fog and smoke, at the silent throng of the roofs of Paris, — steep, numberless, crowded close together, and small as the waves of a calm sea on a summer's night.

The moon shed a faint light, which lent an ashen tint to both heaven and earth.

At this moment the clock raised its shrill, cracked voice; it struck midnight. The priest's thoughts reverted to noon-day; it was again twelve o'clock.

"Oh," he whispered, "she must be cold by this time!"

Suddenly a blast of wind extinguished his lamp, and almost at the same instant he saw, at the opposite corner of the tower, a shadow, something white, a figure, a woman. He trembled. By this woman's side was a little goat, which mingled its bleat with the final bleat of the bell.

He had the courage to look at her. It was she.

She was pale; she was sad. Her hair fell loosely over her shoulders, as in the morning, but there was no rope about her neck; her hands were no longer bound. She was free; she was dead.

She was dressed in white, and had a white veil over her head.

She came towards him slowly, looking up to heaven. The supernatural goat followed her. He felt as if turned to stone, and too heavy to escape. At each step that she advanced, he took one backwards, and that was all. In this way he retreated beneath the dark arch of the staircase. He was frozen with fear at the idea that she might perhaps follow him thither; had she done so, he would have died of terror.

She did indeed approach the staircase door, pause there for a few moments, look steadily into the darkness, but without appearing to see the priest, and pass on. She seemed to him taller than in life; he saw the moon through her white robes; he heard her breathe.

When she had passed him, he began to descend the stairs with the same slow motion as the specter, imagining that he too was a specter,—haggard, his hair erect, his extinguished lamp still in his hand; and as he went down the spiral stairs, he distinctly heard in his ear a mocking voice, which repeated the words,—

"A spirit passed before my face; the hair of my flesh stood up."

CHAPTER II

Deformed, Blind, Lame

Every city in the Middle Ages—and up to the time of Louis XII every city in France—had its places of refuge, its sanctuaries. These places of refuge, amidst the deluge of penal laws and barbarous jurisdictions which flooded the city of Paris, were like so many islands rising above the level of human justice. Every criminal who landed there was saved. In each district there were almost as many places of refuge as gallows. The abuse of a privilege went side by side with the abuse of punishment,—two bad things, each striving to correct the other. Royal palaces, princely mansions, and above all churches, had the right of sanctuary; sometimes an entire town which stood in need of repopulation was given the temporary right. Louis XI made Paris a sanctuary in 1467.

Having once set foot within the sanctuary, the criminal was sacred; but let him beware how he ventured forth: one step outside his shelter plunged him again in the billows. The wheel, the gibbet, and the strappado kept close guard around the place of refuge, and watched their prey unceasingly, like sharks in a vessel's wake. Thus men have been known to grow grey in a convent, on a palace staircase, in abbey fields, under a church porch; so that the sanctuary became a prison in all save name. It sometimes happened that a solemn decree from Parliament violated the sanctuary, and gave up the criminal to justice; but this occurrence was rare. The Parliaments stood in some awe of the bishops; and when cowl and gown came into collision, the priest usually got the best of it. Sometimes, however, as in the matter of the assassins of Petit-Jean, the Paris hangman, and in that of Emery Rousseau, Jean Valleret's murderer, Justice overrode the Church, and proceeded to carry out her sentences; but, without an order from Parliament, woe to him who vio-

lated any sanctuary by armed force! We know what fate befell
Robert de Clermont, Marshal of France, and Jean de Châlons,
Marshal of Champagne; and yet the case in question was
merely that of one Perrin Marc, a money-changer's man, a mis-
erable assassin. But the two marshals broke open the doors of
Saint-Méry; therein lay the crime.

Such was the veneration felt for these refuges that, as tradition goes, it occasionally extended even to animals. Aymoin
relates that a stag chased by Dagobert, having taken refuge
near the tomb of Saint Denis, the pack stopped short, barking
loudly.

Churches had usually a cell prepared to receive suppli-
ants. In 1407 Nicolas Flamel had built for them upon the
arches of Saint-Jacques de la Boucherie, a chamber which
cost him four pounds six pence sixteen Paris farthings.

At Notre-Dame it was a cell built over the aisles under the
flying buttresses, on the very spot where the wife of the present keeper of the towers has made a garden, which compares
with the hanging gardens of Babylon as a lettuce with a palm-
tree, or a porter's wife with Semiramis.

It was here that Quasimodo had deposited Esmeralda after
his frantic and triumphal race through the towers and galleries. While that race lasted, the young girl did not recover
her senses, — half dozing, half waking, conscious only of being
borne upward through the air, whether floating or flying, or
lifted above the earth by some unknown power. From time to
time she heard the noisy laughter, the harsh voice of Quasimodo in her ear. She half opened her eyes; then beneath her
she saw dimly all Paris dotted with countless roofs of slate and
tiles, like a red and blue mosaic; above her head the fearful,
grinning face of Quasimodo. Her eyelids fell; she thought that
all was over, that she had been hanged during her swoon, and
that the misshapen spirit which ruled her destiny had again
taken possession of her and carried her away. She dared not
look at him, but yielded to his sway.

But when the breathless and disheveled bell-ringer laid
her down in the cell of refuge, when she felt his great hands

gently untie the rope which bruised her arms, she experienced that sort of shock which wakens with a start the passengers on a ship that runs aground in the middle of a dark night. Her ideas woke too, and returned to her one by one. She saw that she was still in Notre-Dame; she remembered being torn from the hangman's hands; that Phœbus lived, that Phœbus had ceased to love her; and these two ideas, one of which lent such bitterness to the other, presenting themselves simultaneously to the poor victim, she turned to Quasimodo, who stood before her and who terrified her, saying,—

"Why did you save me?"

He looked anxiously at her, as if striving to guess what she said. She repeated her question. He gazed at her with profound sadness, and fled.

She was amazed.

A few moments later he returned, bringing a packet which he threw at her feet. It contained clothes left at the door of the church for her by charitable women.

Then she looked down at herself, saw that she was almost naked, and blushed. Life had returned.

Quasimodo appeared to feel something of her shame. He covered his eye with his broad hand, and again departed, but with lingering steps.

She hastily dressed herself. The garments given her consisted of a white gown and veil,—the dress of a novice at the Hôtel Dieu, the great hospital managed by nuns.

She had scarcely finished when Quasimodo returned. He carried a basket under one arm and a mattress under the other. In the basket were a bottle, a loaf of bread, and a few other provisions. He set the basket down, and said, "Eat!" He spread the mattress on the floor, and said, "Sleep!"

It was his own food, his own bed, which the bell-ringer had brought.

The gipsy lifted her eyes to his face to thank him, but she could not utter a word. The poor devil was hideous indeed. She hung her head with a shudder of fright.

Then he said,—

"I alarm you. I am very ugly, am I not? Do not look at me; only listen to me. During the day, you must stay here; by night, you can walk anywhere about the church; but do not leave the church by day or night. You would be lost. They would kill you, and I should die."

Moved by his words, she raised her head to reply. He had vanished. Alone once more, she pondered the strange words of this almost monstrous being, struck by the sound of his voice, which was so hoarse and yet so gentle.

Then she examined her cell. It was a room of some six feet square, with a little dormer-window and a door opening on the slightly sloping roof of flat stones. Various gutter-spouts in the form of animals seemed bending over her and stretching their necks to look at her through the window. Beyond the roof she saw the tops of a thousand chimneys, from which issued the smoke of all the fires of Paris. A sad spectacle for the poor gipsy girl,—a foundling, condemned to death, an unhappy creature, without a country, without a family, without a hearth.

Just as the thought of her forlorn condition struck her more painfully than ever, she felt a hairy, bearded head rub against her hands and knees. She trembled (everything frightened her now) and looked down. It was the poor goat, the nimble Djali, who had escaped with her when Quasimodo scattered Charmolue's men, and who had been lavishing caresses on her feet for nearly an hour without winning a glance. The gipsy girl covered her with kisses.

"Oh, Djali," said she, "how could I forget you! But you never forget me! Oh, you at least are not ungrateful!"

At the same time, as if an invisible hand had lifted the weight which had so long held back her tears, she began to weep; and as her tears flowed, she felt the sharpest and bitterest of her grief going from her with them.

When evening came, she thought the night so beautiful, the moon so soft, that she took a turn in the raised gallery which surrounds the church. She felt somewhat refreshed by it, the earth seemed to her so peaceful, viewed from that height.

CHAPTER III

Deaf

Next morning she found on waking that she had slept. This strange fact amazed her; it was so long since she had slept! A bright beam from the rising sun came in at her window and shone in her face. With the sun, she saw at the same window an object that alarmed her,—the unhappy face of Quasimodo. Involuntarily she reclosed her eyes, but in vain; she still seemed to see through her rosy lids that one-eyed, gap-toothed, gnome-like face. Then, still keeping her eyes shut, she heard a rough voice say very kindly,—

"Don't be frightened. I am your friend. I came to see if you were asleep. It does you no harm, does it, if I look at you when you are asleep? What does it matter to you if I am here when your eyes are shut? Now I will go. There, I have hidden myself behind the wall. You can open your eyes again."

The tone in which they were uttered was even more plaintive than the words themselves. The gipsy girl, touched by it, opened her eyes. He was no longer at the window. She went to it, and saw the poor hunchback crouched in a corner of the wall, in a painful and submissive posture. She made an effort to overcome the aversion with which he inspired her. "Come here," said she, gently. From the motion of her lips, Quasimodo thought she was ordering him away; he therefore rose and retired, limping slowly, with hanging head, not daring to raise his despairing eye to the young girl's face. "Do come!" she cried. But he still withdrew. Then she ran out of her cell, hurried after him, and took his arm. When he felt her touch, Quasimodo trembled in every limb. He raised his beseeching eye, and finding that she drew him towards her, his whole face beamed with tenderness and delight. She tried to make him enter her cell; but he persisted in remaining on the threshold. "No, no," said he; "the owl must not enter the lark's nest."

Then she threw herself gracefully upon her bed, with the sleeping goat at her feet. For some moments both were motionless, silently contemplating, he so much grace, she so much ugliness.

Every moment she discovered some additional deformity in Quasimodo. Her gaze roved from his knock knees to his humped back, from his humped back to his single eye. She could not understand why a being so imperfectly planned should continue to exist. But withal there was so much melancholy and so much gentleness about him that she began to be reconciled to it.

He was the first to break the silence: "Did you tell me to come back?"

She nodded her head, as she said, "Yes."

He understood her nod. "Alas!" said he, as if loath to go on, "I am—I am deaf."

"Poor fellow!" cried the gipsy, with a look of kindly pity.

He smiled sadly.

"You think that I only lacked that, don't you? Yes, I am deaf. That's the way I was made. It is horrible, isn't it? And you,—you are so beautiful!"

There was so profound a sense of his misery in the poor wretch's tone, that she had not the strength to say a word. Besides, he would not have heard her. He added:—

"I never realized my ugliness till now. When I compare myself with you, I pity myself indeed, poor unhappy monster that I am! I must seem to you like some awful beast, eh? You,—you are a sunbeam, a drop of dew, a bird's song! As for me, I am something frightful, neither man nor beast,—a nondescript object, more hard, shapeless, and more trodden under foot than a pebble!"

Then he began to laugh, and that laugh was the most heartrending thing on earth. He continued:—

"Yes, I am deaf; but you can speak to me by gestures, by signs. I have a master who talks with me in that way. And then

I shall soon know your wishes from the motion of your lips, and your expression."

"Well," she replied, smiling, "tell me why you saved me."

He watched her attentively as she spoke.

"I understand," he answered. "You ask me why I saved you. You have forgotten a villain who tried to carry you off one night,—a villain to whom the very next day you brought relief upon their infamous pillory. A drop of water and a little pity are more than my whole life can ever repay. You have forgotten that villain; but he remembers."

She listened with deep emotion. A tear sparkled in the bell-ringer's eye, but it did not fall. He seemed to make it a point of honor to repress it.

"Listen," he resumed, when he no longer feared lest that tear should flow; "we have very tall towers here; a man who fell from them would be dead long before he touched the pavement; whenever it would please you to have me fall, you need not even say a single word; one glance will be enough."

Then he rose. This peculiar being, unhappy though the gipsy was, yet roused a feeling of compassion in her heart. She signed him to stay.

"No, no," said he, "I must not stay too long. I am not at my ease. It is out of pity that you do not turn away your eyes. I will go where I can see you without your seeing me. That will be better."

He drew from his pocket a small metal whistle.

"There," said he, "when you need me, when you wish me to come to you, when I do not horrify you too much, whistle with this. I hear that sound."

He laid the whistle on the ground, and fled.

CHAPTER IV

Earthenware and Crystal

O ne day followed another.

Calm gradually returned to Esmeralda's soul. Excess of grief, like excess of joy, is a violent thing, and of brief duration. The heart of man cannot long remain at any extreme. The gipsy had suffered so much that surprise was the only emotion of which she was now capable. With security, hope had returned. She was far away from society, far from life, but she vaguely felt that it might not perhaps be impossible to return to them. She was like one dead, yet holding in reserve the key to her tomb.

She felt the terrible images which had so long possessed her fading gradually away. All the hideous phantoms, Pierrat Torterue, Jacques Charmolue, had vanished from her mind,—all, even the priest himself.

And then, too, Phœbus lived; she was sure of it; she had seen him. To her, the life of Phœbus was all in all. After the series of fatal shocks which had laid waste her soul, but one thing was left standing, but one sentiment,—her love for the captain. Love is like a tree; it grows spontaneously, strikes its roots deep into our whole being, and often continues to flourish over a heart in ruins.

And the inexplicable part of it is, that the blinder this passion, the more tenacious it is. It is never stronger than when it is utterly unreasonable.

Undoubtedly Esmeralda's thoughts of the captain were tinged with bitterness. Undoubtedly it was frightful that he too should have been deceived, he who should have deemed such a thing impossible,—that he should have believed the stab to come from her, who would have given a thousand lives for him. But, after all, she must not blame him too severely; had she not confessed her crime? Had she not, weak woman that she was, yielded to torture? The fault was wholly hers. She should have let them tear out every nail rather than wrest a single word from her. Well, could she but see Phœbus once more, for one moment only, it would need but a word, a look, to undeceive him, to bring him back. She had no doubts in the matter. She also strove to account to herself for various strange facts,—for the accident of Phœbus's presence on the day of her doing penance, and for the young girl with whom he was. Probably she was his sister. An improbable explanation, but one with which she contented herself, because she needed to believe that Phœbus still loved her, and loved her alone. Had he not sworn it to her? What more did she want, simple, credulous girl that she was? And then, in this business, were not appearances much more against her than against him? She therefore waited; she hoped.

Let us add that the church, that vast church which surrounded her on every side, which guarded her, which preserved her, was itself a sovereign balm. The solemn lines of its architecture, the religious attitude of every object about the young girl, the calm and pious thoughts which were emitted, as it were, from every pore of its stones, unconsciously acted upon her. Moreover, the building had sounds of such majesty and blessing that they soothed her sick soul. The monotonous chant of the officiating priests, the people's response to them, sometimes inarticulate, sometimes thunderous, the harmonious quiver of the stained-glass windows, the organ loud as the blast of a hundred trumpets, the three belfries, buzzing and humming like hives of great bees,—all this orchestra, with its gigantic gamut perpetually rising and falling, from the crowd to the belfry, lulled her memory, her imagination, her grief. The bells, particularly, soothed her. Those vast machines poured over her broad waves of mighty magnetism.

Thus, each day's rising sun found her more composed, breathing better, less pale. As her inward wounds were healed, her grace and beauty bloomed again, although she was more reserved and quiet. Her former disposition also returned,—something even of her gaiety, her pretty pout, her love for her goat, her passion for singing, and her modesty. She was careful to dress herself every morning in the corner of her cell, lest the inmate of some neighboring garret should spy her through the window.

When the thoughts of Phœbus gave her time, the gipsy sometimes thought of Quasimodo. He was the only tie, the only bond, the only means of communication left to her with mankind, with the living. Unhappy girl! She was even more completely cut off from the world than Quasimodo. She could not understand the strange friend whom chance had given her. She often reproached herself for not feeling sufficient gratitude to blind her eyes; but, decidedly, she could not accustom herself to the poor ringer. He was too ugly.

She had left the whistle which he gave her on the floor. This did not prevent Quasimodo from appearing now and then during the first few days. She did her best not to turn away with too much aversion when he brought her the basket of food or the jug of water; but he always noticed the slightest movement of the kind, and would then go sadly away.

Once he came up just as she was fondling Djali. He stood for a few moments considering the pretty group of the girl and the goat; at last he said, shaking his heavy, clumsy head,—

"My misfortune is that I am still too much like a human being. I wish I were wholly an animal like that goat."

She looked at him in surprise.

He answered her look:—

"Oh, I very well know why." And he withdrew.

On another occasion he appeared at the door of the cell (which he never entered) as Esmeralda was singing an old Spanish ballad, the words of which she did not understand, but which had lingered in her memory because the gipsies had rocked her to sleep with it when a child. At the sight of his ugly face, coming so suddenly upon her in the midst of her song, the young girl stopped short, with an involuntary gesture of alarm. The wretched ringer fell upon his knees on the door-sill, and clasped his great misshapen hands with a beseeching air. "Oh," said he, sadly, "I pray you, go on, and do not drive me away." She was unwilling to pain him, and, trembling though she was, resumed her song. By degrees, however, her terror subsided, and she gave herself up entirely to the emotions aroused by the slow and plaintive music. He remained on his knees, his hands clasped as if in prayer, attentive, scarcely breathing, his eyes riveted upon the gipsy's sparkling orbs. He seemed to read her song in her eyes.

Another day he came to her with a timid, awkward air. "Listen to me," said he with an effort; "I have something to tell you." She signed to him that she was listening. Then he began to sigh, half opened his lips, seemed just about to speak, looked at her, shook his head, and retired slowly, pressing his hand to his head, leaving the gipsy utterly amazed.[17]

Among the grotesque images carved upon the wall, there was one of which he was particularly fond, and with which he often seemed to exchange fraternal glances. The girl once heard him say to it, "Oh, why am not I of stone, like you!"

Finally, one morning Esmeralda ventured out to the edge of the roof, and looked into the square over the steep top of Saint-Jean le Rond. Quasimodo stood behind her. He stationed himself there to spare the girl as far as possible the annoyance of seeing him. All at once she started; a tear and a flash of joy shone together in her eyes. She knelt on the edge of the roof, and stretched out her arms in anguish towards the square, crying, "Phœbus! Come! Come! One word, only one word, for the love of Heaven! Phœbus! Phœbus!" Her voice, her face, her gesture, her whole person, wore the heartrending expression of a shipwrecked mariner making signals of distress to a ship sailing merrily by in the distance, lit up by a sunbeam on the horizon.

Quasimodo bent over the parapet, and saw that the object of this frenzied entreaty was a young man, a captain, a handsome knight, glittering with arms and ornaments, who pranced and curveted through the square on horseback, waving his plumed helmet to a lovely damsel smiling from her balcony. However, the officer did not hear the unhappy girl's appeal; he was too far away.

But the poor deaf man heard it. A deep sigh heaved his breast; he turned away; his heart swelled with suppressed tears; his clinched fists beat his brow, and when he withdrew them, each of them grasped a handful of red hair.

The gipsy paid no heed to him. He gnashed his teeth, and muttered,—

"Damnation! So that is how one should look! One only needs a handsome outside!"

Meantime, she remained on her knees, crying with great agitation,—

"Oh, now he is dismounting from his horse! He is going into that house! Phœbus! He does not hear! Phœbus! How cruel of that woman to talk to him at the same time that I do! Phœbus! Phœbus!"

The deaf man watched her. He understood her pantomime. The poor bell-ringer's eye filled with tears, but he did not let a single one flow. All at once he plucked her gently by the hem of her sleeve. She turned. He had assumed a tranquil air, and said,—

"Shall I go and fetch him?"

She uttered a cry of joy.

"Oh, go! go! run, quick! that captain! that captain! bring him to me! I will love you!"

She clasped his knees. He could not help shaking his head sadly.

"I will bring him to you," said he in a faint voice. Then he turned his head and hurried quickly down the stairs, choked with sobs.

When he reached the square, he saw nothing but the fine horse tied to the post at the door of the Gondelaurier house; the captain had already entered.

He raised his eyes to the roof of the church. Esmeralda was still in the same place, in the same position. He shook his head sorrowfully, then leaned against one of the posts before the Gondelaurier porch, determined to await the captain's coming.

Within the house, it was one of those gala days which precede a wedding. Quasimodo saw many people go in, and none come out. From time to time he looked up at the roof; the gipsy girl was as motionless as he. A groom came, unfastened the horse, and led him into the stable.

The whole day passed thus,—Quasimodo against the pillar, Esmeralda on the roof, Phœbus, doubtless, at the feet of Fleur-de-Lys.

At last night came,—a moonless night, a dark night. In vain Quasimodo fixed his eyes upon Esmeralda; she soon ceased to be anything more than a white spot in the dusk; then she vanished. Everything faded out; all was dark.

Quasimodo saw the front windows of the Gondelaurier mansion lighted up from top to bottom; he saw the other windows on the square lighted, one by one; he also saw the lights extinguished to the very last, for he remained at his post all the evening. The officer did not come out. When the latest passers had gone home, when all the windows in the other houses were black, Quasimodo was left alone, entirely in the darkness. There were no street lamps in the Parvis then.

But the windows of the Gondelaurier house remained lighted, even after midnight. Quasimodo, motionless and alert, saw countless moving, dancing shadows pass across the many-colored panes. If he had not been deaf, as the noise of sleeping Paris ceased, he would have heard more and more distinctly, within the house, the sounds of revelry, music and laughter.

About one o'clock in the morning the guests began to go. Quasimodo, wrapped in darkness, watched them as they passed beneath the porch bright with torches. The captain was not among them.

He was filled with sad thoughts; at times he looked up into the air, as if tired of waiting. Great, black, heavy clouds, torn and ragged, hung like masses of crape from the starry arch of night. They seemed like the cobwebs of the vaulted sky.

In one of these upward glances he suddenly saw the long window of the balcony whose stone balustrade was just over his head, mysteriously open. Two persons passed out through the glass door, closing it noiselessly behind them; they were a man and a woman. It was not without some difficulty that Quasimodo succeeded in recognizing in the man the handsome captain; in the woman, the young lady whom he had that morning seen wave a welcome to the officer from that self-same balcony. The square was perfectly dark, and a double crimson curtain, which fell again behind the door as it closed, scarcely permitted a ray of light from the room to reach the balcony.

The young man and the girl, as far as our deaf man could judge without hearing a single one of their words, seemed to give themselves up to a very tender *tête-à-tête*. The young girl had apparently allowed the officer to encircle her waist with his arm, and was making a feeble resistance to a kiss.

Quasimodo looked on from below at this scene, which was all the more attractive because it was not meant to be seen. He beheld that happiness and beauty with bitterness. After all, nature was not mute in the poor devil, and his spinal column, wretchedly crooked as it was, was quite as susceptible of a thrill as that of any other man. He reflected on the miserable part which Providence had assigned him; that woman, love, pleasure, were forever to pass before him, while he could never do more than look on at the happiness of others. But what pained him most in this sight, what added indignation to his annoyance, was the thought of what the gipsy must suffer could she see it. True, the night was very dark; Esmeralda, if she had remained at her post (which he did not doubt), was very far away, and it was all he could do himself, to distinguish the lovers on the balcony. This comforted him.

Meantime, their conversation became more and more animated. The young lady seemed to be entreating the officer to ask no more of her. Quasimodo could only make out her fair clasped hands, her smiles blent with tears, her upward glances, and the eyes of the captain eagerly bent upon her.

Luckily,—for the young girl's struggles were growing fee-bler,—the balcony door was suddenly reopened, and an old lady appeared; the beauty seemed confused, the officer wore a disappointed air, and all three re-entered the house. A moment later a horse was pawing the ground at the door, and the brilliant officer, wrapped in his cloak, passed quickly by Quasimodo.

The ringer let him turn the corner of the street, then ran after him with his monkey-like agility, shouting:

"Hollo there! Captain!"

The captain stopped.

"What can that rascal want?" said he, seeing in the shadow the ungainly figure limping quickly towards him.

Meantime Quasimodo caught up with him, and boldly seized the horse by the bridle:—

"Follow me, Captain; there is some one here who wishes to speak with you."

"The devil!" muttered Phœbus, "here's an ugly scarecrow whom I think I've seen elsewhere. Hollo, sirrah! Will you let my horse's bridle go?"

"Captain," replied the deaf man, "don't you even ask who it is?"

"I tell you to let my horse go!" impatiently replied Phœbus. "What does the fellow mean by hanging to my charger's rein thus? Do you take my horse for a gallows?"

Quasimodo, far from loosing his hold on the bridle, was preparing to turn the horse's head in the opposite direction. Unable to understand the captain's resistance, he made haste to say,—

"Come, Captain, it is a woman who awaits you." He added with an effort: "A woman who loves you."

"Arrant knave!" said the captain; "do you think I am obliged to go to all the women who love me, or say they do? And how if by chance she looks like you, you screech-owl? Tell her who sent you that I am about to marry, and that she may go to the devil!"

"Hear me!" cried Quasimodo, supposing that with one

word he could conquer his hesitation; "come, my lord! it is the gipsy girl, whom you know!"

These words did indeed make a strong impression upon Phœbus, but not of the nature which the deaf man expected. It will be remembered that our gallant officer retired with Fleur-de-Lys some moments before Quasimodo rescued the prisoner from the hands of Charmolue. Since then, during his visits to the Gondelaurier house he had carefully avoided all mention of the woman, whose memory was painful to him; and on her side, Fleur-de-Lys had not thought it politic to tell him that the gipsy still lived. Phœbus therefore supposed poor "Similar" to have died some two or three months before. Let us add that for some moments past the captain had been pondering on the exceeding darkness of the night, the supernatural ugliness and sepulchral tones of the strange messenger, the fact that it was long past midnight, that the street was as deserted as on the night when the goblin monk addressed him, and that his horse snorted at the sight of Quasimodo.

"The gipsy girl!" he exclaimed, almost terrified: "pray, do you come from the other world?"

And he placed his hand on the hilt of his dagger.

"Quick! quick!" said the deaf man, striving to urge on the horse; "this way!"

Phœbus dealt him a vigorous kick.

Quasimodo's eye flashed. He made a movement to attack the captain. Then drawing himself up, he said,—

"Oh, how fortunate it is for you that there is some one who loves you!"

He emphasized the words *some one*, and releasing the horse's bridle, added,—

"Begone!"

Phœbus clapped spurs to his horse, with an oath. Quasimodo saw him plunge down the street and disappear in the darkness.

"Oh," murmured the poor deaf man, "to refuse that!"

He returned to Notre-Dame, lighted his lamp, and

climbed the tower. As he had supposed, the gipsy was still in the same place.

As soon as she caught sight of him, she ran to meet him.

"Alone!" she cried mournfully, clasping her lovely hands.

"I could not find him," said Quasimodo, coldly.

"You should have waited all night," she replied indignantly.

He saw her angry gesture, and understood the reproach.

"I will watch better another time," said he, hanging his head.

"Go!" said she.

He left her. She was offended with him. He would rather be maltreated by her than distress her. He kept all the pain for himself.

From that day forth the gipsy saw him no more. He ceased to visit her cell. At most, she sometimes caught a glimpse of the ringer on the top of a tower, gazing sadly at her. But as soon as she saw him, he disappeared.

We must own that she was but little troubled by this willful absence of the poor hunchback. In her secret heart she thanked him for it. However, Quasimodo did not lie under any delusion on this point.

She no longer saw him, but she felt the presence of a good genius around her. Her provisions were renewed by an invisible hand while she slept. One morning she found a cage of birds on her window-sill. Over her cell there was a piece of carving which alarmed her. She had more than once shown this feeling before Quasimodo. One morning (for all these things occurred at night) she no longer saw it; it was broken off. Any one who had climbed up to it must have risked his life.

Sometimes in the evening she heard a voice, hidden behind the wind-screen of the belfry, sing, as if to lull her to sleep, a weird, sad song, verses without rhyme, such as a deaf person might make:—

> "Heed not the face,
> Maiden, heed the heart.

The heart of a fine young man is oft deformed.
There are hearts where Love finds no abiding-
> place.

"Maiden, the pine-tree is not fair,
Not fair as is the poplar-tree
But its leaves are green in winter bare.

"Alas! why do I tell you this?
Beauty alone has right to live;
Beauty can only beauty love,
April her back doth turn on January.

"Beauty is perfect,
Beauty wins all,
Beauty alone is lord of all.

"The raven only flies by day,
The owl by night alone doth fly,
The swan by day and night alike may fly."

One morning, on waking, she saw at her window two vases
full of flowers. One was a very beautiful and brilliant but
cracked crystal vase. It had let the water with which it was
filled escape, and the flowers which it held were withered.
The other was an earthen jug, coarse and common; but it had
retained all its water, and the flowers were fresh and rosy.

I do not know whether it was done purposely, but Esmeralda took the withered nosegay, and wore it all day in her
bosom.

That day she did not hear the voice from the tower singing.

She cared but little. She passed her days in fondling Djali,
in watching the door of the Gondelaurier house, in talking to
herself about Phœbus, and in scattering crumbs of bread to
the swallows.

She had entirely ceased to see or hear Quasimodo; the
poor ringer seemed to have vanished from the church. But

one night, when she could not sleep, and was thinking of her handsome captain, she heard a sigh close by her cell. Terrified, she rose, and saw by the light of the moon a shapeless mass lying outside across her door. It was Quasimodo sleeping there upon the stones.

CHAPTER V

The Key to the Porte-Rouge

Meantime, public rumor had informed the archdeacon of the miraculous manner in which the gipsy had been saved. When he learned of it, he knew not what he felt. He had accepted the fact of Esmeralda's death. In this way, he made himself perfectly easy; he had sounded the utmost depths of grief. The human heart (Dom Claude had mused upon these matters) can hold but a certain quantity of despair. When the sponge is thoroughly soaked, the sea may pass over it without adding another drop to it.

Now, Esmeralda being dead, the sponge was soaked. Everything was over for Dom Claude in this world. But to know that she was alive, and Phœbus too, was to endure afresh the torments, shocks, and vicissitudes of life; and Claude was weary of them all.

When he heard this piece of news, he shut himself up in his cloister cell. He did not appear at the chapter meetings or the sacred offices. He barred his door against every one, even the bishop, and remained thus immured for several weeks. He was supposed to be ill, and indeed was so.

What did he do in his seclusion? With what thoughts was the unfortunate man battling? Was he waging a final conflict with his terrible passion? Was he plotting a final plan to kill her and destroy himself?

His Jehan, his adored brother, his spoiled child, came once to his door, knocked, swore, entreated, repeated his name half a score of times. Claude would not open.

He passed whole days with his face glued to his window-panes. From this window, in the cloisters as it was, he could see Esmeralda's cell. He often saw her, with her goat,—sometimes with Quasimodo. He noticed the attentions of the ugly deaf man,—his obedience, his refined and submissive manners to the gipsy. He recalled,—for he had a good memory, and memory is the plague of the jealous,—he recalled the bell-ringer's strange look at the dancer on a certain evening. He asked himself what motive could have led Quasimodo to save her. He witnessed countless little scenes between the girl and the deaf man, when their gestures, seen from a distance and commented on by his passion, struck him as very tender. He distrusted women's whims. Then he vaguely felt awakening within him a jealousy such as he had never imagined possible,—a jealousy which made him blush with rage and shame. "'Twas bad enough when it was the captain; but this fellow!" The idea overwhelmed him.

His nights were frightful. Since he knew the gipsy girl to be alive, the chill fancies of specters and tombs which had for an entire day beset him, had vanished, and the flesh again rose in revolt against the spirit. He writhed upon his bed at the idea that the dark-skinned damsel was so near a neighbor.

Every night his fevered imagination pictured Esmeralda in all those attitudes which had stirred his blood most quickly. He saw her stretched across the body of the wounded captain, her eyes closed, her beautiful bare throat covered with Phœbus's blood, at that moment of rapture when he himself had pressed upon her pale lips that kiss which had burned the unhappy girl, half dead though she was, like a living coal. He again saw her disrobed by the savage hands of the executioners, exposing and enclosing in the buskin with its iron screws her tiny foot, her plump and shapely leg, and her white and supple knee.

He again saw that ivory knee alone left uncovered by Torterue's horrid machine. Finally, he figured to himself the young girl in her shift, the rope about her neck, her shoulders bare, her feet bare, almost naked, as he saw her on what was to have been her last day on earth. These voluptuous pictures made him clinch his hands, and caused a shudder to run from head to foot.

One night, especially, they so cruelly heated his virgin and priestly blood that he bit his pillow, leaped from his bed, threw a surplice over his shirt, and left his cell, lamp in hand, but half-dressed, wild and haggard, with flaming eyes.

He knew where to find the key to the Porte-Rouge, which led from the cloisters to the church, and he always carried about him, as the reader knows, a key to the tower stairs.

CHAPTER VI

The Key to the Porte-Rouge (continued)

That night Esmeralda fell asleep in her cell, full of peace, hope, and pleasant thoughts. She had been asleep for some time, dreaming, as she always did, of Phœbus, when she fancied she heard a noise. Her sleep was light and restless,—a bird's sleep. A mere trifle roused her. She opened her eyes. The night was very dark. Still, she saw a face peering in at the window; the vision was lighted up by a lamp. When this face saw that Esmeralda was looking at it, it blew out the lamp. Still, the girl had had time to catch a glimpse of it; her eyes closed in terror.

"Oh," said she, in a feeble voice, "the priest!"

All her past misery flashed upon her with lightning speed. She sank back upon her bed, frozen with fear.

A moment after, she felt a touch which made her shudder so that she started up wide awake and furious.

The priest had glided to her side. He clasped her in his arms.

She tried to scream, but could not.

"Begone, monster! Begone, assassin!" she said at last, in a low voice trembling with wrath and horror.

"Mercy! mercy!" murmured the priest, pressing his lips to her shoulders.

She seized his bald head in both hands by the hairs which remained, and strove to prevent his kisses as if they had been bites.

"Mercy!" repeated the unfortunate man. "If you knew what my love for you is! It is fire, molten lead, a thousand knives driven into my heart!"

And he held her arms with superhuman strength. She cried desperately: "Release me, or I shall spit in your face!"

He released her. "Degrade me, strike me, do your worst! do what you will! but have mercy! love me!"

Then she struck him with the impotent fury of a child. She clinched her lovely hands to bruise his face. "Demon, begone!"

"Love me! love me! have pity!" cried the poor priest, clasping her, and returning her blows with caresses.

All at once she felt him stronger than she.

"No more of this!" he exclaimed, gnashing his teeth.

She lay conquered, crushed, and quivering in his arms, at his mercy. She felt a wanton hand wandering over her. She made one last effort, and shrieked: "Help! help! a vampire! a vampire!"

No one came. Djali alone was awakened, and bleated piteously.

"Silence!" said the panting priest.

Suddenly, in her struggle, as she fought upon the floor, the gipsy's hand encountered something cold and metallic. It was

Quasimodo's whistle. She seized it with a convulsion of hope, raised it to her lips, and blew with all her remaining strength. The whistle gave forth a sharp, shrill, piercing sound.

"What is that?" said the priest.

Almost as he spoke he felt himself grasped by a vigorous arm. The cell was dark; he could not distinguish exactly who held him; but he heard teeth chattering with rage, and there was just enough light mingled with the darkness for him to see the broad blade of a knife gleam above his head.

He thought he recognized the figure of Quasimodo. He supposed that it could be no other. He remembered having stumbled, as he entered, over a bundle lying across the outside of the door. But as the new-comer did not utter a word, he knew not what to think. He flung himself upon the arm which held the knife, crying. "Quasimodo!" He forgot, in this moment of distress, that Quasimodo was deaf.

In the twinkling of an eye the priest was stretched on the floor, and felt a heavy knee pressed against his breast. By the angular imprint of that knee, he knew Quasimodo; but what was he to do? How was he also to be recognized by the hunchback? Night made the deaf man blind.

He was lost. The young girl, pitiless as an enraged tigress, did not interpose to save him. The knife came nearer his head; it was a critical moment. All at once his adversary appeared to hesitate.

"No blood upon her!" said he, in a dull voice:

It was indeed the voice of Quasimodo.

Then the priest felt a huge hand drag him from the cell by the heels; he was not to die within those walls. Luckily for him, the moon had risen some moments before.

When they crossed the threshold, its pale rays fell upon the priest. Quasimodo looked him in the face, trembled, relaxed his hold, and shrank back.

The gipsy, who had advanced to the door of her cell, saw with surprise that the actors had suddenly changed parts. It was now the priest who threatened, and Quasimodo who implored.

The priest, who was overwhelming the deaf man with gestures of wrath and reproach, violently signed him to withdraw.

The deaf man bowed his head, then knelt before the gipsy's door. "My lord," said he, in grave, submissive tones, "do what you will afterwards; but kill me first!"

So saying, he offered his knife to the priest. The priest, beside himself with rage, rushed upon him. But the young girl was quicker than he. She tore the knife from Quasimodo's hands, and uttered a frenzied laugh.

"Approach now!" she cried.

She held the blade high above her head. The priest stood irresolute. She would certainly have struck.

"You dare not touch me now, coward!" she exclaimed.

Then she added with a pitiless look, and knowing that her words would pierce the priest's heart like a thousand red-hot irons,—

"Ah, I know that Phœbus is not dead!"

The priest threw Quasimodo to the ground with a kick, and rushed down the stairs quivering with rage.

When he had gone, Quasimodo picked up the whistle which had just saved the gipsy.

"It was getting rusty," said he, returning it to her; then he left her alone.

The young girl, overcome by this violent scene, fell exhausted on her bed and burst into a flood of tears. Her horizon was again becoming overcast.

The priest, on his side, groped his way back to his cell.

That was sufficient. Dom Claude was jealous of Quasimodo.

He repeated musingly the fatal words: "No one else shall have her!"

BOOK X

CHAPTER I

*Gringoire Has Several Capital
Ideas in Succession in the
Rue des Bernardins*

When Pierre Gringoire saw the turn which this whole matter was taking, and that a rope, hanging, and other unpleasant things must certainly be the fate of the chief actors in the play, he no longer cared to meddle with it. The Vagrants, with whom he remained, considering that after all they were the best company to be found in Paris,—the Vagrants still retained their interest in the gipsy. He thought this very natural on the part of people who, like her, had no prospect but Charmolue and Torterue to which to look forward, and who did not, like him, roam through the realms of imagination upon the wings of Pegasus. He learned from their conversation that his bride of the broken jug had taken refuge in Notre-Dame, and he was very glad of it; but he felt no temptation to visit her. He sometimes wondered what had become of the little goat, and that was all. In the daytime he performed feats of juggling for a living, and at night he wrought out an elaborate memorial against the Bishop of Paris; for he remembered being drenched by his mill-wheels, and he bore him a grudge for it. He also busied himself with comments on that fine work by Baudry-le-Rouge, Bishop of Noyon and Tournay, entitled "*De cupa*

413

*petrarum,"** which had inspired him with an ardent taste for architecture,—a fancy which had replaced in his heart the passion for hermetics, of which indeed it was but a natural corollary, since there is a close connection between hermetics and masonry. Gringoire had turned from the love of an idea to love of the substance.

One day he halted near Saint-Germain-l'Auxerrois, at the corner of a building known as the For-l'Evêque, which faces another known as the For-le-Roi. This For-l'Evêque contained a charming fourteenth-century chapel, the chancel of which looked towards the street. Gringoire was devoutly studying the outside carvings. He was enjoying one of those moments of selfish, exclusive, supreme pleasure, during which the artist sees nothing in the world but art, and sees the world in art. All at once he felt a hand laid heavily on his shoulder. He turned. It was his former friend, his former master, the archdeacon.

He was astounded. It was a long time since he had seen the archdeacon, and Dom Claude was one of those solemn and impassioned men a meeting with whom always upsets the equilibrium of a sceptic philosopher.

The archdeacon was silent for some moments, during which Gringoire had leisure to observe him. He found Dom Claude greatly changed,—pale as a winter morning, hollow-eyed, his hair almost white. The priest at last broke the silence, saying in a calm but icy tone,—

"How are you, Master Pierre?"

"As to my health?" answered Gringoire. "Well, well! I may say I am tolerably robust, upon the whole. I take everything in moderation. You know, master, the secret of good health, according to Hippocrates: *'Id est: cibi, potus, somni, cenus, omnia moderata sint.'"†*

The Stone Cup (Latin); Baudry-le-Rouge and *The Stone Cup* are fictional.

†Food, drink, sleep, love—all in moderation (Latin).

"Then you have nothing to trouble you, Master Pierre?" replied the archdeacon, looking fixedly at Gringoire.

"No, by my faith!"

"And what are you doing now?"

"You see, master, I am examining the cutting of these stones, and the style in which that bas-relief is thrown out."

The priest smiled a bitter smile, which only lifted one corner of his mouth.

"And does that amuse you?"

"It is paradise!" exclaimed Gringoire. And bending over the sculptures with the ravished mien of a demonstrator of living phenomena, he added: "For instance, don't you think that metamorphosis in low-relief is carved with exceeding skill, refinement, and patience? Just look at this little column. Around what capital did you ever see foliage more graceful or more daintily chiseled? Here are three of Jean Maillevin's alto-relievos. They are not the finest works of that great genius. Still, the ingenuousness, the sweetness of the faces, the careless ease of the attitudes and draperies, and that inexplicable charm which is mingled with all their defects, make these tiny figures most delicate and delightful, perhaps almost too much so. Don't you think this is entertaining?"

"Yes, indeed!" said the priest.

"And if you could only see the inside of the chapel!" continued the poet, with his garrulous enthusiasm. "Carvings everywhere, crowded as close as the leaves in the heart of a cabbage! The chancel is fashioned most devoutly, and is so peculiar that I have never seen its like elsewhere."

Dom Claude interrupted him,—

"So you are happy?"

Gringoire eagerly replied,—

"Yes, on my honor! At first I loved women, then animals; now I love stones. They are quite as amusing as animals or women, and they are less treacherous."

The priest pressed his hand to his head. It was his habitual gesture.

"Indeed?"

"Stay!" said Gringoire; "you shall see my pleasures!" He took the arm of the unresisting priest, and led him into the staircase turret of For-l'Evêque. "There's a staircase for you! Every time I see it I am happy. It is the simplest and yet the rarest in Paris. Every step is beveled underneath. Its beauty and simplicity consist in the treads, which, for a foot or more in width, are interlaced, mortised, dovetailed, jointed, linked together, and set into one another in a genuinely solid and goodly way."

"And you desire nothing more?"

"No."

"And you have no regrets?"

"Neither regret nor desire. I have arranged my mode of life."

"What man arranges," said Claude, "circumstances disarrange."

"I am a Pyrrhonian philosopher," replied Gringoire, "and I keep everything equally balanced."

"And how do you earn your living?"

"I still write occasional epics and tragedies; but what brings me in the most, is that trade which you have seen me follow, master,—namely, upholding pyramids of chairs in my teeth."

"That is a sorry trade for a philosopher."

"'Tis keeping up an equilibrium all the same," said Gringoire. "When one has but a single idea he finds it in everything."

"I know that!" responded the archdeacon.

After a pause he added,—

"And yet you are poor enough?"

"Poor! Yes; but not unhappy."

At this instant the sound of horses' hoofs was heard, and our two friends saw a company of archers belonging to the king's ordnance file by at the end of the street, with raised lances, and an officer at their head. The cavalcade was a brilliant one, and clattered noisily over the pavement.

"How you stare at that officer!" said Gringoire to the archdeacon.

"Because I think I have seen him before."

"What is his name?"

"I believe," said Claude, "that his name is Phœbus de Châteaupers."

"Phœbus! a queer name! There is also a Phœbus, Count de Foix. I once knew a girl who never swore save by Phœbus."

"Come with me," said the priest. "I have something to say to you."

Ever since the troops passed by, some agitation was apparent beneath the icy exterior of the archdeacon. He walked on; Gringoire followed, accustomed to obey him, like all who ever approached that man full of such ascendency. They reached the Rue des Bernardins in silence, and found it quite deserted. Here Dom Claude paused.

"What have you to tell me, master?" asked Gringoire.

"Don't you think," replied the archdeacon, with a most reflective air, "that the dress of those horsemen whom we just saw is far handsomer than yours and mine?"

Gringoire shook his head.

"I' faith! I like my red and yellow jacket better than those scales of steel and iron. What pleasure can there be in making as much noise when you walk as the Quai de la Ferraille in an earthquake?"

"Then, Gringoire, you never envied those fine fellows in their warlike array?"

"Envied them what, Sir Archdeacon,—their strength, their armor, or their discipline? Philosophy and independence in rags are far preferable. I would rather be the head of a fly than the tail of a lion."

"That's strange," said the priest, meditatively. "And yet a handsome uniform is a fine thing."

Gringoire, seeing that he was absorbed in thought, left him in order to admire the porch of a neighboring house. He came back clapping his hands.

"If you were not so absorbed in the fine uniforms of those soldiers, Sir Archdeacon, I would beg you to take a look at that door. I always said that my lord Aubry's house had the most superb entrance in the world."

"Pierre Gringoire," said the archdeacon, "what have you done with that little gipsy dancer?"

"Esmeralda? What a sudden change of subject!"

"Was she not your wife?"

"Yes, by means of a broken pitcher. We are married for four years. By the way," added Gringoire, regarding the archdeacon with a half-bantering air, "are you still thinking of her?"

"And you,—do you think of her no longer?"

"Seldom. I have so many other things to occupy me. Heavens! how pretty that little goat of hers was!"

"Did not the girl save your life?"

"She did indeed, by Jupiter!"

"Well, what has become of her? What have you done with her?"

"I can't say, I fancy that they hanged her."

"You really think so?"

"I'm not sure of it. When I saw that they had taken to hanging people, I withdrew from the game."

"Is that all you know about the matter?"

"Stay. I was told that she had taken refuge in Notre-Dame, and that she was in safety there, and I am delighted to hear it; and I can't find out whether the goat was saved along with her. And that's all I know about it."

"I'll tell you more," cried Dom Claude; and his voice, hitherto so low, slow, and almost muffled, became as loud as thunder. "She did indeed take refuge in Notre-Dame. But within three days justice will again overtake her, and she will be hanged upon the Place de Grève. Parliament has issued a decree."

"That's a pity!" said Gringoire.

The priest, in the twinkling of an eye, had recovered his coldness and calm.

"And who the devil," resumed the poet, "has amused himself by soliciting an order of restitution? Why couldn't he have left Parliament in peace? What harm does it do if a poor girl takes shelter under the flying buttresses of Notre-Dame, alongside of the swallows' nests?"

"There are Satans in the world," replied the archdeacon.

"That's a devilish bad job," observed Gringoire.

The archdeacon resumed, after a pause,—

"So she saved your life?"

"From my good friends the Vagrants. A little more, or a little less, and I should have been hanged. They would be very sorry for it now."

"Don't you want to do anything to help her?"

"With all my heart, Dom Claude; but what if I should get myself into trouble?"

"What would that matter?"

"What! what would it matter? How kind you are, master! I have two great works but just begun."

The priest struck his forehead. In spite of his feigned calmness, an occasional violent gesture betrayed his inward struggles.

"How is she to be saved?"

Gringoire said: "Master, I might answer, '*Il padelt*,' which is Turkish for, 'God is our hope.'"

"How is she to be saved?" dreamily repeated the archdeacon.

Gringoire in his turn clapped his hand to his head.

"See here, master, I have a lively imagination; I will devise various expedients. Suppose the king were asked to pardon her?"

"Louis XI,—to pardon!"

"Why not?"

"As well try to rob a tiger of his bone!"

Gringoire set to work to find some fresh solution of the difficulty.

"Well!—stop!—Do you want me to draw up a petition to the midwives declaring the girl to be pregnant?"

This made the priest's hollow eye flash.

"Pregnant, villain! do you know anything about it?"

Gringoire was terrified by his expression. He made haste to say, "Oh, no, not I! our marriage was a true *forismaritagium*. I was entirely left out. But at any rate, we should gain time."

"Folly! infamy! be silent!"

"You are wrong to be so vexed," grumbled Gringoire. "We should gain time; it would do no one any harm, and the mid-wives, who are poor women, would earn forty Paris pence."

The priest paid no attention to him.

"And yet she must be got away!" he muttered. "The order will be executed within three days! Besides, even if there were no order, that Quasimodo! Women have very depraved tastes!" He raised his voice: "Master Pierre, I have considered it well; there's but one means of salvation for her."

"What is it? I, for my part, see none."

"Listen, Master Pierre, and remember that you owe your life to her. I will frankly tell you my idea. The church is watched night and day. No one is allowed to come out but those who are seen to go in. Therefore, you can go in. You will come, and I will take you to her. You will change clothes with her. She will put on your doublet; you will put on her gown."

"So far, so good," remarked the philosopher. "What next?"

"What next? She will walk out in your clothes; you will stay behind in hers. Perhaps they may hang you, but she will be saved."

Gringoire scratched his ear, with a very grave look.

"There!" said he; "that's an idea which would never have occurred to me."

At Dom Claude's unexpected proposition, the poet's benign and open face had suddenly darkened, like a smiling Italian landscape when some fatal blast sweeps a cloud across the sun.

"Well, Gringoire, what do you say to the plan?"

"I say, master, that they would not hang me *perhaps*, but they would hang me without the slightest doubt."

"That does not concern us!"

"The Devil it doesn't!" said Gringoire.

"She saved your life. You would only be paying your debt."

"There are plenty of others which I have not paid."

"Master Pierre, it absolutely must be done."

The archdeacon spoke with authority.

"Listen to me, Dom Claude," replied the dismayed poet. "You cling to that idea, and you are wrong. I don't see why I should be hanged in another person's stead."

"What makes you so fond of life?"

"Oh, a thousand things!"

"What are they, if you please?"

"What? The air, the sky, morning and evening, moonlight, my good friends the Vagabonds, our larks with the girls, the architectural beauties of Paris to study, three big books to write,—one of which is directed against the bishop and his mills,—and I know not what else. Anaxagoras said that he came into the world to admire the sun; and besides, I have the pleasure of spending all my days, from morning till night, with a man of genius, to wit, myself, and that is a mighty agreeable thing."

"Rattle-pate!" muttered the archdeacon. "Well, speak; who preserved that life of yours which you find so delightful? To whom do you owe it that you still breathe this air, behold that sky, and are still able to amuse your feather-brain with trifles and nonsense? Where would you be now, but for her? Would you have her die, to whom you owe your life,—have her die, that sweet, lovely, adorable creature, necessary to the light of the world, more divine than God himself, while you, half madman and half sage, a mere sketch of something or other, a sort of vegetable growth which fancies that it walks and fancies that it thinks,—you are to go on living with the life of which you have robbed her, as useless as a candle at high noon? Come, have a little pity, Gringoire; be generous in your turn; she set you the example."

The priest was excited. At first Gringoire listened with an air of indecision; then he relented, and ended by pulling a tragic grimace, which made his pallid face look like that of a new-born baby with the colic.

"You are pathetic!" said he, wiping away a tear. "Well, I will consider it. That's an odd idea of yours. After all," he added, after a pause, "who knows? Perhaps they would not hang me. Betrothal is not always marriage. When they find me in her cell, so ridiculously arrayed, in cap and petticoats, perhaps they'll burst out laughing. And then, if they do hang me, why, the rope is like any other death; or, rather, it's not like any other death. It is a death worthy of the wise man who has wavered and swung to and fro all his life,—a death which is neither fish nor flesh, like the spirit of the genuine sceptic; a death fully impressed with Pyrrhonism and uncertainty, a happy medium between heaven and earth, which leaves one in suspense. It is the right death for a philosopher, and perhaps I was predestined to it. It is magnificent to die as one has lived."

The priest interrupted him: "Is it agreed?"

"What is death, after all?" continued Gringoire, with exaltation. "An unpleasant moment, a turnpike gate, the passage from little to nothing. Some one having asked Cercidas, of Magalopolis, if he was willing to die, 'Why not?' he answered: 'for after my death I shall see those great men,—Pythagoras among the philosophers, Hecatæus among the historians, Homer among the poets, Olympus among the musicians.'"

The archdeacon offered him his hand. "It is settled, then? You will come tomorrow."

This gesture brought Gringoire back to reality.

"Oh, no; by my faith!" said he in the tone of a man awaking from sleep. "To be hanged! That is too absurd. I'll not do it."

"Farewell, then!" and the archdeacon added between his teeth, "I shall see you again!"

"I have no desire to see that devil of a man again," thought Gringoire; and he hurried after Dom Claude. "Stay, Sir Archdeacon; no malice between old friends! You take an interest in that girl,—in my wife, I should say; it is well. You have planned a stratagem for rescuing her from Notre-Dame; but your scheme is a very disagreeable one for me, Gringoire.

Suppose I have another! I warn you that a most brilliant inspiration has just occurred to me. What if I have a suitable plan for getting her out of her evil plight without compromising my own neck in the least of slip-nooses, what would you say? Wouldn't that satisfy you? Is it absolutely necessary that I should be hanged, to suit you?"

The priest impatiently wrenched the buttons from his cassock, saying, "What a flood of words! What is your scheme?"

"Yes," resumed Gringoire, talking to himself, and laying his finger to his nose in token of his absorption, "that's just it! The Vagabonds are brave fellows. The gipsy nation love her! They will rise at a single word! Nothing easier! A sudden attack; amidst the confusion she can readily be carried off. Tomorrow night. They will ask nothing better."

"Your plan! speak!" said the priest, shaking him roughly.

Gringoire turned majestically towards him. "Let me alone! Don't you see that I am in the throes of composition?" He reflected for a few moments more, then clapped his hands in delight, exclaiming, "Capital! success is assured!"

"Your plan!" angrily repeated Claude.

Gringoire was radiant.

"Come close, and let me whisper it to you. It is really a jolly countermine, and one which will get us all out of difficulty. Zounds! you must confess that I am no fool."

He interrupted himself,—

"Oh, by the way! is the little goat still with the girl?"

"Yes. May the foul fiend fly away with you!"

"They were going to hang her too, were they not?"

"What is that to me?"

"Yes, they would have hanged her. They did hang a sow last month. The hangman likes that; he eats the animal afterwards. Hang my pretty Djali! Poor little lamb!"

"Curses on you!" cried Dom Claude. "You are the executioner yourself. What means of saving her have you hit upon, rascal? Must I tear your idea from you with the forceps?"

"Softly, master! It is this."

Gringoire bent to the archdeacon's ear, and whispered to

him, casting an anxious glance up and down the street meanwhile, although there was no one in sight. When he ended,
Dom Claude took his hand and said coldly, "It is well. Until
tomorrow, then."

"Until tomorrow," repeated Gringoire. And as the archdeacon departed in one direction, he moved away in the other,
muttering. "Here's a pretty business, Master Pierre Gringoire!
Never mind! It shall not be said that because a man is little he
is afraid of a great enterprise. Biton carried a full-grown bull
upon his shoulders; wagtails, black-caps, and stone-chats cross
the sea."

CHAPTER II

Turn Vagabond!

The archdeacon, on returning to the cloisters, found his
brother, Jehan du Moulin, awaiting him at the door of
his cell. He had whiled away the fatigue of waiting by
drawing upon the wall in charcoal his elder brother's profile,
enriched with an exaggerated nose.

Dom Claude scarcely looked at his brother; he had other
cares. That merry roguish face, whose radiance had so often
brightened the priest's gloomy countenance, was now incapable of dissipating the clouds which grew daily thicker over
that corrupt, mephitic, stagnant soul.

"Brother," timidly said Jehan, "I have come to see you."

The archdeacon did not even deign to look at him.

"Well?"

"Brother," continued the hypocrite, "you are so good to
me, and you give me such good advice, that I am always coming back to you."

"Well?"

"Alas! brother, how right you were when you said to me, 'Jehan! Jehan! *cessat doctorum doctrina, discipulorum, disciplina!* Jehan, be prudent; Jehan, be studious; Jehan, do not wander outside the college bounds at night without just cause and leave from your master. Do not quarrel with the Picards (*noli, Joannes, verberare Picardos*). Do not lie and molder like an illiterate ass (*quasi asinus illiteratus*) amidst the litter of the schools. Jehan, suffer yourself to be punished at the discretion of your master. Jehan, go to chapel every evening, and sing an anthem with a collect and prayer to our Glorious Lady, the Virgin Mary.' Alas! What excellent counsels were these!"

"Well?"

"Brother, you see before you a guilty wretch, a criminal, a miserable sinner, a libertine, a monster! My dear brother, Jehan has trampled your advice beneath his feet. I am fitly punished for it, and the good God is strangely just. So long as I had money I rioted and reveled and led a jolly life. Oh, how charming is the face of Vice, but how ugly and crooked is her back! Now, I have not a single silver coin; I have sold my table-cloth, my shirt, and my towel; no more feasting for me! The wax candle has burned out, and I have nothing left but a wretched tallow dip, which reeks in my nostrils. The girls laugh at me. I drink water. I am tormented by creditors and remorse."

"What else?" said the archdeacon.

"Alas! dearest brother, I would fain lead a better life. I came to you full of contrition. I am penitent. I confess my sins. I beat my breast lustily. You were quite right to wish me to become a licentiate, and submonitor of the Collége de Torchi. I now feel that I have the strongest vocation for that office. But I have no ink, I must buy some; I have no pens, I must buy some; I have no paper, I have no books, I must buy some. I am in great want of a little money for all these things, and I come to you, brother, with a contrite heart."

"Is that all?"

"Yes," said the student. "A little money."

"I have none."

The student then said with a grave and at the same time resolute air, "Very well, brother: I am sorry to be obliged to tell you that very fine offers and propositions have been made me by another party. You will not give me the money? No? In that case, I shall turn Vagabond."

As he uttered this monstrous word, he assumed the expression of an Ajax, expecting to see the thunderbolt descend upon his head.

The archdeacon said coldly, —

"Turn Vagabond!"

Jehan bowed low and hurried down the cloister stairs, whistling as he went.

Just as he passed through the courtyard of the cloisters, under his brother's window, he heard that window open, looked up, and saw the archdeacon's stern face at the aperture.

"Go to the devil!" said Dom Claude; "this is the last money which you will ever get from me!"

At the same time he flung at Jehan a purse which raised a large lump on his forehead, and with which he departed, at once angry and pleased, like a dog pelted with marrow-bones.

CHAPTER III

Joy Forever!

The reader may remember that a part of the Court of Miracles was enclosed by the ancient boundary wall of the city, many of whose towers had at this time begun to fall into ruin. One of these towers had been made into a pleasure-house by the Vagabonds. There was a tavern in the lower portion, and other things above. This tower was the most lively and consequently the most horrible spot in the Vagrant community. It was a sort of monstrous bee-hive, which buzzed and hummed night and day. At night, when all the surplus beggars were asleep, when there was not a window still lighted in any of the dirty houses in the square, when no sound was longer to be heard from any of the innumerable hovels, the abode of swarms of thieves, prostitutes, and stolen children or foundlings, the jolly tower might always be known by the noise which rose from it, by the red light which, beaming alike from chimneys, windows, and cracks in the crumbling walls, escaped, as it were, at every pore.

The cellar, then, was the tavern. It was reached by a low door, and a flight of stairs as steep as a classic Alexandrine verse. Over the door, by way of sign, there was a marvelous daub portraying a number of coins fresh from the mint and fresh-killed chickens, with these punning words above: "The Bell-Ringers for the Dead."

One evening, when the curfew-bell was ringing from every belfry in Paris, the sergeants of the watch, had they chanced to enter the much-dreaded Court of Miracles, might have observed that there was even more uproar than usual in the tavern of the Vagabonds; that there was more drinking and more swearing than ordinary. Outside, in the square, numerous groups were chatting together in low tones, as if planning some great enterprise; and here and there some scamp squatted on the ground, sharpening a rusty iron blade upon a paving-stone. Within the tavern itself, however, cards and wine proved so powerful a diversion from the ideas which that evening occupied the minds of the Vagrant community that it would have been hard to guess from the remarks of the drinkers what the scheme on foot really was; they merely seemed somewhat more jovial than usual, and between the legs of every man glistened a weapon,—a pruning-hook, an axe, a big two-edged sword, or the hook of an old hackbut.

The room was circular in shape and very large; but the tables were so closely crowded and the topers so numerous that the entire contents of the tavern—men, women, benches, beer-jugs, drinkers, sleepers, gamblers, able-bodied and crippled—seemed to be heaped together pell-mell, with no more order or harmony than a pile of oyster-shells. A number of tallow dips burned on the tables; but the real luminary of the tavern, which played the same part as the chandelier in an opera-house, was the fire. This cellar was so damp that the fire on the hearth was never suffered to go out, even in midsummer. There was a huge fireplace with carved overhanging mantel, bristling with clumsy iron andirons and kitchen utensils, and one of those tremendous fires of wood and turf mixed, which at night, in village streets, cast such red and spectral images on the opposite walls from the window of a forge. A large dog sat soberly in the ashes, and turned a spit laden with meat before the embers.

In spite of the confusion, after the first glance, three principal groups were readily to be distinguished, pressing about three personages with whom the reader is already acquainted. One of these persons, grotesquely decked with various gaudy Oriental rags, was Mathias Hungadi Spicali, Duke of Egypt and Bohemia. The rascal sat upon a table, with crossed legs and uplifted finger, loudly dispensing his store of black and white magic to the many gaping faces around him. Another mob crowded closely about our old friend, the worthy King of Tunis, or lord of blacklegs, Clopin Trouillefou. Armed to the teeth, he was very seriously, and in low tones, superintending the pillage of an enormous cask full of weapons which stood staved in before him, and from which were disgorged quantities of axes, swords, priming-pans, coats of mail, spear-heads and antique lance-heads, arrows and cross-bow bolts, like so many apples and grapes from a cornucopia. Each took from the heap what he chose,—one a helmet, one a sword-blade, and another a *misericordia*, or cross-handled dagger. The very children armed themselves, and there were even legless cripples, crawling about, barbed and cuirassed, between the legs of the topers, like big beetles.

Lastly a third audience—the noisiest, jolliest, and most numerous of all—thronged the benches and tables, in whose midst held forth and swore a flute-like voice issuing from a heavy suit of armor, complete from helmet to spurs. The individual who had thus imprisoned himself in full panoply was so entirely hidden by his warlike habit that nothing was to be seen of him but an impudent, red, snub nose, a lock of light curly hair, a rosy mouth, and a pair of bold eyes. His belt was stuck full of daggers and knives, a huge sword hung at his side, a rusty cross-bow was on the other thigh, and a vast jug of wine stood before him; not to mention a plump and ragged damsel at his right hand. Every mouth in his vicinity laughed, cursed, and drank.

Add to these twenty secondary groups,—the serving men and maids running about with jugs on their heads; gamblers stooping over their marbles, their hop-scotch, dice, vachette, or exciting game of tringlet; the quarrels in one corner, the kisses in another,—and you will have some idea of the scene over which flickered the glare of a huge roaring fire, which made a myriad of monstrous shadows dance upon the walls.

As for the noise, it was like the inside of a big bell ringing a full peal.

The dripping-pan, in which a shower of fat from the spit was crackling, filled up with its constant sputtering the intervals in the endless dialogues going on from one side of the hall to the other.

Amidst this uproar, a philosopher sat at the back of the room on the bench in the chimney-place, musing, with his feet in the ashes and his eyes on the burning brands; it was Pierre Gringoire.

"Come! make haste, arm yourselves! We march in an hour!" said Clopin Trouillefou to his Men of Slang.

A girl hummed,—

> "Good-night, mamma; good-night, my sire;
>   Who sits up last, rakes down the fire."

Two card-players disputed together.

"Knave," cried the redder-faced of the two, shaking his fist at the other, "I will mark you with the club; then you can take the place of the knave of clubs in the king's own pack of cards."

"*Ouf!*" roared a Norman, readily to be recognized by his nasal twang; "we are crowded together here like so many saints at Caillouville!"

"Boys," said the Duke of Egypt to his followers, speaking in falsetto tones, "the witches of France attend their Sabbath without broomstick, or ointment, or any steed, merely by uttering a few magical words. Italian witches always keep a goat waiting for them at the door. All are obliged to go up the chimney."

The voice of the young scamp armed from head to foot rose above the uproar.

"Noël! Noël!" he shouted. "Today I wear armor for the first time. A Vagrant! I am a Vagrant, by Christ's wounds! Give me drink! Friends, my name is Jehan Frollo du Moulin, and I am a gentleman born. It is my opinion that if God himself were a *gendarme*, he would turn plunderer. Brothers, we are about to go on a fine expedition. We are valiant fellows. Assault the church, break open the doors, carry off the lovely damsel in distress, save her from her judges, save her from the priests; dismantle the cloisters, burn the bishop in his palace. We'll do all this in less time than it takes a burgomaster to eat a spoonful of soup. Our cause is just; we will strip Notre-Dame, and that's the end of it. We'll hang Quasimodo. Do you know Quasimodo, ladies? Did you ever see him ring the big bell of a Whit-Sunday until he was out of breath? My word! it's a lovely sight! He looks like a devil astride of a great gaping pair of jaws. Friends, listen to me. I am a Vagrant to my heart's core; I am a Man of Slang in my inmost soul; I was born a Cadger. I have been very rich, and I've devoured my fortune. My mother meant to make a soldier of me; my father, a subdeacon; my aunt, a member of the Court of Inquiry; my grandmother, prothonotary to the king; my great-aunt, a paymaster in the army; but I,—I turned Vagrant. I told my father that I had made my choice, and he hurled a curse at my head;

and my mother,—she, poor old lady, fell to weeping and sputtering, like that log on the fire. A short life and a merry one, say I! I am as good as a whole houseful of lunatics! Landlady, my darling, more wine! I've money enough still to pay for it. No more Surène wine for me; it frets my throat. Zounds! I'd as soon gargle myself with a swarm of bees!"

Meantime, the rabble applauded his words with shouts of laughter; and seeing that the tumult about him increased, the student exclaimed:—

"Oh, what a delightful confusion! *Populi debacchantis populosa debacchatio!*"* Then he began to sing, his eye rolling in feigned ecstasy, in the voice of a canon intoning vespers: *"Quæ cantica! quæ organa! quæ cantilenæ! quæ melodiæ hic sine fine decantantur! Sonant melliflua hymnorum organa, suavissima angelorum melodia cantica canticorum mira—"*† He stopped short: "Here, you devil of a tavern-keeper, give me some supper!"

There was a moment of comparative quiet, during which the sharp voice of the Duke of Egypt was heard in its turn, instructing his followers:—

"The weasel is called Aduine, the fox Blue-foot or the Wood-ranger, the wolf Grey-foot, or Gold-foot, the bear Old Man or Grandfather. The cap of a gnome will make its possessor invisible, and enable him to see invisible things. Every toad that is baptized should be clad in black or red velvet, a bell round its neck and another at its feet. The godfather holds it by the head, the godmother by the legs."

The Vagrants continued to arm, whispering together as they did so, at the other end of the tavern.

---

*The ravings of the people, popular fury! (Latin).

†What canticles! What instruments! What songs! What melodies are eternally sung here! The instruments of hymns, the soft melody of angels, the admirable canticles of canticles resonate softly, like honey (Latin).

"Poor Esmeralda!" said a gipsy; "she's our sister. We must rescue her."

"Is she still at Notre-Dame?" asked a Jewish-looking Cadger.

"Yes, in good sooth, she is!"

"Well, then, comrades," cried the Cadger, "on to Notre-Dame! So much the more, that there are two statues in the chapel of Saint Féréol and Saint Ferrution,—one of Saint John the Baptist and the other of Saint Anthony,—of solid gold, the two together weighing seven golden marks and fifteen sterlings, and the silver-gilt pedestals weigh seventeen marks and five ounces. I know all about this; I am a jeweler."

Here Jehan's supper was served. He exclaimed, as he threw himself back upon the bosom of the girl next him:—

"By Saint Voult-de-Lucques, known to the world at large as Saint Goguelu, I am perfectly happy. Before me stands a fool staring at me with as smug a face as any archduke. And at my left elbow sits another, with teeth so long that they hide his chin. And then, too, I'm like Marshal de Gié at the siege of Pontoise,—my right wing rests upon an eminence. Body of Mahomet! comrade, you look very like a dealer in tennis-balls, and yet you dare to take your seat by my side! I am a noble, my friend. Nobility and trade cannot keep company. Get you gone! Hollo there, you fellows! don't fall to fighting. What! Baptiste Croque-Oison, you who have so fine a nose, will you risk it against the heavy fists of yonder lout? Donkey! *non cuiquam datum est habere nasum.*[*] You are indeed divine, Jacqueline Ronge-Oreille! 'Tis a pity you're so bald. Hollo! my name is Jehan Frollo, and my brother is an archdeacon. May the devil take him! Every word I say is true. When I turned vagabond, I cheerfully renounced the half of a house situated in paradise, which my brother promised me (*Dimidiam domum in paradiso*). I quote the Scriptures. I have an estate in fee in the Rue Tirechappe, and all the women are

---

[*] It is not given to everyone to have a nose (Latin).

in love with me as truly as it is true that Saint Aloysius was an excellent goldsmith, and that the five handicrafts of the good city of Paris are those of the tanners, leather-dressers, baldric-makers, purse-makers, and cordwainers, and that Saint Lawrence was broiled over egg-shells. I swear, comrades,—

> 'That for a year I'll drink no wine
> If there be any lie in words of mine!'

My charmer, it is moonlight; only look yonder, through that loop-hole; how the wind rumples the clouds,—as I do your kerchief! Come, girls! snuff the children and the candles. Christ and Mahomet! what am I eating now, by Jupiter? Ho, there, you old jade! the hairs which are missing on the heads of your women, I find in your omelets. I say, old girl! I like my omelets bald. May the devil put your nose out of joint! A fine hostelry of Beelzebub this, where the wenches comb their heads with forks!"

So saying, he smashed his plate upon the paved floor, and fell to singing at the top of his lungs:—

> "And for this self of mine,
> Now by the Blood Divine!
> No creed I crave,
> No law to save.
> I have no fire,
> I have no hut;
> And I require
> No faith to put
> In monarch high
> Or Deity!"

Meantime, Clopin Trouillefou had finished his distribution of arms. He approached Gringoire, who seemed plunged in deep thought, with his feet upon an andiron.

"Friend Pierre," said the king of blacklegs, "what the devil are you thinking about?"

Gringoire turned to him with a melancholy smile.

"I love the fire, my dear lord; not for the trivial reason that the fire warms our feet or cooks our soup, but because it throws out sparks. I sometimes spend hours in watching the sparks fly up. I discover a thousand things in these stars that sprinkle the black chimney-back. These stars are worlds as well."

"May I be struck by lightning if I understand you!" said the Vagrant. "Do you know what time it is?"

"I do not," replied Gringoire.

Clopin then went up to the Duke of Egypt:—

"Comrade Mathias, this is not a lucky moment for our scheme. They say that King Louis XI is in Paris."

"So much the more reason for rescuing our sister from his claws," answered the old gipsy.

"You speak like a man, Mathias," said the King of Tunis. "Moreover, we will act adroitly. We need fear no resistance within the church. The canons are mere hares, and we muster strong. The officers of the Parliament will be nicely taken in tomorrow when they come to seize her! By the Pope's bowels! I don't want the pretty maid hanged!"

With these words, Clopin left the tavern.

Meantime, Jehan shouted in hoarse tones,—

"I drink, I eat, I am drunk, I am Jupiter himself! Ha! Pierre l'Assommeur, if you stare at me like that, I'll dust your nose with my fist!"

Gringoire, on his side, roused from his meditations, was contemplating the wild, noisy scene before him, muttering between his teeth: "*Luxuriosa res vinum et tumultuosa ebrietas.** Alas! I have good reasons for not drinking; and how aptly Saint Benedict says: '*Vinum apostatare facit etiam sapientes!*'"†

---

*Wine is a thing of luxury, drunkenness of tumult (Latin).
†To abstain from wine also makes men wise! (Latin).

At this instant Clopin returned, and cried in a voice of thunder,—

"Midnight!"

At this word, which had the effect of "Boot and saddle!" upon a regiment at rest, all the Vagrants, men, women, and children, rushed hurriedly from the tavern, with a great clatter of arms and old iron.

The moon was overcast.

The Court of Miracles was quite dark. There was not a light to be seen; and yet it was far from being empty. A crowd of men and women, talking together in low tones had collected. There was an audible buzz of voices and a glitter of all sorts of weapons in the darkness. Clopin mounted a huge stone.

"To your ranks, Men of Slang!" he cried. "To your ranks, Gipsies! To your ranks, Greeks!"

There was a stir in the gloom. The vast multitude seemed to be forming into line. After a brief pause the King of Tunis again raised his voice:—

"Now, silence as we pass through Paris! *'The chive in the cly'** is the password! The torches will not be lighted until we reach Notre-Dame! Forward, march!"

Ten minutes later the horsemen of the watch fled in terror before a long procession of dark, silent men descending upon the Pont-au-Change through the crooked streets which traverse the closely built region of the Halles in every direction.

---

*The dagger in the pocket (thieves' slang).

CHAPTER IV

An Awkward Friend

That same night Quasimodo did not sleep. He had just made his last round in the church. He did not notice, as he closed the doors, that the archdeacon passed, and seemed somewhat vexed at seeing him so carefully bolt and chain the immense iron bars which made the wide leaves as solid as a wall. Dom Claude looked even more preoccupied than usual. Moreover, ever since his nocturnal adventure in the cell he had abused Quasimodo constantly; but though he maltreated him, nay, sometimes even beat him, nothing shook the submission, patience, and humble resignation of the faithful ringer. From the archdeacon he would bear anything and everything,—insults, threats, blows,—without murmuring a reproach, without uttering a complaint. At most he anxiously followed Dom Claude with his eye, as he climbed the tower stairs; but the archdeacon had carefully abstained from appearing again in the gipsy's presence.

That night, then, Quasimodo, after giving a glance at his poor forsaken bells,—at Jacqueline, Marie, and Thibauld— had ascended to the roof of the north tower, and there, placing his well-closed dark-lantern upon the leads, gazed out over Paris. The night, as we have already said, was very dark. Paris, which at this time was but scantily lighted, presented to the eye a confused collection of black masses, intersected here and there by the silvery bend of the Seine. Quasimodo saw but a single light, and that in the window of a distant structure, the dim, dark outlines of which were distinctly visible above the roofs, in the direction of Porte Saint-Antoine. There, too, some one was watching.

While his one eye roamed over the expanse of mist and night, the ringer felt within him an inexplicable sense of alarm. For some days he had been upon his guard. He had constantly seen evil-looking men prowling about the church, and never taking their eyes from the young girl's hiding-place. He fancied that there might be some plot brewing against the unfortunate refugee. He imagined that she was a victim to popular hatred like himself, and that something might come of it soon. He therefore stationed himself upon his tower, on the alert, "dreaming in his dreamery," as Rabelais has it, his eye by turns bent upon the cell and upon Paris, keeping faithful watch, like a trusty dog, with a thousand doubts and fears.

All at once, while scrutinizing the great city with the one eye which Nature, by a sort of compensating justice, had made so piercing that it might almost supply the other organs which he lacked, it seemed to him that the outline of the Quai de la Vieille-Pelleterie looked somewhat peculiarly, that there was something moving at that point, that the line of the parapet darkly defined against the white water was not straight and steady like that of the other quays, but that it rippled, as he gazed, like the waves of a river or the heads of a moving multitude.

This struck him as singular. He redoubled his attention. The movement seemed to be towards the City. There was no light to be seen. It continued for some time, upon the quay; then it subsided gradually, as if whatever might be passing had entered the interior of the Island; then it ceased entirely, and the line of the quay became straight and motionless once more.

While Quasimodo was lost in conjectures, it seemed to him as if the movement had reappeared in the Rue du Parvis, which leads into the City directly opposite the front of Notre-Dame. At last, dense as was the darkness, he saw the head of a column emerge from that street, and in an instant fill the square with a crowd in which nothing could be distinguished in the shadows but that it was a crowd.

The spectacle had its terrors. It is probable that this strange procession, which seemed so desirous of stealing along unseen under cover of darkness, was equally careful to observe unbroken silence. And yet some noise appeared inevitable, were it only the tramp of feet. But this sound could not reach our deaf man's ear, and the vast host, so dimly seen, and wholly unheard by him, yet moving and marching onward so near him, produced upon him the effect of an army of ghosts, mute, impalpable, hidden in mists. He seemed to see a fog-bank full of men advancing upon him; to see shadows stirring amid the shades.

Then his fears revived; the idea of an attempt against the gipsy girl again presented itself to his mind. He had a confused sense that a violent scene was at hand. At this critical moment he held counsel with himself with better judgment and more promptness than could have been expected from so ill-organized a brain. Should he awaken the gipsy; help her to escape? Which way? The streets were infested; the church backed up against the river. There was no boat, no outlet! There was but one thing to be done,—to die if need be on the threshold of Notre-Dame; to resist at least until some help should come, if any there were, and not to disturb Esmeralda's sleep. The wretched girl would be wakened soon enough to die. This resolve once taken he began to scan the enemy with greater composure.

The crowd seemed to increase every moment in the square. He presumed that they must be making very little noise, as the windows in the streets and square remained closed. Suddenly a light shone out, and in an instant seven or eight blazing torches rose above the heads of the multitude, shaking out their tufts of flame in the darkness. Quasimodo then plainly saw an eddying, frightful mass of ragged men and women below him in the square, armed with scythes, pikes, bill-hooks, and halberds, whose myriad blades glistened on every hand. Here and there black pitchforks were reared horn-like above those hideous faces. He vaguely recalled this mob, and fancied he recognized the heads of those who had but a few months previous saluted him as the Pope of Fools. A man, grasping a torch in one hand and a whip in the other, climbed upon a post and seemed to be haranguing the crowd.

At the same time the strange army went through a number of evolutions, as if taking up their station about the church. Quasimodo picked up his lantern and descended to the platform between the towers, to get a nearer view and to consider means of defense.

Clopin Trouillefou, having arrived before the great door of Notre-Dame, had indeed drawn up his troops in line of battle. Although he did not expect to meet with any resistance, he desired, like a prudent general, to preserve such order as would enable him, if necessary, to confront a sudden attack from the watch. He had therefore stationed his brigade in such a way that, viewed from above and from a distance, you would have taken them for the Roman triangle of the battle of Ecnoma, the boar's head of Alexander, or the famous wedge of Gustavus Adolphus. The base of this triangle rested upon the farther end of the square, so that it blocked the Rue du Parvis; one side faced the Hôtel-Dieu, the other the Rue Saint-Pierre-aux-Bœufs. Clopin Trouillefou had placed himself at the head, with the Duke of Egypt, our friend Jehan, and the most daring of the beggar tribe.

Such an attack as the vagrants were now planning to make upon Notre-Dame was no very uncommon thing in the towns of the Middle Ages. What are now known as police did not then exist. There was no central, controlling power in populous cities, or more particularly in capitals. The feudal system constructed these large communities after a strange fashion. A city was a collection of a thousand seigniories, or manors, which divided it up into districts of all shapes and sizes. Hence arose a thousand contradictory police forces; that is, no police at all. In Paris, for instance, independently of the one hundred and forty-one nobles laying claim to manorial rights, there were twenty-five who also claimed the additional right to administer justice,—from the Bishop of Paris who owned one hundred and five streets, down to the Prior of Notre-Dame des Champs who owned but four. All these feudal justiciaries recognized the supreme power of the king only in name. All had right of way; all were on their own ground.

Louis XI, that indefatigable laborer who did such good work in beginning the demolition of the feudal structure, carried on by Richelieu and Louis XIV to the advantage of royalty, and completed by Mirabeau to the advantage of the people,—Louis XI had indeed striven to break this network of seigniories which enveloped Paris, by hurling violently athwart it two or three police ordinances. Thus in 1465 the inhabitants were commanded to light their windows with candles at nightfall, and to shut up their dogs, under pain of the halter; during the same year an order was issued that the streets must be closed with iron chains after dark, and citizens were forbidden to wear daggers or any offensive weapons in the street at night. But all these attempts at municipal legislation soon fell into disuse. People let the wind blow out the candles in their windows, and allowed their dogs to roam; the iron chains were only put up in time of siege; the prohibition of daggers led to but little change. The old framework of feudal jurisdiction remained standing,—an immense number of bailiwicks and seigniories, crossing one another throughout the city, crowded, tangled, interlapping, and interwoven; a useless confusion of watches, sub-watches, and counter-watches, in spite of which brigandage, rapine, and sedition were carried on by main force. It was not, therefore, an unheard-of thing, in the midst of such disorder, for a part of the populace to make a bold attack upon a palace, a great mansion, or a house, in the most thickly settled quarters of the town. In the majority of cases the neighbors did not meddle with the matter, unless the pillage extended to their own houses. They turned a deaf ear to the musketry, closed their shutters, barricaded their doors, left the outbreak to be settled with or without the watch, and next day it would be reported: "Last night Etienne Barbette's house was entered." "Marshal Clermont was carried off," etc. Accordingly, not only royal habitations, the Louvre, the Palace, the Bastille, the Tournelles, but the houses of the nobility, the Petit-Bourbon, the Hôtel de Sens, Hôtel D'Angoulême, etc., had their battlemented walls and their portcullises. Churches were guarded by their sanctity. Certain of them, however, but not Notre-Dame, were fortified. The abbot of Saint-Germain-des-Prés was as strongly intrenched as any baron, and more brass was consumed there in bombards than in bells. His fortress was still standing in 1610. Now the church alone exists, and that in ruins.

Let us return to Notre-Dame.

When the first arrangements had been made (and we must say, to the honor of the discipline of the Vagrants, that Clopin's orders were carried out in silence and with admirable precision), the worthy leader of the band mounted the parapet of the Parvis, and raised his hoarse, surly voice, keeping his face turned towards Notre-Dame, and waving his torch, the flame of which, flickering in the wind, and now and again veiled by its own smoke, first revealed and then hid the front of the church, lit up with a reddish glow.

"To you, Louis de Beaumont, Bishop of Paris, Councillor of the Court of Parliament, I, Clopin Trouillefou, king of blacklegs, king of rogues, prince of slang, and bishop of fools, proclaim: Our sister, falsely condemned for magic, has taken refuge in your church. You owe her shelter and safeguard. Now, the Parliamentary Court desire to recover her person, and you have given your consent; so that indeed she would be hanged tomorrow on the Place de Grève were not God and the Vagrants here to aid her. We have therefore come hither to you, O Bishop. If your church be sacred, our sister is likewise sacred; if our sister be not sacred, neither is your church. Wherefore we summon you to deliver over to us the girl if you would save your church, or we will seize upon the girl, and will plunder the church, which will be a righteous deed. In token whereof I here plant my banner; and may God have you in his guard, O Bishop of Paris!"

Unfortunately Quasimodo could not hear these words, uttered as they were with a sort of sombre, savage majesty. A Vagrant handed the banner to Clopin, who planted it solemnly between two flagstones. It was a pitchfork, from whose prongs hung a bleeding mass of carrion.

This done, the King of Tunis turned and glanced at his army,—a fierce host, whose eyes glittered almost as brightly as their pikes. After an instant's pause he cried,—

"Forward, boys! To your work, rebels!"

Thirty stout fellows, with sturdy limbs and crafty faces, stepped from the ranks with hammers, pincers, and crowbars on their shoulders. They advanced towards the main entrance of the church, mounted the steps, and were soon crouching beneath the arch, working away at the door with pincers and levers. A crowd of Vagrants followed them to help or encourage. They thronged the eleven steps leading to the porch.

Still the door refused to yield. "The devil! how tough and obstinate it is!" said one. "It is old, and its joints are stiff," said another. "Courage, comrades!" replied Clopin. "I'll wager my head against an old slipper that you'll have opened the door, captured the girl, and stripped the high-altar before a single sacristan is awake. Stay! I think the lock is giving way."

Clopin was interrupted by a tremendous din behind him. He turned. A huge beam had fallen from the sky; it had crushed a dozen of his Vagrants on the church steps and rebounded to the pavement with the crash of a cannon, breaking the legs of various tatterdemalions here and there in the crowd, which scattered with cries of terror. In the twinkling of an eye the enclosed portion of the square was cleared. The rebels, although protected by the deep arches of the porch, forsook the door, and Clopin himself retired to a respectful distance.

"I had a narrow escape!" cried Jehan. "I felt the wind of it as it passed, by Jove! but Pierre l'Assommeur is knocked down!"*

It is impossible to picture the mingled consternation and affright which overcame the bandits with the fall of this beam. They stood for some moments staring into the air, more dis-

---

*A play on words, as *l'assommeur* means "he who knocks down."

mayed by that fragment of wood than by twenty thousand of the king's archers.

"Satan!" growled the Duke of Egypt; "that smells of sorcery!"

"It must be the moon which flung that log at us," said Andry le Rouge.

"Why," replied François Chanteprune, "they say the moon is a friend of the Virgin Mary!"

"By the Pope's head!" exclaimed Clopin; "but you are a parcel of fools!" And yet even he could not explain the fall of the plank.

Meanwhile, nothing was to be seen upon the front of the cathedral, to the top of which the light of the torches did not reach. The heavy plank lay in the middle of the square, and loud were the groans of the wretched men who had received its first shock, and who had been almost cut in two upon the sharp edges of the stone steps.

The King of Tunis, his first dismay over, at last hit upon an explanation which seemed plausible to his companions:—

"Odds bodikins! Is the clergy defending itself? Then, sack! sack!"

"Sack!" repeated the rabble, with a frantic cheer. And they discharged a volley of cross-bows and hackbuts at the church.

At this sound the peaceable inhabitants of the houses round about were awakened; several windows were thrown open, and nightcaps and hands holding candles appeared at them.

"Fire at the windows!" roared Clopin. The windows were hastily closed, and the poor citizens, who had barely had time to cast a terrified glance at that scene of glare and tumult, returned to sweat with fear beside their wives, wondering if the witches were holding their revels in the square before Notre-Dame, or if the Burgundians had made another attack, as in '64. Then the husbands thought of robbery, the wives of violence, and all trembled.

"Sack!" repeated the Men of Slang; but they dared not advance. They looked at the church; they looked at the beam.

The beam did not budge, the building retained its calm, deserted look; but something rooted the Vagrants to the spot.

"To work, I say, rebels!" shouted Trouillefou. "Force the door!"

No one stirred.

"Body o' me!" said Clopin; "here's a pack of fellows who are afraid of a rafter."

An old rebel then addressed him:—

"Captain, it's not the rafter that stops us; it's the door, which is entirely covered with iron bars. Our pincers are of no use."

"Well, what would you have to burst it in?" asked Clopin.

"Ah! we need a battering-ram."

The King of Tunis ran bravely up to the much-dreaded beam, and set his foot upon it. "Here you have one," he exclaimed; "the canons themselves have sent it to you." And with a mocking salutation in the direction of the church, he added. "Thanks, gentlemen!"

This piece of bravado proved effective; the charm of the beam was broken. The Vagrants recovered their courage; soon the heavy log, lifted like a feather by two hundred sturdy arms, was furiously hurled against the great door which they had vainly striven to shake. Seen thus, in the dim light cast by the scanty torches of the Vagrants, that long beam borne by that crowd of men, who rapidly dashed it against the church, looked like some monstrous beast with countless legs attacking the stone giantess headforemost.

At the shock of the log, the semi-metallic door rang like a vast drum; it did not yield, but the whole cathedral shook and the deep vaults of the building re-echoed.

At the same moment a shower of large stones began to rain from the top of the façade upon the assailants.

"The devil!" cried Jehan; "are the towers shaking down their balustrades upon our heads?"

But the impulse had been given, the King of Tunis setting the example. The bishop was certainly defending himself;

and so they only beat against the door with greater fury, despite the stones which cracked their skulls to right and left.

It is remarkable that these stones all fell singly, but they followed one another in rapid succession. The Men of Slang always felt two at a time,—one at their legs, the other on their heads. Few of them missed their mark, and already a large heap of dead and wounded gasped and bled under the feet of the besiegers, whose ranks, they being now goaded to madness, were constantly renewed. The long beam still battered the door at regular intervals, like the clapper of a bell; the stones still rained down, and the door creaked and groaned.

The reader has doubtless guessed that the unexpected resistance which so enraged the Vagrants came from Quasimodo.

Chance had unluckily served the brave deaf man.

When he descended to the platform between the towers, his head whirled in confusion. For some moments he ran along the gallery, coming and going like a madman, looking down from above at the compact mass of Vagrants ready to rush upon the church, imploring God or the devil to save the gipsy girl. He thought of climbing the south belfry and ringing the alarm; but before he could set the bell in motion, before big Marie's voice could utter a single shriek, the church door might be forced ten times over. This was just the instant when the rebels advanced with their tools. What was to be done?

All at once he remembered that the masons had been at work all day repairing the wall, timbers, and roof of the south tower. This was a ray of light. The wall was of stone, the roof of lead, and the timbers of wood. (The timbers were so huge, and there were so many of them, that they went by the name of "the forest.")

Quasimodo flew to the tower. The lower rooms were indeed full of materials. There were piles of rough stones, sheets of lead in rolls, bundles of laths, heavy beams already shaped by the saw, heaps of plaster and rubbish,—a complete arsenal.

There was no time to be lost. The hammers and levers

were at work below. With a strength increased tenfold by his sense of danger, he lifted one of the beams, the heaviest and longest that he could find; he shoved it through a dormer-window, then laying hold of it again outside the tower, he pushed it over the edge of the balustrade surrounding the platform, and launched it into the abyss. The enormous rafter, in its fall of one hundred and sixty feet, scraping the wall, smashing the carvings, turned over and over several times like one of the arms of a windmill moving through space. At last it reached the ground; an awful shriek rose upon the air, and the black beam, rebounding from the pavement, looked like a serpent darting on its prey.

Quasimodo saw the Vagrants scatter, as the log fell, like ashes before the breath of a child. He took advantage of their terror; and while they stared superstitiously at the club dropped from heaven, and put out the eyes of the stone saints over the porch with a volley of arrows and buckshot, Quasimodo silently collected plaster, stones, gravel, even the masons' bags of tools, upon the edge of that balustrade from which the beam had already been launched.

Thus, as soon as they began to batter at the door, the hail of stones began to fall, and it seemed to them as if the church were falling about their heads.

Any one who had seen Quasimodo at that moment would have been frightened. Besides the projectiles which he had piled upon the balustrade, he had collected a heap of stones on the platform itself. As soon as the missiles at the edge of the railing were exhausted, he had recourse to the heap below. He stooped and rose, stooped and rose again, with incredible activity. His great gnome-like head hung over the balustrade, then a huge stone fell, then another, and another. Now and again he followed a particularly fine stone with his eye, and if it did good execution he said, "Hum!"

Meantime the ragamuffins were not discouraged. More than twenty times already the heavy door which they were attacking had trembled beneath the weight of their oaken battering-ram, multiplied by the strength of a hundred men. The panels cracked; the carvings flew in splinters; the hinges, at every blow, shook upon their screw-rings; the boards were reduced to powder, crushed between the iron braces. Luckily for Quasimodo, there was more iron than wood.

Still, he felt that the great door was yielding. Although he could not hear, every stroke of the beam echoed at once through the vaults of the church and through his soul. He saw from above the Vagrants, full of rage and triumph, shaking their fists at the shadowy façade; and he coveted, for himself and for the gipsy girl, the wings of the owls which flew over his head in numbers.

His shower of stones did not suffice to repel the enemy.

At this moment of anguish he observed, a little below the balustrade from which he was crushing the Men of Slang, two long stone gutters, or spouts, which emptied directly over the great door. The inner orifice of these spouts opened upon a level with the platform. An idea flashed into his mind. He ran to the hovel which he occupied as ringer, found a fagot, placed upon this fagot a quantity of bundles of laths and rolls of lead,—ammunition which he had not yet used,—and having carefully laid this pile before the mouth of the two spouts, he set fire to it with his lantern.

During this space of time, the stones having ceased to fall, the Vagrants had also ceased to look up. The bandits, panting like a pack of dogs which have hunted a wild boar to his lair, crowded tumultuously about the door, disfigured by the battering-ram, but still holding firm. They awaited, with a shudder of eagerness, the final blow which should shiver it. Each one strove to be nearest to it, that he might be first, when it opened, to rush into that wealthy cathedral, the vast magazine in which were stored all the riches of three centuries. They reminded each other, with roars of joy and greed, of the beautiful silver crosses, the gorgeous brocade copes, the superb monuments of silver-gilt, the magnificences of the choir, the dazzling holiday displays, the Christmas ceremonies glittering with torches, the Easters brilliant with sunshine,—all the splendid and solemn occasions when shrines, candlesticks,

pyxes, tabernacles, and reliquaries embossed the altars with
incrusted gold and diamonds. Certainly at this auspicious
moment every one of the Vagrants thought far less of freeing
the gipsy girl than they did of sacking Notre-Dame. We would
even be willing to believe that to a goodly number of them Esmeralda was but a mere pretext,—if thieves require a pretext.

All at once, just as they gathered together about the battering-ram for a final effort, every man holding his breath and
straining his muscles so as to lend all his strength to the decisive blow, a howl more frightful even than that which had
risen and died away from beneath the rafter, again burst from
their midst. Those who did not shriek, those who still lived,
looked up. Two streams of molten lead fell from the top of the
building into the very thickest of the throng. The sea of men
had subsided beneath the boiling metal which had made, at
the points where it fell, two black and smoking holes in the
crowd, as boiling water would in snow. About them writhed
the dying, half consumed, and shrieking with agony. Around
the two principal jets there were drops of this horrible rain
which sprinkled the assailants, and penetrated their skulls like
gimlets of flame. A leaden fire riddled the poor wretches as
with countless hailstones.

The clamor was heartrending. They fled pell-mell, flinging the beam upon the corpses, the courageous with the
timid, and the square was cleared for the second time.

All eyes were turned to the top of the church. What they
saw was most strange. Upon the top of the topmost gallery,
higher than the central rose-window, a vast flame ascended
between the two belfries with whirling sparks,—a vast flame,
fierce and strong, fragments of which were ever and anon
borne away by the wind with the smoke. Below this flame,
below the dark balustrade with its glowing trefoils, two spouts,
terminating in gargoyles, vomiting unintermittent sheets of
fiery rain, whose silvery streams shone out distinctly against
the gloom of the lower part of the cathedral front. As they approached the ground, these jets of liquid lead spread out into
sheaves, like water pouring from the countless holes of the

rose in a watering-pot. Above the flame, the huge towers, each
of which showed two sides, clear and trenchant, one all black,
the other all red, seemed even larger than they were, from the
immensity of the shadow which they cast, reaching to the very
sky. Their innumerable carvings of demons and dragons assumed a mournful aspect. The restless light of the flames
made them seem to move. There were serpents, which
seemed to be laughing, gargoyles yelping, salamanders blowing the fire, dragons sneezing amid the smoke. And among
these monsters, thus wakened from their stony slumbers by
the flame, by the noise, there was one that walked about, and
moved from time to time across the fiery front of the burning
pile like a bat before a candle.

Doubtless this strange beacon would rouse from afar the
woodcutter on the hills of Bicêtre, in alarm at seeing the gigantic shadow of the towers of Notre-Dame cast flickering
upon his moors.

The silence of terror fell upon the Vagrants, and while it
lasted nothing was heard save the cries of consternation uttered by the clergy shut up in the cloisters, and more restive
than horses in a burning stable, the stealthy sound of windows
hastily opened and more hastily closed, the bustle and stir in
the Hôtel-Dieu, the wind roaring through the flames, the last
gasp of the dying, and the constant pattering of the leaden
rain upon the pavement.

Meantime, the leaders of the Vagrants had withdrawn to
the porch of the Gondalaurier house, and were holding council. The Duke of Egypt, seated on a post, gazed with religious
awe at the magical pile blazing in the air at the height of two
hundred feet. Clopin Trouillefou gnawed his brawny fists
with rage.

"Impossible to enter!" he muttered between his teeth.

"An old witch of a church!" growled the aged gipsy Mathias Hungadi Spicali.

"By the Pope's whiskers!" added a grey-haired old scamp
who had served his time in the army, "here are church-spouts
that beat the portcullis of Lectoure at spitting molten lead."

"Do see that demon walking to and fro before the fire!" exclaimed the Duke of Egypt.

"By the Rood!" said Clopin, "it's that damned bell-ringer; it's Quasimodo!"

The gipsy shook his head. "I tell you that it is the spirit Sabnac, the great marquis, the demon of fortifications. He takes the form of an armed soldier, with a lion's head. He turns men to stones, with which he builds towers. He commands fifty legions. It is surely he; I recognize him. Sometimes he is clad in a fine gown of figured gold made in the Turkish fashion."

"Where is Bellevigne de l'Etoile?" asked Clopin.

"He is dead," replied a Vagrant woman.

Andry le Rouge laughed a foolish laugh. "Notre-Dame makes plenty of work for the hospital," said he.

"Is there no way to force that door?" cried the King of Tunis, stamping his foot.

The Duke of Egypt pointed sadly to the two streams of boiling lead which still streaked the dark façade like two long phosphorescent spindles.

"Churches have been known to defend themselves before," he observed with a sigh. "St. Sophia, at Constantinople, some forty years ago, thrice threw down the crescent of Mahomet merely by shaking her domes, which are her heads. Guillaume de Paris, who built this church, was a magician."

"Must we then go home discomfited like a pack of wretched lackeys?" said Clopin, "and leave our sister here, to be hanged by those cowled wolves tomorrow!"

"And the sacristy, where there are cartloads of gold?" added a Vagabond whose name we regret that we do not know.

"By Mahomet's beard!" cried Trouillefou.

"Let us make one more trial," added the Vagabond.

Mathias Hungadi shook his head.

"We shall not enter by the door. We must find the weak spot in the old witch's armor,—a hole, a back gate, any joint."

"Who'll join us?" said Clopin. "I shall have another try. By the way, where is that little student Jehan, who put on such a coat of mail?"

"He is probably dead," answered some one; "we don't hear his laugh."

The King of Tunis frowned: "So much the worse. There was a stout heart beneath that steel. And Master Pierre Gringoire?"

"Captain Clopin," said Andry le Rouge, "he took to his heels when we had only come as far as the Pont-aux-Changeurs."

Clopin stamped his foot. "By the Mass! he urges us on, and then leaves us in the lurch! A cowardly prater, helmeted with a slipper!"

"Captain Clopin," said Andry le Rouge, who was looking down the Rue du Parvis, "there comes the little student."

"Pluto be praised!" said Clopin. "But what the devil is he lugging after him?"

It was indeed Jehan, running as fast as was possible under the weight of his heavy armor and a long ladder which he dragged sturdily over the pavement, more breathless than an ant harnessed to a blade of grass twenty times its own length.

"Victory! *Te Deum!*" shouted the student. "Here's the ladder belonging to the longshoremen of St. Landry's wharf."

Chopin approached him: —

"Zounds, child! what are you going to do with that ladder?"

"I've got it," replied Jehan, panting and gasping. "I knew where it was, — under the shed at the lieutenant's house. There's a girl there who knows me, who thinks me a perfect Cupid. I took advantage of her folly to get the ladder, and I have the ladder, odds bodikins! The poor girl came down in her shift to let me in."

"Yes," said Clopin; "but what will you do with the ladder now that you have got it?"

Jehan looked at him with a mischievous, cunning air, and cracked his fingers like so many castanets. At that moment he was sublime. He had on his head one of those enormous fifteenth-century helmets, which terrified the foe by their fantastic crests. It bristled with ten iron beaks, so that he might have disputed the tremendous epithet of δεκέμ-βολος,* with Nestor's Homeric vessel.

"What shall I do with it, august King of Tunis? Do you see that row of statues with their foolish faces yonder, above the three porches?"

"Yes; what then?"

"That is the gallery of the kings of France."

"What is that to me?" said Clopin.

"Wait a bit! At the end of that gallery there is a door which is always on the latch, and with this ladder I will climb to it, and then I am in the church."

"Let me go up first, boy!"

"Not a bit of it, comrade; the ladder is mine. Come, you may be second."

"May Beelzebub strangle you!" said the surly Clopin. "I'll not be second to any man."

"Then, Clopin, seek a ladder for yourself"; and Jehan set out at full speed across the square, dragging his ladder after him, shouting,—

"Help, lads, help!"

In an instant the ladder was lifted, and placed against the railing of the lower gallery, over one of the side doors. The crowd of Vagrants, uttering loud cheers, thronged to the foot of it, eager to ascend; but Jehan maintained his right, and was first to set foot upon the rounds. The journey was long and slow. The gallery of the kings of France is in this day some sixty feet above the pavement. The eleven steps leading to the door made it still higher at the time of our story. Jehan climbed slowly, hampered by his heavy armor, clinging to the ladder with one hand and his cross-bow with the other. When he reached the middle, he cast a melancholy glance downwards at the poor dead Men of Slang who bestrewed the steps.

---

*Armed with ten spurs (Greek).

"Alas!" said he, "there's a heap of corpses worthy of the fifth book of the Iliad!" Then he resumed his ascent. The Vagrants followed him; there was one upon every round. As this undulating line of cuirassed backs rose through the darkness, it looked like a serpent with scales of steel rearing its length along the church. Jehan, who represented the head, whistled shrilly, thus completing the illusion.

At last the student touched the balcony, and nimbly strode over it, amid the applause of the assembled Vagrants. Thus master of the citadel, he uttered a shout of joy, and all at once paused, petrified. He had seen behind one of the royal statues Quasimodo and his glittering eye lurking in the shadow.

Before a second assailant could set foot upon the gallery, the terrible hunchback leaped to the top of the ladder, seized, without a word, the ends of the two uprights in his strong hands, raised them, pushed them from the wall, balancing for a moment, amid screams of agony, the long, pliant ladder loaded with Vagrants from top to bottom, and then suddenly, with superhuman force, hurled the clustering mass of men into the square. There was an instant when the boldest trembled. The ladder plunged backward, for a moment stood erect, and seemed to hesitate, then tottered, then all at once, describing a frightful arc of eighty feet in radius, fell headlong on the pavement with its burden of bandits, more swiftly than a drawbridge when the chains which hold it are broken. There was an awful volley of curses, then all was hushed, and a few mutilated wretches crawled away from under the heap of dead.

A clamor of rage and pain followed the first cries of triumph among the besiegers. Quasimodo looked on unmoved, leaning upon the balustrade. He seemed like some long-haired old king at his window.

Jehan Frollo, for his part, was in a critical situation. He was alone in the gallery with the dreadful ringer, parted from his companions by a perpendicular wall eighty feet high. While Quasimodo juggled with the ladder, the student hurried to the postern, which he supposed would be open. Not at all.

The deaf man, on entering the gallery had fastened it behind him. Jehan then hid himself behind a stone king, not daring to breathe, and eyeing the monstrous hunchback with terror, like the man who, making love to the wife of the keeper of a menagerie, went one night to see her by appointment, climbed the wrong wall, and abruptly found himself face to face with a white bear.

For a few moments the deaf man paid no heed to him; but finally he turned his head and started. He had just seen the student.

Jehan prepared for a rude encounter; but the deaf man stood motionless: he had merely turned, and was looking at the youth.

"Ho! ho!" said Jehan, "why do you fix that single melancholy eye so steadfastly upon me?"

As he said this, the young scamp slyly adjusted his crossbow.

"Quasimodo," he cried, "I am going to change your name! Henceforth you shall be called 'the blind!'"

The arrow flew. The winged bolt whizzed through the air, and was driven into the hunchback's left arm. It disturbed Quasimodo no more than a scratch would have done the statue of King Pharamond. He put his hand to the dart, pulled it forth, and quietly broke it across his great knee; then he let the two pieces fall to the ground rather than threw them down. But Jehan had no time to fire a second shot. The arrow broken, Quasimodo drew a long breath, leaped like a grasshopper, and came down upon the student, whose armor was flattened against the wall by the shock.

Then by the dim light of the torches a terrible thing might have been seen.

Quasimodo with his left hand grasped both Jehan's arms, the poor fellow making no resistance, so hopeless did he feel that it would be. With his right hand the deaf man removed from him one after the other, in silence and with ominous slowness, all the pieces of his armor,—the sword, the daggers, the helmet, the cuirass, and the brassarts. He looked like a monkey picking a nut as he dropped the student's iron shell, bit by bit, at his feet.

When the youth found himself stripped, disarmed, naked, and helpless in those terrible hands, he did not try to speak to that deaf man, but he laughed impudently in his face, and sang, with the bold unconcern of a lad of sixteen, the song then popular:—

> "She's clad in bright array,
>   The city of Cambray.
>   Marafin plundered her one day—"

He did not finish. They saw Quasimodo upright on the parapet, holding the boy by the feet with one hand, and swinging him round like a sling over the abyss; then a sound was heard like a box made of bone dashed against a wall, and something fell, but caught a third of the way down upon a projection. It was a dead body which hung there, bent double, the back broken, the skull empty.

A cry of horror rose from the Vagrants.

"Vengeance!" yelled Clopin. "Sack!" replied the multitude. "Assault! assault!"

Then there was an awful howl, intermingled with all languages, all dialects, and all accents. The poor student's death filled the mob with zealous fury. Shame gained the upper hand, and wrath that they had so long been held in check before a church by a hunchback. Rage found ladders, multiplied torches, and in a few moments Quasimodo, in despair, beheld that fearful swarm mounting on all sides to attack Notre-Dame. Those who had no ladders had knotted ropes; those who had no ropes scrambled up by the jutting sculptures. They clung to one another's rags. There was no way to resist this rising tide of awful figures; fury gleamed from their fierce faces; their grimy foreheads streamed with perspiration; their eyes gleamed; all these grimaces, all these deformities beset Quasimodo. It seemed as if some other church had sent its gorgons, its medieval animals, its dragons, its demons, and its most fantastic carvings, to lay siege to Notre-Dame. A stratum of living monsters seemed to cover the stone monsters of the cathedral front.

Meantime, the square was starred with a thousand torches. The scene of confusion, hitherto lost in darkness, was suddenly ablaze with light. The square shone resplendent, and cast a red glow upon the heavens; the bonfire kindled upon the high platform still burned, and lighted up the city in the distance. The huge silhouette of the two towers, outlined afar upon the housetops of Paris, formed a vast patch of shadow amid the radiance. The city seemed to be aroused. Distant alarm-bells sounded. The Vagrants howled, panted, swore, climbed higher and higher; and Quasimodo, powerless against so many foes, shuddering for the gipsy girl, seeing those furious faces approach nearer and nearer to his gallery, implored Heaven to grant a miracle, and wrung his hands in despair.

CHAPTER V

The Retreat Where Louis of France Says His Prayers

The reader may remember that a moment before he caught sight of the nocturnal band of Vagrants, Quasimodo, while inspecting Paris from the top of his belfry, saw but one light still burning, and that gleamed from a window in the highest story of a tall dark structure close beside the Porte Saint-Antoine. This building was the Bastille; that starry light was the candle of Louis XI.

King Louis XI had actually been in Paris for two days. He was to set out again two days later for his fortress of Montilzles-Tours. His visits to his good city of Paris were rare and brief; for he never felt that he had enough trapdoors, gibbets, and Scotch archers about him there.

He had that day come to sleep at the Bastille. The great chamber, five fathoms square, which he had at the Louvre, with its huge chimney-piece adorned with twelve great beasts and thirteen great prophets, and his great bed eleven feet by twelve, were not to his taste. He was lost amid all these grandeurs. This good, homely king preferred the Bastille, with a tiny chamber and a simple bed. And then, the Bastille was stronger than the Louvre.

This tiny room, which the king reserved to his own use in the famous state-prison, was spacious enough, after all, and occupied the topmost floor of a turret adjoining the keep. It was a circular chamber, carpeted with mats of lustrous straw, ceiled with beams enriched with *fleurs-de-lis* of gilded metal, with colored interjoists wainscotted with rich woods studded with rosettes of white metal painted a fine bright green, compounded of orpiment and wood.

There was but one window,—a long arched opening latticed with brass wire and iron bars, and still further darkened by beautiful stained glass emblazoned with the arms of the king and queen, each pane of which was worth twenty-two pence.

There was but one entrance,—a modern door, with surbased arch, hung with tapestry on the inside, and on the outside decorated with a porch of bogwood, a frail structure of curiously wrought cabinet-work, such as was very common in old houses some hundred and fifty years ago. "Although they are disfiguring and cumbersome," says Sauval, in despair, "still, our old folk will not do away with them, and retain them in spite of everything."

The room contained none of the furniture ordinarily found in such an apartment,—neither benches, nor trestles, nor common box stools, nor more elegant stools mounted on posts and counter-posts, at four pence each. There was only one chair,—a folding-chair with arms,—and a very superb one it was: the wood was painted with roses on a red ground, the seat was of scarlet Spanish leather, trimmed with heavy silk fringe and studded with countless golden nails. The solitary chair showed that but one person had a right to be seated in that room. Besides the chair, and very near the window there was a table covered with a cloth embroidered with figures of birds.

Upon this table were a standish spotted with ink, sundry parchments, a few pens, and a chased silver goblet. Farther away stood a stove, and a prayer-desk of crimson velvet embossed with gold. Lastly, at the back of the room there was a simple bed of yellow and carnation-colored damask, without tinsel or lace,—merely a plain fringe. This bed, famous for having borne the sleep,—or sleeplessness,—of Louis XI, might still be seen two hundred years ago, at the house of a councillor of state, where it was viewed by old Madame Pilou, celebrated in "Cyrus," under the name of "Arricidia" and of "Morality Embodied."

Such was the room known as "the retreat where Louis of France says his prayers."

At the moment when we introduce our reader to it, this retreat was very dark. The curfew had rung an hour before; it was night, and there was but one flickering wax candle placed on the table to light five persons grouped about the room.

The first upon whom the direct rays of the candle fell was a nobleman, magnificently dressed in scarlet breeches and jerkin striped with silver, and a loose coat with padded shoulders, made of cloth of gold brocaded in black. This splendid costume, upon which the light played, seemed to be frosted with flame at every fold. The man who wore it had his armorial bearings embroidered on his breast in gay colors,—a chevron with a deer passant at the base of the shield. The escutcheon was supported by an olive-branch dexter and a buck's horn sinister. This man wore at his belt a rich dagger, the silver-gilt handle of which was wrought in the shape of a crest, and surmounted by a count's coronet. He had an evil expression, a haughty mien, and a proud bearing. At the first glance his face revealed arrogance, at the second craft.

He stood bare-headed, a long scroll in his hand, behind the arm-chair in which sat, his body awkwardly bent, his knees crossed, his elbow on the table, a most ill-attired person. Imagine, indeed, upon the luxurious Spanish leather seat, a pair of knock knees, a couple of slender shanks meagerly arrayed in black woollen knitted stuff, a body wrapped in a fustian coat edged with fur, which had far more skin than hair; finally, to crown the whole, a greasy old hat, of the poorest quality of black cloth, stuck round with a circlet of small leaden images. This, with a dirty skull-cap, which showed scarce a single hair, was all that could be seen of the seated personage. His head was bent so low upon his breast that nothing could be distinguished of his face, which was wholly in shadow, unless it might be the tip of his nose, upon which a ray of light fell, and which was clearly a long one. By the thinness of his wrinkled hand, he was evidently an old man. This was Louis XI.

Some distance behind them, two men clad in Flemish fashion chatted together in low tones. They were not so entirely in the shadow but that any one who had been present at the performance of Gringoire's play could recognize them as two of the chief Flemish envoys, Guillaume Rym, the wise pensionary of Ghent, and Jacques Coppenole, the popular hosier. It will be remembered that these two men were connected with Louis XI's secret policy.

Lastly, at the farther end of the room, near the door, stood in the gloom, motionless as a statue, a sturdy man with thick-set limbs, in military trappings, his doublet embroidered with armorial bearings, whose square face, with its goggle eyes, immense mouth, and ears hidden under two broad pent-houses of straight, lank hair, partook at once of the character of the dog and the tiger.

All were uncovered save the king.

The gentleman nearest to the king was reading a lengthy

document, to which his Majesty seemed listening most attentively. The two Flemings whispered together.

"Zounds!" grumbled Coppenole, "I am weary with standing; is there no chair here?"

Rym replied by a shake of the head, accompanied by a prudent smile.

"Zounds!" resumed Coppenole, utterly miserable at being obliged to lower his voice; "I long to sit down on the floor with my legs crossed, in true hosier style, as I do in my own shop at home."

"Beware how you do so, Master Jacques."

"Bless me! Master Guillaume! must we be on our feet forever here?"

"Or on our knees," said Rym.

At this moment the king spoke. They were silent.

"Fifty pence for the coats of our lackeys, and twelve pounds for the cloaks of the clerks of our crown. That's it! pour out gold by the ton! Are you mad, Olivier?"

So saying, the old man lifted his head. The golden shells of the collar of Saint Michel glistened about his neck. The light of the candle fell full upon his thin, peevish profile. He snatched the paper from his companion's hands.

"You will ruin us!" he cried, running his hollow eye over the scroll. "What is all this? What need have we for so vast an establishment? Two chaplains at ten pounds a month each, and an assistant at one hundred pence! A valet at ninety pounds a year! Four head cooks at six-score pounds a year each; a roaster, a soup-maker, a sauce-maker, an under cook, a keeper of the stores, two stewards' assistants, at ten pounds a month each! Two scullions at eight pounds! A groom and his two helpers at twenty-four pounds a month! A porter, a pastry-cook, a baker, two wagoners, each sixty pounds a year! And the farrier, six-score pounds! And the master of our exchequer chamber, twelve hundred pounds! And the comptroller five hundred! And I know not how many more! 'Tis sheer madness! Our servants' wages plunder France! All the treasures of the Louvre will melt away before such a wasting fire of expense! We will sell our plate! And next year, if God and Our Lady [here he raised his hat] grant us life, we will take our tisanes from a pewter pot!"

With these words he cast a glance at the silver goblet which sparkled on the table. He coughed, and continued,—

"Master Olivier, princes who reign over great domains, such as kings and emperors, should never suffer extravagant living in their houses; for thence the fire spreads to the provinces. Therefore, Master Olivier, forget this not. Our expenses increase yearly. The thing displeases us. What, by the Rood! until '79 they never exceeded thirty-six thousand pounds; in '80 they amounted to forty-three thousand six hundred and nineteen pounds,—I have the figures in my head; in '81 they were sixty-six thousand six hundred and eighty pounds; and this year, by my faith! they will come to eighty thousand pounds! Doubled in four years! monstrous!"

He paused for lack of breath; then he went on angrily,—

"I see around me none but people fattening on my leanness! You suck crowns from me at every pore!"

All were silent. His rage must be allowed free vent. He continued:—

"It is like that petition in Latin from the nobles of France, that we would re-establish what they call the charges on the crown! Charges, indeed! crushing charges! Ah, gentlemen! you say that we are not a king to reign *dapifero nullo, buticulario nullo!** We will show you, by the Rood! whether we be a king or no!"

Here he smiled with a sense of his power; his bad humor moderated, and he turned towards the Flemings:

"Mark you, gossip Guillaume, the head baker, the chief cellarer, the lord chamberlain, the lord seneschal, are not worth so much as the meanest lackey; remember that, gossip Coppenole. They are good for nothing. As they thus hang uselessly around the king, they remind me of the four Evan-

---

*No footman, no butler (Latin).

gelists about the dial of the great clock on the Palace, which Philippe Brille has just done up as good as new. They are gilded over, but they do not mark the hour, and the hands go on as well without them."

For a moment he seemed lost in thought, and added, shaking his aged head: —

"Ho! ho! by Notre-Dame, I am no Philippe Brille, and I will not re-gild my lordly vassals! Go on, Olivier!"

The person thus addressed took the scroll from his royal master's hands, and began to read again in a loud voice: —

"To Adam Tenon, clerk to the keeper of the seals of the provosty of Paris, for the silver, fashioning, and engraving of said seals, which have been new made by reason of the others preceding being old and worn out, and no longer fit for use, twelve Paris pounds.

"To Guillaume Frère, the sum of four pounds four Paris pence for his labor and cost in nourishing and feeding the pigeons in the two dovecots of the Hôtel des Tournelles, for the months of January, February, and March of this present year; for the which he hath expended seven sextaries of barley.

"To a Grey Friar, for confessing a criminal, four Paris pence."

The king listened in silence. From time to time he coughed; then he raised the goblet to his lips, and swallowed a mouthful with a wry face.

"In this year have been made by order of the courts and by sound of trumpet, in the public places of Paris, fifty-six proclamations; the account yet to be made up.

"For quest and search in sundry places, both in Paris and elsewhere, for funds said to be concealed there, but nothing found, forty-five Paris pounds."

"A crown buried to unearth a penny!" said the king.

"For setting six panes of white glass at the Hôtel des Tournelles, in the place where the iron cage is, thirteen pence; for making and delivering, by the king's command, on musterday, four escutcheons with the arms of our said lord wreathed all around with roses, six pounds; for two new sleeves to the king's old doublet, twenty pence; for a box of grease to grease the king's boots, fifteen farthings; for rebuilding a sty to lodge the king's black swine, thirty Paris pounds; sundry partitions, planks, and gratings made for the safe-keeping of the lions at the Hôtel Saint-Pol, twenty-two pounds."

"Here be costly beasts," said Louis XI. "Never mind, 't is a luxury which befits a king. There is one big tawny lion that I love for his pretty tricks. Have you seen him, Master Guillaume? Princes need to keep these rare wild beasts. We kings should have lions for lapdogs, and tigers instead of cats. Grandeur beseems a crown. In the time of Jupiter's pagans, when the people offered an hundred sheep and an hundred oxen to the gods, emperors gave an hundred lions and an hundred eagles. That was fierce and very fine. The kings of France have ever had these roarings round their throne; nevertheless, my subjects must do me the justice to say that I spend far less money in that way than my predecessors, and that I am much more moderate as regards lions, bears, elephants, and leopards. Go on, Master Olivier. We merely wished to say this much to our Flemish friends."

Guillaume Rym bowed low, while Coppenole, with his sullen air, looked like one of those bears to which his Majesty referred.

The king did not notice him. He wet his lips with the liquid in the goblet, and spat the brew out again, saying, "Faugh! what a disagreeable tisane!" The reader continued:—

"For feeding a rascally tramp, kept under lock and key in the little cell at the shambles for six months, until it should be decided what to do with him, six pounds and four pence."

"What's that?" interrupted the king; "feed what should be hanged! By the Rood! I will not pay one penny for his keep! Olivier, settle the matter with Master d'Estouteville, and this very night make me preparations for this gallant's wedding with the gallows. Go on."

Olivier made a mark with his thumb-nail against the item of the rascally tramp, and resumed:—

"To Henriet Cousin, chief executioner of Paris, the sum of

sixty Paris pence, to him adjudged and ordered by the lord provost of Paris, for having bought, by order of the said provost, a broadsword for the execution and decapitation of all persons condemned by the courts for their demerits, and having it furnished with a scabbard and all thereunto appertaining; and likewise for having the old sword sharpened and repaired, it having been broken and notched in doing justice upon my lord Louis of Luxembourg, as herein more fully set down—"

The king interrupted. "Enough; I cheerfully order the sum to be paid. These are expenses which I never regard; I have never regretted such moneys. Continue."

"For repairing a great cage—"

"Ah!" said the king, grasping the arms of his chair with both hands, "I knew that I came here to the Bastille for a purpose. Stay, Master Olivier; I desire to see this cage for myself. You may read the costs while I examine it. Gentlemen of Flanders, come and look at it; it is a curious sight."

Then he rose, leaned upon his reader's arm, signed to the mute who stood at the door to go before him, to the two Flemings to follow him, and left the room.

The royal party was increased at the door of the retreat by men-at-arms weighed down with steel, and slender pages bearing torches. It proceeded for some time through the interior of the gloomy keep, perforated with staircases and corridors in the thickness of the walls. The captain of the Bastille walked at the head of the procession, and ordered the gates to be thrown open before the bent and feeble old king, who coughed as he moved along.

At every wicket gate all heads were forced to stoop, except that of the old man bowed by age. "Hum!" he mumbled, for he had lost all his teeth, "we are all ready for the door of the tomb. A low door needs a stooping passenger."

At last, after passing through a final gate so encumbered with locks that it took a quarter of an hour to open it, they entered a lofty, spacious, vaulted hall, in the middle of which they saw, by the light of the torches, a huge and massive cube of masonry, iron, and wood. The interior was hollow. It was one of those famous cages meant for prisoners of state, which were known by the name of "the king's daughters." In its sides were two or three small windows, so closely grated with heavy iron bars that the glass was entirely hidden. The door was a great flat stone slab, such as are used for tombs,—one of those doors used for entrance only. But here, the dead man was a living being.

The king walked slowly around the little structure, carefully examining it, while Master Olivier, who followed him, read aloud:—

"For repairing a great cage of heavy wooden joists, girders, and timbers, being nine feet long by eight in breadth, and seven feet high between the planks, planed, and clamped with strong iron clamps, which has been placed in a room in one of the towers of the Bastille Saint-Antoine, in which cage is put and kept, by command of our lord the king, a prisoner formerly dwelling in a worn-out and crazy old cage. There were used for the said new cage ninety-six horizontal beams and fifty-two uprights, ten girders eighteen feet long. Nineteen carpenters were employed for twenty days, in the court of the Bastille, to square, cut, and fit all the said wood."

"Quite fine heart of oak," said the king, rapping on the timber with his knuckles.

". . . There were used in this cage," continued the other, "two hundred and twenty large iron clamps, of eight and nine feet, the rest of medium length, with the screws, roller-bolts, and counter-bands requisite for said clamps, all the aforesaid iron weighing three thousand seven hundred and thirty-five pounds; besides eight large iron bolts serving to fasten the said cage, with the nails and clamp-irons, weighing all together two hundred and eighteen pounds; not to mention the iron gratings for the windows of the room wherein the cage was placed, the iron bars on the door, and other items—"

"Here's a mighty deal of iron," said the king, "to restrain the lightness of one mind!"

". . . The whole amounts to three hundred and seventeen pounds five pence and seven farthings."

"By the Rood!" exclaimed the king.

At this oath, which was Louis XI's favorite imprecation, some one seemed to waken within the cage: chains rattled loudly against the wood-work, and a faint voice, which appeared to issue from the tomb, cried: "Sire! Sire! Pardon!" But no one could see the person uttering these words.

"Three hundred and seventeen pounds five pence and seven farthings!" repeated Louis XI.

The piteous voice which issued from the cage had chilled the blood of all present, even that of Master Olivier himself. The king alone appeared as if he had not heard it. At his command Master Olivier resumed his reading, and his Majesty calmly continued his inspection of the cage.

"Moreover, there has been paid to a mason who made the holes to receive the window-bars, and the floor of the room in which the cage stands, forasmuch as the floor could not have borne this cage by reason of its weight, twenty-seven pounds and fourteen Paris pence—"

The voice again began its moan:—

"Mercy, Sire! I swear that it was my lord Cardinal of Angers, and not I, who plotted the treason."

"The mason charges well!" said the king. "Go on, Olivier!"

Olivier continued:—

"To a joiner, for window-frames, bedstead, close stool, and other items, twenty pounds two Paris pence—"

The voice continued likewise:—

"Alas! Sire! will you not hear me? I protest that it was not I who wrote that thing to my lord of Guyenne, but his highness Cardinal Balue!"

"The joiner is dear," observed the king. "Is that all?"

"No, Sire. To a glazier, for the window-panes in said chamber, forty-six pence eight Paris farthings."

"Have mercy, Sire! Is it not enough that all my worldly goods were given to my judges, my silver plate to M. de Torcy, my books to Master Pierre Doriolle, my tapestries to the Governor of Roussillon? I am innocent. For fourteen years I have shivered in an iron cage. Have mercy, Sire! You will find your reward in heaven."

"Master Olivier," said the king, "what is the sum total?"

"Three hundred and sixty-seven pounds eight pence three Paris farthings."

"By'r Lady!" cried the king. "What an extravagant cage!"

He snatched the scroll from Master Olivier's hands, and began to reckon up the items himself upon his fingers, looking by turns at the paper and the cage. Meantime, the prisoner's sobs were plainly to be heard. It was a doleful sound in the darkness, and the by-standers paled as they gazed into one another's faces.

"Fourteen years, Sire! full fourteen years! ever since the month of April, 1469. In the name of the Blessed Mother of God, Sire, hear me! You have enjoyed the warmth of the sun all these years. Shall I, poor wretch, never again behold the light of day? Pity me, Sire! Be merciful. Clemency is a goodly and a royal virtue, which turns aside the stream of wrath. Does your Majesty believe that it will greatly content a king in the hour of his death, to reflect that he has never let any offence go unpunished? Moreover, Sire, I never did betray your Majesty; it was my lord of Angers. And I wear about my leg a very heavy chain, and a great ball of iron at the end of it, far heavier than is reasonable. Ah, Sire, have pity upon me!"

"Olivier," said the king, shaking his head, "I observe that these fellows charge me twenty pence the hogshead for plaster, which is worth only twelve. Have this account corrected."

He turned his back on the cage, and prepared to leave the room. The miserable prisoner guessed by the receding torches and noise that the king was departing.

"Sire! Sire!" he cried in tones of despair.

The door closed. He saw nothing more, he heard nothing save the harsh voice of the jailor singing in his ears the song:—

> "Master Jean Balue,
> Has quite lost view

> Of his bishoprics cherished.
> My lord of Verdun
> Has not a single one;
> Every one hath perished."

The king silently reascended to his retreat, and his train followed him, terrified by the prisoner's last groans. All at once his Majesty turned to the governor of the Bastille.

"By the way," said he, "was there not some one in that cage?"

"Zounds, Sire, yes!" replied the governor, lost in amaze at such a question.

"Who, then?"

"The Bishop of Verdun."

The king was better aware of this than any one else; but this was his way.

"Ah!" said he, with an innocent semblance of thinking of it for the first time, "Guillaume de Harancourt, the friend of Cardinal Balue,—a merry devil of a bishop!"

A few moments later the door of the retreat was reopened, then closed again upon the five persons whom we saw there at the beginning of this chapter, and who resumed their places, their low-voiced conversation, and their former attitudes.

During the king's absence a number of dispatches had been laid on the table, and he now broke the seals. Then he rapidly read them one after the other, motioned to Master Olivier, who seemed to perform the office of his minister, to take a pen, and without imparting the contents of the dispatches to him, began to dictate answers in an undertone, the latter writing them down, kneeling uncomfortably at the table.

Guillaume Rym watched him.

The king spoke so low that the Flemings caught but a few detached and scarcely intelligible fragments, such as:—

". . . keep up fertile places by commerce and sterile ones by manufacturers. Show the English lords our four bombards,

the London, Brabant, Bourg-en-Bresse, and Saint-Omer. . . .
Artillery occasions war to be more wisely waged at the present
time. . . . To Monsieur de Bressuire, our friend. . . . Armies
cannot be maintained without tribute," etc.

Once he raised his voice: —

"By the Rood! the King of Sicily seals his letters with yellow wax, like a king of France. We may be wrong to allow him
this privilege. My fair cousin of Burgundy gave no armorial
bearings upon a field gules. The greatness of a house is ensured by holding its prerogatives intact. Note that, gossip
Olivier."

Again: —

"Oho!" said he, "an important message this! What would
our brother the emperor have?" And running his eye over the
missive, he interrupted his reading with constant exclama-
tions: "Surely the Germans are so great and powerful that 't is
scarcely credible. But we are not unmindful of the old
proverb: The finest county is Flanders; the fairest duchy,
Milan; the most beauteous kingdom, France. Is it not so, Sir
Flemings?"

This time Coppenole bowed with Guillaume Rym. The
hosier's patriotism was tickled.

The last dispatch made Louis XI frown.

"What's this?" he exclaimed. "Complaints and requisitions
against our garrisons in Picardy! Olivier, write with speed to
Marshal de Rouault: That discipline is relaxed. That the men-
at-arms of the ordnance, the nobles of the ban, the free-
archers, and the Swiss guards do infinite injury to the
peasants. That the soldiers, not content with the goods which
they find in the houses of the tillers of the soil, constrain
them, by heavy blows of bludgeons and sticks, to seek
throughout the town for wine, fish, spices, and other articles
of luxury. That the king is well aware of all this. That we intend to preserve our people from all unseemly acts, larceny,
and pillage. That this is our sovereign will, by Our Lady!
That, moreover, it likes us not that any minstrel, barber, or
serving man at arms should go arrayed like a prince, in velvet,

silken cloth, and rings of gold. That these vanities are hateful in the sight of God. That we content ourselves—we who are a gentleman of high degree—with one cloth doublet at sixteen pence the Paris ell. That soldiers' servants may well come down to that also. We command and order these things. To Monsieur de Rouault, our friend. Good!"

He dictated this letter in a loud voice, in a firm tone, and by fits and starts. Just as he ended it, the door opened and admitted a new personage, who rushed into the room in extreme alarm, shouting,—

"Sire! Sire! the people of Paris have risen in revolt!"

The grave face of Louis XI was convulsed; but every visible sign of emotion passed away like a flash of lightning. He restrained himself, and said with calm severity,—

"Compère Jacques, you enter somewhat abruptly!"

"Sire! Sire! there is a revolt!" replied the breathless Jacques.

The king, who had risen, took him roughly by the arm, and whispered in his ear in a manner to be heard by him alone, with concentrated rage, and a sidelong glance at the Flemings,—

"Hold your tongue, or speak low!"

The new-comer understood, and began to tell him in a low voice a very incoherent tale, to which the king listened with perfect composure, while Guillaume Rym drew Coppenole's attention to the new-comer's face and dress, his furred hood (*caputia fourrata*), his short cloak (*epitogia curta*), and his black velvet gown, which bespoke a president of the Court of Accounts.

This person had no sooner given the king a few details, than Louis XI cried with a burst of laughter,—

"Indeed! Speak up boldly, Compère Coictier! Why do you talk so low? Our Lady knows that we hide nothing from our good Flemish friends."

"But, Sire—"

"Speak up boldly!"

Compère Coictier was dumb with surprise.

"So," resumed the king,—"speak, sir,—there is a commotion among the common people in our good city of Paris?"

"Yes, Sire."

"And it is directed, you say, against the Provost of the Palace of Justice?"

"It looks that way," said the compère, who still stammered and hesitated, utterly astounded by the sudden and inexplicable change which had been wrought in the king's sentiments.

Louis XI added: "Where did the watch encounter the mob?"

"Moving from the chief haunt of the beggars and vagrants towards the Pont-aux-Changeurs. I met them myself on my way hither to execute your Majesty's orders. I heard certain of the number shouting, 'Down with the Provost of the Palace!'"

"And what is their grievance against the provost?"

"Ah!" said Jacques, "that he is their lord."

"Really!"

"Yes, Sire. They are rascals from the Court of Miracles. They have long complained of the provost, whose vassals they are. They refuse to recognize him either as justiciary or road-surveyor."

"Ay, say you so!" returned the king, with a smile of satisfaction which he vainly strove to disguise.

"In all their petitions to Parliament," added Jacques, "they claim that they have but two masters,—your Majesty and their God, who is, I believe, the devil."

"Hah!" said the king.

He rubbed his hands; he laughed that inward laugh which makes the face radiant; he could not disguise his joy, although he tried at times to compose himself. No one understood his mood, not even Master Olivier. He was silent for a moment, with a pensive but contented air.

"Are they strong in numbers?" he asked suddenly.

"Indeed they are, Sire," replied Compère Jacques.

"How many?"

"At least six thousand."

The king could not help exclaiming, "Good!" He added, "Are they armed?"

"With scythes, pikes, hackbuts, mattocks, and all sorts of dangerous weapons."

The king seemed by no means alarmed at this account. Compère Jacques felt obliged to add,—

"If your Majesty send not promptly to the provost's aid, he is lost."

"We will send," said the king, with an assumed expression of seriousness. "It is well. Certainly we will send. The provost is our friend. Six thousand! They are determined knaves. Their boldness is marvelous, and we are greatly wroth at it; but we have few people about us tonight. It will be time enough in the morning."

Compère Jacques exclaimed, "Straightway, Sire! The provost's house may be sacked twenty times over, the seigniory profaned, and the provost hanged, by then. For the love of God, Sire, send before tomorrow morning!"

The king looked him in the face. "I said tomorrow." It was one of those looks which admit of no reply. After a pause, Louis XI again raised his voice. "Compère Jacques, you must know— What was—" He corrected himself. "What is the Provost's feudal jurisdiction?"

"Sire, the Provost of the Palace has jurisdiction from the Rue de la Calandre to the Rue de l'Herberie, the Place Saint-Michel, and the places commonly called the Mureaux, situated near the church of Notre-Dame des Champs [here the king lifted the brim of his hat], which residences are thirteen in number; besides the Court of Miracles, the lazaretto known as the Banlieue, and all the highway beginning at this lazar-house and ending at the Porte Saint-Jacques. Of these divers places he is road-surveyor, high, low, and middle justiciary, and lord paramount."

"Hey-day!" said the king, scratching his left ear with his right hand; "that is a goodly slice of my city. And so the provost was king of all that?"

This time he did not correct himself. He continued to muse, and as if speaking to himself, said,—

"Have a care, Sir Provost! You had a very pretty piece of our Paris in your grasp."

All at once he burst forth. "By the Rood! Who are all these people who claim to be commissioners of highways, justiciaries, lords, and masters in our midst; who have their toll-gate in every bit of field, their gibbet and their hangman at every cross-road among our people, in such fashion that, as the Greek believed in as many gods as there were fountains, and the Persian in as many as he saw stars, the Frenchman now counts as many kings as he sees gallows? By the Lord! this thing is evil, and the confusion likes me not. I would fain know whether it be by the grace of God that there are other inspectors of highways in Paris than the king, other justice than that administered by our Parliament, and other emperor than ourselves in this realm! By the faith of my soul! the day must come when France shall know but one king, one lord, one judge, one headsman, even as there is but one God in paradise!"

He again raised his cap, and went on, still meditating, with the look and tone of a hunter loosing and urging on his pack of dogs: "Good! my people! bravely done! destroy these false lords! do your work. At them, boys! at them! Plunder them, capture them, strip them! Ah, you would fain be kings, gentlemen? On, my people, on!"

Here he stopped abruptly, bit his lip, as if to recall a thought which had half escaped him, bent his piercing eye in turn upon each of the five persons who stood around him, and all at once, seizing his hat in both hands, and staring steadily at it, he thus addressed it: "Oh, I would burn you if you knew my secret thoughts!"

Then again casting about him the attentive, anxious glance of a fox returning by stealth to his earth, he added,—

"It matters not; we will succor the provost. Unfortunately, we have but few troops here to send forth at this moment against so large a populace. We must needs wait until tomorrow. Order shall be restored in the City, and all who are taken shall be strung up on the spot."

"By-the-bye, Sire!" said Compère Coictier, "I forgot it in my first dismay,—the watch has caught two stragglers of the band. If it please your Majesty to see these men, they are here."

"If it please me to see them!" cried the king. "Now, by the Rood! do you forget such things! Run quickly, you, Olivier! go and fetch them."

Master Olivier went out, and returned a moment after with the two prisoners, surrounded by archers of the ordnance. The first had a fat, stupid face, with a drunken and astonished stare. He was dressed in rags, and bent his knee and dragged his foot as he walked. The second was a pale, smiling fellow, whom the reader already knows.

The king studied them for an instant without speaking, then abruptly addressed the first:—

"Your name?"

"Gieffroy Pincebourde."

"Your business?"

"A Vagabond."

"What part did you mean to play in this damnable revolt?"

The Vagabond looked at the king, swinging his arms with a dull look. His was one of those misshapen heads, where the understanding flourishes as ill as the flame beneath an extinguisher.

"I don't know," he said. "The others went, so I went too."

"Did you not intend outrageously to attack and plunder your lord the Provost of the Palace?"

"I know that they were going to take something from some one. That's all I know."

A soldier showed the king a pruning-hook, which had been found upon the fellow.

"Do you recognize this weapon?" asked the king.

"Yes, it is my pruning-hook; I am a vine-dresser."

"And do you acknowledge this man as your companion?" added Louis XI, pointing to the other prisoner.

"No. I do not know him."

"Enough," said the king. And beckoning to the silent, motionless person at the door, whom we have already pointed out to our readers:—

"Friend Tristan, here is a man for you."

Tristan l'Hermite bowed. He gave an order in a low voice to two archers, who led away the poor Vagrant.

Meantime, the king approached the second prisoner, who was in a profuse perspiration. "Your name?"

"Sire, Pierre Gringoire."

"Your trade?"

"A philosopher, Sire!"

"How dared you, varlet, go and beset our friend the Provost of the Palace, and what have you to say about this uprising of the people?"

"Sire, I had naught to do with it."

"Come, come, rascal! were you not taken by the watch in this evil company?"

"No, Sire; there is a mistake. It was an accident. I write tragedies. Sire, I entreat your Majesty to hear me. I am a poet. It is the melancholy whim of people of my profession to roam the streets after dark. I passed this way tonight. It was a mere chance. I was wrongfully arrested; I am innocent of this civil storm. Your Majesty sees that the Vagabond did not recognize me. I conjure your Majesty—"

"Silence!" said the king, betwixt two gulps of his tisane. "You stun me."

Tristan l'Hermite stepped forward, and pointing at Gringoire, said,—

"Sire, may we hang this one too?"

It was the first time that he had spoken.

"Pooh!" negligently answered the king. "I see no reason to the contrary."

"But I see a great many!" said Gringoire.

Our philosopher was at this moment greener than any olive. He saw by the king's cold and indifferent manner that his only resource was in something very pathetic, and he threw himself at the feet of Louis XI, exclaiming with frantic gestures,—

"Sire, your Majesty will deign to hear me. Sire, let not your thunders fall upon so small a thing as I! The thunderbolts of God never strike a lettuce. Sire, you are an august and very mighty monarch; have pity on a poor honest man, who would find it harder to kindle a revolt than an icicle to emit a spark. Most gracious lord, magnanimity is a virtue of kings and of royal beasts. Alas! rigor does but anger the minds of men; the fierce blasts of winter could not make the traveler doff his cloak, while the sun shining down, little by little warmed him to such a degree that he stripped to his shirt. Sire, you are the sun. I protest to you, my sovereign lord and master, that I am not of the company of the Vagrants. I am neither disorderly nor a thief. Rebellion and brigandage are not of Apollo's train. I am not one to rush into those clouds which burst in thunders of sedition. I am a faithful vassal of your Majesty. A good subject should feel the same jealousy for the glory of his king that the husband feels for the honor of his wife, the same affection with which the son responds to his father's love; he should burn with zeal for his house, for the increase of his service. Any other passion which possessed him would be mere madness. Such, Sire, are my political maxims. Do not, therefore, judge me to be a rebel and a plunderer, by my ragged dress. If you will but pardon me, Sire, I will wear it threadbare at the knees in praying to God for you night and morning! Alas! I am not exceeding rich, 'tis true. I am indeed rather poor; but not vicious, for all that. It is not my fault. Every one knows that great wealth is not to be derived from literature, and that the most accomplished writers have not always much fire in winter. Lawyers get all the grain, and leave nothing but the chaff for the rest of the learned professions. There are forty most excellent proverbs about the tattered cloak of the philosopher. Oh, Sire, clemency is the only light which can illumine the interior of a great soul! Clemency bears the torch for all the other virtues. Without her, they are but blind, and gropers after God. Mercy, which is the same thing as clemency, produces those loving subjects who are the most potent body-guard of princes. What matters it to you,—to you whose majesty dazzles all who behold it,—if there be one poor man the more upon the earth, a poor innocent philosopher floundering in the darkness of calamity, with an empty stomach and an empty purse? Besides, Sire, I am a scholar. Great kings add a pearl to their crown when they encourage letters. Hercules did not disdain the title of Musagetes. Matthias Corvinus favored Jean of Monroyal, the ornament of mathematics. Now, it is a poor way of protecting letters, to hang the learned. What a blot upon Alexander's fame if he had hanged Aristotle! The deed would not have been a tiny patch upon the visage of his reputation to enhance its beauty, but a malignant ulcer to disfigure it. Sire, I wrote a most fitting epithalamium for the Lady of Flanders, and my lord the most august Dauphin. That is no fire-brand of rebellion. Your Majesty sees that I am no mere scribbler, that I have studied deeply, and that I have much natural eloquence. Pardon me, Sire. By so doing, you will perform an act of gallantry to Our Lady; and I vow that I am mightily frightened at the very idea of being hanged!"

So saying, the much distressed Gringoire kissed the king's slippers, and Guillaume Rym whispered to Coppenole, "He does well to crawl upon the floor. Kings are like Jupiter of Crete,—they have no ears but in their feet." And, regardless of the Cretan Jove, the hosier responded, with a grave smile, his eye fixed on Gringoire: "Oh, 'tis well done! I fancy I hear Councillor Hugonet begging me for mercy."

When Gringoire paused at last for lack of breath, he raised his head, trembling, to the king, who was scratching with his nail a spot on the knee of his breeches; then his Majesty drank from the goblet of tisane. He spoke not a word, however, and the silence tortured Gringoire. At last the king looked at him. "What a dreadful bawler!" said he. Then, turning towards Tristan l'Hermite: "Bah! let him go!"

Gringoire fell backwards, overcome with joy.

"Scot-free!" grumbled Tristan. "Don't your Majesty want me to cage him for a while?"

"Friend," rejoined Louis XI, "do you think it is for such birds as these that we have cages made at an expense of three hundred and sixty-seven pounds eight pence three farthings? Let this wanton rascal depart incontinently, and dismiss him with a beating."

"Oh," cried Gringoire, "what a noble king!"

And for fear of a contrary order, he hastened towards the door, which Tristan opened for him with a very bad grace. The soldiers followed, driving him before them with sturdy blows, which Gringoire bore like the true Stoic philosopher that he was.

The king's good humor, since the revolt against the Provost was announced to him, appeared in everything he did. This unusual clemency was no small proof of it. Tristan l'Hermite, in his corner, wore the surly look of a dog who has seen a bone, but had none.

The king, meantime, merrily drummed the march of Pont-Audemer with his fingers on the arm of his chair. He was a dissembling prince, but more skilled in hiding his troubles than his joy. These outward manifestations of delight at any good news sometimes went to extraordinary lengths,—as on the death of Charles the Bold, when he vowed a silver balustrade to Saint-Martin of Tours; and on his accession to the throne, when he forgot to order his father's obsequies.

"Ha, Sire!" suddenly exclaimed Jacques Coictier, "what has become of that sharp fit of illness for which your Majesty summoned me?"

"Oh," said the king, "indeed, I suffer greatly, good compère. I have a ringing in my ears, and cruel pains in my chest."

Coictier took the king's hand, and began to feel his pulse with a knowing air.

"See, Coppenole," said Rym in a low voice; "there he is, between Coictier and Tristan. They make up his entire court,—a doctor for himself, a hangman for the rest of the world!"

As he felt the king's pulse, Coictier assumed a look of more and more alarm. Louis XI watched him with some anxiety. Coictier's face darkened visibly. The king's feeble health was the worthy man's only source of income, and he made the most of it.

"Oh, oh!" he muttered at last. "This is serious enough."

"Is it not?" said the frightened king.

"*Pulsus creber, anhelans, crepitans, irregularis,*"* added the physician.

"By the Rood!"

"This might take a man off in less than three days."

"By'r Lady!" cried the king. "And the remedy, good compère?"

"I must reflect, Sire."

He examined the king's tongue, shook his head, made a wry face, and in the midst of these affectations said suddenly,—

"Zounds, Sire, I must tell you that there is a receivership of episcopal revenues vacant, and that I have a nephew."

"I give my receivership to your nephew, Compère Jacques," replied the king; "but cool this fire in my breast."

"Since your Majesty is so graciously inclined," rejoined the doctor, "you will not refuse me a little help towards building my house in the Rue Saint-André des Arcs."

"Hey!" said the king.

"I have come to the end of my means," continued the doctor, "and it would really be a pity that my house should have no roof; not for the sake of the house, which is very plain and ordinary, but for the paintings by Jehan Fourbault, which enliven the walls. There is a Diana flying in the air, so excellently done, so delicate, so dainty, so natural in action, the head so nicely coifed and crowned with a crescent, the flesh so white, that she leads into temptation all those who study her too curiously. There is also a Ceres. She, too, is a very

---

*Pulse rapid, full, intermittent, irregular (Latin).

lovely divinity. She is seated upon sheaves of grain, and crowned with a gay garland of wheat-ears intertwined with purple goat's-beard and other flowers. Nothing was ever seen more amorous than her eyes, rounder than her legs, nobler than her mien or more graceful than her draperies. She is one of the most innocent and perfect beauties ever produced by mortal brush."

"Wretch!" groaned Louis XI; "what are you driving at?"

"I must have a roof over these paintings, Sire; and although it will cost but a trifle, I have no more money."

"How much will your roof cost?"

"Why, a roof of copper, embellished and gilded, two thousand pounds, at the utmost."

"Ah, the assassin!" cried the king; "he never draws me a tooth that is not priceless."

"Am I to have my roof?" said Coictier.

"Yes; and go to the devil! but cure me first."

Jacques Coictier bowed low and said,—

"Sire, a repellant alone can save you. We will apply to your loins the great specific, composed of cerate, Armenian bole, white of egg, vinegar, and oil. You will continue your tisane, and we will answer for your Majesty."

A lighted candle attracts more than one moth. Master Olivier, seeing the king so liberally inclined, and thinking the moment opportune, advanced in his turn: "Sire!"

"What is it now?" said Louis XI.

"Sire, your Majesty knows that Master Simon Radin is dead?"

"Well?"

"He was King's Councillor for the Treasury."

"Well?"

"Sire, his post is vacant."

As he said this, the haughty face of Master Ohivier lost its arrogant look, and assumed a mean and groveling expression. This is the only change of which a courtier's features are capable. The king looked him full in the face, and said dryly, "I understand."

He added,—

"Master Olivier, Marshal Boucicaut once said, 'There are no good gifts save those from the king, no good fishing save in the sea.' I see that you are quite of his opinion. Now, hear this; we have an excellent memory. In '68, we made you groom of our chamber; in '69, keeper of the castle of the Pont Saint-Cloud, at a salary of one hundred pounds Tours (you wished them to be Paris pounds); in November, '73, by letters given at Gergeole, we appointed you keeper of the woods at Vincennes, in place of Gilbert Acle, esquire; in '75, warden of the forest of Rouvray-lez-Saint-Cloud, in the place of Jacques le Maire; in '78, we graciously settled upon you, by letters-patent sealed with green wax, a rental of ten Paris pounds, for yourself and your wife, to be derived from the Place-aux-Marchands, situated in the Saint-Germain School; in '79, warden of the forest of Senart, in place of that poor Jehan Daiz; then, captain of the Château de Loches; then, governor of Saint-Quentin; then, captain of the Pont de Meulan, of which you style yourself count; of the five pence fine paid by every barber who shall shave a customer upon a holiday, three pence go to you, and we take the remainder. We were pleased to change your name of Le Mauvais,* which too strongly resembled your face. In '74, we granted you, to the great displeasure of our nobles, armorial bearings of countless hues, which make your breast shimmer like that of a peacock. By the Rood! are you not sated yet? Is not the draught of fishes fine enough, and miraculous enough; and do you not fear lest another salmon should sink your boat? Pride will be your ruin, my friend. Pride is always hard pressed by ruin and shame. Consider this, and be silent."

These words, uttered in a severe tone, restored its former insolence to Master Olivier's face.

"Good!" he muttered almost audibly; "it is plain that the king is ailing today; he gives the doctor everything."

---

*Epithet meaning "the wicked one."

Louis XI, far from being irritated by this offense, replied with much gentleness. "Stay; I forgot that I had also made you my ambassador to Mistress Marie at Ghent. Yes, gentlemen," added the king, turning to the Flemings, "this fellow has been an ambassador. There, my compère," he continued, addressing Master Olivier, "let us not quarrel; we are old friends. It is very late; we have finished our work. Shave me."

Our readers have doubtless ere now recognized in Master Olivier the terrible Figaro whom Providence, the greatest of all dramatists, so artistically added to the long and bloody comedy of Louis XI's reign. This is not the place for us to attempt any portrait of this strange figure. The royal barber went by three names. At court he was politely termed Olivier le Daim; by the people, Olivier le Diable: his real name was Olivier le Mauvais.

Olivier le Mauvais, then, stood motionless, casting sulky glances at the king, and scowling at Jacques Coictier.

"Yes, yes; the doctor!" he muttered.

"Well, yes, the doctor!" rejoined Louis XI, with rare good-nature; "the doctor has more influence than you. That is natural enough; he has a hold upon our whole body, while you only take us by the chin. There, my poor barber, cheer up. Why, what would you say, and what would become of your office, if I were such a king as King Chilpêric, whose favorite trick it was to pull his beard through his hand? Come, gossip, look to your work; shave me! Go, fetch the necessary tools."

Olivier, seeing that the king was in a jesting mood, and that it was impossible to put him out of temper, left the room to obey his orders, grumbling as he went.

The king rose, stepped to the window, and suddenly opening it with strange agitation, clapped his hands, exclaiming,—

"Oh, yes, there is a red glow in the sky over the City! The provost is burning; it can be nothing else. Ah, my good people! 'tis thus at last you help me to crush their lordships!"

Then turning to the Flemings: "Gentlemen, come and look. Is not that a fire which flares so high?"

The two men of Ghent approached.

"A great fire," said Guillaume Rym.

"Oh," added Coppenole, whose eyes flashed, "that reminds me of the burning of the lord of Hymbercourt's house! There must be a fine riot yonder!"

"Do you think so, Master Coppenole?" And the face of Louis XI was almost as full of joy as that of the hosier. "'T will be hard to suppress it, eh?"

"By the Mass, Sire! your Majesty will make great gaps in many a company of troops in doing it."

"Oh, I! that's quite another thing," rejoined the king. "If I chose—"

The hosier answered boldly,—

"If this rebellion be what I suppose, you may choose to no purpose, Sire."

"Friend," said Louis XI, "two companies of my ordnance and the discharge of a serpentine would win an easy victory over the groundlings."

The hosier, in spite of the signs made to him by Guillaume Rym, seemed determined to oppose the king.

"Sire, the Swiss were groundlings too. My lord duke of Burgundy was a great gentleman, and he despised that vulgar mob. At the battle of Grandson he cried, 'Gunners, fire upon those low-lived villains!' and he swore by Saint George. But magistrate Scharnachtal fell upon the proud duke with his club and his people, and at the onslaught of the peasants with their bull-hides, the brilliant Burgundian army was broken like a pane of glass by a stone. Many knights were killed that day by base clowns; and my lord of Château-Guyon, the grandest noble in Burgundy, was found dead beside his great grey charger in a small marshy meadow."

"Friend," replied the king, "you talk of battles. This is only a mutiny; and I will quell it with a single frown whenever it pleases me."

The other answered indifferently,—

"That may be, Sire. In that case it will merely be because the people's hour has not yet come."

Guillaume Rym felt obliged to interfere:—

"Master Coppenole, you are speaking to a powerful king."

"I know it," gravely answered the hosier.

"Let him talk, friend Rym," said the king. "I like such frankness. My father, Charles VII, said that Truth was sick. I, for my part, thought she had died, without a confessor. Master Coppenole has undeceived me."

Then, laying his hand familiarly upon Coppenole's shoulder, he added,—

"You were saying, Master Jacques—"

"I was saying, Sire, that perhaps you were right,—that the people's hour had not yet come in this land."

Louis XI looked searchingly at him:—

"And when will that hour come, sirrah?"

"You will hear it strike."

"By what o'clock, pray?"

Coppenole, with his homely, peaceful face, drew the king to the window.

"Listen, Sire! Here you have a donjon, a bell-tower, cannon, burghers, soldiers. When the bell rings, when the cannon growl, when the donjon falls with a crash, when burghers and soldiers shout and slay one another, then the hour will strike."

The king's face became dark and thoughtful. For an instant he stood silent; then he gently patted the thick donjon wall, as he might have caressed the flank of his favorite horse.

"Oh, no!" he said; "you will not crumble so easily, will you, my good Bastille?"[18]

Then, turning with an abrupt gesture to the daring Fleming,—

"Did you ever see a revolt, Master Jacques?"

"I made one," said the hosier.

"And how," said the king, "do you set to work to make a revolt?"

"Ah!" replied Coppenole, "it is not very difficult. There are a hundred ways of doing it. In the first place, discontent must be rife in the town; that is not an uncommon occurrence. And then you must consider the character of the inhabitants.

The men of Ghent are always ready to rebel; they always love the prince's son, never the prince. Well, I will suppose that one morning somebody comes into my shop and says: Friend Coppenole, this thing or that thing has happened,—the Lady of Flanders is resolved to maintain the Cabinet; the high provost has doubled the tax on vegetables or something else; whatever you please. I drop my work on the spot; I leave my shop, and I run out into the street, crying, 'Storm and sack!' There is always some empty hogshead lying about. I mount upon it, and I proclaim aloud, in the first words that come to me, all that distresses me; and when you belong to the people, Sire, there is always something to distress you. Then there is a gathering of the clans; there are shouts; the alarm bell rings; the people disarm the troops and arm themselves; the market-men join in; and so it goes on. And it will always be so, so long as there are nobles in the seigniories, burghers in the towns, and peasants in the country."

"And against whom do you rebel in this way?" asked the king. "Against your provosts; against your liege-lords?"

"Sometimes; that depends on circumstances. Against the duke, too, at times."

Louis XI reseated himself, and said with a smile,—

"Ah! here they have got no farther than the provosts."

At this instant Olivier le Daim returned. He was followed by two pages carrying various articles of the king's toilet; but what struck Louis XI was the fact that he was also accompanied by the provost of Paris and the captain of the watch, who seemed dismayed. The spiteful barber also looked dismayed, but was inwardly pleased. He was the first to speak:—

"Sire, I crave your pardon for the disastrous news I bring!"

The king turned so quickly that he tore the matting on the floor with the legs of his chair.

"What do you mean?"

"Sire," replied Olivier le Daim, with the malicious look of a man who rejoices to strike a severe blow, "this rising of the people is not directed against the Provost of the Palace."

"And against whom, then?"

"Against you, Sire."

The old king rose to his feet as erect as a young man.

"Explain yourself, Olivier! And look to your head, my friend; for I swear by the cross of Saint-Lô that if you lie to us at this hour, the same sword which cut off the head of my lord Luxembourg is not too dull to chop off yours!"

The oath was a tremendous one; Louis XI had never but twice in his life sworn by the cross of Saint-Lô.

Olivier opened his lips to answer.

"On your knees!" fiercely interrupted the king. "Tristan, watch this man!"

Olivier knelt, and said coldly,—

"Sire, a witch was condemned to death by your parliamentary court. She took refuge in Notre-Dame. The people desire to take her thence by force. The provost and the captain of the watch, who have just come from the scene of the insurrection, are here to contradict me if I speak not truly. The people are besieging Notre-Dame."

"Indeed!" said the king in a low voice, pale and trembling with rage. "Notre-Dame! So they lay siege to my good mistress, Our Lady, in her own cathedral! Rise, Olivier; you are right. I give you Simon Radin's office. You are right; it is I whom they attack. The witch is in the safe-keeping of the church; the church is in my safe-keeping; and I was foolish enough to believe that they were assaulting the provost. It is myself!"[19]

Then, made young by fury, he began to pace the floor with hasty strides. He laughed no longer; he was terrible to behold; he came and went; the fox was turned to a hyæna. He seemed to have lost all power of speech; his lips moved, and his fleshless hands were clinched. All at once he raised his head, his hollow eye seemed filled with light, and his voice flashed forth like a clarion:—

"Do your work well, Tristan! Do your work well with these scoundrels! Go, Tristan my friend; kill! kill!"

This outburst over, he sat down again, and said with cold and concentrated wrath,—

"Here, Tristan! There are with us in this Bastille Viscount de Gif's fifty lances, making three hundred horse: take them. There is also M. de Châteaupers' company of archers of our ordnance: take them. You are provost-marshal; you have your own men: take them. At the Hôtel Saint-Pol you will find forty archers of the Dauphin's new guard: take them. And with all these soldiers you will hasten to Notre-Dame. Ah, you commoners of Paris, so you would attack the Crown of France, the sanctity of Notre-Dame, and the peace of this republic! Exterminate them, Tristan! exterminate them! and let not one escape but for Montfaucon."

Tristan bowed. "It is well, Sire."

After a pause he added, "And what shall I do with the witch?"

This question gave the king food for thought.

"Ah," said he, "the witch! D'Estouteville, what was the people's pleasure in regard to her?"

"Sire," replied the provost of Paris, "I fancy that as the people desire to wrest her from her shelter in Notre-Dame, it is her lack of punishment that offends them, and they propose to hang her."

The king seemed to muse deeply; then, addressing Tristan l'Hermite: "Very well, compère; exterminate the people, and hang the witch!"

"That's it," whispered Rym to Coppenole, "punish the people for their purpose, and then fulfill that purpose."

"It is well, Sire," answered Tristan. "If the witch be still in Notre-Dame, shall we disregard the sanctuary, and take her thence?"

"By the Rood! Sanctuary!" said the king, scratching his ear. "And yet this woman must be hanged."

Here, as if struck by a sudden thought, he fell upon his knees before his chair, doffed his hat, put it on the seat, and gazing devoutly at one of the leaden images with which it was loaded, he exclaimed, with clasped hands: "Oh, Our Lady of Paris, my gracious patroness, pardon me! I will only do it this once. This criminal must be punished. I assure you, Holy Virgin, my good mistress, that she is a witch, and unworthy of your generous protection. You know, madame, that many very pious princes have infringed upon the privileges of the Church for the glory of God and the needs of the State. Saint Hugh, Bishop of England, allowed King Edward to capture a magician in his church. Saint Louis of France, my master, for the same purpose violated the church of St. Paul; and Alphonso, son of the King of Jerusalem, the Church of the Holy Sepulchre itself. Forgive me this once, Our Lady of Paris! I will never do so again, and I will give you a fine new silver statue, like the one I gave Our Lady of Ecouys last year. Amen."

He made the sign of the cross, rose, put on his hat, and said to Tristan,—

"Make haste, friend; take Châteaupers with you. Ring the alarm! Quell the mob! Hang the witch! That is all. And I expect you to pay the costs of hanging. You will render me an account thereof. Come, Olivier, I shall not go to bed tonight; shave me."

Tristan l'Hermite bowed, and left the room. Then the king dismissed Rym and Coppenole with a gesture, and the words,—

"God keep you, my good Flemish friends. Go, take a little rest; the night is passing, and we are nearer morn than evening."

Both retired, and on reaching their apartments under the escort of the captain of the Bastille, Coppenole said to Guillaume Rym,—

"Ahem! I have had enough of this coughing king. I have seen Charles of Burgundy drunk, and he was not so bad as Louis XI sick."

"Master Jacques," replied Rym, "'tis because the wine of kings is less cruel than their tisane."

CHAPTER VI

"The Chive in the Cly"

On leaving the Bastille, Gringoire ran down the Rue Saint-Antoine with the speed of a runaway horse. On reaching the Porte Baudoyer, he walked straight up to the stone cross in the middle of the square, as if he had been able to distinguish in the darkness the figure of a man in a black dress and cowl, who sat upon the steps of the cross.

"Is it you, master?" said Gringoire.

The black figure rose.

"'Sdeath! You make my blood boil, Gringoire. The man on the tower of Saint-Gervais has just cried half-past one."

"Oh," rejoined Gringoire, "it is not my fault, but that of the watch and the king. I have had a narrow escape. I always just miss being hanged; it is my fate."

"You just miss everything," said the other; "but make haste. Have you the password?"

"Only fancy, master, that I have seen the king! I have just left him. He wears fustian breeches. It was quite an adventure."

"Oh, you spinner of words! What do I care for your adventure? Have you the watchword of the Vagrants?"

"I have; never fear. It is 'the Chive in the Cly.'"

"Good! Otherwise we could not make our way to the church. The Vagrants block the streets. Luckily, it appears that they met with considerable resistance. We may yet be there in time."

"Yes, master; but how are we to get into Notre-Dame?"

"I have the key to the towers."

"And how shall we get out?"

"There is a small door, behind the cloisters, which opens

upon the Terrain, and thence to the water. I have the key, and I moored a boat there this morning."

"I had a pretty escape from being hanged!" repeated Gringoire.

"Come, be quick!" said the other.

Both went hurriedly towards the City.

CHAPTER VII

Châteaupers to the Rescue

The reader may perhaps recall the critical situation in which we left Quasimodo. The brave deaf man, assailed on every hand, had lost, if not all courage, at least all hope of saving not himself (he did not think of himself), but the gipsy. He ran frantically up and down the gallery. Notre-Dame was about to be captured by the Vagrants. Suddenly, the gallop of horses filled the neighboring streets, and with a long train of torches and a broad column of horsemen riding at full speed with lances lowered, the furious sound burst into the square like a whirlwind:—

"France! France! Hew down the clodpolls! Châteaupers to the rescue! Provosty! provosty!"

The terrified Vagrants wheeled about.

Quasimodo, who heard nothing, saw the naked swords, the torches, the pike-heads, the horsemen, at whose head he recognized Captain Phœbus. He saw the confusion of the Vagrants,—the alarm of some, the consternation of the stoutest-hearted,—and he derived so much strength from this unexpected succor, that he hurled from the church the foremost assailants, who were already bestriding the gallery rails.

The king's troops had actually arrived.

The Vagrants fought bravely; they defended themselves desperately. Taken in flank from the Rue Saint-Pierre-aux-Bœufs, and in the rear from the Rue du Parvis, driven close against Notre-Dame, which they were still assailing, and which Quasimodo was defending, at once besiegers and besieged, they were in the singular situation in which Count Henro d'Harcourt afterwards found himself at the famous siege of Turin, in 1640,—between Prince Thomas of Savoy, whom he was besieging, and the Marquis de Leganez, who was blockading him. *"Taurinum obsessor idem et obsessus,"** as his epitaph says.

The conflict was frightful. As Père Mathieu puts it, "wolf's flesh needs dog's teeth." The king's cavaliers, among whom Phœbus de Châteaupers comported himself most valiantly, gave no quarter, and the edge of the sword slew those who escaped the thrust of the lance. The Vagrants, ill-armed, foamed and bit. Men, women, and children flung themselves upon the cruppers and breast-pieces of the horses, and clung to them like cats with tooth and nail. Others blinded the archers by blows of their torches; others again struck iron hooks into the rider's necks and pulled them down, cutting into pieces those who fell.

One man had a large shining scythe, with which he mowed the legs of the horses. It was a frightful sight. He sang a nasal song, and swept his scythe ceaselessly to and fro. At every stroke he cut a broad swath of dismembered limbs. He advanced thus into the thickest of the cavalry, with the calm deliberation, swaying of the head, and regular breathing of a mower cutting down a field of grain. This was Clopin Trouillefou. A shot from an arquebus at last laid him low.

Meantime, windows were again opened. The neighbors, hearing the battle-shouts of the king's men, joined in the skir-

---

*He oppressed the people of Turin and was oppressed by them (Latin).

mish, and from every story bullets rained upon the Vagrants. The square was filled with thick smoke, which the flash of musketry streaked with fire. The front of Notre-Dame was vaguely visible through it, and the decrepit hospital the Hôtel-Dieu, with a few wan patients looking down from the top of its roof dotted with dormer-windows.

At last the Vagrants yielded. Exhaustion, lack of proper arms, the terror caused by the surprise, the musketry from the windows, the brave onslaught of the king's men, all combined to crush them. They broke through the enemy's ranks, and fled in every direction, leaving the square heaped with corpses.

When Quasimodo, who had not stopped fighting for a single instant, saw this rout, he fell upon his knees and raised his hands to heaven; then, mad with joy, he ran, he climbed with the swift motion of a bird to that little cell, all access to which he had so intrepidly defended. He had but one thought now: that was, to kneel before her whom he had saved for the second time.

When he entered the cell he found it empty.

BOOK XI

CHAPTER I

The Little Shoe

When the Vagrants attacked the church, Esmeralda was asleep.

Soon the ever-increasing noise about the building, and the anxious bleating of her goat, which waked before she did, roused her from her slumbers. She sat up, listened, looked about; then, alarmed by the light and commotion, hurried from her cell to see what it all meant. The aspect of the square, the vision which she beheld, the disorder and confusion of this night attack, the hideous rabble bounding hither and thither like an army of frogs half seen in the darkness, the croaking of the hoarse mob, the few red torches moving and dancing in the darkness like will-o'-the-wisps sporting on the misty surface of a marsh,—the whole scene produced upon her the effect of a weird battle waged by the phantoms of the Witches' Sabbath and the stone monsters of the church. Imbued from infancy with the superstitious notions of the gipsy tribe, her first thought was that she had surprised the strange beings of the night in their sorceries. Thus she ran back to her cell in affright to hide her head, and implore her pillow to send her some less horrid nightmare.

Little by little, however, the first fumes of fear vanished; from the ever-increasing tumult, and from various other tokens of reality, she felt that she was beset, not by specters, but by human beings. Then her terror, without being augmented, changed its nature. She reflected upon the possibility of a popular revolt to tear her from her refuge. The idea of again losing life, hope, and Phœbus, whom she still hoped to win in the future, her own absolute defenselessness, all flight cut off, no help at hand, her forlorn condition, her isolation,— these thoughts and countless others overwhelmed her. She fell upon her knees, her face buried in the bed-clothes, her hands clasped above her head, full of agony and apprehension, and, gipsy, pagan, and idolater though she was, she began with sobs to entreat mercy of the good Christian God, and to pray to her hostess, Our Lady. For, believe in nothing though one may, there are moments in life when one belongs to the creed of whatever church is nearest.

She lay thus prostrate for a very long time, trembling indeed, far more than she prayed, chilled by the ever-advancing breath of that frantic mob, wholly ignorant of the meaning of their unbridled rage, knowing not what was on foot, what was being done, what object that throng had in view, but foreseeing some terrible issue.

In the midst of her anguish she heard steps close at hand. She turned. Two men, one of whom carried a lantern, entered her cell. She uttered a faint shriek.

"Fear nothing," said a voice which was not unknown to her; "it is I."

"Who are you?" she asked.

"Pierre Gringoire."

That name calmed her fears. She raised her eyes, and saw that it was indeed the poet; but beside him stood a black figure veiled from head to foot, which silenced her.

"Ah!" replied Gringoire in reproachful tones, "Djali knew me before you did!"

The little goat, in fact, did not wait for Gringoire to pronounce his name. He had no sooner entered, than she rubbed herself fondly against his knees, covering the poet with caresses and white hairs,—for she was shedding her coat. Gringoire returned her caresses.

"Who is that with you?" said the gipsy in a low voice.

"Never fear," replied Gringoire; "it's a friend of mine."

Then the philosopher, placing his lantern on the ground, crouched upon the flagstones, and enthusiastically exclaimed, as he clasped Djali in his arms,—

"Oh, 'tis a pretty creature, doubtless more remarkable for her neatness than her size, but ingenious, subtle, and learned as any grammarian of them all! Come, my Djali, let us see if you have forgotten any of your cunning tricks! Show us how Master Jacques Charmolue does—"

"The man in black would not let him finish. He stepped up to him and gave him a rude shove on the shoulder. Gringoire rose.

"True," said he; "I forgot that we are in haste. Still, that's no reason, master mine, for handling people so roughly. My dear child, your life is in danger, and Djali's too. They want to hang you again. We are your friends, and are come hither to save you. Follow us."

"Is it true?" cried she, distractedly.

"Yes, quite true. Come quickly!"

"I will," she stammered. "But why doesn't your friend speak?"

"Ah!" said Gringoire, "that's because his father and mother were queer people, and brought him up to be silent."

She was forced to rest content with this explanation. Gringoire took her by the hand; his companion picked up the lantern and went on before. The girl was dizzy with dread. She let them lead her away. The goat followed them with leaps of delight, so rejoiced to see Gringoire once more that she made him stumble every moment by thrusting her horns between his legs.

"Such is life," said the philosopher at each escape from falling; "it is often our best friends who cause our downfall!"

They rapidly descended the tower stairs, traversed the church, full of solitude and gloom, but echoing with the din without in frightful contrast to the peace within, and came into the cloister courtyard by the Porte-Rouge. The cloister was deserted; the clergy had fled to the bishop's palace to pray

together; the court was empty, save for a few timid lackeys
hiding in dark corners. They made their way towards the door
which led from this courtyard to the Terrain. The man in
black opened it with a key which he had about him. Our
readers know that the Terrain was a strip of ground enclosed
with walls on the City side, and belonging to the Chapter of
Notre-Dame, which formed the extreme eastern end of the island in the rear of the church. They found this enclosure
quite forsaken. Here there was already less noise in the air.
The sound of the Vagrants' assault reached them more faintly,
less harshly. The fresh wind which followed the course of the
stream stirred with a perceptible rustle the leaves of the one
tree planted at the tip of the Terrain. However, they were still
very close to the danger. The nearest buildings were the Episcopal palace and the church. There was plainly great commotion within the palace. The gloomy mass was furrowed
with lights, which flew from one window to another, as when
you burn paper a dark structure of ashes remains, upon which
bright sparks trace countless grotesque figures. Beside it the
huge towers of Notre-Dame, thus viewed from the rear with
the long nave upon which they are built, outlined in black
against the vast red light which filled the square, looked like
two monstrous andirons for a fire of the Cyclops.

In all directions, so much of Paris as could be seen shim-
mered in blended light and shade. Rembrandt has just such
backgrounds in some of his pictures.

The man with the lantern walked straight to the end of the
Terrain. There, on the very edge of the water, were the worm-
eaten remains of a picket-fence with laths nailed across, to
which a few withered branches of a low vine clung like the
fingers of an open hand. Behind, in the shadow of this trellis,
a small boat was hidden. The man signed to Gringoire and
his companion to enter it. The goat followed them. The man
stepped in last; then he cut the hawser, shoved off from the
shore with a long boat-hook, and seizing a pair of oars, seated
himself in the bow, rowing with all his strength towards the

middle of the stream. The Seine runs very swiftly at this point, and he had some difficulty in clearing the end of the island.

Gringoire's first care on entering the boat, was to take the goat upon his knees. He sat down in the stern; and the young girl, whom the stranger inspired with indescribable fears, took her place close beside the poet.

When our philosopher felt the boat moving, he clapped his hands, and kissed Djali between her horns.

"Oh," said he, "here we are all four saved!"

He added, with the look of a deep thinker, "One is sometimes indebted to fortune, sometimes to cunning, for the happy issue of a great undertaking."

The boat proceeded slowly towards the right bank. The young girl watched the stranger with secret dread. He had carefully covered the light of his dark-lantern, and was but dimly visible, in the gloom, like a ghost in the bow of the boat. His cowl, still drawn down, formed a sort of mask over his face; and every time that he opened his arms, with their wide hanging black sleeves, in rowing, they looked like the broad wings of a bat. Moreover, he had not yet breathed a word. The only sound in the boat was that of the oars, mingled with the ripple of the water against the side of the boat.

"By my soul!" suddenly exclaimed Gringoire, "we are as gay and lively as so many owls! We're as silent as Pythagoreans or fishes! By the Rood! my friends, I wish one of you would speak to me. The human voice is music to the human ear. I am not the author of that remark, but Didymus of Alexandria is, and famous words they are. Certes, Didymus of Alexandria is no mean philosopher. One word, my pretty child,—say one word to me, I implore. By the way, you used to make a queer, funny little face; do you still make it? Do you know, my darling, that Parliament holds jurisdiction over all sanctuaries, and that you ran great risks in your cell in Notre-Dame? Alas! the little bird trochylus builds its nest in the jaws of the crocodile. Master, there's the moon peeping out again. How I hope they won't see us! We are doing a laudable deed in saving the damsel, and yet we should be hanged in the

king's name if we were caught. Alas! human actions may be
taken two ways. I am condemned for the same thing for
which you are rewarded. Some admire Cæsar and blame
Catiline. Isn't that so, master mine? What do you say to that
philosophy? For my part, I possess the philosophy of instinct,
of Nature (*ut apes geometriam*).* —What! nobody answers
me! What disagreeable tempers you both have! I must needs
talk to myself. That's what we call in tragedy a monologue. By
the Rood!—I must tell you that I've just seen King Louis XI,
and that I caught that oath from him,—by the Rood, then,
they're still keeping up a fine howling in the City! He's a
wicked old villain of a king. He's all muffled up in furs. He
still owes me the money for my epithalamium, and he came
precious near hanging me tonight, which would have bothered me mightily. He is very stingy to men of merit. He really
ought to read the four books by Salvien of Cologne, '*Adversus
avaritiam.*'† In good sooth, he is a very narrow-minded king in
his dealings with men of letters, and one who commits most
barbarous cruelties. He's a sponge to soak up money squeezed
from the people. His economy is like the spleen, which grows
fat upon the leanness of all the other members. Thus, complaints of the hardness of the times become murmurs against
the sovereign. Under the reign of this mild and pious lord, the
gallows crack with their weight of victims, the headsman's
blocks grow rotten with blood, the prisons are filled to bursting. This king takes in money with one hand and hangs men
with the other. He is pander to my lady Taxes and my lord
Gibbet. The great are stripped of their dignities, and the small
are ceaselessly loaded with new burdens. 'Tis an extravagant
prince. I do not love this monarch. And how say you, my master?"

The man in black suffered the babbling poet to prate his

---

*As the bees do geometry (Latin).

†*Against Avarice* (Latin); this satirical work was written in the fourth
century by Salvien of Cologne, a priest.

fill. He continued to struggle against the strong and angry current which divides the prow of the City from the stern of the Ile Notre-Dame, which we now know as the Ile Saint-Louis.

"By the way, master," suddenly observed Gringoire, "just as we made our way into the square through the angry Vagabonds, did your reverence note that poor little devil whose brains your deaf friend was about dashing out against the railing of the gallery of kings? I am near-sighted, and did not recognize him. Do you know who it could be?"[20]

The stranger made no answer, but he ceased rowing; his arms fell powerless; his head drooped upon his breast, and Esmeralda heard him heave a convulsive sigh. She shuddered; she had heard similar sighs before.

The boat, left to itself, drifted with the current for some moments. But finally the man in black drew himself up, again seized the oars, and began again to pull against the stream. He rounded the end of the Ile Notre-Dame, and bent his course towards the landing-place of the Hay-Market.

"Ah!" said Gringoire, "there's the Logis Barbeau. There, master, look: that collection of black roofs which form such strange angles; there, beneath that mass of low, stringy, streaked, and dirty clouds, where the moon looks like the yolk of a broken egg. 'Tis a handsome house. It contains a chapel capped by a tiny dome full of daintily wrought decorations. Above it you may see the bell-tower with its delicate tracery. There is also a pleasant garden, consisting of a fish-pond, an aviary, an echo, a mall, a labyrinth, a house for wild beasts, and a quantity of shady alleys most agreeable to Venus. There is also a rascally tree, which goes by the name of the Lovers' Retreat, because it once hid the meetings of a famous French princess and a gallant and witty constable of France. Alas! we poor philosophers are to a constable what a bed of cabbages and radishes is to the gardens of the Louvre. What does it matter, after all? Human life, for the great as well as for us, is made up of mingled good and ill. Grief goes ever hand in hand with gladness, as the spondee with the dactyl. Master, I must tell you the story of this Logis Barbeau. It ends in tragic fashion. It was in 1319, during the reign of Philip V, the longest of all the French kings. The moral of the story is, that the temptations of the flesh are hurtful and pernicious. Do not look too often at your neighbor's wife, much as your senses may be tickled by her beauty. Fornication is a very libertine thought. Adultery is curiosity about another's pleasure. Hollo! The noise seems to be growing louder over yonder!"

The din around Notre-Dame was indeed increasing rapidly. They paused and listened. They distinctly heard shouts of victory. All at once a hundred torches, which lit up the glittering helmets of men-at-arms, appeared upon all parts of the church,—upon the towers, galleries, and flying buttresses. These torches seemed searching for some one or something; and soon distant cries of, "The gipsy! The witch! Death to the gipsy!" fell plainly on the ears of the fugitives.

The wretched girl hid her face in her hands, and the unknown boatman began to row frantically for the shore. Meantime our philosopher reflected. He hugged the goat in his arms, and edged very gently away from the gipsy, who nestled closer and closer to him, as her only remaining protector.

Gringoire was certainly cruelly perplexed. He considered that the goat too, "according to the existing law," would be hanged if she were recaptured, which would be a great pity,— poor Djali! that it was quite too much of a good thing to have two condemned prisoners clinging to him at once; and, finally, that his companion asked nothing better than to take sole charge of the girl. A violent conflict went on within him, in which, like Jupiter in the Iliad, he alternately weighed the merits of the gipsy and the goat; and he gazed first at the one, then at the other, with tearful eyes, muttering, "After all, I cannot save you both!"

A shock warned them that the boat had reached shore. The ominous uproar still pervaded the City. The stranger rose, approached the gipsy, and tried to take her by the arm to help her to land. She repulsed him, and clung to Gringoire's sleeve, while he, in his turn, absorbed in the goat, almost pushed her from him. Then she sprang from the boat unaided. She was so distressed that she knew not what she was doing, or where she was going. She stood thus stupefied an instant, watching the water as it glided by. When she had somewhat recovered her senses, she was alone upon the wharf with the stranger. It seems that Gringoire had taken advantage of the moment of their landing, and stolen away with the goat into the throng of houses in the Rue Grenier-sur-l'Eau.[21]

The poor gipsy shuddered when she found herself alone with this man. She tried to speak, to cry out, to call Gringoire; her tongue clove to the roof of her mouth, and no sound issued from her lips. All at once she felt the hand of the unknown upon her arm. It was a cold, strong hand. Her teeth chattered, she turned paler than the moonbeams which illumined her face. The man said not a word. He strode rapidly towards the Place de Grève, holding her firmly by the hand. At that moment she vaguely felt that fate is an irresistible power. She had lost all control of her limbs; she suffered him to drag her along, running while he walked. The quay at this point rises abruptly from the river, but it seemed to her is if she were going down hill.

She looked in every direction. Not a single passer. The quay was absolutely deserted. She heard no sound, she perceived no stir save in the tumultuous and blazing City from which she was separated only by an arm of the Seine, and whence her name came to her joined with threats of death. The rest of Paris lay spread around her in great masses of shadow.

Meantime, the stranger drew her on in the same silence and with the same speed. She recognized none of the places through which she passed. As she went by a lighted window she made an effort, suddenly resisted him, and cried, "Help!"

The owner of the house opened the window, appeared in his shirt with his lamp, looked out upon the quay with a drowsy face, pronounced a few words which she did not catch, and closed the shutter. Thus her last glimmer of hope faded.

The man in black did not utter a syllable; he held her fast, and began to increase his speed. She resisted no longer, but followed him helplessly.

From time to time she mustered a little strength, and said in a voice broken by the unevenness of the pavement and the breathless haste with which she was borne along: "Who are you? Who are you?" He made no reply.

In this way they proceeded along the edge of the quay to an open square of considerable size. The moon shone faintly. They were in the Place de Grève. In the middle stood a sort of black cross; it was the gallows. She recognized all this, and knew where she was.

The man stopped, turning to her, and lifted his cowl.

"Oh!" stammered she, frozen with fear; "I was sure that it must be he."

It was the priest. He looked like the ghost of himself. This was due to the moonlight. It seems as if by that light one could see only the specters of things.

"Listen!" said he; and she trembled at the sound of that fatal voice which she had not heard for so long a time. He went on, with the short, quick gasps which betray deep mental emotion: "Listen! We have reached our goal. I must speak with you. This is the Place de Grève. This is a decisive point in our lives. Fate has delivered us over to each other. Your life is in my hands; my soul rests in yours. Beyond this place and this night all is dark. Hear me, then. I am going to tell you— But first, speak not to me of your Phœbus." (As he said this he came and went, like a man who cannot remain quietly in one place, dragging her after him.) "Speak not of him. If you but mention his name, I know not what I shall do, but it will be something terrible."

This said, like a body which has found its center of gravity, he again stood still, but his words revealed no less emotion. His voice grew lower and lower.

"Do not turn away your head. Listen to me. It is a serious business. In the first place, I will tell you what has happened. It is no laughing matter, I assure you. What was I saying? Remind me! Ah! There is an order from Parliament which returns you to the scaffold. I have rescued you from the hang-man's hands; but even now they are in pursuit of you. See!"

He stretched his arm towards the City. The search did indeed seem to be continued. The noise drew nearer; the tower of the lieutenant's house, directly facing the Place de Grève, was full of light and bustle, and soldiers were seen running along the opposite quay with torches, shouting: "The gipsy! Where is the gipsy? Death! Death!"

"You see that they are in pursuit of you, and that I do not lie. I love you. Do not open your lips; rather, do not speak to me, if it be to tell me that you hate me. I am resolved never again to hear that. I have saved you. — Let me finish first. — I can save you wholly. Everything is ready. It is for you to choose. I can do as you would have me."

He interrupted himself excitedly: "No, that is not what I meant to say."

Then, running, and making her run after him, — for he did not loose his hold, — he went straight to the gibbet, and pointed to it.

"Choose between us," said he, coldly.

She tore herself from his grasp, and fell at the foot of the gibbet, throwing her arms about that dismal support; then she half turned her lovely head, and looked at the priest over her shoulder. She seemed a Holy Virgin at the foot of the cross. The priest remained motionless, his finger still raised to the gallows, his gesture unchanged as if he were a statue.

At last the gipsy said, —

"It is less horrible to me than you are."

Then he let his arm drop slowly, and gazed at the pave-ment in deep dejection.

"If these stones could speak," he murmured, "yes, they would say, 'There is a very miserable man.'"

He went on. The girl, kneeling before the gibbet, and veiled by her long hair, let him speak without interruption. He had now assumed a gentle, plaintive tone, in painful con-trast with the proud severity of his features.

"I love you. Oh, it is indeed true! Is there then no visible spark of that fire which burns my soul? Alas! girl, night and day; yes, night and day,—does this deserve no pity? It is a love which consumes me night and day, I tell you; it is torture. Oh, my suffering is too great to be endured, my poor child! It is a thing worthy of compassion, I assure you. You see that I speak gently to you. I would fain have you cease to feel such horror of me. After all, if a man love a woman, it is not his fault! Oh, my God! What! will you never forgive me? Will you always hate me? Is this the end? It is this that makes me wicked, I tell you, and horrible in my own sight! You do not even look at me! You are thinking of other things, perhaps, while I stand and talk to you, and both of us are trembling on the verge of eternity! But do not talk to me of your soldier! What; I might throw myself at your knees; what! I might kiss, not your feet, for that you would not suffer, but the ground beneath your feet; what! I might sob like a child: I might tear from my bosom, not words, but my heart and my very life, to show you how I love you; all would be in vain,—all! And yet your soul is full of gentleness and tenderness; you are radiant with the most beauteous mildness; you are all sweetness, goodness, mercy, and charm. Alas! you are unkind to me alone! Oh, what a freak of fate!"

He buried his face in his hands. The young girl heard his sobs. It was the first time she had seen him weep. Standing thus, shaken by sobs, he appeared more miserable and more suppliant than had he been on his knees. He wept thus for some time.

"Ah, well!" he added, his first tears over, "I can find no words to express my feelings; and yet I pondered well what I should say to you. Now, I tremble and shudder; I give way at the decisive moment; I feel that some superior power surrounds us, and I stammer. Oh, I shall fall to the ground if you do not take pity upon me, upon yourself! Do not condemn us both! If you knew how much I love you; what a heart mine is! Oh, what an abandonment of all virtue! what a desperate desertion of myself! A scholar, I scoff at science; a gentleman, I disgrace my name; a priest, I make my missal a pillow of foul desires, grossly insult my God! All this for your sake, enchantress! to be worthy of your hell! And you reject the damned soul! Oh, let me tell you all! more still, something yet more horrible, oh, far more horrible—"

As he pronounced these last words, his look became quite wild. He was silent an instant, then resumed as if talking to himself, and in a firm voice,—

"Cain, what hast thou done with thy brother?"

There was another pause, and he added,—

"What have I done with him, Lord? I took him in my arms, I brought him up, I fed him, I loved him, I idolized him, and I killed him! Yes, Lord, for they have just now dashed his head, before my very eyes, against the stones of your temple, and it was because of me, because of this woman, because of her—"

His eye was haggard. His voice died away; he still repeated mechanically, over and over, at considerable intervals, like a bell prolonging its last vibration, "Because of her; because of her—"

Here his tongue ceased to articulate any distinct sound, although his lips still moved. All at once he gave way, and sank in a heap, lying motionless upon the ground, his head upon his knees.

A slight movement made by the girl to pull her foot from under him revived him. He slowly drew his hand over his hollow cheeks, and looked in amazement at his fingers, which were wet. "What!" he muttered, "have I wept?"

And turning quickly to the gipsy with indescribable anguish:—

"Alas! and you could coldly see me weep! Child, do you know that those tears are burning lava? Is it then really true,—in the man we hate, nothing moves us? You would see me die, and still laugh! One word,—only one word of pardon! Do not tell me that you love me, only tell me that you will try; that shall suffice, and I will save you. If not,—oh, time passes. I conjure you! by all that you hold sacred, do not wait until I am once more turned to stone, like that gibbet which also claims you! Think, that I hold the destinies of both in my hand; that I am mad,—it is terrible!—that I may let all fall; and that beneath us yawns a bottomless pit, wretched girl, wherein my fall shall follow yours through all eternity! One word of kindness,—but a single word!"

She opened her mouth to answer him. He threw himself upon his knees before her, to receive with adoration the words, perhaps relenting, which were about to fall from her lips. She said to him, "You are an assassin!"

The priest caught her fiercely in his arms, and began to laugh an abominable laugh.

"Well, yes, an assassin!" said he; "and you shall be mine. You will not have me for your slave, you shall have me for your master. You shall be mine! You shall be mine! I have a den whither I will drag you. You must follow me, you must needs follow me, or I will give you up to justice! You must die, my beauty, or be mine,—be the priest's, the apostate's, the assassin's! and that this night; do you hear me? Come! rejoice; come, kiss me, foolish girl! The tomb, or my bed!"

His eyes flashed with rage and desire. His impure lips reddened the neck of the young girl. She struggled in his arms. He covered her with frantic kisses.

"Do not bite me, monster!" she shrieked. "Oh, the hateful, poisonous monk! Let me go! I will tear out your vile grey hair, and throw it by handfuls in your face!"

He flushed, then paled, then released her, and looked at her gloomily. She thought herself victorious, and went on:—

"I tell you that I belong to my Phœbus, that 'tis Phœbus I love, that Phœbus alone is handsome! You priest, are old! you are ugly! Begone!"

He uttered a violent cry, like the wretch to whom a red-hot iron is applied. "Then die!" he said, gnashing his teeth. She saw his frightful look, and strove to fly. He overtook her, shook her, threw her down, and walked rapidly towards the corner of the Tour-Roland, dragging her after him over the pavement by her fair hands.

Reaching it, he turned to her:—

"For the last time, will you be mine?"

She answered emphatically,—

"No!"

Then he called in a loud voice,—

"Gudule! Gudule! here is the gipsy girl! Avenge yourself!"

The young girl felt herself suddenly seized by the elbow. She looked. A fleshless arm was thrust from a loop-hole in the wall, and held her with an iron grip.

"Hold her fast!" said the priest; "it's the runaway gipsy. Do not let her go. I will fetch the officers. You shall see her hanged."

A guttural laugh from the other side of the wall replied to these bloody words: "Ha! ha! ha!" The gipsy saw the priest depart in the direction of the Pont Notre-Dame. The tramp of horses was heard coming from that quarter.

The girl recognized the spiteful recluse. Panting with terror, she tried to release herself. She writhed, she twisted herself in agony and despair; but the woman held her with unnatural strength. The thin bony fingers which bruised her flesh fastened about her arm like a vise. That hand seemed riveted to her wrist. It was stronger than any chain, stronger than any pillory or iron ring; it was a pair of intelligent and living pincers issuing from a wall.

Exhausted, she sank back, and the fear of death took possession of her. She thought of the beauty of life, of youth, of the sight of the sky, of the various aspects of Nature, of the love of Phœbus, of all that was behind her and of all that was rapidly coming upon her, of the priest who would denounce her, of the hangman who would soon arrive, of the gallows which was already there. Then terror rose to the very roots of her hair, and she heard the melancholy laugh of the recluse, as she whispered in her ear,—

"Ha! ha! ha! You shall be hanged!"

She turned, almost fainting, to the window, and saw the savage face of the *sachette* through the bars.

"What have I done to you?" she asked feebly.

The recluse made no answer; she began to mumble in angry, mocking sing-song, "Gipsy girl! gipsy girl! gipsy girl!"

The luckless Esmeralda veiled her face with her hair, seeing that it was no human being with whom she had to deal.

All at once the recluse exclaimed, as if the gipsy's question had taken all this time to penetrate her troubled brain: —

"What have you done to me, do you say? Ah! What have you done to me, indeed, you gipsy! Well, listen, and I will tell you. I had a child, even I! Do you hear? I had a child, — a child, I say! A pretty little girl! My Agnès," she repeated, her wits wandering for a moment, and kissing something in the gloom. "Well, are you listening, gipsy? They stole my child; they took my child from me; they ate my child! That is what you have done to me."

The young girl answered, as innocently as the lamb in the fable, —

"Alas! I probably was not even born then!"

"Oh, yes!" rejoined the recluse, "you must have been born. You had a hand in it. She would have been about your age! There! For fifteen years I have been in this hole; for fifteen years I have suffered; for fifteen years I have prayed; for fifteen years I have dashed my head against these four walls. I tell you, 'twas the gipsies who stole her from me, — do you hear? — and who gnawed her bones. Have you a heart? Fancy what it is to have a child who plays at your knee; a child who sucks your breast; a child who sleeps in your arms. It is such a helpless, innocent thing! Well, that, — that's what they took from me, what they killed for me! The good God knows it well! Now it is my turn; I will slaughter the Egyptians. Oh, how I would bite you, if the bars did not prevent me! My head is too big to pass through them! Poor little thing! they took her while she slept! And if they waked her when they snatched her up, all her shrieks were vain; I was not there! Ah, gipsy mothers, you ate my child! Come, look at yours!"

Then she began to laugh, or gnash her teeth, for the two things were much the same in that frenzied face. Dawn was at hand. An ashen light faintly illumined the scene, and the gallows became more and more distinctly visible in the center of the square. From the other side, towards the Pont Notre-Dame the poor prisoner imagined she heard the tramp of approaching horsemen.

"Madame," she cried, clasping her hands and falling on her knees, disheveled, frantic, mad with fright,— "Madame, have pity! they are coming. I never harmed you. Would you see me die so horrible a death before your very eyes? You are merciful, I am sure. It is too awful! Let me save myself! Let me go! Have mercy! I cannot die thus!"

"Give me back my child!" said the recluse.

"Mercy! mercy!"

"Give me back my child!"

"Let me go, in Heaven's name!"

"Give me back my child!"

Upon this, the girl sank down, worn out and exhausted, her eyes already having the glazed look of one dead.

"Alas!" she stammered forth, "you seek your child, and I seek my parents."

"Give me my little Agnès!" continued Gudule. "You know not where she is? Then die! I will tell you all. I was a prostitute; I had a child; they took my child from me. It was the gipsies who did it. You see that you must die. When your gipsy mother comes to claim you, I shall say, 'Mother, look upon that gibbet!—Or else restore my child!' Do you know where she is,—where my little girl is? Stay, I will show you. Here's her shoe,—all that is left me. Do you know where the mate to it is? If you know, tell me, and if it is only at the other end of the world, I will go on my knees to get it."

So saying, with her other hand, stretched through the bars, she showed the gipsy the little embroidered shoe. It was already light enough to distinguish the shape and colors.

"Show me that shoe," said the gipsy shuddering. "My God! my God!"

And at the same time with her free hand she hastily opened the little bag adorned with green glass beads, which she wore about her neck.

"That's it! that's it!" growled Gudule; "search for your devilish spells!"

All at once she stopped short, trembled from head to foot, and cried out in a voice which came from her inmost soul, "My daughter!"

The gipsy had drawn from the bag a tiny shoe, precisely like the other. A strip of parchment was fastened to the little shoe, upon which these verses were written:

> "When the mate to this you find,
> Thy mother is not far behind."

Quick as a flash of lightning the recluse compared the two shoes, read the inscription on the parchment, and pressed her face, beaming with divine rapture, to the window-bars exclaiming, —

"My daughter! my daughter!"

"Mother!" replied the gipsy.

Here we must forbear to set down more.

The wall and the iron grating parted the two. "Oh, the wall!" cried the recluse. "Oh, to see her and not to kiss her! Your hand! your hand!"

The girl put her arm through the window; the recluse threw herself upon the hand, pressed her lips to it, and stood lost in that kiss, the only sign of life being an occasional sob which heaved her bosom. Yet she wept torrents of tears in silence, in the darkness, like rain falling in the night. The poor mother poured out in floods upon that idolized hand the dark, deep fountain of tears within her heart, into which all her grief had filtered, drop by drop, for fifteen years.

Suddenly she rose, flung her long grey hair back from her face, and without a word began to shake the bars of her cell more fiercely than a lioness. They held firm. Then she brought from one corner a large paving-stone which served her as a pillow, and hurled it against them with such violence that one of them broke, flashing countless sparks. A second blow utterly destroyed the old iron cross which barricaded her window. Then with both hands she pulled out and demolished the rusty fragments. There are moments when a woman's hands seem endowed with supernatural strength.

A passage being cleared,—and it took less than a minute to do the work,—she seized her daughter by the waist and dragged her into the cell. "Come, let me draw you out of the abyss!" she murmured.

When her daughter was in the cell, she placed her gently on the ground, then took her up again, and bearing her in her arms as if she were still her little Agnès, she paced to and fro in the narrow space, frantic, mad with joy, singing, shouting, kissing her daughter, talking to her, bursting into laughter, melting into tears, all at once, and with the utmost passion.

"My daughter! my daughter!" she cried. "I've found my daughter! Here she is! The good God has restored her to me. Come, all of you! Is there no one here to see that I've found my daughter? Lord Jesus, how beautiful she is! You made me wait fifteen years, my good God, but it was to make her more beautiful for me! Then the gipsies did not eat her! Who told me so? My little girl! my little girl! kiss me. Those good gipsies! I love gipsies. It is really you. Then that was why my heart leaped within me every time you passed; and I thought it was hate! Forgive me, Agnès, forgive me. You thought me very cruel, didn't you? I love you. Have you still the same little mark on your neck? Let us see. She has it still. Oh, how beautiful you are! It was I who gave you those big eyes, miss. Kiss me. I love you. I care not now if other mothers have children; I can laugh them to scorn. They may come. Here is mine. Here's her neck, her eyes, her hair, her hand. Find me another as lovely! Oh, I tell you she'll have plenty of lovers, this girl of mine! I have wept for fifteen years. All my beauty has left me and gone to her. Kiss me."

She made her a thousand other extravagant speeches, their only merit being in the tone in which they were uttered, disordered the poor girl's dress until she made her blush, smoothed her silken hair with her hand, kissed her foot, her knee, her forehead, her eyes, went into ecstasies over each and all. The young girl made no resistance, but repeated ever and anon, in a low tone and with infinite sweetness, "Mother!"

"Look you, my little one," went on the recluse, interrupting each word with kisses, — "look you; I shall love you dearly. We will go away; we shall be very happy. I have inherited something at Rheims, in our native country. You know, at Rheims? Oh, no! you don't remember; you were too little. If you only knew how pretty you were at four months old! Tiny feet, which people, out of curiosity, came all the way from Epernay, full seven leagues off, to see! We will have a field and a house. I will put you to sleep in my bed. My God! my God! who would ever have believed it? I've found my daughter!"

"Oh, mother!" said the girl, at last recovering sufficient strength to speak in spite of her emotion, "the gipsy woman told me it would be so. There was a kind gipsy woman of our tribe who died last year, and who always took care of me as if she had been my nurse. It was she who hung this bag about my neck. She always said to me, 'Little one, guard this trinket well. It is a precious treasure; it will help you to find your mother. You wear your mother around your neck.' The gipsy foretold it!"

The *sachette* again clasped her daughter in her arms.

"Come; let me kiss you! You said that so prettily. When we are in our own country, we will give these little shoes to the Child Jesus in the church; we surely owe that much to the kind Blessed Virgin. Heavens! what a sweet voice you have! When you spoke to me just now, it was like music. Oh, my Lord God, I have found my child! But is it credible, — all this story? Nothing can kill one, for I have not died of joy."

And then she again began to clap her hands, to laugh, and cry,

"How happy we shall be!"

At this moment the cell rang with the clash of arms and the galloping feet of horses, which seemed to come from the Pont Notre-Dame, and to be advancing nearer and nearer along the quay. The gipsy threw herself into the arms of the *sachette* in an agony.

"Save me! save me, mother! I hear them coming!"

The recluse turned pale.

"Heavens! What do you say? I had forgotten; you are pursued! Why, what have you done?"

"I know not," replied the unhappy child; "but I am condemned to die."

"To die!" said Gudule, tottering as if struck by lightning. "To die!" she repeated slowly, gazing steadily into her daughter's face.

"Yes, mother," replied the desperate girl, "they mean to kill me. They are coming now to capture me. That gallows is for me! Save me! save me! They come! Save me!"

The recluse stood for some moments motionless, as if turned to stone; then she shook her head doubtingly, and all at once burst into loud laughter; but her former frightful laugh had returned:—

"Ho! ho! No; it is a dream! Oh, yes; I lost her, I lost her for fifteen years, and then I found her again, and it was but for an instant! And they would take her from me again! Now that she is grown up, that she is so fair, that she talks to me, that she loves me, they would devour her before my eyes,—mine, who am her mother! Oh, no; such things cannot be! The good God would not suffer them."

Here the cavalcade seemed to pause, and a distant voice was heard, saying,—

"This way, Master Tristan; the priest says that we shall find her at the Rat-Hole!" The tramp of horses began again.

The recluse sprang up with a despairing cry.

"Save yourself! save yourself, my child! I remember now! You are right; it is your death! Horror! Malediction! Save yourself!"

She thrust her head from the window, and rapidly withdrew it.

"Stay!" she said in a low, curt, and mournful tone, convulsively clasping the hand of the gipsy, who was more dead than alive. "Stay! do not breathe! There are soldiers everywhere. You cannot go; it is too light."

Her eyes were dry and burning. She stood for a moment speechless; then she strode up and down the cell, pausing at intervals to tear out handfuls of her grey hair. Suddenly she said: "They are coming; I will speak to them. Hide yourself in this corner; they will not see you. I will tell them that you have escaped; that I let you go, by my faith!"

She laid her daughter—for she still held her in her arms—in a corner of the cell which was not visible from without. She made her crouch down, carefully arranged her so that neither hand nor foot protruded beyond the shadow, loosened her black hair, which she spread over her white gown to hide it, put before her her jug and paving-stone,—the only articles of furniture which she had,—imagining that they would conceal her; and when this was done, feeling calmer, she knelt and prayed. Day, which was but just breaking, still left many shadows in the Rat-Hole.

At that instant the voice of the priest—that infernal voice—passed very close to the cell, shouting,—

"This way, Captain Phœbus de Châteaupers!"

At that name, at that voice, Esmeralda, huddling in her corner, made a movement.

"Do not stir!" said Gudule.

She had hardly finished speaking when a riotous crowd of men, swords, and horses, halted outside the cell. The mother rose hastily, and placed herself before the window in such a way as to cut off all view of the room. She saw a numerous band of armed men, on foot and on horseback, drawn up in the Place de Grève. The officer in command sprang to the ground and came towards her.

"Old woman," said this man, who had an atrocious face, "we are looking for a witch, that we may hang her. We were told that you had her."

The poor mother assumed the most indifferent air that she could, and answered,—

"I don't know what you mean."

The other replied, "Zounds! Then what was that frightened archdeacon talking about? Where is he?"

"Sir," said a soldier, "he has disappeared."

"Come, now, old hag," resumed the commanding officer, "don't lie! A witch was left in your care. What have you done with her?"

The recluse dared not deny everything, lest she should rouse suspicion, and answered in a surly but seemingly truthful tone,—

"If you mean a tall girl who was thrust into my hands just now, I can only tell you that she bit me, and I let her go. There. Now leave me in peace."

The officer pulled a wry face.

"Don't lie to me, old scarecrow!" he replied. "I am Tristan l'Hermite, and I am the friend of the king. Tristan l'Hermite, do you hear?" he added looking round the Place de Grève, "'Tis a name familiar here."

"You might be Satan l'Hermite," responded Gudule, whose hopes began to rise, "and I could tell you nothing more, and should be no more afraid of you."

"Odds bodikins!" said Tristan, "here's a vixen for you! Ah, so the witch girl escaped! And which way did she go?"

Gudule answered indifferently,—

"Through the Rue du Mouton, I believe."

Tristan turned his head, and signed to his troop to prepare to resume their march. The recluse breathed more freely.

"Sir," suddenly said an archer, "pray ask this old sorceress how the bars of her window came to be so twisted and broken."

This question revived the miserable mother's anguish. Still, she did not lose all presence of mind.

"They were always so," she stammered.

"Nonsense!" rejoined the archer; "only yesterday they formed a beautiful black cross which inspired pious thoughts in all who looked upon it."

Tristan cast a side-glance at the recluse.

"It seems to me that our friend looks embarrassed."

The unfortunate woman felt that everything depended upon her putting a good face on the matter, and, with death in her soul, she began to laugh. Mothers have such courage.

"Pooh!" said she, "that man is drunk. 'Twas more than a year ago that the tail of a cart full of stones was backed into my window and destroyed the grating. And, what's more, I scolded the carter roundly."

"That's true," said another archer; "I was here at the time."

There are always people everywhere who have seen everything. This unexpected testimony from the archer encouraged the recluse, who during this interrogatory felt as if she were crossing a precipice on the sharp edge of a knife.

But she was condemned to a continual alternation between hope and fear.

"If it was done by a cart," returned the first soldier, "the broken ends of the bars would have been driven inward; but they are bent outward."

"Ho! ho!" said Tristan; "your nose is as sharp as that of any inquisitor at the Châtelet. Answer him, old woman!"

"Good heavens!" she cried, at her wits' end, and in a voice which despite all her efforts was tearful, "I swear, sir, that it was a cart which broke those bars. You heard that man say he saw it; and besides, what has that to do with your gipsy?"

"Hum!" growled Tristan.

"The devil!" added the soldier, flattered by the provost's praises; "the fractures in the iron are quite fresh!"

Tristan shook his head. She turned pale.

"How long ago did you say this affair of the cart occurred?"

"A month,—perhaps a fortnight, sir. I'm sure I don't remember."

"She said it was a year, just now," observed the soldier.

"That looks queer!" said the provost.

"Sir," she cried, still pressing close to the window, and trembling lest their suspicions should lead them to put in their heads and examine the cell,—"sir, I swear it was a cart that broke these bars; I swear it by all the angels in paradise!

If it was not a cart, may I be damned forever: and may God renounce me."

"You seem very ready to swear!" said Tristan, with his searching glance.

The poor woman felt her courage sink. She was in a state to commit any folly, and with terror she realized she was saying what she ought not to say.

Here another soldier ran up, shouting,—

"Sir, the old fagot lies. The witch did not escape through the Rue du Mouton. The chain has been stretched across the street all night, and the chain-keeper has seen no one pass."

Tristan, whose face grew more forbidding every instant, addressed the recluse:—

"What have you to say to this?"

She still strove to brave this fresh contradiction.

"I don't know, sir; I may have been mistaken. I dare say, indeed, that she crossed the water."

"That is in the opposite direction," said the provost. "However, it is not very likely that she would wish to return to the City, where she was closely pursued. You lie, old woman!"

"And then," added the first soldier, "there is no boat either on this side of the water or on the other."

"Perhaps she swam across," replied the recluse, disputing the ground inch by inch.

"Can women swim?" said the soldier.

"Odds bodikins! old woman! you lie! you lie!" angrily rejoined Tristan. "I have a great mind to let the witch go, and hang you in her stead. A quarter of an hour of the rack may wring the truth from your lips. Come! follow us!"

She seized eagerly upon his words:—

"As you like, sir. So be it, so be it! The rack. I am willing. Take me. Be quick; be quick. Let us be off at once. Meantime," thought she, "my daughter may escape."

"Zounds!" said the provost; "so greedy for the rack! I don't understand this mad-woman!"

An old grey-headed sergeant of the watch stepped from the ranks, and addressing the provost, said,—

"Mad, indeed, sir! If she let the gipsy go, it was not her fault, for she has no liking for gipsies. For fifteen years I have done duty on the watch, and I have heard her curse the gipsy women nightly with endless execrations. If the girl of whom we are in search is, as I suppose, the little dancer with the goat, she particularly detests her."

Gudule made an effort, and said,—

"Particularly."

The unanimous testimony of the men belonging to the watch confirmed the old sergeant's statement. Tristan l'Hermite, despairing of learning anything from the recluse, turned his back upon her, and with unspeakable anxiety she saw him move slowly towards his horse.

"Come," he muttered, "we must be off. Let us resume our search. I shall not sleep until this gipsy girl be hanged."

Still, he hesitated some time before mounting his horse. Gudule trembled between life and death as she saw him glance about the square with the restless air of a hunting-dog, which scents the lair of the wild beast and refuses to depart. At last he shook his head and leaped into his saddle. Gudule's terribly overladen heart swelled, and she said in a low voice, with a glance at her daughter, at whom she had not dared to look while the soldiers were there, "Saved!"

The poor girl had crouched in her corner all this time, without moving or breathing, staring death in the face. She had lost none of the scene between Gudule and Tristan, and each of her mother's pangs had found an echo in her own soul. She had heard the successive snappings of the thread which held her suspended over the abyss; twenty times she had felt that it must break, and now at last she began to breathe freely, and to hope that her footing was secure. At this instant she heard a voice say to the provost,—

"'Sblood! Mr. Provost, it is no business for a soldier to hang witches. The mob still rages yonder. I must leave you to your own devices. You will not object to my rejoining my company, who are left without a captain."

This voice was that of Phœbus de Châteaupers. She underwent an indescribable revulsion of feeling. So he was there,—her friend, her protector, her stay, her refuge, her Phœbus! She rose, and before her mother could prevent her, flew to the window, crying,—

"Phœbus! help, my Phœbus!"

Phœbus was no longer there.[22] He had just galloped round the corner of the Rue de la Coutellerie. But Tristan was not yet gone.

The recluse flung herself upon her daughter with a roar. She dragged her violently back, digging her nails into her neck. A tigress does not look twice when the safety of her young is in question. But it was too late. Tristan had seen her.

"Ha! ha!" cried he, with a laugh which bared all his teeth, and made his face look like the muzzle of a wolf, "two mice in the trap!"

"I thought as much," said the soldier.

Tristan clapped him on the shoulder, "You are a famous cat! Come," he added, "where is Henriet Cousin?"

A man who had neither the dress nor the manner of a soldier stepped from the ranks. He wore a motley garb of brown and grey, his hair was smooth and lank, his sleeves were of leather, and in his huge hand was a bundle of rope. This man always accompanied Tristan, who always accompanied Louis XI.

"My friend," said Tristan l'Hermite, "I presume that this is the witch we are seeking. You will hang her for me. Have you your ladder?"

"There is one yonder under the shed of the Maison-aux-Piliers," replied the man. "Are we to do the business on this gallows?" he continued, pointing to the stone gibbet.

"Yes."

"Ho! ho!" rejoined the man, with a coarse laugh even more bestial than that of the provost; "we sha'n't have far to go."

"Despatch!" said Tristan; "you can laugh afterwards."

Meantime, since Tristan had seen her daughter, and all hope was lost, the recluse had not spoken a word. She had cast the poor gipsy, almost lifeless, into the corner of the cell, and resumed her place at the window, her hands clinging to the sides of the frame like two claws. In this position her eyes wandered boldly over the soldiers, the light of reason having once more faded from them. When Henriet Cousin approached her refuge, she glared so savagely at him that he shrank back.

"Sir," said he, returning to the provost, "which am I to take?"

"The young one."

"So much the better; for the old one seems hard to manage."

"Poor little dancer with the goat!" said the old sergeant of the watch.

Henriet Cousin again advanced to the window. The mother's eye made his own fall. He said somewhat timidly,—

"Madame,—"

She interrupted him in very low but furious tones:

"What do you want?"

"Not you," said he; "it is the other."

"What other?"

"The young one."

She began to wag her head, crying,—

"There's nobody here! there's nobody here! there's nobody here!"

"Yes, there is!" rejoined the hangman, "and you know it well. Let me have the young one. I don't want to harm you."

She said with a strange sneer,—

"Ah! you don't want to harm me!"

"Let me have the other, madame; it is the provost's will."

She repeated with a foolish look,—

"There's nobody here!"

"I tell you there is!" replied the hangman; "we all saw that there were two of you."

"Look then!" said the recluse, with a sneer. "Put your head in at the window."

The hangman scrutinized the mother's nails, and dared not venture.

"Despatch!" cried Tristan, who had ranged his men in a ring around the Rat-Hole, and himself sat on horseback near the gibbet.

Henriet returned to the provost once more, utterly out of countenance. He had laid his rope on the ground, and awkwardly twirled his hat in his hands.

"Sir," he inquired, "how am I to get in?"

"Through the door."

"There is none."

"Through the window."

"It is too small."

"Then make it bigger," angrily exclaimed Tristan. "Have you no pickaxes?"

From the back of her den, the mother, ever on the alert, watched them. She had lost all hope, she knew not what she wished, but they should not have her daughter.

Henriet Cousin went to fetch his box of tools from the shed of the Maison-aux-Piliers. He also brought out the trestles, which he at once set up against the gibbet. Five or six of the provost's men armed themselves with picks and levers, and Tristan moved towards the window with them.

"Old woman," said the provost in a stern voice, "surrender that girl with a good grace."

She looked at him like one who does not understand.

"'Sblood!" added Tristan, "why should you prevent that witch from being hanged, as it pleases the king?"

The wretched woman began to laugh wildly.

"Why? She is my daughter!"

The tone in which she uttered that word made even Henriet Cousin shudder.

"I am sorry," replied the provost, "but it is the king's good pleasure."

She shrieked with redoubled laughter, —

"What is your king to me? I tell you she is my daughter!"

"Make a hole in the wall," said Tristan.

It was only necessary to remove one course of stones under the window, in order to make an opening of sufficient size. When the mother heard the picks and levers undermining her fortress, she uttered an awful scream; then she began to pace her cell with frightful speed,—one of the habits of a wild beast which she had acquired in her cage. She said no more, but her eyes flamed. The soldiers were chilled to the marrow.

All at once she caught up her paving stone, laughed, and hurled it with both hands at the workmen. The stone, ill aimed (for her hands trembled), struck no one and fell at the feet of Tristan's horse. She ground her teeth.

Meantime, although the sun had not yet risen, it was broad daylight; a lovely pink tint illumined the worm-eaten old chimneys of the Maison-aux-Piliers. It was the hour when the windows of the earliest risers in the great city open joyously upon the roofs. Some few country people, some fruiterers going to market on their donkeys, began to pass through the Place de Grève; they paused a moment at sight of this cluster of soldiers huddled in front of the Rat-Hole, looked at them in surprise, then went their way.

The recluse had seated herself beside her daughter, covering her with her body, her eye fixed, listening to the poor girl, who never stirred, but murmured softly the one word, "Phœbus! Phœbus!" As the work of the destroyers progressed, the mother mechanically moved back, pressing the young girl closer and closer against the wall. All at once she saw the stones (for she was on the watch and never took her eyes from them) quiver, and she heard Tristan's voice urging the laborers on. Then she woke from the stupor into which she had sunk, exclaiming,—and, as she spoke, her voice now pierced the ear like a saw, then stammered as if all the curses which she uttered crowded to her lips at once:

"Ho! ho! ho! But this is horrible! You are robbers! Do you really mean to take my daughter from me? I tell you it is my daughter! Oh, cowards! Oh, base hangmen! Vile assassins! Help! help! Fire! Will they thus take my child? Then, what is he whom men call the good God?"

Then turning to Tristan, with foaming mouth, haggard eyes, on all fours like a panther, and bristling with rage:—

"Come and take my daughter! Do you not understand that this woman tells you it is her daughter? Do you know what it is to have a child of your own? Have you no mate, O lynx? Have you never had a cub? And if you have little ones, when they howl does nothing stir within you?"

"Down with the stones," said Tristan; "they are loosened."

The levers lifted the ponderous course of stone. It was, as we have said, the mother's last bulwark.

She threw herself upon it, tried to hold it up. She scratched it with her nails; but the heavy block, set in motion by six men, escaped from her grasp and slid gently to the ground along the iron levers.

The mother, seeing that an entrance was effected, fell across the opening, barricading the breach with her body, wringing her hands, beating her head against the flagstones, and shrieking in a voice hoarse with fatigue and scarcely audible,—

"Help! Fire! fire!"

"Now, seize the girl," said Tristan, still unmoved.

The mother glared at the soldiers in so terrible a fashion they would much rather have retreated than advanced.

"Come, come," repeated the provost. "Here, Henriet Cousin!"

No one stirred a step.

The provost swore:—

"By the Cross! my soldiers! Afraid of a woman!"

"Sir," said Henriet, "do you call that a woman?"

"She has a lion's mane!" said another.

"Come!" resumed the provost, "the gap is broad enough. Go in three abreast, as at the breach of Pontoise. Have done with it, by the head of Mahomet! The first who recoils I'll cut in two!"

Thus placed between the provost and the mother, both alike menacing, the soldiers hesitated an instant; then, making their choice, they advanced upon the Rat-hole.

When the recluse saw this, she rose suddenly to her knees, shook her hair back from her face, then let her thin, bleeding hands fall upon her thighs. Great tears started one by one from her eyes; they trickled down a wrinkle in her cheeks, like a torrent down the bed which it has worn for itself. At the same time she spoke, but in a voice so suppliant, so sweet, so submissive, and so full of pathos, that more than one old fire-eater about Tristan wiped his eyes.

"Gentlemen! soldiers! one word. I must say one thing to you. She is my daughter, you see,—my dear little daughter whom I lost! Listen. It is quite a story. You must know that I was once very friendly with the soldiers. They were always kind to me in the days when little boys threw stones at me because I led a light life. Do you see? You will leave me my child, when you know all! I am a poor woman of the town. The gipsies stole her away from me. I kept her shoe for fifteen years. Stay; here it is. That was the size of her foot. Paquette Chantefleurie, at Rheims,—Rue Folle-Peine! Perhaps you knew her once. That was I. When you were young, you led a merry life; there were fine doings then. You will take pity on me, won't you, gentlemen? The gipsies stole her from me; they kept her hidden from me for fifteen years. I thought she was dead. Only fancy, my kind friends, I thought she was dead. I have spent fifteen years here, in this cave, with never a spark of fire in winter. That was hard to bear, that was. The poor, dear little shoe! I have shed so many tears that the good God heard me. Last night he gave me back my girl. The good God wrought a miracle. She was not dead. You will not take her from me, I am sure. If it were only myself, I would not complain; but for her, a child of sixteen! Let her have time to see the sun! What has she done to you? Nothing at all. No more have I. If you only knew that I have nobody but her, that I am old, that she is a blessing sent down to me by the Holy Virgin! And then, you are all so kind! You did not know that she was my daughter; now you know it. Oh, I love her! Mr. Provost, I would rather have a hole through my heart than a scratch on her finger. You look like a good, kind gentleman!

What I tell you, explains the whole thing, doesn't it? Oh, if you ever had a mother, sir! You are the captain; leave me my child! Remember that I pray to you on my knees, as one prays to Jesus Christ! I ask nothing of any one; I am from Rheims, gentlemen; I have a little field there, left me by my uncle, Mahiet Pradon. I am not a beggar. I want nothing, but I must have my child! Oh, I must keep my child! The good God, who is master of us all, never gave her back to me for nothing! The king! you say the king! It can't give him much pleasure to have my little girl killed! And besides, the king is good! It's my daughter! It's my daughter, my own girl! She is not the king's! she is not yours! I will go away! we will both go away! After all, they will let two women pass,—a mother and her daughter! Let us pass! we are from Rheims! Oh, you are very kind, sergeants! I love you all. You will not take my dear little one from me; it is impossible, isn't it? Utterly impossible! My child, my child!"

We will not try to give any idea of her gestures, of her accent, of the tears which she swallowed as she spoke, of her hands which she clasped and then wrung, of the heartrending smiles, the pathetic glances, the groans, the sighs, the agonizing and piercing cries which she mingled with her wild, incoherent, rambling words. When she ceased, Tristan l'Hermite frowned, but it was to hide a tear that dimmed his tigerish eye. However, he conquered this weakness, and said curtly,—

"It is the king's command."

Then he bent down to Henriet Cousin and said in a low voice,—

"Put an end to this!"

Perhaps the terrible provost himself felt his heart fail him.

The hangman and his men entered the cell. The mother made no resistance. She only dragged herself towards her daughter and threw herself heavily upon her.

The gipsy saw the soldiers coming. The horror of death revived her.

"My mother!" she cried in tones of unspeakable distress; "my mother! They are coming! Defend me!"

"Yes, my love. I will defend you!" replied her mother, in a feeble voice; and clasping her closely in her arms, she covered her with kisses. The two, prostrate on the ground, mother and daughter, were a sight worthy of pity.

Henriet Cousin seized the girl just below her beautiful shoulders. When she felt his hand, she shrieked and fainted. The hangman, whose big tears fell drop by drop upon her, tried to raise her in his arms. He strove to loose her mother's hold, she having, as it were, knotted her hands about her daughter's waist; but she clung so closely to her child that it was impossible to part them. Henriet Cousin therefore dragged the girl from the cell, and her mother after her. The mother's eyes were also closed.

At this moment the sun rose, and there was already a considerable crowd of people in the square, looking on from a little distance to see who was being thus dragged over the pavement to the gallows,—for this was Provost Tristan's way at hangings. He had a mania for hindering the curious from coming too close.

There was no one at the windows. Only, far off, on the top of the Notre-Dame tower overlooking the Place de Grève, two men were to be seen darkly outlined against the clear morning sky, apparently watching the proceedings.

Henriet Cousin paused with his burden at the foot of the fatal ladder, and, scarcely breathing so strongly was he moved to pity, he passed the rope around the girl's beautiful neck. The unhappy creature felt the horrible contact of the hemp. She raised her eyelids, and saw the fleshless arm of the stone gibbet stretched above her head. Then she shook off her torpor, and cried in a sharp, shrill voice, "No, no, I will not!" Her mother, whose head was buried and lost in her child's garments, did not speak a word; but her entire body was convulsed by a shudder, and she lavished redoubled kisses upon her child. The hangman took advantage of this moment quickly to unclasp her arms from the prisoner. Whether from exhaustion or despair, she submitted. Then he took the girl upon his shoulder, over which the charming creature fell gracefully, bent double over his large head. Then be put his foot upon the ladder to ascend.

At this instant the mother, crouching on the pavement, opened wide her eyes. Without a cry, she sprang up with a terrible look; then, like a wild beast leaping upon its prey, she threw herself upon the hangman's hand, and bit it. It was a flash of lightning. The hangman yelled with pain. They ran to his aid. With some difficulty they withdrew his bleeding hand from between the mother's teeth. She maintained a profound silence. The men pushed her away with some brutality, and observed that her head fell heavily on the pavement. They lifted her up; she fell back again. She was dead.

The hangman, who had not let go his hold of the girl, resumed his ascent of the ladder.

CHAPTER II

La Creatura Bella Bianco Vestita*

When Quasimodo saw that the cell was empty, the gipsy gone, that while he was defending her she had been carried off, he tore his hair, and stamped with rage and surprise; then he ran from end to end of the church in search of his sovereign lady, uttering strange howls as he went, scattering his red hair upon the pavement. It was just at

---

*The beautiful creature clad in white (Italian). In the second section, entitled "Purgatory," of Dante's *Divine Comedy*, the angel of humility, described this way, serves as one of the poet's guides.

the moment when the royal archers entered Notre-Dame in triumph, also in search of the gipsy. Quasimodo helped them, without suspecting—poor deaf fellow!—their fatal purpose; he supposed that the enemies of the gipsy were the Vagrants. He himself guided Tristan l'Hermite to every possible hiding-place, opened secret doors, false altar-backs, and inner sacristies for him. Had the wretched girl still been there it would have been Quasimodo himself who betrayed her.

When the fatigue of unsuccessful search discouraged Tristan, who was not easily discouraged, Quasimodo continued to search alone. Twenty, nay, a hundred times he went the round of the church, from one end to the other, from top to bottom, upstairs, downstairs, running, calling, crying, sniffing, ferreting, rummaging, poking his head into every hole, thrusting a torch into every vault, desperate, mad. No wild beast which had lost its mate could be wilder or more frantic.

Finally when he was sure, very sure, that she was no longer there, that all was over, that she had been stolen from him, he slowly climbed the tower stairs,—those stairs which he had mounted with such eagerness and delight on the day when he saved her. He passed by the same places, with hanging head, voiceless, tearless, almost breathless. The church was again deserted, and had relapsed into its usual silence. The archers had left it to track the witch into the City. Quasimodo, alone in that vast cathedral, so crowded and so noisy but a moment previous, returned to the room where the gipsy had for so many weeks slept under his watchful care.

As he approached it, he fancied that he might perhaps find her there. When, at the turn of the gallery opening upon the roof of the side-aisle, he caught sight of the narrow cell with its tiny door and window nestling under a huge flying buttress, like a bird's nest under a branch, his heart failed him,—poor man!—and he leaned against a pillar lest he should fall. He imagined that she might perhaps have returned; that a good genius had undoubtedly brought her back; that the cell was too quiet, too safe, and too attractive for her not to be there; and he dared not take another step for fear of destroying his illusion. "Yes," he said to himself, "she is asleep, or saying her prayers. I won't disturb her."

At last he summoned up all his courage, advanced on tiptoe, looked, entered. Empty,—the cell was still empty. The unhappy deaf man slowly walked about it, lifted the bed and looked under it, as if she might be hidden between the mattress and the stones; then he shook his head, and stood staring stupidly. All at once he trampled his torch furiously under foot, and without a word, without a sigh, he threw himself headlong against the wall, and fell fainting on the floor.

When he came to his senses, he flung himself upon the bed; he rolled upon it; he kissed frantically the place, still warm, where the young girl had slept; he lay there for some moments as motionless as if about to die; then he rose, streaming with perspiration, panting, insensate, and began to beat his head against the wall with the frightful regularity of the clapper of one of his own bells, and the resolution of a man who is determined to dash out his brains. At last he fell exhausted for the second time; he dragged himself from the cell on his knees, and crouched before the door in an attitude of wonder.

Thus he remained for more than an hour without stirring, his eye fixed upon the empty cell, sadder and more pensive than a mother seated between an empty cradle and a coffin. He did not utter a word; only at long intervals a sob shook his whole body convulsively; but it was a dry, tearless sob, like summer lightning, which is silent.

It seems that it was then that, seeking in his desolate thoughts to learn who could have been the unlooked-for ravisher of the gipsy, his mind reverted to the archdeacon. He remembered that Dom Claude alone had a key to the staircase leading to the cell. He recalled his midnight attempts upon the girl,—first, in which he, Quasimodo had helped him; the second, which he had foiled. He remembered a thousand details, and soon ceased to doubt that the archdeacon had stolen the gipsy from him. However, such was his respect for the priest, his gratitude, his devotion, his love for the man were so deeply rooted in his heart, that they resisted, even at this moment, the claws of jealousy and despair.

He considered that the archdeacon had done this thing, and the thirst for blood and murder which he would have felt for another were turned in the poor deaf man to added grief where Claude Frollo was concerned.

Just as his thoughts were thus concentrated upon the priest, as dawn whitened the flying buttresses, he saw on the upper story of Notre-Dame, at the angle formed by the outer railing which runs round the chancel, a moving figure. The figure was walking towards him. He recognized it. It was the archdeacon.

Claude advanced with grave, slow pace. He did not look before him as he walked. He was going towards the north tower; but his face was turned aside towards the right bank of the Seine, and he held his head erect, as if trying to see something over the roofs. The owl often carries its head in this crooked position; it flies towards one point, and looks in another. The priest thus passed above Quasimodo without seeing him.

The deaf man, petrified by this sudden apparition, saw him disappear through the door of the staircase in the north tower. The reader knows that this tower is the one from which the Hôtel de Ville is visible. Quasimodo rose, and followed the archdeacon.

Quasimodo climbed the tower stairs, intending to go to the top, to learn why the priest was there; yet the poor ringer knew not what he, Quasimodo, meant to do or say, or what he wished. He was full of fury, and full of fear. The archdeacon and the gipsy struggled for the mastery in his heart.

When he reached the top of the tower, before issuing from the shadow of the stairs and stepping upon the platform, he looked carefully about to see where the priest was. The priest stood with his back to him. There is an open balustrade around the platform of the belfry tower; the priest, whose eyes were riveted upon the city, leaned against that one of the four sides of the railing which overlooks the Pont Notre-Dame.

Quasimodo, stealthily advancing behind him, gazed abroad to see what he was watching so closely.

But the priest's attention was so fully absorbed that he did not hear the deaf man's step at his side.

Paris is a magnificent and charming sight, and especially so was the Paris of that day, viewed from the top of the towers of Notre-Dame in the cool light of a summer dawn. The day might have been one of the early days of July. The sky was perfectly clear. A few tardy stars were fading out at different points, and there was a single very brilliant one in the east, in the brightest part of the sky. The sun was just rising. Paris began to stir. A very white, very pure light threw into strong relief all the outlines which its countless houses present to the east. The monstrous shadows of the steeples spread from roof to roof from one end of the great city to the other. There were already certain quarters filled with chatter and noise,—here the stroke of a bell, there the blow of a hammer, yonder the intricate jingle and clatter of a passing cart. Already smoke rose here and there from the sea of roofs, as from the fissures in a vast volcano. The river, whose waters wash the piers of so many bridges and the shores of so many islands, was rippled with silvery folds. Around the city, outside the ramparts, the view was lost in a wide ring of fleecy vapors, through which the indefinite line of the plains and the graceful swell of the hills were vaguely visible. All sorts of sounds floated confusedly over the half-awakened city. Towards the east, the morning breeze chased across the sky a few white flakes torn from the fleece of mist upon the hills.

In the cathedral square certain good women, milkjug in hand, pointed with amaze to the strange dilapidation of the great door of Notre-Dame, and the two rivulets of lead congealed in the crevices of the sandstone. These were the only remaining signs of the tumult of the night. The bonfire kindled by Quasimodo between the towers had gone out. Tristan had already had the square cleared and the dead bodies thrown into the Seine. Kings like Louis XI are careful to wash the pavement quickly after a massacre.

Outside the tower rail, exactly under the point where the priest had paused, there was one of those fancifully carved gutters with which Gothic edifices bristle; and in a chink of this gutter were two pretty gilly-flowers in full bloom, waving and seeming almost alive in the breeze, as they playfully saluted each other. Above the towers, aloft, far away in the depths of the sky, were little twittering birds.

But the priest heard and saw none of these things. He was one of those men for whom there are no day-dreams, or birds, or flowers. In all that immense horizon, which assumed so many and such varied aspects about him, his gaze was centered on a single point.

Quasimodo burned to ask him what he had done with the gipsy; but the archdeacon seemed at this instant to have left the world far behind him. He was evidently passing through one of those critical moments of life when a man would not feel the earth crumble beneath him. His eyes fixed constantly upon a certain spot, he stood motionless and silent; and there was something so fearful about his silence and his motionlessness, that the shy bell-ringer shuddered before it, and dared not disturb him. Only—and this was one way of questioning the archdeacon—he followed the direction of his glance, and in this manner the eye of the unfortunate deaf man fell upon the Place de Grève.

Thus he saw what the priest was watching. The ladder was reared beside the permanent gallows. There were a few people in the square, and a number of soldiers. A man dragged across the pavement a white object to which something black was fastened. This man stopped at the foot of the gallows.

At this point something took place which Quasimodo could not quite make out. Not because his one eye had not retained its great range, but there was a knot of soldiers which hindered him from seeing everything. Besides, at this instant the sun rose, and such a flood of light burst from the horizon that it seemed as if every pinnacle in Paris, spires, chimneys, and gables, were set on fire at once.

Meantime, the man continued to climb the ladder. Then

Quasimodo saw him again distinctly. He had a woman across his shoulder,—a young girl dressed in white; this girl had a knotted rope around her neck. Quasimodo recognized her.

It was she!

The man reached the top of the ladder. There he arranged the noose. Here the priest, to see the better, knelt upon the balustrade.

All at once the man pushed the ladder quickly from him with his heel; and Quasimodo, who had scarcely breathed for some moments past, saw the unfortunate girl dangling from the end of the rope, a dozen feet from the ground, the man crouching above her, pressing his feet against her shoulders to weigh her down. The rope revolved rapidly several times, and Quasimodo saw a horrible shudder run through the gipsy's frame. The priest, on his part, with outstretched neck and starting eyes, watched that dreadful group of man and girl,— of the spider and the fly.

At the most awful moment a demoniac laugh—a laugh impossible to a mere man—broke from the livid lips of the priest. Quasimodo did not hear this laughter, but he saw it.

The ringer shrank back a few paces behind the archdeacon, and then, suddenly rushing furiously upon him, with his huge hands he hurled Dom Claude into the abyss over which he leaned.

The priest cried, "Damnation!" and fell.

The gutter below arrested his fall. He clung to it with desperate hands, and, as he opened his mouth for a second shriek, he saw, looking over the edge of the balustrade, above his head, the terrible, avenging face of Quasimodo.

Then he was silent.

The abyss was beneath him. A fall of more than two hundred feet,—and the pavement.

In this dreadful situation the archdeacon said not a word, uttered not a groan. He merely writhed about the gutter making incredible efforts to climb up it, but his hands had no grip upon the granite, his feet scratched the blackened wall without finding a foothold. Those who have visited the Towers of

Notre-Dame know that the stone projects directly below the balustrade. It was against this swell that the wretched archdeacon exhausted himself in frantic struggles. He was working, not upon a perpendicular wall, but upon a wall which sloped away from beneath him.

Quasimodo had only to stretch forth his hand to save him from the gulf; but he did not even look at him. He looked at the Place de Grève; he looked at the gibbet; he looked at the gipsy girl.

The deaf man leaned his elbows on the railing, in the very place where the archdeacon had been the moment previous, and there, never removing his gaze from the only object which at this instant existed for him, he stood motionless and mute as if struck by lightning, and a river of tears flowed silently from that eye which until then had shed but a single tear.

Meantime, the archdeacon gasped. His bald head streamed with perspiration, his nails bled against the stone, his knees were flayed against the wall.

He heard his cassock, by which he hung to the spout, crack and rip at every jerk that he gave it. To complete his misfortunes, this spout terminated in a leaden pipe which was bending beneath the weight of his body. The archdeacon felt this pipe slowly giving way. The miserable creature said to himself that when his cassock was torn through, when the lead bent completely, he must fall; and terror took possession of him. Sometimes he gazed wildly at a sort of narrow platform some ten feet below him, formed by certain carvings which jutted out; and he implored Heaven, from the depths of his distressed soul, to permit him to end his life upon that space two feet square, were it to last a hundred years. Once he looked down into the abyss, into the square; when he raised his head his eyes were shut and his hair was erect.

There was something frightful in the silence of the two men. While the archdeacon, a few feet beneath him, was agonizing in this horrible fashion, Quasimodo wept, and watched the Place de Grève.

The archdeacon, seeing that all his struggles merely weakened the frail support which remained to him, resolved to move no more. He clung there, hugging the gutter, scarcely breathing, never stirring, his only movement being that mechanical heaving of the chest experienced in dreams when we think that we are falling. His eyes were fixed in a wide stare of anguish and amaze. Little by little, however, he lost ground; his fingers slipped from the spout; the feebleness of his arms and the weight of his body increased more and more. The bending lead which supported him, every moment inclined a notch nearer to the abyss.

He saw below him a fearful sight,—the roof of Saint-Jean le Rond as small as a card bent double. He gazed, one after another, at the impassive sculptures on the tower, like him suspended over the precipice, but without terror for themselves or pity for him. All around him was of stone: before his eyes, gaping monsters; below, far down in the square, the pavement; above his head, Quasimodo weeping.

Groups of curious citizens had gathered in the square, calmly trying to guess what manner of madman it might be who amused himself in so strange a manner. The priest heard them say,—for their voices reached him clear and shrill,— "But he will break his neck!"

Quasimodo was weeping.

At last the archdeacon, foaming with rage and fright, knew that all was in vain. However, he summoned up his remaining strength for a final effort. He braced himself against the gutter, set his knees against the wall, hooked his hands into a chink in the stones, and succeeded in climbing up perhaps a foot; but this struggle made the leaden pipe upon which he hung, bend suddenly. With the same effort his cassock tore apart. Then, feeling that everything had failed him, his stiffened and trembling hands alone retaining a hold upon anything, the unfortunate wretch closed his eyes and loosened his grasp of the gutter. He fell.

Quasimodo watched him fall.

A fall from such a height is seldom perpendicular. The

archdeacon, launched into space, at first fell head downward, with outstretched arms; then he rolled over and over several times; the wind wafted him to the roof of a house, where the unhappy man broke some of his bones. Still, he was not dead when he landed there. The ringer saw him make another effort to clutch the gable with his nails; but the slope was too steep, and his strength was exhausted. He slid rapidly down the roof, like a loose tile, and rebounded to the pavement. There, he ceased to move.

Quasimodo then raised his eye to the gipsy, whose body he could see, as it swung from the gibbet, quivering beneath its white gown in the last death-throes; then he again lowered it to the archdeacon, stretched at the foot of the tower, without a trace of human shape, and he said, with a sob which heaved his mighty breast, "Oh, all that I ever loved!"[23]

CHAPTER III

Marriage of Phœbus

Towards evening of the same day, when the bishop's officers came to remove the mangled body of the archdeacon from the pavement, Quasimodo had vanished from Notre-Dame.

Many rumors were rife concerning the accident. No one doubted that the day had come when, according to their compact, Quasimodo—that is to say the devil—was to carry off Claude Frollo,—that is to say the sorcerer. It was supposed that he had destroyed the body in taking the soul, as a monkey cracks the shell to eat the nut.

Accordingly the archdeacon was not buried in consecrated ground.

Louis XI died the following year, in the month of August, 1483.

As for Pierre Gringoire, he succeeded in saving the goat, and he achieved some success as a tragic author. It seems that after dipping into astrology, philosophy, architecture, hermetics, and all manner of follies, he returned to writing tragedies, the most foolish of all things. This he called "making a tragic end." In regard to his dramatic triumphs, we read in 1483, in the Royal Privy Accounts: "To Jehan Marchand and Pierre Gringoire, carpenter and composer, who made and composed the mystery performed at the Châtelet in Paris, on the entry of the legate, ordered the personages, dressed and habited the same as the said mystery required, and likewise made the necessary scaffoldings for the same, one hundred pounds."

Phœbus de Châteaupers also came to a tragic end: he married.[24]

CHAPTER IV

Marriage of Quasimodo

We have already said that Quasimodo disappeared from Notre-Dame on the day of the death of the gipsy and the archdeacon. Indeed, he was never seen again; no one knew what became of him.

During the night following the execution of Esmeralda, the hangman's assistants took down her body from the gibbet, and carried it, as was customary, to the vaults at Montfaucon.

Montfaucon, as Sauval states, was "the most ancient and most superb gibbet in the kingdom." Between the suburbs of the Temple and Saint-Martin, about three hundred and twenty yards from the walls of Paris, a few cross-bow shots from the village of La Courtille, at the top of a gentle, almost imperceptibly sloping hill, yet high enough to be seen for a distance of several leagues, was a building of singular shape, looking much like a Celtic cromlech, and where human sacrifices were also offered up.

Imagine, at the top of a chalk-hill a parallelopipedon of masonry fifteen feet high, thirty broad, and forty long, with a door, an outer railing, and a platform; upon this platform sixteen huge pillars of unhewn stone, thirty feet high, ranged in a colonnade around three of the four sides of the base which supported them, connected at the top by stout beams from which at intervals hung chains; from all these chains swung skeletons; round about it, in the plain, were a stone cross and two gibbets of secondary rank which seemed to spring up like shoots from the central tree; above all this, in the sky, a perpetual flight of ravens: such was Montfaucon.

At the close of the fifteenth century the awful gibbet, which dated from 1328, was already very much decayed; the beams were worm-eaten, the chains rusty, the pillars green with mold; the courses of hewn stone gaped widely at the joints, and grass grew upon the platform where no foot ever trod; the structure cast a horrid shadow against the sky, particularly at night, when the moon shone feebly upon those white skulls, or when the breeze stirred chains and skeletons, and made them rattle in the darkness. The presence of this gibbet was enough to give the entire neighborhood an evil name.

The stone base of the odious structure was hollow. It had been made into a vast vault, closed by an antique grating of battered iron, into which were cast not only the human remains taken from the chains at Montfaucon, but the bodies of all the unfortunates executed upon the other permanent gallows throughout Paris. In this deep charnel-house, where so many mortal remains and so many crimes rotted together, many of the great ones of the earth, many innocent beings, have laid their bones, from Enguerrand de Marigni, who was the first victim of Montfaucon, and who was an upright man, down to Admiral de Coligni, who was the last, and who was likewise a good man.

As for the mysterious disappearance of Quasimodo, all that we have been able to discover is this:—

Some two years or eighteen months after the events which close this story, when search was made in the vault at Montfaucon for the body of Olivier le Daim, who had been hanged two days previous, and to whom Charles VIII had accorded permission to be buried at Saint-Laurent in better company, among all those hideous carcasses two skeletons were found locked in a close embrace. One of the two, which was that of a woman, still had about it some fragments of a gown, of stuff once white, and about its neck was a necklace made of beads of red seeds, with a little silk bag, adorned with green glass beads, which was open and empty. These articles were doubtless of so little value that the hangman had not cared to remove them. The other skeleton, which held this in so close an embrace, was that of a man. It was noticed that his spine was curved, his head close between his shoulder-blades, and one leg shorter than the other. Moreover, his neck was not broken, and it was evident that he had not been hanged. The man to whom these bones belonged must therefore have come hither himself and died here. When an attempt was made to loose him from the skeleton which he clasped, he crumbled into dust.[25]

AUTHOR'S NOTE

Added to the Definitive Edition

It was through error that this edition was announced as enlarged by several *new* chapters. They should have been spoken of as *unpublished*; for if by "new" we understand "recently made," the chapters added to this edition are not new.[26]

They were written at the same time as the rest of the work; they date from the same epoch, and came from the same idea; they have always been part of the manuscript of *Notre-Dame de Paris*. Furthermore, the author does not understand how any one can add new developments to a work of this character. That cannot be done at will. A novel, in his opinion, is born, in a way in a certain sense necessary, with all its chapters; a drama is born with all its scenes. Do not believe that there is anything arbitrary of which this whole is composed,—this mysterious microcosm that you call a drama or a novel. Grafting and soldering act unfortunately upon works of this nature, which should spring into being at a single leap and remain such as they are. Once the thing is done, do not revise or retouch it. Once the book is published, and its sex—virile or not—recognized and proclaimed, once the child has uttered its first cry, it is born; here it is; it is made thus; neither father nor mother can alter it; it belongs to the air and the sun; let it live or die as it is. Is your book immature? So much the worse. Never add chapters to an immature book. Is it incomplete? You should have completed it when you brought it forth. Is your tree crooked? Do not attempt to straighten it. Is your novel sickly; is your novel to be short-lived? You cannot give to it the breath which it lacks. Is your drama born limping? Believe me, you cannot give it a wooden leg.

The author, then, attaches a particular value to this, that

the public should know that the chapters added here have not been made expressly for this reprint. That they were not published in earlier editions of the book was for a very simple reason. At the time when *Notre-Dame de Paris* was printed for the first time, the package which contained these three chapters was lost. It was necessary to rewrite or omit them. The author concluded that the only two chapters which would have been important by their scope were those chapters on art and history whose loss would detract nothing from the drama and the novel; that the public would be none the wiser concerning their disappearance; and that he alone, the author, would be in the secret of this gap. He decided to go on without them; and besides—to tell the whole truth—his indolence recoiled before the task of re-writing the three lost chapters. He would have found it less work to write a new novel.

Today the chapters are found, and he seizes the first occasion to replace them where they belong.

Here, then, is his entire work, as he dreamed it, as he wrote it, good or bad, lasting or fleeting, but such as he wished it.

Without doubt these recovered chapters will have little value in the eyes of persons, in other respects very judicious, who have sought in *Notre-Dame de Paris* only the drama, only the novel; but there are perhaps other readers who have not found it unprofitable to study the æsthetic and philosophic thought hidden in this book, who would have been glad, in reading *Notre-Dame de Paris*, to detect under the novel something besides novel, and to have followed, if we may be allowed somewhat ambitious expressions, the system of the historian and the object of the artist through the creation, such as it is, of the poet.[27]

It is for such readers especially that the added chapters of this edition will complete *Notre-Dame de Paris*, if we admit that *Notre-Dame de Paris* is worth being completed.

The author expresses and develops in one of these chapters the actual decline of architecture, and, according to him, the almost inevitable death today of this art king,—an opinion unfortunately very firmly rooted in him, and thoroughly reflected upon. But he feels the need of saying here that he eagerly desires that the future may prove him to have been in error. He knows that art under all its forms may hope everything from the new generations whose genius, still in the bud, can be heard springing forth in our studios. The seed is in the ground; the harvest will certainly be fine. He fears only, and in the second volume of this edition one can see why, that the sap has been entirely withdrawn from the old soil of architecture which during so many ages has been the best garden for art.

However, there is today so much life in our artistic youth, so much power, and, as it were, predestination, that in our architectural schools in particular, at the present time, the professors, who are detestable, make not merely unwittingly, but even in spite of themselves, scholars who are excellent,—the reverse of that potter of whom Horace speaks, who would have made amphoræ and produced only saucepans. *Currit rota, urceus exit.* *

But, at all events, whatever may be the future of architecture, in whatever way our young architects determine some day the question of their art, while waiting for new monuments, let us keep the ancient ones. Let us, if possible, inspire the nation with the love of national architecture. That, the author declares, is one of the principle objects of this book; that, one of the principal objects of his life.

Notre-Dame de Paris has perhaps opened some true perspectives in the art of the Middle Ages, in that marvelous art not as yet understood by some, and, what is worse, misunderstood by others. But the author is far from considering as accomplished the task which he voluntarily assumed; he has already pleaded, upon more than one occasion, for our ancient architecture; he has already denounced loudly many of the profanations, many of the destructions, many of the impious alterations. He will never cease to do so. He has pledged

---

*The wheel turns, why does a jug come out? (Latin).

himself to return often to this subject. He will return to it. He will be as indefatigable in defending our historic buildings as our iconoclasts of the schools and the academies are in attacking them; for it is a sad thing to see into what hands the architecture of the Middle Ages has fallen, and in what way the bungling plasterers of the present day treat the ruins of that great art. It is even a shame for us, intelligent men who see it done, and who content ourselves in crying out against it. And I am not speaking here only of what goes on in the provinces, but of what is done in Paris, at our gates, under our windows, in the great city,—this city of letters, of the press, of free speech, and of thought. We cannot resist pointing out as they deserve,—to end this note,—a few acts of vandalism which are every day projected, debated, begun, continued, and carried out peaceably under our very eyes, under the eyes of the artistic public of Paris, in face of criticism that is disconcerted by so much audacity. They have just pulled down the archbishop's palace,—a building in poor taste, and the evil is not great; but at one blow with the archbishop's palace they have demolished the bishop's, a rare ruin of the fourteenth century, which the demolishing architect could not distinguish from the rest. He has rooted up the wheat with the tares; it is all the same to him. They are talking of tearing down the admirable Chapelle de Vincennes, to make from its stones some sort of a fortification, I know not what, of which Daumesnil* has no need whatever. While they repair at great expense the Bourbon Palace,—that hovel,—they allow the magnificent windows of the Sainte-Chapelle to fall in before the force of the equinoctial gales. There has been for some days past a scaffolding around the tower of Saint-Jacques de la Boucherie, and one of these days the pickaxe will be applied to it. There has been found a mason to build a small white house between the venerable towers of the Palace of Justice;

---

*General who protected the Château de Vincennes both at the end of the First Empire (1814–1815) and during the uprising of 1830.

another has been found to maim Saint Germain-des-Prés, the feudal abbey with the three bell-towers. There will be found, no doubt, another to lay low Saint-Germain-l'Auxerrois. All these masons pretend to be architects, are paid by the prefecture, or from the royal treasury, and wear green coats. All the evil that bad taste can inflict upon good taste they have done. At the moment we are writing,—deplorable sight!—one of them has possession of the Tuileries, another has made a deep gash directly across the beautiful face of Philibert Delorme; and it certainly is not one of the least scandals of our time to see with what effrontery the clumsy architecture of this gentleman has sprawled across one of the most delicate façades of the Renaissance.[28]

Paris, October 20, 1832.

THE END.

ENDNOTES

1. (p. xxxix) *book is based:* In drawing attention to anankè, this "absent" word, Hugo inscribes two themes that are central to *The Hunchback of Notre Dame* and that will be central to his subsequent novels: the potentially destructive effects of the passage of time and the weight of fatality.

2. (p. 2) *Epiphany . . . Feast of Fools:* Emphasis on the convergence of these two feasts, one religious and one popular, falls perfectly in line with the principle of totality—that is to say, the coexistence of the sublime and the grotesque—which Hugo outlined in the preface to his play *Cromwell* (1827).

3. (p. 21) *"Pierre Gringoire":* Pierre Gringoire was indeed a poet who lived from 1475 to 1538. Hugo ages him by about twenty years to fit the time frame of his novel and has little concern for historical accuracy regarding Gringoire's life. While the real Pierre Gringoire was a successful poet protected by Louis XII, Hugo renders his poet as a starving artist of mediocre quality whose greatest (pre)occupation is saving his own skin.

4. (p. 66) *thieves' brotherhood:* Hugo borrowed the majority of this description from the seventeenth-century French historian Henri Sauval but augmented it by his imagination and fascination with the clandestine organization and working of the underworld. Vagrants, their world, and the "secret" language of slang are themes that Hugo will take up again in *Les Misérables*; these themes will also be addressed by other nineteenth-century novelists such as Honoré de Balzac and Eugène Sue.

5. (p. 71) *classic and romantic schools:* The narrator's tongue-in-cheek comment makes reference to the state of drama in 1831, when a battle is waging between the supporters of classical theater and its tenets and the new romantic school. In this battle, Hugo, author of the Romantic manifesto prefacing his play *Cromwell*, is no small player.

6. (p. 76) *their neighbors' sleep:* The literary type of the gamin, which Hugo sketches here, will find its fullest form with the cre-

ation of the unforgettable man-child Gavroche in *Les Misérables*.

7. (p. 102) *"heaven itself"*: In all of Hugo's novels, romantic love and the formation of a couple mean the complete fusion of the two individuals into one organic whole. This (desired) state is, however, rarely attained. With the exception of Marius and Cosette in *Les Misérables* and Déruchette and Ebenezer in *The Toilers of the Sea*, Hugo's characters most often do not succeed in creating or sustaining ties (romantic or familial) that would bind them to the fictional world. This failure to connect underscores the isolation and exclusion that the majority of these characters face.

8. (p. 159) *of living bronze*: The sexual undertones of the virginal Quasimodo's ardor for the cathedral bells has been noted often. What is more significant, however, than this displaced passion is that the cathedral represents everything to the hunchback: It is his protector, his mother, his lover, his universe. As the narrator observes, so much is Quasimodo a part of the cathedral and the cathedral a part of him that, as a result of the cathedral's "mysterious influences" upon him, he even comes "to look like it" (p. 154).

9. (p. 222) *"a young mother"*: In all of Hugo's fiction, maternity is depicted as a sublime state that transforms the woman both physically and spiritually through redemption of present or past transgressions. In this way, the marks of Paquette's past prostitution are literally erased once she becomes a mother ("She grew handsome again"), as her subsequent existence turns uniquely around her child.

10. (p. 245) *for the third time. . . . ever shed*: In addition to solidifying the Christian and, in this case, specifically biblical frame of reference (in imitating Mary Magdalene's gesture to Christ during his torture and crucifixion), this response to Quasimodo's thrice-repeated cry for water releases Quasimodo's soul from its state of dormancy. This transfiguration is highlighted by the release of a different kind of water from Quasimodo's eye—a tear—"perhaps the first that the unfortunate man had ever shed."

11. (p. 248) *weeks had passed:* In the chronology of the novel, which covers a period of approximately six months in the year 1482 and then shoots ahead a year and a half or two in the final chapter, time moves forward unevenly. Gaps, parallel accounts of the same moment, and flashbacks are some of the narrative techniques of acceleration and deceleration that Hugo employs to build suspense.

12. (p. 254) *only the historian:* The term "historian" was often employed by nineteenth-century French novelists as a way of lending veracity to their works through the illusion of objectivity. In reality, Hugo's narrator alternates between moments of God-like omniscience and moments of distance in which he consciously draws attention to what he—and consequently the reader—cannot know. This destabilized quality of the narration both adds a dimension of autonomy to the characters and forces the reader to participate actively in a decoding of the text.

13. (p. 262) *spelled this word:—"PHŒBUS":* From her first introduction, Djali, with her remarkable grace, beauty, and mystery, is figured as Esmeralda's double in every way. Yet in spite of their sororal complicity, Djali works against Esmeralda here, setting in motion a chain of events that will lead to disaster.

14. (p. 295) *"do its work!":* In this image of the spider and the fly, we see *anankè* (the French rendition of the Greek word for "fate") at work. A metaphor for his own unstoppable path toward calamity, this image will repeatedly come back to Frollo during the course of the novel.

15. (p. 352) *"pity upon me!":* After the slow revelation of Frollo's secret obsession with Esmeralda, this frenzied confession of his love reveals the depth of Frollo's "misery." The antithetical discourse employed by Frollo (abhorred/loved, torture/caress) further emphasizes the abyss that divides—and that will continue to divide—the priest from the gypsy.

16. (p. 376) *strength of God:* No longer the passive participant that he was during the Feast of Fools, his trial, and his torture, Quasimodo, with foresight and purpose, saves Esmeralda here from her imminent death. From this point on, he will remain active

and even proactive in his behavior, seeking to protect Esmeralda at all costs.

17. (p. 399) *gipsy utterly amazed*: Like all of Hugo's heroes, Quasimodo is unable to communicate in a way that allows him to connect to others. With the exception of Frollo, with whom Quasimodo converses using a rudimentary mixture of signs and gestures, he is literally (as a result of his deafness) cut off from the world around him. The failure of this effort to express his feelings to Esmeralda underscores his isolation, as his only recourse is to silence.

18. (p. 484) *"my good Bastille"*: The answer to this question will, of course, come during the Revolution, when this Bastille, from which Louis XI so confidently monitors the vagrants' uprising, is the location of a "successful" assault, one that signals the beginning of the end for the French monarchy.

19. (p. 486) *"It is myself!"*: With the threat of fissure ever present in his mind, Louis XI will be merciless in his repression of the vagrants. The difference in his attitude between the moment when he approves of the revolt (believing it to be against the Provost of the Palace and thus furthering his goal of eliminating decentralized power) and the moment when he does not (learning that it is against the Church, which is under his protection) highlights the unwavering tyranny of this king, who uses the people as a political instrument.

20. (p. 499) *"your deaf friend . . . who it could be?"*: Once the unique object of Frollo's love, Jehan, whose gruesome death at the hands of Quasimodo is relived here, has been all but forgotten by the priest during his increasingly relentless pursuit of Esmeralda. Yet no more than he could force his brother to yield to his wishes can he force Esmeralda to yield to his advances: Frollo—even when disguised, as he is here—continues to inspire only horror in her.

21. (p. 501) *stolen away with the goat . . . Rue Grenier-sur-l'Eau*: Gringoire's escape with Djali instead of Esmeralda again underscores the fact that the goat is her mistress's double. But Djali represents for Gringoire a more "attainable" version of Esmeralda, one who will return his affection. This burlesque cou-

ple will be among the few to survive the mass evacuation of characters that is about to occur.

22. (p. 519) *was no longer there:* In spite of Esmeralda's plea, no "help" will come from the guardsman. This final appearance—and disappearance—of Phoebus, which leads directly to Esmeralda's perdition, accentuates, on the contrary, her complete and utter insignificance to him.

23. (p. 536) *"all that I ever loved!":* Even if Frollo's death is at Quasimodo's own hand, this loss, coupled with that of Esmeralda, is overwhelming and indeed insurmountable for Quasimodo, who has received so little love in his life and knows nothing outside the protective enclaves of the cathedral.

24. (p. 537) *tragic end: he married:* This ironic commentary on Phoebus's "fate" speaks to the moral emptiness, criminal indifference, and bourgeois mediocrity that define him. In opposition to the "marriage" that is the subject of the novel's concluding chapter, this loveless union, through which Phoebus will link his name to Fleur-de-Lys's fortune, cements Phoebus's place and role in the social world depicted in the novel.

25. (p. 539) *crumbled into dust:* This "erasure" of all traces of Quasimodo—as his skeleton fantastically disintegrates into dust—brings the novel full circle back to the "absent" word *anankè* on which the story is "based."

26. (p. 540) *are not new:* The chapters added to this eighth edition in 1832 are: "Unpopularity" (book 4, chapter 6), *"Abbas Beati Martini"* (book 5, chapter 1), and "The One Will Kill the Other" (book 5, chapter 2).

27. (p. 541) *creation . . . of the poet:* In all of Hugo's fiction, he cultivates the "other readers" to whom he refers in this paragraph—those who look beyond the plot to uncover the ideological content of the work. In a proposed dedication to *The Man Who Laughs* (1869), Hugo christens this reader *le lecteur pensif* ("the thoughtful reader") and promises greater rewards to any reader who seeks to apprehend the meaning of the multiple and sometimes contradictory layers of his writing.

28. (p. 544) *clumsy architecture . . . Renaissance:* This theme will be further amplified in Hugo's "Guerre aux démolisseurs"

("War on Those Who Demolish"), published in 1834 in *Littérature et philosophie mêlées* ("Literature and Philosophy Mingled"), which builds upon his 1825 musings in "Sur la destruction des monuments en France" ("On the Destruction of Monuments in France"), a piece on the unnecessary demolition of historical monuments.

INSPIRED BY *THE HUNCHBACK OF NOTRE DAME*

Victor Hugo's *The Hunchback of Notre Dame* has been brought to the screen an extraordinary number of times, including two silents titled *Esmeralda* (1905 and 1922), Jean Delannoy's 1957 version starring Anthony Quinn, a BBC TV play (1977), a 1982 made-for-television production starring Anthony Hopkins as Quasimodo and Derek Jacobi as Claude Frollo, and another television adaptation simply titled *The Hunchback* (1997), starring Mandy Patinkin and Salma Hayek.

The first full-screen production of Hugo's classic was the silent 1923 film *The Hunchback of Notre Dame*, starring Lon Chaney as Quasimodo. Director Wallace Worsley faithfully re-creates medieval Paris, in particular the majestic cathedral of Notre Dame. But the one-eyed Chaney, wearing a hairy body suit, a leather harness to prevent him from standing upright, and a seventy-pound hump on his back, is the film's most memorable spectacle, giving a sensitive performance as the grotesque, misshapen bell ringer. Chaney's portrayal of the deaf, hideous, but ultimately kind "monster" predicts the pathos of later films centered around an outsider—especially those in the golden age of horror such as *Frankenstein* (1931) and *Dracula* (1931). The scene of Quasimodo's public flogging, followed by Esmeralda's (Patsy Ruth Miller) offering him water to drink, is particularly moving.

The next exemplary film of *The Hunchback of Notre Dame* was William Dieterle's lavish, all-star adaptation of 1939. Shot on location in Paris, with large-scale fifteenth-century sets, the film features grand camera sweeps of Notre Dame Cathedral and captures the swarming crowds and the ominous public square, perfectly setting the medieval stage on which Church and State grapple for dominance.

In the role of Quasimodo is a terrifically made-up and stooped Charles Laughton, who also appeared in another Hugo film adaptation, *Les Misérables* (1935). The grotesque Laughton cuts a stunning figure as he peers out from the spires of Notre Dame sandwiched between gargoyles. Nineteen-year-old Maureen O'Hara, in her screen debut, shines as the gypsy Esmeralda, charming the audience along with Quasimodo, Claude Frollo (Cedric Hardwicke), and even King Louis XI (Harry Davenport), who watches, positively enthralled, as she dances. Hardwicke's Frollo, with his ghastly pallor and ghoulish repugnance, emerges as the story's true monster, who, surprisingly for the period in which this film was made, threatens Esmeralda with decidedly licentious intent. Supporting these actors are Edmond O'Brien (another film debut) as the poet-playwright Gringoire and Walter Hampden as Frollo's brother.

The year 1939 is often remembered as the grandest moment in American cinema with the release of such renowned films as *Gone with the Wind*, *The Wizard of Oz*, *Stagecoach*, and *Wuthering Heights*. Yet even with this stiff competition, Dieterle's *Hunchback* garnered Oscar nominations for sound and Alfred Newman's score.

Exceedingly popular is Disney's 1996 animated feature *The Hunchback of Notre Dame*, featuring the vocal talents of Tom Hulce, Kevin Kline, and Demi Moore. Directors Gary Trousdale and Kirk Wise, who explored a nearly identical theme in Disney's *Beauty and the Beast* (1991), struggle to carry off a production interesting to both children and adults. Hulce (best known for his virtuosic performance as Mozart in 1984's *Amadeus*) lends his voice to Quasimodo, playing him more youthfully than his predecessors. When "Quasi" finds himself pelted with objects at the Feast of Fools celebration, the fiery Esmeralda (Moore) comes to his rescue, forever endearing herself to the hunchback. Kevin Kline portrays the film's other hero in love with Esmeralda: the punning Phoebus, captain of the Guard. Together they lead a heroic crusade against prejudice and persecution.

Typical of Disney's safe approach to classics is a chorus of three gargoyles, animated to provide a bit of forced comic relief. And not surprising is the removal of Hugo's bleak-hearted pessimism from the tale's conclusion. However, the animation, aided by some computer-generated imaging, is wonderful, particularly the pleasingly dark landscapes and Notre Dame's intricate architecture. Disney's *Hunchback of Notre Dame* was nominated for an Academy Award in the Original Musical or Comedy Score category for its roster of songs by Alan Menken and Stephen Schwartz.

COMMENTS & QUESTIONS

In this section, we aim to provide the reader with an array of perspectives on the text, as well as questions that challenge those perspectives. The commentary has been culled from sources as diverse as reviews contemporaneous with the work, letters written by the author, literary criticism of later generations, and appreciations written throughout the work's history. Following the commentary, a series of questions seeks to filter Victor Hugo's The Hunchback of Notre Dame *through a variety of points of view and bring about a richer understanding of this enduring work.*

Comments

FOREIGN QUARTERLY REVIEW

Notre Dame de Paris has already, within a few months of its publication, run through several editions; and as long as a taste remains for the extraordinary, or perhaps it should be called the tremendous, such works must be popular. They appeal to an appetite which is shared by the peer with the peasant. Victor Hugo is not a writer in whose hands the power of moulding the human sympathies is likely to be idle. He is eloquent, his fancy is active, his imagination fertile; and passion, which gives life and energy to the conceptions of a writer, and which, acting upon ideas as fire does upon the parched woods of America, sets the whole scene in a flame, is in him readily roused. Hugo may be called an affected writer, a mannerist, or a horrorist, but he can never be accused of the great vice, in modern times, the most heinous of all—dullness. A volume of Hugo is an active stimulant.

—July 1831

THE ATHENÆUM

It is especially in *Notre Dame de Paris*—a terrible and powerful narrative, which haunts the memory with the horrible dis-

tinctness of a nightmare—that M. Victor Hugo displays, in all
their strength, at once the enthusiasm and self-possession, the
boldness and flexibility of his genius. What varieties of suffering are heaped together in these melancholy pages—what
ruins built up—what terrible passions put in action—what
strange incidents produced! All the foulness and all the superstitions of the middle ages are melted, and stirred, and
mixed together with a trowel of mingled gold and iron. The
poet has breathed upon all those ruins of the past; and, at his
will, they have taken their old forms and risen up again, to
their true stature, upon that Parisian soil which toiled and
groaned, of yore, beneath their hideous weight, like the earth
under Etna. Behold those narrow streets, those swarming
squares, those cut-throat alleys, those soldiers, merchants, and
churches; look upon that host of passions circulating through
the whole—all breathing, and burning, and armed!

—July 8, 1837

ROBERT LOUIS STEVENSON

The moral end that the author had before him in the conception of *Notre Dame de Paris* was (he tells us) to "denounce" the external fatality that hangs over men in the form
of foolish and inflexible superstition. To speak plainly, this
moral purpose seems to have mighty little to do with the artistic conception; moreover it is very questionably handled,
while the artistic conception is developed with the most con-
summate success. Old Paris lives for us with newness of life:
we have ever before our eyes the city cut into three by the two
arms of the river, the boat-shaped island "moored" by five
bridges to the different shores, and the two unequal towns on
either hand. We forget all that enumeration of palaces and
churches and convents which occupies so many pages of admirable description, and the thoughtless reader might be inclined to conclude from this, that they were pages thrown
away; but this is not so: we forget, indeed, the details as we forget or do not see the different layers of paint on a completed

picture; but the thing desired has been accomplished, and we carry away with us a sense of the "Gothic profile" of the city, of the "surprising forest of pinnacles and towers and belfries," and we know not what of rich and intricate and quaint. And throughout, Notre Dame has been held up over Paris by a height far greater than that of its twin towers: the Cathedral is present to us from the first page to the last; the title has given us the clew, and already in the Palace of Justice the story begins to attach itself to that central building by character after character. It is purely an effect of mirage; Notre Dame does not, in reality, thus dominate and stand out above the city; and any one who should visit it, in the spirit of the Scott-tourists to Edinburgh or the Trossachs, would be almost offended at finding nothing more than this old church thrust away into a corner. It is purely an effect of mirage, as we say; but it is an effect that permeates and possesses the whole book with astonishing consistency and strength. And then, Hugo has peopled this Gothic city, and, above all, this Gothic church, with a race of men even more distinctly Gothic than their surroundings. We know this generation already: we have seen them clustered about the worn capitals of pillars, or craning forth over the church-leads with the open mouths of gargoyles. About them all there is that sort of stiff quaint unreality, that conjunction of the grotesque, and even of a certain bourgeois smugness, with passionate contortion and horror, that is so characteristic of Gothic art. Esmeralda is somewhat an exception; she and the goat traverse the story like two children who have wandered in a dream. The finest moment of the book is when these two share with the two other leading characters, Don Claude and Quasimodo, the chill shelter of the old cathedral. It is here that we touch most intimately the generative artistic idea of the romance: are they not all four taken out of some quaint moulding, illustrative of the Beatitudes, or the Ten Commandments, or the seven deadly sins? What is Quasimodo but an animated gargoyle? What is the whole book but the reanimation of Gothic art?

—*The Cornhill Magazine* (August 1874)

ALGERNON CHARLES SWINBURNE

[Hugo,] the greatest poet of this century[,] has been more than such a force of indirect and gradual beneficence as every great writer must needs be. His spiritual service has been in its inmost essence, in its highest development, the service of a healer and a comforter, the work of a redeemer and a prophet. Above all other apostles who have brought us each the glad tidings of his peculiar gospel, the free gifts of his special inspiration, has this one deserved to be called by the most beautiful and tender of all human titles—the son of consolation. His burning wrath and scorn unquenchable were fed with light and heat from the inexhaustible dayspring of his love—a fountain of everlasting and unconsuming fire.

—*Victor Hugo* (1886)

VICTOR BROMBERT

The principle of effacement in Hugo's work has far-reaching implications. It not only signals a steady displacement of the historical center of gravity but corresponds to the dynamics of undoing that Hugo reads into the process of nature and of creation. It also denies the priority, and even the status, of the historical event. History itself—both as event and as discourse on the event—must ultimately be effaced in favor of transhistorical values. To be historically committed is a moral responsibility. But more important still is the need to understand that beyond history's inability to provide meaning, there is history as evil. What is involved is not a banal inventory of history's horrors—the brutalities, contusions, fractures, mutilations, and amputations attributed to man throughout history by the narrator of *Notre-Dame de Paris* as he considers the historical ravages that disfigured gothic architecture. More fundamentally, evil is linked to the very notion of sequentiality.

—*Victor Hugo and the Visionary Novel* (1984)

Questions

1. Through the character of Pierre Gringoire, how does Hugo represent the figure of the writer/artist? What kinds of conclusions can we draw from this vision?

2. Who is the villain of the novel? Claude Frollo? Phoebus de Châteaupers? The king, Louis XI? What does this ambiguity suggest?

3. In the French original, the titular hero (so to speak) of this novel is the cathedral of Notre-Dame, not the "hunchback." Which title—*Notre-Dame de Paris* or the title given in the English translation, *The Hunchback of Notre Dame*—more accurately names the novel's thematic core?

4. In the manifesto-like preface to his play *Cromwell*, Hugo called for a new aesthetic that brought together the grotesque and the sublime. Clearly, *The Hunchback* is informed by this aesthetic. Is the result to be admired or deplored? What, for example, is the effect on characterization?

5. *The Hunchback of Notre Dame* has been popular for roughly 170 years. It has generated many movies, musicals, plays, and a library of commentary. How would you explain this enduring popularity?

FOR FURTHER READING

Biography and General Interest

Bloom, Harold, ed. *Victor Hugo*. Modern Critical Views. New York: Chelsea House, 1988.

Frey, John Andrew. *A Victor Hugo Encyclopedia*. Westport, CT, and London: Greenwood Press, 1999.

Georgel, Pierre. *Drawings by Victor Hugo: Catalogue*. London: Victoria and Albert Museum, 1974.

Peyre, Henri. *Victor Hugo: Philosophy and Poetry*. Translated by Roda P. Roberts. Tuscaloosa: University of Alabama Press, 1980.

Porter, Laurence. *Victor Hugo*. Twayne's World Authors Series, no. 883. New York: Twayne Publishers, 1999.

Robb, Graham. *Victor Hugo: A Biography*. New York and London: W. W. Norton, 1998.

Ward, Patricia. *The Medievalism of Victor Hugo*. University Park: Pennsylvania State University Press, 1975.

Criticism

Brombert, Victor. *Victor Hugo and the Visionary Novel*. Cambridge, MA: Harvard University Press, 1984.

Grant, Richard B. *The Perilous Quest: Image, Myth, and Prophecy in the Narratives of Victor Hugo*. Durham, NC: Duke University Press, 1968.

Grossman, Kathryn M. *The Early Novels of Victor Hugo: Towards a Poetics of Harmony*. Geneva: Librairie Droz, 1986.

Works Cited in the Introduction

Hugo, Victor. *Oeuvres complètes*. 18 vols. Edited by Jean Massin. Paris: Le Club français du livre, 1967–1970.

Timeless works. New scholarship. Extraordinary value.

Look for the following titles, available now and forthcoming from
BARNES & NOBLE CLASSICS.

Visit your local bookstore for these fine titles.
Or to order online go to: WWW.BN.COM/CLASSICS

Adventures of Huckleberry Finn	Mark Twain	1-59308-000-X	$4.95
The Adventures of Tom Sawyer	Mark Twain	1-59308-068-9	$4.95
Aesop's Fables	Aesop	1-59308-062-X	$5.95
The Age of Innocence	Edith Wharton	1-59308-074-3	$4.95
Alice's Adventures in Wonderland and Through the Looking Glass	Lewis Carroll	1-59308-015-8	$5.95
Anna Karenina	Leo Tolstoy	1-59308-027-1	$8.95
The Art of War	Sun Tzu	1-59308-016-6	$3.95
The Awakening and Selected Short Fiction	Kate Chopin	1-59308-001-8	$4.95
The Call of the Wild and White Fang	Jack London	1-59308-002-6	$4.95
Candide	Voltaire	1-59308-028-X	$4.95
A Christmas Carol, The Chimes and The Cricket on the Hearth	Charles Dickens	1-59308-033-6	$5.95
The Collected Poems of Emily Dickinson	Emily Dickinson	1-59308-050-6	$5.95
The Complete Sherlock Holmes, Volume I	Sir Arthur Conan Doyle	1-59308-034-4	$7.95
The Complete Sherlock Holmes, Volume II	Sir Arthur Conan Doyle	1-59308-040-9	$7.95
The Count of Monte Cristo	Alexandre Dumas	1-59308-088-3	$5.95
Cyrano de Bergerac	Edmond Rostand	1-59308-075-1	$3.95
David Copperfield	Charles Dickens	1-59308-063-8	$7.95
The Death of Ivan Ilych and Other Stories	Leo Tolstoy	1-59308-069-7	$7.95
Don Quixote	Miguel de Cervantes	1-59308-046-8	$9.95
Dracula	Bram Stoker	1-59308-004-2	$4.95
Emma	Jane Austen	1-59308-089-1	$4.95
Ethan Frome and Selected Stories	Edith Wharton	1-59308-090-5	$5.95
Frankenstein	Mary Shelley	1-59308-005-0	$3.95
Great Expectations	Charles Dickens	1-59308-006-9	$4.95
Grimm's Fairy Tales	Jacob and Wilhelm Grimm	1-59308-056-5	$7.95
Gulliver's Travels	Jonathan Swift	1-59308-057-3	$3.95
Heart of Darkness and Selected Short Fiction	Joseph Conrad	1-59308-021-2	$4.95
The House of Mirth	Edith Wharton	1-59308-104-9	$4.95
Howards End	E. M. Forster	1-59308-022-0	$6.95
The Hunchback of Notre Dame	Victor Hugo	1-59308-047-6	$5.95
The Idiot	Fyodor Dostoevsky	1-59308-058-1	$7.95
The Importance of Being Earnest and Four Other Plays	Oscar Wilde	1-59308-059-X	$6.95
The Inferno	Dante Alighieri	1-59308-051-4	$6.95
Jane Eyre	Charlotte Brontë	1-59308-007-7	$4.95

BARNES & NOBLE CLASSICS

(continue

Jude the Obscure	Thomas Hardy	1-59308-035-2	$6.95
The Jungle	Upton Sinclair	1-59308-008-5	$4.95
The Last of the Mohicans	James Fenimore Cooper	1-59308-065-4	$4.95
Les Misérables (ABRIDGED)	Victor Hugo	1-59308-066-2	$9.95
Little Women	Louisa May Alcott	1-59308-108-1	$6.95
Main Street	Sinclair Lewis	1-59308-036-0	$5.95
The Metamorphosis	Franz Kafka	1-59308-029-8	$6.95
Middlemarch	George Eliot	1-59308-023-9	$8.95
My Ántonia	Willa Cather	1-59308-024-7	$4.95
Moby-Dick	Herman Melville	1-59308-018-2	$9.95
Narrative of the Life of Frederick Douglass, an American Slave	Frederick Douglass	1-59308-041-7	$4.95
Notes From Underground, The Double and Other Stories	Fyodor Dostoevsky	1-59308-037-9	$4.95
O Pioneers!	Willa Cather	1-59308-019-0	$4.95
The Odyssey	Homer	1-59308-009-3	$5.95
Oliver Twist	Charles Dickens	1-59308-030-1	$4.95
The Origin of Species	Charles Darwin	1-59308-077-8	$7.95
Persuasion	Jane Austen	1-59308-048-4	$4.95
The Picture of Dorian Gray	Oscar Wilde	1-59308-025-5	$4.95
The Portrait of a Lady	Henry James	1-59308-096-4	$7.95
A Portrait of the Artist as a Young Man and Dubliners	James Joyce	1-59308-031-X	$7.95
Pride and Prejudice	Jane Austen	1-59308-020-4	$4.95
The Prince and Other Writings	Niccolò Machiavelli	1-59308-060-3	$5.95
The Red Badge of Courage and Selected Short Fiction	Stephen Crane	1-59308-010-7	$3.95
Robinson Crusoe	Daniel Defoe	1-59308-011-5	$4.95
The Scarlet Letter	Nathaniel Hawthorne	1-59308-012-3	$3.95
Selected Stories of O. Henry	O. Henry	1-59308-042-5	$5.95
Sense and Sensibility	Jane Austen	1-59308-049-2	$4.95
Sons and Lovers	D. H. Lawrence	1-59308-013-1	$7.95
The Souls of Black Folk	W. E. B. Du Bois	1-59308-014-X	$5.95
The Strange Case of Dr. Jekyll and Mr. Hyde and Other Stories	Robert Louis Stevenson	1-59308-054-9	$3.95
A Tale of Two Cities	Charles Dickens	1-59308-055-7	$4.95
The Three Musketeers	Alexandre Dumas	1-59308-079-4	$6.95
The Time Machine and The Invisible Man	H. G. Wells	1-59308-032-8	$4.95
Uncle Tom's Cabin	Harriet Beecher Stowe	1-59308-038-7	$5.95
The Varieties of Religious Experience	William James	1-59308-072-7	$7.95
Walden and Civil Disobedience	Henry David Thoreau	1-59308-026-3	$4.95
The War of the Worlds	H. G. Wells	1-59308-085-9	$3.95

BARNES & NOBLE CLASSICS

If you are an educator and would like to receive an
Examination or Desk Copy of a Barnes & Noble Classic edition,
please refer to Academic Resources on our website at
WWW.BN.COM/CLASSICS
or contact us at
B&NCLASSICS@BN.COM.

All prices are subject to change.